DIVIDED ALLEGIANCE

THE DEED OF PAKSENARRION

BOOK 2

BAEN BOOKS
by ELIZABETH MOON

The Deed of Paksenarrion
Sheepfarmer's Daughter
Divided Allegiance
Oath of Gold

The Deed of Paksenarrion (omnibus)

The Legacy of Gird
Surrender None
Liar's Oath

The Legacy of Gird (omnibus)

The Serrano Legacy
Hunting Party
Sporting Chance
Winning Colors
Once a Hero
Rules of Engagement
Change of Command
Against the Odds

Heris Serrano (omnibus)
The Serrano Connection (omnibus)
The Serrano Succession (omnibus

The Planet Pirate Series
Sassinak with Anne McCaffrey
Generation Warriors with Anne McCaffrey

The Planet Pirates with Anne McCaffrey
& Jody Lynn Nye (omnibus)

Remnant Population

Short-Fiction Collections
Lunar Activity
Phases

DIVIDED ALLEGIANCE

THE DEED OF PAKSENARRION

BOOK 2

ELIZABETH MOON

BAEN

DIVIDED ALLEGIANCE

A Baen Books Original

Baen Publishing Enterprises
P.O. Box 1403
Riverdale, NY 10471
www.baen.com

ISBN: 978-1-6680-7362-9

Cover art by Todd Lockwood

First printing, June 1988
First trade paperback printing, January 2019
Second trade paperback printing, September 2026

Distributed by Simon & Schuster
1230 Avenue of the Americas
New York, NY 10020

Library of Congress Control Number: 2026941090

Printed in the United States of America

10 9 8 7 6 5 4 3 2 1

DIVIDED ALLEGIANCE INTRODUCTION

By Elizabeth Moon

What's your writing process? How do you come up with all that stuff and how do you keep track of it? These questions come up naturally considering the middle book of a trilogy, where there are more complications than resolutions.

The writing process is deceptively simple (even simpler now, with a computer and printer, because I don't have to put a sheet of paper in the typewriter every few hundred words, use white-out, or literally cut and paste to make changes). Seat of pants on seat of chair, fingers on keys, GO. And keep going. For hours. For more hours. For days, weeks, months. Stagger up now and then to use the facilities or input water and food. Until it's done. Then edit, and edit again, and then start the next one. Scream loudly when the power goes off in the middle of a backup, when a hard drive decides to self-destruct, when the backup hard drive is corrupted, when the roof leaks onto the computer (yes, it did) and then start again. And again. Until it's done.

Everything else is a refinement. Music: I write to music a lot, mostly classical music, which generates writing rhythm for me. I need it less now (my mind can play music though not as well). Food: dark chocolate is particularly useful when the writing is harder than usual, otherwise something that doesn't need time spent to prepare it. Time: I started out writing in long solitary stretches, but learned, when we adopted an infant, to write long books in short (even five-minute) bursts, holding a paragraph in my head while changing a diaper or feeding or cuddling the baby, then—the moment he was down for a nap—running in to write as fast as I could. That had not been my plan—my plan was that the baby would love being in a sling snuggled against my front while I typed. That was not the baby's plan, and writing epic fantasy (or anything much) while a struggling screaming infant is whacking you with that tiny little fist destroys concentration on anything but the baby.

Remember: you don't FIND time to write; you MAKE time to write, whatever it takes in terms of lost sleep, undone chores (other than feeding and cleaning that relate to the baby), no recreation (other than writing), no social life (other than baby/toddler/child). If you want the book written, it's up to you to figure out how, because nothing but doing it will get it done. You can (I did) write a book a year while caring for and home-schooling an autistic kid. And you can enjoy both. (No, I'm not saying it's easy. Just doable.)

I do my best first-drafting if I start fairly early in the morning, because I wake up at or just before dawn, completely awake and hungry. I want food, some exercise (mucking out a stall will do; a short ride will do more—or, lacking a horse, a bike ride or swim or brisk walk) and then the story is live and nudging me to get in there and write. Some days I could write straight through until late evening, but now I need a long break and a nap as well, before the evening surge of energy. For the entire first volume, I had long mostly empty days to write in and a horse to care for and ride. Even with the old typewriter and those uncooperative sheets of paper, it went fast.

Keeping track of the details was another issue. I had charts (Paks's recruit cohort: names, and who died when). Although I had technical-looking small maps of each combat encounter, I didn't have area maps until the second campaign year, when one of my first readers commented that no matter which way an army approached a certain city, it had to cross a river. Was the city on an island, she asked, and if so, shouldn't I mention that? It wasn't. I had created a city that jumped from side to side of its river. A map fixed that. That first map grew to cover all of Aarenis, and then spread north to cover the Eight Kingdoms.

I kept lists of character names, place names, names of plants and animals, words specific to this story-world, short bits about legends, myths, religions, customs. All these went into a three-ring binder. Many of these names required searching through various dictionaries (we have quite a few) to find what I needed, and some required the help of a friend who spoke Latvian. (Why Latvian? Old language believed to have very close ties to the original Indo-European. Some wonderful root words in there.)

In November 1983, when our son arrived, I was partway through the second book, had my reference notes tucked into the notebook, and a brand new computer (IBM PC with two floppy drives and 256K RAM) to replace the old Corona half-electric typewriter I'd inherited from my step-grandmother. I had chosen WordStar for its versatility, and loved it. Would still be using it, if it would run on newer machines. Baby and all, having a computer to write on saved me a lot of time in both writing and editing, almost enough to keep on at the same pace. Sleep was overrated, I thought.

Since my brain thought the story was all one thing (though too long to fit easily in a normal-size volume) I had no "second book slump" with *Divided Allegiance*. And that brings up the issue of a series versus a multi-volume story. A series has separate standalone stories, each in one volume. Detective series with the same detective/team in each are an example. The story arc is complete in each volume, though elements (detective, sidekick, office politics) may carry through. Each book, standing alone, is rather like one in a row of storage units. In contrast, a true multi-volume work has one main story arc that needs several volumes to complete, while each volume has sub-arcs in support of the main one (think Gothic architecture).

This means that the middle part of a multi-volume work holds the keystone of the work—the volume that holds the entire story together. It's where the infinite possibilities of the rising curve are controlled, limited, and forced back down in a definite shape toward a definite end. Which means the middle volume is where you find out if the initial concept has what it takes to center and control that long an arc.

Is there enough "stuff" in the story—not just wordage, but complexity, both in characters and plot—to sustain the tension of such a long arc? A middle book may seem weaker (a less defined beginning and end for that volume) but have the strength, when the reader finishes the whole, to show that it's the right middle, a true keystone. Or it can fail, by not tying the others together—and the failure is usually a matter of attempting a perfect internal arc with too little connection to the larger one.

So, deep in the story as it developed through *Divided Allegiance*, I was excited to realize that it was behaving like a very strong keystone indeed. Writing the actual keystone and the downward arc, however, was anything but the same fun I had had with *Sheepfarmer's Daughter*. Unlike readers (who had to survive the end of it to get to the final volume) I knew as I wrote that what seemed to be desolation would not last forever but it was still hard when the characters' flaws—clearly there in the first book—had their inevitable outcome in the second. It's still hard for me to read, years later. But it would have been dishonest to make it easy.

Once into *Oath of Gold* I could see more of where the story was going. I hurried on, in my increasingly short periods of writing, as we entered the home stretch of the race between my first book and his becoming able to walk. He beat me by five days, in early January 1985—but close enough. The story was complete, all the parts in the right place. Now it was time to turn 2500 sheets of paper covered with words into separate manuscripts ready for submission. I would have had a nice long nap—but I had a very active toddler in the house.

DIVIDED ALLEGIANCE

THE DEED OF PAKSENARRION

BOOK 2

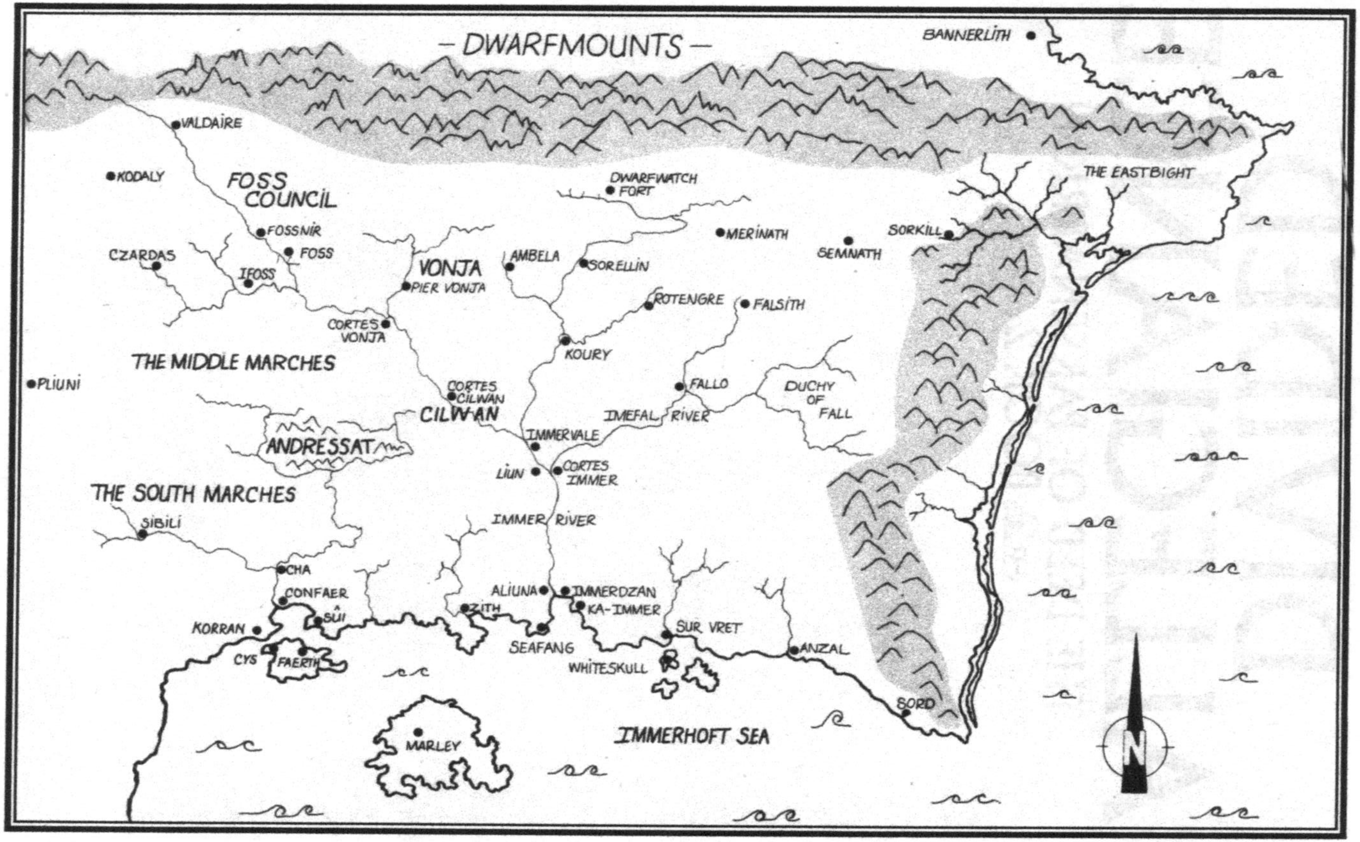

- DWARFMOUNTS -
BANNERLITH
VALDAIRE
KODALY
FOSS COUNCIL
DWARFWATCH FORT
THE EASTBIGHT
FOSSNIR
FOSS
CZARDAS
IFOSS
VONJA
PIER VONJA
AMBELA
SORELLIN
MERINATH
SEMNATH
SORKILL
ROTENGRE
FALSITH
CORTES VONJA
KOURY
THE MIDDLE MARCHES
PLIUNI
CORTES CILWAN
CILWAN
FALLO
DUCHY OF FALL
IMEFAL RIVER
IMMERVALE
ANDRESSAT
LIUN
CORTES IMMER
THE SOUTH MARCHES
SIBILI
IMMER RIVER
CHA
CONFAER
SUI
ALIUNA
IMMERDZAN
ZITH
KA-IMMER
SUR VRET
KORRAN
SEAFANG
ANZAL
CYS
FAERTH
WHITESKULL
SORD
MARLEY
IMMERHOFT SEA
N

PROLOGUE

Long ago, before the elder folk were driven from the lands south of the Hakkenarsk, the elves who dwelt in those heights had found a valley more lovely than any other. The shape of its rock and the clarity of its water brought joy to all who saw it. There for a time the elves lived, and built as they rarely build, while the greatest among them sang to the taig of that place, and wakened it to its own power. Over long years they shaped it, singing one song of beauty after another, and the taig responded, willing itself to flourish as the elves suggested. Very dear was this valley to all who could sense the taigin, both elder and younger folk, and it was known as the *elfane taig,* the holy place and living banner of the elves and their powers.

Then troubles came: the tales are lost that tell who brought them, or how those who fled sought refuge far away. Even to the elfane taig the evil came, and the elves fled, driven out by a power they could not resist for all their songs. The taig remained, crippled in its resistance to that evil by corruption placed at its heart, no longer truly *elfane* but *banast,* or wounded. Most of its great strength was spent in containing that corruption. The taig could not attack the embodied evil without loosing the worse danger, the periapt which would leave it permanently defiled.

Few travelers went that way at first, for its hazards were well known. The elves, when they were asked, warned all. No dwarf would venture so near the Ladysforest, and humans, for the most part, preferred the easier pass at Valdaire, or the shorter one over Dwarfwatch. So for long years the contending powers in the valley had only each other to feed on. A stray orc here, a wolfpack there—these nourished the conflict ill. And of the travelers that passed, not all were apt for use. Some, when the visions came, woke quickly and fled, leaving packs and animals behind. Others, greedy for treasure, stormed into the ruins without sense, and fell to the first of the traps and creatures, ending as servants of evil, or its food.

But ages passed, and time dulled human memories, and ever the contending powers sought lives and souls to serve them, to war in their long and bitter strife. As elven influence waned in Lyonya, the nearest settled land, few asked elves for advice; fewer still obeyed. Bold explorers, half-brigand, wandered the northern slopes. From time to time, an entire band disappeared below the valley's ruins, to live in the eternal light of the old halls, and fight for whichever power could enchant each separate soul. There they died, for none came alive from the banast taig. So the treasure accumulated, over the years: most of it the weaponry and armor of wandering mercenaries or brigands, but also odd bits of magical equipment, scholars' scrolls—whatever a lost traveler might be carrying.

Then two more travelers entered the valley.

CHAPTER ONE

When all Siniava's troops had been marched away under guard, most of the Phelani assumed they'd be going back to Valdaire—even, perhaps, to the north again. Some were already making plans for spending their share of the loot. Others looked forward to time to rest and recover from wounds. They were more than a little surprised, then, to be marched south, along the Immer, in company with Alured's men, the Halverics, and several cohorts of the Duke of Fall's army. These last looked fresh as new paint, hardly having fought at all, except to turn Siniava away from Fallo.

"I don't understand it," muttered Keri to Paks as they marched. "I thought we were through—Siniava's dead. What more?"

Paks shook her head. "Maybe the Duke has a contract."

"Contract! Tir's bones, it'll take us the rest of the season just to get back to Valdaire. Why do we need a contract?"

"Have you ever seen the sea?" asked Seli.

"No—why?"

"Well, that's reason enough to go south. I've seen it—you'll be impressed."

"What is it like?" asked Paks.

"I don't think anyone can tell you. You have to see it. I've heard the cliffs are lower here, at the Immer's mouth, than at Confaer, where I was. But even so—"

As they marched south beyond the forest, the river beside them widened. They passed through a few small towns and villages. Alured stationed some of his troops in each of these. Word trickled down from the captains that Alured was claiming the title of Duke of Immer. This meant nothing to Paks or the younger soldiers, but Stammel knew that the title had been extinct for several hundred years, since the fall of the old kingdom of Aare across the sea.

"I'm surprised that the Duke of Fall and the other nobles are accepting it," he said one night.

"That was the price of his help this year," said Vossik. All the sergeants were gathered around one fire for an hour or so. "I heard talk in Fallo's cohorts about it. If the Fallo, Andressat, and Cilwan would uphold his claim—and our Duke, of course—then he'd turn on Siniava."

"But why would they, even so?"

"It's an odd story," said Vossik, obviously ready to tell it.

"Go on, Voss, don't make us beg," growled Stammel.

"Well, it's only what I heard, after all. I don't know whether those Fallo troops know the truth, or if they're telling it, but here it is. It seems that Alured used to be a pirate on the Immerhoft—"

"We knew that—"

"Yes, but that's the beginning. He'd captured another ship, and was about to throw the prisoners over, the way pirates do—"

"Into the water?" asked Paks.

Someone laughed. Vossik turned to her. "Pirates don't want a mess on their ships—so they usually do throw prisoners overboard—"

"But don't they swim or wade to shore?" asked Natzlin.

"They can't. It's too far, and the water is deep."

"I can swim a long way—" said Barra.

"Not that far. Tir's gut, Barra, you haven't seen the sea yet. It could be a day's march from shore, the ship, when they toss someone out." Vossik took a long swallow of sib and went on. "Anyway, one of the prisoners was a mage—or said he was. He started calling to Alured, telling him he should be a prince by rights."

"I'd have thought Alured wouldn't listen to prisoners' yells," said Stammel. "He doesn't look the type.'

"No," agreed Vossik. "He doesn't. But it seems he'd had some sort of tale from his father—about being born of good blood, or whatever. So he had the man brought to him, and the mage told him a long tale about his ancestors. How he was really heir to a vast kingdom, and was wasting his time as a pirate."

"He believed that?" Haben snorted and reached his own mug into the sib. "I'd heard pirates were superstitious, but—"

"Well, the man offered proof. Said he'd seen scrolls in old Aare that proved it. Offered to take Alured there, and prove his right to the kingdom."

"To Aare? That heap of sand?"

"How do you know, Devlin? You haven't been there."

"No, but I've heard. No one's ever said anything was left in Aare but ruins."

"That's what the mage told Alured—that he'd been in the ruins, and could find the proof of Alured's ancestry."

"It seems to me," said Erial, "that it's extra trouble to hunt up ancestors like that. What difference does it make anyway? Our Duke's got his steading without dragging in hundreds of fathers and fathers' fathers."

"Or mothers," muttered Barra.

"You know they're different here in Aarenis," said Stammel. "Think of Andressat."

"That stuffed owl," said Barra.

"No—don't be that way, Barra. He's a good fighter, and a damn good count for Andressat. Most other men would have lost Andressat to Siniava years ago. He's proud of his ancestors—true—but he's someone they could be proud of as well."

"But go on about Alured, Voss," said Stammel. "What happened?"

"As I said, he already had some idea that he was nobly bred. So he listened to this fellow, and sailed back to old Aare with him. Then—now remember, I got this from the Fallo troops; I don't say it's true—then the mage showed him the proof. They say that Alured believed it—an old scroll, showing the marriages, and such, and proving that he was in direct descent from that Duke of Immer who was called back to Aare in the troubles."

"But Vossik, it wouldn't take much—any decent mage could fake something like that!" Erial looked around at the others; some of them nodded.

"I didn't say I believed it, Erial. But Alured did. It fitted what he wanted, let's say. If Aare had been worth anything, it would have meant the throne of Aare—if it was true. It certainly meant the lands of Immer."

"And so he left the sea, and settled into the forest to be a land pirate? How was that being a duke?"

"Well—again—this is hearsay. Seems he came to the Immer ports first, and tried to get them to swear allegiance—"

"But he'd been a pirate!"

"Yes, I know. He wasn't thinking clearly, perhaps. Then he hired a lot of local toughs, dressed them in the old colors of Immer, and tried to parley with the Duke of Fall."

"Huh. And came out with a whole skin?"

"He wasn't stupid enough to put it in jeopardy—this took place on the borders of Fallo. The Duke reacted as you might expect, but—well—he didn't much care what happened in the southern forest, as long as it didn't bother him. And, so his men say, he's longsighted—won't make an enemy unnecessarily."

"But what about Siniava?"

"Well, Alured wasn't being accepted as Duke of Immer any more than Siniava was accepted as Count of the South Marches. Now this bit I got from one of Alured's men. Siniava promised Alured the dukedom if he'd break up the Immer River shipping, and protect Siniava's movements in the area. That's why no one could trace him after Rotengre."

"Yes, but—"

"But a couple of things happened. First, Andressat. Andressat didn't accept Alured's claim, but he was polite: read the scroll, said he could understand Alured's feelings, but pushed the decision off on the Duke of Fall. He let Alured look at his archives, and said if Fallo was ever convinced, he'd back him. So when Siniava tried to get Alured to move on Andressat's flank, he wouldn't. Then the wood-wanderers: you remember that old man we met in Kodaly, that time?" Stammel nodded. "Alured had befriended them when he moved into the forest, so they were on his side. Same time, our Duke had befriended them for years in the north, and northern Aarenis. From that, our Duke knew what Alured wanted. And he knew what Fallo wanted, which was to marry into a northern kingdom—and he knew that Sofi Ganarrion had a marriageable child—"

"But Sofi's not a king—"

"Yet. Remember what he's always said. And with Fallo behind him—"

"Gods above! You mean—"

"Somehow our Duke and the Halveric convinced the Duke of Fall that Alured's help in this campaign was worth that much to him. So the Duke of Fall agreed to back Alured's claim, and Andressat fell into line, and we got passage through the forest and Siniava didn't."

Paks shivered. She had never thought of the maneuvering that occurred off the battlefield. "But is Alured really the Duke of Immer?"

Vossik shrugged. "He has the title. He will be ruling. What else?"

"But if he's not really—by blood, I mean—"

"I don't see that it matters. He'll be better as a duke than a pirate: he'll have to govern, expand trade, stop robbing—"

"Will he?" Haben looked around the whole group before going on. "I wouldn't think, myself, that a pirate-turned-brigand would make a very good duke. What's the difference between taxes and robbery, if it comes to that?"

"He's not stupid, Haben." Vossik looked worried. "It will have to be better than Siniava—"

"That's my point. Siniava claimed a title—claimed to be governing his lands—but we all saw what that meant in Cha and Sibili. He didn't cut off trade entirely, as Alured has done on the Immer, no—but would any of us want to live under someone like him? I remember the faces in those cities, if you don't."

"But he fought Siniava—"

"Yes—at the end. For a good reward, too. I'm not saying he's all bad, Vossik; I don't know. But so far he's done what any mercenary might—gone where the gold is. How will he govern? A man who thinks he's nobly born, and has been cheated of his birthright—what will he do when we reach the Immer ports?"

They found out at Immerdzan, where the Immer widened abruptly into a bay. It sheltered four ports: Immerdzan and Aliuna, across the river from each other, Ka-Immer, seaward of Immerdzan, and Seafang, high on the last rocky point of the bay on Aliuna's side. Seafang alone had not been controlled by Siniava in the past few years; it was more a pirates' lair than a port anyway. But Immerdzan, Ka-Immer, and Aliuna had been governed by Siniava's minions.

Immerdzan required no formal assault. It had never been fortified on the land side, beyond a wall hardly more than man-high with the simplest of gates. The army marched in without meeting any resistance. The streets were crowded and dirty; the air stank of things Paks had never smelled before. Paks got her first look at the bay, here roiled and murky from the Immer's output. The shore was cluttered with piers and wharves, with half-rotted pilings, the skeletons of boats, boats sinking, boats floating, new boats, spars, shreds of sail, nets hung from every available pole, and festooned on the houses. She saw small naked children, skinny as goats, diving and swimming around the boats. Most of them wore their hair in a single short braid, tied with bright bits of cloth.

Beyond the near-shore clutter, the bay lay wide and nearly empty under the hot afternoon sun. A few boats slid before the wind, their great triangular sails curved like wings. Paks stared at them, fascinated. One changed direction as she watched, the dark line of the hull shortening and lengthening again, now facing another way. Far in the distance she could see the high ground beyond the bay, and southward the water turned green, then blue, as the Immer's water merged with the open sea.

Around the Duke's troops, a noisy crowd had gathered—squabbling, it seemed to Paks, in a language high-pitched and irritable. Children dashed back and forth, some still sleek and wet from the water, others grimy. Barefoot men in short trousers, their hair in a longer single braid, clustered around the boats; women in bright short skirts and striped stockings hung out of windows and crowded the doorways. One of Alured's captains called in the local language, and a sudden silence fell. Paks heard the water behind her, sucking and mumbling at the pilings, slurping. She shivered, wondering if the sea had a spirit. Did it hunger?

Alured's captain began reading from a scroll in his hand. Paks looked for Arcolin and watched his face; surely he knew what was going on. He had no expression she could read. Now the announcement, whatever it was, was finished: Alured's captain spoke to the Duke, saluted, and mounted to ride away. The crowd was silent. When he rounded the corner, a low murmur passed through them. One man shouted, hoarsely. Paks looked for him, and saw two younger men shoving a graybearded one back. Another man near them called in accented Common:

"Who of you speaks to us?"

"I do." The Duke's voice was calm as ever.

"You—you are pirates?"

"No. What do you mean?"

"That—that man—he says is now our duke—he is a pirate. You are his men—you are pirates."

"No." The Duke shook his head. Paks saw Arcolin give the others a hand signal, saw the signal passed from captains to sergeants. It was unneeded; they were all alert anyway. "We are his allies, not his men. He fought with us upriver—against Siniava."

"That filth!" The man spat. "Who are you, then, if you fight Siniava but also with pirates?"

"Duke Phelan, of Tsaia.'

"Tsaia? That's over the Dwarfmounts, all the way north! What do you here?"

"I have a mercenary company, that fights in Aarenis. Siniava—" The Duke's voice thinned, but he did not go on. "We fought Siniava," he said finally. "He is dead. Alured of the forest has been granted the Duchy of Immer, and as he aided us, so I am now aiding him."

"He is no duke!" yelled the man. "I don't know you—I heard something maybe, but I don't know you. But that Alured—he is nothing but pirate, and pirate he will be. Siniava was bad, Barrandowea knows that, but Alured! He killed my uncle, years back, out there in the bay, him and his filthy ship!"

"No matter," said the Duke. "He is the Duke of Immer now, and he rules this land—including this city. I am here to keep order until his own officers take over."

The man spat again, and turned away. The Duke said nothing more to the crowd, but set the cohorts on guard along the waterfront, and had patrols in the streets leading to and from their area. All was quiet enough, that first day. Paks felt herself lucky to be stationed on the seawall. She could look down at the boats, swaying on the waves, and catch a breath of the light wind that blew off the water. Strange birds, gray and white with black-capped heads, and large red bills, hovered over the water, diving and lifting again.

It was the next day that the executions began. Paks heard the yells from the other side of the city, but before they could get excited, the captains explained what was going on.

"The Duke of Fall and the Duke of Immer are executing Siniava's agents." Arcolin's face was closed. "We are to keep order here, in case of rioting—but we don't expect any." In fact, nothing happened in their quarter. The men and women went about their work without looking at the soldiers, and the children scampered in and out of the water freely. But the noise from across the city did not quiet down, and in the evening Cracolnya's cohort was pulled out to join the Halverics in calming the disturbance. They returned in the morning, tired and grim; Paks did not hear the details until much later. But the Duke's Company marched out of Immerdzan the following day, and the bodies hung on the wall were eloquent enough.

In Ka-Immer, the word had arrived before they did. The gates were closed. With no trained troops for defense, and only the low walls, the assault lasted only a few hours. This time the entire population was herded into the market square next to the seawall. While the Halverics and Phelani guarded them, Alured's men searched the streets, house by house, bringing more and more to stand with the others. When they were done, Alured himself rode to the edge of the square. He pointed at a man among the others. His soldiers seized him, and dragged him out of the mob. Then two more, and another. Someone yelled, from across the square, and a squad of Alured's men shoved into the crowd, flailing them aside, to seize him as well. The first man had thrown himself down before Alured, sobbing. Alured shook his head, pointed. All of them were dragged to a rough framework of spars which Alured's troops had lashed together.

A ripple of sound ran through the crowd; the people crammed back against each other, the rear ranks backing almost into Pak's squad. She and the others linked shields, holding firm. She could hardly see over the crowd. Then the first of the men lifted into sight, stretched on ropes slung over the framework. Paks stiffened; her belly clenched. Another. Another. Soon they hung in a row, one by the feet and the others by their arms. Alured's men pelted them with mud, stones, fish from the market. One of them hung limp, another screamed thinly. Paks looked away, gulped back nausea. When her eyes slid sideways, they met Keri's, equally miserable. She did not see the end, when Alured himself ran a spear into each man. She felt, through the movement of the crowd, that an end had come, and looked up to see the bodies being lowered.

But it was not the end. Alured spoke, in that strange language, gesturing fiercely. The crowd was still, unmoving; Paks could smell the fear and hatred of those nearest her. He finished with a question: Paks recognized the tone of voice, the outflung arm, the pause, waiting for an answer. It came as a dead fish, flung from somewhere in the crowd, that came near to its mark. His face darkened. Paks could not hear what he said, but his own soldiers fanned out again, coming at the crowd.

Before they reached it, the crowd erupted into sound and action. Jammed as they were against a thin line of Phelani and Halverics holding the three landward sides of the market, they somehow managed to turn and move at once. Paks' squad was forced back, by that immense pressure. They could hear nothing but the screams and bellows of the crowd; they had been ordered to guard, not attack. But they were being overwhelmed. Most of the people had no weapons; their weapon was simply numbers. Like Paks, they were reluctant to strike unarmed men and women—but equally, they did not want to be overrun.

Behind, in the streets that led to the market, Paks could hear other troops coming, and shouted commands that were but pebbles of noise against the stone wall around them. She tried to stay in contact with the others, tried to fend off the crowd with the flat of her sword, but the pressure was against them all. A man grabbed at her weapon, screaming at her; she raised it, and he hit her, hard, under the arm. Almost in reflex, Paks thrust, running the sword into his body. He fell under a storm of feet, that kept coming at her. She fended them off as best she could, pressing close to the rest of the squad as they tried to keep together and keep on their feet.

A gap opened between them and the next squad; the crowd poured through, still bellowing. Paks was slammed back into the building behind her; she could feel something—a window ledge, she supposed—sticking into her back. Faces heaved in front of her, all screaming; hands waved, grabbed at her weapon. She fought them off, panting. She had no time to look for Stammel or Arcolin; she could hear nothing now but the crowd. They had broken through the ring in many places, now, and streamed away from the market, lurching and falling in their panic. A child stumbled into her and fell, grabbing at her tunic as he went down, screaming shrilly. Paks had no hand to spare for him, and he disappeared under the hurrying feet.

By the time she could move again, most of the crowd was gone. She could see Alured riding behind his soldiers as they tried to stop those in the rear. She finally saw Arcolin, and then Stammel, beyond the tossing heads. Then she could hear them. The cohort reformed, joined the others, and was sent in pursuit of the fugitives. But by sundown, barely a fifth had been retaken, mostly women and children too weak to run far, or too frightened. Paks, shaken by the morning's events, was upset still more by the treatment of those she helped recapture. Alured was determined that none of Siniava's sympathizers would survive, and that all would acknowledge his rank and rule. To this end, he intended, as he explained to Phelan in front of the troops, to frighten the citizens into submission.

Paks expected the Duke to argue, but he said nothing. He had hardly seemed to smile since Siniava's death, and since reaching the coast had spent hours looking seaward. She did not know—none of them knew—what was troubling him. But more and more Paks felt that she could not live with what was troubling her. The looks of fear and loathing turned on them—the muttered insults, clear enough even in a foreign tongue—the contempt of Alured's troops, when the Phelani would not join them in "play," which to them meant tormenting some poor citizen—all this seemed to curdle her belly until she could hardly eat, and slept but little, waking from troubled dreams.

Paks tried to smother these feelings. She had spoken out once—that was enough for any private. As long as she wore the Duke's colors, she owed him obedience. He had done a lot for her, had honored her more than most. Surely, the Duke's service was worth a little discomfort, even this unease. When they marched out of Ka-Immer, leaving a garrison of Alured's men behind, Paks tried to tell herself the worst was over. But it wasn't. In town after town, along the Immerhoft coast, the same scenes were played. Alured, it seemed, knew of Siniava's agents in every one. Or they refused his lordship, remembering him as a pirate, and he had to enforce his will. The mercenaries did not participate in the executions and tortures, but without them Alured lacked the troops to force so many towns.

None of them knew how long it would last—where the Duke was planning to stop. Surely he would, they thought. Any day he would turn back, would march to Valdaire. But he said nothing, staring south across the blue endless water. Uneasiness ran through the Company like mice through a winter attic.

Paks thought no one had noticed her in particular until Stammel came to her guardpost one night. He stood near her, unspeaking, for a few minutes. Paks wondered what he wanted. Then he sighed, and took off his helmet, rumpling up his hair.

"I don't need to ask what's wrong with you," he began. "But something has to be done."

Paks could think of nothing to say.

"You aren't eating enough for someone half your size. You'll be no good to any of us if you fall sick—"

"I'm fine—" began Paks, but he interrupted.

"No, you're not fine, and neither am I. But I'm keeping my food down, and sleeping nights, which is more than you're doing. And I don't want to lose a good veteran in all this. We don't have that many."

Paks nodded slowly. "So many of us aren't—aren't really the Company."

"Yes—all those new people we've picked up here and there. They aren't the same." Stammel paused again. He put his helmet back on, and rubbed his nose. "I don't know if they ever will be—if we ever will be—what we were." His voice trailed away.

"I keep—keep seeing—" Paks could not go on.

"Paks, you—" Stammel cleared his throat. "You shouldn't be in this."

She was startled enough to make a choked sound, as if she'd been hit. "What—why—"

"You don't." His voice gathered firmness as he went on. "By Tir, I can't stand by and see you fall apart. Not for this. You've served the Duke as well as anyone could. D'you think he doesn't know it? Or I?" Now he sounded almost angry. "You don't belong here, in this kind of fighting. That Marshal was right; even the Duke said you might be meant for better things." He stopped again, and his voice was calmer when he resumed. "I think you should leave, Paks."

"Leave the Company?" Despite the shock, she felt a sudden wash of relief at the thought of being out of it.

"Yes. That's what I came to say. Tir knows this is hard enough on me—and I'm older, and—But you leave, Paks. Go back north. Go home, maybe, or see if you can take knight's training somewhere. Don't stay in this until you can't stand yourself, or the Duke either."

"But I—how can I ask—I can't go to him—"

Stammel nodded forcefully. "Yes, you can. Tell Arcolin. The captain'll understand—he knows you. He'll tell the Duke—or you can. They'll recommend you somewhere, I'm sure of it."

"But to leave the Duke—"

"Paks, I've got nothing to say against him. You know that. He's been my lord since I started; I will follow him anywhere. But—you stopped him once, when he—he might have made a mistake. Maybe—if you leave, maybe he'll look again—"

Paks was speechless, faced again with the decision she thought she'd settled in Cortes Immer. How could she leave the Company, how could she return to the north, alone? It was closer to her now than family, more familiar than the rooms of the house where she'd been born.

"Paks, I'm serious. You can't go on the way you have been. Others have noticed already; more will. Get out of this while you still can. Will you?"

"I—I'll have to think—"

"Tonight. We'll be in Sord tomorrow—more of the same, I don't doubt."

Paks found that her eyes were full of tears. She choked down a sob. Stammel gripped her shoulder. "That's what I mean, Paks. You can't keep fighting yourself, as well as an enemy. Tir knows I know you're brave—but no one can fight inside and outside both at once."

"I gave my word," she whispered.

"Yes. You did. And you've already served your term, and more. You've seen Siniava die, which ends that oath, to my mind. I don't think you're running out—and I don't think Arcolin or the Duke will, either. Will you talk to them?"

Paks stared up at the dark sky spangled with stars. Torre's Necklace was just rising out of the distant sea. She thought of the distant past, when she had dreamed of being a soldier and seeing far places, and of the last town they had been through. "I—can't—go into another—"

"No. I agree."

"But it's too late. It—"

His voice was gentle. "Would you if it weren't so late?"

"Oh, I—I don't know. Yes. If the Duke would let me—"

"He will," said Stammel. "Or I don't know Duke Phelan, and I think I do." He called back toward the lines for one of the newcomers. "He'll take your place. Come on. If I know you, you'll convince yourself by morning that you owe it to the Duke to work yourself blind, deaf, and crazy."

The following hour was not as difficult as Paks had feared. Four of the captains had been talking in Arcolin's tent; the others melted away when Stammel asked Arcolin for a few minutes of conference. Arcolin himself looked at Paks steadily, but with no anger or disappointment.

"I had been thinking," he said, "that you were overdue for leave. And this isn't your kind of fighting—mine, either, for that. But yes, if you want either leave, or to quit the Company entirely, you have the right to do so. I would hate to see you leave us for good; you've done well, and I know Duke Phelan is pleased with you. Would you consider a year's leave, with the right to return?"

Paks nodded. "Whatever you say, Captain."

"Then we'll speak to the Duke about it. I think you should come, too. He may wish to speak to you about your service."

The Duke also had not gone to bed. His gaze sharpened when he saw Paks behind Arcolin, but he waved them into his tent. Arcolin explained what Paks wanted, and the Duke gave her a long look.

"Are you displeased with my command, Paksenarrion?"

"No, my lord." She was able to say that honestly. It was not his command, but his alliances, that bothered her.

"I'm glad for that. You have been an honest and trustworthy soldier. I would hate to think I had lost your respect."

"No, my lord."

"I can see that you might well wish to leave for a while. A northern girl—a different way—but do you wish to leave the Company forever, or for a while?"

"I—don't know—I can't imagine living another way, but—"

"How could you? I see. Well, you perhaps should know that the Marshal we met outside Sibili had a discussion with my captains and me—" he glanced at Arcolin, who nodded. "You refused to leave, once—perhaps this is the right time. You would benefit from advanced training, I think. If you decide to enter another service, I will be glad to recommend you. My own recommendation would be that you seek squire's training somewhere, or the equivalent. You're already good with single weapons—learn horsemanship as well, and you might qualify for knight's training." He stopped, and looked at Arcolin. "She'll need maps for the journey north; I suppose you've already arranged about pay and settlements—"

"Not yet, my lord. She came just this evening."

"Well, then. You might stay with the Company, Paksenarrion, until you have decided how you will travel. The state Aarenis is in, going alone would not be wise. If you can find a caravan—you could hire on as a guard—that might work. I'll be sending someone back to Valdaire a little later, if you wanted to wait—" There was more of this discussion, but none of what Paks had feared. The Duke seemed more tired than anything else, a little distracted, though kind. She shook his hand, and returned to the cohort area with ArcoHn, a little let-down at how easy it had been.

Stammel was waiting. "You go on to bed. Tomorrow—"

"But tomorrow is Sord—"

"No. That's the day after. And you won't march with us. I'll have something for you to do."

"But—"

"Don't argue with me! I'm still your sergeant! By the time you get into Sord, you'll be free of all this. Now get over there and go to sleep."

To her surprise, Paks slept all night without waking.

CHAPTER TWO

"From Duke Phelan's Company, eh?" Paksenarrion nodded. The guard captain was a burly dark man of middle height. "Leaving the Company?"

Paks shrugged. "Going home for awhile."

"Hmm. Wagonmaster says you want to leave the caravan halfway—?"

"It's shorter."

"Mmm. Wagonmaster talked to your sergeant, didn't he?"

"Yes, sir."

"It'll do, then, I suppose. Do you handle a crossbow?"

"Not well, sir. I have used a longbow, but I'm no expert."

The guard captain sighed. "Can't have everything, I suppose. Now listen to me—the caravan starts making up day after tomorrow, and we'll leave the day after that or the next, depending on how many merchants join up. I'll want you here by high noon day after tomorrow, ready to work. You come in drunk, and I'll dock your pay. We have to watch the wagons as close in the city as on the trail. Don't plan on sleeping that night. Be sure to get some armor; the caravan doesn't supply it. I'd recommend chainmail. The brigands we'll run into along the coast use powerful bows. That leather you're used to won't stop arrows. You can buy mail from us, if you want." He cocked his head at her. "Clear so far?"

"Yes, sir. Be here at noon day after tomorrow, with armor."

"And not drunk."

Paks flushed. "I don't get drunk."

"Everyone gets drunk. Some know when. And by the way, no bedding with the merchants; it's bad for discipline."

Paks bit back an angry retort. "No, sir."

"Very well. See you day after tomorrow." He waved her off. As she left the room, she passed two armed men in the hall outside; one of them carried a crossbow.

"I can't believe you're going." Paks had hoped to slip out quietly, but Arne, Vik, and other friends had found her. "What'll you do by yourself?"

"I won't be alone," she said. "I'm doing caravan work—"

"Caravan work! Tir's gut, Paks, that's—"

"Some years the Duke does some. You know that."

"Yes, but that's with us—with the Company. To go out there with strangers—"

"Arne, think. How many strangers are in the Company this year?"

"You're right about that. But still, we're—we're your friends, Paks. Since I came in, you've been my friend. Is it that Gird's Marshal? Are you going to join the Girdsmen?"

"I don't know. No, I don't think so. I'm just—" Paks stared past them, trying to say it. "I'm taking leave—we're all owed leave—and I might come back or I might not."

"It's not like you." Vik scowled. "If it was Barra, leaving in a temper, I could understand it, but you—"

"I'm leaving." Paks glared at him. "I am leaving. I have talked to Stammel and Arcolin and the Duke himself, and I'm leaving."

"You'll come back," said Arne. "You have to. It won't be right." Paks shook her head and walked quickly away.

As she was leaving the camp, one of the Duke's squires caught her. "The Duke wants to see you before you go," he said. She followed him to the Duke's tent. Inside, the Duke and Aliam Halveric were talking.

"—And I think that will—Oh, Paksenarrion. The Halveric has a request to make of you."

"My lord?"

"Since you are going north—I understand you are planning to cut across the mountains?"

"Yes, my lord."

"If you'd be willing to delay your journey home long enough to carry this scroll to my steading in southern Lyonya, I will pay you well. It won't be much out of your way if you take the eastern pass."

"I would be honored, sir." Paks took the scroll, in its protective leather case, and tucked it into her belt pouch.

"Come look at this map. You should come out of the mountains near here. If you go north, you'll come to an east-west trail that runs from southern Fintha all the way to Prealith. You'll find Lyonya rangers, if you're in Lyonya, or traders on it in Tsaia, and any of them can tell you how to find it." He pointed it out on the map. "Tell them Aliam Halveric's, or they'll send you north to my brother or uncles. You don't want to go that far out of your way. When you come there, be sure you give it to my lady: Estil, her name is, and she's several hands higher than I am. Your word will come to her sooner than a courier going back up the Immer, I think."

"Yes, sir."

"And I can trust you, I'm sure, to tell no one of this. There are those who would be glad to steal that scroll, and cause trouble with it."

"No, sir, I will tell no one."

"I thank you. Will you trust my lady to pay you, or would you take it now?"

"Of course I will trust you—your lady, sir. I have not delivered it yet, though I swear I will."

"Phelan says you may seek work in the north; is that so?" Paks nodded. "Well, then, Estil may be able to help. She will do what she can, I promise you."

"Paksenarrion," said the Duke, extending his hand. "Remember that you are welcome in my hall, and in my Company, at any time. May the gods be with you."

"Ward of Falk," said the Halveric. Paks left the tent half-unwillingly. It was hard to think that she had no right here anymore. If anyone had stopped her then and asked her to stay, she might have changed her mind. But she saw none of her friends, and passed through the sentries without challenge. As she neared the city gates, the thought of the journey ahead drew her on.

She moved quickly through the crowded streets of Sord. Now that she was out of the Duke's colors, in rough brown pants and shirt with a pack on her back and a longsword at side, she heard no more of the catcalls that bothered her so. It felt very strange, being in trousers again after so long. Her legs were hot and prickly. The longsword, too, rode uneasily at her hip. She pushed it farther to the back, impatient. The pack was heavy... she had thought it was too hot to wear the chainmail shirt, and warm woollen clothes as well were folded into the pack. She cocked an eye at the sun, and strode on.

At the inn, the caravan master bustled about the court; three wagons were already loaded. He grunted as he saw her, and jerked his head toward the inn door. Paks looked and saw the guard captain there.

"Ha," he said. "You're on time." He looked her up and down critically. "Where's your mail?"

"In my pack, sir," said Paks.

"Best wear it," he said. "With all the confusion around here, I wouldn't trust leaving it anywhere. Then you can put your gear in that wagon—" he pointed. "For now, just patrol around the packed wagons. As soon as some of the others arrive, I'll organize guard shifts."

By the time they had been on the road a few days, Paks felt a little more comfortable with the other guards. She still did not feel like trusting them in a bad fight, but she found them much like other soldiers she had known. A few were outcasts of this company and that militia, but most were reliable and hard-working. Some had never been anything but caravan guards, and had no skills beyond aiming a crossbow. Others were well-trained, and had left respectable military units for all sorts of unimportant reasons.

Days passed. It was hotter on the Copper Hills track than any place Paks had yet been; the others told her this was the hottest part of the year.

"The smart ones take the spring caravans," said one, hunkered in the shade of a wagon one noon.

"When there is a spring caravan."

"Yes, well, what can you expect of merchants?"

"High prices." A general laugh followed this. Paks sweltered in her chainmail and looked east, toward the distant line of ocean. On some of the higher ground, when the heat haze didn't blur it, she could see the sand and water form long, intricate curves. It looked cool out there. Finally she asked someone why they didn't travel closer to the ocean.

"Where are you from?"

"The north," she said. "Northwest of Vérella."

"Oh. That's inland, isn't it? You don't know much about the sea. Well, if we went closer to the sea, we'd get down in the worst country you can imagine. Sand—have you ever tried walking through sand?"

"I walked on a little bit of beach, between Immerdzan and—"

"No, not a beach. Dry sand—loose sand. It's—oh, blast. It's—it's worse than a dry plowed field." That Paks could understand, and she nodded. He went on. "So think about these wagons—the wheels sink in, and the mules labor. We labor. And then it's swamp. Sticky, wet, salt marsh. And more sand. And it's not cool—its beastly hot, and the water is salt, and everything stinks. Yech."

"And don't forget the pirates," put in another of the guards.

"I was coming to that. Pirates—they call it the robber's coast, you know."

"But how do pirates live there?"

"Some people like eating crabs and clams and things. There's plenty of that shellfish. There are freshwater springs here and there, so they say. A few miserable shacky villages. And the pirates have ships, and can sail away."

Despite the ominous name of robber's coast, and the caravan master's precautions—or because of them—no bandits showed their faces, and the caravan crawled steadily northward without any trouble. Paks practiced the crossbow, and impressed the other guards with her fencing. She, in turn, spent plenty of time spitting out dirt after trying unarmed combat with the others. They had tricks she had never seen in the Company.

Finally, she saw the smudge on the horizon ahead, where the Dwarfmounts crossed the line of the Copper Hills. As they came closer, she could see that they ran east of the present coast line, and saw the angle of shore change from sand and mud to rock again.

"That's the Eastbight," said a merchant, when he saw her looking. "If you sail, you have to get well out for the best currents."

"And where you don't ever want to go," added one of the guards, "is over there—" He pointed to a wide bay that lay in the angle. "That's Slaver's Bay. If there's a robber on the coast, there's ten in Slaver's Bay. It'd take a Company the size of your Duke's to keep you safe in that place."

"I've traded there," objected another merchant. The guard looked at him.

"Well," he said finally, "they must not have liked your face—or your fortune."

The caravan had reached the crossroads, and turned west for the pass through the Copper Hills into the Eastmarches of Aarenis. Paks began to look at her map again, hoping she could find the trail that led to the eastern pass of the Dwarfwatch. The other guards kept suggesting that she find a companion, but she was reluctant to ask anyone; she didn't want everyone on the caravan to know where she was going. Finally they took it on themselves to look.

"If you want a traveling companion, there's another that's leaving us at the Silver Pass."

"Oh?" Paks kept working at the crossbow mechanism. "Who is it?"

"That elf." She looked up, startled. She hadn't known there was an elf with the caravan. Jori grinned wickedly. "Proud as elves are, you won't have to worry about 'im bothering you."

Paks ignored that. "What's he leaving for?"

Jori's smile faded. "Oh—says he's going to the Ladysforest. You know, the elf kingdom. But he'd be going part of the way with you."

"Huh." Paks set the crossbow down and stood up, stretching. "Where is he?"

"Over there." Jori cocked his chin at the group around the big fire. "I'll introduce you, eh?"

"Not yet. I want to see him first."

"In the gray cloak, then," said Jori.

He looked to be a fingersbreadth shorter than she was, Paks thought, and he didn't look like the elves she had seen, but for something a little alien in the set of his green-gray eyes, and his graceful way of moving. His voice held some of the elven timbre and music.

"No, I have business in my own kingdom," he was saying to a merchant of spice.

"But don't you fear the high trails alone?" asked another.

"Fear?" His voice mocked them and his hand dropped lightly to the golden hilt of a slender sword. The merchants nodded and murmured. Paks looked closely at the sword. Very slender—a dueller's blade, she thought. If he had not been elvish, she would have suspected bravado rather than confidence in that word. He was slender and moved lightly. She could not tell, for the strange billowing style of his tunic, whether his shoulders were broad enough for a practiced warrior. His hands were sinewy, but she saw no training scars or calluses. Was it the firelight, or did elves not callus? One of the merchants looked up then and noticed her.

"Ho, a guard! It's that tall wench—come to the fire, girl, and be warm." He waved an expansive arm. Paks grinned and stayed where she was.

" 'Tis warm enough here, by your leave. But I heard talk of the high trails, and came near to listen."

"What do you want with that? Are you planning to skip the caravan and go north?"

"I'd heard of several trails," said Paks. She didn't want to say exactly how much she knew. "And I knew someone who'd been over Dwarfwatch. But if there's a shorter way—"

"Oh, shorter," said another merchant. "That's with where you're going in the north—" He looked closely at Paks, but she didn't say anything. After a moment he shrugged and went on. "If you go straight across at Silver Pass, you come out between Prealith and Lyonya, but there's a good trail on the north side that will bring you west again and out near the southeast corner of Tsaia." Paks nodded. She felt rather than saw the elf watching her. "That trail meets the one crossing from Dwarfwatch; there's a cairn at the crossing, and a rock shelter. If you're headed for Tsaia, the distance isn't less, but you can travel faster alone, and the passes themselves are easier than the Dwarfwatch route. That high one—" he broke off and shook his head.

Paks followed this with interest. "I thank you, sir," she said. "I have no great knowledge of mountaincraft; I had heard only that the pass was short."

The merchant laughed. "Aye—it's short enough. If you get over it. Ice in midsummer, and blizzards—dangerous always, and for one alone—well, were I you, I'd take the eastern passes, the ones we spoke of. You'll be in mountainous country longer, but none of it as high or as cold. Does the Wagonmaster know you're leaving?"

"Of course, sir!" Paks was angry, but she saw by the reactions of the others that no insult was meant.

"I would ask him to free you for the eastern pass," said the merchant seriously. "Especially since you're traveling alone."

Paks nodded and said no more. The merchants returned to their usual topics: what product they had found in this or that port, and how well they sold; who ruled what cities, and what the recent war would do to the markets.

"What I worry about," said one enormous man in a heavy yellow cloak, "is what it will do to the tolls. They say the Guild League spent and spent for this last year's fighting—they'll have to get it back somehow, and what easier than by raising the tolls?"

"They need us too much," said another. "And they were founded to give trade a chance. The Guild League won't rob us, take my word for it."

"If they do, there's the river," suggested another. "Now Alured's settled down to play Duke, he'll be letting us use the river again—"

"Ha! That old wolf! By Simyits, you can't believe a pirate's changed by gaining a title, can you? And what have we ever got, come to that, from the noble lords and their kind? They want our gold, right enough, when a war's brewing, but after that it's—oh, those merchanters: no honor, no loyalty—tax 'em down, they're getting too proud." Paks found herself laughing along with the rest, though she, too, thought of merchanters as having no honor—like the militia of Vonja. It had never occurred to her before to wonder what the merchanters thought of anyone.

When she came off watch that night, and stopped by the guards' fire for a mug of sib, a cloaked figure rose across the circle of light to greet her. She caught a flash of green from wide-set eyes.

"Ah. Paksenarrion, is it not?"

Paks stood stiffly, uncertain. "Yes. And you, sir?"

He bowed, gracefully, but with a curious mocking style. "Macenion, you may call me. An elf, as you see." Paks nodded, and reached for the pot of sib. "Allow me—" he said softly, and a tin mug rose from the stack beside the pot, dipped into the liquid, and rose to Paks' hand. She froze, her breath caught in her throat. "Go on," he said. "Take it." She looked at the mug, then her hand, then folded her fingers gingerly around the mug's handle. She nearly dropped it when it sank into her grip. She let her breath out, slowly, and sipped. It tasted like sib—she wondered if he had put anything into it. She froze again as another mug rose from the pile, filled itself, and sailed across the fire to Macenion. He plucked it from the air, bowed again to her, and took a sip himself. "I apologize," he said lightly, "if I frightened you. I had heard you were a warrior of some experience."

Paks drank her sib, wondering what to make of this. She certainly did not want to admit being frightened of a little magic, but he had seen her reaction. She set the mug down firmly, when she finished, and sat down slowly. "I had not seen that before," she said finally.

"Evidently," he replied. He brought his own mug back to the stack and sat near her. "When I asked," he began again, "everyone assured me that you had an excellent reputation." Paks felt a tingle of irritation; what gave him the right to ask about her? "You were in Phelan's Company, I understand." He looked at her and she nodded. "Yes. One of the other guards had heard about you. Not the usual sort of mercenary, he said." Again Paks felt a flickering anger. "And this evening past, you said you were going north over the mountains before we reached Valdaire. Alone, I assumed—?" Paks nodded again. "I might," he said, looking down at his hands clasped in his lap. "I might be able to help you. I know those trails—difficult for one with no mountain experience, but safe enough."

"Oh?" Paks reached out and refilled her mug.

"Unless you prefer to travel alone. Few humans do."

Paks shrugged. "I have no one to travel with. I'd appreciate your advice on the trail." She was remembering Stammel's warning about those who might seek to travel with her.

The elf moved restlessly. "If you are willing, I thought we might travel together—as far as the borders of the Ladysforest, at least. I could tell you about the trails from there." He sat back, and looked at her from under dark brows. "It would be far safer for you, Paksenarrion, and a convenience to me. While the trails are not as dangerous as these caravan roads, all trails have their hazards, and it is as well to have someone who can draw steel at your back."

Paks nodded. "I see. It is well thought of. But—forgive me, sir—you seem to know more of me than I of you."

He drew himself up. "I'm an elf—surely you know what that is."

"Yes, but—"

His voice sharpened. "I fear I have no relatives or friends nearby that you can question. You will have to trust my word, or go alone. I am an elf, a warrior and mage—as you have seen—and I am returning to my own kingdom of the Ladysforest."

"I'm sorry to have angered you, sir, but—"

"Have you been told bad tales of elves? Is that it?"

Paks thought back to Bosk. "Yes—some."

His voice eased. "Well, then, it's not your fault. You must know that elves are an elder race, older far than men. Some humans are jealous of our knowledge and our skills. They understand little of our ways, and we cannot explain to those who will not listen. But elves, Paksenarrion, were created by the Maker himself to be the enemy of all evil beings. It is elves that orcs hate most, for they know their destiny is on the end of our blades: the dark powers of the earth come never near the elven kingdoms."

Paks said nothing, but wondered. She had heard that the elves were indeed far older than men, and that elves never died of age alone. But she had not heard that elves were either good or evil, as orcs and demons were clearly evil, and saints like Gird and Falk were clearly good.

In the next few days, she found out what she could of elves in general and Macenion in particular. It was not much. But as the higher slopes closed in on the caravan track, she saw how easy it would be to miss her trail. Traveling with someone who had been there before seemed much wiser.

Paks saw the last of the caravan winding away to the west, higher into Silver Pass, with great relief. She had not felt at home with the other caravan guards; she had not been able to give them her trust, as she had her old companions. But now she was free—free to go north toward home, to adventure as she would. She imagined herself, as she had so often, riding up the track from Three Firs to her home, with gifts for everyone and money to spend at a fair. She could almost hear her mother's gasp of delight, the squeals of her younger brothers and sisters.

She imagined her father struck silent, awed at her wealth and the sword she bore. She turned to grin at Macenion beside her, whose long-sighted gaze lingered on the caravan's dust.

"Well, they're all gone by the smell. Let's get moving."

He turned his gray-green eyes away from the pass and glared at her. "Must you be in such hurry? I want to be sure no thief drops out to trail us."

Paks loosened her sword in its sheath. "Unlikely now. And with your magic arts, and this sword, we shouldn't have much to fear. I wanted to find a good camping spot before dark."

"Very well. Come along, then, and keep a good watch. Move as quietly as a human can."

Paks bit back an angry retort. It wouldn't do to quarrel with her only companion for the trip across the mountains; she had no other guide, and elves made dangerous enemies. She turned to the sturdy pack pony she'd bought from the Wagonmaster and checked the pack a last time, then stroked Star's neck, and started up the narrow trail that forked away from the caravan route. She hoped Macenion would mellow as they traveled. So far he had been scornful, sarcastic, and critical. It seemed obvious that he knew a great deal about the mountains and the various trails across them, but he made his superior knowledge as painful as possible for anyone else. Now he walked ahead, leading his elven-bred horse whose narrow arched neck expressed disdain for the pack on its back.

But at the campfire that night, Macenion seemed to have walked out part of his bad temper, and was once again the charming elf she had first met. He lit the fire with one spell, and seasoned their plain boiled porridge with another. He set a spell to keep the horse and pony from wandering. Paks wanted to ask if he could not set one to guard the camp, so that they could both sleep through the night, but thought better of it, and offered to take the first watch instead.

Though it had been hot that afternoon, the night was cold, with the feeling of great spaces in movement that comes only on the flanks of mountains. Nothing threatened them that Paks could see or hear, but twice the hair on her arms and neck stood straight, and fear caught the breath in her throat. Macenion, when she woke him at the change of watch, simply laughed lightly. "Wild lands care not for humans, Paksenarrion—neither to hunt nor hide. That is what you feel, that indifference." She surprised herself by sleeping easily and at once.

For two days they climbed between the flanks of the mountain. Midway of the second, they were high enough to see once more the caravan route below and behind them, and the twist where it crossed the spine of the Copper Hills. Paks could barely discern the pale scar of the route itself, but Macenion declared that he could see another caravan moving on it, this time from west to east. Paks squinted across the leagues of sunlit air, wavering in light and wind, and grunted. She could not see any movement at all, and the brilliant light hurt her eyes. She turned to look up their trail. It crawled over a hump of grass-grown rock—what she would have called a mountain, if the higher slopes had not been there—and disappeared. In a few moments, Macenion too turned to the trail.

To her surprise, the other side of the hump was forested; all that afternoon they climbed through thick pinewoods smelling of resin and bark. Paks added dry branches to Star's pack. They camped at the upper end of that wood, looking out over its dark patchwork to the east, where even Paks could see the land fall steeply into the eastern ocean. Macenion gazed at it a long time.

"What do you see?" Paks finally asked, but he shook his head and did not answer. She went back to stirring their porridge. Later that night, he began to talk of the elves and their ways—the language and history—but most of it meant little to Paks. She thought he seemed pleased that she knew so little.

"My name's elven," she said proudly, when Macenion seemed to be running down. "I know that much: Paksenarrion means tower of the mountains."

"And I suppose you think you were named that for your size, eh?" Macenion sneered. "Don't be foolish; it's not elven at all."

"It is, too!" Paks stiffened angrily. She had always been as proud of her name as its meaning.

"Nonsense! It's from old Aare, not from elves. Pakseenerion, royal tower, or royal treasure, since they used towers for their treasuries."

"That's the same—" Paks had not clearly heard the difference in sounds.

"No. Look. The elven is—" Macenion began scratching lines in the dust. "It has another sign, one that you don't use. Almost, but not quite, the same as your 'ks' sound—and the first part means peak or high place. The elven word enarrion means mountain; the gnomes corrupted it to enarn, and the dwarves to enarsk, which is why these mountains are the dwarfenarsk—or in their tongue, the hakkenarsk. If your name were really elven, it would mean peak or high place in the mountains. But it doesn't. It's human, Aaren, and it means royal treasure."

Paks frowned. "But I was always told—"

"I don't care what you were told by some ignorant old crone, Paksenarrion; neither you nor your name is elven, and that's all." Macenion smirked at her, then pointedly lifted the kettle without touching it and poured himself another mug of sib.

Paks glared at him, furious again. "My grandmother was not an ignorant old crone!"

"Orphin, grant me patience!" Macenion's voice was almost as sharp as hers. "Do you really think, Paks, that you or your grandmother—however worthy a matron she may have been—know as much about the elven language as an elf does? Be reasonable."

Paks subsided, still angry. Put that way she could find no answer, but she didn't have to like it.

Relations were still strained the next day when they came to the first fork of the trail. Macenion slowed to a halt. Paks was tempted to ask him sharply if he knew where he was going, but a quick look at the wilderness around her kept her quiet. Whether he knew or not, she certainly didn't. Macenion turned to look at her. "I think we'll go this way," he said, gesturing.

"Think?" Paks could not resist that much.

His face darkened. "I have my reasons, Paksenarrion. Either path will get us where we wish to go; this one might provide other benefits."

"Such as?"

"Oh—" He seemed unwilling to answer directly. "There are ruins on some of the trails around here. We might find treasure—"

"Or trouble," said Paks.

His eyebrows went up. "I thought you claimed great skill with that sword."

"Skill, yes. I don't go looking for trouble." But as she spoke, she felt a tingle of anticipation. Trouble she didn't want, but adventure was something else. Macenion must have seen this in her face, for he grinned.

"After these peaceful days, I daresay you wouldn't mind a little excitement. I don't expect any, to be sure, but unless you're hiding a fortune in that pack, you wouldn't mind a few gold coins or extra weapons any more than I would."

"Honestly—no, I wouldn't." Paks found herself smiling. Ruins in the wilderness, and stray treasure, were just the sort of things she'd dreamed of as a girl.

Macenion's chosen path led them back west, by winding ways, and finally through a narrow gap into a rising valley, steep-sided, where the trail led between many tall gray stones. These stood about like tall soldiers on guard.

"What are those?" asked Paksenarrion, as they began to near the first ranks of them. The stones gave her an odd feeling, as if they were alive.

"Wardstones," said Macenion. "Haven't you ever seen wardstones before?"

Paks gave him a sharp look. "No. I wouldn't have asked, if I had." She didn't want to ask, now, what wardstones warded, or whom. But Macenion went on without her question.

"They're set as guardians, by the elder peoples," he said. "Humans don't use them, that I know of. Can't handle the power, I suppose."

Paks clamped her lips on the questions that filled her mind. How did they guard? And what?

"It's the patterns they make," Macenion went on. "Patterns have power; even you should know that—" He looked at her, and Paks nodded. "If intruders come, then, it will trouble the pattern, and that troubling can be sensed by those who set the stones."

"Are we intruders?" asked Paks.

Macenion laughed, a little too loudly. "Oh my, no. These are old, Paksenarrion, very old. Whatever set them is long gone from here."

"But are they still in those—those patterns you spoke of?" Paks felt something, an itch along her bones.

Macenion looked around. "Yes, but it doesn't matter."

"Why not?" asked Paks stubbornly. "If it's the patterns that have the power, and they're still in the patterns, then—"

"Really, Paksenarrion," said Macenion loftily. "You must realize that I haven't time to explain everything to you. But I do know more about this sort of thing than any human, let alone a very young soldier. You must simply take my word for it that we are in no danger from these stones. The power is long past. And even if it weren't—" he fixed her with a glance from his brilliant eyes, then tapped his wallet suggestively. "I have spells here to protect us from such as these."

Paks found nothing to say to this. She could not tell whether Macenion really knew about such magic, or whether it was all idle boasting, but her bones tingled as they passed between the wardstones, rank after rank. Did Macenion not feel it because of his greater powers? Or perhaps because of his duller perceptions? She did not care to find out. For the next glass, as they climbed between the stones, she thought as little as possible, and resisted the temptation to draw her sword.

They were nearly free of the stone ranks when Paks heard a sharp cry from behind. Before she thought, she whirled, snatching her sword free of the scabbard. Macenion was down, sprawled on the rocky trail, his face contorted with pain. When he saw her standing with naked sword in hand, he gave another cry.

"No! No weapons!" He was pale as milk, now. Paks felt, rather than heard, a resonant thrum from around them. She spared a quick look around the valley, and saw nothing but the shimmer of the sun on many stones. She moved lightly toward Macenion.

"Don't worry," she said, grinning at him. "It's not drawn for you. What happened?"

"Sheathe it," he said. "Hurry!"

Paks was in no mood to listen to him. She felt much better with her sword in hand. "Why?" she asked. "Here, let me help you up." But Macenion had scrambled away from her, and now staggered to his feet, breathing hard. She noticed that he put little weight on his left foot. "Are you hurt?"

"Paksenarrion, listen to me. Sheathe that sword. At once." He was staring behind her, over her shoulder.

"Nonsense," said Paks briskly. "It's you that's being silly now." She still felt a weight of menace, but it was bearable as long as she had her weapons ready. "Come—let's be going. Or shall I bring Star, and let you ride?"

"We must—hurry, Paksenarrion. Maybe there will be time—" He lurched toward her, and she offered her left arm. He flinched from it, and started to circle her. Paks turned, scanning the valley again. Still nothing. Sun glittered off the wardstones, seemed to shimmer as thick as mist between them. She shook her head to clear her vision. Macenion was already a few yards ahead of her.

"Wait, now—" she called. "Let me lead, where I can guard you." But at her call Macenion stumbled on even faster. He reached the horses, and clung to Windfoot's saddle as he clapped Star on the rump. Paks lengthened her stride, angry now, and muttering curses at cowardly elves. The quality of light altered, seeming to match her mood, ripping across the stones. Paks was too angry to be frightened, but she moved faster. For an instant, Macenion turned a white face back towards her; she saw his eyes widen. Then he screamed and flailed forward. Paks did not look back; she broke into a run as Macenion and the animals took off up the trail. She felt a building menace behind her, rising swiftly to a peak that demanded action.

As they passed the last pair of stones, the light seemed to fail for an instant, as if someone had filled the valley with thick blue smoke. Then a blaze of white light, brighter than sunlight, flashed over them. Paks saw her shadow, black as night, thrown far ahead on the trail. A powerful blow in the back sent her sprawling facedown on the trail; she had no time to see what had happened to Macenion or the horses. Choking dust rose in clouds, and heavy thunder rumbled through her body. Then it was gone, and silence returned. From very far away, Paks heard the scream of a hawk.

When Paks caught her breath and managed to rise to her feet, she saw nothing behind or before her on the trail. Afternoon shadows had begun to strip the narrow valley; the trail itself was latticed with shadows from the stones. Ahead, upslope, the trail was scuffed and torn where Macenion and the horses had fled. Paks scowled at the place the trail disappeared behind a fold of mountain. Alone, in unknown wilderness, without supplies or her pony . . . She looked back at the valley and shook her head. She knew without thinking about it that she had no escape that way. And perhaps she could catch up to Macenion—he had been limping.

In fact, by the time she reached the turn that left the valley safely behind, she could hear him, coaxing the horses to come. When she trudged around the last rocks, she saw him, limping heavily and trying to grab Windfoot's rein. The horse edged sideways, nervous, keeping just out of reach. Paks eyed the situation for a moment before speaking.

"Would you like some help, Macenion?"

He whipped around, nearly falling, his mouth open. Then he glared at her. "You fool!" he said. Paks had not expected that; she felt her ears burning. He went on. "What did I tell you—and you had to keep waving that sword!"

"You told me there wasn't any danger," snapped Paks, furious.

"There wasn't, until you drew your sword," he said. "If you had only—"

"What did you think I'd do, when you let out a yell?"

"You?" He sniffed, twitching his cape on his shoulders. "I should have realized the first thing a fighter would do would be draw steel—"

"Of course," said Paks. "You hadn't said a word about not drawing, either."

"I didn't think it was necessary," muttered Macenion. "I never dreamed you would, for no reason like that—" Paks snorted, and he went on hurriedly. "If we went through quietly, nothing would happen—"

"You told me nothing could happen." Paks felt the length of her blade, lightly, to see that it was unharmed, then slid it into the scabbard. "If you'd warned me, I wouldn't have drawn. I don't like liars, Macenion." She looked hard at him. "Or cowards. Did you even look to see if I was still alive?"

"I'm no liar. I just didn't think you needed to know." He looked aside a moment. "And I was coming back as soon as I caught Windfoot or Star, to find you—or bury you."

Paks was not at all sure she believed that. "Thanks," she said drily. "Why did you choose this path—the real reason, this time."

"I told you: it's shorter. And there are ruins—"

"And?"

"And I'd heard of this place."

Paks snorted again. "I'll warrant you had. So you wandered in to see what it looked like, eh?"

"I knew what it looked like." He glared at her. "Don't look at me like that, human. You nearly got us both killed—"

"Because you didn't tell me the truth."

"Because all you thought of was fighting—weapons. I knew what it looked like because I'd spoken to someone who was here—a cousin of mine. She said it was quite safe for peaceful folk." He emphasized peaceful. Paks had nothing more to say for the moment. She looked at Windfoot, and spotted Star behind a screen of trees. She clucked softly, holding out her hand. Windfoot looked from her to Macenion, and took a few steps back down the trail. Paks stepped into the middle of it, and clucked again. Windfoot's ears came up; the horse looked at her.

Paks walked forward, and took the dangling rein in her hand. The other rein was broken near the bit ring. Macenion was staring at her strangely; she handed him the rein without comment, and called Star. The pony nickered, pushing through the undergrowth. Once out of the trees, she came to Paks at once, pushing her head into Paks' chest.

"All right, all right." Paks untied one side of the pack and pulled out an apple. They were going soft anyway. "Here." The pony wrapped her lips around the apple and munched, dribbling pungent bits of apple from her mouth. Windfoot whuffled, watching Star, and Paks dug out another apple for the horse. "How's your foot?" she asked Macenion, who had watched this silently. "I saw you were limping."

"Not bad," he said. "I can walk." Paks started to say he could run, but decided not to. She turned back to Star, checking her legs and hooves for injuries and the packsaddle for balance. Everything seemed to be in place. Macenion, meanwhile, mended the broken rein. They traveled until nearly dark, hardly speaking.

CHAPTER THREE

More than ever Paks realized how she had depended on the plain honesty of her friends in the Duke's Company. Perhaps they were not magicians or elves with mysterious powers—but they did not pretend to powers they did not have. What they promised, they performed. And in a fight of any kind, they would never leave her behind, possibly injured or dead. Now, wandering in the mountain wilderness with Macenion for a guide, she wondered if he even knew where they were. He had said nothing more about the wardstones—nor had she. He seemed as confident as ever. But she felt almost as trapped as if she were in a dungeon.

Their way—or the way Macenion led them—continued upward, day by day. The distant sea was hidden behind the shoulders of mountains now. Paks had asked if that meant they were across the pass, but Macenion had laughed. He tried to show her, on the map, how far they had come. But to Paks, the intricate folds of the mountains and the flat map had little to do with each other. Most of the time the trail ran through open forest, broken with small meadows. Paks thought it might be good sheep country. Macenion said no one farmed so far away from any market.

Wild animals had been scarce. Macenion told her of the wild sheep, the black-fleeced korylin, that spent the summers just above timberline. He had pointed out an occasional red deer in the trees, but Paks lacked the experience to spot them. They had seen plenty of rock-rabbits and other small furry beasts, but nothing dangerous. Nor did Macenion seem especially worried. Wolves, he'd said, were scarce in this region. The wild cats were too small to attack them, at least until they were high above timberline. If they saw a snowcat, he said—but Paks had never heard of snowcats.

"I'm not surprised," said Macenion, with his usual tone of superiority. "They are large—very large. I suppose you've seen the short-tailed forest cats?" Paks had not, but hated to admit it. "Humph. Well, snowcats are about three times that size, with long tails. They're called snowcats because they live high in the mountains, among the icepacks and snow; they're white and gray."

"What do they live on, up there?"

Macenion frowned. Paks saw his shoulders twitch. Finally he answered. "Souls," he said.

"Souls?"

"And anything else they can find, of course. Wild sheep, for meat. But—I don't think we'll have much trouble, at this season, Paksenarrion. The pass should not be snowed in. But if we do see one, remember that they're the most dangerous wild creature in the mountains. I don't except men—a snowcat is more dangerous than a band of brigands."

"But how? Are they—"

"I'm telling you. The snowcat is a magical beast, like the dragon and the eryx. It lives on both sides of the world, and feeds on both sides. For meat it eats wild sheep, or horses, or men. For delight it eats souls, particularly elven and human, though I understand it takes dwarven souls often enough that the dwarves fear it."

"I thought elves didn't have souls—"

Macenion suddenly looked embarrassed. "I didn't know you knew so much about elves."

"I don't, but that's what I heard—they don't have souls because they don't need them—they live forever anyway."

"That's not the reason—but in feet, you're right. Elves don't have souls—not full-blooded elves. But—" he gave her a rueful smile. "I don't like to admit it, Paks, but in fact I am not pure elven."

"But you said—"

"Well, I'm more elven than human—I do take after my elven ancestors much more. You yourself wouldn't call me human—"

Paks had to agree with that, but she still felt affronted. "Well, if you're not elven—"

"I am. I am—well—you could say—half-elven. Human-elven. If you must know, that's how I gained my mastery of human wizardry as well as elven magic." He drew himself up, and took on the expression she found most annoying.

"Oh," Paks left this topic, and returned to the other. "But the snowcat—can't we fight it off? We have a bow, and—"

"No. It is truly magical, Paksenarrion. It can spell your soul out of you before you could strike a blow. I am a mage and part elf; it will desire mine even more."

Paks thought about it. It seemed to her that this meant nothing more than death. She started to ask Macenion, and he turned, startled.

"No! By the First Tree, you humans know nothing, even of your own condition! It is not the same thing as being killed. When you die, your soul goes—well, I don't know your background, and I'd hate to upset your beliefs—" Paks glared at him, and he went on. "You have a soul, and it goes somewhere—depending on how you've lived. Is that plain enough? But if a snowcat eats your soul, it never gets where it should go. It's trapped there, in the snowcat, forever."

"Oh. But then—what does it want with a soul?"

"Paksenarrion, it's magical. It does magic with souls. I don't know how it started, or why; I only know it does. Somehow the souls it eats feed its magic powers. If we see a snowcat, we'll flee at once—try to outrun it. Whatever you do, don't look into its eyes." He walked on quietly some hundred paces. Then: "Paksenarrion, how did you make Windfoot come to you?"

She had not thought about his surprise since that day. "I don't know. I suppose—he knows me now. He knows I have apples. Horses have always liked me."

Macenion shook his head. "No. It must be something more. He's elfbred; our horses wouldn't go to humans unless—do you have any kind of magical tools? A—a bracelet, or ring, or—"

Paks thought of Canna's medallion; surely that wouldn't have moved an elfbred horse. "No," she said. "Not that I know of."

"Mmph. Would you mind if I checked that?"

"What?"

"I could—um—look for it."

"For what?"

Macenion turned on her, eyes blazing. "For whatever you used, human, to control my horse!"

"But I didn't! I don't have anything—"

"You must. Windfoot would never come to a human—"

"Macenion, any horse will come to anyone kind. Look at Star—"

"Star is a—a miserable, shaggy-coated, cow-hocked excuse of a pack pony."

Paks felt the blood rush to her face. "Star is beautiful! She's—"

Macenion sneered. "You! What do you know about—"

"Windfoot came to me. I must know something." Paks realized that her hand had found her sword-hilt. She saw Macenion glance at it. He sighed, and looked patient.

"Paksenarrion, I'm sorry I abused Star. But she is a pony, and human-bred; she is not an elfbred horse. There's a difference. Just look at Windfoot." They both looked. Windfoot cocked an ear back and whuffled, whether at Star or Paks was uncertain. Paks could not sustain her anger, with Windfoot's elegant form before her. Macenion seemed to recognize the moment her anger failed, because he went on. "If you're carrying a magical item, without knowing it perhaps, it could be dangerous—or very helpful. Magical items in the hands of the unskilled—"

Paks bristled again. "I'm not giving you anything."

"I didn't mean that." But Paks thought he had meant exactly that. "If you have such an item, I can show you how to use it. Think, Paksenarrion. Perhaps it's something that would call danger to us—wolves, say—or—"

"All right." Paks was tired of the argument. "All right; look for it. But, Macenion, what I have is mine; I'm not giving it up. If it calls danger, we'll just fight the danger."

"I understand." He looked pleased. "We can camp here—I know it's early, but I'll need time. And the horses could use the rest. They can graze in this meadow."

Shortly they had the camp set up, and both animals had been watered and fed. Macenion withdrew to one side of the fire, and brought out his pouch. Paks watched with interest as he fished inside it. He looked up at her and glared.

"Don't watch."

"Why not? I've never seen a mage—"

"And you won't. By Orphin, do you want to get your ears singed? Or your eyes burnt out? Can't I convince you that magic is dangerous?" Paks did not move. She was tired of being sneered at. Macenion muttered in what she supposed was elven, and turned his back. She thought of circling the fire to see what he was doing, but decided against it. Instead she lay back, staring up at the afternoon sky bright overhead. So far they had had good travel weather; she hoped it would continue. She shifted her hips off a sharp fragment of rock and let her eyes sag shut. She could hear the horses tearing grass nearby; to her amusement, she could distinguish Star and Windfoot by sound alone. Star took three or four quick bites of grass, followed by prolonged chewing; Windfoot chewed each bite separately. She opened her eyes to check on them and glanced at Macenion. His back still faced her. She closed her eyes again and dozed off.

"I found it." Paks opened her eyes to see Macenion's excited face. She rubbed her face and sat up.

"You found what?"

"The magic ring you're wearing." Macenion sounded as smug as he looked.

"What? I don't have any magic ring!"

"You certainly do. That one." He pointed to the intricate twist of gold wires that Duke Phelan had given her in Dwarfwatch.

"That's not magic," said Paks, but with less assurance. The Duke had said nothing about magic, and surely he would have known.

"It is. Its power is over animals; that's why you could use it on Windfoot."

"I didn't use it on Windfoot. I just called him and held out my hand . . ."

"That's all it would take. You touched it—perhaps accidentally, since you say you didn't know about it."

"I didn't—and I don't believe it." But Paks was already half-convinced.

"Where did you get it?"

"It was—my commander gave it to me, after a battle."

"As a reward?"

"Yes"

"Was it part of the loot from Siniava's army?"

"Yes."

"Well, then. He and his captains used magic devices often, so I heard. Perhaps your commander didn't know. It is magic and it is how you controlled Windfoot. You can prove it—call him now, with the ring. Don't say anything, or move, but touch the ring and think that you want him to come."

Paks looked across the meadow to see Windfoot and Star grazing side by side. She clenched her hand around the ring, and thought of Windfoot. She didn't like the idea that a ring—a ring she had received from the Duke—could have such power. She had always liked horses; horses had always liked her. She thought of Windfoot: his speed, his elegance. A quick thudding of hooves made her look up. Windfoot came at a long swinging trot, breaking to a canter. Star followed, her shorter stride syncopating the beats. Windfoot stopped a few feet away, and came forward, ears pricked.

"All right," said Paks quietly, holding up her hand for Windfoot to sniff. Star pushed in and shoved her head in Windfoot's way. "But I didn't call Star—"

"No, she came for company, I think. But that is definitely a magic ring, with the power to summon animals. See if you can make Windfoot go away."

Paks wrinkled her brow. It did not seem fair to control Windfoot this way. She flipped her hand, and the horse threw up his head and backed.

"Not that way," said Macenion, annoyed.

"Yes." Paks pushed Star's head away. "Go on, horses! Go eat your own dinners." She stood up. "I believe you; it's magic. But I don't like the idea."

"You'd rather have the power in yourself?"

"Yes. No—I don't know. It just doesn't feel right, to be able to call and send them like that."

"Humans!" snorted the elf. Paks glared at him, and he modified it. "Non-magicians don't understand magicians, that's all. Why involve right and wrong in it? The ring is magic, it's useful magic, and you should use it."

Paks had had no idea what a mountain pass would be like. Macenion told her that the pass at Valdaire wasn't really a mountain pass at all. Now, as they climbed past the forested slopes to open turf and broken rock, she wondered how, in this jumble of stone, anyone could find the way. It was a gray morning, and she felt the cold even through her travel cloak. Macenion pointed out marking cairns.

"But it's just another pile of rock."

"No, it's not just a pile of rock. It's a particular pile of rock. Look—do you see anything else like that?"

Paks looked. Rocks everywhere, but nothing that tall and narrow. "No."

"Now, look here." He pointed to a smaller pile on one side. "This is the direction."

"What is?"

"This—Paksenarrion, pay attention. The big pile tells you that this is the trail, and the little pile tells you which way is downhill."

"But are we across the pass? Aren't we going uphill?" Then she realized the simple answer, and felt her face burning. "I see," she said quickly, before Macenion could tell her. "I know. We go the other way."

"Yes. And we know it's the right trail because of the runes."

"Runes?"

"Look at this." He lifted the top rock of the small pile and turned it over. On the under face were angular marks gouged in the rock. "That's the rune for silver, which means that this is the way to Silver Pass."

"Oh." Paks looked around again. "But that only says what's downhill. Can we tell where this will come out?"

"Easily." Macenion's smile was as smug as ever. He turned over the top rock of the big pile and showed her another rune. "This means gnomes, and means that this trail ends at the rock shelter on the border of Gnarrinfulk, the gnome kingdom south of Tsaia."

"I didn't know there was one."

"Gods, yes. And you don't want to wander in there without leave." Macenion replaced the stones carefully. "It's simple, really. The big pile points uphill and has the uphill trail-end rune, and the small one points downhill and has the downhill trailend rune. Can you remember that?"

"Yes," said Paks shortly.

"Good. Let's hurry. I don't like the smell of this weather." Macenion looked at the sky above the peaks, which was, as they had often seen from below, thickened into cloud. As if his words had been a signal, a cold rain began to leak down, thin at first. They started upward.

As they climbed, forty paces at a time, Paks watched the stones near the trail darken in the rain. Instead of the rustle of rain on leaves, the water tinkled, as if a thousand thousand tiny bells rang in the stillness. The slopes around them closed in, and the trail became steeper. It was more like a stairway than a trail. When they stopped for rest, Paks looked up. The clouds seemed lower. She looked back down the trail. The cairn had disappeared into a hollow behind and below them. She was surprised at how far they had climbed.

Macenion shivered beside her. "It's getting colder—we'd better keep climbing. There's no good place to stop until we're over the top."

"You mean, this is the actual pass?"

"Yes—didn't you know? What I'm afraid of is snow—it can snow all year up here. We've been lucky with weather so for, but this rain—and if it gets colder—"

"What if it does?"

"Then we keep going. There are some undercut ledges near the top, but they aren't good shelter. We won't stop if we can possibly make it through."

But as mountain weather changes from minute to minute, so it thickened around them. Rain changed to sleet which coated their cloaks and the horses' packs, and made the trail treacherous. Paks did not even suggest stopping to eat. She fumbled a strip of meat from under her cloak and chewed it as they climbed. Wind began to funnel the sleet, now mixed with snow, down the trail. Macenion showed Paks how to wrap a cloth around her face to keep it from freezing.

All too soon the rocky slopes around them whitened as snow flurried past. They climbed higher, leaving clear tracks that filled quickly behind them. Rocks disappeared under the snow. Macenion had to shout in Paks' ear that he thought the snow had been falling at this height for more than a day. As they came around a shoulder of mountain on their right, the pitch flattened. Paks expected a change to a downhill slope, but instead met a blast of wind that nearly took her off her feet. Macenion, ahead of her, disappeared in a white fog of snow. She stumbled, and forced her way on, dragging Star behind her.

Paks finally found Macenion by stumbling into him. Windfoot was sideways to the wind, trying to turn. Macenion grabbed her arm and yelled into her ear.

"Paks! We can't go any farther this way. Drifts! Go back!"

"Where?"

"Back!" He pushed her a little, and Paks turned carefully, bracing against the wind. Star had already turned, and Paks followed her back the way they had come. At least, she hoped it was the way, for nothing remained of their tracks. With the wind at her back, shoving her along like a giant hand, she could see a little way. A dark smudge to one side caught her eye; before she could ask, Macenion's arm on her shoulder pushed her that direction. "It's one of those overhangs," he yelled in her ear.

Star and Windfoot shouldered their way to the back of the shelter and stood, heads down and together, their breath making a cloud in the gloom. Paks swiped the snow off Star's pack and rump, and wiped the pony's face clear. Ice furred her eyelashes and muzzle. Both animals were quivering with cold and exhaustion. Macenion, meanwhile, was doing what he could for Windfoot. When he had the saddle off, he turned to Paks.

"We need to block the ends of this completely," he said. "Snowdrift will help, but we'll have to work hard before we dare rest."

Paks groaned inwardly; she wanted to fall on the ground and sleep. She looked where he pointed. Snow blocked most of the uphill end of the overhang, but some blew in above the drift. Wind roared through the gap, swinging the horses' tails wildly and freezing their sweat.

"We'll use the cover off your pack," Macenion went on. "Anchor it with rocks—" He was picking rocks off the floor of the shelter as he spoke. "If we're lucky, we won't have to compress the snow much—that's the hardest work." Paks began wrestling the pack off Star, and tried to unwrap the cover. The knots were frozen, and the rope stiff as iron, but she dared not cut it. She took off her gloves to fight with it, and muttered a curse as the rope scraped her fingers raw.

"Here—" said Macenion suddenly. "Let me help with that. Get your gloves on; you don't need frozen hands." Paks sat back. Macenion glared at her and she backed farther away. He moved his body between her and the pack, and said a few words she did not know. When he stepped back, the knots were untied, and the ropes were supple again. Paks shook out the pack cover, and Macenion reached for it.

By the time Macenion was satisfied that their campsite was safe, Paks felt she could not move another inch. They had managed to secure the pack cover in the upwind gap. Snow drifted against it quickly, and now—so Macenion said; Paks had not gone back out in the wind to see—covered it several feet deep. The other end of the shelter was still open; they had nothing large or strong enough to block it. Macenion wanted to form blocks of snow, but finally gave up when Paks simply stared at him, exhausted. He managed to light a small fire of the wood they had packed along, despite the wind that still gusted in and out of their overhang. Paks helped steady their smallest pot above it. She thought longingly of hot food, hot mugs of sib. But the snow that finally melted and boiled was hardly hot enough to warm her.

"It's the cold demons," explained Macenion. "They're jealous of their territory; they hate the warm-bloods who come up from the plains. So they steal the heat from fire, up on these heights."

Paks drank the lukewarm sib, and decided she might never be warm again. Marching in a cold rain now seemed like a pleasant excursion. Only a few feet away, the wind whirled veils of snow past their shelter. She huddled in every scrap of clothing and blanket she could find. But as the afternoon wore away, she regained both strength and warmth. The horses, too, seemed to recover. Paks gave them some of the warm water, and dampened Star's grain. Macenion claimed that elven horses didn't need such coddling, but Paks noticed that Windfoot tried to push Star away from hers. She poured warm water on the pile of grain Windfoot had been ignoring, and the horse ate eagerly. Macenion glared, but said nothing more. He ventured outside several times, trying to judge the weather. As the light faded, he reported that both snow and wind were lessening.

"We might get through tomorrow, if the drifts downhill on the other side aren't too bad. It'd be easier without the beasts—"

"You wouldn't leave them!" said Paks, horrified.

"No, of course not. We need the supplies. But we can walk over drifts they'll stick in. Anyway, get what sleep you can. If we can get out tomorrow, it will be early—as soon as it's light. I'll watch tonight—I'm more used to the cold and the height."

Paks resented his usual tone, but was too tired to resist. She fell quickly into a light doze, waking as Macenion replenished the fire. She squinted around the shelter. The horses stood head-to-tail near the rock wall; she could see the firelight reflecting from Star's eyes. Hardly man-high, the ledge of rock overhanging them glittered as if it were full of tiny stars. Paks blinked several times, and decided the rock itself had shiny fragments to catch the light. Firelight turned the snowdrifts into glittering gold and orange—pretty, she thought, when you didn't have to be out in it. She snuggled deeper into her blankets, took a long breath, and slid back into sleep.

Macenion's choked cry brought her halfway out of her blankets before her eyes were open. She had her sword in hand. He stood rigid beside the fire, mouth open. Paks tried to see beyond him, to the outside. Nothing but a wavering dark. She glanced back at the horses. Both of them were alert, heads high, nostrils flared. Star's ears were back; Windfoot's tail was clamped tight. Paks began to untangle herself from the blankets as unobtrusively as possible: she felt they were both easy targets, in the firelight.

It was then she saw the pale blue glow of eyes.

"Paksenarrion!" Macenion's whisper was hoarse and desperate.

"I'm awake," she said softly. What, she wondered, had eyes like that? Farther apart than human eyes, that was all she could tell. Big eyes.

"Paks, it's a—" he choked, and then recovered. "It's a snowcat."

"Holy Gird," said Paks without thinking. When she realized what she had said, she wished she'd kept quiet.

"What?" asked Macenion.

Paks felt herself blushing in the dark. "Nothing," she said. "Now what?"

"Can't you see it?"

"No—nothing but eyes."

"I don't know what we can—" Macenion's voice suddenly sharpened. "Paks! Your ring!" For a moment Paks had no idea what he meant. Macenion spared a glance at her, furious.

"Your ring, human! Your special ring," he went on. Paks nodded, then, stripped off her glove to touch it.

"But are you sure it will work? Maybe the thing—the snowcat—will just go away if we let it alone."

As if in answer to that suggestion, the glowing eyes moved closer. Now Paks could see a suggestion of the body's outline, a long, powerful catlike form, crouching as if to spring.

"You fool!" cried Macenion. "It knows we're here! It's about to jump. Stop it! Hold it!"

Paks thought she could see a twitch in that long tail, like the twitch she had seen in the mousers at the barn, the last instant before they sprang on a rat. She pressed her thumb hard on the ring and thought, "Hold still, cat." She wondered if those words would work.

"Are you?" asked Macenion hoarsely.

"Yes," said Paks. "How long does it—"

"As long as you concentrate. Keep holding it."

Paks tried to concentrate. She wished she could see the snowcat better. Macenion turned to rummage among his things. She was afraid to look sideways at him, lest the cat jump. She forced her eyes back to the shadowy cat-form. Suddenly light flared around her, and she jumped.

"Don't look," said Macenion harshly. The light was clear and white, brilliant enough to show true colors. Now she could see the snowcat clearly. Its body was man-long; it would stand almost waist-high on her at the shoulder. As Macenion had said, its fur was white and blue-gray, patterned with dapples that reminded Paks of snowflakes enlarged. The ears bore long tufts of white, and it had a white beard and short ruff. The eyes, despite the blue glow they'd shown before, were amber in Macenion's spell-light.

"Macenion, it's beautiful. It's the most beautiful—"

"It's spelling you," he said firmly. "It seems beautiful because it's trying to use magic on you."

"But it can't be. It's—" she stopped as Macenion came forward into her field of view. "Macenion, what are you doing?"

"Don't be silly, Paks. I'm going to kill it."

"Kill it? But it's helpless—it can't move while I—"

"That's right. Just keep holding it still. It's the only way I have a chance—"

"But that's not fair—it's helpless—" Paks let her concentration waver, and at once the snowcat moved, shifting in a kind of constricted hop, as she caught her control back. She was distracted again by this evidence of her power and its limitations, and the cat managed to rear, swiping at Macenion's head with one massive paw. He ducked, and Paks forced the cat to stillness again.

"Damn you, human! Hold that beast, or we're both dead. Worse than dead—you remember what I told you!" Macenion glared back at her, then turned, raising his sword.

Paks felt a wave of fear and pain sweep through her mind. It was wrong, terribly wrong—but what else could she do? "Macenion—" she tried again, staring into the snowcat's huge amber eyes. "It's not right—"

"It's not right for us to end up soul-bound to a snowcat, no," he said roughly. "It's easy enough, though, if you forget yourself one more time. If that's what you want, go ahead."

Paks looked down, biting her lip. She could not watch, and then she thought she must. The snow cat made no resistance—could make no resistance—but it could cry out, in fury and pain, and so it did. That wailing cry, ending in an almost birdlike whistle, brought tears to her eyes. She blinked them back. He came back to the fire almost jauntily.

"A snowcat. That's quite a kill, even if you don't think it was fair. I'll just take the pelt before it freezes—"

"No." Paks glared at him.

"What d'you mean, no? Snowcat pelts are nearly priceless, it's so rare to take one—you noticed how careful I was not to damage it when I killed—"

Paks erupted in fury. "By the gods, Macenion, I wonder if you ever tell the truth! You dare pride yourself on killing a helpless animal? It might as well have been a sheep trussed up, for all the courage and skill it took—"

"I didn't notice you out there—"

"You told me to stay here—"

"I told you to hold it still. You could have helped me, if you were able to hold more than one thought in mind at a time. As it was you nearly killed me—"

"I!" Paks flourished her own sword. She noticed with some satisfaction that Macenion backed up a step. "I but tried to save your honor and mine—not that I would have thought an elf would care so little for it—"

"You know nothing about elven honor, human!" Macenion seemed to swell with rage. "You are my travel companion, oath-bound to defend me—as I defended you just now—against all dangers. As for the snowcat having no defense, it was trying to spell you the entire time."

Paks felt her anger leak away into the cold. Had she been half-spelled? Had she nearly failed her oath because of it? Macenion took quick advantage of her hesitation. "I don't blame you," he said more quietly. "You are human, unused to magicks of any kind, and this may be the first magical beast you've seen." She nodded unwillingly. "It would have killed all of us, and feasted many days while our souls were enslaved to it, if we had not managed to kill it. Or send it away." He cocked his head and gave her a sly grin. "If you'd been quick enough thinking, o lover of animals, you might simply have sent it away."

"Sent it—it would have gone?"

"Oh, yes. I'm surprised it didn't occur to you, Paksenarrion. Just as you sent Windfoot—oh, that's right. You didn't. But you could have."

"Then you didn't have to kill it," Paks cried, angry again. "You told me—"

"I told you what seemed best to me. Kill it and it's gone forever. Send it away and it might come back—though you could have laid a compulsion on it to avoid us. Besides, this way we have a valuable pelt." Macenion turned again to his pack, and pulled out a short wide skinning blade. Paks moved between him and the snowcat; when he rose and saw her, he frowned.

"I won't let you," said Paks, fighting back tears. "You told me I had to hold it, or it'd kill both of us—and you lied about that. It isn't the first lie, either. You're not going to profit by it, Macenion—I was wrong to hold it that way, and that's the worst thing I've done. I won't let you do more."

"You mean you'd waste a perfectly good pelt—already back in winter coat—just because you didn't think of sending it away?"

"No—because you lied to me." Paks had backed slowly and carefully across the ledge outside their shelter, until she bumped her heels into the snowcat's corpse. Now she turned, and with a powerful heave pushed the snowcat over the edge.

"You're a stubborn fool," said Macenion, but without the anger she had feared. "That's enough gold for both of us to live on for a month, that you threw away. But—" he shrugged, "I suppose it meant something to you. Now don't stand there and freeze, Paksenarrion—we still have to cross the pass tomorrow."

It was not the next morning, but the one after that, when they finally ventured from their shelter. Dawn that day was clear, the wind hardly moving, and nothing in the white drifts below looked like the remains of a snowcat. They had said little to each other in the storm-whitened hours between—only what must be said about the fire, the care of the animals, and packing up their campsite. Now they moved through a pale rose and blue world, leaving blue-shadowed tracks behind. Once through the pass, Paks could see—not the rolling forests of the Eight Kingdoms she had hoped for—but more ridges and steep valleys. Far below and ahead, forests clothed the slopes. Somewhere beyond, the mountains ended. She hoped to make it there.

CHAPTER FOUR

Paks had not slept well since the killing of the snowcat. Despite Macenion's sarcastic reassurance, she knew that she had dishonored her sword, and the ring that she had used. She had stayed with him only because she had no other guide out of the mountains. Now, as they came through a gap in the trees into yet another narrow valley, she wondered whether she should refuse to accompany him any farther. Surely here, with the bulk of the mountains behind her, she could find her own way north.

"Well, indeed—" said Macenion, in a tone that meant he wished to be asked what he meant.

"Well, what?" Paksenarrion turned half-away from him, and bent to check her pony's hooves.

"It's what I hoped to find—the right valley."

Paksenarrion looked at the valley, this time, and saw, in its widest span, a group of stone piles. "More of your ruins?" she asked sourly.

"Much more important," said Macenion. He was grinning again, and when he caught her eye he winked. "Didn't I say there was treasure to be won in these mountains?"

"You've said a lot." Paks had turned back to Star, and was adjusting the ropes on her pack.

Macenion sighed. "Come now, don't be tiresome. You're carrying a new sword, for one thing, and—"

Paks knew Macenion had parted with the elf-wrought blade (if it was one) only because he wanted to soothe her after the snowcat's murder. The sword felt well enough—it was better than the one she'd bought—but she resented the whole incident. And she wasn't about to be grateful.

"And you say there's more. And, as usual, you want me to bodyguard you while we get it—right?"

"I will need your help." Macenion sighed again. "Paks, I'm sorry about the snowcat. I didn't know you'd feel that way."

"I'd have thought an elf would—"

"So my human parentage betrayed me. It's not the first time. But listen, at least, before you stalk off in outrage."

Paks looked around at the tree-clad slopes. She thought she saw a faint trail across from them, leading south, but she knew the ways of apparent trails that appeared and disappeared and tangled together. She shrugged and stared down at the ruins while Macenion talked.

"This valley," he said, "is forbidden to elves. My mother's cousin told me that, and also told me how to find it. He meant the directions to keep me away. But here is a great treasure—the stories are clear on that—and much of it is magical. Something happened here that the elves don't want to talk about, and so they went away and never came back."

"Elves lived here?" Paksenarrion frowned. "I thought they lived in forests, not stone buildings."

"It's true that elven cities are surrounded by trees and water, but they're constructed, nonetheless."

Despite herself, Paksenarrion was interested. "What happened, then? Why did the elves leave?"

"I don't know." The answer had come so fast that Paks disbelieved it and gave Macenion a sharp look. He spread his hands. "It's true—I don't know. I suspect, but I don't know. They say they haven't come back because the valley is haunted by evil, but I'm fairly sure that they just don't like to admit mistakes."

"You were more than fairly sure that the wardstones wouldn't work any longer," Paks reminded him. Macenion scowled.

"This is different," said Macenion loftily. "Those were human artifacts. This is elven. My elven blood will sense the truth—and my magic will enable us to pass safely what might be perilous for others." He patted the pouch that held his magical apparatus. Paksenarrion said nothing. "And the treasures here are worth a risk. Elf-made weapons, Paks, and magic scrolls and wands: I've heard about them. They were all abandoned when the elves fled. My relatives—well, I hate to say anything bad about the elves, but they haven't been any too generous with their goods. I feel I have a right to whatever I can find in there." He nodded toward the ruins.

"But what about the evil whatever-it-is?"

"That's why I've waited this long. First, my power as a mage is much greater now; I've spent years in study and practice, and I have some powerful new spells." He showed her the polished end of a scroll-case. "And, as well, I'm traveling with a very experienced and able warrior—you."

"I see."

"I'm quite sure that whatever is there—if anything—will be no match for the two of us."

"What do you think is there?"

"Oh—if the underground passages are still open, some animals may have moved in. Perhaps even an orc or two. As for an evil power—" Macenion tilted his hand back and forth. "If it were very strong, I'd be aware of it here. And I'm not."

Paksenarrion looked around again. She felt nothing. After the wardstones, she thought she might, if anything like that were going on. She touched her sword hilt for comfort. "Well, then, I suppose we could take a look."

Macenion smiled, and turned to lead the way down.

It was farther than it looked. The path they had followed from the slopes above disappeared in a tangle of undergrowth that cloaked tumbled rocks as big as cattle. The sun had long disappeared behind the western peaks when they hacked their way free of the thorny stuff and found themselves on short rough turf still several hours away from the ruins. In fact, these were no longer visible; the floor of the valley was uneven.

"Let's make camp," said Paksenarrion. "It'd be full dark by the time we came to the ruins. The horses could use a rest, too." Star had a long bleeding scratch down one leg, and Windfoot was streaked with sweat.

"I suppose so." Macenion was staring toward the ruins. "I wish we could go right on, but—"

"Not in the dark," said Paks firmly. He seemed to shake himself.

"You're right." Still he sat, facing west, silent, while Paks gathered wood from the brushy edge for a fire. She touched his arm when it was ready to light, and he jumped.

"The fire's ready," she said, pointing.

Macenion looked around at the gathering darkness, and threw back his cloak. He glanced up at Paks. "Perhaps tonight we should use the tinderbox."

"You? The great magician?" Paksenarrion turned to the horses. "I thought you were sure it was safe."

"There's no sense making it obvious we're here—just in case."

"Then we shouldn't have a fire at all." Paks pulled her own pack near the stacked wood. "That's fine with me; I know fires draw trouble."

"Yes. Well—let's not, then." Macenion pulled his cloak around him again, and began to unload his horse. Paks eyed the hollow they were in. It was not particularly defensible, if Macenion thought they might be attacked. But when she asked, he was disinclined to move. Paks shrugged, and pulled her sword from its sheath. As the darkness closed in, the rasp of her whetstone on the blade seemed louder and louder. When she tested the blade, and found it well enough, she noticed how still a night it was.

Paksenarrion woke in the first light of dawn; the peaks behind were just showing light instead of dark against the sky. For a moment or so she was not sure where she was. The visions of her dream were still brilliant before her eyes. She shook her head vigorously and rolled on her side, hardly surprised to find that she held her sword hilt in her hand. She looked toward Macenion, a dark shape in darkness. Was he stirring? She spoke his name softly.

"I'm coming!" His answer was a shout, and he sprang to his feet. "Begone, you foul—" She heard a gasp, and then, in a different voice, "By all the gods of elf and man, what was that?"

"I don't know. I thought you were waking, and called, and you jumped up—"

"A dream." Paks heard Macenion's feet on the grass. "It must have been a dream."

"What dream?" Paks wondered if this were a haunted place, a place that gave dreams. Hers had been vivid enough.

"It was—it's hard to say. I felt something—almost as if—" He paused for a long moment. Paks tried to see his face in the dimness, but could not.

"I dreamed too," she said finally. "A—I don't know what to call it—a spirit of some sort, I suppose—was imprisoned, and calling for help—"

"Yes—and was there a yellow cloud that stank of evil?" Macenion's voice sounded alert and eager.

"I saw no cloud," replied Paks. "But something tall, in a yellow robe, with a staff. I wondered if it was an elf."

"That was no elf, whatever it was. I must have seen the aura of power, and you saw the physical form. But it was evil, and the—" Macenion paused again as if searching for a word. "I can't think," he said finally. "I should know what it was, that was calling. Something to do with elves, and the places they've lived for long. It needs our help."

"So that was a sent dream," said Paks. "Not something we dreamed on our own."

"It was sent, certainly," said Macenion. "The question now is—"

"Who sent it."

"No, I wasn't worried about that. The question is, what do we do? I know what we should do, but—"

"I still want to know who sent it."

"One of the gods, of course. Sertig or Adyan, probably. Who else would?"

"The—the thing itself? The one that needs our help? It might want us to come, and caused the dream."

"Nonsense. If it's strong enough to do that, it wouldn't need our help against a mere sorcerer or wizard."

"I don't know..." Somehow Paksenarrion could not believe Macenion's explanation. He had been wrong about so many things. She wished, not for the first time, that she knew more herself about the world beyond the Duke's Company. She had not realized, until she left it, how little she had learned in three years of soldiering. For all she knew, Macenion himself could have caused the dream, to ensure that she would be willing to enter the ruins. She pushed that thought aside. Until they were clear of the mountains, she had no real choice; Macenion was the only available guide. Her hand found its way to the pouch that held Canna's medallion. She stopped herself from taking it out, and squatted down to reroll her blankets.

"In your dream, did you—did it offer you any treasure?" Macenion, too, was packing up.

Paks nodded, realized it was still too dark for him to see that gesture, and spoke instead. "Yes. I didn't know what all of it was, but the weapons and armor were beautiful."

"It can't hurt, Paksenarrion, to take a look—" His voice was almost pleading.

Paks laughed despite her worries. "No, I suppose not. Don't worry, Macenion, your hired blade won't leave you. I've got more loyalty than that. But I hope you really do have the skill to handle whatever magic comes up."

"I think so. I'm sure of it." He didn't really sound sure.

It took them four hours to reach the ruins. As they came nearer, Paks recognized that the grassy mound before them was the ruin of a defensive wall. They entered through a gap that had once been a gateway. Two of the stones that had formed the framework were still standing. Although they were scarred as if they had been scorched, much of the decorative carving was still visible. Paks stood bemused, enjoying the intricacy of the interlacing designs, until Macenion touched her arm.

"It's meant to do that," he said, grinning. "Elves use patterns for control. In fact, elves taught men how to set the patterns for the wardstones. You'd better not let yourself look at any of the decoration that remains, just in case."

Paks felt herself flush with embarrassment. She said nothing, but followed Macenion deeper into the complex of ruins, her hand on her sword.

Little remained but irregular mounds overgrown with grass and weeds. Here and there a bit of stone showed through, and a few doorways still stood wreathed in ivy. Although Paks could hear birdsong in the distance, the ruins themselves were quiet. No lizards sunned themselves on the mounds, to scuttle away as they passed. No rabbits found shelter in the occasional briar. Macenion moved almost as carefully as Paks could have wished, pausing beside each mound before crossing the next open space. As they went deeper into the complex, the silence grew more intense. The horses' hooves made no noise on the turf. Paks could not bring herself to speak. The breath caught in her throat, but she could not cough. At last Macenion raised his hand for a halt. When he turned to look at her, his face was paler, she thought, than it had been. He swallowed visibly, then spoke, his voice soft.

"We'll leave the horses here. They won't stray. They have grass, and there's a fountain ahead. I'll put a spell on them, as well."

Now that the silence had been broken, Paks found she could speak, though it was still an effort. "Have you found the way to what we're looking for?"

"Yes. I think so. Look there—" Macenion pointed out one of the mounds ahead, and Paks saw that under an overgrowth of ivy and flowering briar (flowering? she thought) it was almost intact: a curious round structure with columns on the outside and a bulbous roof. She could see, as well, the fountain that lay before it, a clear pool whose surface rippled as if in a breeze. "I've heard that such a building lay in the center of this place," Macenion went on. "From it, passages lead to the vaults below and to other buildings. I'm sure that the being we are to help is trapped somewhere below; this is the surest way down."

Paks frowned. "If so, it's surely known to others, as well. To the enemy of that being, for instance. I'd rather not go in by such a public entrance."

"Scared?" Macenion's face twisted in a sneer. He glanced at her sword, then back at her face.

Paks fought back an angry retort. "No," she said quietly. "Not any more scared than you, with your pale face. But you brought a soldier along for a soldier's skills, and I learned in my first campaign that you don't go in the door that the enemy expects. Not if you want to live to have your share of the loot."

Macenion flushed in his turn, and scowled. "Well, that's the only way down that I know how to find. Besides, in my dream, this was shown as the way."

"Did your dream show both of us going in that way?"

"How else?"

"You hadn't thought we might need a rear guard?"

"What for?"

"What for?" Paks glared at Macenion. "Haven't you any experience? Suppose that whatever-it-is, that evil thing, has its own way to the surface. It could come after us, and attack from the rear, or trap us underground."

"Oh, I'm sure it wouldn't—couldn't—"

"Like you were sure about the other things? No, Macenion, I'm not going down there without knowing a little more about it. Surely your magic can show you something, or guard the way behind us."

Macenion looked thoughtful. "If you insist, I suppose I can think of something. It might be better, after all—" He burrowed into his tunic, then gave Paks a sharp look. "You can walk around a bit—look for another entrance—"

"I wish you'd quit worrying. I'm not another magician, and I couldn't use anything I might see."

Macenion drew himself up. "It's a matter of principle."

Paks snorted, but moved away. She decided to take the packs off Star and see if there was anything she might want to take underground. Macenion, she noticed, hadn't thought of that. As she went through their gear, she wondered again what she was doing following such a person. She did not like the thought of going underground, in a unknown place against unknown dangers, at all. Especially with someone like Macenion. Perhaps with a squad of the Duke's Company, but a single half-elf? But a scene from her dream recurred: after victorious combat, she was receiving the homage of those who had asked her help—she was given a new weapon, of exquisite workmanship, and a suit of magical armor. Honor—glory—her reputation made as a fighter. She shook her head, driving the vision away. A chance for glory, Stammel had always said, was a chance to be killed unpleasantly. Still—she had left the Company to seek adventure and fame and a chance to fight for such causes as now lay before her. Could she miss the chance? She piled on one side the things she thought would be useful, and made the rest into a small bundle.

"We'll need something to light the way," said Macenion suddenly. "Whatever the elves used may not be working, and I don't want to use magical light until it's needed." He was going through his own pack. "This should do. This oil—these candles—and yes, I can set a spell at our backs that will keep out any trouble—at least give us warning. We probably won't be that long, but I suppose we should take water and some food."

"How about the fountain? Is it safe?"

"I should think so. Try it." Macenion held out his water bottle to Paks. She frowned.

"If it's elvish, you try it first."

"What a brave warrior! Very well, then." Macenion dipped his bottle in the fountain pool. Nothing happened. "You see? Just water."

"Good." Paks, too, filled her water bottle from the fountain pool, then bent to drink directly from it. The water was cold and had a faint mineral tang. Although the water seemed perfectly clear, she could not see the bottom of the pool. Somehow, after drinking, she no longer considered not following Macenion under the ruins.

Macenion led the way through a tangle of ivy into the building. From within, Paks could see that the original domed roof had been pierced by a number of skylights, each with an ornamental molding around it. The interior walls were still covered with inlay of many-colored stones that formed a dazzling array of designs. The floor was a mosaic of cool grays and soft greens, rounded pebbles that looked like those in any mountain stream, but chosen carefully to match in size and shape.

"Here it is," said Macenion, pointing to a circle of darker stones laid in the center of the room.

"What?"

Macenion looked smug. 'The door—the way in."

"That?"

"Yes." He drew out a short black rod; Paks looked down, more frightened than she cared to admit. Something sizzled, and she looked quickly at the circle: it was gone. A hole in the floor revealed a spiral stair. Dust lay thick on the stone steps.

Paks took a deep breath. "Do you think we're the first to come this way? The first to be asked for help?"

"I don't know. Probably not. Only a magician could find this way down, you know. Perhaps others couldn't find a way to help and went away. You stay here a moment, while I take a quick look down." Macenion set a careful foot on the first step. Nothing happened. He went down several more, bending to look beneath the floor. Paks looked out the way they had come in, half-expecting some monster to appear on their trail, but there was nothing. As she watched, Macenion's horse moved past the opening to drink at the fountain; she heard it sucking the water up. When she looked back at the hole in the floor, Macenion was coming back up. "Just below, the ceiling's much higher; we won't have any problem. And I don't see that anything's disturbed the dust. The only thing is, the stair is only one person wide—"

Paks suppressed a last shudder of doubt about the wisdom of this whole project, and grinned at him. "I suppose you'd like the fighter to go in front, eh? Well, I can't see behind myself; I'd just as soon know who's at my back." She drew her sword as she spoke. "But I'll have this out, just in case. What about light? Must I carry a candle or torch?"

"No-o—" said Macenion, climbing out of her way onto the floor. "There's light."

"What sort of light?"

"I'm not sure. It may be the same the elves used. But it's easily light enough to see."

"What if it goes out? You'd best keep some sort of flame alight, Macenion."

"Why should it go out if it's lasted this long? Oh, all right—" he answered her look of disgust. "But you're so suspicious."

"I'm alive," said Paks, "and I intend to stay that way."

"As a fighter, an adventurer?"

"Some do," said Paks, starring down the stairs. "And from what I hear, those that do stay suspicious. Magicians, too."

The stair dropped steeply, and curved to the right, back under the floor. Paks found that she did not have to duck at all; when she thought about it, she remembered that elves were, in general, taller than humans. Light filled the stairwell as far as she could see, a gentle, white light with no apparent source. She looked back once, to see the deep scuffing footprints she had made in the dust. Macenion was just in sight, several steps higher. After what she judged was the first half-turn, the steps were not so steep. She could move more easily now, and, of course, anything coming up could do so as well. She glanced back again, for Macenion, and thought of the spell he had promised to put at their backs.

"What did you do up there?" she asked softly, nodding upward.

"It's open," he said. "If I'd closed it, and anything happened to me, you couldn't get out that way. But I put a spell on the opening that should repel anything from outside trying to get in. And just in case, I put another spell on it to give us an alarm if something does go through."

All that sounded impressive to Paksenarrion. She hoped it would work. "Do you know how far this goes down?"

"No. It should open into a wide hall at the bottom, though."

Paks went on. The mysterious light bothered her. The silence bothered her. She felt her hand grow sweaty on her sword hilt, and that bothered her. Nothing had happened; no danger appeared, and yet her breath came short, just as if she were a recruit in her first battle. She concentrated on the construction of the stair: pale gray stone underfoot, and slightly darker gray stone on the walls and vaulted ceiling. The stair treads were ribbed, under the dust, and when she reached to feel the walls, she found that they were lightly incised with an intricate design. Remembering Macenion's warning, she took her fingers off the wall. She looked back over her shoulder again. Macenion, too, had one hand on the wall; when he met her eyes he smiled at her.

"It's decoration and information both," he said. "I can read some of it, though I'd have to stand here a long time to figure it out. But for those who lived here, it would be a way of telling how far they had come, though that's not what it says, exactly." He moved his hand along the section of wall nearest him. "This, for example, is part of an old song: The Long Ride of Torre. Do you know it?"

Paks nodded. "If that's the same Torre as Torre's Necklace."

"Of course. Do you know the story?"

"Yes." Paks turned again and kept stepping down. The dust seemed no thicker, and with no changes in light or silence, she had a hard time figuring out how far they had come. At last she saw an opening ahead, rather than a curving wall. As she came to the last step, and waited for Macenion to close in behind her, she could see a space of dusty stone paving, and nothing else. Although it was light beyond the opening, any walls were too far away to show.

"Now this, I believe, was the Winter Hall," said Macenion, peering past her. "Go on, Paksenarrion."

"And have whatever's waiting beside the door take my head off? Let's be careful." Paks unslung her small shield and reached for Macenion's walking staff.

He jerked it away. "What?"

Paks sighed. "Remember what I just said about doorways? Better a piece of wood than my neck."

"Oh, all right." Macenion handed over his staff grumpily. Paks tied the shield quickly to one end, and stuck it through the door. Nothing happened. She pulled it back, handed Macenion his staff, tightened the shield on her arm, and slipped quickly through the doorway, putting her back to the wall beside it.

She was in a large bare hall, lit by the same mysterious means as the stair. It stretched away on either side of the doorway she'd come through for twice the distance of its width. No furniture remained, and dust covered the broad floor. Macenion came through after her, and looked up. Paks followed his gaze. Far overhead the arched ceiling was formed into intricate branches and vaults, a tracery of stone such as Paks had never seen. Between ribs of dark stone, patterns of smaller colored ones gave almost the effect of a forest overhead.

"That's—beautiful—" she whispered, hardly aware of speaking.

For once, Macenion did not take a superior tone. "It's—I've never seen the like myself. I knew this was once the seat of the High King, but I never imagined—" He took a few steps out into the hall, and looked at his footprints. "Certainly this has not been disturbed for many years—perhaps not since they left."

Paks had noticed, at the right end of the hall, a darker alcove. "What's that?"

"That should lead to other passages. But I can't understand why there are no signs at all." Macenion stopped and shook his head. "We won't find out anything by standing here. Let me think—"

Paks scanned the walls again. At the left end of the hall was a dais, four steps up from the main level, and at the back of it an arched doorway. Two heavily patterned bronze doors closed the opening. Across from her, on the other long wall, were four doorways, also closed with heavy doors. At the right end, no doors showed save the alcove, if that was, as Macenion said, an opening.

"Do you know where any of these doors lead?" she asked.

"The door on the dais leads to the royal apartments. The others—no, blast it, I can't remember. We'll have to look and see."

"Would the doors be locked?"

"I doubt it. They may be spelled, though. Luckily I have ways of handling that. Perhaps we should start with the royal apartments. We might find something worthwhile there."

Paks felt a twinge. "We're here to help that trapped thing, first. I don't think treasure hunters would be lucky here."

"I was thinking we might find something that would help us free the spirit, Paksenarrion. It wasn't just greed."

Paks was not convinced. She turned from one side to the other, trying to feel which way to go. Was that a pull toward the right end? Or the door directly across from her? And if it was, did it come from the one they wanted to help or from the enemy? She shook her head, as if to clear it, and watched Macenion approach the royal doors. A feeling of wrongness grew stronger. He reached the foot of the dais.

"Macenion! No!" She surprised herself as much as him with her shout.

He whirled to face her. "What?"

"Don't go that way." She was utterly certain of danger. She moved quickly to his side, and lowered her voice. "That's wrong; I'm sure of it. If you go up there, we'll—"

"Paksenarrion, you're no seer. I assure you that we may very well find, in the royal apartments, clues to what sort of spirit may be locked here. We'll certainly find information about the layout of the underground passages."

"That may be, but if you open that door, Macenion, you'll wish you hadn't."

He looked at her closely. "Have you had some sort of message? From a—a god, or something like that?"

"I don't know. But I know you shouldn't go that way. And I may not be a seer, Macenion, but I have had warning feelings before, and they've been true."

"A fighter?" He arched his brows.

"Yes, a fighter! By the gods, Macenion, carrying a sword in my hand doesn't mean I don't carry sense between my ears. If a warning comes, I heed it."

"I wish you'd told me before about your extra abilities. It comes hard to believe in them now, when I've never seen them." He gave her a superior smile. "Very well, then . . . since you're so sure. We'll wander about down here with no other guidance than your intuition. Perhaps you're turning into a paladin or something."

Paks glared at him, angry enough to strike, but relieved that he had turned away from the dais. Macenion looked around the hall.

"Which door would you suggest, since you don't like my choice?"

"What about that alcove?" asked Paks. "Or the center doors on the long side there?"

Macenion shrugged. "It doesn't matter to me. Why not the alcove?

It's as far as possible from those you fear." Paks flushed but held her peace as they walked the length of the hall.

The alcove was deeper than it looked; the light was deceptive. Within it were two doors, both bronze. One had a design on it that reminded Paks of a tree; the other was covered with interlacement bands that enclosed many-pointed stars. Macenion looked at her. "Do you have any feelings about either of these? My own preference would be for the stars; stars are sacred to elves."

Paks felt, in fact, a stubborn desire to use the door with the tree, but she felt no special menace from the other one. With Macenion grinning at her in such a smug way, she didn't want to press a mere preference. "That will do. I don't have anything against it, anyway." When Macenion simply stood there, she asked sharply, "Aren't you going to open it?"

"As soon as I figure out how. It's locked, spell-locked—if you laid a hand on it, you'd be flat on your back. I'm surprised your intuition didn't tell you that."

Paks wondered herself, and thought that if her intuition worked on bigger things, they'd better pay attention to it. She said nothing, however, and as Macenion stood in apparent thought, she turned to keep watch on the rest of the room.

When she looked the length of the room toward the dais, she thought she saw a faint glow around the doors there. She looked at the other doors in the room. They looked the same. When she looked back at the dais, the glow was more definite. It had an irregular shape, and seemed to be coming from the joint between the doors—as if it were seeping through.

"Macenion!"

"What now?!" He turned to her angrily. Paks pointed toward the dais. "I don't see—by the gods! What's that?"

"I don't know. I don't like it. Did you step up on the dais?"

"No. You yelled, and I—I may just have touched the lower step with my foot—"

"I hope not. It's brighter, now."

"So I see. I wonder if it's—by Orphin, I'd better get this spell correct."

"What is it?"

"Not now! Just watch. Tell me if it gets more than halfway down the hall."

"But what can I do to hold it back?"

"If it's what I think, nothing. Now let me work."

Paks turned to stare at the mysterious glowing shape, which grew slowly as she watched. It seemed to spread, widening itself to the width of the dais, and slowing its forward movement as it did so. At first she had been able to see through it clearly, but as it grew and thickened, she could no longer see the doors behind it. She felt sweat crawling through her hair. Her intuition had been right, but what was this thing? Surely there was a way to fight it. Now it reached the forward edge of the dais. Paks could hear Macenion muttering behind her. She heard a faint sizzle, then a little pop. Macenion cursed softly and went back to muttering. The glowing shape extended along the front edge of the dais, and began to grow taller. Slowly it filled the space above the dais, from the doors behind to the lowest step in front, rising higher and higher to the canopy that hung between the dais and the ceiling. When this space was full, the glow intensified again. It seemed more and more solid, as if it were a definite shape settling there. As it solidified, it contracted a little, no longer so regular. Just as Macenion's triumphant "Got it!" broke her concentration, Paks thought she could see the shape it was condensing toward.

"Come on, Paks. Quickly!" Macenion grabbed her arm to hurry her through the now-open door, and looked back. "Great Orphin, protect us, it is a—Come on!"

Paks tore her eyes from the glowing shape, and darted through the door after Macenion. He waited on the other side and threw his weight against the heavy panel. As it swung closed, a curious hissing noise came from the hall they had left.

"Help me—close it!" Macenion looked as frightened as Paks had ever seen him. She, too, leaned on the door, as Macenion fumbled for something in his pouch with one hand. It seemed reluctant to stay closed, as if pressure were on it from the other side. "Don't let it come open," warned Macenion. "If that gets out, we're dead."

"What is it?"

"Not now! I'm trying to—" Macenion grunted suddenly, and began to mutter in a language Paks didn't know. Suddenly Paks felt a great shove from the other side of the door. "Blast! Wrong one." Macenion began muttering again, as Paks held the door with all her strength. She heard an abrupt click, and found that she needed no strength to hold the door. Macenion sighed. "That should do it," he said. "I expect it will. You can let go now, Paks."

"What was that?" Paks noticed that Macenion still looked worried.

"I don't know how to explain it to you."

"Try."

"A sort of evil spirit, then, that can take solid form, and attack any intruder, elves preferred. It has many ways of attacking, all of them unpleasant."

"And a sword would be no use against it?"

Macenion laughed. "No."

"Is it the thing we came to find? What's holding the other thing prisoner?"

"No. Unlikely. I fear, though, that it may be in league with it. This may prove harder than I thought. And we certainly can't risk returning this way to the surface."

"Unless we've destroyed that thing." Paks felt better. Her intuition had been right after all, and, as always, the joining of the fight roused her spirits. Macenion looked at her curiously.

"Don't you understand? We can't destroy that—and we don't know any other way out. If what we're looking for is as bad or worse, we may never get out."

Paks grinned. "I understand. We took the bait, and we're in the trap, and we don't even know the size of the trap. But they, Macenion, don't know the size of their catch." She drew her sword and looked along the blade for a moment. "You managed to shut the door against that thing. I can deal with more fleshly dangers. And—I've been in traps before."

"Yes, but—Well, there's no help for it. We'd better keep moving. We want to be well away from that door if it breaks through."

They were in a short corridor, lit as the stairwell and hall had been, and ahead of them was an archway into a larger room. Here, too, the floor was thick with dust. Paks led the way forward, sword out and ready. Macenion followed.

The room had obviously been a kitchen. Not a stick of furniture remained, but two great hearths, blocked up with hasty stonework, told the tale of many feastings. On the left, a narrower archway led to another corridor. On their right, a short passage led to another room, just visible beyond it.

"That should have been the cellar," said Macenion. "I wonder if any of the wine is left."

Paks chuckled. "After so long? It wouldn't be worth trying."

"I suppose not. We'll go this way, then." He gestured to the left. As they crossed the kitchen, Paks looked around for any sign of recent disturbance but saw nothing.

"Was that thing back there what drove the elves out?" asked Paks.

"No. I don't think so. Enough high elves together would be able to drive it away. It's—well, you humans know of gods, don't you? Good and evil gods?"

"Of course." Paks glared at him for an instant.

"Do you know of the Court of Gods? Their rankings, and all that?"

Paks shook her head. "Gods are gods."

"No, Paksenarrion, they are not. Some are far more powerful than others. You should have learned that in Aarenis, even as a soldier. You fought in Sibili, didn't you? Yes—and didn't you see the temple of the Master of Torments there? I heard it was sacked."

Paks shivered as she remembered the assault on Sibili. "I was knocked out," she said. "I didn't see it."

"Well, you've heard of the Webmistress—"

"Of course. But what—"

"Liart—the Master of Torments—and that other, they're both fairly low in the court of evil. Between the least of the gods and the common evils of the world, there are still beings—they have more power than any human or elf, but not nearly so much as a god."

Paks was suddenly curious. "What about the heroes and saints like Gird and Pargun?"

"Who knows? They were humans once; I don't know what, if anything, they are now. But that creature, Paks, is more powerful than any elf, and yet is far below the gods. Our gods—the gods of elves."

The corridor they traveled curved slightly to the left. Paks glanced back and saw that the kitchen entrance was now out of sight. Ahead was a doorway blocked by a closed door, this one of carved wood. As they neared it, Paks noticed that the dust on the floor was not nearly so deep; their footsteps began to ring on the stone and echo off the stone walls. She wondered what had moved the dust. Macenion, when she pointed it out, looked around and shook his head.

"I don't know. Draft under that door, possibly—"

"Underground?" Paks remembered that she didn't know much about underground construction, and put that thought aside. She moved as quietly as possible toward the door.

In the cool white light of the corridor, its rich red and black grain and intricate carving seemed warm and alive. She reached out to touch it gently. It felt a slightly warm under her hand. "That's odd. It's—"

The door heaved under her hand; Paks jumped backward just in time to avoid a blow as it swung wide. Facing them were several armed humans in rough leather and woolen clothes; the leader grinned.

" 'Ere's our bonus, lads!" he said. "The ears off these'll give us something to show the lord—"

Paks had her sword in motion before he finished; his boast ended in a howl of pain. She took a hard blow on her shield, and dodged a thrust meant for her throat. Behind her, she heard Macenion draw, then the ring of his blade on one of the others. The noise brought two more fighters skidding around the corner ahead to throw themselves into the fight. Paks and Macenion fought almost silently; they had no need for words. Paks pressed ahead, finding the attackers to be good but not exceptional fighters. She had the reach of most of them, and she was as strong as any. Macenion yelped suddenly, breaking her concentration; as she glanced for him, a hard blow caught her in the side. She grunted, grateful for the chain shirt she wore, and pushed off from the wall to skewer her opponent. Macenion's arm was bleeding, but he fought on. Paks shifted her ground to give him some respite. She took a glancing blow on her helmet that gashed her forehead as it passed. She could feel the blood trickling down toward her eye. Macenion lunged forward, flipping the sword away from one of their attackers; Paks downed the man with a blow to the face. They advanced again; the other attackers seemed less eager. Finally, only two were still fighting. The others, dead or wounded too badly to fight, lay scattered on the corridor floor. Paks expected them to break away and flee, but they didn't; instead, they fought doggedly on, until she and Macenion managed to kill them.

CHAPTER FIVE

Paks leaned against the wall breathing heavily. Her side ached, and she could feel a trickle of blood running down the side of her face. Her shield had broken; she pulled the straps free and dropped the pieces. Macenion had ripped a length of cloth from his tunic, and was wrapping the wound on his arm. As he moved, she caught a glimpse of the bright mail under his outer clothing.

"If I'd known you wore mail," she said finally, "I wouldn't have worried so much. I was sure you were being skewered."

Macenion glanced up. "I nearly was. By Orphin, you're a good fighter in trouble. I wouldn't have made it alone, even with mail." He looked at her more closely. "You're bleeding—is it bad?"

"I don't think so. Just a cut on the head, and they always bleed—a mess." Paks swiped at her face with her free hand, and found the cut itself, a shallow gash near the edge of her helmet.

"Here—" Macenion sheathed his sword and came over. "Let me clean that out." Paks looked at the bodies on the floor as he wiped out the cut with something from a jar in his pack. It burned, but the bleeding stopped. The bodies did not move, this time. When Macenion finished, she pushed herself off the wall, grunting at the pain in her side, and wiped her sword clean on the dirty cloak of the nearest enemy. She wished they could stop and rest, but she distrusted the flavor of the air down here.

"I suppose we ought to keep going," she said, half hoping that Macenion would insist on rest and food.

"Definitely. Whatever sent these guards will know, soon enough, that we've passed them. If we're to have any surprise at all, we'll have to go on. Why? Are you hurt?"

"No." Paks sighed. "Bruised, but no more. I wish we were out of here."

"As do I." Macenion gave a short laugh. "I begin to think that my elven relatives have more wit than I gave them credit for—they may have been right to tell me that I would find more trouble here than treasure."

But along with her fear and loathing of the underground maze in which they were wandering, Paks felt a pull of excitement and interest. With each encounter they were pressed more closely, but so far they had won, penetrating deeper and deeper into their enemy's lair. In a corner of her mind, Paks saw herself telling this tale to Vik and Arne in an inn somewhere. She checked her sword for damage, finding none, and turned to Macenion. He nodded his readiness, and she set off carefully, sword ready.

They passed an open door into an empty room on their right, and another like it a few feet down on the left. Ahead of them, the corridor turned again. Paks looked at Macenion and he shrugged. She flattened against the wall and edged forward to the turn. She could hear nothing. She widened her nostrils, hoping for a clue to what lay ahead. Her own smell, and Macenion's, overwhelmed her nose. Finally, with a mental shrug, she peeked around the corner. An empty corridor, its dusty floor scuffed and disturbed. Four doorways that she could see in the one quick look she allowed herself. A crossing corridor a short run ahead.

"Do you have any of your feelings about any of this?" asked Macenion when she described what she'd seen.

"No. Not really. The whole things feels bad, but nothing in particular."

"Nor can I detect anything. I wish our friend who wants our help would give us some guidance."

Paks felt around in her mind to see if anything stirred. Nothing but a faint desire to get moving. She sighed. "Let's go, then."

The doors that opened off the corridor were all of wood; all bore the scars of some sort of fire. One was burned half-through, and they could see into a small room with stone shelves built into the walls. At the cross corridor, Paks took one corner and Macenion the other. To the right, her way, the corridor ended in a blank stone wall perhaps fifty paces away. To the left, it opened after perhaps thirty paces into a chamber whose size they could not guess. Macenion cocked his head that way, and Paks began to edge along the wall of the cross corridor toward the chamber door. Macenion stayed where he was.

As she neared the opening, Paks felt a wave of confidence. Surely they were going the right direction. Macenion was being too cautious, as usual. She hesitated only a moment before putting her head around to see what the chamber was like.

Here, for the first time, was something not desolate and ruined. The floor had been laid of colored blocks of stone, pale green and gold, and was swept clean of dust so that the pattern was clearly visible. At the far end of the chamber, a great ring of candles seemed to hover in midair. After a moment, Paks realized that they were attached to a metal framework suspended from a chain that ran to a ringbolt in the high ceiling. Candlelight warmed the cool white light of the corridors to a friendlier hue. In that warm glow, on a brilliantly colored carpet, stood a tall figure robed in midnight blue. Its face was subtly like Macenion's, and yet different; Paks knew at once that she stood in the presence of an elf, and someone of high rank. Along the far wall of the chamber were several motionless figures: humans, for the most part, clad in rough garments of gray and brown like poor servants.

Paks looked at the elf's face. Its bones showed clearly under the skin, yet there was no hint of age or decay. The eyes were a clear pale green. She felt no fear, though she was fully aware of the elf's power, so much greater than Macenion's. The elf's wide mouth curved in a smile.

"Welcome, fair warrior. Was your companion too frightened to come so far with you?"

Paks shook her head, uncertain how to answer. She had the vague thought that no elves should be here. But perhaps this was the person they had come to help? She could not seem to think clearly. The elf was not frightened of her, and did not seem angry—and elves were, if uncanny, at least not evil. As she thought this, she realized that she was walking forward, moving out into the chamber.

"Excellent," the elf continued. "I shall be glad to receive you both into my service." He gestured to the line of servants. "You see how few I have, and you have just killed some of my best fighters. It is only fair that you take their place."

Paks found her voice at last. "But, sir, I have a deed to perform before I can take service with another." She tried to stand still; her feet crept forward despite her efforts. She knew she should be afraid but she could feel nothing.

"Oh?" The silvery elven voice was amused. "And what is that?"

Paks found it difficult to say, or even think. A confusion of images filled her mind: the Halveric's face as he handed her a sealed packet, the Duke's parting words, the images of victory and glory that had come in the dream of the night before. She had advanced to the edge of the carpet. This close to the elf, she noticed a distinct, slightly unpleasant odor. Even as her nose wrinkled in distaste, the odor changed, becoming spicy and attractive. She drew a deep breath.

"Now—" the elf began, but at that moment, Macenion cried out from the far end of the chamber.

"Paks! What are you—"

Only for a moment those green eyes shifted from Paks; then the elf chuckled. "Well, so your companion finally gathered his courage. Stand near me, fair warrior, and show him your allegiance." And Paks stepped onto the soft carpet and stood silent beside the elf, unable to move or speak. She could just see Macenion from the corner of her eye. The elf went on. "You think yourself a mage, I understand—you have scarcely the powers to match me, crossbred runt."

Macenion reddened at this reference to his human ancestry. "You don't know what I might have—" he began.

"If you had any abilities I need worry about, you'd not have let yourself walk into this trap. You sensed nothing, at the last turn—you said so."

Macenion glared, and slid his hand stealthily under his cloak.

The elf nodded. "Go ahead—try your little spells if you wish. It won't do any good. Nor will that wand. But try it, if you like—" He laughed. "Do you not even wish to know who it is that you face, little mage? Are you in the habit of loosing spells on chance-met strangers?"

"We are not chance-met, I fear," said Macenion. He came forward a short distance, then stopped. "And if I cannot put a name to you, still I have a good idea what you are."

"What and not who? What erudition! And what makes you think I cannot charm you to obedience, as I did your—delightful—companion, here?"

Macenion smiled in his turn. "Charm a mage? You well know what that would get you. If you would use me as a mage, you need my mind unclouded—"

"But not unbroken, little one. Remember that."

Macenion bowed, as arrogantly as Paks had ever seen him. "Yet a pebble," he said, "may be harder to break than a pine, though insignificant beside it."

"Are you to quote dwarvish proverbs to me?" The elf sounded slightly less amused than before. Paks, listening to all this, could scarcely pay attention to it; her mind seemed to float at a slight distance.

Macenion bowed again, even more elaborately; as he rose, he made a complicated movement of his right hand, and said a few strange words loudly. Paks heard the hiss of breath indrawn beside her as the elf gasped. Before he could move, she felt a wave of nausea and fear. She whirled, sword at ready, before she even knew she could move. Where she had seen elven beauty, she now saw the ruin of it, and the stench stung her nose.

"Paks!" shouted Macenion. He was cut off by a great shout from the elf. A blast of energy poured down the chamber. Paks thrust at the elf, but her sword met another in his hand.

"Cross blades with me, will you?" The green eyes blazed. Paks tore her gaze from them to watch the sword hand. "No human has skill to match an elf—and I am no common elf." Indeed, the first ringing strokes revealed his ability. Paks fought on a rising wave of anger. Elves were never evil, ha! She avoided a quick trapping ploy, and thrust again. The tip of her blade seemed to hesitate an instant—an instant that let the enemy escape. She pressed on, furiously. Macenion had probably been killed by the blast, but he had won her freedom from whatever spell had bound her. She would fight to the end, and show this creature what human skill could be.

Again and again she managed to slip aside from a deadly blow, and just as often her own attacks fell short. Sweat rolled down her ribs, and she found herself grunting with every stroke. The elf did not seem to tire. The same smile curved his lips; the same arrogance arched his brows. Now her wrist began to ache, as he used every advantage of height and reach. She was usually taller than those she drilled with; she was not accustomed to adjusting to a longer reach. One of his blows fell true; the force of it drove her to one knee. She felt the links of mail sink into her flesh; she barely ducked the next blow and staggered back. She wanted to look for Macenion, but dared not. The elf's smile widened.

"You are outclassed, human fighter," he said lightly. "You are quite good, for a human, but not good enough. But look at my eyes, and acknowledge me your lord, and this can end."

Paks shook her head, as much to clear it as to refuse. Was that a movement behind the elf? She lunged again, her blade struck, but she narrowly avoided his. He seemed not to notice her blow. Suddenly a bit of hot wax fell on her face. As quick as the thought that followed, almost before she knew what she meant to do, Paks leaped high, grabbing the framework the candles were set on with one hand, and jerking her legs away from the elf's astonished stroke. The frame swung wildly, spattering them both with wax. With one arm over the ring, Paks swung at the elf from above. He grabbed at her leg and missed as she kicked out. She heard a squeal from above and glanced up to see the ringbolt slipping from the ceiling. She threw herself to one side, trying to clear the frame as it fell. The elf, pursuing, was struck. Before he could free himself from the ring, Paks attacked. Hampered by the framework and the candles, which caught his robe afire, he parried her blows weakly.

And then Macenion came up, panting and pale, and threw the whole of their oil supply on the elf. Paks jumped back as the candle flames flared on this fuel. A foul stench filled the chamber, and a black cloud swirled up from the fire, denser than smoke. Paks felt a wave of cold enmity that sent her staggering to her knees. The flames roared, now more blue than any fire of oil could be. Air rushed into the chamber, whistling round the corners. Paks realized that Macenion was tugging at her arms, pulling her away. She could hardly move. She managed to look around, and saw that the others in the room, the servants, were shuffling out a door in one corner as fast as they could.

When the flames died down, Paks still crouched helplessly where Macenion had dragged her. The elf's body had not been consumed in the fire, though it was horribly blackened, and all the clothing was gone. Macenion stood by it, frowning.

Paks tried several times before she could speak. "What's—wrong? He's dead, isn't he?"

"I wish I knew. That kind of power—it was some spirit of evil, Paks, that took over the body of an elf. Of an elf lord. And the body is here still. I wonder if he is dead—truly. I've heard tales of such—"

Paks didn't want to move. Every muscle hurt. She managed to flex her hand, and found she still held her sword. She took a deep breath, which also hurt, and forced herself to her feet. She felt as if her legs and body were only loosely connected. Another deep breath. It was hard to believe that she and Macenion were still alive, and the elf was dead. Or dead in some way. She walked over to see.

"Your magic has done well so far, Macenion. We wouldn't be here without it. Can't you do something to make sure he stays dead?"

For once Macenion did not seem complacent. "No," he said soberly. "That's beyond my abilities. I wish my old master were here. We are fortunate that he chose a simple spell to bind you. Perhaps he wanted to have plenty left for me, or perhaps he had more in use than we know. But now—"

"Couldn't we put a stake through his heart?"

"What do you think he is, a kuerin-witch? Are you thinking of dragging his corpse to a crossroads, too?"

Paks flushed. "I don't know. I just remembered some old stories . . ."

"That won't work for him. Whatever took him over won't be withheld by any simple measures."

"We could—" Paks swallowed hard, then went on. "We could cut—dismember him."

"You? I? I know what you would think of such. As for me, I tell you, Paksenarrion, I don't even wish to touch that corpse, if corpse it is. Nor should you. That power may still dwell in it, and could reach out to us. You see that the body was not consumed by the fire as it should have been; the skin is blackened but unblistered."

"Well, then? Do we wait to see what comes of it, or what?"

Macenion shook his head. "I don't know. I wish I knew a spell to free this body from whatever power holds it so."

"But since elves are immortal, do their bodies burn or decay?"

"Elves do not die of age alone, but they can, as you saw, be killed. And yes, their bodies can burn or decay or return to earth in many ways."

Paks shifted her shoulders, easing the stiffness. Suddenly she was hungry—and thirsty. She put up her sword and fumbled to unhook her water flask. After a couple of swallows, she felt much better. "It's too bad," she said, "that you don't know what's in that fancy scroll you're so proud of."

Macenion scowled and opened his mouth for a quick retort, then paused. "I never thought of that," he said. "I wonder if—" and he rummaged around inside his tunic until he came out with the tooled scroll case Paks had commented on. "It's difficult—" he went on, as he flicked off the lid and slid the scroll out. "You remember I told you how expensive it was?" Paks nodded. "Thing is, a magical scroll—one that has on it a workable spell—can be written only by a magician who can cast the spell without it. I don't know why; it seems a silly rule, and it certainly gives far too much power to men who do nothing but study, but there it is. Usually a scroll belongs to the man who wrote it, or to someone he trusts; his journeyman, say, or a brother mage. He knows which scroll is which—or he sets his private mark on each—and all's well. But for someone who comes across one of these scrolls—far away from the person who wrote it—it's difficult to tell what it is without reading it."

"Then read it," said Paks, gnawing on a slab of dried meat. It was delicious. "You can read—?"

"Of course, I can read! That's not the point. That's how it's used—by reading it. If I read it, whatever it is happens."

"Oh. But if it's not the right thing, can't you just read another?"

"No. Think! In the first place, suppose it's a spell to turn everyone but me in the room to stone. I read it, and there you are: stone."

"Right away?" Paks was startled.

"Yes, right away. And before you ask: no, I don't have any spell to turn you back—if one exists, and if I cared to use it. Contrary to popular belief, reading the spell backwards doesn't make it reverse. And in the second place, once it's read, it's gone. Poof!"

"Gone how?"

"Gone from the scroll. The magic is used up, and it—leaves."

"Oh. So there's no way to—to peek?"

Macenion allowed himself to look amused. "No. Not that I ever heard of. There are a lot of teaching tales for young apprentice magicians that tell of attempts to peek and what happened afterwards. No, I must decide, by examining all the marks on the outside of the scroll and by my own abilities, whether it's worth chancing that the spell or spells on it will do us any good." He peered at the scroll itself, then at the case, and then back at the scroll.

"I might just take a look into the corridors," said Paks casually. "In case someone is coming—"

"Good idea. Then you'll be out of range if something does happen." Paks had not realized that Macenion would find her motive so obvious. She said nothing, but looked into the corridor diagonally opposite to that from which she'd entered the chamber. This was the way the "servants" had left. She could see no one before the corridor turned, some twenty paces away. She looked back at Macenion. He was still examining the scroll, but he looked up at her and nodded. "Go on—not too far. I think I'll try one of these; for what I paid for them, they should be fairly powerful." Paks went on as far as the turn.

It seemed a long time before he called. His voice was high and excited. Paks swept out her sword and ran back to the chamber. She was just in time to see a blue flare lance to the ceiling from the elf's body. A dry clatter brought her eyes back to the floor; bones lay scattered there, and as she watched, they crumbled to dust. A draft scattered the dust. She looked up to meet Macenion's eyes. He was pale and trembling.

"It worked," she said unnecessarily,

"Yes, It—by Orphin, I'm tired. That—even reading it—that was beyond my powers—" He reeled, and Paks moved quickly to catch him before he fell. He lay some time unmoving. She could feel a pulse beating in his neck, so she folded her cloak under his head and let him rest. Some time later he opened his eyes and blinked. "What—? Oh yes. That." Silently Paks offered him water and food. He took a long drink, and shook his head at the food. After another swallow, he rolled up to a sitting position and shook his head sharply.

"Do you think, Macenion, that that creature was what we came here to fight?" Paks had been worrying about this; if it were the servant of some greater evil, she had little hope of escape.

"I think so. That—was a considerable power. If it had chosen a better spell for you, or been more practiced at swordplay—we wouldn't be here."

"Then what were we to free? The elf's body? That couldn't have called us. What else is there?"

Macenion rubbed his face with both hands. "No. You're right. We haven't been greeted with cries of joy and armfuls of reward, have we? Something still to be done—by Orphin, I don't know if I can manage any more spells today." He reached for the food and started eating slowly.

"Maybe you won't need to. If whatever it was is trapped somewhere, all we need to do now is find it."

"I hope it's that easy." Macenion stood up, swaying slightly at first. "I just had a thought. I hope whatever it is wasn't trapped in a jewel or something worn by the elf. Some magicians do that sort of thing. If so, we're out of luck."

"If only we get out of this," said Paks, "we'll be in luck."

"True. Did you see anything down that corridor?"

"No. Nothing."

Paks was never afterwards sure what had guided their choice, with so many ways to go, and no knowledge. At first, as they walked the bare stone corridor, Macenion continued to eat, reaching out now and again to touch the walls as if for balance. Then the corridor sloped down, and he paused.

"Wait—" Macenion's face, when Paks turned, was grim. He pulled out his own sword, and tested the balance. "I sense something—"

"Not that thing in the Winter Hall!"

Macenion shook his head. "No. Not so dire as that. But it's as if my blood tingled—some enemy is below, and coming nearer."

Paks looked around for a good place to fight. The corridor was slightly too wide for two to hold. "We'd better go on, then, and hope for something we can use."

Macenion nodded, and came up beside her as they started off again.

"Don't you want to stay back and prepare your spells?"

"I told you—I can't do that again today. I'd never be able to cast a simple fire spell, let alone anything useful."

The corridor turned right, and continued downward. Paks felt edgy; she was increasingly aware of the weight of stone and earth above her. She found herself whispering words from a Phelani marching song. Macenion looked at her curiously, and she blushed and fell silent.

Suddenly Paks caught a foul whiff that stopped her short. "What's that?"

Macenion looked eager. "Ah, I might have known. Orcs, that's what. They would move in when the elves were driven away."

"Orcs?" Paks had heard of orcs; they had raided Three Firs in her great-grandfather's day, but she had not expected to meet any.

"Ugly but cowardly," said Macenion briskly. "If that was their master, they'll want nothing better than escape. They won't be looking for experienced fighters like us—"

"If they want to escape, we can let them," suggested Paks.

"Let orcs loose? Are you crazy? They're disgusting. Vermin, killers, filthy—"

"How many are likely to be in a group?" Paks didn't care how disgusting they were; enough orcs could kill them.

"Oh—not more than seven or eight. We can handle that many. I killed three by myself one time."

"But Macenion—"

"Paksenarrion, I've seen you fight, remember? We have nothing to worry about. If we can handle that thing up there—" he jerked his head back where they'd been, "—we can handle a few orcs. Trust me. Haven't I been right on this so far?"

"I still think we should wait until we know how many there are. Let's find a hiding place, and—"

"Where?"

Paks looked around. Ahead, the corridor turned again twenty paces away, still going down. They had passed no doors for the last two hundred paces. She shrugged, and went on.

Around that corner the stench was stronger. Trash littered the floor. Paks looked for someplace to hide. Halfway to the next turn a doorway shadowed one wall. They had nearly reached it when they heard a harsh voice from somewhere ahead. Paks darted forward. The doorway was an empty gap opening into a tiny bare room. She grabbed Macenion's arm and pulled him in. He glared at her, but said nothing as the voice came nearer in the corridor.

The first orcs were uglier than Paks had imagined. Greasy leather armor covered their hunched torsos; long arms banded with spiked leather hung nearly to the floor. The first carried a curved blade, badly nicked along the inner curve, and the second dragged a short spear, short enough not to impede a fighter in the corridor. Paks noted the spare knives in sheaths on both hips, and helmets that came low over the nose. Behind the first pair came another, whose voice they had heard. It wore a filthy fur cloak over its armor, and carried a spiked whip as well as a sword. Whatever it was saying to the others must have been unpleasant, for the spear carrier turned suddenly and growled back at it. Paks flattened herself into the angle of wall away from the door, and hoped the orcs would quit arguing and go on. Macenion, however, leaned toward the door. She realized suddenly that he was about to attack. He looked back at her and cocked his head at the door.

If he attacked them and was killed, they'd be sure to look in the room. Paks cursed the stupidity of all magicians, and moved to the other side of the door, sword ready.

"It's only three," hissed Macenion. "We can take them easily." Paks hoped so. The argument outside was even louder. At least they could surprise the orcs. She took a deep breath and crouched. Now!

Her first blow caught the third orc low, in the thigh. His leg was harder than she'd expected, but she got her sword back, and he went down, bellowing. Macenion had gone for the spear carrier and missed; the other sword bearer took one wild swipe at Macenion's head, then turned to Paks. The orc she had wounded flung its whip at her sword, and she dropped the tip just in time. The orcs were faster than she'd expected. She parried the curved blade on one side and danced back from the wounded orc's whip. Macenion was trying to get past the guard of the spear carrier. She didn't envy him.

Once out of reach of the wounded orc, she found fencing with the other one strange but not as hard as she'd feared. Its reach was almost as long as hers, but low; it couldn't match her height. She had little trouble defending herself. Attack was harder. Her overhead blows fell on heavy armor. Paks abandoned that tactic and tested its quickness. Perhaps she could get behind it. She heard a yelp from Macenion, then a guttural command from the fallen orc. When she looked, Macenion was fencing left-handed, shaking blood from his right hand. That was the second wound to that arm. She attacked her own orc with sudden ferocity, and made a lucky stab under the right shoulder. The orc fell, snarling, and stabbed at her legs. Paks skipped back and ran to Macenion's opponent. He could not use a spear in two directions at once. Paks ran him through when he thrust at Macenion. But before they could do anything about the first orc she had wounded, it was bellowing even louder.

"Gods above!" gasped Macenion. "There's more of them!"

Paks heard the clamor almost as he spoke. "Which way?"

"I don't know! I—" He stared wildly around.

"Here!" Paks ripped a length of cloth from his cloak and wrapped it around his arm. "If we've got more to fight, you don't need to be dripping like that." She still could not tell where the sound came from; the corridor echoed confusingly.

"We'll go down," said Macenion suddenly.

"Down! But—"

"Come on!" He whirled away from her and strode down the corridor; the noise was much louder. Paks looked after him an instant, and ran to catch up.

"How do you know they're not—" But Macenion wasn't listening. He hurried ahead, and again she had to stretch her legs to catch him. "Macenion!" She caught at his arm as he neared the next turn.

It was too late. From around the turn erupted a wild band of orcs, stinking and dressed in filthy leather armor. Before she could guess how many of them they faced, she was engulfed in a deadly lacework of iron: swords, knives, and axes swung around her. The harsh clamor of their voices and the ring of blades filled her ears; it seemed all she could see was weapons and armor. Then she realized that Macenion was nearby, fencing with skill she had not suspected. That slender blade he bore had more strength than she'd thought.

"This way, Paks!" he yelled. He seemed to be edging ahead, still, and downward. Paks grunted and lunged toward him, taking a solid blow in one side as she came away from the wall. She felt the rings of her chainmail shirt dig in to the same place she'd been hit earlier, but it held whatever blade that was. She caught one orc under the chin, and dodged another. The place was full of them—she saw a doorway, now, and another doorway, and orcs in both. She slipped on something underfoot and staggered. Luckily they couldn't all reach her at once, and she hacked on, grimly determined to kill as many as she could before they killed her. She couldn't see Macenion, now.

Suddenly, the orcs gave way in front of her, and she plunged through them to find herself in a circular chamber. In front of her, Macenion lay face down as he had fallen, an axe standing out of his back. Beyond his body rose a focus of light that changed color as she looked. She whirled to face the orcs. They blocked the doorway, grinning and muttering. One at the rear of the mass yelled out, and they started toward her. She gave one quick glance to the chamber—no other door. And entirely too many orcs: no hope of winning through them all. She took a deep breath and laughed, at peace with her fate.

Afterwards she was never sure how she came to move into the light. As the orcs came forward, she ran to fight them over Macenion's body. They were too many, and pressed her back, and back again. Someone or something was calling her—wanted her to do something—but she had no time, no hands, for anything but the fight. As in a dream, she felt one ragged blade catch her arm, and another stabbed deep into her leg. Orc stench choked her nose; she gasped for breath, with a sudden memory of the young soldier in her first battle, a wry grin for the girl who would never get home. Back, and back again, a step at a time. She kept expecting a blow from behind, but it never came. Her arm felt heavy and clumsy; her sword slid off an orc helmet as the dagger in her left hand parried another blade. She took a deep breath—her last, she thought—and lunged hard at the orc in front of her.

She could not reach him. He stood as close as her own arm, but his sword, thrusting at her, jabbing wildly, touched her not at all, nor hers, him. And a pressure filled her head, as if a river poured itself in one side and found no outlet. She felt herself falling under that pressure, her hand loosening, losing its grip on the dagger.

—Take—It was more of a picture than a word: a hand, grasping.

Paks stared at her own hand, open as if it were reaching for something.

—Take . . . this . . . thing—The pressure moved her eyes; she looked as it directed, and saw a blue egg-shaped object. She could not tell how far away it was, or how big, or even what it was. She tried to frame a question. Instead, the command returned, and filled her whole head; she felt it would burst.—TAKE IT—

She reached toward the object, and felt an unpleasant oily sensation on the insides of her fingers, as if they were sinking slightly into it. But her hand closed around the object firmly. It felt disgusting, in ways she could not describe, and had never imagined. She would have dropped it, thrown it far away, but it clung to her hand. When she tried to open her fingers, they wouldn't move. All at once she felt the pain of all her wounds, the exhaustion of all the fighting, a great heaving wave of sickness that seemed to cut her legs from under her. She tried to raise her sword for one last blow.

And the pressure within suddenly burst out in a vast roar, a vibration so deep she felt it in her bones and hardly at all in her ears. The light was gone—darkness churned around her—she caught a last confused glimpse of orcs screaming, falling stones, Macenion's body glowing blue as fire—then a deafening, whirling confusion.

And silence.

CHAPTER SIX

When she managed to lift her head, she was lying on the turf near the well. The building they had entered was down, collapsed in a heap of stones. It was broad daylight, with the sun's warmth filtered through high clouds. Paks took a breath, and sneezed. She was stiff and sore, and it was hard to think what had happened. Her head felt empty; her ears rang like a bucket. She looked at her hands—the one still cramped around the hilt of her sword, and the other empty, but with the feel of something filthy on it. She scrubbed it in the grass. Her eyes watered, and she swiped at them clumsily with her sword hand.

She knew she should get up, but she wished she could lie there and rest forever. After a moment, sighing, she forced herself up: elbows, knees—she rested there for a bit. Her legs felt shaky and uncertain. She looked at her sword; blood and dirt were caked on it. She shuffled on her knees to the well and took a handful of water to clean it. After a mouthful or two of that clear water, she began to feel more alert. The sword slid back in its scabbard sweetly—it feared nothing near. She looked around for the horses. Macenion's had disappeared; that seemed right. Star grazed unconcernedly across the well from her. There were the packs, lying open outside the ruins of the little building. Whatever had happened, there below, was over. She could do nothing for Macenion now. She must go on.

Even so, she might have sat beside the well for the rest of the day if something had not moved her. The pressure she had felt before seeped back into her mind. This time it was more delicate: she was aware of it as a separate being. There were thanks, for her and Macenion. There were directions, specific and detailed. Slowly she rose to her feet, and slowly she gathered up her belongings. She wondered what to do with Macenion's things, and the being told her. This to the well, and that under a stone, and those to lie open on the grass, for the wind and sun to play with. Star came to her quietly, and she tied her pack to the frame.

Before she left, the being demanded one thing more. She was tired and found it hard to think, but the pressure gave her no ease until she obeyed. In that mound, through that gap—and take those things. She packed, vaguely aware that much of it was treasure: weapons decorated with gold and jewels, coins, rings, and baubles. But why the scrolls? She didn't understand, but she obeyed, picking up what she was bid, and stowing it away in Star's pack. As she worked, the clouds thickened overhead, and a chill wind rolled down from the mountains. She didn't notice. She felt no triumph, only a great tiredness.

As she stumbled away on the narrow track she had been nudged to follow, the first dancing flakes of snow fell from the thickening clouds behind her. Soon a light dusting whitened the tops of the mounds in the valley, outlined the limbs of trees and clung to the cedars in little furry clumps. The clouds reached out, northwards, and gathered in the trail Paks had taken. Snow hung in the air around her, filling her lungs with its damp clean smell. She hardly noticed. It was harder and harder to walk. Every step seemed to take the last of her strength, as if she were pulling her legs out of the ground. Her left hand still felt dirty, and she rubbed it on her trousers as she walked, without realizing it. Uphill—it was all uphill, trying to clear the ridge on the far side of the valley. Paks caught at Star's pack, clung to it, and the sturdy pony plowed on, through the deepening snow, ears flat and tail clamped down. Paks' left side caught the blast of wind off the mountains. Soon it was numb, and she stumbled, lurching into Star, and then back, to fall facedown in the snow. A wave of nausea swept over her, but she had nothing to heave. Her stomach cramped. She couldn't push herself up; she felt the snow on the back of her neck, and then nothing.

The elfane taig, having won, settled back into place with satisfaction. Its rule ran to the boundary stones placed by the elves when first they came. If it could do something, for the one who freed it from such contamination, it might do so—but beyond the stones it could not go. And, as well, the troubles of weak mortals are of little interest to such as the elfane taig. Even less when it had suddenly been restored to its powers, and had much to do. She had received her reward. The elfane taig had no notion, of course, of the human value of what she had been given; gold, it knew, was prized by humans. Some of the other objects had come from humans in the first place. The elfane taig thought their return appropriate.

In the darkness, the first elf mistook her snow-covered body for a drift of snow, and stumbled over it. His muffled curse disturbed the pony, huddled in a thicket nearby, and she snorted.

Quickly the next elves found the pony and soothed her, whisking the snow from her back and running deft hands over the pack straps. Meanwhile the first elf felt what was under the drift, and called for more light. Torches flared in the windy darkness.

"A human." Contempt laced the silver voice.

"A robber by the look of it—her," said another, holding out the patched cloak.

"Robber indeed," said one of the elves near Star. "This little one is loaded with such treasure that she can hardly walk. And more than that, it comes from the banast taig. '

"Mother of Trees! I had not thought even the humans bold enough to rob there. Or skilled enough to escape." The leader of the group looked at a dagger and sheath from the pack and shook his head. "With such to carry, it must not be escape, but something worse."

"She is alive," said the first elf, after finding a pulse.

"Not for long," said the leader. "We may not be able to challenge *that* evil, but we can deal with its minions. We can leave—"

"Look at this," said one of those going through the pack. He held out to the leader the sealed message from the Halveric. "Is this stolen as well?"

"We must know what we have here, before we decide what to do," added the one at Pak's side. "I feel no great evil in her." He had brushed the snow off her, and now caught his breath as he saw the rings on her hand. He worked off the one with the Duke's seal, and read the inscription inside. "This is no common robber, cousins. Here is a ring given for honor to a soldier of the Duke Phelan—Halveric's friend, and—"

"And we all know of Kieri Phelan. Yes. If she did not steal that as well. We shall wake her, then, and see what she says. I doubt that any fair tale can be told resulting in such a one bringing treasure out of the banast taig. But we shall see."

Paks was vaguely aware of voices talking over her head before she woke fully. They were strange-sounding voices, musical and light but carrying power nonetheless. Light glowed through her eyelids. She struggled toward it, and finally managed to raise her heavy lids.

"You waken at last," said one of the strange beings before her. He turned to speak to another, and Paks saw torchlight play over the planes of his face. It was clearly unhuman, and in it she saw full strength the strangeness that Macenion had shared. These must be elves. He looked back at her, his expression unreadable. "You were very cold. Can you speak now?"

Paks worked her jaw around, and finally managed to say yes, weakly.

"Very well. We have many questions for you, human warrior. It would be well for you to answer truthfully. Do you understand?"

"Who—are you?" Paks had no idea of elven politics, if any.

"Do you not know elves, human, when you see them?"

"I thought—elves—but who?"

Arched eyebrows rode up his forehead. "Do humans now concern themselves with the genealogy of elves, having so little themselves? If you would know, then, I am of the family of Sialinn—do you know what that means?" Paks shook her head. "Then you need know no more of my family. Who are you, and what lineage gives you the right to question elves?"

Paks remembered now Macenion's pride, and how Bosk had always said elves were haughty and difficult.

"I am Paksenarrion Dorthansdotter," she began. "Of Three Firs, far to the north and west—"

"Far indeed," said one of the other elves. "I have seen that place, though not for many years. Is there a birch wood, a day's ride west of it, in the side of a hill?"

"I don't know, sir; I never traveled so far before leaving to join the Duke's Company. Since then, I have never been home, or near it."

"Whose company was this you joined?"

"Duke Phelan's. He has a stronghold in northern Tsaia, and fights in Aarenis."

"A red-haired man?" Paks nodded, and the elf went on. "This packet sealed by the Halveric, in your baggage: how came you by that?"

"I was given it, by the Halveric, to take to his home." Even as she spoke, Paks felt the cold darkness rolling over her again. One of the elves exclaimed, and she felt an arm under her shoulders. A cold rim touched her lips, and fiery liquid trickled into her mouth. She swallowed. Warmth edged its way along her bones.

"Not too much of that," said the first elf who had spoken to her. "In case we must—" He broke off and looked at her again. "You have come to a strange place, soldier of Duke Phelan and messenger of the Halveric. You have come to a strange place, and you seem—forgive me—weaker than I would expect such a soldier to be. Give us now an account of how you came here, and what you were doing in the valley of the banast taig."

Paks found it difficult to tell a coherent story. Events and places were tangled in her memory, so that she was hard put to distinguish the encounters of the last day or so from those in the past. Still she managed to convey the call she and Macenion had received, and the outline of their adventures undergound. The elves listened attentively, interrupting only to ask for clarification. When she finished, they looked at each other in silence. Then a burst of elven; it sounded to her like an argument. The leader turned to her again.

"Well, Paksenarrion Dorthansdotter, you have told an unlikely tale, to be sure. Yet on the chance that it is true, I am sending one of my party into the banast taig to find out. Should he not return, or return in jeopardy, it will go hard with you."

In the snowy darkness, Paks could not tell how long the elf was gone. She lapsed into a doze, hardly aware of her surroundings. She was roused by a hand on her shoulder.

"Awake, warrior. You will need this—" and a hot mug pressed against her lips. She swallowed, still half-asleep, and found the taste strange but pleasant. Slowly her drifting mind came back to her. She tried to sit up on her own, but was still too weak. The elves had pitched a shelter over her, and a tiny fire flickered in one corner, under a pot.

"You still need healing," said the elf leader. "I admit surprise, Paksenarrion. I would not have believed such a thing without proof.

The banast taig freed to be the elfane taig again, and the pollution gone from its heart! We rejoice to know that. But you have taken more damage from that combat than you know: humans cannot fight evil of that power unscathed. Without healing, you would die before daylight."

Paks could not think what to say. She felt weak, and a little sick, but no worse than that. As the elf seemed waiting for something, she finally asked. "Was—did you find out about Macenion?"

"Macenion!" It was very nearly a snort. "That one! The elfane taig buried him cleanly with his orcish murderers; he is well enough."

"But he was an elf—half-elf, I meant. I thought you would—"

"Macenion a half-elf? Did he tell you that?" Paks nodded, and the elf leader frowned. "No, little one, he was not half-elven—not a quarter-elven, either. He had so much elvish as might your pack pony have of racing blood."

"But he said—" Paks broke off. It was hard to talk, and she realized that Macenion's behavior made more sense the less elven he was.

"He lied. What did he tell you, Paksenarrion, to get you into that valley?"

"That—his elven cousins—denied him his rights to elvish things. That he knew of—treasure there—that should be his."

"Did he not warn you of evil at all?"

"Yes—but he said nis magical talents could fight that; he needed a warrior for protection against—physical things. Like the orcs."

"I see that you speak truly. I apologize, Paksenarrion, for the untruth of this distant cousin; it shames me that any elven blood could lie so."

"That's—all right." Paks felt as if she were slipping down a long dark slope.

"No! By the gods of men and elves, we shall redeem the word of our cousin." And the elf shook her again, lifting her up until she could drink from a cup one of the others held. The darkness crept back. The elven faces came back into focus. Then one of them laid his hand on her head, and began to sing. She had never heard anything like that, and in trying to follow the song she forgot what was happening. Suddenly she felt a wave of strength and health surge through her. The elf removed his hand, and smiled at her.

"Is that better now?"

"Yes—much better." Paks sat up, and stretched. She felt well and rested, better than she'd felt in days.

"Good. It will be day, soon, and we must be going. We have much to say to you in the few hours left us."

The snow had stopped before dawn. A light wind tore the last clouds to shreds and let the first sunlight glitter on the snowy ground. In daylight, the elves bade her farewell, and Paks saw their beauty clearly. She felt ashamed to have thought Macenion elvish-looking. One of them caught her thought, and laughed, the sound chiming down the long slope.

"No—don't be sorry, fair warrior. Your eyes saw truly, to find what was there in so little. Remember what we have told you, and fare well."

And as she turned to climb the slope upward to the ridge and the trail the elves had spoken of, she felt far distant from the self of yesterday. She felt a surge of the same spirit that had sent her away from home in the first place, a sense of adventure and excitement. Anything might happen—anything had happened. She still found it difficult to think clearly what it was—what nature of thing she and Macenion had fought against, and what had helped her at the end. The words elfane taig meant nothing to her. The elves' explanation meant very little more.

But she was on a trail once more, alive and eager to be going. Star moved slowly, burdened heavily by the gifts of the elfane taig. Paks had transferred some of that to her own back. The pony snorted a little with each heave of her hindquarters. Paks grinned to herself. No more mountains, they had told her. These, that would have been mountains anywhere else, counted but as foothills, and in another two days she would be on the gentler lowland slopes.

On the far side of the ridge, only a few patches of snow whitened the trail, and by noon these had melted. Now other trees mingled with the pointed evergreens—duller greens, more rounded shapes. Paks did not need her cloak for warmth. She was alert for danger, but the elves had told her that they sensed nothing dire moving in the area. She hoped they were right. As far as she could see, the forested slopes wove into each other endlessly, the trail angling down one and up another, always edging west and north.

Her solitary camp that night was almost too silent. She had

resented Macenion's lectures—yet to sit alone, in the middle of a vast wilderness, was worse than anything he had ever said to her. She doused her tiny fire early, and sat awake a long time, staring at the stars. The night was half-gone when she realized that she was missing more than Macenion. She had never, in her life, spent an entire night alone like this. Not even once had she slept outside, out of hearing or sight of others. The thought itself made her shiver, and she got up to check on Star. The pony's warm rough mane reassured her. She looked at the stars again, her hands still tangled in Star's mane. The night sky seemed to go on forever, up and up without ending, as if the stars were sewn on veils that lay one behind another. She looked for Torre's Necklace; it was still behind the mountains. Of the other stars she knew nothing.

A breeze began to move lightly along the ground. Star moved away from her hand, and lowered her head to graze. Paks went back to the blankets she'd laid out. A wild animal cried out in the distance; she stiffened, but no sound followed. Paks felt an urge to take out Canna's medallion; her hand found her pouch before she thought. Her fingers touched it, smoothed the crescent shape. When she pulled it out, Saben's little horse came along; the thongs were tangled. She woke stiff and cold in the morning, with Star nosing her face, and the horse and crescent still clutched in her hand.

That day warmed quickly. Paks looked over the whole treasure she had been given, and made her first estimate of its value. She had not realized what she'd taken—it was too much—it shouldn't be hers. But she was not going to return to the elfane taig with it, that was certain. She thought the elves must have examined it as well, and if they said nothing about it, she would not. Sunlight glittered on the items she'd laid in the grass—the ruby-decorated dagger and sheath, the gold-and-jewel-inlaid battleaxe, gold and silver coins, both familiar in stamp and strange, a set of chainmail that was oddly light when she lifted it, and looked as if it would fit. She thought about that, looked around, and tried it on. It did fit—perfectly—which made her scowl, thinking. Where had she heard of enchanted mail, evil stuff—? But when she reached for Canna's medallion, nothing happened; it felt easy in her hand. Was it dress mail, then, good for nothing? She tried her own dagger on the sleeve, notching the dagger. Lightweight, the right size—she scowled again, but kept it on. Over it she put on the best clothes she had—not that any of them looked like much, she thought ruefully, remembering the money she'd spent in Sord to outfit herself.

It was late when she started moving again, and she traveled slowly as much for her own benefit as the pony's. She was beginning to wonder what she would find when she came out of the wilderness into settled lands again. The elves had been quite specific in their directions—go to Brewersbridge, they had said, by this trail, and tell the Master Oakhallow and Marshal Deordtya about the elfane taig. But they would say no more about either Master Oakhallow or the Marshal, or why these would want to know about events so far away.

As Paksenarrion came around the slope of the hill, she could see cleared fields and orchards some miles ahead, their straight edges easily visible against the broken forest and meadowland. The track's gradient lessened as she descended; she saw sheep grazing on the slopes to her right, and a barelegged child with a crook watching them from a rock. Gradually the track changed from rock to dirt. Star stepped out more easily. Paks lengthened her own stride to keep up. She saw smoke rising from the center of the cleared area; perhaps it was the village the elves had spoken of. She wondered if the people were friendly. At least it was the north again: home.

In an hour, she was among the fields and orchards. She had passed two farmsteads set back from the road. The farms looked prosperous; she noted tight barns, well-made stone walls, sleek livestock. A boy picking early apples from a tree near the track told her the village ahead was Brewersbridge; when she'd passed she looked back and saw him running for the farmhouse. Now the track joined a lane, bordered on either side by a wall, wide enough for wagon traffic. She noted wheelruts grooving the surface. On the right, a wedge of forest met the road; she could not tell how large it was. Ahead were a cluster of buildings and another road coming in from the right.

Two cottages now on the left, one opening directly on the road. Beyond them was a large two-story building with a walled courtyard to one side. A bright green and yellow sign hung over the road, and a paved area fronted it. Paks squinted at the sign: The Jolly Potboy. It must be an inn; it was too big for a tavern. She looked around.

The inn sat at the crossroad, facing north. The road Paks had come on continued generally west, wandering among houses and shops. The north road was straighter, with buildings along its west side and forest on the east. The ground floor of the inn had a row of tall windows facing the road; these were open, and Paks heard the murmur of many voices from inside. She wondered if she had enough money to stay there. The treasure—but she didn't know what it was worth, or if they would accept the old coin.

As she hesitated, a stout man in a big apron came out and spoke to her.

"Just arrived?"

"Yes, sir."

"Will you be wanting a room?"

"I don't know, sir. How much are they?"

"A silver in the common loft; that includes bread and beer for breakfast. A gold crown for a private room; two for the suite. A silver a day for stabling, including grain, hay, grooming, and safe storage for your tack."

Paks thought a moment. It seemed high, but she had enough southern money for a night or two. She could always find a cheaper place the next day. Star could use a good bait of grain. "I'd like a private room," she said. "And stabling for Star."

"That'll be in advance, please," said the man. "I'm Jos Hebbinford, the landlord."

Paks wrapped Star's lead around her arm and dug into her belt pouch. "Here—" she handed over the money. "I'm Paksenarrion Dorthansdotter, from Three Firs."

The landlord looked closely at the coins she had given him. "Hmm. From Aarenis—that your home?"

"No, sir. Three Firs is north and west of here. I was with Duke Phelan's company hi the south, and I'm headed home."

"I see. A fighter, are you?" Paks nodded. "Are you a Girdsman, too?"

"No. I've known those who were."

"Hmmm. We don't think much of brawling, here."

Paks flushed. "I'm not a brawler, sir."

"Good. Just a moment—Sevri! Sevrienna!" At his call, a short stocky redheaded girl came out of the courtyard and ran up. "My daughter, Sevrienna," said the landlord. "Sevri, this is Paksenarrion, who will be staying this night. This is her horse—" he glanced at Paks.

"Her name's Star," said Paks. "She's gentle."

"Sevri will take her to the stable," said Hebbinford. "If you'd like to see your room—?"

"If you don't mind, sir," said Paks, "I'll just give Star a rubdown first, and check her hooves. She's come a long way over rocks."

"Very well. Sevri will help you. When you come in, I'll take you to your room."

"Come on—this way," said Sevri. Paks followed. The walled courtyard was large, paved in flat slabs of gray stone. A flock of red and black hens scratched and pecked in the entrance of the stable that ran along one side; a black cock with gold on his throat and a green tail stood atop the dungheap. Along other sides of the courtyard were barns full of hay and an open shed with two wagons and a cart beneath it.

Sevri led Paks to a box stall big enough for a warhorse; all the stalls were big. "I can rub her down," Sevri offered. "You're paying for grooming."

Paks smiled at the child. "I want to check her and make sure she hasn't hurt her hooves on the rocks. If you want to rub her down—"

Sevri nodded. "Surely. She'll be easier than the big horses, and I do them. Do you want her to have grain, or would a mash be better?"

"A mash would be good for her, if it's not too much trouble."

"I'll put one on, then come back and start on her. If you want water to work on her feet, here's a bucket, and the well is out there." Sevri jerked her head toward the courtyard.

When Sevri had gone, Paks untied the bundles from the saddle, and lifted them down. Star sighed. "Poor pony," said Paks. "That was a load. Here now—" She uncinched the pack saddle and lifted it from Star's back. Underneath, Star's coat was matted and damp. Paks moved the bundles to one side of the stall, and bent to feel Star's legs. Then she took the bucket Sevri had pointed out, and filled it at the well. Back in the stall, she lifted Star's feet, one at a time. They were dry and hot. Paks found a rag in her pack that she'd used for a headcloth and dipped it in the water. She washed out each hoof and dampened the coronary band. The pony reached down and mumbled Paks' hair. "No, Star; stop that." Paks shoved the pony's head away. She found a cut on the off hind pastern, and cleaned it out carefully.

"You must like her a lot," said Sevri. Paks jumped.

"I didn't hear you come."

"That's because I'm barefooted," said Sevri. "Are her feet all right?"

"Yes, but for one little cut. Just dry from the rocks."

"She is wet. You want me to start rubbing her now?"

"Yes. Just let me get these things out of the stall." Paks grunted as she hoisted the bundles. She dumped them in the aisle. Sevri was watching her.

"That must be awfully heavy."

"It is," said Paks shortly.

Sevri had brought two lengths of coarse woolen cloth and a brush. When she picked up one cloth and started work on Star's sweaty back, Paks took the other and began the other side.

"You don't have to help me," said Sevri. "I can do it by myself."

"Do you mind, though? I'm used to doing her."

"No-o. But I am strong enough."

"I don't doubt that," said Paks, though she did. Star turned her head and nudged Sevri with her soft nose. Sevri stopped and stroked Star's head.

"She's gentle," said Sevri. "Have you had her long?"

"Not very. She is a good pony, though—seems to like everyone. Only don't come near her with apples unless you want to lose a few."

Sevri laughed. "I'll bring her one. Is she greedy about other things?"

Paks shrugged. "She's a pony. I've never known a pony that wouldn't eat anything it could find, have you?"

"That's true." Sevri looked across Star's back at Paks. "Are you a fighter?"

Paks paused before answering. "It depends on what you mean by fighter. Your father seems to think a fighter is the same as a brawler, a troublemaker. That's not what I am. I was a mercenary, a soldier in the Duke's Company."

"But you can use that sword?"

"Oh, yes. I can use a sword. That's how I've earned my keep since I left home. But that doesn't mean I go picking fights everywhere."

"I see." Paks thought by the tone of Sevri's answer that she didn't see. She decided to change the subject.

"Sevri, I have a message for two people here: can you tell me where to find them?"

"Surely."

"One is a Master Oakhallow—" she stopped as Sevri gasped audibly.

"You—you know Master Oakhallow?"

"No, I don't know him; I've never been here before. But someone I met a few days ago gave me a message for him. What's wrong?"

"Nothing. He's the Kuakgan, that's all."

Paks felt a chill. "Kuakgan? I didn't know that."

Sevri nodded. "He's a good man, it's just—he's very powerful, Master Oakhallow. My father's told me about him; he helped in the troubles."

Paks said, "Well, I must speak to him, at least. Where is he?"

"In his grove, of course. I'll show you, when we're through. Which way did you come in?"

"From the southeast," Paks pointed.

"Well, then, you saw part of the grove on your right, as you came into town."

"I remember. I was surprised to see uncleared forest so near the town."

"Don't go in except by the entrance," said Sevri. "It's dangerous. Now, who else was it you wanted to find?"

"There's a grange of Gird here, isn't there?" Sevri nodded. "I must speak to a—a Marshal, I think it was, by the name of Deordtya."

Sevri stared. "She isn't here anymore. We have a new Marshal now, called Cedfer, and a Yeoman-marshal called Ambros. But what kind of message can you have for the Kuakgan and the Marshal?"

"I'm sorry, Sevri, but I must speak with them first."

"Oh. Of course, I shouldn't have asked."

"That's all right. Now, where can I put the packsaddle, and where's a safe place for these bundles?"

"Here—" Sevri ducked around Star and led Paks down the aisle. "Put your things here—and I'll be around watching, if you'll trust me. You can leave your bundles here, too."

Paks looked at the freckled face and wondered.

"They'll be safer here than in your room," said Sevri frankly. "The rooms have locks, but Father's fairly sure we have a thief staying with us. Nothing's happened yet, but—I can watch your things, out here."

Paks sighed. "All right, Sevri. I'll be back when I've made my visits."

"Don't miss supper," said Sevri, grinning. "We have good food."

Paks smiled back at her. "I won't miss dinner, not after my journey." She left the stable and entered the inn. The landlord saw her at once and came forward.

"Sevri taking care of you?"

"Yes, sir. She's most helpful."

"Come this way—upstairs—to your room." He turned and led the way across the main room to a broad stone stair. Paks followed, glancing about. The main room evidently served as both tavern and dining room; it was furnished with tables and benches. Half a dozen men were scattered about the tables drinking; two were men-at-arms in blue and rose livery, one was dressed all in black, with a black cloak over trousers and tunic, two looked like merchants, in long gowns, and one was a huge burly fellow in a patched leather tunic over russet hose. Two women sat near the fireplace: the gray-haired one drew out yarn on a hand spindle, while the dark one marked something in a book. Paks went on up the stairs.

A landing at the top of the stairs opened onto a passage on one side and a fair-sized room with pallets in it on the other. The landlord led the way down the passage, past two doors on the left, and three on the right, to stop at the third on the left. He took a ring of keys from his belt and fitted one to the lock. The door swung open silently.

The room was compact but not cramped. A sturdy wooden bedstead with a thick straw pallet on it stood against the left-hand wall. Linen sheets were stretched over the pallet, and two thick wool blankets were folded at the foot. A three-legged stool stood at the foot of the bed, and a low chair (leather stretched on a wood frame) stood under the window. A row of pegs ran down both walls of the room, and a narrow clothespress stood beside the door. The walls were whitewashed, the wooden floor scrubbed, and the room smelled as clean as it looked. Paks looked out and saw the window overlooked the crossroads.

"Will this do?" asked the landlord.

"Oh, yes. It's very nice," said Paks.

"Good." He worked the key to the room off his ring and handed it to her. "Return this, please, before you leave. Is there anything more?" Paks shook her head, and he turned away. Paks shut the door, then took down her hair and combed it. If she was to see a Kuakgan and a

Gird's Marshal, she would be neat, at least. She brushed her cloak as well as she could, rebraided her hair, and left the room, locking it carefully behind her.

CHAPTER SEVEN

Paks left the inn, wishing she didn't have to go. She felt eyes watching her from the inn's wide windows; her shoulders twitched. Evening light glowed in the changing foliage of the trees on her right; a few shrubs were already brilliant crimson. She saw two men-at-arms in the local livery coming toward her. They stared, and she returned the stare coolly, hand near the hilt of her sword. One opened his mouth, but his companion nudged him in the ribs and they passed by in silence.

Ahead on the right she saw a break in the wall of trees and leaves. As she came closer, she saw that it was an arch of sorts: vines binding branches, with a narrow path winding away toward the wood. Paks paused before the opening. She could go in the morning, she thought, and started to turn away—but there on the road were more men-at-arms, and these moved towards her. She stepped under the arch and went in.

She had taken only a few steps when she became aware of the silence. Voices from the road did not penetrate the grove. Her own breathing seemed loud. She slowed, and looked around. Trees, irregularly spaced. More light than she would have expected under the trees, but—she looked up—the leaves were worn and frayed with autumn. Golden light spilled through. The path, though narrow, was easy to see, picked out in rounded white stones that looked like river cobbles. She moved on, alert and watchful. Sevrienna had not had to warn her about Kuakkganni and their groves. Everything she had ever heard of them was danger.

A gust of wind stirred the dry leaves around her. As the rustling faded away, she heard somewhere ahead the gentle laughter of falling water. The path twisted once, then again. The trees framed more light: a glade, open to the sky. Almost in the center was a simple fountain, water welling up in a stone basin and trickling over the edge to fall into another, and then another. The last was a small pool from which Paks could see no outlet. Beside the fountain was a rough block of stone with a wide bronze basin on top. Paks moved towards it, eyes scanning the clearing. Now she could see a low gray house, close under the trees on the far side of the clearing; it looked almost like a fallen tree trunk, it was so rough. Paks made out a door and windows, shuttered, but nothing else. The clearing was otherwise empty.

Still nervous, Paks neared the fountain. Its water was perfectly clear, a silken skin that rippled with every breath of air; the falling drops from one level to the next sparkled like jewels. Paks looked back to see if the sun was still that high. It had gone behind the trees but scattered rays, she assumed, lit the fountain. She tore her gaze from the water and approached the bronze basin on its pedestal of stone. An offering basin, she was sure, but what offerings were acceptable to Kuakkganni? Childhood memories of the dark tales her grandfather told clouded her mind. Blood, he'd said. Kuakkganni follow the oldest gods, and blood they demand.

"It is customary to place one's offering in the basin." The voice was deep and resonant, complex. Paks jerked her head up and found herself face to face with a tall, dark-faced man in a hooded robe of greens and browns. Her heart leaped against her ribs; she felt sweat spring out on her back. She had heard nothing.

"Sir, I—" she swallowed, as her voice failed, and tried again. "Sir, I know not what offerings would be acceptable—to a Kuakgan."

The heavy brows arched. "Oh! And why would one with no knowledge of Kuakkganni come seeking one?"

Paks found it hard to meet those dark eyes. "Sir, I was told to."

"By whom?"

"By the elves, sir." Paks did not miss the sudden shift of shoulders, the movement of brows and eyelids.

"Go on, then. What elves, and why?"

"Sir, the elves of the Ladysforest. The one who sent me said that he was of the family of Sialinn."

"And his message?"

"That the elfane taig had woken again, the lost elf been freed."

"Ahh. That is news indeed. And did he chance on you, to be his messenger, or had he other reasons?"

"I had been there—" Paks began to shiver, remembering as if it were happening, the final conflict in the round chamber.

"Hmmm. So there is more reason than chance. Well, then, I'll have your name, wanderer, and you shall indeed offer something to the peace of the grove which you displace."

"My name is Paksenarrion Dorthansdotter—"

"From the northwest, by your patronymic. And for an offering, what have you?"

Paks pulled the little pouch out of her tunic. "Sir, as I said, I do not know what would please—but I have these—" She poured out on her palm the largest jewels from the treasure."

"Any would be acceptable," said the Kuakgan. "Place your offering in the basin." Paks wondered why he did not simply take one, but chose a green stone from them and set it carefully at the base of the bowl. The others she returned to the pouch.

"And I," said the Kuakgan as if continuing a sentence, "am Master Oakhallow. As you knew, a Kuakgan. But I think you must have strange ideas, child, of what Kuakkganni are—what, then?"

To her surprise, Paks found herself telling her grandfather's lore. "And he said, sir, that—that Kuakkganni ate babies—sir—at the dark of midwinter."

"Babies!" The Kaukgan sounded more amused than angry. "That old tale still! No, child, we don't eat babies. We don't even kill babies. In fact, if you use that sword you're wearing for anything but decoration, I daresay you've spilled more blood than I have."

Paks stared at him. Despite the undertone of amusement, he still radiated power. She wondered if he could tell what she was thinking. Macenion had said that wizards could—were Kuakkganni the same?

"Are you a warrior?" he pursued.

"Yes, sir."

"Hmm. And involved somehow in the wakening of the elfane taig. Well, then, tell this tale: where are you from that you came to that dread valley, and what happened?"

Paks looked again at his face, trying to gauge his mood. It was impossible. His dark eyes seemed to compel her to go on. She began, haltingly enough, to explain that she had left a mercenary company in

Aarenis to return to the north. When she came to tell of her companion, the Kuakgan stopped her abruptly.

"Who did you say? Macenion? He said he was an elf?"

"Yes, sir." Paks wondered at his expression. "Later he said he was but half-elven—"

"Half-elf! Hmmph! No wonder the elves sent you here." He motioned for her to continue. She went on to tell of the early part of their journey, at first slowly, but warming up to it when describing Macenion's behavior among the wardstones. Her resentment flared again: he had lied to her, he had pretended to knowledge he didn't have, he might have gone on and left her... She stopped abruptly, at the look on the Kuakgan's face. Suddenly that quarrel seemed silly, like the attempt of a half-drunken private to explain to Stammel that a drinking companion was really to blame. She rushed on, skimping on the other adventures. This was no time to bring up the snowcat. Then she came to Macenion's decision to enter the valley of the elfane taig.

"He said whatever was there wouldn't hurt me, because I was human, and the power was elvish. He said that the elves had tried to keep him away out of jealousy, but he knew he could control whatever evil was there, and regain his inheritance."

"And what did you think, human warrior?" Paks could not tell if the deep voice was scornful or merely interested. She felt the same confusion at his questions as at the elves' persistent interrogation. Why would anyone expect her to have an opinion about something like the elfane taig? She explained about the dreams, and Macenion's confidence in his own wizardry.

"Did you trust him?" asked the Kuakgan, in the same tone.

Paks remembered too well the sinking feeling she'd had as they entered the outer wards. But he had died well. "Yes," she said slowly. "He could be good with a sword. And he could make light, and windshift, and that."

The Kuakgan looked at her closely. "Don't lie to me, child. Did you truly trust him, as you would have trusted a member of your old company?"

"No, sir." Paks stared down at the grass blades between her feet.

"And yet you went with him, knowing that danger, and powers a human should not face, lay below?"

"Not knowing, sir. I felt danger, and was worried, but I didn't know what we faced. And we had traveled together for weeks. Besides, he knew more than I—"

The Kuakgan frowned. "You said that before. You seem to be convinced of it. And you followed this so-called half-elf, whom you did not trust, into unknown dangers. Followed him, it seems, even to the depths of that ruin?"

"Yes, sir." She went on with her story, not quite sure how much detail to put in. When she came to her first sight of the old elf-lord, she stopped short, trembling and sweating. She could scarcely get her breath, and her vision blurred.

"No," came a firm voice, like a command, and a sharp scent tickled her nose. She took a long breath, and saw the Kuakgan's brown hand beneath her face, the tough fingers twisting some gray herb. "You must tell this tale," he said, "but I will make it easier. Sit there, on the pool's edge." Paks sank down, her sword banging against her leg. The Kuakgan scattered more leaves on the pool, and their scent seemed to clear her head. "Now," he said above her. "Now go on."

She was able to continue by clenching her mind to the task, forcing out the words phrase by phrase. Since her wakening to the elves' care, she had carefully avoided those memories, and they lay bright and sharp as shards of glass, still capable of injury. She could see the elf-lord's ravaged face, the strange blue flames, the very chips and notches on the orcs' weapons. Their stench stung her nose; their hoarse cries rasped her ears. Macenion's body lay once more dead at her feet.

"We couldn't stay together," said Paks bleakly, unaware of the tears that ran from her closed eyes. "I tried to stay near him, but—"

"Enough." A strong hand gripped her shoulder. "And what of the elfane taig?"

"The elfan taig?"

"That which you freed."

She had never understood what happened at the end; describing it clearly was impossible. But again the disgusting touch of whatever she had had to take shriveled her mind. And then, with relief, she told of the escape, of the journey from the valley, and the falling snow.

"When did the elves find you?" asked the Kuakgan.

"That night, I think. I don't remember. I woke, and it was cold, and snowing, and dark. I couldn't move. The elves were there; at first they seemed angry, and then suddenly they were kind."

"Hmmm." The Kuakgan sat, suddenly, in front of her. "Paksenarrion Dorthansdotter, you give your name freely—look at me." Paks looked, and could not look away. She could not say afterwards how long she met the Kuakgan's gaze. He broke it at last, rose, and offered a hand up. "Well," he said briskly, "you're an honest warrior, at least. Kuakkganni rarely have to do with warriors, but I've been known to make exceptions." Paks stood, once more aware of the glade's silence. "Are you planning to be here long?" he asked.

"I don't know, sir. I might be, if someone hired me; otherwise I'll be going on when Star has rested from the mountains."

"You're looking for work? As a fighter?"

"Yes, sir. At least—I want to send my father what he paid on my dowry before I left."

The Kuakgan's eyes shifted to look at the jewel winking in the offering basin. "Hmmm. If you've many of that quality, I'd think they would cover most dowries. Was your father a wealthy man?"

"No, sir. A sheepfarmer, near Three Firs. He had his own land and flocks, but he wasn't rich. Not the way people are in cities."

"I see. You should have those things valued, then. I think you have enough for repayment of any likely sum. But tell me, what sort of employment were you hoping for, after the mercenaries?"

Paks flushed at the tone of his question. "It was an honorable company, sir," she said firmly. "I wasn't sure—I thought a guard company perhaps. The Duke suggested that."

"Duke? What Duke?"

"Duke Phelan, of Tsaia—"

"Ah," he broke in. "The Halveric's friend? A redhead?" When Paks nodded, the Kuakgan went on. "So that's the company you've been in. Why did the Duke suggest you leave, young warrior?"

Paks did not want to get into that question, least of all to a Kuakgan. Her confusion and reluctance must have shown, because the Kuakgan shook his head. "Never mind, then. I have no right to ask that, unless the answer poses a danger for those under my care, and I judge it does not. But tell me, did the elves give you any other message here?"

"Not to you, sir. They did say I should speak to Marshal Deordtya, but the innkeeper's daughter said that she was no longer here. She said a Marshal Cedfer had taken her place."

"The elves sent you to Girdsmen?" the Kuakgan seemed surprised at this.

Paks didn't want to answer any more questions. "Yes, sir, and I'd better be going now—"

"You just arrived this afternoon. Are you in such a hurry?"

Paks sensed more behind the simple question. She took refuge in stubbornness. "Yes, sir. They told me to come to you, and to the Marshal. I should do that as soon as I can."

"Well, then, Paksenarrion, I expect I'll see you again. You may come here, if you want to, and you need not bring such an offering each rime. One of Jos Hebbinford's oakcakes will do."

"Yes, sir. Thank you." Paks was not sure why she was thanking the Kuakgan, but she felt much less afraid of him, though she didn't doubt his power. When he nodded dismissal, Paks turned and went back along the path to the north road. As she stepped through the arch of vines and trees, the village noises returned. A boy and a small herd of goats were jogging toward the crossroads, the goats baaing loudly. Somewhere nearby a smith was at work; the cadenced ring of steel on anvil made Paks think of Star's worn hooves. She wondered if it was a farrier or a weaponsmith. She looked about, but the sound came from behind the first row of buildings, and she decided not to look for it right away. At the crossroad, she turned right, as Sevri had told her, toward the Gird's grange, and followed a curving lane past one small shop after another. Faces glanced out at her, curious; those she passed in the street looked sideways: she felt the looks.

The lane angled around a larger building, set back in a fenced yard, and dipped toward a small river. Over the river was a stone bridge, unexpectedly large, with handsome carved endposts on the parapets. Upstream a millwheel turned slowly; downstream on the near bank was a large building and yard. At first Paks thought it was another inn, for a group of men sat on its wide veranda drinking ale, but the sign over the gate said "Ceddrin and Sons: Brewmasters" with a picture of a tapped barrel. Across the river from the brewery, and a little downstream, was a yard full of hides hung on frames, and stinking tubs: the tanner's. Paks crossed the bridge, and saw a great barnlike building looming over the cottages between. If Sevri was right, that was the grange.

As Paks came nearer, she noted the construction of the Girdsmen's meeting place. It was very much like the barns she'd seen in grain-growing regions: stone-walled to twice a man's height, and closely fitted boards above that. Tall narrow windows began in the top course of stones and rose to the eaves of a steeply pitched roof. On the end nearest the road, wagon-wide doors of heavy dark wood barred with iron were tightly closed. Above them was a square hay-door with the hoist in place. Paks wondered what they could possibly use that for. Along one side of the grange was a space closed off by a stone wall half again as tall as Paks. A narrow gate of iron palings barred the way in, but she could see that it was nothing but a bare yard, beaten hard by heavy traffic. Across from the outer gate was another, of wood. She wondered what was behind it.

"It's not the time for meeting," said a voice close behind her. Paks whirled, her hand dropping to her sword hilt. The man who had spoken led a donkey, its back piled high with sticks. He wore no weapon, but his brawny shoulders and muscular arms were no stranger to fighting; he had training scars on both arms, and a long scar on his leg that had come from a spear.

"How would I find the Marshal?" asked Paks. She had noticed that he had not flinched when she reached for her sword; his eyes met hers easily.

"Oh. You're a traveler, aren't you? Well, the Marshal—" he cocked his head at the sky. "This time of day he'll be just finishing his drill with the young'un, I don't doubt. Go round the side there, past the barton, and ask at the door you'll come to. Gird ward you, traveler." He nodded and stepped away before Paks could answer.

The walled yard, or barton, was not quite as long as the grange itself. Despite what she knew of Girdsmen, Paks was not happy to find that the door she was to find was out of sight of the road, in an angle behind the barton wall. It too was shut, but she gathered her nerve and knocked.

Nothing happened for a few moments, then the door was swept open and she found herself facing a red-faced young man in a sweaty homespun tunic. The red lumps of fresh bruises marked his arms; he had a rapidly blackening eye. For an instant, they stared at each other, silent, until a voice called from within.

"Well? Who is it, Ambros?"

"Who are you?" asked the young man quietly. "Did you want to see the Marshal?"

"I'm Paksenarrion Dorthansdotter," began Paks. "I have a message for the Marshal."

"Wait." The young man turned and called her name to the interior. In a moment an older man, a hand shorter than Paks, came into the room. He had brown hair, streaked with gray and matted with sweat, and a short brown beard. The younger man stepped back to let him come to the door.

"Paksenarrion, eh? A fighter, I see. Yeoman, are you, or yeoman-marshal?"

"Not either, sir," said Paks. He grunted and looked her up and down.

"Should be, with your build. Well, let's have your message. Come on in, don't stand dithering in the door." He turned abruptly and strode into the room, leaving Paks to follow. "You got those boots in Aarenis, I'll warrant," he said over his shoulder. "I hear it's been lively over the mountains this year." Paks did not answer, but followed him into a narrow passage, and then a small room fitted with desk and shelves on one side, and two heavy chairs on the other. The man dropped into the chair nearest the desk. "Have a seat. So—you're not a Girdsman at all?"

"No, sir."

"Who sent you?"

"The elves, sir, that I met—"

"Elves!" He looked at her sharply. "You run with elves? Dangerous company you keep, young warrior. So, what message did they have for the Marshal of Gird in this grange?"

"To tell you, sir, that in a high valley east and south of here the elfane taig had been wakened, and the lost elf-lord had been freed."

The Marshal sat straight up. "Indeed! That old evil gone, eh? And they had done this, the elves? I thought they claimed they could not."

"Sir, they hadn't done it. They—we—it happened, sir, while I and another were there—"

"Happened! Such things do not happen, they are caused. Are you the cause? Did you fight in that valley and live to return?"

"I fought there, yes. But they did not say the evil was gone, only that the elf-lord was freed."

"I understand. But the evil has lost its body; it will have some trouble to find a new one that will serve so well. And the elfane taig awake. Hmmph. That will please none but elves and Kuakkganni. But tell me more. You were there; you were a fighter. What was your part in this?"

For the second time that afternoon Paks found herself telling over what had happened. It was not so hard, talking to the Marshal: almost like telling Stammel or Arcolin back in the Company. When she finished, the Marshal looked grave, his lips pursed.

"Well," he said finally. "You have been blessed by the gods—and I would think by Gird himself as well—to come through that alive and free of soul. I'd not dare call it luck that a party of elves found you, and knew what to do. For all I've just finished drill, we'll go into the grange and give you a chance to show your appreciation. Unless your allegiance forbids—?" Paks had no idea what he meant, but saw no harm in entering the grange. She had been curious about them since the events in Aarenis.

Marshall Cedfer led the way into the grange, first along a passage, past the door to the outer room, and through another door set at an angle. Inside, the vast room was already dim in the fading light. Paks could see the glint of weaponry here and there along the walls. The Marshal struck a spark and lit a candle, then lifted the candle toward a torch set in a bracket above him. Paks saw that most of the floor was stone paving blocks, worn smooth.

But at the near end of the room a platform of wood rose knee-high, floored with broad planks. It was six or eight spans long and the same wide, easily large enough for many men to stand on. The Marshal, meanwhile, had lit several more torches. Paks wondered what the platform was for, and then noticed Ambros' face in the doorway. So did the Marshal.

"Come on in, Ambros. Good news! Paksenarrion, here, brings word that the elf-lord possessed by the demon is freed. She's a little travel weary, but I just finished drill, so that will be fair." He went over to a rack on the wall and took down a sword. "This should do. Now, Paksenarrion, since you are not a Girdsman, I suppose I should explain. You know that Gird is the patron of fighters?" Paks nodded. "Good. Well, for thanks and praise we honor him with our skill, such as it is, in fighting. You have escaped not only death, but great evil; you owe the High Lord and Gird great thanks. We shall cross blades, therefore, and by the joyous clash of them the gods will hear our thanks. Unless—" he paused suddenly. "Do you have a wound that would pain you? I should have asked before."

"No," said Paks. "I have none. But what is the purpose to which we fight? Am I to wound you, or—?"

"Oh no. It's like weaponsdrill. We are not enemies, to draw blood. Gird is no blooddrinker, like some gods. This will not take long; just spar with me."

Paks drew her sword and stepped onto the platform with the Marshal, who had thrown off his robe to reveal a tunic as drab and worn as Ambros'. He eyed her thoughtfully. "Are you sure you won't take off your cloak? You might find it troublesome." At that, Paks realized that she was still wearing her chainmail shirt; she hardly thought of it these days.

"Sir, it will not trouble me, but is it right that I wear mail? If I must change—" She wondered as she said it why she was so willing to please him by this exercise.

"Oh no. Oh no, that's no problem. I'm a Marshal, after all; if I can't face mail without it, I'm a poor follower of Gird, who fought in an old shirt and a leather apron, or less than that. Now, Ambros, turn the quarterglass, and we'll begin."

And with a quick tap of greeting, the Marshal began testing Paks' control of her weapon. When she proved strong, he tried quickness. When she proved quick—and he smiled broadly when his lunges failed—he tried movement. Paks met his attacks firmly, but concentrated on defense: she did not want to know what would happen should she injure a Marshal of Gird in his own grange.

He was skilled indeed, as skilled as any human she had faced but for old Siger, perhaps. Still, he did not penetrate her defenses, though she had to shift ground more than once. She sensed the sand passing through the quarter glass, and changed her tactics slightly, pressing the Marshal a bit. Was he just a little slower to the right? Were his returns to position sluggish there? She felt the impact in the blades through her wrist. It had been long since she had such good practice.

Suddenly, the Marshal quickened his pace, surprising her; she'd thought he was slowing. She gave back, turning, her rhythm slightly off, but fending him off as much by reach as stroke. She took a breath, and stepped back to gain room for her own attack, but her foot found nothing to step on: she had come to the edge of the platform.

Instantly, she threw herself sideways and tucked, hitting the stone floor on her left side, and rolling up to a fighting position. But the Marshal had not followed up her fall.

"Forgive me!" he cried when he saw her up. "I had forgotten, Paksenarrion, in the fighting, that you were not one of us, and did not know the platform well. It was illdone of me to press you so close to the edge." He racked his sword and came to her side. "Were you hurt in the fall?"

Paks took a breath. Her side hurt, but that was as much the old bruises as the new ones. "No, sir. It's all right, truly it is. I've had harder falls."

"Oh, aye, I'm sure you have. But you're not a yeoman here for training. I should have warned you—glad you're not hurt." As Paks sheathed her blade, he picked up his robe. "Its customary," he said, "to make an offering toward the armory, too. Though as you're not a Girdsman, it isn't strictly required—" Paks found that Ambros had come to her side with a slot-lidded box. She fished out the pouch from her tunic again, thinking to herself that it seemed hard to be dumped on the floor and then asked for money. She took the first jewel at random and dropped it into the box. The Marshal did not appear to be watching.

"You're very good with that longsword," he commented. "Don't most mercenary companies use a short one?"

"Yes, sir, we do, but we had the chance to learn other weapons. And out of formation a longsword has great advantage."

"Yes, of course. With your height, too. I was surprised to see that you moved so freely with it, though. Most who come from formation fighting are used to depending on the formation, and are static. Though you're not a Girdsman, you're certainly welcome to drill with us here at the grange, as long as you're in Brewersbridge. We have open drill three nights a week, in the barton usually. You'll find most of the local yeomen fairly good at basic things, though few of them are up to your standard. And I'd be honored to partner you for advanced swordsmanship—or Ambros, here; he's certainly up to a bout with you. Have you had any training at unarmed combat?"

"Yes, some. And some with polearms," added Paks, hoping to forestall further questions.

"Excellent! I certainly hope you'll come; you'll be most welcome.

Tonight's a beginner's class in marching drill—I hardly think it would interest you—but tomorrow?"

"Perhaps, sir. I thank you for your invitation." Despite herself, Paks was curious to see the sort of drill a Marshal of Gird would conduct. And she needed to keep her own skills honed; it couldn't hurt to come once or twice.

Outside the grange it was full dusk; stars shone overhead to the east. She made her way quickly back to the inn, where the great open windows laid bars of yellow lamplight across the crossroad. As she entered, Jos Hebbinford caught her eye.

"I thought you weren't going to make it back for the meal," he said, half-laughing.

"Mmm. My errands took longer than I thought." Paks looked around the common room, now crowded with men-at-arms and other guests of the inn. "Where—?"

"I've no single tables left. How about over here?" He led her to a round table where two men were already halfway through a substantial meal. "Master Feddith is a stonemason, a local here, and that's his senior journeyman." Feddith, a burly man in a velvet tunic, looked up and nodded briefly as the innkeeper introduced Paks, then went back to his conversation with the journeyman. Paks ordered roast and steamed barley and looked around the room while waiting for her meal. Nothing Feddith was saying made much sense—it had to do, she assumed, with stonework—she had never heard of coigns or coddy granite or buckstone.

Few other women were in the common room besides serving wenches. One, the same white-haired woman Paks had seen in the afternoon, sat knitting by the fire with a glass of wine beside her. At another table, two women in rough woollen dresses sat with men dressed like farm laborers. And a group of youths, drinking a bit too much ale together, included a sulky-faced girl whose dress was tight across the shoulders and loose everywhere else. Paks watched Hebbinford go to their table in response to another shout for ale, shaking his head. One of the youths started to argue, and a hefty man with a short billet appeared beside the innkeeper. They all subsided, and after a moment threw coins on the table and left. The girl looked quickly at Paks before she went out the door.

"Here, miss," said a serving wench at Paks' shoulder. She turned to find a platter piled high with roast mutton and a mound of barley swimming in savory gravy. With it came a loaf of crusty bread and a bowl of honey. "And will you take ale, miss, or wine?"

"Ale," said Paks. She drew her dagger to slice the bread and found the master mason watching her.

"You're not from around here," he challenged.

"No, sir."

"Are you a Girdsman?"

"No, sir."

"Ummph. A free blade, then; that's not any livery I know."

"Yes, sir."

"Humph. Were I you, young woman, I'd keep my blade sheathed here. We're not partial to troublemakers."

Paks flushed. "I've no wish to make trouble, sir, wherever I am."

"Maybe not, but free blades are trouble as often as not. What gods do you serve?"

Paks put both hands on her thighs and looked him steadily in the eyes. "The High Lord, sir, and the gods my father served, back where I came from."

His gaze flickered. "Well enough. But if you're planning to stay here long, you'd best find a master who can vouch for you." Before Paks could think of anything to say, he had pushed back his stool and gone, his cloak swirling. Her stomach clenched with anger. Why did they all think she was a brigand, trying to cause trouble? Then she thought of the wandering fighters in Aarenis—perhaps they had had trouble here, though she had not heard of such in the north. She took a deep breath to calm herself and settled to her meal.

Hebbinford, as he came back past her table, had a smile for her. "Did I hear Master Feddith growling at you? Don't take offense; he's on the Council here, and we've had some trouble. I hear you visited our Master Oakhallow and Marshal Cedfer this afternoon—no wonder you were late. Marshal Cedfer alone can take up half a day, with his drills and lectures."

"Does everyone here think fighters are bad?" asked Paks.

"Well—no. Not all fighters. But we've had those come through that were: got drunk, broke things, started fights with local boys, even robbed. You've known some like that, surely."

Paks nodded.

"So, you see, we've got careful. As long as nothing happens, you're welcome, but we don't want the street full of idle blades looking for mischief."

"I can see that."

"Now, Sevri tells me you're quiet-spoken even to servants, and Master Oakhallow had nothing against you, so—" He broke off as someone yelled across the room, smiled again, and left. Paks finished eating. The food was good. It had been too long since she'd eaten well-cooked food. She finished with a slice of bread drenched in honey. The room was much emptier. Most of the men-at-arms were gone, and the rest were leaving, throwing down coppers and silvers as their boots scraped on the stone. Paks decided to check on Star before going to bed.

The bed was so soft that at first she could not sleep. Her room was far enough from the common loft that she heard nothing from it, but boots rang on the stone outside the inn from time to time. Even with the window open to the cold night air, it seemed strange to be sleeping inside again.

CHAPTER EIGHT

She woke at first light, aware of the clatter of small hooves in the road below. Looking out, she saw a herd of goats skittering along the north road. She looked east, at a clear dawn lightening over the hills, and shivered in the cold. Minutes later she was downstairs. The innkeeper was poking in the fireplace, and she could smell fresh bread from the kitchen.

"You're an early one," he said, surprised. "Did you want breakfast now?"

Paks grinned. "Not yet. I want to check on Star."

"Sevri'll feed her—"

"Yes, but she's used to me. And I'm used to being up early." Paks went out the side door of the common room into the stable yard. The green-tailed rooster was racing after a hen, and a group of cats crouched near the cowbyre. Paks watched as a stream of milk shot out the door, neatly fielded by one of the cats. She went into the stable, and found Star looking over the top of the stall door. The pony looked well-rested, and Paks rubbed her behind the ears and under the jaw. When she checked her tack, the packbags were intact.

"Is it all right?" asked Sevri, who had come into the passage.

"Yes, fine. I didn't realize I'd gotten up too early for you."

"It's not. Most of the travelers sleep late, that's all. Some of them sleep through breakfast. Star doesn't get much grain, does she?"

"Not when she's not working. Let's see your measure—oh, half of that, and tell me where your hay is—I'll bring it."

"Over there—" Sevri nodded toward a ladder that rose to the loft. "You can just throw it down, if you want."

Paks was already up the ladder. "Why don't I throw down what you need for all of them?"

"You don't have to—but if you wish—" Sevri looked up as Paks tossed down an armload for Star.

"It's no trouble; I'm already up here."

Sevri peered up at her. "I didn't think soldiers knew how to care for animals."

"I grew up on a farm," said Paks shortly. "How much more hay?"

"Just pitch it down, and I'll tell you." Sevri disappeared from the hold, and Paks threw down several armloads. "That should do it. We have just the two big horses in." Paks climbed down, brushing off the hay.

"Who does your milking?" she asked, wondering if Sevri did everything but the inside work.

"My brother Cal," said Sevri. "He's got bigger hands; it takes me too long, and Brindle is a crabby cow." Paks laughed.

"We milked our sheep," she said.

"Sheep?"

"Yes. I've never milked a cow, but I've milked my last sheep. I hope." Paks watched as the girl dumped hay into each feeder. She noticed a blaze-faced black horse that laid its ears back when Sevri neared the stall: obviously one of the "big horses" she'd mentioned. "When can I ask for breakfast, without being rude?"

"There won't be anything cooked, yet," said Sevri doubtfully. "The bread's out, and you could have eggs and cold roast and bread, if that's enough."

"It's plenty." Paks felt her stomach churn in anticipation.

"Just tell Father, then."

"Thanks." Paks returned to the common room to find the innkeeper waiting.

By the time she had finished breakfast, the other guests were stirring. First down was a man in dark tunic and trousers over soft boots. He gave Paks a look up and down that lingered on her sword-hilt, and sat down to his meal with no comment. Then came two heavily built men that Paks classified as merchants, followed by a tall man in a stained leather tunic over patched trousers. He had a longsword at his hip, a dagger at his belt, and the hilts of two daggers sprouted from his boot tops. Paks noticed that he chose a seat against a wall, far from the others.

After breakfast, she managed a private word with Hebbinford. He was willing to tell her about the moneychangers in town, and described them for her.

"Well," he began slowly, "as you ask me, I'd say Senneth. He's a Guild member, but the northern guild's not the same as that in Aarenis, if that means anything to you."

"Which guild?" asked Paks.

"The moneylenders, of course. I've heard that down south they were mixed up in a lot of—well—all sorts of trouble, let's say. But Master Senneth is as honest as any of that sort, say what you will. He's given me honest weight, at least. Or there's Master Venion—some prefer him. He's not a Guild member, but some say his commission's less. But for myself, I'd see Senneth."

Paks did not know what he meant by commission, and asked.

"Well, if he takes your raw gold and gives coin, say, or changes southern coin for local, he's got to make something on the trade. Or if he arranges a transfer far away—you said you wanted your dowry to go home. If you don't want to take it yourself, he could arrange it for you. But it would cost you. Now Venion might charge you less, but—how would you know it got there? The Guild, now, it'll see things are done right. It's whether you want to pay for it, that's all."

Paks nodded. "Where is Master Senneth?"

"Just across from the Hall." Paks looked blank, and he explained. "When you went to the Grange last night, before you crossed the bridge, did you see the large building on your left with a fenced yard?"

"Yes."

"Well, that's the Hall. Master Senneth is right across from it. It's easy to find. He's got a guard at the door." Paks raised her eyebrows. "And you won't be able to take your weapons in, either. The guard stacks them for you."

Master Senneth was a brisk, trim man in a tight-sleeved gown of black wool. He smiled at Paks as she came through the door. "Yes? What may I do for you?"

Paks explained her needs.

"Hmmm. Valuation, yes. It would be better for you, actually, to take anything really valuable to a larger town, or to Vérella. For one thing, you can get several appraisals, and for another, they can offer more who have a market to hand. I'll tell you frankly that I probably can't give you the best price you could get, except for southern coin. That's because we trade coin across the mountains each year. Some items I may not be able to take at all; those, of course, I'll note as we go along. Now transfer—if it's money alone, that's the easiest. If it's specific items, that can be quite expensive. Have you brought it all along?"

"Yes," said Paks. "But most of it's outside; your guard said he would watch the packs." She had tied Star to the railing outside.

"Well, let's bring it in and take a look, if you wish." Paks nodded and he came from behind his counter to the door. "Arvid, bring this lady's packs in, please." The guard unloaded Star, staggering a bit at the weight, and carried the packs inside. As he left, Master Senneth called after him. "And see that we're not disturbed until we're through, Arvid." Then to Paks. "I suppose you don't want half the town wandering in as we're counting, and knowing just what you have."

"I hadn't thought of that," admitted Paks.

"Ah, they would," he said darkly. "They saw you come in yesterday, and watched you come here with a loaded pony. If they could look through walls—" He made a warding sign. "But they can't. Now, what's first?"

Paks began unstrapping the packs. "I don't know what—some of this is weapons, but fancier ones than I'd use." She pulled out the pair of jewelled daggers sheathed in silver. Senneth caught his breath.

"My—those are lovely. Where did you say—no. No matter. Only—" he looked at her sharply. "Were these stolen, somewhere in Aarenis?"

"No." Paks shook her head. "I didn't steal them. You can ask Marshal Cedfer or Master Oakhallow, if you like."

"You're not a Girdsman nor a kuakkgannir."

"No, I'm not. But they know where they are from, and how."

"I see." He returned to the daggers. "What lovely tracings. And these gems are valuable in themselves, not just in this design."

Paks pulled out the small battle-axe. She had forgotten the gold inlay tracing runes along the blade.

"That's dwarfwork!" Senneth shook his head. "A rare piece, though I don't know where I'd find a buyer. That's the sort of thing you'd get a better price for in Vérella." Looking at it again, Paks wished she could keep it. But she knew she had no use for a battleaxe, one weapon she'd never handled. She pulled out the ivory-handled dagger with a red stone set in the pommel, and the matching sheath with the dragon carved around it, and two red stones for eyes. Laying these aside, she pulled out one of the sacks of coins.

Master Senneth looked at the treasure, then at Paks, with dawning respect. "Young lady, that's a remarkable amount of wealth you have there. Are you sure you're not an elf princess in disguise, checking to see if humans are still greedy? I assure you, my honest commission for handling all this will well repay my time."

Paks sat back on her heels, grinning. "No, Master Senneth, I'm no princess, elf or human. A very lucky young warrior, yes. And my old sergeant said, if ever we got a chance to set some aside, to do it. If there's enough, after sending my dowry home, that's what I'll do."

"Not spend it all on new clothes and wine, eh? Wise head on young shoulders—and a fighter, at that. You're a new one on me. What was your name again?"

"Paksenarrion."

"Lady Paksenarrion, what other surprises have you?" He smiled over the coins, sorting them quickly into heaps of like kind, while Paks pulled out everything else. When all the coins had been counted, he turned to the jewels, rolling them out on a square of black velvet on his counter, and angling a mirror to catch sunlight from the window. His fingers moved among them deftly, turning them this way and that. At last he looked up.

"Unless your father was a very wealthy man, I'd say you have ample to repay any dowry, and my commission for the transfer, and enough over to live well for a long time. Let me start making notes. If you don't accept my value for anything, just retrieve it; as I said, you can get more for many of these things in a city. Now—" He opened a tall book, fetched a pen and a soft piece of chalk to mark the slate that topped one end of his counter. "Let me start with the coins. You realize that those are all quite old. I don't even know the issue on the ones where the imprint is visible. They have value only for the metal content; they'll have to be melted and restruck. So I use the weight to determine the value—" He pulled out a set of scales.

As Paks walked back toward the inn, leading Star, she tried to think how much money she actually had. She was hungry; by the sun it was long past time for lunch. How many hours, then, had she been closeted with the moneychanger? She had seen the spiky columns of figures climb up the pages of his account-book, as he added the value of coins, jewels, the small pieces of weaponry. But she couldn't make sense of it in terms of her salary in the Duke's Company. He spoke of gold crowns and silver coronets and halflings instead of the natas and nitis she was used to. She couldn't manage to convert it, in her head. But it seemed she could send home twice what she thought her dowry had been and have plenty left. She need not take the first guard job that came along. She could buy a riding saddle for Star—perhaps even a full-sized horse. She had left most of her money on deposit with Master Senneth, but she had enough with her to order a few new clothes, and eat the best the Jolly Potboy offered for that night's dinner.

On the way back, she remembered Sevri's directions to the smithy, where Master Doggal shod all the horses for miles around. Now she turned from the main road, and led Star between two small stone buildings down an alley that led to the forge. In the paved courtyard before the blacksmith's shop, the tall, rough-looking man from the inn was haggling with the smith over the cost of shoes; his black warhorse, its ears twitching nervously, stamped and shifted, the shoes in question ringing on the stones. Paks recognized it by the blazed face; it had tall white stockings on all four legs.

"I charges fair," the smith rumbled. "Nobody says but what I charges fair. That beast of yours has feet so big, and stands so bad—aye, he come near tearing loose, that he did, and kicked me as near as maybe. It's not the shoes being set wrong has him tittupy like that: he's a wrong 'un, and too handy with them white socks." The smith was a head shorter than the other, but his massive arms and shoulders made his hammer look small.

The tall man put his hand to the hilt of his sword, but the smith hefted his hammer.

"You just pay me, now," the smith went on. "Pay as you ought, and we'll have no trouble."

"And if I don't?" The black horse shied at that harsh voice; the tall man jerked the bridle viciously. Neither man had noticed Paks, but the horse winded Star and stood still, head high and ears pricked, snuffing.

"Well, if ye don't I'll have the law on ye—"

"The law, is it?" The tall man laughed contemptuously. "In this town? What law here could touch me?"

"This," said the smith, and quick as a snake's tongue his hammer tapped the man's shoulder.

With an angry snarl, the big man dropped the reins, drew his sword, and swung at the smith. The black horse walked over to Star as Paks dropped the lead and whipped out her own blade. Only then did the smith see her.

"Another one of ye, eh?" He blocked one swipe of the big sword with his hammer; she noted that he handled it as if it were weightless. "Well, I can take two of ye, no doubt, but still—Aieeeh! By the Maker!" His bellow split the early afternoon stillness. Paks heard a startled outcry in the distance, as she ran forward.

"Not against you, Master Smith," she said as her sword rang against the other. "But you, you coward. I can see that horse has new shoes—and you owe the smith—and you've no business attacking an unarmed man with a sword!" The swordsman had turned, furious, with her first blow, and now concentrated on her.

"Unarmed, is it?" cried the smith. "And you a woman? Is any smith unarmed that has his hammer and the strength of the forge in his arm?" Paks made no answer; the tall man was skilled, and she saved her breath for the fight. The smith threw his hammer on the ground and bellowed at them both. "Is it a barton of Gird you think I have here, and not a smithy? By the Maker, is a smith to be reft of his fight by any wandering female? I can collect my own debts, you silly girl, without your help. I was just teaching this fellow a lesson—" Paks quit listening. The tall man had the reach of her, and his blade was the heavier. She missed her helmet and shield; he had a round iron pot on his head, and heavy bracers on both arms. His black eyes gleamed from under the helmet.

"Eh—the girl from over the mountains! A wild one, I see. I like wild ones." He grunted as her sword pricked his shoulder. "I'll tame you, little mountain-cat, and then I'll see to him—" He jerked his head at the smith, without giving Paks an opening.

"You will, will you?" yelled the smith. "By the Maker, you're a fine one, if you think you can!" And before Paks realized what he was about, he darted behind the tall man and brought the hammer down on his head with a resounding clang. The tall man sagged to his knees and fell over in a heap. The smith glared at Paks over the crumpled body. "A sword," he said severely, "is a pitiful weapon, young woman, and only fit for those that don't have the strength for a hammer. It was by the hammer that Sertig the Maker forged the world on the Anvil of Time. The hammer will always win, with the strength of the faithful behind it."

Paks had dropped the tip of her sword and stood panting. "Uhm—yes—"

"Don't forget that."

"No—" She took a deep breath and wiped her sword on her leg before sheathing it.

"Not that yours isn't a fine bit of work," the smith went on. "It's just that swords are inferior weapons." Paks did not feel like arguing with him. She was, however, a bit disgruntled. She'd only tried to help someone.

"Doggal!" A shout from the alley. "Need help?" Paks could see two hefty men, armed with clubs.

"Nay, nay. 'Twas a bit of trouble with a fellow from outside, that's all." The smith sounded smug. "He'll have a headache, if he wakes at all."

"Will you need someone to take him away?"

"He's not dead yet. He's still snorting. If this lady will lead his horse back to the inn, I can throw him over—" He turned to Paks. "If you're going that way, that is." The men waved and turned back up the alley.

"I was coming here," said Paks. "To get my pony shod. But if—"

The smith suddenly grinned, and looked like a different man. "Oh? That's no problem. He'll keep a bit, just there. I did wonder what you were doing up my alley, to be sure, but if it was on business, then—" He looked around. "That's your pony, with the star?"

"Yes. Just a moment." Paks started toward Star, who stood stiffly nose-to-nose with the black horse. Both shifted away from her, eyes wide.

"Come on, Star," said Paks crossly. She felt the smith was laughing at her. "Come on, pony." She rubbed her thumb on the gold ring. The wildness left Star's eyes, and the pony minced toward her. The black horse, too, lowered his head and stretched his neck.

"Catch up that fancy-socks, if you can," called the smith. "Be careful; he's a mean one, but he'll do no good running loose." Paks caught Star's lead, and rubbed the ring again, talking softly to the black.

"Come on, then, big one. Come on. I'd like to have one like you someday." The black horse came forward step by slow step until she could reach the reins. She talked on as she led them toward the smithy itself. She could feel the horse's fear trembling in the reins as they neared the building.

"Well!" The smith sounded surprised. "You've a rare way with a horse, that you have. I'll take the pony, then, if you'll hold that one. What sort of shoes? Are you going into the mountains again?"

Paks shook her head. "No. And she won't be carrying as much weight. I'll be going toward Vérella, I think."

"Umph." He had one of Star's feet up, then another. "I'd still say low caulks in front. It'll frost before these wear out."

By the time Star was shod and the shoes paid for, the tall man had grunted and groaned and shifted around on the stones. His eyes were still closed, though, and he had said nothing coherent.

"You wanted to help," said the smith with a bit of his earlier belligerence. "Suppose you take him back to the inn for me. I'll tell the watch about it, and Jos can ask me, if he wants. And look—" The smith bent down with a grunt and opened the man's belt pouch. "You know he owes me for the shoeing of that devil there; see, I'm taking just what he owes." Paks nodded, and the smith heaved the man upright and slung him over one broad shoulder. "Now, I think your pony would carry him better than his horse. Can you lead both?"

"Yes—" Paks was reluctant, nonetheless, to go out on the streets leading another man's horse, with the man himself slung unconscious over her pony. "But don't you think that—I mean, since you hit him, shouldn't—?"

"A warrior like you doesn't want credit for defeating him?" The smith's voice was scornful, and his look more so. Paks reddened. Nothing and no one in this town was as she had expected. "I'd have thought," the smith continued, "that such as you were quite used to hauling bodies around. Or did you just leave them?"

Paks opened her mouth and shut it again. There seemed nothing to say to that. But as the smith folded the man over Star's back, the Gird's Marshal walked into the courtyard. His glance rested on Paks, then on the smith and his burden.

"I heard, Master Doggal, that you had had a disturbance."

The smith stopped, with a hand on the tall man's back where he lay across the pony. "If you heard that, Marshal, you heard I needed no help."

The Marshal glanced at Paks again. The smith caught the look and raised his voice. "No, and I didn't need her, either. Is that it, is she one of your precious yeoman?"

"No. I merely wondered."

The smith began tying the man to Star's pack pad with the thongs. "Took you long enough. If I had needed help, I'd have been dead long since." He turned to Paks. "Now, lady, just you work whatever magic you used on that horse, and take him and this fellow back to the inn for me." Paks saw the Marshal give her a sharp look at the word magic, but he turned back to the smith as that individual kept talking. Paks started to move away, but the Marshal raised his hand to stop her.

"You seem to think, Marshal, that we'd have no order here without you Girdsmen. I'm not denying you're a brave bunch, and useful when we have trouble too big for one man or two. But I can hold my own with any single man, and most two or three. As I was telling this lady—" Paks wondered why she had been promoted from "girl" and "female" to "lady." "As I said to her, the Maker's hammer wielded by a faithful arm will stand over a sword any time."

"Yet the Maker is said to have made many a blade, in the old tales," said the Marshal, with a kindling eye. "And you, I know, have made most of the blades in this village—"

"Oh, aye, that's true. When I have time. And it's a test of the art, that it is, to make a fine-balanced blade that will hold an edge and withstand a hard fight. I won't say against that. But I will say—"

"That you can hold your own in a fight. And I'll agree to that, Master Doggal. But the captain did ask me to keep an eye on things, after that last trouble, and the Council as well—"

The smith had calmed down a lot, and the discussion seemed, to Paks, to be working over well-plowed ground. "That's so. If it's for the Council, then I might as well tell you all that happened. Saves seeing the watch. This fellow came to have his horse shod—that black one there—and quarreled with my price, after. The beast is vicious; doesn't look it now, I'll admit, but just you try and put a shoe on it. I charged more for it. Always do, as you know. If I'm to risk my head, I must have gain for it." He paused and the Marshal nodded. "Well, then, he said as much as that I'd no way to make him pay. I tapped his arm to show I meant my words, and he drew on me. Then this lady—I'd not seen her come—she drew as well. I thought they were together, and raised a yell. Then it seemed she thought to aid me—but, you see, I'd already raised a cry—so I thought I'd let her fight, was she so eager to. They were well-matched. He'd the reach of her, and was heavier, but she was quicker and her blade had more quality. Then—well—it's hard to stay out of a fight, so I broke his head with the hammer, after all."

"Mmm." The Marshal looked at Paks. "I'd have told you our smith can handle himself in a fight. It's not well for newcomers to brawl in the streets."

Before Paks could answer, the smith was defending her. " 'Tis not her fault, Marshal. I'd think you'd be pleased, even if she's not one of yours. She thought she saw an old man"—he rumpled his thin gray hair—"beset by an armed bully. She did well."

"Hmm. Well, I suppose—if you have no complaint against her—" the Marshal was frowning.

"Not at all. Not at all. Suppose I had slipped and fallen? She was trying to help. And, you might notice, on the side of that law and order you praise so highly. I've no complaint. In feet—but go on, now, and get that lummox out of my yard." He turned abruptly and dove back into the forge.

"I'll walk with you to the inn," said the Marshal to Paks in a neutral tone. Paks followed him down the alley, leading both animals. She kept her thumb firmly on the ring.

They were almost to the crossroad when the Marshal spoke again. "If I'd defended you," he said without preamble, "old Doggal would be lodging a complaint to the Council somehow. He won't agree with me on anything but smithing itself if he can help it."

"Then—you aren't angry with me for this?"

"For going to his aid? Of course not. You might wait, another time, to see whether your aid is needed, or someday you'll be killed over some little thing, and nothing gained. I'll just have a word with Hebbinford," he said as they came to the inn door. "You take that horse around back."

Paks found herself leading the tall black warhorse to the stable before she quite realized the Marshal had taken Star's lead. She heard, behind her, the innkeeper's voice and the Marshal's, and the exclamations of the serving wenches.

CHAPTER NINE

When she came in to supper that night, the common room stilled. Someone dropped a dish, and it clattered on the floor. She could hear the rustle of cloth as someone bent to pick it up. Paks carefully did not meet any of the eyes in the room, but picked her way to an empty table. As she sat down, a muted hum resumed. She heard a phrase here and there, but tried to ignore the voices. They all knew, as she did, that the tall man lay unconscious in his room upstairs. She didn't know what stories were going around, but obviously she was in them. She ordered the special dinner: roast beef, mushrooms, hot bread, and pastry. She was halfway through it before she remembered that she'd thought of going to weapons-practice at the Girdmen's that evening. If she ate all that—she sighed and pushed the dishes away.

"Is something wrong with your meal?" asked Hebbinford, pausing by her table.

"No, not at all. I thought I'd go to the grange this evening, though, and drill—and not on a full stomach."

"I see. Well, we can put that by for you, for when you get back, if you like."

"Thank you." Paks had not thought of that. "I'd like that—this is too good to waste. If it's not too much trouble—?"

"Not at all. Marshal Cedfer mentioned that you might be visiting this evening. I suppose, a warrior must always practice, eh?"

"Yes, if we want to stay good. And it's been too long since I had a proper drill.'

"Fights don't count?"

"No. Not really. A fight may not last long enough, or call out what you need to practice. I should drill every day—we did in the Duke's Company. But no one can practice well on a full belly." Paks leaned back and fished into her pouch for the correct silver piece. As she stood and turned to leave, she noticed several of the diners watching her.

Although it was full dark, she had no trouble making her way along the street. Uncurtained windows were open to the cool evening air, and torches burned at either end of the bridge. Ahead, the grange was ablaze with light; torches flared atop the barton wall as well. As Paks came nearer, she could see that the gate to the barton and door to the Grange both had sentries before them. She saw two dark shapes enter the barton ahead of her, pausing to exchange greetings with the sentries.

Up close, she realized that the sentries were very young. They carried long billets of wood, and struggled to maintain the dignity of their posts. Paks wondered which entrance to use. She heard the mutter of voices through both. Finally she decided on the barton gate. The youth there stared up at her, eyes wide.

"I'm Paksenarrion Dorthansdotter," she said. "The Marshal invited me to come to weapons-practice."

"Oh—eh—you're the lady as has come over the mountains, eh?"

"Yes," said Paks. "May I pass?"

"Oh—well—if the Marshal said—yes, lady, go on in. Are—are you really a fighter, like they say?" This last, as she was nearly past.

Paks turned back to him, hand on the hilt of her sword. "Yes. Did you doubt it?"

"Oh, no, lady. I—I just wondered, like."

Paks turned back to the barton itself and looked about her. The bare little yard was ringed with torches set high on the wall. One man was stretching, arching his thick back with a grunt. Two more were looking over a pair of pikes, smoothing the shafts with pumice. Out of the side door of the grange came Ambros with an armful of short clubs that reminded Paks of hauks. She heard more men coming in the gate behind her, and a confused sort of clatter and mumble from the grange itself. She watched, uncertain, as Ambros dumped the clubs in a heap near the wall. When he straightened, he saw her.

"Ah, Paksenarrion. Welcome. Marshal Cedfer will be glad to see you. Will you come in? Or he'll be out here in a few moments."

"I'll wait," said Paks. "I can warm up out here." She unbuckled her sword and laid it by the wall, then began limbering exercises. Others were busy with the same. One man belched repeatedly; a cloud of onion followed him.

"Eh, Gan," said another. "If you've ate as much as I smell, you won't last the night."

"Air and onion won't slow any man," retorted Gan, grinning. "Might just set off my opponent—"

Paks ignored them. It was much like drill in the Company—the familiar mixture of joking and criticism. She finished her exercises and went to buckle on her sword. The barton was half-full of men—she saw no other women—and they were all mature and well-muscled. Most had picked up one of the short clubs; four had pikes, and one had a sword of medium length.

A bell rang, a single mellow stroke. Everyone stilled, and Marshal Cedfer came into the barton, followed by five other men.

"Are you ready, yeomen of Gird?" he asked.

"We are ready, Sir Marshal," they answered in unison. Paks was silent.

"Then may Gird strengthen your arms and your hearts, and keep them strong for the safety of our land."

"In the name of St. Gird, protector of the innocent," came the response.

"We have a guest here tonight," said the Marshal less formally. "Paksenarrion, come forward. I want all our yeomen to know you." Paks edged past the others to stand near the Marshal under the torches. "Though she is not a Girdsman, Paksenarrion is an experienced warrior. She has accepted my invitation to drill with us. Those of you who drill with swords will have a chance to cross blades with her if you wish. Now, bring your weapons and let me see—" The Marshal began to look over the weapons, commenting on their condition. He was as thorough as any of the Duke's armsmasters. Ambros explained that some of the weapons belonged to the men, and the rest were stored in the grange. Then the Marshal began assigning drills: some to one-on-one, others to two-on-one, and others to more basic exercises. When they were all occupied, he led

Paks to a corner of the barton where Ambros waited with two short swords.

"If you don't mind," said the Marshal, "I'd like to work with these short swords. I suspect you are far more skilled with a short blade than I am. It would be best for the yeomen, I think, to learn the short. Of course, you'll want a chance to work with your own, but—"

"That's fine," said Paks. "But I haven't drilled with a short sword in several months. I may be clumsy with it."

"Not as clumsy as I am," said the Marshal. "I haven't been able to teach the men to fight in lines with it."

Paks unbuckled her long sword, racked it, and took one of the short ones from Ambros. "We used a small shield with these, in formation," she said. "Do you have shields?"

"Yes, but we rarely practice with them. As I said, most of our men are not at all skilled with swords. Once they learn that, then we'll try adding the shields." The Marshal, too, had taken a short blade; he gestured at another man to come over. He looked closely at Paks. "You aren't wearing your mail."

"No. I didn't think all of you would have mail." Paks wished she had a banda, but was not about to ask for one.

"Mmm. I always say, the stripes you take in training reinforce the lesson." The Marshal looked pleased, and the other two grinned. "Now—we'll warm up in pairs, then go two-against-two. Is that all right?"

"Surely." Paks moved the sword around, feeling its balance. It was subtly different from the one in the Duke's Company. Lighter, she finally decided.

As she had expected, the Marshal was not nearly as inexperienced as he'd claimed. They tested each other's ability and strokes, without either making a touch, for a few minutes. Then the Marshal gestured a pause.

"Yes, indeed," he said. "I see you have much to teach us. Now, Ambros, you stand with her, and Mattis, you take my right."

Paks shot a look at the young man who came to stand beside her. She felt queer, standing in formation with a stranger against strangers. But if she joined a guard company somewhere, this is what it would be like. Again the blades came up in salute, and the drill began.

Ambros, she saw at once, wanted to move around too much. He

shifted from side to side with each stroke, alternately crowding and leaving her flank uncovered. The Marshal's partner, Mattis, looked as if he couldn't shift at all, but at least he was keeping some sort of line. Paks managed to cover Ambros' lapses at first, but finally the Marshal's blade leaped in and rapped his side sharply. Paks had managed two touches on Mattis, but none on the Marshal. He signalled another halt.

"I think I see our problem," he said. "Ambros, you aren't holding your position. Isn't that it, Paksenarrion?"

She was not sure how critical she could be without angering them. "Well—yes, part of it. A line works only if it holds together. But I think those who learn a long blade first have more trouble. It seems to me that you, sir, and Ambros both are trying strokes more suited to a long blade. More wrist, and less elbow and shoulder."

"Ah. I see. Suppose you stand out, and watch us, and give corrections." The Marshal lined up with Ambros this time, and a nervous Mattis braced himself to meet both of them. Paks shook her head.

"No, sir, by your leave. Let all of you line up, and go slowly—do you ever count the cadence for a slow drill? Yes? Good. If those of your men with the short clubs use much the same strokes, they can partner you, and the line can be long enough to work. I can anchor the center of the opposing line." The Marshal agreed, and soon they had a line of four swords (for another man took up a blade, a little uncertainly) against Paks and three men with clubs. At first the drill was very ragged, but in a few strokes they all caught on, and Paks was able to talk them through it.

"You see," she said, as the blades met clubs with light taps, "if you are in close formation you'll hurt your partners if you shift too much. And leave yourself open, as well. There is a rhythm—and a trust—that your partner will be there. Not so much turn to the side—yes—and if you have a shield as well, you can foul your partners blade if you turn." As practice went on, they grew used to the limited sideways movement, and Paks encouraged them to increase the tempo. After some minutes, the Marshal called a halt.

"Very good!" he exclaimed. "Very good indeed. Anything else?"

"I didn't notice it in the others, sir," said Paks, "but you and Ambros still seem to have too much flex in the wrist. You are trying to do more with the point than a short sword allows—it's the quick thrust you want, not fencing about." She expected him to be angry, but he was not.

"So. Each craft has it masters, and a knight's training ill-suits an infantry soldier. I'll try to remember that. Perhaps you'll give us the benefit of your training again. And now, since you carry a long blade by choice, you should have the chance to practice with it, if you will." He handed Ambros his short blade and gestured to Paks. She handed over the short sword and went to pick up her own blade. When she had settled it to her satisfaction,the Marshal had also armed himself, and awaited her.

"I suggest we go into the grange itself," he said. "The light is better."

Paks followed him in. So, she noticed, did many of the other men.

"I don't suggest the platform, since you aren't used to it. But here—" his glance cleared a space in the crowd, and he drew.

"Now," said Paks, smiling, "I expect you will have plenty to teach me."

The Marshal grinned. "I should hope so. You have some good strokes; I noticed that yesterday, but—" He moved to attack.

For the next few minutes, they circled first one way then the other, blades ringing with stroke after stroke. Paks had to use everything she knew and all her size, to keep from being pricked again and again. She could feel the sweat pouring down her back and burning her eyes. The Marshal was much more a swordsman than Macenion. Every thrust was met with a firm repulse, and she found herself more often defending than attacking. She found no weakness she could exploit, and wondered what old Siger would do against him. That thought almost made her laugh—she'd still back Siger against anyone, even a Marshal of Gird.

"Very good," the Marshal said finally, still hard at work. "You certainly have a thorough grounding in long blades. I have a few tricks, but as far as plain fighting goes, you do very well." Paks said nothing, needing all her concentration. Despite her best efforts, he made a touch the next moment, ripping her left sleeve from shoulder to elbow. "There, now," he said. "I have regained the respect of our yeomen. Would you rest a bit?" He stepped back, and Paks lowered her weapon.

"I could stand to," she said ruefully, wiping her face. "I see I still have a lot to learn—just as I thought."

"The willing student learns quickly," he said. "You need naught but experience to master this weapon as well as the other. Common swordsmen you could defeat now, quite easily I imagine."

"Ah, but I like learning weaponcraft," said Paks. She thought of Saben's teasing with a pang. "I always have."

"Good, then. You're welcome here, any time. I'll be glad to drill with you; you're good enough to give me practice. Ambros, too. And mind—" he said briskly, fixing her with a sharp glance, "mind, I intend to have you a Girdsman before long. Such skill as yours should be dedicated to a good cause. We need such fighters on the side of right, not running loose after idle gain." Paks felt a flicker of anger at that, and her chin came up. "No—" He stopped and nibbed his head. "I shouldn't say that of you, when I don't know your allegiance, but Gird knows we've trouble enough coming, and few to meet it." He grinned at her suddenly. "I still think you'll make a fine Girdsman someday—even a Marshal, who knows?"

The others milled about, replacing weapons in racks on the grange walls, and taking their leave. Paks sheathed her sword, and turned to go. The Marshal was talking seriously to two men, low-voiced.

A hand touched her arm. It was Ambros. "If—if you'd come again, I'd like to drill with you—"

"Oh, I'll come again, while I'm here. It's good practice. But—don't you have any women drilling with you?"

Ambros shook his head. "No. Not at this level. We'd had some in the beginner's class—in fact, we have two there now. But those who want to go on, the Marshal sends elsewhere for more training."

"I see."

"Were there many women in your company?"

"Maybe a quarter of us. One of the cohort captains."

"I've heard of Duke Phelan. Isn't his title from the court of Tsaia?"

"Yes. He has lands in the north of the kingdom, on the border." Paks sighed. "I might—I might be going back there."

"But you left the company, didn't you? We thought you were a free sword."

"Well—I was due leave, and—and the Duke thought perhaps I should try another company—another service—for a time. But I miss it; I've thought of going back."

"Oh." Paks could hear the unasked questions. Ambros stopped at the door, starting to say something and stopped, and finally said, "Well—Gird go with you. We'll be glad to see you again."

It was late. Most torches in the village were out. Paks made her way down the dark streets with care, following some distance behind several others from the Grange.

Cold night air, damp from the river, soothed her hot face. She caught a whiff from the tanner's crossing the bridge. As she neared the crossroad, she saw light spilling from the inn's windows. She slipped in the door, ignoring the few who sat late in the common-room, and went up the stairs to her own room. Her shoulder ached pleasantly. She pulled off her tunic and washed the sweat off, then remembered her unfinished dinner. She put on her other shirt and went back downstairs. Hebbinford rose from his place near the fire.

"Do you want the rest of your dinner?"

"Yes, if it's not too much trouble." Paks settled at an empty table. Hebbinford brought a candle; a serving wench came with a tray. They had heated the leftovers by the kitchen fire, and the gravy was bubbling hot. She cut a slice of bread and began eating.

Several of those who had been at the drill clustered at one table over mugs of ale, chatting. One caught her eye and grinned and waved. The man in black that Paks had seen the previous night sat across the room, a flagon of wine at his elbow. Two men in merchants' gowns diced idly nearby. One of them, looking around the room, saw her and nudged the other. They both rose and came to her table.

"I'm Gar Travennin," said the older. "A merchant, as you see, from Chaya. Could we talk with you?"

Paks nodded; her mouth was full. They sat across from her. Travennin was balding, with a gray fringe. The younger man was blond.

"We hear you came over the mountains, from Aarenis." Paks nodded again. "I heard there was more fighting than usual down there, and no trade this year. Is that so?"

Paks took a sip of her ale. "Yes. That's so. Had you heard of Lord Siniava?" The man nodded. "Well, he tried open war against the Guild League cities and the northern mercenaries all at once. He lost."

"Ah . . . so. Do you think, then, that trade will be back to normal by next spring? I held off this year, but I've a caravan of fine wool that needs a buyer."

Paks thought back to the turmoil in Aarenis. She spread her hands. "I can't say, sir, for certain. I came north with a late caravan, as far as the Silver Pass, but whether they made it safe to Valdaire I don't know."

"Were you with a regular company?" Travennin asked as if he had heard already.

"Yes. Duke Phelan's Company. The Duke was—much involved." Paks was not sure how much to say; the old habit of silence held her still.

"Mmm. And why did you leave?"

Paks felt irritated. "Why, sir, I enlisted for two years. My time was up."

"I see. You had had no trouble—?"

Merchants! she thought disgustedly. No honor at all. "No, sir. No trouble." She went on eating.

"I heard the Duke and Aliam Halveric were much in each other's pockets," said Travennin, his eyes roaming around the room.

Paks gave him a hard look and returned to her meal. "Oh? I couldn't say."

"After some kind of trouble last year—over the pass? Some border fort, I forget the name—"

She thought of Dwarfwatch at once, and said nothing. The smell of that mountain wind came to her, and her last sight of Saben and Canna in the rain, and Captain Ferrault's dying face.

"—do you know it?" the merchant persisted.

Paks stopped eating and slowly put both hands flat on the table. He glanced at her and froze as she glared at him. "Sir," she said finally, in a voice she hardly recognized. "I have nothing to say about our—the Duke's—Company. Nothing. And by your leave, sir, I'll finish my supper in peace." She stared at him until he reddened and pushed back his stool. She had lost her appetite. All those deaths, that grief and rage—The merchants she had traveled with had not been so crass. But of course, they had been in Aarenis during the war. They knew. Her breathing slowed; she took another sip of ale. The merchants were back at their own table, heads together. The man in black was watching her. As he met her eyes, he lifted his glass in salute and grinned. She looked away. All at once she wished she were anywhere but here. No, not anywhere, but back with the Company, laughing with Vik and Arne, talking with Stammel or Seli or Dev.

Tears stung her eyes and she blinked them back angrily. She drew a long breath and drank more ale.

She had thought she'd feel at home in the north; she was northern. But Brewersbridge was far from home. Maybe that was it. She thought of Vérella, thought of going straight on to Three Firs. She had money enough now; she could make more show than even her cousin. She imagined her mother's smile, her father's scowl—but he might not be angry, with the dowry repaid. She wondered what she would tell them, and what they would ask. Her musings ended there. She could not tell them anything they would understand. They would see her as these folk did: dangerous, wild, a stranger. She started to pour more ale, and found the tankard dry. She was still thirsty. She beckoned to Hebbinford, but when he came she doubted the steadiness of her voice and asked for water. His expression approved that choice. The merchants left the room and went upstairs.

Paks drank the water and thought of what she would do the next day. She needed new clothes, at least a new shirt. A saddle for Star. She knew where the tailor's shop was, and the leatherworker's—if he made saddles. She would order a shirt or two, and then think about how long to stay. Suddenly she remembered the tall man the smith had felled. How was he? She was unwilling to ask the innkeeper. She picked up the pastry from a dish she had pushed aside and bit into it absently. It had been a long day.

CHAPTER TEN

Next morning she woke again at dawn. This time Hebbinford seemed to expect her when she padded down the stairs and out to the stableyard. There she stretched and twisted, working the stiffness out of her shoulder. When Sevri came out, they fed the horses together. Paks stopped to watch the black horse eat. She wondered what would happen to it if its master died. She imagined herself riding away on it—then wondered if she could even mount it.

The tailor, she found after breakfast, was away on a trip. "Buying cloth up at the Count's fair," said his wife. "He's got a commission to make cloaks for the new council members, and has gone to buy cloth. He won't be home for a sennight or more. But what did you need, lady? Perhaps I could serve?"

"Well—some shirts, at least. I'd wanted a cloak, a heavy traveling cloak for winter."

"Fur? I couldn't do fur, nor does he, without it being paid in advance."

"No, not fur. Just good warm wool, weatherproofed—"

"Plain shirts, or fancy ones?"

Paks thought of her money. "Plain. Maybe one fancy one."

"The plain shirts I can do. And here—here's our silks, from the south. They say you've been there; you'll know these are good."

Paks looked at the goods. The silk was so soft—she decided on a silk shirt, green, with gold embroidery on the yoke. For that, the woman said, she'd have to await the tailor's return. In the meantime, a linen shirt—Paks explained the cut she wanted, to free her arms for sword-play. The tailor's wife took her measurements.

"You're as big as a man," she said, a little nervously. "Even in the neck—"

Paks laughed. "It comes of the fighting," she said. "Wearing a helmet every day would thicken anyone's neck. Makes it harder to cut through." But the woman didn't take the joke, and only looked frightened. Paks sighed, and ordered trousers as well, of the local wool, thicker and softer than she'd found in Aarenis. The tailor's wife knew someone who knitted for sale, and by noon Paks had ordered new socks and gloves for the coming winter.

As she came back to the inn, well satisfied with her morning's work, she noticed a crowd round the door. She slowed. A group of men came out, carrying something on a plank. Boots, scuffed and worn, poked out from under a blanket. The tall man. Paks shivered. Marshal Cedfer, walking with the carriers, nodded shortly to Paks as he led the group toward the Grange. Paks went on to the door, staring after them.

Just inside the inn door, Hebbinford was talking to Master Oakhallow.

"—doesn't do the inn any good," he was saying. "And besides—Oh. Paksenarrion. Master Oakhallow was looking for you."

Paksenarrion felt a tremor in her gut. The Kuakgan was looking at her without expression. She opened her mouth to say something about lunch, and thought better of it.

"For a simple warrior," said the Kuakgan, "you certainly have managed to make a stir in our quiet village." Hebbinford moved away, into the common room. Paks thought of several things to say, and decided against all of them. "You were about to eat?" Oakhallow went on.

"Yes, sir." Paks tried to judge his expression. "But if you needed—"

"No. I think I'll join you for lunch, if that's acceptable."

Paks wondered what he would say if she said no. Instead she nodded, and followed him into the common room. He murmured something to Hebbinford, and the innkeeper waved them on into the kitchen. The serving wenches were wide-eyed. The Kuakgan moved to a table at the kitchen window, overseeing the courtyard, and sat down. Paks hesitated, then sat opposite him. Hebbinford brought a platter of sliced meat, a loaf of bread, and a round of cheese to the table. One of the girls brought a pitcher of water and two mugs.

"You might as well know," the Kuakgan began, as he pulled out a dagger and sliced the round of cheese, "that you're causing a stir. I don't mean that dead bully, necesarily, though that's part of it. Not your fault, I agree with the Marshal, but you were involved. Then Master Senneth, after you left his place, has had a—how shall I put it?—a complacent look. And he called you 'lady,' I hear. In his vocabulary, that means rich. Folk here know the Halveric Company, and most have heard of your duke. After your comments last night, to the Chaya merchants, no one has much doubt that he's still your duke. You gave both to me and to the Grange a jewel worth a knight's ransom—apparently without knowing their worth. You walked off with a horse that the smith claimed was an outlaw." He paused to eat a slice of cheese.

Paks was still staring at her food; she shook herself and speared a slice of meat. Put that way, it almost seemed that she'd tried to show off. She finished that slice, and tore off a hunk of bread. She had no idea what was coming, or what to do.

"Marshal Cedfer says," the Kuakgan went on, after pouring himself some water, "that you're uncommonly good with that sword, and also good with the short sword—which I'd expect, where you've been—and also good at instructing in weapons. We didn't expect that of one so young, a mere private. Sevri tells me you're good with all the animals, and helpful as well. Fighters aren't, as a rule. In fact—" Paks looked up and was caught by his dark gaze. "In fact, Paksenarrion Dorthansdotter, you are very different from the usual ex-mercenary. Now Kuakkganni—" he gave a slow smile that changed his whole face. "Kuakkganni have their own ways of learning things. From what I know, I judge that you're as honest as most youngsters are, and mean no harm—not that no harm comes of it. You have some secrets rankling in your heart which must come out—and soon, I judge—if they're not to hurt you later. But unless you choose to confide in me, it's not my business." Paks thought of the snowcat with a mental wince, and looked down. "Marshal Cedfer thinks you need only join the Grange to be a fine addition to our town. That's a compliment; he's hard to please. But you've come to the notice of our local Guard, and the Council, and it's best you know the eyes they have on you."

Paks stirred restlessly. "But, sir—Master Oakhallow—why should they be so interested? I won't be here long—"

"No? Are you sure? The simple answer, child, is that they can't fit you in. You aren't one of the Count's Guard at the new Keep. You aren't an ordinary soldier on leave. You aren't a Girdsman, which would put you under command of Marshal Cedfer, or a kuakkgannir, which would put you under mine. You have no skill but war, isn't that so?" Paks nodded. "And you come from war, from Aarenis, where I hear the whole land is one great bubbling stew of fighting. Where an army might come over the pass, the short way, and be on us before we could send for aid. Can you imagine a southern army up here?" Paks thought of it and nodded. "And you come with treasure—how much, only you and Master Senneth know, but I can guess. Agents carry such treasure, Paksenarrion. Agents hiring troops, or buying loyalty ahead of invasion."

Paks stared at him, shocked. She couldn't speak. Finally she choked out: "Agent? But—but I never thought—"

"No," said the Kuakgan grimly. "You didn't think. That much is obvious. An agent would think, would have acted very differently. But the Council can't know what I know. They are concerned. So they should be. Your tale of the elfane taig, and the elves' aid, and having to meet me and Marshal Cedfer, and treasure—well, it would be stupider men than our Council that could see where that might come from." He went back to his meal. Paks sat frozen, her appetite gone, the food she had already eaten a cold lump in her belly. She watched him eat. Finally, he pushed his plate away. "And on top of all," he said, "a green shirt. With gold embroidery. I suppose you don't know what that means?" She shook her head. "Hmmph. You must have gone straight from your sheepfarm into the Company, and straight into Aarenis from there."

"Yes, sir."

"Well, child, Brewersbridge is near the border of Tsaia and Lyonya. Our local Count, such as he is, is a vassal of Tsaia. His colors are blue and rose. Green and gold are the colors of the royal house of Lyonya."

"Oh." Paks thought suddenly of the Halveric colors: dark green and gold. She did not even consider asking.

"I told them you didn't mean anything by it. I assume you just like the colors? Yes. They'll be asking you anyway. There's a Council meeting tonight, and you're summoned. I'll be there, and Marshal Cedfer. You met our Master Mason the other night. Captain Sir Felis Trevlyn, the Count's military representative, and commander at the new Keep. Probably his mage, Master Zinthys. Jos Hebbinford you know, and Master Senneth. Our mayor is Master Ceddrin, the Brewmaster. You'll be asked for a clear account of yourself, and for news of what's happened this past year in Aarenis." He stopped again. Paks nodded, and he went on.

"I thought you might give a clearer account, if you had the afternoon to think about it. If there's anything you haven't told the truth about, you'd better be prepared to tonight. You'll probably be asked to submit to an Examination of Truth—"

"What's that?" asked Paks.

"A spell. Under its influence, you cannot lie. You can refuse to answer questions, however, should you wish. The Council consented to my telling you this, because of my judgement of you. I think you have nothing to fear from the Examination or the Council, but you must expect sharp questioning: don't get angry. If you are unwilling to come before the Council, you must leave Brewersbridge at once. You can't go north, deeper into the Count's lands, without Sir Felis' permission, which you won't get. You could go west, if you went fast, and were beyond the bounds by sundown. East, as you know, has its own hazards, and south is back up the mountains. And if you go, they'll assume you've lied. I advise you to stay."

"I wouldn't have run away," said Paks.

"Good. Jos Hebbinford will tell you what time to come. After supper. You might want to dress for it, if you can." He stood, and Paks scrambled to her feet. "You are, you know, as welcome at the Grove as at the Grange." He turned away. Paks thought of the snowcat again. Should she tell him? She wondered what he would say.

By midafternoon, Paks had bathed and washed her hair. Her good shirt, mended, was drying in the stableyard; she wore the ragged one in her room. She had oiled her boots, and was working on her sword belt while her hair dried in the breeze from the window. She heard boots coming down the passage, stopping before her door. She froze, and reached for the sword, where she'd laid it on the bed. Someone knocked, and called her name softly.

Paks glanced around the room, then at the door, conscious of her loose hair, the mail shirt hanging on a peg. She shrugged, and answered.

"Yes?"

"I'm Arvid Semminson, lady, a traveller also staying here. You've seen me in the common room, in black trousers. I heard you were staying in this afternoon, and I've been wanting to speak with you. May I come in, or could we meet downstairs shortly?"

Paks thought of the man in dark clothes. She had no idea what his profession was, which itself made thief most likely. She thought of the Council meeting that night, and decided that she didn't want to meet anyone privately. "I'll be downstairs a little later, if that will suit."

"Very good," came the voice through the door, a mellow and pleasant voice. "I shall be honored to buy you a tankard of Hebbinford's best ale, or wine, whichever you prefer." The footsteps went away, back toward the stairs. Paks ran her hands through her hair, which was almost dry, and began to comb it. Somehow it was much worse to be found with loose hair: she did not feel like a fighter with hair down her back and wisping into her face. She braided it tightly, then finished her work on the sword belt. Her sword was clean and sharp, as always. She took off her trousers and looked them over. The previous mending still held. She could do nothing more for the shirt she had on. She had patched the worst rents, but the other holes and scorches remained. She had brushed and aired her cloak, but it, too, was stained and worn. The leather tunic, though bloodmarked, was better over her shirt than nothing. She slipped it over her head, decided against the mail, and felt her boots. Still damp and oily. It would be another hour or so before they were dry. She pulled out the thin leather liners she'd worn in the high mountains, and put them on. More respectable than socks or bare feet. She strapped her sword belt on over the tunic, made sure she could get her dagger easily, and went downstairs.

Arvid Semminson had chosen a table with a good view of the stairs. He smiled as he saw her, and waved. Paks came to his table. Only one other person was in the common room, a great cheerful youth she had seen before, happily downing a tankard of ale at a swallow. He was leaning on the wall behind his table, and looked half-asleep.

Semminson's clothes, Paks noticed as she came closer, were, if not new, at least unpatched and whole. By the drape of the shoulder and sleeve, the cloth was of fine quality. The belt at his waist was polished black leather, new enough that the edges had not curled; his dagger's sheath was well-oiled and unscarred. He himself had neatly trimmed dark hair, a smooth-shaven face, and bright black eyes. His mouth quirked in amusement.

"Do I pass your inspection, lady?" he asked pleasantly.

Paks thought of her own ragged shirt and patched trousers, and reddened. "I've no right to inspect," she muttered.

"No, but you were. Everyone does. I expect that. See here, lady, I'll be straight with you—no secrets. I'm no merchant, nor mercenary fighter. Our esteemed innkeeper thinks I'm a thief, though I haven't robbed him. That's neither here nor there. But you, either you're—how shall I say?—in a business related to mine, or you're simply unaware of the situation. Either way, I can't let such an attractive young woman wander into a trap without warning. Do you follow me?"

Paks shook her head. She felt a certain distaste for his attempt at flattery. After the tailor's wife's comments, she had no illusions about being "an attractive young woman" by local standards.

"Well—" he looked her up and down. "It might be that our interests would lie together. Or if not, a favor done might earn a favor later, who knows? But you know there's a Council meeting set for tonight?"

"Yes, but—"

"And you've agreed to go."

"Yes."

He snorted. "Then either you're a great deal more knowing than you act, or you know nothing at all." He leaned closer to her. "You can't hope to come out of that easily, you know. They'll get you one way or the other."

"What do you mean?"

He ticked off the points on his fingers. "A stranger in town, with plenty of money, and no liege to worry about angering, and under no protection they know of? Don't be silly. They'll find some excuse, and then pfft! You're in trouble."

"But I haven't—"

"—done anything," he finished for her, and laughed again. "And just what do you think that has to do with it, eh? No, let me give you some advice. It's too late to escape, if you would. But be very careful. After they back you in a corner, they'll probably offer you some sort of deal, if they can't find anything to imprison you for at once. Consider it very carefully, whatever it is. Very carefully. Make no promises you can avoid. Beware of that wizard, if he's there. He'll try to bind you with some sort of spell, if you aren't careful."

"But why are you telling me all this?" asked Paks, thinking hard.

"As I told you. A favor. I may need one from you someday. You can't do me any good if you're in a cell, or dead. And if they do offer you a deal, I'd like to know about it. Before I came here, I'd heard the Council had hired outsiders for some kind of interesting work. Since I arrived, no one will tell me anything. Maybe they'll tell you, if they think they have a hold on you. And if you end up taking a job—well, you might want someone with you who wasn't one of theirs, if you know what I mean."

Paks was both fascinated and repelled. What he said almost made sense, almost fit with the Kuakgan's words. She still could not understand what sort of hold anyone could have on her, or why they would want to find her guilty of something. In Aarenis, they might have wanted an excuse to seize her for the slave market, but not in Tsaia. She wondered if Semminson was the kind of agent that the Kuakgan had been talking about. Would anyone, ever, try to help a southern army invade the north? She was sure not, until she remembered that Sofi Ganarrion was planning to come north to fight for his throne. She said nothing, rubbing her toe against the top of the other foot. Semminson was watching her.

"Well," she said finally. "Whatever comes, I'll be meeting with the Council tonight."

"Just keep what I said in mind," he urged.

"Mmm. I will." She noticed Hebbinford watching her from the kitchen door. She looked away and stood.

"Good luck to you," said Semminson softly. "I fear you'll need it." Paks went on out to the stableyard to gather her clean clothes from the line.

All in all, she had little appetite for supper that night. Her clean shirt had only the one tear, which she had mended, and everything was as neat as she could make it, but she still felt shabby. She wondered whether to wear her mail. If Semminson was a thief, she hated to leave it behind, but she didn't want them to think she was looking for trouble, either. She thought it over, and finally cornered Hebbinford to ask him.

"It doesn't matter," he said. "It's valuable, and you're a fighter—wear it if you wish. You can't carry a sword into Council, but the guards will keep it for you. Whatever you're comfortable with."

She wasn't comfortable at all, but decided to go upstairs and put on the mail. Semminson was coming out of a room farther along the hall, and he gave her a knowing look. She put on the heavy jingling shirt, buffed her helmet on the blanket, and put that on as well. With a captain of soldiers coming, she might as well look like a soldier.

Hebbinford sent one of the girls to her room to call her; she came down the stairs with a sort of muddled determination to do the right thing and not be trapped. He was waiting at the door, dressed in a long blue gown under a far-collared cloak instead of his usual tunic and apron. He smiled and they set off for the Hall together. Paks heard horses behind them, and moved to the edge of the street automatically. Hebbinford turned to look, and waved to the lead rider.

"Ah, Sir Felis. You haven't been in town these past few days."

"No. There's enough to do at the keep." Paks looked up at the mounted figure, his face lit by his escorts' torches. He wore chainmail and helmet, and she could tell nothing about him except that he sat his horse like a soldier. He looked down at her and spoke to Hebbinford. "Is this the person I've heard of?"

"Yes, Sir Felis. This is Paksenarrion Dorthansdotter."

"Hmmph." She saw the glitter of his eyes as they scanned her. "You look more like a soldier than a free blade, young woman. You were with Duke Phelan's Company?"

"Yes, sir."

"What rank?"

"As a private, sir. File leader, my last year."

"I see. What—? No, I'll wait until we're in session." He gave a casual wave of the hand to Hebbinford, and rode on past them.

The hall, when they reached it, was lighted by torches in brackets along the front, as well as inside. Two of the captain's escorts stood guard at the door. Paks felt sweat spring cold on her forehead; she wanted to yawn for no reason. Semminson's veiled warnings seemed suddenly appropriate. She heard voices inside. Hebbinford nudged her, and she surrendered her sword to the guard on the right, and went on through the door.

At the far end of a large room, much larger than the common room at the inn, a knot of people clustered around the one table. Paks recognized Marshal Cedfer, now in mail, and looking much more like the Marshal she'd seen in Aarenis. His surcoat bore the crescent of Gird on a dark blue field. Master Oakhallow, in the same long robe he had worn in the afternoon, was already seated, and talking to one of the other men. Another man in mail—Paks assumed it was Sir Felis—stood at the end of the table, lips folded tightly as he listened.

Paks heard someone come in behind her, and turned to see the stonemason, Master Feddith. He gave her a cold look and stumped over to the table at once. Hebbinford, too, moved to that side of the room, and Paks followed slowly. A man she had not seen in town before, tall, with a generous belly, sat behind the table and looked up as the master mason and Hebbinford approached.

"Ah," he said. "We're all here, then. Have a seat, Councillors, have a seat. Let's get on with this." He looked at Paks. "So you're the young woman I've heard so much about? Paks—" He looked down at a sheet before him. "Paksenarrion Dorthansdotter? Of Three Firs?"

"Yes, sir," said Paks. The others were all taking seats around the far side and end of the table.

"Good. Let me introduce you to the Council. I'm the mayor, Brewmaster Ceddrin. You saw my place on your way to the grange. You know Marshal Cedfer, and Master Oakhallow, and Master Hebbinford already. Captain Sir Felis Trevlyn, our count's military representative—" Sir Felis nodded shortly; in this light Paks could tell that he was a lean, weatherbeaten man somewhat shorter than Duke Phelan. His beard was carefully trimmed. "—and Master Zinthys, the mage—" Paks looked at the slender, handsome young man in a long velvet robe lavishly banded with braid. He had rings on both hands, and a great polished crystal hanging by a silver chain on his chest. Master Zinthys smiled. The mayor went on. "This is Master Feddith, the stonemason, and I believe you also know Master Senneth, the moneychanger." He looked up and Paks nodded. "Also with us tonight are past Councillors: Master Hostin, our miller, Trader Garin Garinsson, and Master Doggal, the smith. Eris Arvidsdotter is here representing the farmholders." Trader Garin wore merchants' robes, and Eris Arvidsdotter wore a wool gown and cloak. She was as tall as Paks, and broad-shouldered; her gray hair was in a braided coil. The mayor paused until Paks had nodded at each of these. Then he picked up a heavy gavel lying on the table and rapped three times; the table boomed.

"The council of Brewersbridge is in session," he said loudly. "I ask the protection of all the gods, and the guidance of all good spirits, to be over us in this meeting. May wisdom and truth prevail. In the name of the High Lord, and all the powers of light." It sounded stilted, as if he didn't open the council formally that often.

"May it be," responded the others.

"We are met," he said in a lower tone, "to learn what we can of a traveler here, one Paksenarrion Dorthansdotter. We have heard disturbing things all this year of trouble in Aarenis. We will examine this person to see what her business is here, and how it may be bound in with what has happened there." He waited, and Paks noticed that both the mage and the Marshal were taking notes. "Does anyone object to my asking the questions?" asked the mayor. Heads were shaken around the table. "Very well, then. If you have other questions, when I'm through, just say so. Now—is Paksenarrion Dorthansdotter your true name?"

"Yes, sir, but I'm called Paks, since I left home."

"I see. And you come from Three Firs? Where is that? In Tsaia?"

"I—I'm not sure. The closest larger town was Rocky Ford; that's where I joined Duke Phelan's Company—"

The Marshal cleared his throat. "Excuse me, Mayor, but Rocky Ford is just within Tsaia, near the Finthan border in the north."

"I see. Three Firs was small, then?"

"Yes, sir. Much smaller than Brewersbridge. My father's land was a half-day's sheep drive out on the moors. We went to Three Firs rarely."

"And Rocky Ford?"

"I'd never been there before I—I ran away to join the Company."

"So you went directly from home to Duke Phelan's Company—hmm. And what was your father?"

"A sheep farmer," said Paks. "I learned about mercenary companies from my cousin, Jornoth; he'd left several years before, and came back with a horse and gold, and said he was in the guard."

"Where? In Tsaia?"

"He didn't say, sir. But he said I couldn't go directly to a job that good. He said I'd have to start somewhere else, and he told me what to do."

"Hmm. Not common, for a girl from a remote farm to join an army."

"No, sir. But I'd always wanted to be a warrior—"

"As a mercenary?" put in the Marshal.

Paks blushed. "Not—exactly, sir. But Jornoth said that was the way to start."

The mayor took control again. "You say you were trained at Duke Phelan's stronghold, and went from there to the wars in Aarenis?"

"Yes, sir."

"How long were you in Aarenis?"

"I was there for three campaign seasons, and in winter quarters in Valdaire. Only a few come back north in the winters."

"You must have had a short season this year," he said, looking at her sharply. "Why did you leave your Company?"

Paks hesitated. "The war—Siniava had been killed, and my two years were up."

"You have told Marshal Cedfer and Master Oakhallow what happened to you; we also would like to know, from your own lips."

"Yes, sir." Paks gathered her wits. She hurried over the first part of the trip with Macenion, merely mentioning his half-elf ancestry and the knowledge he claimed of the mountains. Then she described the valley of the elfane taig as they had first seen it, and the dream that came to both of them. The Councillors listened without interrupting as she described the underground passages, and the chamber where they'd found the elf-lord. Through the battle with him, the burning, and the running fight with the orcs, and the last struggle that ended, beyond her comprehension, with her alone on the surface, no one spoke or stirred. "Some sickness came on me," she said finally. "I couldn't go far along the trail; a snowstorm came down off the mountains, and I fell. Then it was that the elves came. They healed me, and entered the valley to see whether I had told them the truth. When they returned, they told me how to find my way here, and gave me messages to Master Oakhallow and Marshal Deordtya. I was to say that the elfane taig has awaked, and the elf-lord was freed." Paks stopped, and looked up and down the table. The faces were intent, but no longer hostile.

After a moment's silence, Sir Felis turned to the mayor. "If you don't mind, I'd like to ask a few questions."

"Go ahead."

"Paksenarrion, you say you served three campaign seasons. How soon after you joined the regular company were you made private from recruit?"

"The first battle, sir."

"What was your file position?"

"File second, the first year, sir, and the second. This past year we moved around a lot, but at the end I was file leader."

"I'm not clear on something. You've spoken both of leaving the Company, and of being on some sort of long leave. Are you still the Duke's soldier, or not?"

Paks sighed. "Sir, the Duke had reason to give me a long leave. He and others had suggested that I might leave the Company for a year or so. For other training, or experience, they said. But the Duke said I would be welcome back any time. I hadn't decided yet, sir, how soon to return."

"But you have no complaints against Duke Phelan, or he against you?"

"I have none against him, sir, and as far as I know he has none against me. And the Company is all I've known. I miss them."

"Have you any sort of token or pass from your Duke that might prove what you say of his opinion?"

Paks remembered the ring he had given the survivors of Dwarfwatch, and reached into her pouch to get it. "Here is a ring—" She handed it to the mayor, who peered at it, and passed it along the table. When they had all looked at it, the mayor passed it back.

"Dwarfwatch," the mayor said. "Isn't that the name of that Sorellin fort on the south end of Hakkenarsk Pass?"

"So the traders say," said Master Senneth.

"So. Those rumors, last spring, of a major battle there—" mused Hebbinford. "You must have been there. Why were you so angry with the merchants, Paksenarrion, for mentioning it?"

Paks glanced quickly at Sir Felis and the Marshal, then back to Hebbinford. "Sir, it is the Duke's business. I don't talk of it with merchants. But—by treachery, most of my—of a—cohort was lost at Dwarfwatch, to Lord Siniava. Most of a cohort of Halveric's, too. For those of us who lived, the Duke had these rings made."

"So he's fought understrength this past year," commented Sir Felis. "And the Halveric, too, I presume."

The Marshal was not deflected from the original story. "What was it, a siege, or what?"

"If she considers it her Duke's business, Cedfer—" began the Kuakgan.

"Nonsense. Anything that's happened almost a year ago is public knowledge in Aarenis, and we'll know the details here sooner or later."

Paks took a deep breath and tried to shove her private memories back into hiding. All the mercenary companies in the south knew the story; Cedfer was right. She gathered her wits and began. "One cohort of the Duke's Company was detached from the siege of Rotengre—the Guild League cities had joined in that—and garrisoned Dwarfwatch while the Sorellin militia, who had been there, helped with the grain harvest." She paused, and they all nodded. They listened intently as she described Halveric Company's approach, the surrender, the departure of all but a guard cohort of Halveric's and Siniava's attack, the fate of the prisoners marched away toward Rotengre, and the desperate defense of the few who held the fort.

"And you were in that. I see." Marshal Cedfer glanced at the Kuakgan and back to Paks. "Were you one of those sieged in the fort, or were you taken prisoner?"

"Neither, sir. Three of us were not taken—by chance, we were gathering berries in the brambles and they didn't see us. We took word to the Duke." Paks stopped there and looked at them. Sir Felis was leaning forward, alert and eager; the Marshal's eyebrows were up; the Kuakgan was frowning slightly. The rest merely looked interested. "How far did you go?" asked Sir Felis. "Where was the Duke?"

"Outside Rotengre, with the rest of the Company," said Paks. She wished they would go on to something else. She didn't want to think about that journey, about Saben and Canna.

"I can see," said the Marshal, "why you would be trusted by Duke Phelan. Remarkable. Well, then—so the Duke relieved his force at the fort. And where was the Halveric? I should think he'd have been there, too."

"He had taken most of his Company toward Merinath," said Paks. "They arrived the next day, too late to fight there, but they came to Rotengre."

"And how many troops did Siniava have?"

"We thought about eight hundred, altogether—"

"But Phelan's force is what—three cohorts altogether?"

"Yes, sir. He had help from the Claris and Count Vladi—"

"And Gird, no doubt," said the Marshal firmly. "Well, indeed. That's quite a tale, but straight enough. Now, what's happened this last year?

We've heard of widespread fighting, open war from the mountains to the sea, armies marched clear from the Westmounts to the Copper Hills. What about it?" The mayor was watching the Marshal closely, but did not interfere.

Paks wondered where to start. "Sir, after the year before, the Duke and the Halveric were certain that Siniava meant to conquer all of Aarenis. The Guild League cities blamed him for the piracy of Rotengre, and other things as well. My lord Duke pledged to spend himself on a campaign against Siniava, for what he had done to us. He gathered most of the northern mercenaries to his aid. And the Guild League cities fought on their own lands, and sometimes marched abroad as well."

"Aha!" Master Senneth was rubbing his hands together. "I always suspected the like, sirs, I did indeed. Too many caravans were robbed on the trade roads between Merinatn and Sorellin, and none of the goods ever showed up here. They must have been taken on south. And I'd heard through—well, I'd heard that Siniava had bought into some of the guilds."

Paks nodded. "We heard the same, sir, after Cortes Cilwan fell."

"Cilwan fell?" asked Sir Felis sharply. "What happened to the Count?"

"He was killed," said Paks. "But Vladi's men got his heir out, the boy, and he's safe in Andressat, the last I heard."

"Succession wars," muttered the Marshal. "They'll have succession wars, as well as everything else."

"Go on," said the mayor, with a gesture that silenced the others. "What then?"

Paks shrugged. "I don't know it all, sir; I was only a private, after all." She described the campaign as best she could. Sir Felis and the Marshal listened intently, their fingers moving as if on maps. The others reacted more to descriptions of cities fallen, battles fought, factions implicated in this plot or that. Finally, dry-throated with the length of the tale, she came to that last few days, when Siniava's remaining soldiers were neatly trapped with the help of Alured the Black. "We caught up with the last of them," Paks explained, "in an old ruin where the Immer and Imefal meet."

"Cortes Immer," said the Kuakgan softly. "No one's held that since the old duke's line died."

Paks looked at him. “Is that what it is? It’s still a great citadel, built into the living rock like Cortes Andres. Anyway, Siniava was killed, trying to escape secretly from the citadel, and after that his army surrendered to the militia.”

“I can hardly believe Siniava is truly dead,” mused the mayor. “How many years have we worried that he might gain control of Aarenis and come over the mountains? I remember the first word we had of him, don’t you, Master Oakhallow?”

“Indeed yes.”

“And now he’s gone. And no more agents of his will come through, trying to spy out defenses, such as they are.”

CHAPTER ELEVEN

"*If* she's telling the truth," said Feddith harshly. "If. 'Twould be months before we could check her tale. She might be an agent herself."

Paks tensed, but Sir Felis answered. "I don't think so," he said. "She carries the duke's ring, and showed it willingly. I know that crest."

"It could have been stolen," said Feddith stubbornly.

"She fights like a soldier trained in Phelan's company," commented the Marshal. "I know what training Phelan's soldiers would have, and she has it."

"And as well," said the mayor, with a look at the mage, "we have a way to tell if she lied. If Master Zinthys is willing—"

The mage looked at Paks, and smiled disarmingly. "I should say, if the lady is willing. Without any special arts, sirs, I see no liar there. An honest soldier, it seems to me, and I daresay to Captain Sir Felis." He caught Felis' eye, and the captain nodded. "I would not wish to cast a spell on her if she's opposed, sir; I would not indeed."

The tradesmen of the Council looked taken aback. Master Oakhallow smiled faintly. Marshal Cedfer spoke up, brisk as always.

"I'm sure she'll have no objection; it's an honorable request. Isn't that right, Paksenarrion?"

Paks felt the tensions in the room, and wondered what to do. She wished they'd agreed with the mage to let her alone. What was this truth spell like? Even with the Kuakgan's assurance in the afternoon, she feared to be involved in more magic.

"Sirs," she began cautiously, "the only time I know of that I've been spelled, it was by the elf-lord. Could I ask what the spell is, that Master

Zinthys would use? I have no wish to put myself in another's power for anything but the truth alone."

"Well said," murmured the Kuakgan. The others nodded, and Master Zinthys smiled at her.

"It's not like that at all—or rather, it may be a bit like that, but this spell is quite limited. You're absolutely right, not to let yourself be spelled without safeguards. I'll explain it to you. The power of this spell is that you cannot lie while it is active. Nor, for that matter, can anyone standing very close to you. I could, of course, cast it so that no one in the room could lie, but that takes a great deal of power. The limit of the spell is that while you cannot lie, you are not compelled to say anything at all. Nor does it affect acts other than speech—either compulsion or prevention. And when the spell wears off, you can lie at will. As a practical matter, the spell will wear off fairly soon; I see no reason to expend the power for a longer duration. Is all that clear?" He seemed quite proud of his explanation.

"Yes," said Paks slowly. "But—" she looked around at them all. All strangers. "Forgive me, sirs and lady," she said, trying to be very polite, "but I know none of you well, and at most have known you for a few days only. How do I know that you—?" Her voice trailed off as they reacted. Some of the faces went red at once. The mason began to sputter, but the smith laughed out loud.

"She's got you there," he chuckled. "Ah, lady, you have hit on it. I should have known that anyone who could lead that black devil away would think in the end. You don't trust us to say truth, and no wonder."

"That's right," said Master Zinthys quickly. "I hold no rancor, lady, for your doubts. Nonetheless, the Council has a reason to make sure of you, and your tale."

"Is it that thief, Paks?" asked Hebbinford. "I saw him talking to you this afternoon."

"Sir, I don't know. I didn't believe much that he said, no. But—Master Oakhailow said I had caused so much talk—I've been foolish, it seems. It may be late in the day, but I think I should be careful now, however I've acted. I never traveled alone before, as I told you. I never thought how it would seem, coming alone from the mountains with a load of treasure. I can understand your suspicions. But still—I don't want to be magicked into anything."

The mayor, still red-faced, nodded. "I see. You don't know me at all; no use to tell you how my family founded this town, generations back. You've no call to trust me. Are there any here you could trust? Did you know any Girdsmen before? Or were you kuakkgannir?"

Paks thought about it. "Sir, I didn't mean to insult you, but I did, didn't I? Yes, I have known Girdsmen, and the elves sent me to both the Marshal and the Kuakgan. If they say it is all right, I am willing."

The mayor looked at her shrewdly. "You may simply be as inexperienced as you seem. We'll see. Well, Master Oakhallow? Marshal Cedfer?"

"To my knowledge," said the Kuakgan, "Master Zinthys is an honest mage, and the spell he speaks of works just as he said it did. Certainly I pledge that we are not planning any other magic on you."

"And I the same," said the Marshal. "I assure you that Master Oakhallow and I are quite competent to prevent anything else, too."

"Yes, sir," said Paks miserably. "I just wanted to ask." She looked at Master Zinthys, fighting a hollow feeling in her belly. "Whenever you're ready, sir."

"You'd best sit down," said the mage. He rose and dragged a chair over for her. "It might make you dizzy for a moment. Now, try to relax." Paks had the feeling that he enjoyed showing his skill before the others, as he gestured fluidly with his long graceful hands.

Once she was seated, the mage took from his robe a small pouch and from that a pinch of colored dust, which he tossed at Paks. It spread in the air, and seemed to hang a long time before settling. Then he took four wands from up one sleeve, and set them on the floor around her chair. Finally he stood back and began to chant in a language Paks had never heard before, while gesturing with one hand in front of her face. Behind him, the faces of the others at the Council table were intent. Only the Kuakgan's showed amusement in the quirk of his mouth. She wondered why. At last the mage finished, and said in the common tongue: "Speak truth, or be silent, until the spell is done." Paks was surprised to feel nothing. No tingles, no pain, nothing at all different from before. She did not plan to lie, but what would happen if she did? Had the spell worked?

The mayor began the questioning, asking the same things as before: her name, background, reasons for leaving the Duke, reasons for coming to Brewersbridge. He asked little about the conflicts she'd described, and no details she had not already given. She answered, as before, honestly. It went more quickly, since no one interrupted. When he was done, the mayor sat back and looked at the others.

"She's not lied. Her story's unusual, but true."

"Then why did she resist being spelled?" asked the mason, still hostile. "And how do we know the spell is working?"

The mage flushed and sat up straight, but Master Oakhallow's deep voice forestalled what he might have said. "Master Mason, Zinthys is a competent wizard. The spell is good."

"If you say so," muttered the mason.

"I wonder myself," said the Marshal, "that a soldier of her experience would show fear of a simple spell. But if the sorcery she suffered before were severe enough—"

The Kuakgan looked at him sharply. "Come, Marshal, you know as well as I the power in that place. Only a witless fool would want to risk that again."

"True—true."

"How long, Master Zinthys, will the spell last?" the Kuakgan asked.

"Not long. Another quarter-glass, perhaps, though I can counteract it now, if you wish."

"It would be more courteous," he murmured, and the rest of the Council nodded.

Paks watched as the mage came near. He picked up the wands and stowed them up his sleeve, then began another incantation. When he finished, he grinned at her.

"There. That wasn't so bad, was it?"

"No, sir." Paks still felt nothing. Foolish, maybe. She wished she'd agreed at once to the spell, since it had done her no harm. The mayor cleared his throat.

"We've been here for some time, and there's more to come." Paks tensed again. "Let's take a short break now, and ease our throats with a bit of ale. Is that all right with you, Paksenarrion?"

"Yes, sir." Paks wondered what was coming next, and thought of Semminson's warning. What might they want her to do? Meanwhile, she stood when the others did, and followed them out to the yard before the building. The mayor spoke to a man in servant's clothes standing there, and told him to fetch ale. It was quite dark out, and cool; Paks shivered. Sir Felis came up to her.

"I'm more than glad to know Siniava's dead," he began. "One reason the count had me down here is in case an army came over the pass. It will be a year or more before the keep is finished. But you haven't seen that, have you?"

"No, sir."

"That's my command. When it's finished, we'll have a place to fight from, if it's necessary. The last time there was a battle near here, we had no fortified position. No place to store arms, or haven for those who couldn't fight—nothing."

"We've built the grange since then," put in the Marshal.

"Oh, yes. But then, it's not designed as a keep, though it is stone. You couldn't hold it against assault."

"No, you're right. Not against a trained force. It would hold against bandits, though—we've used it for that."

"Before my time, Marshal—and wasn't it before yours?"

"Oh, yes. That was Deordtya's doing, not mine, years back. I suppose I shouldn't say 'we' when I mean Gird's grange; it's just habit."

The servant appeared at their side with a tray of tankards; each took one.

"This will be Ceddrin's private brew," commented the Marshal. "I doubt you've tasted as good, Paksenarrion."

Paks blew away the foam and sipped. It was rich and hearty. "It's very good," she said.

"Just what sort of training did Duke Phelan suggest you look for?" asked Sir Felis. "I'd have thought he could offer anything you or he might need."

"He thought, sir, that I might learn mounted warfare, and something of fortifications and defense—"

"Huh. Sounds as if he were planning the education of a squire, not a man-at-arms. Had he suggested you work toward a knighthood, or something like that?" His voice hinted at the unlikeliness of this.

Paks nodded. "He said, sir, that nothing was certain, but that I might have the ability to become a cohort captain, or some such, years from now."

Sir Felis frowned. "The land's full of captains; I wonder that he'd risk losing a good soldier. Had he ever given you any command?"

"I was temporary corporal for awhile, sir, when one of ours was injured. And at the end of the campaign, when Siniava was trapped in—Cortes Immer, was it?—I led those who watched the bolthole."

"Did Siniava come that way?"

"Yes, sir." Paks offered no details. "He was captured and killed."

"I see. Phelan obviously thought well of you. I must tell you that there's not much chance my count would hire you, if you were hoping for that. He's done no recruiting this past year. You could, of course, go and ask him directly."

"I hadn't thought of it, sir. I know little of this country, or who holds which keep."

"Mmmm. I'll show you a map—can you read maps? Good. I've one of the kingdom, showing the principal fiefs. It may give you some idea where you could hope to hire on. Marshal Cedfer can tell you of opportunities of the grange and Hall. The Fellowship of Gird, you know, maintains several training centers for fighting men at every level. For that matter, they have fighting orders, as do followers of Falk and Camwyn."

"Is that where paladins come from?" asked Paks. "We saw a paladin in Aarenis."

Sir Felis choked on his ale. "Is that what you—!? Sorry. No, not exactly. The Marshal can tell you more than I, if you're interested in that. There's an order of knights, the Knights of Gird, just as there are Knights of the Dragon's Breath, followers of Camwyn Dragonmaster."

Paks was confused. "I thought knights were—were knights, all the same. Noblemen born, or those knighted for service."

Sir Felis stared. "Oh, no. Whatever gave you that idea? Oh dear, no. Where did you say you were from? A small border village, wasn't it? Now let me try to explain."

His explanation was hardly enlightening to Paks, since she knew few of the places and none of the rulers he mentioned. He finished his lecture with a gesture to the small gold device on his collar, shaped like a peal of bells.

"Now," he went on, after wiping his mustache, "members of my order may be followers of any honorable god or hero. I myself am a Girdsman, but my father's brother is Falkian, and so are my cousins. Our loyalty is to the crown of Tsaia—or, more accurately, to the heir of the House of Mahierian. But Knights of Gird swear their loyalty to the Marshal-General of Gird, through their Knight Commander. The—er—rules governing admission to each order depends—er—on the order, and the circumstances." He looked her up and down, doubtfully, as if she were an unpedigreed horse at a sale.

"I see," said Paks, more to stop him than because she did. She was still confused. She was actually relieved when the mayor tapped her arm.

"Let's get back; we have yet a good bit of business to talk over."

This time they asked her to sit down at the beginning of the session, and the rest spread themselves around the table on all sides. Only the master mason seemed stil! faintly hostile.

"We appreciate your cooperation," began the mayor. "Now that we know something of your background, let me explain how things stand in Brewersbridge. We're on a major trade route from the west to the sea. We have a lot of traffic through, and want it—we depend on it. Nonetheless, I hope you won't be insulted when I say that the Council is opposed to having free blades hanging around town. Some of them, like you, are honorable folk, and cause no trouble intentionally. Others, like the fellow who died, pick quarrels everywhere. We've learned it's best to insist that soldiers and warriors either find a local lord or commander, to be responsible for their behavior, or move on." He smiled, as he said this. Paks wondered what was coming next.

"Now you," he said, "are perhaps a special case. While Master Senneth, even for the Council's peace of mind, won't divulge how much treasure you desposited with him, he has assured us that you will not need to rob anyone for the price of a meal before Midwinter Feast." A chuckle went around the table. Even the mason smiled. "So, since you've given honest account of yourself, we have one less thing to worry about. Nonetheless, our tradition is clear, and since Sir Felis has no employment for you, we would not willingly have you stay too long idling about. That would mean more than a few weeks, in your case: I understand that you've ordered goods from some of our local tradesmen. Certainly you may stay until they're completed, as long as nothing happens. On the other hand, we are prepared to offer you certain employment—the Council is, I mean. If you took it, we would not consider you in the same class as an adventurer."

Paks remembered Semminson's warning. "What sort of employment, sir, did you have in mind?"

"Work suitable for your abilities and training, I believe. And so says Marshal Cedfer. I think Sir Felis would now concur, would you not?"

Sir Felis nodded. "We have been plagued, hereabouts, with brigands preying on caravans in the region. You can understand why that is critical for us; we depend on their trade. Sir Felis has swept the area several times, finding nothing. He has direct orders from the count to concentrate his time and men on the building of the keep north of town. We need someone to search out the brigands' hiding place, and lead a force against them. None of us have the training—or, to be frank, the time to take away from our trades. Would you be willing to take this commission?"

Paks could not suppress a grin. It sounded like fun, at least the part about rinding the brigands' camp. But as for killing or catching them... "Sir, it is an interesting proposal. But, whatever Marshal Cedfer may think, I am hardly able to defeat a band of brigands on my own."

"Not at all," said the mayor. "Of course not. We would expect you to lead a force, including some of the local militia. And you could confer, perhaps, with the Marshal or Sir Felis, on the best method for defeating them, once you had found their camp. It is that we cannot do."

Put that way, it sounded even more attractive. Whenever Paks thought of brigands, she thought of those who had killed Saben and Canna. She nodded at the mayor. "I have no love for brigands," she said. "I'll be glad to hunt them for you."

"Good. What we propose is this: we will authorize you to call on members of the local militia who have free time, and they—or the town—will supply their weapons. We will not pay you, but we will grant you a share of any recovered goods, and a head-price for each robber killed or captured. If you need extraordinary aid, come to Marshal Cedfer, and he will arrange it as he sees fit. Is that satisfactory?"

Paks had no idea what such contracts were usually like, but it seemed reasonable. If many caravans had been robbed, surely the plunder would make a fair return. "Yes," she said. "That will do. But do you have any idea where they might be?"

The mayor leaned forward. "An idea, yes, but we aren't sure. Caravans have been attacked on all the roads around. But Eris"—he nodded to the farm woman, who nodded to Paks—"Eris tells us that farms have been robbed, too and one or two wiped out—west of here. None close in, but those farther out have lost livestock. There are several ruins out that way which might be useful to brigands, though Sir Felis found no one there—"

"That's not to say they might not use them," Sir Felis broke in. "We've had no time for more than a fast sweep—they could have been hiding nearby, if they were clever."

"We think," the mayor went on, "that they must have some spy in town. More caravans are robbed on their way out—especially those that have come on a market day, and sold things in our market. I won't conceal the fact that these men—if it's humans—are dangerous. Typically they kill all the caravaners, merchants and guards alike. That's ten to twenty guards, and say five merchants or so, and the drivers. They've killed two farm families we know of—I suppose they surprised them robbing—"

"But," Sir Felis interrupted again, "it may be that some farmer out there is in league with them." Eris Arvidsdotter shook her head angrily, but Paks remembered the setup at "uncle's" in Aarenis. It would make sense. "Northwest of here," Sir Felis continued, "was Baron Anseg's land, but he died without a close heir years ago, and the title of that land is still being argued in Vérella. Once you're away from the river, and well into the woods beyond Brewersbridge, there's no lord for two days' travel, until Baron Velis' outside Bingham."

"The merchants' guilds," put in the mayor, "naturally have an interest in the safety of the roads. We have no Guild League, as in Aarenis, with real authority, but the guilds will support any effort to keep the roads safe where no lord has the responsibility."

"I see," said Paks. She was becoming confused again, and clung to what she did understand. "So you want me to hunt around and find where the brigands are hiding, and get a small force to drive them out? Do you want them driven away, or killed, or captured, or what?"

"Killed or captured, definitely," said Marshal Cedfer. "Drive them out, and they'll return as soon as you're gone."

"I say kill them," put in the mason. "What good are brigands anyway?"

Paks wondered if he'd ever killed anyone. Himself.

"And if you find out who is—I mean, who may be giving information here in Brewersbridge—" added the mayor.

Paks grinned. "You expect a stranger to find out what's going on when you, who know everyone, can't? I might be able to find the brigands, sir, and I know I can fight, but I've no experience in finding out secrets like that."

"Well, but if you should happen to learn—"

"I would tell—Marshal Cedfer, you wished me to report to? Is that right?"

"Yes, that's right. Or me. But Marshal Cedfer is best."

Paks looked around the table. Everyone was watching her. The mage gave her a bright smile, as if to encourage her. The Marshal and Sir Felis looked impatient, as if she were a slightly stupid recruit. Master Oakhallow's level gaze held a challenge. She felt, suddenly, very tired. To fight brigands was well enough, and she'd be glad of an honest, above-ground battle again, but she had the feeling that they all expected something more. Something more.

"Yes," she said finally. "I'll do that—or try to. I suppose the first thing is to look for the places they might be. Do you have a map, perhaps, of the local—"

But at that they all began to talk.

"How good of you—"

"No need for that tonight, now that you've—"

"Perhaps tomorrow you can meet with Marshal Cedfer—"

"—out to the keep, and I'll introduce you to my sergeants—"

The mayor banged his gavel once, and everyone quieted. "One last thing. The town, as I said, will supply the militia, their food and weapons. But do you have what you need for yourself? I see you have armor—" He waited for her answer. Paks thought about her gear. To move about the countryside, as far as he had mentioned—a day's ride away?—she would need a horse of some kind.

"I could use a horse or mule," she said. "My pony's not the right animal for prowling around."

Sir Felis frowned. "I haven't any spares, right now. We've thrush in the stable, and horses lame."

The mayor shook his head. "It's so late in the season. The horses in town now are work horses—and in use every day. Marshal Cedfer?"

"No. Sorry, my own mount, and Ambros', that's all I've got. If you wanted to buy one, perhaps Sir Felis could send to the count's stable—"

"There's one spare horse," said Hebbinford. "In my stable—that black horse."

Paks felt a surge of excitement. She had not thought of the black, but that was the sort of horse she had dreamed of in the past. A true warrior's horse. She looked at the mayor, and Hebbinford, and back again. "What about that one, then? No one else is using it."

"I suppose that's all right," said the mayor slowly. "I can see you need a horse, to go looking all over the country. If the rest of you agree—"

"What of the man's heirs?" asked Master Feddith. "He looked a friendless man, but if he had heirs, they'd have some right to the beast."

"What of the fines he'd have owed, for trying to rob the master smith, if he'd lived?" asked Senneth sharply. "I say the Council can claim his horse for damages, and sell it to Paksenarrion if we choose."

"Perhaps, sirs," said Paks, uncertain if she should speak, "I could but have the use of the horse at first—paying Master Hebbinford for his keep, of course. It may be that I have not the skill to master such an animal—" she paused as the smith snorted loudly, and all eyes went to him. "Even if I do, I will not need it after this, I think."

"That's well-spoken," said the smith abruptly. "Twould do that beast good to be worked, that it would, and the trying of him out would be a reason for her to ride about the countryside. But as for skill—" He looked hard at Paks. "You've either skill of a horse-breaker, girl, or magic in your fingers, and that's a fact." Paks saw both the Kuakgan and the Marshal give her hands a quick glance. She was glad they were clasped to cover the ring.

"Well, then," said the mayor, "how think you? I see no harm in that, and it saves Master Hebbinford risking his own neck to keep the beast exercised, for I doubt you'd let Sevri try it, would you Jos?"

"Never," said Hebbinford, with a ghost of a grin. "Nor is my lass that crazy. I'm for it."

"And I," said the other Council members.

"And I hope you'll decide to buy that horse," said Senneth, as they rose. "If you go, and leave it here, the Council will be left with the care of it all winter until the spring fairs. We'll give you a good price, I swear."

"We can do better than that, Senneth," said the mayor, clapping him on the shoulder. "Should she succeed in routing all the brigands, we might call it a reward. Then she could not refuse, and we need not worry about the feed."

The others laughed, and gathered around Paks for a few words each before leaving. When she had retrieved her sword from the guard at the door, she found Hebbinford and the Kuakgan waiting to walk with her. The night had turned even colder, and she looked forward to the new cloak the tailor would make.

CHAPTER TWELVE

After so late a night, Paks would have been glad to sleep later than usual, but anticipation of the black horse woke her at dawn. She felt sure of the power of the ring, but once mounted she could not concentrate on her ring finger. She knew she should be thinking of the brigands, and less of the horse, but the black horse seemed far more important this day.

She had hoped to work with him in privacy first, but everyone in the inn seemed to have business in the stableyard, early as it was. Sevri had not groomed the beast, for he had nearly caught her with one of his powerful kicks on the first day, and his owner had done it after that. Paks kept her thumb firmly on the ring as she picked up a brush and eased into the stall by his head. The ears were alert but not flattened, and the great dark eye watched her calmly as the horse worked on its ration of grain.

"There now," crooned Paks, setting the brush to that massive shoulder. "There, quiet, stay calm, black one." She began to brush, more gently than would do for a thorough grooming, and with a wary eye on the ears. The horse was taller and more heavily built than the Duke's warhorses, as tall as Arcolin's favorite. She worked her way along the ribs, the croup, the rump. Dust and scurf flew; the horse had not been well groomed for some time. She brushed down the haunches, saw them tense, and concentrated on the ring for a moment. "Nothing's wrong, horse. I won't hurt you. Quiet, now, easy—" The bunched muscles relaxed; she saw the fetlock sink deeper in the straw. "You'd like to be out of here, wouldn't you? Go for a ride? Out in the open air—along the roads—good horse—" Soon she had brushed both sides, the belly (another pause for the ring's action there), brushed out the heavy tangled mane. She looked up and saw Sevri's awed face over the stall wall.

"I didn't think you could really do it," said Sevri.

Paks grinned at her, thumb firm on the ring. "I wasn't sure I could myself. Can you bring me a pick?"

"You're going to touch his feet?'

Paks shrugged. "What if he has a stone? If he's taken this much, he should take that."

Sevri handed over the hoofpick. "I just finished Star. Here."

Paks leaned down beside the near fore, impressed again by the size of those platter-like hooves. "Come on, black one—let's have a hoof." She could feel the tension above her, and glanced up to see the horse watching, ears stiffly turned back. "No—come on, now—" She pinched the tendons as she'd been taught, wondering briefly if she should have done this outside a stall, just in case. But the hoof came up, at last, and she cleaned around the frog with her pick. The other front hoof went as well, but as she bent near the rear, the horse squealed and slammed a kick into the stall wall, narrowly missing her. Paks thought a loud NO through the ring, and the horse froze, trembling. She could see the cracked board where the hoof struck, and heard a murmur of voices at the stable door. Sevri was urging watchers away.

Slowly, concentrating on the ring, Paks slid her hand down the hind leg, over slick black hide to the white feather below the hock, and through that heavy hair felt along to the fetlock. The scar was hidden by the thick hair above it—a deep scar, and still sensitive, for the horse blew a rattling breath, despite the ring's compulsion, as she touched it. Paks straightened. "Easy—I'd warrant you have another on the off side as well. No wonder you don't like having your legs handled. I wonder what did that? Nothing good. Well, perhaps we can leave that a day, until you trust me more." She came back to the horse's head, and scratched under his jaw until the strained look left his eyes. "Surely the smith didn't do that, holding you to shoe you?" The horse relaxed enough to stretch its neck. Paks slipped out of the stall, shaking a little with the strain of using the ring for so long.

"Will you ride today?" asked Sevri, who was waiting by the door.

"He needs exercise," said Paks. "But he's got some injury to his back legs—that's why he's so touchy, I think. I hate to ride him out until I can handle those legs, but he's had as much as he can take, for now. Maybe later."

Paks went in to breakfast, trying to ignore the curious looks of the others. If she was going to lead a group out against brigands, and train a horse, she needed several things from the shops. She made a list during breakfast, and asked Hebbinford where she could find some of the items. When she returned, everyone seemed to be out of the way but Sevri.

"If you want me to leave, as well—" she said shyly.

"No, but don't get too close. I don't know what he'll do. Tir's bones, I don't even know how to rig that saddle." She went into the stable. The black horse nosed over the stall wall; she had not yet touched the ring. Perhaps it was not a true outlaw. Sevri brought the bridle, red leather decorated with copper rings that had tarnished green. The reins were broad and heavy, and the bit—Paks shook her head.

"I can't use that! Look at those spikes, Sevri."

"The warhorses we see here all have bits like that," said Sevri. "Are you sure?"

"I'm sure of this—I won't use that bit. The Duke didn't use anything like that. Where can I buy another one?"

"You can use my father's old one, if it'll do. He had a hauling team once, before he sold it to a caravaner that was short. Try this—" Sevri brought out an old, rusty-linked bit like those Paks had seen on cart horses. While Sevri shook it in a sandbag to get the rust off, Paks worked at the stiff lacings of the bridle. At last she had the old bit off, and the smooth one in place.

"If he's used to that mess in his mouth, he won't take the bit easily," said Paks. "Let's see—" And as she walked up with the bridle, the black horse threw up its head, snorting. Again she thumbed the ring, which quieted the noise. Sevri darted off for an apple.

"Will this work?"

"It might." Paks was glad of anything that would conceal the action of the ring. She offered it, concentrating on the ring, and in a moment slid the bit in place, and the crownpiece over the horse's ears as its teeth crunched the apple. She waited to fasten the noseband and throatlatch until the apple was finished, and the last lumps passed down the black throat.

"I hope you can hold him with that," said Sevri doubtfully.

"With what?" came a brisk voice from the door, and they all jumped. Paks clenched her left hand on the ring and turned. Marshal Cedfer stood there, with Ambros just behind him.

"She changed bits," said Sevri, before Paks could think what to say. "She wouldn't use that old one." She nudged it with her toe, where it lay in the aisle.

"That's a mouthful indeed," said the Marshal, picking it up. "But what are you using instead, Paksenarrion? That 'magic' Doggal mentioned?"

"No," said Sevri again. "It's one of my father's old bits, a smooth one that he used when he had a team. But I thought warhorses had to have spiked bits."

The Marshal's face relaxed. "Good, Paksenarrion, very good. No, Sevri, a horse can be trained to any bit, but the smooth ones are better. Hasty warriors try to use rough bits instead of training to get their horses' attention. A good horseman uses as smooth a bit as he may." He took a step forward to look at the horse more closely. "As I recall, Duke Phelan's troops use horses for transport only. I'm sure you ride—perhaps well—but I thought I could help you with the commands peculiar to warhorses, not traveling mounts."

"Thank you, Marshal," said Paks. "I realized this morning that even the saddles we used are not like this one—" she gestured at the heavy saddle with its tangle of rigging, on a peg nearby.

"You haven't cleaned it yet," said the Marshal, frowning.

"No, sir." Paks flushed as if Stammel had found her with dirty equipment.

"Hmm. Clean tack, Paksenarrion, is very important. Sevri, bring us a fresh pad, at least. Lead him out to the yard, Paksenarrion."

With her hand clenched around the ring, Paks led the black horse out. He followed as calmly as Star, for which she was grateful. Her neck prickled as she placed the sheepskin pad. The Marshal handed her the saddle.

"I see you know how to work with a bridled horse—see, Ambros. She's got her arm in the rein, just as I keep telling you. Now, Paksenarrion, let me explain all those extra straps." Paks needed the help, but wished it were someone else's. "That—yes, that one—is the foregirth. Fasten it first. Good. Now the breastband—see those hooks on the saddle? Yes. Not tight—just lying smoothly. That's so the saddle cannot slip back under any strain. Now the rest of that—by Gird himself! That fellow didn't know how to stow his gear. Roll that mess slowly out over his rump—be careful girl! Yes. Now see that loop on top? The tail goes through that. Wait, though—" The Marshal moved to the horse's rump and felt of the loop. "Heh. I might have known. Feel this. It's too stiff; it's probably rubbed him raw already. We'll take all this off—" and he began to work at fastenings on the back of the saddle as he talked. "You don't really need it yet. Oil and clean it—get it all soft—and I'll show you how to put it back on. In a fight, or traveling in rough country, it keeps the saddle from slipping forward, just like the breeching strap on a pack animal." He went to the other side, and finished there. "Here, Sevri, take these away." He watched as Paks checked the stirrup length; she left it unchanged. "Do you want me to hold him while you mount?"

Paks looked at the horse, which suddenly seemed very tall. Yet she had ridden Arcolin's horse, that once. Her mouth was dry. If the Marshal had not been there, she could have led the horse to a field, where she could hope to land soft. Instead, she sighed inwardly, and thanked him. "I must admit, sir, that this is the biggest horse—"

"You've ridden," he finished. "Yes, I thought it might be." He took the rein and the horse stiffened. Paks got her foot in the stirrup, and tried to swing up, but the horse shifted suddenly with her weight. She fell into the saddle with an ungraceful scramble. It was built high and close to her body; she had almost landed on, and not in, it.

"With a horse like this," said the Marshal, "you need to be quicker. Or else train him to stand." He stepped back, releasing the rein, as Paks straightened.

The saddle felt strange, as if it were hovering over the horse's back, and the ground was very far away. Paks nudged the horse lightly with her heels, and it lunged forward. She thumbed the ring, thinking "Easy!" and it settled again, ears flicking. Paks saw eyes at the inn door, and cursed silently. She could feel the horse tensing under her, the hump in its back that kept the saddle too high. "Settle down, horse," she said softly. "Settle down, and we'll go for a walk somewhere." It took one stiff step, then another. She laid the rein against its neck, to turn it around the dungheap, and it whirled on its hind legs, almost unseating her. "Easy!" she said. Arcolin's horse had been nothing like this! For a moment, she longed for gentle little Star, but she was conscious of the Marshal and Ambros watching. She was a warrior, and this was a warrior's horse. If she was ever to be a knight—she talked the horse forward, hardly daring to touch it with her heels. Nearly to the cowbyre: she had to turn. Again the light touch of rein, and the lightning spin, but this time she was ready for it.

"You might see what happens if you pull one rein lightly," called the Marshal. "Those that are trained to spin on one cue usually turn slowly on the other."

Paks tried a gentle pull, and the horse veered left. It was walking more freely now, and she finally managed a circle around the stable yard.

"Now the other way," commanded the Marshal. This, too, went well, though Paks could still feel a knot of tension in the horse's back. They walked around the yard once, then twice. She pulled back for a halt, feeling more confident, and the horse reared. Paks lurched backward and grabbed for mane. Someone in the inn door laughed, and cut it off. The horse stayed up—and stayed up—she felt like a fool. How could she get him down? She closed her legs on him, and the horse leaped forward, snapping her head back. He landed charging, whirling about the stableyard as Paks fought to stay on. The saddle, so uncomfortable before, seemed to grip her. She could hear frantic yells, and the clatter of shod hooves on stone. At last she remembered the ring, and thought, "Whoa!" The horse skidded to a stop and stood rigid. Paks was breathless; pain stabbed her side, and her hands were shaking. She had been sure she'd fall. It was hard to believe anything so ponderous had moved so fast. It had seemed easy when she'd seen others riding—she grinned at the memory.

"You can stay on, at least," The Marshal's voice broke into her thoughts. "But that beast may still be too much for you. Best not ride through town until you have better control."

"I—I won't, sir. I had—no idea—"

"Not well-trained, either." The Marshal was walking around the horse. "He's got the makings of a fine animal, Paksenarrion, but he's been ill-trained, and I would judge ill-used. If you can retrain him, you'll have a formidable mount."

"I'm not sure," said Paks ruefully, "that I'll be able to figure out how to ride down the road, let alone fight on him."

"You're a long way from that, but—a stableyard is not the best place to learn. If you can get him as far as the grange, you can ride in the drillfields behind, and I'll be glad to instruct you. If you go behind the inn, and ride south of town, there's a ford upstream of the bridge."

"Thank you," said Paks. "I'll try. But how will I stop him? If a pull on the reins doesn't work, what will?"

"May I try?"

"Of course, sir." Paks slid off, finding it harder than she'd thought to clear the unfamiliar saddle. She held the rein for the Marshal, who mounted in one smooth motion.

As she stepped back, the black horse exploded in a fit of bucking. Paks flattened herself beside Ambros, near the stable door, appalled at the unleashed power.

"Don't worry," said Ambros. "The Marshal's good with horses." And indeed, after scattering a good part of the dunghill over the yard, the horse trotted stiffly around, neck bowed, obedient to the Marshal's rein and legs. Paks could not see what the Marshal had done when the horse stopped, but he told her.

"To halt him, you'll need to stiffen your back and sit back slightly. That's all. Right now I wouldn't use the rein at all; we can retrain him later. Think you can manage?"

Paks wasn't at all sure, but she nodded. She would try, at least. The Marshal swung off as easily as he'd mounted, and handed her the rein. He grinned after a look around the stableyard, and spoke to Ambros.

"Well, I made a considerable mess, didn't I? We'd best get at it, Ambros, if we want to keep our welcome—"

"No, Marshal, that's all right—" Sevri looked dismayed, nonetheless.

"No, it isn't. Ambros and I will take care of it." And to Paks' surprise, and the obvious surprise of other watchers, the Marshal took the shovel from Sevri, and Ambros found another. They began shoveling the scattered dung back into a heap. Paks led the black horse to his stall, and returned with another shovel to help. The Marshal smiled, but said nothing as he worked. Soon the yard was tidy once more. "There now." The Marshal wiped sweat from his forehead, and handed Sevri the shovel. "Paksenarrion, early morning is a good time to train horses. Bring him along after feeding tomorrow."

"Yes, sir." Paks hoped she wouldn't fall off before she got to the grange. The Marshal waved and left. Only after he was gone did she realize that she now had a perfect excuse to ride around the countryside and spend hours with the Marshal. No one would wonder, after hearing about the black horse's performance, why she rode alone, or why she went to the grange every day.

By that afternoon, the tailor's wife had one shirt ready for her to try on. Paks would gladly have taken it then, but the woman insisted that she must do more work. "See on the inside, lady? The edges there? I'll turn those down, and they'll not ravel or be rough—"

"But—"

"Nay, we're proud of our work, my husband and me—we won't let such as this leave our hands. But I'll have it tomorrow, by lunchtime, and the other plain shirts in two days—unless you'd rather have the trousers first?"

Paks thought of all the riding she'd be doing, and asked for the trousers next. Outside the shop, she headed for the saddler's, and bought a jug of the heavy oil he used on his leathers. In Doggal's yard, she found the smith forging heavy wagon fittings, and waited outside until he paused.

The next morning, she was able to bridle and saddle the black horse without help—but with constant support from the ring. Sevri offered to hold the rein, but Paks feared the horse might hurt her. Instead, she faced him into a corner. Her attempt at a quick mount was as rough as the day before, but she had gained the saddle before he moved out from under her. She pulled the left rein gently, and he turned toward the gate. Once out from between the walls, the horse seemed slightly calmer. Paks turned him along a path between the back of the inn yard and a cottage garden, and then through the fields behind the village. She found the ford the Marshal had mentioned by following a cow path, and the black horse pranced gingerly through the swift shallows, rocks rolling under his hooves. Now she was at the lower end of the grange drilling fields; she could see someone standing near the grange. As she thought, it was the Marshal. Ambros, mounted on a rangy bay, rode around the barton wall from the street as she came up.

"You made it safely, I see," said the Marshal. "Ambros rides three times a week, and this will give both of you practice in riding with others."

Paks said nothing. The black horse had laid his ears back flat at the sight of the other horse.

In the next few days, Paks acquired a whole new set of bruises. The Marshal was as hard a riding master as Siger had been in weapons training. Like all occasional riders, Paks hated to trot—but the Marshal insisted that they trot most of the time. He was particular about the placement of her feet, and way she held the rein, the angle of her head. But the black horse no longer jumped out from under her. She could control his pace, and stop him, turn and return, without difficulty. Much of the time she did not need the action of the ring, except for grooming and mounting.

She was able to ride along the roads, now, and spent several hours a day learning where they led. The Marshal had told her that such quiet slow work was excellent for a high-strung mount.

But at night she dreamed of the snowcat, and woke, sweaty and trembling. Once it was the black horse's neck that Macenion hacked at, instead of the cat. Another time a shadowy spotted creature followed her along the trails she'd ridden that day, disappearing when she tried to turn on it. Every time she used the ring on the horse, she felt a pang of remorse. At last she decided to talk to the Kuakgan about it.

This time, as she came in sight of the clearing, she saw the Kuakgan talking to another near the fountain. Uncertain, she paused. She could hear nothing from where she stood, and wondered whether to intrude or go back. She turned to look the way she had come, and froze. No path lay behind her. The white stones that should have marked one had disappeared, and a tree rose inches from her back. She shuddered, sweat springing out on her neck and back, crawling down her ribs. She looked forward, and the clearing was open before her. Master Oakhallow, facing her, beckoned. She saw no one else. Paks took a deep breath and stepped out of the trees. As she came nearer the fountain, she felt the quiet deepen. She laid the oatcake Hebbinford had given her in the basin.

"It is well," said Master Oakhallow in his deep voice, "that you did not try to leave again. The unsteady of purpose find my grove unsettling."

"Sir, it is not that," said Paks. "But you were speaking to another. I would not intrude."

He smiled. "Your courtesy is appreciated. But you could not have come nearer than I wished. Enough you came with a purpose. What troubles you?"

Paks did not want to meet his eyes. "Sir, I did not take the time to tell you all that happened on our way across the mountains—'

"You had no need to tell me all, or anything you would not," he interrupted. "But you shied from some part of your tale, and it speaks in your eyes yet. Is it this you came for?"

Paks felt her heart begin to hammer against her ribs. She wished she had gone to Marshal Cedfer. She wished she had done nothing at all. From everything she had heard of the Kuakkganni—their deep love of wild things, their distaste for men's arts, their contempt for war and soldiery—she was in danger now, danger against which her sword was no protection. She ducked her head lower yet.

"Yes, sir. It is. I—did something, sir, and I—I can't—I don't know what to do."

"Are you sure," he asked, "that I am the one you wish to talk to? You have spent much time lately with Marshal Cedfer. You are not kuakkgannir; I have no claim on your actions."

"I'm sure," said Paks, fighting the tremor in her voice. "It—has to do with—with the elf, and wild things, and he—Marshal Cedfer—he would think it silly, I think."

"Hmm. By elf, I presume you mean Macenion? Yes. And wild things. I doubt, Paksenarrion, that he would think it silly, but I am more used to dealing with those than he. Now—" his voice sharpened a little, and Paks flinched at the tone. "If you can spit out your tale, child, and let us see what it is, perhaps I can be of some use."

Paks took a deep breath, and began, haltingly, to tell of the night in the pass. The Kuakgan did not interrupt, or prompt her. When she told of the coming of the snowcat, she felt through the bones of her head the sharpening of his gaze and struggled on.

"Then he—Macenion—told me to use the ring—"

"The ring?" His voice might have been stone, from the weight of it.

Paks held out her hand and withdrew it. "This ring, sir. He said it was made to control animals. He said that after I caught his horse when it ran away, and he looked at it."

"You did not know that before?"

"No, sir."

"Where did you get it?"

"From the Duke, sir. He—he gave it to me, at Dwarfwatch last year, for bringing the word to him." Suddenly tears ran from her eyes as she thought of the honor of that ring, and how she'd used it.

"Did he know what it was, do you think?"

"No, sir. It was part of the plunder from Siniava's army that we'd beaten. He said he chose it for the form—the three strands for the three of us that went—"

"The others?"

"Died, sir."

"Mmmm. So, you had a ring to control animals, and you used it on a horse. Knowingly?"

"No, sir. I thought the horse came because—well—I like horses. Star always came to me."

"So why did Macenion think it was the ring?"

"He said his was an elf-bred horse, and that elf horses would not come to humans without magic. He said I had been wearing the ring, and wanting the horse to come." In telling this, Paks had calmed a little.

"So then you were faced with the snowcat. Had you heard of one before? No? And Macenion told you to use the ring. How?"

"He said, sir, to make—make the cat hold still. Not jump at us or the horses. And it worked—" Paks could feel, in memory, the surprise of that. She had still not believed her ring was magic, until the great beast crouched still on the trail before them, the snowflake dapples on its coat blending with the falling snow. "And then he—told me how dangerous it was—"

"You didn't see that for yourself?" The Kuakgan's voice was edged with sarcasm.

"Sir, I could see that it was a hunting creature, and big—but it was so beautiful. I didn't know about the magic it had, until Macenion told me. He said we had no chance—and—" Paks faltered again.

"Go on." The Kuakgan was implacable.

"He told me to—to hold it still—and—" Paks squeezed her eyes shut against the memory. "And he took his sword—and killed it."

There was a long silence. Paks dared not move or speak. Her skin prickled all over.

"You held it still, by magic, while Macenion killed it? Helpless?"

"Yes, sir," said Paks faintly. "I—I knew it was wrong. I asked him—"

"What!" The word shook the ground with power.

"I asked him not to," whispered Paks. "But he said—he said it was the only way—then—and I—I shouldn't have, sir, I know that, but what can I do now?"

Another long silence. "And men wonder," the Kuakgan said finally, in a quiet voice worse than a shout, "why evil roams the land. I should hope you knew it was wrong. Wrong, yes, bitterly wrong. And I assure you, Paksenarrion, that Marshal Cedfer would not think light of this. It was an evil deed, and whatever else they may be, the Marshals of Gird abhor evil. Do you claim, as your defense, that it was Macenion's fault, because he told you to do so?"

"No, sir," said Paks. "I should have thought—he told me, later, when I spoke of it, that I could have used the power to send the beast away—"

"Macenion said that? After telling you to do it in the first place?"

"Yes, sir. I know it was my doing. I know it was wrong. But—what now? I thought you would know what to do."

"To make amends?"

Paks nodded. "I thought—even—I had dishonored my sword. I should—give it up, if you said so: not be a warrior."

"Look at me." Paks could not resist the command, and met the Kuakgan's dark eyes, her own blurred with tears. He looked every bit as angry as she had expected. "You would give that up? Your own craft in the world? You take the injury so seriously?"

"Yes." Paks fought again for control of her voice. "Sir, it was wrong. I have not slept well since. How can I be—what I want, if I could do that?"

"But you are a soldier," he mused. "I judge you are a good one, as soldiers go. Have you any other skill?"

"No, sir."

"I think, then, that you must stay so. Kuakkganni do not hate soldiers, but the necessity of war. If you have dishonored your sword, you must cleanse it with honorable battles. As for amends—the snowcat is dead, and by now the eagles have feasted. Nothing can change that." He looked closely at her, and Paks nodded. "As I said, I have no responsibility for your actions. But if you will be bound by me, I will take a blood payment from you."

"Yes, sir."

"Give me the ring, with which you bound the snowcat, so that you cannot misuse such power again."

Paks froze. Give up the ring? Her hand closed on it. She could hear again the Duke's voice as he gave it, feel again the throb in her injured leg.

"I will not compel," said the Kuakgan. She could feel, however, the withdrawal behind his words. She unclenched her hand, staring at the ring, its twisted strands that meant so much more than power over animals. Then she pulled it from her finger, feeling the tiny ridges for the last time, and laid it in the Kuakgan's waiting palm. His hand closed over it. She felt a cold wave sweep through her heart: that ring she had never meant to lose, save with her life.

"Child, look at my face." She looked again; he was smiling gravely. "You did well, Paksenarrion. I think the evil was not rooted too deeply in you, and this may have it out. Choose your companions with more care, another time, and trust your own honor more. No one can preserve it but you."

"Yes, sir."

"Go now. You have much to do, if you would accomplish what the Council set you—and train that black horse you've been busy with."

Paks started. She had forgotten, until then, that she had been using the ring on the black horse.

The Kuakgan gave her an open grin. "We will see whether Macenion was right, and all your skill with horses mere ring-magic. I think myself you have a way with animals, ring or no. And you can trust yourself, now. Is it not so?"

"Yes, sir." Suddenly Paks felt much better. She had not known how much it bothered her to control the horse with the ring.

"You may take a few extra bruises, but—I heard from Sevri the care you gave your pack pony when you arrived. Such care, Paksenarrion, and not magic, will accomplish what you hope for." He took her shoulders and turned her away from the fountain. "And there's your path out. Don't stray from it—and don't look back."

"Thank you, sir," said Paks. She walked toward the white stones, and along them to the lane.

Lighter in heart, Paks headed for the inn, thinking of what had passed. Her finger felt sore and empty without the Duke's ring. She would not have bartered it for food if she had been starving, it was that dear. But the Duke, she felt, would rather have had her give it up, under the circumstances, than keep it in dishonor. She turned aside from the inn door and went around by the stableyard. Sevri was currying a trader's heavy cart horse outside. Paks went into the stable. Star pushed her head up over the stall side, and Paks scratched her absently, watching the black. He seemed more relaxed; he stood at ease, nose resting on the stall door, tail switching at intervals. Paks fed Star half an apple and took the rest to him.

He stiffened as she neared the stall, then caught the scent of apple. Paks held it on the flat of her hand. His nostrils quivered; his lip twitched. Slowly he reached out and lifted it from her palm. She reached up and scratched him, just as she would Star. Still crunching, he leaned into the caress. Paks murmured to him, the meaningless, friendly talk that soothes, and watched his eyes slide shut. She heard Sevri behind her in the aisle, leading the cart horse to its stall.

All at once Paks decided what to do. "Sevri?"

"Yes? Do you need something?"

"Only to tell you something." Paks paused. It wasn't going to be easy. She liked the girl. "Sevri, I—haven't been fair with you." The girl's face was puzzled. "The smith was right, Sevri, about this horse. I was using magic on him. To quiet him."

"What kind of magic?" She seemed more interested than surprised.

"A ring. It worked to quiet animals—to control them. That's why I could work on him at all."

"Oh. Are you using it now? Which ring is it?"

Paks spread her hand. "I don't have it any more. It was the gold one. I'm sorry, Sevri, I should have told you—"

"Why? All horse trainers have their secrets. And you weren't using it to hurt him. What happened to your ring? Was it stolen?"

"No. I gave it to Master Oakhallow." Paks was surprised at the girl's reaction. "But Sevri—your family are kuakkgannir, aren't they? I thought you would think it wrong."

Sevri shrugged. "I don't think you needed it. Master Oakhallow says the heart shows in all things. You were always kind to Star and the black, and that's what works with horses. If you used the ring to quiet him until he could trust you—it shortened your work, that's all."

Paks felt a wave of relief. She had feared the girl's disapproval more than she knew. "I—I thought you should know, that's all."

"I'm glad you trust me," said Sevri seriously, older than her years. "But I wouldn't tell those others. Let them think what they will. If they knew you'd had one magic ring, they might come looking for others. I learned that working here in the inn."

"I hadn't thought of that," said Paks. "Thank you. But now I suppose we might as well see how the training has gone, and bring him out."

To her surprise, the black horse was no worse than any other morning. Paks had just finished grooming him and turned to reach for the saddle, when she saw the Kuakgan beside her.

"You are doing well with him," said the Kuakgan. Paks could find nothing in his voice but polite interest. "Have you been able to cure the injuries he received earlier?"

Paks laid a hand on the horse's shoulder to steady herself. She had not thought to see the Kuakgan again so soon; her breath came short. "Sir, his mouth healed quickly, but—there's one thing. He has deep scars on his hind legs, and I don't know what can be done for them."

"I'll take a look." At the Kuakgan's touch, the horse relaxed even more, and did not flinch even when the Kuakgan ran his strong hands down the hind legs. He paused when he came to the scar on the near leg. "A rope or wire cut him deeply here; it's a wonder he was not crippled by it. The wound healed cleanly, but the scar has grown to hamper the action of the joint a little. Do you find he sometimes seemed to drag his hoof there?"

Paks shook her head. "I've never seen it myself. But Marshal Cedfer says he does so, when I'm training with him."

"Hmmm. Perhaps I can ease that for him." Paks did not see him do anything, but he laid his hand over the scar a long moment, and then on the other leg. "Now," he said, as he straightened up, "I would see you ride, young woman."

Paks felt her belly clench. Would he make the horse rear and buck? Run away? She was sure he could do that. Or would he criticize what Marshal Cedfer had taught her? Her fingers felt huge and clumsy as she set the saddle on the horse's back, arranged the crupper and breastband, girthed up, and bridled. The Kuakgan inspected the tack, running the leather through his hands, touching the bit with his fingers. At last there was nothing to do but mount. The horse had picked up Paks' tension, and stiffened his ears, but he stood still while she gained the saddle.

Once up, habit reasserted itself, and she gave to the horse's movement. She rode around the stableyard twice, then made a few circles and other figures around the dungheap. She looked at the Kuakgan; he gestured for her to ride outside. Paks sighed, nodded, and guided the black through the gate. He had already passed it himself, and was walking out of town on the south-east road. Paks followed it, the black horse stepping along lightly. He turned as she caught up with him.

"I think you have done well so far," he said. "Ride ahead, now, and turn back when you come to the edge of the grove."

Paks nudged the horse into a slow trot, halted and turned where she was bid, and rode back.

"He should have no more trouble with those scars," said the Kuakgan. "He's moving easier. Could you feel it?"

"It seemed springier, somehow."

"Yes, and he will be able to do some of those fancy things the Marshal would like to teach you. It's too bad they're used for fighting only. If it did not risk his death or yours, I'd be happier about it." He smiled up at her. "But you and he were meant to be so, perhaps. I wish you well, Paksenarrion. You may come again to the grove, if you wish; you have a definite talent with animals. That is, in part, what hurt you so when you misused it." He waved and turned away. Paks sat still, and watched him cross the road and enter the grove by leaping the wall. She almost called a warning, then realized that it would hold no perils for him. He had disappeared among the trees when she lifted the reins and roae to the grange, along the street for the first time.

CHAPTER THIRTEEN

In the next two days, Paks rode along most of the roads near town, and began to explore the small lanes and paths that led to outlying farmsteads. She found nothing; she was not even sure what she was looking for. But at least, she thought, she had a better idea of the surrounding land. It was richer than the land around Three Firs. Most farm folk had an orchard of apples and pears; for grain they grew wheat as well as northern barley and oats. Redroots, onions, and other vegetables grew in every kitchen garden. Paks saw the local hogs, hefty red beasts with yellow eyes, rooting in the roadside woods and hedges. Cattle were sleek, mostly dun-colored, with dark horns.

She was trotting the black horse along the west road one afternoon when she got her first clue. Low sun behind her threw her shadow far ahead. In that slanting light, she saw something glint on a treetrunk beside the road. She rode toward it, suddenly alert, her hand dropping to her swordhilt.

As she came nearer, she saw that it was nothing but the tree itself—instead of dark furrowed bark, pale underbark lay open to the sun from a narrow gash. Paks halted the black horse, her brow furrowed in thought. She'd heard of such signs—the scouts in the Duke's Company had had a system of marks on trees and wayside rocks. But she had no idea what this one meant—if indeed it were anything but an accident.

She turned the black horse off the road, and made a half-circle in the woods around the marked tree. Nothing but a game trail, that ended a few yards from the road. She came out to the road again, and thought about it. Game trail? Why would a game trail stop suddenly?

She had seen others that crossed the road. Her neck prickled, and she looked around at the silent trees. Nothing. She thought of returning to the mysterious trail, but decided to ride on as if she had found nothing. As she jogged on toward town, she heard a distant call off to her right—a herdsman, perhaps, or perhaps someone else.

That night was drill night again. Paks drank a quick bowl of soup in the crowded common room, then went upstairs to change. When she came downstairs, the tall young man she'd noticed the first day in the common room called to her.

"Lady Paks! Going to drill! Walk with us, why don't you?" His grin was nearly as wide as his shoulders. Two other men who Paks remembered, but vaguely, from the first night's drill smiled at her.

Paks nodded at them. She wondered who they were.

"I'm Mai Argonist," said the one who had called her. "I'm the forester here, since my brother went away. I saw you the day you came in."

"Amisi," said the dark one at his side. "I'm a farmer, just east there—beyond the Grove, those grain fields."

"Adgan," said the redhead. "I work for Amisi, right now."

"He's my senior herdsman."

"They're just learning sword drill," said Mai. "I told 'em they should use an axe, but—"

"Mai, for Gird's sake don't start on that—"

"What?" asked Paks.

"Axes. Mel thinks everyone should fight with an axe. It's all right for him, as big as he is, and using an axe every day. But—"

"In formation?" Paks tried to imagine it. She knew that some knights fought with small axes; the smaller head was said to be easier to handle than a long blade. But she'd never heard of a foot soldier using one.

"Nah—not formation exactly." Mel laughed loudly. "It's a right Girdish weapon, that's all, being taken from our tools, you see. And I've killed wolf with it—"

"With an axe?" Paks stared at him.

"Oh, aye. Just you swing it from side to side, see—like the Master Smith does his hammer, that's all. It's the very thing. Won't break like a sword will." He laughed again, and Paks eyed him narrowly. If she had seen him in a tavern in Aarenis, she'd have thought him a stupid lout. He was two fingers taller than she, and built like an ale barrel. She'd seen him drain a tankard at one swallow. Yet he didn't move like a drunkard, and his size was more solid than fat.

Several more yeomen had joined them, hurrying out of side lanes. For a few moments, Paks felt almost at home, almost as if she was going somewhere with Stammel and other friends. Then one of them nudged another and spoke.

"Is it true, lady, that the Council has hired you?"

Paks was too surprised to make a good pretence of ignorance. "Why do you ask?" she said finally.

"Well—you've got money enough, that's obvious, and you make no sign of leaving. Could be you bribed them, or could be they hired you."

"Doryan!" Mai's bellow startled Paks as much as the statement.

"Don't yell at me, Mai. I've a right to ask, as much as anyone." Doryan shifted away from Mai, nonetheless, and winked at Paks. He was middle-aged, slightly stooped, and she had no idea what his trade was. "If you don't want to say, that's all right. Just asking."

Paks thought what she could say. The Council had not told her to keep her mission quiet, but she had planned to say nothing. How else could she find the spy they thought lived in Brewersbridge? "The Council decided," she said, "that I was no threat to the peace here. I had ordered goods, and they gave me leave to stay until these were made up. They did say that you'd had trouble with brigands attacking caravans. Since I have been a soldier, they asked me to consider leading some volunteers against them."

"Huh!" Mai grunted and rubbed his neck as he walked. "Have to find them first, don't you? We all know they're out there, but no one's seen them."

"But who would go with you?" asked Doryan. He had an irritating whine in his voice. "We don't know you—the militia don't—and they don't think you could fight all those brigands yourself, do they?"

Paks answered Mai first. "You're right, no one can say where they are. I don't even know where to start looking. If I ever get that black horse tamed down—"

"I've seen you riding out," said Adgan. "One time I saw him shy, and you nearly went over his ears."

Paks blushed, grateful for the evening gloom. "Yes—the Marshal's teaching me, but I still fall off now and then. Anyway, I thought I could ride around and look for the brigands that way, but not until I can look at something besides his ears."

"You rode though town today," said Doryan. Paks began to dislike him very much.

"Yes," she said shortly.

"You don't want to go looking for brigands alone," said Mai, more quietly than she'd heard him speak. "What if you found them?"

"I'd ride away," said Paks. "Very quickly."

"That's right; you're not a Girdsman." Doryan managed a sneer. Before Paks could react, Amisi and Adyan took him up on it. "Doryan, that's stupid—"

"What's she to do, be hogstuck by a dozen brigands? That's not Gird's way; you know the Marshal says Girdsmen have to think as well as fight."

"I still think—" began Doryan. Mai punched his shoulder hard enough to make him gasp.

"Doryan, you don't think. You just talk. The Lady Paks is our guest in the grange, and if you treat her like this she never will join the fellowship of Gird. We've all seen her drill; we know she'd be a good Girdsman. Marshal hopes she'll join the grange, and so do I. Leave her be, man. You haven't caught any brigands yourself."

By this time they were approaching the barton gate. This time the boy on guard recognized Paks and grinned at her as she entered. Drill went much as it had before, with most of her time spent teaching the few swordsmen to use the short blades in formation. Ambros and the Marshal did much better; Paks decided they must have been practicing in private. As he was dismissing them from drill, the Marshal asked Paks to carry a message to Sir Felis.

"Cal or Doryan could take it," he said, as some of the men turned to listen. "But even though they live on that side of town, it's an extra couple of miles for either of them—and they start work early in the morning. It wouldn't take you long, to ride out there—"

"I'll be glad to," said Paks honestly. She had been looking for a good reason to talk to Sir Felis in privacy.

"And I can't work with you for a couple of days," the Marshal went on. "That's why the message must go tonight. I'm leaving for barton court rounds immediately. Ambros here will handle matters at the grange. Drill as usual," he said to the others. "I expect I'll be back in a few days, but Ambros will take drill if I'm not. Paksenarrion, I suggest that you and Ambros ride together an hour or more a day—but don't try mounted drill until I return. And if you can give him a couple hours of swordplay, it'll be good for both of you."

The other men left at last, and the Marshal ushered Paks back to his study. On his desk was a leather tube; Paks could see the paper rolled inside. He nodded at it. "That's for Sir Felis; it explains what I'm doing. Now—you seemed uneasy tonight. What have you found?"

Paks told him about the blazed tree, and the "game" trail that ended a few yards from it and the road. The Marshal nodded. "I think you've found something important. If you'll take my advice, don't ride that way tomorrow. If you were seen pausing there—well, it could be very dangerous. Right now a single arrow could end your campaign. Anything else?"

Paks hesitated. She glanced at Ambros, leaning against the door. He shrugged and moved back into the passage. "I—I'm not sure. One of the yeomen said something—

"Asked or said?"

"Asked, at first, about my business with the Council. He asked if I'd been hired or if I'd—I'd bribed them."

The Marshal's face stiffened. "Who?"

"Sir, I don't think he meant insult—"

"I didn't ask that. I asked who it was."

"I think his name is Doryan."

The Marshal nodded. "That doesn't surprise me. Doryan is—difficult, sometimes. He became a Girdsman after he moved here. Anything more?"

Paks thought of Doryan's words and decided none of them were important. "Not really, no."

He looked thoughtfully at her before going on. "Paksenarrion, it's my business to defend my yeomen, if they need it. Don't be afraid to tell me what they say."

"But I don't want to be—" she couldn't think how to say what she meant, that no soldier held another to close account for every word, or told even a sergeant what a friend had said.

"You are not of our fellowship yet," said the Marshal with a smile. "Now—I meant what I said about you and Ambros riding out together. Race the horses, if you will—anyone will understand that.

Ride north and east for a day or so. Wear your mail, and keep alert. If you find where the brigands are hiding out, talk to Sir Felis before you do anything. Don't wait for my return, if you need to take action, but don't rush things, either. Ambros will not be able to go with you on an attack; until I return, his primary responsibility must be the grange."

A little later, Paks rode north out of town toward the keep. Most of the houses were dark; the black horse's hoofbeats echoed in the quiet streets. She had put on her mail shirt, and kept one hand close to her dagger.

At the keep, torches burned at the perimeter fence and on the building itself. An alert sentry challenged her; she waited while he took her name in, and returned to escort her to the entrance. There another soldier led her upstairs to Sir Felis' workroom, a long room with two tables littered with papers and maps. Sir Felis and Master Zinthys, standing together near one table, looked up as she entered.

"You have an urgent message from the Marshal?"

"Yes, sir." Paks pulled the leather tube from her tunic and passed it over. Zinthys smiled at her, as Sir Felis, frowning, worked the paper out of the tube and unrolled it. Zinthys wore a different, but equally rich-looking velvet robe, trimmed in white fur around the shoulders. Paks noticed, once again, the graceful movements of his hands.

"Why don't you sit down, Paksenarrion. We have spiced wine ready on the fire—would you care for some?"

Paks shook her head, not certain what courtesy demanded, but sat in the chair Zinthys pointed out. He moved to the one next to her, and sat down with a sigh, stretching his legs.

"I'll have some then, if you permit." He hooked a potlift in the handle of a can on the hearth, and poured the wine into his mug. "Ah. These chill autumn nights make the best of wine. You should try it." He slid his eyes sideways at her. "Or perhaps you drink only ale?"

"I—most soldiers drink ale," said Paks. "Wine—we had that with an herb in it, if we were wounded."

"Numbwine. Yes. Not as good as a potion, but good enough. But you're hardly a common soldier now, lady, and you might find you liked spiced wine." Zinthys poured another mug full and passed it to her. Paks took it, and sipped. Zinthys watched her, his eyebrows raised. "Well?"

"It's—very good." She looked down, and sipped again. It was good, a red wine flavored with her favorite spices.

"Have you found any trace of our brigands?" asked Zinthys.

"No, sir, unless something I saw today—" She told him about the blazed tree, and answered his questions. She started to add what the Marshal had explained about the possible uses of such a blaze in setting an ambush, but remembered in time that Sir Felis probably already knew that. He nodded.

"Fresh blazes. There's that merchant from Chaya in town now—wasn't he planning to leave tomorrow, Zinthys?"

"That's right. Master merchant Cobai Trav-something, and his gnome partners—"

"Gnomes?" asked Paks, sitting up.

"Yes. What is it, haven't you seen gnomes before?"

"No. I've heard of them." She remembered Bosk talking about gnomes, elves, and dwarves on her first trip south.

"Well, around here you'll see gnomes fairly often. I'm surprised you didn't see these at the inn today. Two of the gnome kingdoms are less than a three days' ride from here. If you meet them, remember that they're very strict."

"Strict?"

Zinthys laughed. "They make a court judge look like a juggler, Paksenarrion. They are full of dignity, and pride, and the right way to do everything—Ashto help you if you laugh at a gnome, or fail to complete a contract."

"They don't like wizards," said Sir Felis drily. Paks glanced at him, and he grinned slightly, cocking his head at Zinthys. Zinthys flushed.

"It's not that, Sir Felis—it's that they're so—so—" he waved his hands in the air. "Sober," he finished. "Dead serious all the time, that's gnomes."

"Anyway," Sir Felis went on, "there's a west-bound caravan in town now—headed for the gnome kingdoms next, and then Vérella. And if that blaze is fresh, it could mean that the brigands are planning to attack."

"It won't do any good to tell gnomes," said Zinthys.

"No, perhaps not. But I will send word to the caravan master. Not you, Paks—" he said, as she opened her mouth. "I don't want you to ride with this caravan—you weren't hired as a guard. If the brigands do strike, they should leave some trace you can follow to find their lair."

Sir Felis agreed with the Marshal's advice to ride out in other directions for the next day or so. Paks took this chance to look at his maps one more time, and fix in her mind the location of the ruined buildings he thought might harbor brigands.

The next morning when Paks went out to care for the black horse, the inn yard was busy. The day before she had been so excited about the blaze that she had not noticed the wagons and teams in the yard. Now teamsters were hitching teams of heavy mules to wagons. Paks realized that the short fellows she'd dismissed as someone's boys were actually not human—gnomes, she assumed. They were not so stout as the dwarves she'd seen; they wore plain clothes of gray and brown. Sevri merely nodded to her, darting quickly from one stall to another as she finished her morning's work. Paks decided to eat breakfast at the inn, after feeding the horses, so that she could watch the caravan leave.

It was not nearly so large as the one she had been with in Aarenis: seven wagons loaded with barrels and bales, with two guards besides the driver on each. The merchants—a blond human and two gnomes in sober colors but richer cloth than the gnome teamsters—rode saddle mules. Paks noticed that none of the gnomes smiled, though the human merchant grinned a farewell to Hebbinford, and promised to bring a barrel of "Marrakai red" on the way back. She went on with her breakfast, and was just washing down the last crumbs of it when Ambros appeared outside. She leaned out the window and called to him.

"I thought I'd come here," he said, dismounting. "If we're riding east today—"

"Just a moment—" Paks gestured to Hebbinford, who came to take her coins. "I know I'm late, but I thought I'd have time to breakfast before work today."

"Don't rush." Ambros did not seem in any hurry. "Shall I saddle your horse for you?"

"No. I don't know how he'd behave." Paks hurried up to her room, remembering the Marshal's injunction to wear mail every day. She was startled to see the black-clad man lounging in the upper passage. Had he been trying her door? But he smiled and nodded, as if glad to see her. Paks unlocked her door thoughtfully and latched it behind her.

Everything seemed to be in place. She donned the lightweight mail the elfane taig had given her, pulled her shirt back over it, and caught up her old cloak. With that rolled into a bundle under her arm, she came back into the passage, and found it empty. She had heard no footsteps passing.

By the time she was back downstairs, Ambros had led his horse into the inn yard. He was munching a hot pastry, and grinned at her as she went into the stable. Sevri was busily cleaning out stalls; Paks thought of telling her about the black-clad man, but decided against it. She saddled the black horse without trouble, led it into the yard, and mounted. Ambros swung into his own saddle and they rode out, turning right onto the east road.

"How far out this way have you ridden?" he asked.

"Not very. I came in this way—on a trail that joins the road from the south."

"I know the one."

"I've ridden that far—no more."

"Let's go to the border, then," said Ambros. Paks looked at him. He seemed happy and younger, like a child at a fair. She wondered what the life of a yeoman-marshal was like.

"How far is that?"

"Oh—if we keep moving, we can be there and back by tonight. Late tonight."

"Should we?"

Ambros grinned at her. "Probably not. But it would be fun. I grew up near the border; I know the country. We won't get lost, and I don't think anything this way will bother us."

"Well, the Marshal said—"

"The Marshal said ride other ways than west. This is other. By Gird, Paks, I haven't had a day to myself since—" he stopped suddenly, and ran his hand through his hair. Paks remembered suddenly that she had not brought her helmet, and felt stupid. What good was mail, when a head-blow was easy and deadly? "Anyway," he went on, more calmly, "I don't see that it will hurt to ride all day. If we don't make it that far by noon, then we'll turn back. Why not?"

Paks wondered if he really wanted to visit his home. She did not want to ask. She wondered what Ambros would say if she turned back for her helmet. Would he think she was a coward? Was he even wearing mail himself? She tried to see, and could not tell. The mail from the elfane taig, she had found, did not jingle as her other mail shirt had; she thought perhaps good mail did not. In the end she said nothing, and they jogged on together, into the morning sun.

When nothing happened for some time, Paks quit thinking so much about an arrow in the head, and instead enjoyed the ride. A thin haze covered the sun, thickening to a gray ceiling as they rode. Ambros frowned at the sky.

"If that keeps up, we'd better turn back."

"Why?"

"From that direction, it means rain, or even an early snow." He sighed. "I might have known that Gird himself would shorten my leash, with the Marshal gone."

Paks stared at him; he looked both unhappy and slightly worried. "Ambros, what is it?"

"I—I'll tell you, Paks, but please don't tell everyone. I'd hoped to—to go as far as my father's farm. It's been over a year, now, and it less than a day's ride away. And I wonder if I'll ever see them again."

"But if it's that close, why haven't you—?"

"Because the Marshal hasn't allowed it," said Ambros shortly, reining his bay around to the west. "It's been one thing after another—chores, drills, whatever. My father's been in to Brewersbridge, of course, to the markets. My mother came once, last spring. But it'll be spring before either of them come again. I just wanted to see them one more time before winter." He sighed again. "It was a foolish idea."

"But why? I mean, just because it's going to rain—I don't melt in the rain, Ambros—not even in snow. How far is it?"

He shook his head. "No. Paks, you're not a Girdsman; I can't explain. But I tried to go on my own, and it's not what I should do. With Marshal Cedfer gone, the grange is my responsibility. The clouds are another warning; the first was in my own heart. We'll go back. I pray Gird that no more will be required."

Puzzled, and a little put out, Paks followed Ambros back toward Brewersbridge. The clouds did not lift, but thickened, and soon a fine drizzle wet her face. It was not enough to penetrate her cloak. She nudged the black horse and rode up beside Ambros.

"Ambros, do you really think Gird made it rain because you wanted to see your family?" She thought even less of Gird if that was his sort of action.

"No, not exactly." Ambros spoke slowly, as if more lay behind his words than he wanted to say. "I don't know, to be honest, where the clouds came from—the High Lord may grant the wind's keys to any he wishes, I daresay. But Marshal Cedfer did say the grange was my responsibility—even if you find the brigands, he said, I cannot fight them with you."

"But did he tell you not to visit your family?" Paks persisted.

"No. I think—I think he knew I would want to go, but did not insult me by telling me my duty." Ambros gave a short laugh. "He should have."

"But you—"

"Paks," said Ambros, with a look that stopped the words in her mouth. "Paks, you have been a soldier in many battles—have you ever had a dream of death?"

She stared at him, surprised into long silence. "Not—exactly," she said finally. "Some of my friends have . . . I have had disturbing dreams, though, if that's what you mean."

"Have you—did you ever know someone to have a true dream like that?"

"Once." Paks swallowed with difficulty. She wondered what dream had come to Ambros. When she glanced at him, he was staring at his horse's mane, fists clenched on the reins.

"I—I saw myself," he said softly. She could barely hear him. "I saw myself fighting—and struck—and dying. And then nothing. I know—" he said, turning to meet her eyes. "I know that all Girdsmen train for this, to fight evil to the death. But—but Paks, it was so soon. You know this cut—" He pushed back his sleeve to show a cut she had dealt him in practice the night before. "It wasn't healed yet; I could see it, under the other marks."

Paks shivered violently. Ambros' face seemed to waver, changing from the ruddy living countenance before her to the pale fixed expression she had seen on so many dead. "It was a dream," she managed to say. "And not all dreams are true."

"I know." He nodded, seeming more at ease. "I know that. But I thought—I thought I'd like to see my father and mother again." He looked sideways at her. "Do you think less of me for that?"

"No. Of course not."

"I wondered—you being a soldier, and all. You've seen more fighting than I have. To be honest, I've never faced an actual enemy."

Paks did not know what to say. She did not feel like boasting of her experience. She thought, as she often did these days, of her own home, and wondered for the first time if she would see her own family again. But she had had no troubling dreams, and had no fears. She smiled at Ambros, hoping to reassure him. "You fight well, Ambros, in practice; I expect you'll fight well when need comes. I hope it is not as soon as you fear. Will you tell the Marshal of this dream?"

"I would have, if he had not left already. Yes, he must know, in case it is an evil sending. I thank you, Paks, for not laughing at me."

They were back at the inn in time for a late lunch; Paks persuaded Ambros to eat with her. She had decided to show him the scrolls from the elfane taig; if she had not laughed at his bad dreams, perhaps he would not laugh at her slow reading. But they ate slowly, and it was near midafternoon when she started upstairs to get the scrolls. She had them in her hand when a disturbance in the street below brought her to the window.

A yelling crowd surrounded a blood-stained man bareback on a fat mule. As Paks watched, Ambros erupted from the inn door, followed by Hebbinford. The crowd spotted him, ran to him.

"Robbers!" she heard. "Robbers! The caravan!" The man on the mule slid off sideways; two men caught him, half-carried him toward the inn. Paks saw Sevri's red head move through the crowd and take the mule by the bridle. She waited to see no more, but turned away and moved quickly downstairs.

Hebbinford and Ambros bent near the man, who half-lay in a chair near the fireplace, his clothes torn and bloody. Paks saw the black-clad man leaning quietly against the wall behind several others, who were chattering loudly. He caught her eye and smiled; Paks felt herself blushing. Ambros glanced up and saw her.

"Paks, good. Come here, will you?" Paks moved through the group, aware of curious glances. She had seen, from above, that Ambros commanded more of their respect than she'd thought—at least when the Marshal was away.

"What is it?" she asked.

"This man says he was a teamster on the caravan that left this morning. They were attacked by brigands on the west road, and all the guards were killed."

Paks looked at the man—a stocky, darkly tanned man of medium height—and wondered just where on the west road. Ambros was asking more questions; she could not hear the soft answers. Hebbinford began clearing the others out of the room. Over his shoulder he said, "I'll tell the mayor." Paks wondered who would be sent to Sir Felis.

With the room empty and quiet, Paks could hear the man's replies to Ambros' questions—hundreds of bandits, he said shakily. Hundreds and hundreds, with horses and bows and swords. They took the whole caravan, every animal and wagon, and killed all the guards, and—

"How did you escape?" asked Ambros. "Isn't that one of the caravan mules?"

Paks would not have thought the dark face could darken, but it did. "I was the last wagon, sir. I heard a noise—that stretch of road has an evil name, you know—and so I cut the lead offside mule free, and—"

"Ran for it," finished Ambros, with the same tone Paks thought the Marshal would have used.

"Well, I tried." Paks watched the man's face as he took a long difficult breath. "But that Simyits-damned son of a Pargunese jackass bucked me off, that he did. And ran away, after dumping me flat in the midst of it all. So I lay there too stunned to run or fight, and I reckon that was best, in the end. One of 'em poked me a little, but I made shift to lie still and be quiet. I heard 'em talking, telling each other to be sure all the guards were dead. Then they tried to catch my mule, but they couldn't lay a finger on him, so they went off. I waited a bit—and I was some sore, too, sir—and then when I did sit up there was that damned mule not a length away, heehawing at the blood smell. Then he came to me, and thank the luck for that. I counted all the guards' bodies, sir, and so I know—"

"What about the merchants, and the other teamsters."

"The teamsters are all dead, gnome and man alike. I didn't see the merchants' bodies, but I doubt they live."

"Hmm." Ambros sounded, again, very like the Marshal. "Where was this? It seems to me you're back soon and luckily with such a tale."

The man paled a little. "Sir, please! I swear it's the truth. We left early this dawn, the landlord can tell you. And the road was dry; we made good time. Old Cobai—that's the master—he didn't want to stop for nooning in that stretch of woods, so we pressed on, eating on the seat as we drove. I had just finished my pickle when I heard the noise. Coming back, sir, I fair beat that mule to a lather."

Ambros gave Paks a quick look; she could not tell his meaning. But something made her speak up. "How badly are you hurt, can you tell?"

The man looked at her gratefully. "They poked me some, lady, and I fell hard before that. I wrapped my own shirt on it—this is off a guard—" He indicated his blood-stained shirt.

"Well, you'd best let us see. Yeoman-marshal, is there a surgeon in town?" She hoped she was right to use his title.

"Yes," said Ambros. "At the keep, with Sir Felis." He looked aside. "We'll need clean cloths, and water—it's too bad the Marshal is gone."

"That's what they counted on, no doubt," said the driver.

Paks, meanwhile, had unwrapped the rag he had bound to his head; underneath was an ugly gash. She thought it looked bone-deep.

"It's no wonder they thought you dead with that head wound," she commented. "What's your name?"

"Jeris, lady. Jeris Angara, of Dapplevale in Lyonya. Do you know it?"

"No. Be steady, now." Paks helped Ambros uncover the man's other injuries—mostly bruises but for two shallow gashes in side and back. "You're lucky, Jeris. They could easily have killed you."

"I know it." He shifted uneasily as they began to clean the wounds. "It—ouch!—sorry. If that mule hadn't bucked, they might have got me sure; they had horses. I don't deserve it, that's the truth, but that's luck. It comes as Simyits pleases—"

"You think Simyits has more power than the High Lord?" asked Ambros. "Is that what you learned in Lyonya?"

"Oh sir—in Lyonya, I was a boy, and had a boy's faith. But I've been on the roads near twenty years, now, and I've seen good luck and bad come to all. As for the High Lord, he made the whole world, so I hear, if it wasn't Sertig instead, but what does he have to do with a mule driver? The good men, you might say, died today—they that was brave, and tried to fight. And here I am, alive a bit longer, and able to give you word, because a mule bucked me off on my hard head. Does the High Lord extend his power to make a mule buck?"

Paks stifled a laugh. She had heard of Simyits only as the thieves' god, and the gambler's patron, but the muleteer seemed honest if not brave. Ambros, however, was sober, and crouched down to meet the man's eyes.

"If the High Lord wanted your mule to buck, Jeris, be sure he could do it. But there is one more near us than that—Gird Strongarm, a man once, like you. He had a hard head himself, and it's said he knows how to convince another. I would not call it luck alone, if I found myself alive, when my companions were all dead—and a mule nearby to ride on, despite the blood-smell. Does your mule love you so, to buck you off, escape capture, and then return to you?"

Jeris' face furrowed as he tried to think. "Well—now—I see what you mean. To be honest, I wouldn't have thought that donkey-spawn would stay near new dead like that. But why would Gird, if he wanted me alive, dump me on my head first? Why not save the whole caravan and set fire to the brigands?"

"Why is there winter? Why does water flow downhill only?" Ambros sounded even more like a Marshal. "The High Lord lets men deal with men, as often as not. As for you, perhaps Gird knew your mule could not outrun their horses—or perhaps he was seeking an entrance into your hard head, and tried knocking it first."

"Peace, Ambros," said Sir Felis from the doorway. "You can convert the man later, but for now I'd like to know what happened." Behind him a surgeon carried a cloth bag of gear; Master Zinthys, in still another robe, followed him, and smiled at Paks.

When the man had told his tale again, and the surgeon had settled him in one of the inn's rooms, Sir Felis, Zinthys, Ambros, and Paks conferred in a small room opening off the kitchen.

"Hundreds of brigands I simply do not believe," said Sir Felis. "They haven't stolen enough food and forage for anything like that number. In this case they killed twenty, and captured several—we aren't sure how many. But out of ambush, that wouldn't take more than a score of well-armed, disciplined troops. Perhaps fewer. Certainly I don't think they can have more than—" he paused, looked up at the lamp, and thought a moment. "Thirty, I'd say. And fewer horses than that. Most of the caravans they've hit have been carrying dry goods, weapons, that sort of thing—not food."

"Yes, but now what?" asked Ambros. "You know Marshal Cedfer said I couldn't go—what do we do now?"

Sir Felis looked at Paks. "It's your choice, since you accepted the task—but if you want advice—"

"Yes, sir."

"Then I would say let me take a troop out there, as everyone expects, and pick up the bodies. Contrive some reason for riding that way yourself tomorrow—not just riding, something else—and see if you can find a trace of the wagons' movement. I won't even look; it'll be dark by the rime I get out there with my men. If you find it, don't be in too much hurry to follow it up. They'll be watching the road pretty closely for a day or so, I expect. Give them time to relax. Then—if it's where we think—go after them."

Paks shook her head. "By your leave, sir, I have another thought. An assault on a keep—even a ruined keep—is no easy matter. We tried that once in Aarenis. Why not try to frighten them out—catch them at their bolthole?"

"The game trail you're thinking of?"

"Yes, but close by the keep. If a show of frontal assault—"

"With what?" asked Sir Felis. "I can't give you a troop."

"No, but Master Zinthys might have some magical means." She glanced at him. "Macenion—the part-elf I was traveling with—had some illusions. I thought perhaps—"

Zinthys looked pleased, though Ambros frowned. "In fact, Lady Paksenarrion, illusions are a specialty of mine. Far less dangerous to the onlooker than, say, real firebolts."

"And easier to do," muttered Ambros softly. Zinthys glared at him.

"Young sir, if you think it is easy to produce even illusory fire, I suggest you try. My old master, who is well known in the arts, always said that a fine, convincing illusion was far more difficult—because reality carries its own conviction, and saves its own appearances. If you make a flame, it is a real flame, and you don't have to worry, once you've got it. But an illusory flame can go wrong in many subtle ways—even such a thing as forgetting which way the wind is blowing, so that it flickers the wrong direction."

"Sorry," said Ambros, staring at the table. Paks thought he didn't sound sorry at all. She smiled at Zinthys.

"I don't know anything about it," she said, "but could you make something to scare them out—something to make them think a large force was coming at them?"

"I might do," said Zinthys, still obviously ruffled. He twitched his shoulders and glanced at Sir Felis. "It would be easier if I had a small matrix to work on, as a pattern."

"A what?"

"A form—a framework—or, in plain terms, if I had a few real men-at-arms, that I could simply multiply in illusion, rather than creating the whole thing out of my head. It's easier to keep them in step, you see."

Paks didn't see, but nodded anyway. Sir Felis made a steeple of his hands. "How many, Zinthys?"

The mage looked at him, considering. "Oh—a half-dozen, say?"

"Four." Sir Felis set down his mug. "Four is plenty to save your hide if it doesn't work, and I can't waste the time of more."

"Four," repeated Zinthys cheerfully. "You'll see, Lady Paksenarrion—I'll do you an illusion that'll have them running out the back door for cover—by the way, how do you know there is a back door?"

"Never saw a keep without one," said Paks cheerfully, thinking of Siniava's many tricks. "Gods grant we choose the right place."

"That," said Zinthys with satisfaction, "is up to you soldiers. Just tell me when and where you want them frightened—I'll take care of that."

CHAPTER FOURTEEN

Mai, when Ambros explained the plan, seemed shrewder than Paks had expected. He spoke quietly enough, with a rumbling chuckle when amused. Paks began to think he might be an asset after all.

"So we're to find the place first, and find sign—then she'll lead a troop?" He gave Paks a sharp look. "Have you led troops before, lady? I don't mean to be like Doryan, but—"

"I was acting corporal in one of the cohorts," said Paks.

"That means yes, I take it." He turned back to Ambros. "And what if their place is fortified? Do we try to take it?"

"No. There's a plan to get them out—if it's the place we think it might be, or one like it. Have you been out near the old Seriyan ruins lately?"

"Gird, no! I told the Marshal a few years ago that was a bad place—unlucky, that is. Is that where you think they are?"

"It could well be—considering the sign Paks saw a few days ago."

"Then they're a brave bunch, that's all I can say. I wouldn't stay there for a silver a day. Not even for a cask of ale."

"And for you, that's saying a lot. All right, Mai—I know you don't like it. But if they're wicked enough, it might not bother them."

"What is it?" asked Paks. "Why are the ruins so bad?"

Mai and Ambros looked at each other. Ambros broke the silence. "It's from before my time—I was just a boy, living over near the Lyonyan border. But there was a wizard who settled in there—built a stronghold all in one year, by magic, some said. Like most wizards, he didn't care more for bad and good than a deaf man cares for music."

"I don't know as that's fair," Mai broke in. "Master Zinthys is a nice enough fellow."

"Who buys you ale every quarterday. But would you trust him, Mai, at your back in a fight?"

Mai considered. "Well—yes. If Sir Felis or the Marshal were there, at least."

"I like him myself," said Ambros. "I think he's as honest as any wizard, but they care more for magic and money than anything else—it's their nature. But this other wizard, Seriyan, wasn't much like Zinthys. No. He came here, so I was told, because he wanted to rule. That's not what he said; he said he had come to study. But he had a small horde of magical creatures that he let loose, and then he threatened worse if people didn't pay 'taxes' for protection from them. Brewersbridge had no keep then, just the grange."

"It wasn't Marshal Cedfer here then," Mai put in, grinning at Paks. "Nor yet Deordtya, but the one before her. I don't recall his name."

"It doesn't matter," said Ambros shortly. "He made the mistake of believing the wizard harmless when he came, and it ended with a lot of lives lost when the yeomen had to storm the place. He blew himself up, at the end, rather than be taken."

"I hope he blew himself up," said Mai darkly. "The way that place feels, I'm not so sure."

"He may have left spells," said Ambros. Paks found herself hoping that the brigands were hiding somewhere else. She did not want to meet a wizard who had only pretended to blow himself up. But she had to agree that Seriyan's old keep was the closest of the known ruins to the blaze she'd found, and Mai agreed to go out with her the next day to take a look at the trail sign.

Mai arrived at the inn driving a sturdy two-wheeled cart with a large shaggy pony between the shafts. His big axe stood head-down in the corner beside him. Two more wheels filled the bed of the cart.

"This way," he said quietly, downing the tankard of ale which Hebbinford brought him without being told. "This way I'm just hunting a good straight bole of limber pine for the Town Hall extension. With these extra wheels, I can haul anything we find." Paks wondered how; she had never seen foresters at work. Mai saw her confusion and laughed loudly. Paks noticed others watching and listening. "See, lady, you don't know everything yet." Now his voice was louder, and more accented. "What I do is cut a short heavy piece for the axle, to bind these wheels together, and then tie them near the end of the bolt. With the front end resting in the cart, and the other held by the wheels—now do you see?" Paks nodded. She started to ask why the second set of wheels didn't fall out from under the tree trunk, and then realized that he could tie it securely to the wood that held the wheels together.

"Ride along with me," said Mai, as if she had planned something else, "and I'll show you some more things you don't know about."

"I should find Ambros—" she said doubtfully, as they had arranged. Mai laughed again.

"Oh, Ambros! By Gird, you don't want to spend every day with him, do you? He's a yeoman-marshal, after all. Come on, now—" He gave her an enormous wink, and swaggered back to his cart after handing one of the serving wenches his tankard. Someone laughed. Paks grinned.

"You go on ahead; I'll catch up when I've got my horse ready. Which way are you going?"

"Oh, west again. I remember a few years ago, out that way, there was a straight, tall, limbless bole right near the road. Not so hard, you see, if the trees I want are next to the road."

"Good," said Paks. "That way I can tell Ambros I won't be riding with him this morning." Mai waved and went on, and she ducked into the stable to saddle the black horse. She hoped their act had gone off well. She hated to think of a spy in the village, but the evidence for such was persuasive.

She caught up with Mai before he was well into the forest on the far side of Brewersbridge; he had stopped to chat with the woman at the last roadside farm. He waved her to a stop.

"Paks, do you know Eris here?" It was the same woman Paks had met in Council. Paks began to think Mai was even smarter than she'd thought.

"Yes, I remember you," said Paks, swinging down from the saddle. She was no longer afraid to mount and dismount in front of witnesses; the black was learning manners. "I didn't know this was your farm."

"It wasn't, a few years ago," said Eris, with a slow smile. "We used to be out there—" she pointed southwest. "But raiders—bandits—

something—kept breaking our fences, and running off stock. Finally after my husband died, and the boys married, I bought this farm from a cousin, just to be closer to town."

"It looks good," said Paks. The small farmhouse looked in good repair, and the orchard next to it was obviously flourishing.

"Oh, it's a good farm," said Eris. "I miss the spring we had before—the best water I ever had, and only a few steps from the door. But when you find dead animals in it, day after day—"

"Ugh—" Paks shuddered.

"Do you like apples?" she went on. "The good ones are coming ripe now—I'd be glad for you to have some."

"Between me and the horses," said Paks, "we'd eat half your crop. I'll buy a measure of good ones for me, and a double measure of bruised ones for the horses."

"I would have given—"

"Eris," said Paks, wondering as she said it whether she should have given her the council title, "I grew up on a farm myself. Right now I have the money, and you have apples to sell."

"Very well," said Eris. "When you come back by this evening—or whenever—I'll have them near the gate, under the hedge."

"And you know I want some, Eris," said Mai.

"You! I thought you lived on ale, Mai!" But she was laughing as she said it.

They continued down the road, chatting freely. Paks continued to lead the black horse, since Mai was walking beside the cart. He pointed out different trees, but Paks quickly grew confused with it: colors and patterns of bark, and shapes of leaves, and the form of the tree meant little to her. She could tell a star-shaped leaf from a lance-shaped one, and both those from the ferny-looking compounds, but that was her limit. Mai teased her gently. In the meantime, they both watched the road for the signs of the caravan—the fresh wheel ruts and narrow mule hoofmarks. These they did not mention.

Paks wondered what would be left at the ambush site, since Sir Felis had sent a troop of his soldiers out to retrieve the bodies. Would she even notice it? As the sun neared its height, she began to worry that they'd missed it. But it was clear, when they came to it. Deeper tracks, round-hoofed, of ridden horses, and the mules' tracks veering from side to side. Bloodstains on the fallen leaves, and on the rocks that edged the road. A few spent arrows, mostly broken. Mai pointed out the traces she missed, chatting the while about trees. In the end, Paks found the way the wagons had been taken. Freshly cut boughs, the leaves hardly withered, disguised the wagons' track into the woods; the brigands had chosen a stony outcrop for the turn off the road. It led, or so Paks thought, the wrong direction—north—but Mai looked grim when he saw it.

"There's a farm to the northwest," he said. "Or was, until it burned. If they're using it, they may be using the old form lane to bring the wagons back, and cross this road farther along. As I remember, that other farm lane hits this road in about the same place."

"Well, do we follow this?' asked Paks.

"No. Not with horses. We'd make a noise like an army in there, with a third of the leaves down as they are. If you'll take my advice, we'll go along the road and look for that other place, where the lane comes in."

Paks could just see the lane coming in ahead when Mai stopped abruptly. "Ha," he said loudly. "There's the tree I come for." She stared at him, surprised, and he winked. "You'd best go on up the road a ways," he went on. "I want to drop it right here in the road. Tell you what. You take these two wheels along with you, eh? Go on—yes—right along up there, at least as far as that lane. This 'un'll fall long, I tell you." Paks finally caught on, and wandered slowly up the road as he bade her. Behind her, the axe rang on the tree. She wondered if it really was a "limber pine" or whatever.

It was hard to roll the wheels along with one hand and lead the black horse with the other. Several times a wheel got loose, and she had to bend to pick it back up. When she got both wheels as far as the lane crossing, she dropped them with a grunt and wiped her hands on the fallen leaves. The black horse nudged her, and she scratched his chin idly. She could just see Mai bending to his work.

"How long will you be?" she called back to him. The rhythmic axe blows stopped, and he stood up.

"Eh?"

"How long will you be?" She made it loud and distinct. "I thought I'd ride on and find water for my horse."

"Oh—say—a finger or two of sun. Not longer. There's a spring up that lane—used to be a farm there, some years back. You could bring me some—my can's back here; this fellow won't fall till I drop him."

Paks mounted and rode back, to another of Mai's winks, and he handed her a tall can with a wire bail. "It's good water, or used to be," he said. "Look out for wild animals, though. I've heard of wolves using it."

"I'll be careful," said Paks, and drew along the black horse's neck the tracks she'd seen: wagons and teams both. Mai nodded and waved her away.

Paks made no attempt at silence as she rode along the lane that led south. She found a thread of water beside the lane, and then a cobble-walled springhouse. Beyond was a half-overgrown clearing with the ruins of a farmhouse and outbuildings. She didn't look at it, but dipped the can in the spring, and let the black horse drink afterwards. It was not really thirsty, and wanted to sniff at fresh droppings a few feet away. Paks reined it around slowly, and rode back, glad of her helmet and mail shirt.

Mai had the tree down by the time she got back, and loudly directed her in placing the wheels under one end of it. He had trimmed the ends of the axle log into rough rounds, and once the wheels were in place split the ends and placed cross-wedges in them.

"Thing is," he said, "the wheels have to turn on the axle, not with it—else it'd walk right off the end of the tree." Paks hadn't thought of that problem. Nor had she noticed the can of grease he'd brought to put on the axle. She did wonder how he'd gotten the large end of the tree into the cart. Surely he wasn't that strong. She glanced overhead for something he might have slung a line from.

"Don't look up," he warned quietly. Paks froze. "If you want to know how I lifted that monster," he said more loudly, "I used its own limbs for levers. Trimmed 'em after, that's how I do it. Some men use lines, but then they have to have a taller tree nearby. Not always handy. By Gird, I'm thirsty!" He drained the can at one swallow.

The journey back was slower; Mai's pony moved the tree at an easy foot-pace. The black horse fretted. Paks got off again and walked alongside. When they reached Eris', they picked up the apples; Mai told Paks what the current price was, and she left it wrapped in the cloth Eris had put over the baskets. From there into town they talked softly of what Paks had seen. Mai said he had spotted a watcher in the trees. They agreed it would be too dangerous to scout the game trail if the brigands were still so alert.

It was nearly dark when they passed the grange; Ambros and several other yeomen were talking in the barton gateway, and called greetings.

"You can come help me on the bridge," Mai yelled back. "Paks here isn't much of a teamster."

"That's not a team," Paks retorted, sure by now that such joking was acceptable.

"I'd be glad to hitch your black up and let him do some work," said Mai.

"I doubt that." Ambros came up to them. "You weren't there the first time she saddled him. He'd be impossible in harness. Come on Jori, give us a hand here." Ambros and the other yeoman helped Mai get the wheels aligned on the bridge. Still talking, they followed along. Mai untied the log beside the Council Hall, and drove it off the back wheels. Then he let the weight drag it out of the cart. His pony gave a heavy sigh as the log fell, and the men laughed.

"Come on to the inn," said Mai. "I'll buy a mug for you."

They nodded and walked along; Jori and Ambros returned to some grange matter; Paks did not know what grange-set was, or what it had to do with a farm's sale. She hardly listened, intent instead on figuring out just what Mai Argonist really was—not a simple forester, that was clear. She was beginning to wonder if anyone was actually a simple anything. Until Brewersbridge, she had not considered that an innkeeper might be a Council member as well—that many people had more than one role, and considered them all important.

The common room was moderately busy, but quiet. News of the attack made solemn faces. Paks stabled the black horse, and went back in to find that the others expected her at their table. She shook her head at Mai's offer of ale, and asked Hebbinford for supper instead.

"I eat before I drink," she said in answer to Mai's question. "I don't have your—" she paused and looked at him with narrowed eyes, as the others laughed. "—capacity," she said finally. Mai shook the table with his laughter.

"You didn't start young enough," he said. "When I was scarce knee high, my old dad had me down tankards at a time."

"Of ale?" asked Ambros.

"No—ale costs too much. Water. But it's the habit, Ambros, of an open throat. The feel of it sliding down—"

"Then why didn't you stick with water?"

"Oh, that was my brother." His face grew solemn, but Paks thought she could sense the laughter underneath. "He said a yeoman of Gird must learn to drink like a man. So I did."

"If that's your reason," said Ambros, "you should be a kuakkgannir—you don't drink like a man, you drink like a tree."

They all laughed. Hebbinford brought Paks her platter of sliced meat and gravy. Mai grabbed a slice and stuffed it in his mouth. She looked at him.

"It's luck," he said. "It's your good luck if someone else eats the first bite."

Paks shook her head, and began eating. By the time she had eaten, the room had almost emptied. Ambros and Mai had gone out together. Sir Felis, Paks knew, would be coming in later for her report. She asked Hebbinford for another of the apple tarts, and settled back comfortably. The black-clad man was still in the room, and met her eyes. She had not talked to him since the afternoon before the Council's summons; now he came to her table.

"May I sit?"

Paks nodded, her mouth full of apple tart. She reached for her mug to wash it down.

"I don't mean to pry," he said. "You seem in good favor now; I hope for your sake that is true. But if anything is going to be done about that attack on the caravan—and if you are going to be part of it—I wish you'd consider my offer to come along. You might well want someone who was not—let's say—from here."

Paks looked at him a moment before answering. "Sir—Arvid, didn't you say?—" He nodded, smiling slightly. "You seem to be telling me that these people can't be trusted. Is that so?"

"I don't think I'd put it like that. I do think that those who live in small villages are more trustworthy to others of the village than to strangers. Haven't you found that to be true, in your travels? That these village folk stick together?"

"I suppose." Paks took another swallow from her mug, and prodded the remains of the tart. "It might be a reason not to trust them fully, but—pardon me—why should I trust you?"

He gave her a suggestion of a wink. "All—I knew you knew more than you showed at first. That mountain traveling is enough to scramble anyone's wits. Now I don't have anything to say about their character—everyone knows how honest the Girdsmen are—at least to Girdsmen." When Paks didn't rise to this, he smiled a little and went on. "But you aren't Girdish. Or of this village. I don't think they'd lie, exactly, but they might shade the truth. And if it came to your skin or theirs—?"

"I see your point," said Paks quietly. "But you have still to answer mine."

"My dear," he began, as he drew his dagger and carefully trimmed his fingernails with it. "You should trust me only because it is in your interest, as well as mine. I am neither Girdish nor a native here—therefore I am unlikely to sacrifice you for a brother's reputation or a friend's life. I don't expect you to trust me as you trusted your companions in Duke Phelan's Company—of course not. But I have no good reason to kill you—and several to keep you alive."

"And they are?" asked Paks curiously. She picked up the rest of her tart and ate it, waiting for his answer. His eyes narrowed. He resheathed his dagger.

"I told you before that our interests might march together. I think they do. I wish the brigands no luck; I would be glad to see them dead. You need not know why. Obviously, no one official is going to encourage me to go after them—I'm not an experienced soldier, and that's what it takes. But if that is the charge they gave you, then I would be glad to assist. Perhaps to make sure it is done thoroughly.'

"Have you a grudge against them?" asked Paks, honestly curious now. "Have they done you or your family an injury?"

"I will not tell you that at this time." Arvid turned a little, and signalled Hebbinford, who came over with a sharp glance for both of them. "Wine, sir, if you please." Paks shook her head, and the innkeeper moved away. "I perceive, lady, that you are of sufficient experience to have caution—but insufficient to recognize an honest offer. Nonetheless, it stands. My word you would have no reason to trust—but I will tell you honestly that I will not kill you, and I will defend you within reason, if you accept me as one of your company. If you were wise enough to know what I am, you would know what that is worth."

Paks frowned, not liking the bantering tone or the subtle insults. It reminded her too much of Macenion. She looked up at him again. "If such a command is offered me, and if I accept you, what other suggestions would you have?"

His brows arched. "You ask much, with nothing given."

"I do? What of you—you ask my trust, with no evidence of your character. I have had such chances, sir, as make me distrust most strangers."

"But Girdsmen." His tone was sour.

"Most soldiers have found Girdsmen to be honest, at the least, and usually brave as well. I don't know your allegiance, either to gods or lords."

Arvid sighed. "I am a guild member in good standing. As such I obey my guildmaster, in Vérella. It is an old guild, long established there—"

"What craft?" asked Paks.

He laughed. "What—do you think the Master Moneychanger here tells everyone when he travels what his guild affiliation is? Don't you know that some guilds bind their traveling members to secrecy? Do you want to bring down on me that very plague of thieves you think I represent?"

"No—" Paks flushed, confused.

"I'm sorry," he said quickly. "I shouldn't have laughed. I understand your suspicion—and it does you credit. Any experienced adventurer is suspicious. But I cannot tell you my guild—at least not without asking—at this time. I cannot tell anyone here. I can only tell you what I have told you. In my judgement—and I am not without experience in the world myself—it is in both our interests to cooperate. I have an interest in those brigands—I want to see them removed. Does that sound like a thief or worse? You, I believe, have the Council's permission to mount an attack on them. And you could use someone at your back who has no reason to wish an honest witness dead. Suppose they are actually living in town—related to one of the Council members. Do you honestly think they'll thank you for capturing such as that? Let you take the risk, yes. Let you kill and capture them, yes—perhaps. But let you live to take the credit, when it's their own? I doubt that much. If the brigands really are strangers, then you have no problem. But otherwise—"

Paks nodded slowly. She was not truly convinced, but she had worried that the spy the Council wanted her to find might turn out to be someone they liked. And, as well, they had asked her to involve the other adventurers in town if she could. Surely this Arvid Semminson was an adventurer.

From the hill west of the keep, the crooked path down the moat was clearly visible, as were the signs of age and decay: stones from the outer wall tumbled into the moat, leaving ragged gaps in the wall through which the battered interior could be seen. Paks, concealed behind a thick-leaved but prickly shrub, stared down at the broken walls and waited for the diversion Sir Felis had promised. She had ended up with a motley group: Mai and several other yeomen of Gird, including Doryan; the two traders she'd met some days before, who said they wanted to avenge the attack on the caravan; a servant of theirs whom they said was a good bowman; one of Eris' sons (a Falkian, Mai had reported sadly, but a good man), and Arvid. The sun rose higher, burning off the last of the mist from the moat and swamp around. Paks insisted that her group stay well back in cover, and refused to let them talk or light pipes. A subdued grumble followed these commands.

"Stands to reason," muttered the heavy-set bowman, "that if they could see us, we could see them. We can't see a thing, through these leaves. We could smoke, at least."

Paks shook her head fiercely. "Sun's in our eyes. They've got the better light. Think: how far can you see a shepherd's breakfast firesmoke? There could be a dozen eyes looking out of that gap, from the shadow, and we'd never know it. Be still."

Someone cursed, but softly, and they rested as best they could in the positions Paks had chosen for them. The sun rose higher. Paks had to force herself to stay still. She wanted to walk back and forth, from post to post. Was this why the captains had so often walked the line before battle? She could hardly believe that she, the same old Paks, was commanding a group like this—a group of strangers.

She looked again at the keep, which seemed a different shape as the shadows shifted with the sun, and wondered if the magician who built it had, indeed, left a curse. A light wind sifted through the trees, shuffling the leaves and making the shadows dance. She wondered if the militia had left Brewersbridge on time. They were supposed to have left just enough time for her to get her group into position. It had been too long. She squinted at the sun, feeling the sweat spring out on her neck, chill as it was. She swallowed against the fear, and glared around at the others. Someone had shifted carelessly, and a rock clattered. She turned back to the keep. Nothing moved there but a cloud of midges over the moat, a shimmer in the sun.

At last she heard the rhythmic noise of marching men and horses. She eased forward to the edge of the wood, trying to see the north side of the keep, where the forest stood back a ways. The sound came louder, eddying in the uncertain wind. Now she could hear it distinctly. A movement in the distance caught her eye. A horn call swam through the air, mellow and long. She looked back at the keep. There: a flicker, quick as a lizard's tail, on the highest part of the ruin. The horn call came again, louder. She could hear a bellowed command from the oncoming force. She looked back at her group; they were all alert. Mai grinned at her, shifting his broad shoulders. She realized that he had moved forward, coming between her and the others. But she had no time to think of that. The front of the captain's "show of force" was out of the trees now. She could not tell from this distance how many of them were illusion. Nor could she tell which was Zinthys. None of them wore the kind of robes she had seen on him so far.

"There's one," said Mai, so softly she almost missed hearing it. Then she, too, saw the brown-clad man peering from a low gap in the keep wall. He passed through, carrying a plank and laid it on the edge of the moat. It extended to one of the fallen blocks farther out. He moved out onto the plank and at once another came, this one in a heavy mailed shirt, and dragging another plank. The second plank bridged the moat from the stone to the near shore. A third man appeared, carrying bows, and the three slipped across the bridge and spread to cover it. After a glance upslope, they concentrated on the corners of the keep.

Noise from the north side increased. Paks could not tell if it was a fight, or just noise. Suddenly a gout of flame rose up, and a thunderous boom echoed across the woods. Birds flew up screaming. The bowmen below did not flee, though one of them half stood, to be pulled back by the others. Another gout of flame, and another, followed. The noise was appalling, even though Zinthys had warned them. A deer broke cover and bounded through the woods, crashing and snorting. A hurrying file of men slipped from the gap and teetered across the bridge. Paks saw the glint of mail on most of them; they had their swords out, and bows slung to their backs. She counted as they came, hoping that Sir Felis' estimate was right.

She knew the last had come when the bowmen moved. The entire group—just over a score—started up the hill, as she had expected. The archers stayed in the rear, and two swordsmen took the lead, several strides ahead of the rest. Paks frowned. With that spread, some of them could escape, if they were quick. She thought they would be quick.

She turned to the stocky bowman. "Shoot low. Just in front of 'em."

"Why?" But he complied. Two arrows thudded into the ground, and the two brigands in front slowed and peered up the slope.

"So they'll bunch up," said Paks. "As they are now."

He gave her a quick look. "Hunh. That's quite a trick. Where'd you learn—?" But they were all together now, and Paks called for another volley, from this man and the Girdish archers as well. Four of the brigands fell; Paks saw one of them struggle up and begin to crawl away along the slope. The others, furious and frightened, charged up the slope.

The bowmen shot as fast as they could, and seven more were hit before Paks led the others to break the charge. Some of them fell; others turned aside, limping, or jerked the arrows free and kept with the main group. She herself was in the lead, full of the same delight she often felt in battle. The sword she had carried since the elfane taig balanced easily in her hand. She met the first brigand with a sweeping blow that broke his sword at the hilt. He jerked out his dagger and thrust, but she was past him, the sword carving into another man's side. A blade she didn't see caught her in the ribs; she felt the blow, but rolled off it to take another brigand in the neck. She heard the yeomen of Gird call his name as they followed her. But compared to the battles she'd been in with the Duke's company, it was short and easy. Almost before she knew it, the clash of weapons ceased.

She looked around. Arvid Semminson was wiping the blade of his narrow sword; it was stained to the hilt. One of the merchants nursed a wounded arm; his bowman stood guard over him, dagger drawn. Mai had one brigand down, and was tying his arms; two of the other yeomen were guarding the remaining brigands who could stand. Ten of them were down, dead or dying of serious wounds. In the distance, Paks thought she saw two or three huddled forms limping away. None of her own force seemed badly hurt, barring the merchant. Paks walked over to look. He had a long, deep gash on the arm, but not a killing wound, though he seemed dazed. She hadn't expected much from him anyway.

"What now, Paks?" asked Mai. "Do we kill them, or take them back, or what?"

Paks glared at him, before she remembered the agreement. For an instant she had thought he might seriously mean to kill the prisoners. In that moment, the other merchant spoke. "We ought to kill them."

"No." Paks shook her head for emphasis. "We'll take them to Sir Felis. He's the Count's representative."

"But they killed—"

"We've killed enough. How many do you want?" Paks turned away, and squatted beside Mai's prisoner. She recognized the man who had led the others up the hill. He was bleeding from a cut on his head that had split the leather helm, and from a deep gash in one leg. "Better bandage that," she said to Mai, who nodded. She wiped the blood off her own sword and sheathed it. The prisoner watched her, dark eyes alert. He flinched when Mai touched his leg, then held still as it was bandaged. Paks said nothing, looking around at the others as she caught her breath. Then she met the prisoner's eyes.

"Your name?" she asked.

"Why should I tell you? We're just going to be killed—"

"Probably," said Paks. "Any reason why not?"

"Reasons!" His mouth worked and he spat blood. "Being poor's reason enough—that and going looking for work. That'll get you killed, that will—going along, trying to find a place, and nothing—nothing." He twisted his neck, wincing, to look around.

Paks felt an obscure sympathy she had not expected with this weatherworn robber. He did not look as if he'd enjoyed his life. For that matter, he didn't look as if he'd profited by it. "How many of you were there?"

"They're the lucky ones," he said sourly. "Dead and over with. Gods above, what chance did we have—"

"Chance?" rumbled Mai, coming back to confront him. "About the chance you gave Eris at her farm, I suppose. Poor, eh? You think we're all rich?"

The prisoner closed his eyes briefly. "I don't—dammit, man, I never thought to be a robber. Not back when I—I had land once myself. A few cattle, enough. If I hadn't come here—"

"What about 'here'?" asked Arvid, who had come up softly behind Paks. "What's so special here?"

"I—" The man seemed to choke, shook his head, and said no more. Paks pushed herself up. All of her group could travel as they were; of the brigands, four that might live could not walk. Those whose wounds were mortal she despatched herself, not trusting the others to give a clean deathstroke. But she told the others to gather the weaponry, such as it was: she had always hated stripping the bodies, and had avoided it most of the time. She had the yeomen supervise the prisoners in making litters for those who could not walk.

"Paks, what about those that got away?" Mai swung his bloody axe slowly in his hand.

"We'll have to track them. They're all wounded." Paks sighed. "I don't know how many—"

"I thought four or five. There's a couple down there still—" he jerked his head toward the slope.

"I'd better go—"

"No. You stay here—I'll take Doryan. You don't need him here." Paks started to protest, but thought better of it. She was sure Mai was trustworthy.

He had just started down the hill when five horsemen broke from the woods on the south side of the keep. Paks saw a flurry of motion in the bushes near them, and then four of the horsemen charged, driving out the remnant of the robbers. That was over in a few seconds. Zinthys rode across the slope to greet her.

"Well done, Lady Paksenarrion," he said cheerfully. "Sir Felis will be pleased."

"You too. That was a real show, that—" Paks stopped short, wondering if she should reveal his work as illusion. Zinthys grinned at her confusion, and spoke up.

"Most people find a fireblast alarming," he said casually. "I sent the rest of the troops back when we found the main keep empty—you seemed to have everything well in hand back here."

Paks wondered what he would have said if she'd blurted out the truth, but merely smiled. "I'm glad you thought to send a few around back for the stragglers."

"Oh, of course. I see you have quite a few prisoners—how about transport?"

"If you could have someone send a cart or wagon out from town—and Master Travannen is wounded. It would be better for him to ride—"

"Certainly. Why don't I see to moving your mounts back along the road—then you can come out the way we came in. It's easier traveling."

"Fine." Paks looked around. The prisoners had rough litters ready, covered with their cloaks. They loaded the wounded and prepared to march out. Zinthys rode off with a wave of his hand; the soldiers from Sir Felis' command joined her, flanking the party. One of them offered his horse.

"No, thank you," said Paks. "I'll walk to the road." He shrugged and moved back into position. She wondered if she should have taken his offer.

"I wonder," said Arvid quietly at her side, "that you are unhurt. Didn't you know that a sword broke on your armor?"

Paks thought back to the fight—it hardly deserved the name of battle. "I don't—oh—I remember a blow in the side—"

"Yes. I was just behind you then. It was a fair blow, and the man was as heavy as you, or more. I thought you'd get a broken rib out of it, at the least."

Paks took a deep breath, feeling nothing. "No," she said. "It must have caught at an angle."

Arvid shook his head. "I saw it. Either you're a good bit tougher than I thought—which is unlikely—or your armor has great virtue. Where did you get it?"

Paks gave him a straight look. "I found it," she said. "In a ruin."

"Hmm. That's a good sword, too."

"Yes." Paks looked around. Everything seemed to be secure. Mai was moving up beside her. He had wiped the axe blade on something; it was clean.

"The others are dead," he said. "Too bad hurt to make it; the riders trampled some of 'em. I did it quick." He looked past Paks at Arvid. "You fight good, for a city man."

Arvid laughed easily. "Do you think all soldiers begin in a farmyard?"

Mai's forehead creased. "Nay, not that, sir. But the ones I know all did, and the city men I know are mostly merchants. This lady, now, says she comes from a farm. Isn't that so?" Paks nodded.

"Many good things come from cities," said Arvid.

"Oh, I didn't mean any different. I know that. Fine clothes, and jewels, and that. But there's more thieves in cities, too. My brother always said that wealth draws thieves like honey draws bees."

"I suppose." Arvid didn't sound interested; he turned to Paks. "What are you going to do now?"

Paks shrugged. "First things first. Get the prisoners to Sir Felis. Then he can find out how they've been operating, and if they've had contacts in town."

CHAPTER FIFTEEN

Sir Felis met the party coming into town. Ambros was with him, as were several other yeomen. Some of the townspeople cheered; Paks felt her face redden. She was glad she had the black horse; at least she didn't have to look up at Sir Felis.

"You've done well," he said, after a quick look at the group. "None of your men killed—or even badly hurt—"

"My arm—" began the merchant. Sir Felis gave Paks a quick look of amusement, soldier to soldier, before speaking to the man.

"I'm sorry, sir; I didn't see. The surgeon has been alerted; he's at the inn."

"God. It was a terrible fight—"

Paks saw one of Sir Felis' men roll his eyes. She choked down a laugh. Her knees felt shaky. In the stir around them, the black horse began to fidget. She met Ambros' gaze.

"How was it?" he asked.

"Went well." She worked the black horse over to the side of the road near him. "They all came out the bolthole, just as we thought. Your yeomen are good fighters—steady."

Ambros smiled. "I know. The Marshal's trained them well. I'm glad they were willing to go with you."

"What now?"

"Well, Sir Felis will take them to the keep. I suppose he'll ask you along. The Council's heard; of course they're happy about it. Do you think you got them all?"

"Twenty-one came out; we left eleven dead and have ten prisoners.

Unless some stayed in the keep—and I wouldn't have, with what Zinthys did." Mindful of spies, Paks did not elaborate on that.

"They don't—they don't look so bad," said Ambros thoughtfully.

"Who, the brigands?"

"Yes. I thought—"

Paks glanced at him. "They'd all look like orcs?"

He flushed. "I know I don't have your experience—"

"Don't be silly. I didn't mean that." Paks found herself annoyed with his sensitivity. "I was surprised myself, if you want to know. The only brigands I'd seen, in Aarenis, looked as vicious as they were. These men look like any poor farmer or soldier. The leader—that one in the litter there—he said something about not wanting to be a robber—"

"Eh, once he's caught, what'd you expect him to say?" The uninjured merchant had pressed close to Paks' side. "He's not likely to admit he's been a thief from birth."

"He hasn't been," said Arvid, with a certainty that made Paks wonder.

"How do you know?"

"Lady, I, like Master Zinthys, prefer not to reveal all the sources of my knowledge. But I will tell you that had he been a thief from birth, he would not have been in that keep."

"But how do you know?" Both Paks and Ambros stared at Arvid. He smiled, bowed, and passed on toward the inn.

"That one," muttered the merchant, idly putting his hand on the black horse's neck. It jerked aside; by the time Paks had it calm again, the merchant and most of the group had passed. Sir Felis beckoned; Paks moved the black horse beside his at the tail of the procession.

"Come on out with me to the keep, will you?" he asked. "I'd like to hear what happened. My cook should have something ready, too."

Paks nodded. She realized that Sir Felis might want her to be present when he questioned the prisoners. She wondered what the customs were.

"And you, too, Yeoman-marshal, if your duties permit," said Sir Felis smoothly. "Since the Marshal is not here, I would like a representative from the grange to be present."

"The grange's honor, Sir Felis," said Ambros. "May I ask how long this might take? It is customary for the yeoman of Gird to give thanks in the grange for the success of such a mission; I would like to tell them when—"

Sir Felis pursed his lips. "I am not certain, Yeoman-marshal, but surely by dark. These men do not look so desperate as I thought."

Paks had feared that Sir Felis might, like Alured the Black of Aarenis, torture his prisoners; he did not need to. By the time Sir Felis, trailed by Paks and Ambros, came down the stairs to question them, the brigand leader had decided to tell what he knew.

"We was all honest men once, sir," he said weakly. "I was a farmer, myself. Some of the others was trade or craft, but most was farmers. But that bad drought three years ago, in Verrakai lands—that's what drove me out. The taxes—and then no grass, and the cows dying—so my lord Verrakai put me out, and I went wandering. No one had honest work, sir, and that's the truth of it." He closed his eyes a moment; Paks looked around at the other brigands. The wounded lay quietly; the rest squatted against the dungeon wall, heads down. "I suppose Elam and I were the first," the man went on after a long pause. "He and I'd known each other back home. We traveled together. We come on this place in a storm—went in to get dry—and then—seems we couldn't leave."

"What stopped you?" asked Ambros.

"I don't know. Something. It—it called, like. We stayed there a couple of days—shot a bird for food, Elam was a good bowman. I stuck one of those things in the moat, but we couldn't eat that."

"What thing?" asked Sir Felis.

"You know. One of them—big things, like a frog only near man-sized. Smell rotten. They have teeth, too. Anyway we stayed there. Took a goose from a farm nearby—I'd asked for work, and they drove us off. Called us robbers, they did, and we hadn't robbed before that. Made me mad." He stopped again, and rubbed his nose. "Elam wanted to go on somewheres else, but when we got an hour or so away, we both got the cramps bad. Had to come back. Then the others came." He nodded toward the other men. "One or two at a time, every week or so. Soon we'd hunted out all the woods around. If we took from the farms—well, most of us had farmed. We didn't want to."

"So then he said take caravans," put in one of the others, leaning back against the wall and tilting his head up to look at Sir Felis. "He says what's a caravan to you—them merchants are all rich, and what has rich done for you? That's what he says. Steal from caravans, and get rich yourself." The man spat. "Rich! Heh! All we ever see's enough to eat, and that not all the time. A few coppers now and then—a new cloak—that's all."

"You shouldn't talk about *him*," said the first robber, pushing himself up. "It's bad luck. Hell—"

"He can't do much here," said the other. "Teriam, think! It's listening to him has got us here—in jail, when we were born honest men. Robbers, we are, and it's him as profits by it."

"But you know what he said. He can reach us anywheres—that's why we couldn't leave. He could touch us here—right now—and—"

"And what? Kill us deader than they will, when they're through talking?" The man gave Sir Felis a bitter grin. "Tell you the truth, sir, if you can kill that devil, you'll do yourself more good than killing us. And I'll be glad of it."

Paks saw that some of the other brigands seemed very frightened, but they said nothing. The leader had fallen back, and now lay silent with eyes closed and jaw clenched.

"Who is this man that ordered you to rob?" asked Sir Felis. "Was he captured or killed?'

"Not him," said the spokesman angrily. "Not him. He's got his own place, safe and deep, and all we know's his orders. I don't know his name, sir, or who or what he is—and I'm not sure he's a man, even. Teriam knows, I think—" he glanced at the leader.

"I don't." It came out as a harsh whisper. "I swear I don't know—I never seen him but the one time, and after that I couldn't—I couldn't—" He gripped his head, rocking back and forth. "He—he had black robes, that's all, and some kind of—of thing on a chain—it—like a hand spread out, only it had too many fingers—"

Paks felt, rather than saw, Ambros stiffen beside her. "Gird's arm!" he said softly. Then more loudly, "Like a spider, maybe?"

The man's head turned towards him. "It—it might be—if—NO!" He began to flail about on the straw. "No! Don't let him—not here—!"

Sir Felis swore, a soldier's curse Paks had heard many times. She could see nothing but the frightened man, waving his hands at nothing and trying to flee something no one could see. Ambros moved forward before the others shook off their surprise, and caught his arm.

"Be still, man—Teriam's your name? Be still; Gird will ward you from that evil."

"No one can—he said he could—"

"Gird's grace on you, Teriam. Gird Strongarm will ward you; give him a chance."

"You—you're a Marshal? Of Gird?"

"I'm the yeoman-marshal of this grange," said Ambros. "I am sworn to Gird's service, and known to him. I give you my word that I place your name before Gird."

"Please—" the man's eyes were open now, and fastened on Ambros. "Please, sir—I'm not afraid to die—just not that filth, please sir—"

Ambros freed one hand and held out his medallion. Teriam touched it with the tips of his fingers. "You have been spelled by some evil, is that not so?' asked Ambros. "You fear that it will take your soul?"

Teriam nodded. "He said—he said he could do that. Wherever we tried to run, whatever we did—he would find us, and see us in—" He stopped, and lowered his voice. Paks could not hear what he said to Ambros, but she saw the sudden twitch of Ambros' shoulders.

"Well, and do you believe that the High Lord and Gird are stronger than that one?"

"I—I know I should, sir, but I'm feared—I'm feared they won't be for me—"

Ambros looked around at the other robbers. "And you? What do you think of the power of that evil one, when you are here? Do you think the High Lord is weaker?"

Some shook their heads; some simply stared. The man who had spoken so boldly before pushed himself to his feet. "Sir—Yeoman-marshal—I was a yeoman of Gird once. Not a good one, you'll say, and I won't argue that. I never thought to find myself bound by such evil—just a drover like me. I don't know what that black-cape can do, but I will say the High Lord is right, if he kills me for it."

Ambros gave him a bleak smile. "Yeoman of Gird, you must face the Count's judgement, but the High Lord knows his own servants."

The man's face lighted. "I swear, Yeoman-marshal, that it was not fear of the Count's court that kept me there. Whatever the grange-court demands—"

"Gird will have somewhat to say in that, yeoman."

"Aye, Yeoman-marshal." He turned to Sir Felis. "Sir, if you will, if the court demands my life, permit the grange to report the death of a yeoman." Sir Felis looked at Ambros, brows raised. Ambros nodded.

"The Marshal would say the same, Sir Felis. A yeoman may be spelled into evil deeds; I judge it was so with him, and perhaps with some others. The punishment must fall, but their names remain on the grange rolls. Only those who willingly serve evil, and refuse to repent, are cast out."

"He won't tell you," said Teriam softly, "but I will. He tried to get away more than once—we kept him until the curse softened him."

"I pray the High Lord's mercy on you, Teriam, for your deeds and your confessions."

Back upstairs, in Sir Felis' conference room, Ambros reddened under their gaze. Zinthys was studiously ignoring the others, setting wine to heat on the hearth. Sir Felis simply watched Ambros, his weathered face fixed in a neutral expression. Paks tried to see, behind that youth and inexperience, the power he had seemed to have with the prisoners.

"Well," said Sir Felis suddenly, as if he'd made a decision. He looked at Paks. "I say again, Paksenarrion, that you did very well. Very well indeed. I am not now surprised that your Duke recommended you for advanced training. I do not think many novice commanders could have taken over a score with a dozen, and had no casualties."

"I could not, without Master Zinthys' help," said Paks. "And your soldiers caught the stragglers."

"Even so," said Sir Felis. He looked her up and down. "And you, yourself, have no injury? I see your tunic is slashed."

"No, sir," said Paks. "I wear armor, of course."

"Hmmph. Yes. Well, then, I think we'd better have a formal report to the Council—you know the sort of thing—I'll speak to the mayor, and I expect we'll meet tonight. You'll be summoned. Yeoman-marshal—" Sir Felis turned to Ambros.

"Yes, Sir Felis?"

"Since some of the prisoners claim to be yeomen, I will delay trial until the Marshal returns."

"Thank you, Sir Felis."

"I will not promise that it will make any difference—"

"Of course not, Sir Felis. The grange understands that."

"Good. I'll see you later, then—will you be at Council in the Marshal's place?"

"Yes, Sir Felis."

"Good. Paksenarrion, do you wish to make your own reckoning of the arms recovered?"

"No, sir." Paks saw no reason to distrust Sir Felis' count.

"Then I'll see you later. If you'll excuse me—" He shrugged into his heavy cloak.

"Certainly, sir." Paks and Ambros followed Sir Felis down the winding stairs and out to a sunny afternoon. A soldier brought their horses forward; Sir Felis was already mounted and riding off.

They were almost back to the Jolly Potboy when Ambros turned to Paks. "Can I have a talk with you?"

"Me?" Paks had been thinking about the report she would have to give to the Council; she dreaded it. "Of course—but what about?"

"Come on to the grange; I don't want to talk about it here."

Paks sighed. She had been up since long before dawn, and she had looked forward to a hot bath. She had not had time for more than a brief handwash before the simple lunch Sir Felis had served. But Ambros looked so concerned that she nodded finally and turned the black horse away from the inn.

"I should have thought—" Ambros said quietly, nodding to a child in the street. "You're tired, aren t you?"

"I'm dirty and stiff as much as tired. And don't you still have to do whatever ceremony you were talking about?"

"Oh—yes. I'd forgotten, Gird forgive my thick head. Blast. But you'll want to see that, even you aren't Girdish. The Marshal would want you to be there."

"All right." Paks wished he'd get to the point. She saw Sir Felis' horse and escort outside the Brewmaster's gate as they passed.

Once at the grange, Ambros took charge quickly. "I'll rub down the black, and put him up—with the Marshal away, we have plenty of space. You can wash up if you want—there's plenty of water in the scullery—and if you need any bandages or anything—"

"No," said Paks, abandoning the idea of a good soaking bath. "Just to get this dust off—" She took off her helmet and sluiced her head as Ambros led horses away. The cold water woke her up; she wiped her neck with a wet cloth and had most of the grime off her hands and arms before Ambros returned.

"Now," he said, leading the way into the grange proper. "I expect the other yeomen will be here soon—they saw us ride by. What I want to know is whether you'll come with me when I go to seek that blackweb priest."

"What?" Paks was completely confused.

"Didn't you hear him? There's a blackweb—a priest of Achrya—somewhere in that keep. I've got to go and—"

"Wait—Ambros, didn't the Marshal tell you not to go after the brigands?"

"The brigands, yes. And I didn't. This is different. A true evil, Paks—something like this—I can't let it alone."

"But, Ambros, you're not a marshal. Can you fight such a thing? Wouldn't it be better to wait for the Marshal to come back? He said to stay with the grange."

Ambros shook his head. "What if he moved? Now we know where he is—the center of evil for this whole area—and it's my responsibility."

"What about your dream?"

"That's just it." Ambros looked sober but determined. "Paks, such a dream could be an evil sending—to keep me from doing what I should. If I don't try—for fear of dying—what kind of Girdsmen am I?"

"It could be a warning from Gird, couldn't it?"

"Yes—but I can't tell."

"Then I think you should wait." Paks stuck her hands in her sword belt. "Ambros, you don't know anything about what's there except what a robber said. How do you know he's telling the truth? Even if he is, you don't know enough. A priest of Achrya—very good so far. But alone? With other troops? Human or other?"

Ambros had been pacing back and forth; he stopped. "I—see. I hadn't thought of that. It's your experience, I suppose."

"Not just that. I would go with you—but you said, the other day, that you had to obey the Marshal."

"I have to obey Gird. Ordinarily that means the Marshal, but—" He stopped as the yeomen who had been with Paks that morning came into the grange. Paks noticed that none of them had changed from their blood-stained clothing; she wondered why. Mai winked at her, as they all came to the platform. Ambros climbed onto it.

What followed seemed strange to Paks. He called on each one to give an account for his own actions. After each recital, Ambros crossed his blade with the man's weapon. When it came to Mai, the big man grinned as Ambros' sword tapped his axe blade. Then Ambros inspected all the weapons, and supervised their return to the grange racks—for only Mai had carried his own. After that, they all repaired to the inn for a round of ale.

Here the others who had been involved joined them. Paks slipped upstairs for a bath and change of clothes. She put on the new clothes, enjoying the feel of good cloth. It was hard to believe that she'd been in a battle that morning—she thought back to the Duke's Company, and laughed to herself. Very different indeed. No Company chores, no guard duty at night. And the others had fought well. Perhaps she could get used to having strange companions at her side—or none. Even so, she slipped the mail shirt back on and pulled her best leather tunic over it.

She opened the door to find a girl leaning on the wall opposite. Paks recognized her as one of the junior yeoman. The girl stood away from the wall as Paks came out.

"Please—lady—could I speak to you?"

"Yes," said Paks. "What is it?"

"You're a fighter, aren't you? I mean—I know you are, but isn't that—I mean, don't you make your living that way?" All this in a rush.

"Yes," said Paks, trying not to laugh. "Why?"

"Well—" The girl looked down, then back at Paks. She was as tall, Paks realized, and nearly as broad-shouldered. "I want to be a fighter, too," she said finally. "I—they laugh at me here, the people in town. I want to show them—the Marshal says I'm good—"

"Umm." Paks looked at her wrists. They were strong, already marked with training scars. "Well, I can tell you it's possible. I did it. But—"

"I know—I know. They say—those who saw you fight today—they say you're good. The senior yeomen told us, too, after they'd drilled with you. I know I can do it, too. But will you let me?"

"Let you? How do you mean?"

"I want to—to train with you. Like a—a squire, or something."

"But I'm not a knight." Paks stared at her, bewildered. "I don't need a squire—"

"I'll earn my way," the girl went on, heedless. "I swear I will. I'm a hard worker, and I'll do anything you say, if you'll let me fight beside you."

"Listen—" began Paks, then stopped. She remembered too well how much she had wanted what she now had. What could someone have said to her, at that age? "I don't even know your name."

"Suli."

"Suli, it's not that easy—I don't know what I'll be doing next—"

"You're not going to quit fighting!"

"No. But I don't know when—or what—yet. I don't even know what training you've got. What if you can't—"

"You could talk to the Marshal—or even Ambros. They know me. Please, Lady Paks—I'll do exactly what you say. I can groom your horse, and take care of things—"

"If you want to learn to fight, Suli, why don't you join a mercenary company? The Halverics recruit around here, don't they?"

Suli shook her head. "I've heard about that—all marching and drill, and the same old thing day after day. I could do that here—just drilling with the yeomen. I want—" she looked down the passage as if across a field. "I want excitement. Battles. Travel. Like you've had."

Paks grinned. "Suli, I started as a mercenary. Gods above, I had as much travel and excitement as I could take. It's the best training—I swear it."

Suli shook her head again. "And you left. Why should I do it at all, when it's not what I want in the end? Please, please let me fight with you. If you don't like me, after a while, then you can send me away. But give me a chance." Her eyes held a look that Paks could not name—she was flattered and disturbed at once.

"I'll think about it." Paks started down the passage; Suli was at her shoulder. She started to speak, but Paks held up her hand. "No, I didn't say yes. What does your family think about this?" She could hardly believe she had asked that. She, who knew only too well what families thought.

Suli scowled. "My family—they don't get along here. My dad's a trapper. He does a bit of day work in the tanner's sometimes. He's gone mostly, expects me to take care of everything. But my brothers—they're old enough to work, and all that. I don't care what he thinks."

"Mmm." Paks turned to the stairs. "My father didn't want me to leave either."

"You see? I said we were alike. Please—"

"Enough, Suli. I said I'd think about it." Paks could see the others still clustered around two tables pulled together. Arvid and one of the yeomen were arm wrestling. Mai looked up and waved to her; she came to the table, aware of Suli watching her back.

"We were wondering if you'd decided to leave us for good," said Mai.

"No. Suli wanted to talk to me."

"Oh." Mai and several of the others exchanged glances. "Is she bothering you?"

"Bothering me? No. She has an exalted idea of my achievements." Paks snatched the top of a pile of fried cakes a serving girl put in front of Mai. "Good luck for you," she reminded him; the others roared.

"By Gird's arm, you're quick," said Mai, slightly redder than usual. "I never had anyone turn that trick back on me."

Paks smiled with her mouth full. A tankard appeared in front of her. She picked it up and took a sip.

"Seriously," began Ambros, "if Suli pesters you too much, I'll speak to her."

"I should speak to you, rather. She wants to train with me—and work with me. As a squire, she said—but you know I'm not a knight, what would I do with a squire?"

"As for that, you know much more than she does. She fights well, for the little training she's had—but she's got no more experience in actual fights than I have."

"Not exactly," said Mai. "She's been in some rows."

"Brawls," said Ambros. "That's not the same."

"No, I know that. She's an interesting girl, though." Mai took a long pull at his tankard; one of the other men shook his head. "Seriously—she's one of the best of the junior yeomen."

"As far as fighting goes—but fighting's not all of it," said Ambros.

"Well, it's the most important part, isn't it? For Girdsmen, anyway. You know she's not happy here, Ambros—not since Deordtya left. She wants—"

"She wants excitement and glory," said Ambros tartly. "She's more apt to get a broken head. Or don't you agree, Paks?"

Paks nodded slowly. "I told her she should join a mercenary company for more training. I haven't seen her fight; I don't know what she can do. Still, I can understand—I couldn't wait to get away from home. If someone like me had come through Three Firs, I'd have walked on fire to talk to her."

"I can't recommend her exactly," said Ambros, looking at his hands, "but I think she'd be honest and loyal. If you want someone—"

"I hadn't thought about it." Paks took another fried cake off Mai's platter. She wondered what it would be like to have a squire. The Duke had squires—she tried to imagine herself coming down that trail from the ruined wall, and someone like Suli throwing herself between an enemy and her own shield. It didn't seem right. She was not a knight; she had never been a squire herself; she didn't know what a squire should do, or how to teach it.

"Many free swords travel in pairs or trios," said Mai. "Then they have someone they can trust." He leaned back to let the other yeomen past—they nodded to Paks and Ambros, and went out.

"Sometimes." Ambros shook his head. "Not always. But if you wanted to hire her, Paks, go ahead. I don't think you'd do her any harm, and though she's a little wild, she'll serve you honestly."

"Is she a Girdsman?"

"Well—not exactly. She's not old enough for the final oaths, and her family isn't Girdish. She's sworn to the local grange only. Of course I'd rather she found a Girdish patron—"

"I wondered about that."

"But you seem honest enough yourself. Master Cedfer hopes you'll end up a yeoman of Gird."

"I might," said Paks thoughtfully.

"If it's permitted to answer," broke in Arvid, "I'd like to know if you found how those robbers were fencing their spoils."

"Fencing—?" Paks didn't know the term. Ambros did, and looked sharply at Arvid.

"He means, Paks, selling stolen goods somewhere—thieves call that fencing them."

Arvid smiled. "So do others, young sir—I see that you know the term."

Ambros scowled. "Indeed—honest men must learn thieves' speech or lose by it. But to answer your question, as much as I may—no, we didn't find out where the goods are being sent, or how."

"I told Paks, Yeoman-marshal, that I did not believe those men had been thieves for long." Arvid sipped his ale, and went on. "I know you are suspicious of me—but that is the truth. And if I'm right, then someone else is running them—taking the stolen goods, fencing them—and that person, not those poor men, is the dangerous one. Until that person is caught, these attacks will continue." Paks saw a gleam of interest in Mai's eyes, but he was apparently relaxed and half-asleep, leaning on the wall.

Ambros was clearly interested. "How, if Paks has killed or captured all the active robbers?"

Arvid snorted. "How hard is it to fool poor men? How were those men trapped into thievery? As long as the world holds men whose arms are stronger than their wits or will, just so long will subtle men find simple ones to risk and die for them." Paks thought that could have more application than Arvid intended; she glanced at him and met a sardonic glint that set her mind on edge. Ambros missed it.

"I think, sir," he said quietly, "that you and I—and Paks, perhaps—should have a quiet word together."

"I think that indeed, young sir. Yet I would not have it noticed—for I am convinced that someone in this town is telling dangerous tales."

"You may be right."

"I am," said Arvid with calm authority. "We must meet—and we must meet quietly."

Mai sat forward. "Isn't that the way to be noticed, sir, in this town?"

Arvid glanced at him. "You would know, I expect."

Mai grinned broadly. "Oh yes . . . I would know. And if you're speaking to our yeoman-marshal, I guess I'd like to be there."

"Mal!"

"No offense, Yeoman-marshal, but I've seen his swordwork, remember? You know I can keep quiet."

Arvid smiled the same charming smile at Mai. Paks noticed that Mai simply absorbed it, without changing expression—he looked very much like a stupid country lout. "That's fine with me, sir. I am not intending assassination of your yeoman-marshal—or corruption, either—and you are welcome to watch me as closely as you wish."

The Council meeting that evening was straightforward. Paks, seconded by Mai, gave her account of the attack. Sir Felis reported his interview with the captured robbers, and turned over a list of the captured arms and other valuables. Paks was asked why she had not entered and explored the keep, but accepted her explanation without surprise or comment. Even the Master Stonemason seemed content. They argued a bit over the arms, and finally awarded her a third of their value. Hebbinford recommended that the black horse be given to her outright, and after some discussion it was done. No one mentioned the master-thief that Ambros, Arvid, and even Sir Felis believed to be still lurking in the ruins.

Afterwards, Ambros, Paks, Mai, Sir Felis, and Arvid all gathered at the grange. Arvid lagged behind them, and when they were all sitting down in the chairs Ambros fetched from the Marshal's study, he lounged against the door.

"I have endured quite a bit of your suspicion," he said calmly. "I think perhaps I should tell you precisely what I'm doing here—though I should prefer that you don't tell everyone else."

"Why not?" asked Sir Felis, looking grim.

"Because I can be a great help to you," said Arvid. "If you choose to spread my fame too widely, I'll simply leave."

"Well, then?"

Arvid looked pointedly at Ambros. "The yeoman-marshal is the one I'd like to speak to. Will you, young sir, swear to say nothing of my guild or mission?"

"I—I don't know." His hand was on his medallion. "If you're evil—"

"Evil!" Arvid laughed. "Sir, I am not what you would call good, but I serve no evil deity—that I will swear, and on your Relic, if you demand it." He looked at Paks. "I am no more evil than this warrior—she is not Girdish, nor am I, but we have both spilled robbers' blood today alongside your yeomen."

Ambros flushed. "I will keep your secrets, sir, as long as they do not dishonor Gird. But as to that, I will be the judge."

"Fair enough. I trust the honor of the Fellowship of Gird." Arvid glanced around, gathering all their eyes on him. "Now, some of you—and many others—have thought I was a thief. I am not. I am, however, acquainted with the Thieves Guild." He paused, and the silence thickened. "I am, in fact, on a mission for them at this time."

"And you ask me, a yeoman-marshal of Gird, to keep silence?" Ambros jumped up. Arvid's hand rested on his sword.

"Wait, sir. Hear me out. Your own yeomen will tell you I was happy enough to attack robbers this morning; I am no thief myself. The situation is more complicated than that." He waited until Ambros was seated again, and then pulled a chair near the door for himself. "Now, be attentive. The Thieves Guild, however little you like its craft, is like any guild designed to keep the craftsman in order. As far as its power runs, and that is far, it controls not merely the theft out also the sale of stolen goods. Some time ago, the Guild Headquarters in Verélla realized that caravans were being robbed near here—and their goods appeared distantly, sold without Guild authority. Or taxation." He looked around to be sure they were all listening. "You see the problem. It could not be permitted to continue. A renegade thief is a danger not only to you, but to other thieves. The Guild Council determined to find out who was responsible. They sent—investigators, I suppose you could call them. Your amiable Marshal, young sir, being a most diligent worker for good, caught one and scared another two out of town. Yet another disappeared entirely. So at last," he smiled at them all, "they sent me."

"And you are?" asked Sir Felis in a low growl.

"I am, as I said, Arvid Semminson. A man hired to find the false thief in charge of this operation, and either force him into the Guild, with full payment of dues and fines owed, or kill him."

"But you're not a thief."

"Oh, no. Never. Or at least, let's say that I am not presently in need of anything which it would be worth my while to steal. And I have no joy in theft, as some of our weaker members have. I have stolen a few items in my time—I suppose most people have—but does it make this lady a thief that she stole a ham in Aarenis while in flight from Siniava?"

Paks was amazed that he knew about that—then remembered that she had mentioned "uncle's" establishment to the Marshal and Ambros. The others looked at her for a moment, a little confused by the change of emphasis.

"Of course not," barked Sir Felis. "But—"

"What I am saying, Sir Felis, is that I want this ringleader dead as much, if not more, than you do. It was obvious at once to me that the robbers we captured were not in charge. They had not been fencing caravans of goods anywhere—they were poorly dressed and dull of wit. Whoever has been running this operation is not stupid. So we all have an enemy still at large—an enemy, moreover, who knows that we know where he's hiding—and who is responsible for his defeat. I think he's powerful, and probably either a magician or something worse—he probably spelled those poor men to keep them in his power."

"How would you know about that?"

"Please—I am a man of experience in the world. All kinds of experience. Why should I not know of wizardry, and the greed of those who live by it? And, for that matter, something of the evil ones, as well. I judge we must move quickly against the ringleader, before he can gather new forces. I can help you—I am a skilled fighter, and I have other skills that you will find helpful. Underground in that old keep, for instance, you would find me a good tracker, and wary of traps. If you choose to let him go, you will shortly find that he is more powerful and dangerous—even deadly—to this whole community."

"I thought of that," said Ambros suddenly. "I was telling Paks—if it's a priest of Achrya, say, then we must move quickly. Every day may be important."

"Well, we can't do anything until the Marshal comes back," said Sir Felis. "You can't hope to go against anything like that by yourself, Ambros."

"I don't know when he'll be back, Sir Felis. He said I wasn't to go chasing robbers, that's true—but this is different."

"I don't see that. Orders are orders."

Ambros sat up straight. "Sir Felis, with all respect, my orders come from Gird, as well as Marshal Cedfer."

Paks saw a gleam of satisfaction in Arvid's eyes. Sir Felis shook his head stubbornly.

"It wouldn't be the first time a junior officer thought he had divine guidance when he was simply aching for an adventure. I tell you, Ambros, that you're a fool if you tackle Achrya with a thief and a mercenary for aid." He gave Paks a hard look. "Assuming you're thinking of going with him. I think you're honest, but—"

Paks felt a burst of anger. "Sir Felis, if you have cause for that—"

"No. All right, I'll admit you've done well so far—I said it earlier. But you're all young, and like any young fighters, you've got the sense of a clatter of colts. Wait for the Marshal, Ambros. Don't drag others into your romantic dream." Sir Felis pushed himself up and made for the door, pausing beside Arvid. "And you, master thief-not-a-thief, if you push that boy into rash action, I'll not forget who started it."

"Sir Felis," said Arvid coolly, "I'll not forget who was unwilling to root out the deepest evil." He moved aside from the door, as Sir Felis spat where his feet had been and went out.

CHAPTER SIXTEEN

Arvid's black-clothed form seemed to melt into the shadows as they moved farther away from the stairway, where a dim light came from above. Paks felt a tightness in her chest. She did not like dark underground places, and wondered for a moment why she had agreed to come. Ambros nudged her in the back. She waved a hand at him, and took another careful step. Another. Surely it was ridiculous to come on something like this with only six, one of them an untried junior yeoman, an eager girl who would be all too likely to do something silly trying to prove herself. Arvid signalled, a wave of his arm, and Paks moved lightly toward him. He was the scout, accustomed, he said, to noticing traps. Paks, the most experienced sword fighter, came second. After her, Suli and Ambros together. Paks hoped the yeoman-marshal would be steadied by steadying the junior yeoman. Mai brought up the rear with Tori, a friend of his.

"Door," said Arvid quietly in her ear. "I'll try it. Hinges right. Swings out." Paks flattened herself to the left of the door; she saw a gleam of teeth as Arvid smiled. He ran his hands over the door for a moment, then did something Paks could not see to the lock. A nod of satisfaction; he drew his own blade and slowly pulled the door open. Paks waited, ready to strike. Nothing happened. She craned her neck and looked. Within was deeper blackness. A sour smell wafted out, a stench like old rotting leaves and bones. Arvid put his sword through the door. Nothing. With a shrug, he leaned around the frame, poking at the darkness as if it were a pillow.

"Light?" asked Ambros softly. He had come quite close.

"Not yet. It makes a target of us."

"Yes, but we aren't cats—"

"Quiet. Wait." Arvid had told them their main danger at this level would be haste. Make a noise, he had said, clatter around like a horse fair, and our quarry will be ready for us. Paks waited, trying to see into the darkness by force of will. Spots danced before her eyes. Gradually she found she could see a little better. The room ahead was clearly a room—all shades of darkness, but smaller than the banquet hall above them. She tried to see if anything lurked in it. It seemed as if something—a pile of something—obscured the floor, but without light she could not tell.

"Go now," said Arvid, in Pak's ear. Together they moved under the lintel, separating at once on the inside to flatten against the inner wall. The others waited outside.

In here the smell was stronger. Paks wrinkled her nose, trying to decide what it was. It smelled—meatier, she decided. Rotting straw, bones, meat, and something like the inside of a dirty boot. She shook her head, trying to clear it, but the smell seemed stronger every second. Arvid sniffed, a tiny sound she could hear clearly.

"That smell—" she heard from outside. She thought it was Mai.

"Quiet," said Ambros. Paks stood still, trying to hear anything past the pulse in her ears.

"We'll go forward five paces," said Arvid quietly, "and then if nothing happens, we'll try a light."

Paks heard the scrape of his boot on the stone flags as he took the first step, and moved with him. One step. Two, three—and she stumbled over something, staggering on soft, springy, uneven footing. A yelp got out before she closed her throat; Ambros behind her scraped flint on steel at once. As the spark caught, that little light showed that she'd caught her root on the edge of a pile of garbage. Dirty straw, old clothes, leftover bones chewed clean, a broken pot—she started to laugh with relief. Ambros' candle seemed brighter than she'd expected. She turned to Arvid; his eyes were wide with surprise.

"Just trash," she said, waving her sword at the heap. It was half her height, and easily three times her length. "They must have—"

Part of the pile heaved up—and up—a vast hairy shoulder topped by an equally hairy and vast face. A rheumy eye glared at her from under shaggy brows. And the mouth opened on a double row of very sharp teeth. By reflex, Paks struck at the arm that swiped down from the darkness. Her sword bit into it, slicing deep, but the arm's strength nearly cost her the grip. A deep bellow split the air, and the entire pile shuddered. Paks nearly lost her footing as the creature trampled its bed and attacked.

She had no time to wonder what it was. Taller, broader, and apparently stronger than any human, it had roughly a human shape. Heavy pelt over thick skin—it turned Ambros' first stroke—long arms ending in clawed hands, and a surpassingly ugly face—Paks noticed these without trying to classify them. Its deep-voiced bellows shook the air around them.

"Get back, Ambros!" cried Arvid. "Keep the light—this thing can see in the dark."

Ambros made a noise, but moved back. Suli had come up beside Paks, and was doing a creditable job with her sword—except that she couldn't penetrate the thick hide. Paks had wounded the creature several times, while dodging raking blows from its claws, but it was still strong. Arvid, she saw in a quick glance, was trying to attack its flank, but it was quick—he couldn't seem to get a killing blow in. Paks had just begun to wonder where Mai and his friend were, when she saw him working his way around the creature to its back. Once there, he swung his big axe in a mighty arc and sank it into the creature's back. It screamed, a hoarse, high-pitched sound, deafening in that space.

"The axe does it," he yelled. "It's got—" But the creature heaved backwards; Paks heard the axe-haft smack into something, and Mai grunted. She jumped forward, unsteady on the piled trash, and sank her sword deep in its belly. Now it lurched forward, bending. She dodged. Arvid got a stroke in on its left arm. Mai pulled the axe out of its back and swung again, this time higher. It went to its knees, moaning. Paks aimed a blow at the neck, and blood spurted out, drenching her arm. Still writhing, it sank to a heap, its eyes filming.

"So much for silence and caution," said Arvid tartly, when they had caught their breath. Mai and Suli had lit candles now as well, and they all took a close look at what they had killed. Half again as tall as Paks, and heavily built, it was like nothing she had ever seen.

"What is it?" she asked, wiping blood off her hands and face. The blood had an odd smell, and tasted terrible. Ambros shook his head. Arvid looked at her.

"I'm not sure, Paks, but it might be a hool. I've never seen one myself, but I've heard."

"A hool?"

"Big, tough, stupid, dirty, likes to lair underground. If you can imagine a solitary giant orc—"

"I thought hools were water giants," said Ambros.

Arvid shrugged. "Maybe I'm wrong. Whatever it is, it's dead. And we have just announced ourselves to the entire underground."

"I never did think trying to sneak in was a good idea," said Ambros. "Gird is not subtle."

Arvid raised one brow, and smiled. "No. That's why I'm not a Girdsman. But don't worry—you'll have every chance for a suicidal frontal assault now."

Paks had been poking gingerly through the trash heap that the creature had laired on. A copper armband gleamed; she picked it up. "Look. This is human-size."

"Hmm. Not worth much," said Arvid.

"No, but—I wouldn't have thought the robbers would throw it away."

"That's true. I—" Suddenly he stopped. They had all heard the sound: a rhythmic pounding, not loud, but distinct. Paks looked around. In flickering candlelight, the room was large, dim in the corners. A doorway opened across from the way they'd come in, and another door, closed and barred, centered the right-hand wall. Otherwise the room seemed empty.

"It's that door—the closed one," said Mai. He wrenched his axe free of the creature's backbone and started for it. Paks was there first, sword drawn. Arvid and Mai levered the heavy bars up and threw them aside. Then they pulled the door open.

Candlelight showed a small room, hardly more than a cell. A gnome, one shoe off, was poised by the door; his shoe was in his hand, where he'd been pounding the door. Another gnome lay on the bare stone floor, covered in cloaks.

The standing gnome nodded stiffly and put his shoe back on. Then he addressed Paks in gnomish. She shook her head, and he frowned, then spoke in clipped accented Common.

"It is that you lead this rescue? Or do you claim us prisoners?"

"I—" Paks looked sideways at Arvid. He spoke.

"Lady Paksenarrion commanded us for the capture of the robbers, and now we have come to see what else hides in this keep."

The gnome bowed from the waist, and met Paks' eyes as he stood upright. "It shall be that you have the reward of the Aldonfulk, lady. For this indeed shall value be given. It is that our partner of Lyonya is eaten by that monster, true?"

"We haven't seen him," said Paks, thinking of the armring with a shudder. "Is that what you think happened?"

"It took him. It seemed hungry. We heard cries. We could see nothing; I will not say what happened when I have not knowledge, but that is logical."

"Is your friend hurt?" The gnome on the floor had not moved.

"Only slightly—he was hit by arrow of robbers. He sleeps to gain strength."

Paks was surprised by the gnome's composure. Despite days of imprisonment in a dark cell, the death of one companion and the wounds of another, the gnome was calm and matter-of-fact. He turned to the other gnome, and spoke loudly in gnomish. Paks could not understand a word of it. She looked around to see if the others did, but they looked as blank as she felt. The gnome on the floor stirred, and opened his eyes.

"Surely you are hungry or thirsty," said Paks, counting how many days they'd been imprisoned. "We have water and food."

The response was less than she'd expected; the unwounded gnome nodded and came forward. "It is not so bad as you thought. The robbers brought food the first day or so. They fed the creature something too. Then they were gone. Then we had nothing. You will take us back to Brewersbridge?"

Paks handed him her water flask; the gnome uncapped it carefully and carried it to the other, who drank a few swallows. Then the first gnome drank. "We need not so much food as you," he said, returning the flask. "If you take us now—"

"But we haven't found the priest," said Ambros.

"Priest?" asked the gnome.

"We believe that a servant of Achrya is nearby—perhaps deep in this place—and directed the robbers."

"Oh." The gnomes looked at each other. "It is a matter for humans. We are not daskdusky, to search after the webspinner's lair. If return to Brewersbridge, the return of your favor will be granted."

"We might as well," said Arvid. "We've lost all chance of surprise."

"And we can't leave these behind us," said Paks. "They can't defend themselves, with one of them wounded, and weakened as they are. We should get them to safety."

"I agree," said Mai. He had a large swelling bruise across his forehead. Paks realized that the axe-haft must have hit him on the face. "I don't know as I can fight as good as most days." Ambros looked at him in surprise, then concern. His voice seemed slurred.

"Will your friend need to be carried?" asked Paks.

The gnome bowed again, and gave Paks a small tight smile. "It is generous of the lady to think of that. If it is possible, he should not walk so far."

In the end, they came back to Brewersbridge that same evening, with the two gnomes alive and well, and clear evidence of the human trader's death. Ambros and Mai hacked off the creature's right hand and an ear as proof of what they'd found. The gnomes took rooms at the Jolly Potboy—they were well-known enough that Hebbinford trusted their credit. Paks, her clothes still stained with blood, found Suli dogging her every step.

"Did I—I mean, I couldn't get through the hide, but did I do all right otherwise? I didn't scream, or anything—"

Paks felt tired. "No. You did fine, Suli—I said that—"

"Yes, but—you are going back, aren't you? You'll let me come? And I can take your clothes, now, and get Sevri to wash them—"

"No!" It came out harsher than she meant it, and Suli looked worried. Not frightened, Paks noticed, but worried.

"But—"

"Sevri has her own duties—she's not a washing maid. I'll do it; any soldier learns to keep her own gear clean." Paks could see that this was not pleasant news to Suli. She nodded, remembering her own feelings during training. "I told you before, Suli—being a warrior's not what you thought. Most of it is like this—cleaning gear, and keeping weapons in trim, and practice. If you don't do it yourself you can't be sure it's done right."

The girl nodded, and leaned against the wall, evidently planning to stay until she was tossed out.

"Your own sword, for instance," said Paks severely. "Have you inspected it yet? Is it clean? Have you taken care of any nicks or dents? It's the grange's sword—you should return it in perfect condition."

Suli reddened, and pulled it from the scabbard—sticky with drying blood and hair.

"Go clean that," said Paks. "When you've got all the blood off, then polish it, and clean the scabbard. If you leave all that muck in the scabbard, then—"

"But how?" asked Suli. "It's inside, and—"

Paks took the scabbard and looked. Unlike hers, this one was a simple wood casing, pegged in several places and glued along the edges. The upper end was notched for attachment to a belt.

"You're lucky. This is all wood. Take some wet grass or sedge—sedges are better—and tie them to a limber switch, and scrub inside with that. Then run clean water in and out of it. That should do. Set it in a cool place to dry—don't put the sword back inside, or it'll rust. If it smells clean tomorrow, you're done. Otherwise you may have to take it apart."

"Seems a lot of trouble, just to get a bloodstain off," grumbled Suli. Paks glared at her, sure now of her ground.

"Trouble! You don't know what trouble is, until you leave something to rot in your scabbard, and then nick yourself with dirty steel." She remembered the surgeons talking about wound fever, and poisoned weapons. "It's the way some tribes of orcs poison weapons, Suli. Store 'em in rotting flesh and blood." She was glad to see the girl turn green and turn to go without further argument. "Check with Ambros at the grange later this evening—you'll need to pick up another scabbard, and he can tell you where and when to meet us."

"Yes, Paks," said Suli, subdued.

Paks had just finished cleaning up, with her wet clothes hanging behind the kitchen, and her wet hair still chilly on her head, when Hebbinford came to tell her the gnomes wanted a word with her.

"Why?" she asked.

"Gird knows," he said. "Being as it's gnomes, it's some trading matter, I'd say. Remember that they're as full of pride as bees of sting—and as quick with it, too. They don't like jokes, and they don't like someone misjudging them on their size. Gnomes see everything as exchange—good for good, and blow for blow. They don't do favors, but they're perishing fair, if you can understand their idea of fair. And they never forget anything, to the ends of the world."

"Oh." Paks hoped they would understand ordinary courtesy as courtesy.

Both gnomes were seated before the fire in one of Hebbinford's private rooms when Hebbinford announced her. One jumped up and bowed. Paks made a sketchy bow in return. She thought she could see a gleam of satisfaction in that flat dark eye.

"Master Hebbinford if you would bring ale." The gnome gestured to a chair, and Paks sat; he returned to his own seat. His speech lacked the pauses and music of human language; Paks found it hard to follow, even though the words were pronounced correctly. "Is it that you were hired for our rescue?"

"No," said Paks, "not exactly."

"Then this rescue was in hope of reward?"

"No—what is it?"

"That is what I try to find out. For what service were you hired, if not for our rescue?"

Paks wondered how much she should say of the Brewersbridge Council's affairs. "Sir—pardon, if I do not know the correct address—" He took her up at once.

"Lady, it is our mistake. We thought you would not care to be precise. I am Master-trader Addo Verkinson Aldonfulk, sixth son of my father's house. The polite address in Common would be Master-trader Addo Aldonfulk, or Master Addo if in haste. This my companion is journeyman-trader Ebo Gnaddison Gnarrinfulk, the fourth son of my father's third sister. He should be styled Journeyman Ebo. And thine own naming?"

"Master-trader Addo—" Paks got that far before losing track. The gnome nodded anyway.

"That will do."

"—I am Paksenarrion Dorthansdotter of Three Firs—"

"Three Firs is thy clan?"

"No, Master-trader Addo, it is the place of my father's dwelling." Paks found her own speech becoming both stilted and formal.

"Ah. We know that some humans have no clans." He paused as Hebbinford himself returned with a large flagon of ale and three tankards. "Be welcome to ale as the guest of Aldonfulk, Paksenarrion Dorthansdotter; no obligation is thine for partaking of this gift."

Paks stared, then caught her wits back. "I thank you, Master-trader Addo." She took the tankard he offered, and sipped cautiously. "You asked of my employment, sir. The Council of Brewersbridge has, as you may know, a policy against idle swordsmen in the town."

The gnome nodded. "An excellent policy. Human towns are too lawless as it is and human vagabonds cause trouble. We allow no masterless humans in the gnome kingdoms."

Paks reddened, but went on. "Master-trader Addo, the Council examined me, and decided that I might stay some time, but they asked a favor."

"Favor! What is a favor?"

She remembered Hebbinford's warning. "Sir, my—my vows are to another; I am traveling from Aarenis to the far north." That seemed safe enough. The gnome relaxed in his chair. "But they asked my aid in finding the hiding place of a band of robbers—the same who attacked you—and asked that I lead a force against them if I could find them."

"And what pay did they offer for this?"

"Well—that I could stay longer than they would otherwise allow, and the use of a horse, and a share of goods recovered from the hideout, if there were any."

"Hmmph." The gnome chattered in gnomish with his companion. Paks could not tell how old they were, or if the journeyman were younger than the master. They had earth-brown, unwrinkled faces, and thick dark hair. Addo turned back to Paks. "It seems little payment for an uncertain task. How many days were you bound to stay and work at it?"

"No time was set. But I had money enough, and reason to dislike brigands."

"Hmm. And after our caravan was taken did they say aught about rescue?"

"No, Master-trader Addo. It was thought you had been killed with the others. One man escaped to tell of the attack. Many bodies were found."

"I see. Why then were you in the keep? To look for goods?"

"No. The robbers we captured said that someone else took over the goods. Ambros, the yeoman-marshal, thinks it is a priest of Achrya. Arvid Semminson says the goods are being sold at a distance."

"And you did not expect to find us."

"No, sir. But we were glad to find any that had survived."

Another conversation in gnomish. Paks finished the ale in her tankard, and thought about pouring another. But she felt constrained to wait until it was offered. Finally Addo turned to her again.

"If you did not come and search the keep would anyone else have come?"

"No, Master-trader Addo. Most people around here think it is bad luck."

"Superstition. Luck is a fallacy of humans; things either are or are not. That creature who ate our companion—was it dangerous to armed men?"

"Yes, sir. It was very large, and fought well; it took several of us to kill it."

"It is true you command this force?"

Paks frowned. "I would not want to mislead you, sir. I was asked to command, and did command, the force which killed and captured the robbers themselves. Today's foray was not entirely my idea—Yeoman-marshal Ambros insisted that it must be made at once. But because I have experience, I was at the head of the party."

Addo shook his head. "Even among humans, one must take command, and be responsible for all—I ask again if that was you or another. If another who would it be?" "I—in that way, sir, you could say I commanded." Paks thought it was not too great a boast—they had followed her orders, such as they were.

"You are not boastful as many human fighters are," he commented; she wondered if he could read her thoughts. "It is important to know who commands. It is the person the clans owe thanks to." He took a ring off his finger, and reached out to her. "At this time we have been robbed; we have nothing. But this is in earnest of your just claim on Aldonfulk and Gnarrinfulk; it shall be redeemed fairly, on my word as master-trader." Paks took the ring; it was black, like iron, and heavy. She nodded, wondering what to say.

"I thank you, Master-trader Addo Aldonfulk—and Journeyman Ebo."

"It is but right. You had no obligation; you had not been hired for this task. I ask your trust that this will be redeemed."

"Master-trader Addo, you have that trust. But I would free anyone from such captivity—"

"Oh?"

"It is right—"

"You have an obligation to a god? Are you sworn to such deeds, then?" He looked almost as if he might ask for the ring back.

"No, sir," said Paks. "But I serve the gods of my father's house, and they oppose evil."

"Umph. That is well, to stand with tradition. And such belief does not interfere with our owing. Keep the ring, Paksenarrion Dorthansdotter. You returned our lives."

"It was my pleasure to do so." Paks sat a moment; the gnomes were silent. "Would you," she ventured, "be my guest for another flagon of ale? With—with no obligation?" Both gnomes nodded.

"We would not willingly owe thee more," said Addo, "but it is mannerly of thee to offer. We will be thy guests."

Their brush with death had not discouraged Ambros at all. He insisted that they go again the next day. Mai grunted; he was purple from hairline to jaw where the axe-haft had caught him, and he breathed noisily.

"I wouldn't have said it before, Yeoman-marshal, but I'm still head-thick from this, and I don't trust my speed. A thick eye's bad enough in daylight."

"Then you can stay," said Ambros tartly. "I've other yeomen."

Mai sighed loudly. "By Gird's arm, Ambros, I'm willing enough, but—"

"Mai, I can't wait. I can't. Something bad is going on here—I have to deal with it."

"Ambros, we did well by scouting around before attacking the robbers," said Paks. "Why not look for the place where the goods are moving out? That might be a better way in." She was thinking of the tunnel at Rotengre.

"No." Ambros shook his head stubbornly. "It takes too long—let the priest think we were frightened back by that monster. It's a door-guard, I imagine."

"Certainly so," said Arvid.

"Then, when he knows we've killed it but have gone away, he may be careless for a space. A short space, in which we must strike."

Arvid looked at him curiously. "Are you angry, Yeoman-marshal, that I bade you stay back with the light?'

"I was," said Ambros frankly. "Then I realized that you had to have light to fight. This time we'll let another carry the flint—and another be prepared to light candle or torch for us as it's needed. Now—to plans."

The gnomes had told Paks the little they knew of the keep. They had seen only the passage and stairs which Paks had used. When one of the robbers banged on the door, a shuddering howl had arisen, and shortly after that six armed men in dark clothes had opened it from within, taken the prisoners, and shoved them in the cell. The gnomes thought these were the robber chiefs servants or personal guard. Ambros suspected they were servants of whatever power had snared the fugitives and forced them to banditry.

The next day, the stench from the open door was much worse. The dead creature was already swarming with vermin—in the light of the candles, a flurry of rats scuttered away, squeaking. Beyond, the open doorway gaped. Again, Paks and Arvid were in the lead. Ambros had found six yeomen to come with them, including Mai. Two of them carried lighted candles. Suli followed Paks closely.

Beyond the empty doorway, a passage sloped downhill, its rough stone floor heavy with dust churned by many feet. Paks could see and hear nothing. She glanced at Arvid.

"Let me lead," he said quietly. "Stay close, but don't pass me, and be ready to stop on my signal. It's the very place for some trap." He stepped forward. Paks waited until he was three paces ahead, and then followed. The passage went on for twenty paces—twenty more—then Arvid stopped. Paks caught his hand signal and froze in her tracks. Suli bumped her from behind. The others' footsteps seemed loud. Then silence, as they all stood still. Arvid was touching the side walls lightly. He looked back at Paks, and gestured her forward—one step. She took it. He pointed at the floor. She could see nothing, until he pointed again. A slight ridge in the dust, a ripple she would never have noticed. Where the feet had passed it, she could see an edge of stone.

"It's the trigger," he said softly. "If someone steps on that, then—" he pointed up. "That will fell." In the dimness overhead, Paks could make out a dark slit, and shining points. "A portcullis. It probably makes a noise, as well. There should be a safety block on one side, though, if they carry heavy goods through here. Ah-h." Paks could not see what he did, but a small block of stone suddenly slid out of the wall a handsbreadth. "That should do it. We might want to come out this way in a hurry. Meanwhile, make sure no one steps on the trigger stone."

Paks passed this information along, and everyone stepped carefully over the ridge. Arvid had gone on. He disarmed another such trap thirty paces farther on. "I expect," he said quietly to Paks, "that both would close together, and open arrow-slits in the walls as well. But we shall hope not to find out." After that, Paks kept her eyes roving on all sides, trying to spot traps—but she missed the next, after the passage turned and dipped steeply. Arvid halted at the top of the steepening ramp.

"Now this," he said, "may be a chute trap."

"What?"

"If you step on the trigger of a chute trap," he said, "it tips up and dumps you in someone's pot—or prison cell. It's the same. We're meant to go on—but you don't see footprints in that dust, do you?"

"No—but it's been disturbed—"

"Umm. More like something's been dragged on it. They may use it for the caravan goods—saves carrying. I'd rather arrive on my feet. We need another door."

Paks could see nothing but stone-walled passage. Arvid went over every stone with his long fingertips. The others fidgeted; Paks shushed them. Finally he tapped one section of wall and smiled. "This is the entrance. The trouble is that I don't know what's on the other side. They may have a guard right there—in which case, we're in trouble. It may be trapped to sound an alarm—I can't tell. But I judge it's a safer way down than that." He nodded at the chute.

"Well—we have to try something," said Paks. "Can you tell which way it opens?"

"No. I don't think it will rotate, like an ordinary door. It should either come forward or sink in, and then slide sideways. I can't tell which." He looked at her, challenging. Paks was determined to figure it out for herself.

"Well, then—you're the one who can open it. I'll cover you, on your left side. The rest of you move three paces back and stay flat against this wall—you won't get hit by arrows, if there's an archer, and you can see how it works. Shield the candles with your hands, in case of a strong draft. Anything else?" She looked at Arvid. He shook his head.

"You've a feel for this, lady," he said.

She heard a click as he worked the mechanism. The stone before him sank back; faint light came through the gap. Soundlessly the stone slid to the left. Behind it was a landing; stairs went down to the left, where the light brightened, and up to the right. Across the landing was an alcove; four cross-bows hung from pegs. Paks moved quickly through the opening, and looked both ways. Nothing. She signed to Arvid, who nodded and motioned the others in. He did something to the touchstone lock, and murmured that he hoped he'd jammed it open. His eyes slid to the crossbows. Paks quickly cut their strings. The two quivers of bolts she simply took and tied to her belt.

Down toward the light they crept, stair by stair. Halfway down, Paks could see that a passage led away ahead and another to the right. She motioned those behind her to the right-hand wall of the stair. Now she could see a door, closed, at the foot of the stairs to the left. Arvid stayed in the lead, one stair before her. At the foot, he stopped a long moment to scan the passage ahead and the foot of the stair itself. The forward passage ended in another closed door not twenty paces away, heavy wood bound with iron. Neither hinges nor bars showed on this side. The light they had seen came from torches in brackets on both sides of the passage: four ahead, and obviously more to the right. The flame-tips bent toward the left-hand door, and even on the stairs Paks could feel the draft that kept the air fresh.

Arvid put the tip of his sword past the corner. Nothing happened. Very slowly he eased his face to the corner. Paks waited, feeling her heart race. He drew back, and motioned her back a step. Then he spoke softly in her ear. "It goes twenty-thirty paces, then turns left. Wide enough for four fighters. Torch every four paces. Mark on floor, good for bow."

"Run it," suggested Paks.

"Only way," he agreed. "Got to be quiet and fast." Paks did not see how they could all be fast and silent, but she told the others. Ambros and another yeoman moved up beside her; she told Suli to stay in the second rank.

They started off at a quick jog, as quietly as possible. Paks saw the pale stripes on the floor, four of them, and stepped over the first. Then she heard a noise from somewhere ahead, and leaped into full speed, the others with her. Four crossbowmen appeared at the far end of the passage; the first flight of crossbow bolts whirred by. Paks heard a yelp from behind; something clicked on her helmet. Behind them four more, shooting even as the first four dropped their bows and leaped forward with shortsword in hand. Paks did not hesitate; it would be suicide to stop in that bare passage. She reached the first swordsmen before they were set in position; Arvid and Ambros were hardly behind her, and they forced the line back into the others. Now all eight defenders had dropped their bows. Paks had never faced a shortsword formation with a longsword. She found herself fighting as if she had her Company weapon. At least they didn't have shields—she smiled as her sword went home in one of them. He folded over, to lie curled on the floor. The man behind thrust at her, and she raked his arm. She noticed that Arvid, beside her, had downed another. The first man down tried to stab at her legs; Paks edged by, and Suli got him in the throat. Paks and Arvid were one step ahead of Ambros and the yeoman. Paks was beginning to think they might get through without too much trouble when four more men appeared.

"Blast!" said Arvid. "I'd hoped this was the first wave."

Paks said nothing, fighting her way forward a step at a time. She was beginning to use the longsword more freely, with effect. Another man went down before her, and those behind seemed less eager to engage. But the noise in the passage was considerable. Ambros was yelling Girdish slogans, as was the yeoman; each had now defeated his man, and they were back in line. The clash of steel rang from the walls.

Then the torches went out as if they'd been dipped in water. Paks felt something rake across her torso; the mail held. She thrust hard ahead of her, and heard someone grunt, then sigh. She shook the weight off her blade and thrust again. Nothing.

"Arvid?" she asked.

"Here." His voice beside her was calm. She wasn't.

Ambros cursed, off to Arvid's right. Paks could hear heavy breathing in front of them somewhere. She moved forward a step, and her boot landed on something soft and moving. She kicked, hard, and stepped back.

"Light," said Ambros testily. She could hear the scrape of flint and steel, but saw no spark.

"You want light, servant of Gird?" came a silky voice out of the dark ahead. "I thought you Girdsmen claimed the knowledge of lightspells."

Paks tried again to move toward the voice, but Arvid grabbed her arm. She froze in place. She could sense that he was fumbling in his cloak. As her eyes adjusted to the darkness, she could tell that somewhere around the bend torches were still burning—vague shapes stood out against that dim glow. She could not tell how many. If they were reloading crossbows—if they had spears—we're crazy to stand here, she thought, like sheep in a chute. With a wild yell, she jumped forward, a standing leap that took her to the first of the dark shapes. She heard Arvid's curse, the others jumping after her. Her sword clashed against another, suddenly glowing blue. She heard other weapons striking, and pressed her own opponent hard by instinct, since she could scarcely see. She felt a blow on her shoulder, and another on the ribs. Her own blade flickered, a dancing blue gleam that lit only its target. Something raked her free hand, burning like fire or ice. She shook it, still fencing.

Their surprise attack brought them around the turn of the passage, over bodies now crumpled beneath the fighters. Ahead was a short stretch with a door to the right. Against the golden glow from that door stood a tall, slender robed figure. They were within four paces of it, when that same smooth voice spoke, a word Paks had not heard before. Her muscles slackened, as if she had been hit in the head; she nearly dropped her sword. Arvid fell back a pace. Even Ambros stopped where he was, and dropped the tip of his blade. The defenders leaped forward.

"Gird!" cried Ambros, in that instant. Paks felt her body come alive again; she covered Arvid's side with a desperate lunge, and took a glancing blow on her helmet. Suli pushed past Arvid, throwing a quick glance at Paks, and lunged at the man before her. Paks had time to notice that she was indeed quick, and quite good. Then the defenders retreated past the door, and turned to run. Paks faced the doorway. It was empty.

Within, the steady glow of lamplight revealed a chamber hung with rich tapestries in brilliant colors. In the center of the chamber stood a handsome young man in long black velvet robes edged with black fur. He smiled at them, and held out empty hands.

"Don't you think you're being discourteous?" he asked. His voice was mellow as old ale. "It is friendlier to announce oneself, don't you think?"

"You—!" began Ambros. Paks noticed Suli edging forward and plucked at her sleeve. Suli turned, frowning, but obeyed when Paks gestured her back. "Spawn of Achrya," Ambros went on. The man laughed easily.

"Alas, young sir yeoman-marshal of Gird, I am not Achrya's spawn—if I were, you might have found another welcome. 'Tis true I have done her some service, but—what is that to thee?"

"I am the yeoman-marshal—"

"Yes, of Brewersbridge. This is not Brewersbridge. This is my keep, and you have broken in, attacking and killing my men—and you are not even the Marshal. It's not your grange."

"It is. It was left in my care. And you—corrupting men, robbing caravans, killing and looting—Gird's teeth, it's my business!" Ambros took a step forward, toward the doorway.

"So you really think a yeoman-marshal of Gird is a match for me? Or are you relying on your muscle-bound women for protection?" Suli lunged forward, and Paks caught her in the midriff with a stiff elbow. Suli gasped, and Paks spoke over her shoulder.

"Don't be a fool, he's trying to anger us. Stay back."

The man looked directly at her. Something about his gaze warned her, and she dropped her eyes. "My," he said sweetly, "a wise head rules that magic sword. Perhaps you are not what you seem, eh? I had heard of a strange lady swordfighter in Brewersbridge—a veteran of Phelan's Company, they said, who left because she would not see evil done. Is that you, then?" Paks fought back a surge of rage that roared in her ears and threatened to haze her vision. "Defeated that elven mage, and freed the elfane taig, that's what I heard. Near enough a paladin, I should think—not a Girdsman yet, what a shame—if, that is, you defeat me. Do you think to defeat me, pretty one?"

This too Paks ignored, fixing her gaze on his throat. She thought how she would like to sink her sword in it. But she heard what he said. Near enough a paladin? The thought beckoned, like a finger in the mist. But Arvid spoke up, having regained his position beside her.

"You, sir, seem to have some power of enchantment, or why do we stand here speaking to you? For me, I would see your blood on that handsome rug, and put an end to such delay." He moved forward a handsbreadth and stopped, as if he'd hit a wall.

"Enchantment? Yes, indeed. And, since you've robbed me of robbers and guards alike, I'm in need of servants. You, I believe, will do nicely. And the women; Achrya will be pleased if I interfere in the growth of a paladin of Gird. I hope, indeed, to convert all of you. How pleasant it will be to have spies in the grange of Brewersbridge."

"No! By Gird!" Ambros leaped forward, sword high. Paks shook herself, suddenly alert to her musings, and followed him. She was not surprised to see a sword appear in the man's hand, a dagger in the other. Ambros met the sword with his own, narrowly missing a dagger thrust. Paks came in on the Achryan's sword side. She turned his blade and thrust. Her blade seemed to stick in his robes; she jerked it free with an effort. Meanwhile his blade had raked her shoulder. She could feel the links of mail along that track.

No one else came to join them. As the priest of Achrya turned, Paks had time for a quick glance back. The others stood motionless, clearly unable to break free. Meanwhile the priest fought superbly, sweeping away their blades again and again. It seemed impossible to wound him. Every thrust that Paks thought went home caught in his robes, and he fought on unhindered. She did not notice that he worked them toward a corner of the room where dark blue velvet rose behind a carved black chair. He backed, backed again, turned, and grabbed for the chair arm. Paks, hearing a rustle above, jerked back and looked up. A tangled mass of black webbing fell down, catching her off balance. Where it touched her clothes, they turned black, charring. She slashed at the cords, her sword hissing as it sliced them. But they were tough and sticky; she could not free herself quickly.

Ambros had jumped forward, a long lunge at the priest, and the web caught only one foot. Before the priest could strike, he had cut himself free. Now they fought behind the chair, great sweeps of sword parting the air and ringing together.

"You might as well quit," the priest said. "You can't win now—two of you couldn't defeat me."

"Gird's grace," said Ambros between clenched teeth. "I won't quit—I will kill you."

"I think not, boy," said the priest with a smile. He made a gesture toward Ambros' face, and a length of something gray flicked at him.

Ambros blinked but kept fighting. "You're a stubborn fool, boy—are you hunting your death?" Paks struggled with the web, hardly aware of the Company curses she shouted. She could see the blisters rising on Ambros' face, like the mark of a fiery whip. The priest spared her a look. "You won't get clear of that in a hurry, sweetling. 'Tis made of Achrya's own webs. As is this—" He lashed once more at Ambros' face. The yeoman-marshal screamed, one hand clawing at his face. "You see, boy, what you drive me to? Why will you not submit?"

Somehow Ambros had kept hold of his sword; Paks could see that the blow had caught his eye. He fought on, with less skill now, his movements jerky. Paks sawed frantically at the web, cursing again when it touched her bare skin; it burned like fire. The priest said something, a string of words she did not know, and the web moved, shifting around her, so that the cut strands were out of reach. Ambros called to her.

"Paks—call on Gird! With me—" he gave a sharp cry of pain as the priest's gray whip touched him again.

Paks opened her mouth to say something else, and found herself yelling, "By the power of Gird Strongarm, and the High Lord, and all the gods of right—" Ambros, too, was yelling, holding his Girdish medallion now with one hand, as he flung himself on the priest. Light flared around them; Paks could hardly see, in the flurry of movement, what happened. Then the web lay still around her, and nothing moved in the heap of robes behind the chair. And the rest of the party, suddenly freed, ran forward full of questions and noise.

CHAPTER SEVENTEEN

Suli grabbed the web strands that bound Paks, then yanked her hand back as welts rose on her palm. Arvid ran past Paks to look at Ambros and the priest.

"He's dead," he said shortly.

"Both?" asked Mai.

"Yes. Both." Arvid sighed, then turned back to help Paks and Suli hack the web apart. "Lady, that's a dire trap you're caught in."

"I know." Paks was hardly able to speak for mingled anger and shame—Ambros was dead, and she had not been able to fight. She kept cutting grimly, until finally she could step out of the web. Her clothes were charred to rags, and Arvid looked at her mail with respect.

"That's . . . very good mail you're wearing."

"Yes—" Paks touched one of the burns on her face gingerly, and went to look at Ambros' body. The priest's gray lash had laced blistered welts across his face. Together, she and Mai straightened his body, wrapping his cloak around it. Arvid and the other yeoman stood watch at the door, but no sound came from the corridor. Paks suspected that with their master dead, and his control broken, the men they'd fought had fled, either to the surface at once, or to deeper hiding places. Suli roamed the room idly, staring at the tapestries, then stooped over the dead priest's body.

"Look at this," she said, lifting a silver chain around the dead priest's neck. "It's got—"

"Drop that!" Paks remembered the cleric of Achrya in Rotengre. "It's magic."

Suli looked startled, and dropped it less quickly than Paks intended. But nothing happened.

Paks could not define what she felt. She had not wanted to go back underground; she had not wanted to meet another evil mage. But she liked Ambros, had gotten used to his cheerful face. When he told her the dream, she felt his trust in her—and as always, gave trust for trust in return. In a vague way, she had hoped—and made herself believe—that what they might face under the keep was not nearly so bad as the possessed elf-lord had been. She thought Ambros' dream was the dream of an untried soldier, a recruit thinking too much of the coming battle.

Now he was dead. She had failed him. She, the seasoned soldier, had not been able to fight. The untried recruit, the boy (as she thought of him), had fought on, alone, and died without her aid. He was as dead as Macenion, as Saben, two others she had not saved. As she took the precautions she knew to take—setting a watch, planning their return to the upper level—her mind was roiling with confusion. Only after they were on their way did she start thinking what her position might be. What Sir Felis would think. What the Marshal would think. What everyone would think, when their yeoman-marshal was dead and the experienced fighter let herself be trapped in a net. She did not know how grim her expression was until Arvid spoke.

"Lady? Do you foresee some trouble I do not? Your sorrow for the yeoman-marshal, yes, but—what else?"

Paks shook her head. "I did it all wrong."

"All wrong?" Arvid looked at her with obvious surprise. "We went against a larger force, on their ground, and lost one dead and a few are wounded, and you think you did it all wrong? By Simyits' eyebrow, lady, we could all be dead."

"No thanks to me that we aren't."

"Nonsense. You forget that you fought that priest, too. Quite well, I might add—and you were right to jump lead in the dark when you did. I only thought afterward that if flint and steel wouldn't spark, then my oil flask robably wouldn't burn anyway. That young man died bravely, but not because you failed. Though I expect you won't miss an overhead net trap again."

Paks shook her head, but felt a little better. The others said nothing, but smiled at her shyly when she looked at them and tried to smile herself. They were at ground level again when Arvid beckoned her aside.

"I'll be saying farewell," he said with a smile. "Good luck to you, Lady Paksenarrion—you have the makings of a great warrior. You're already a good one. Keep thinking on all sides of a question—"

"But what do you mean, are you going?"

"Yes."

"But why?"

"My work is done," he said with a shrug. "I was hired, as I said, to kill or convince the fellow to join the Guild. In my judgement, he would have made a poor member, even if he had been willing to join. I have seen him dead, and I have taken enough value to repay the Guild some of what it lost by his unlicensed theft." Paks had not seen him take anything; while she was still sorting that out, he dipped into a pocket and handed something to her. "Here—a gift for you. Unlike your gnomish friends, I prefer to pay my debts at once." Paks felt a handful of small round objects through the thin leather of her glove. "No—don't look now. Gratitude bores me. You see, I don't think I'd like to explain everything to the Marshal—or have another talk with Sir Felis. You have enough witnesses to your actions; I need none for mine, if I go now." He lifted her hand, still clenched around his gift, to his lips; Paks had never seen or imagined such a gesture. Before she could say anything, he had dropped it and moved lightly away, not looking back. She stuffed the handful, still unseen, into a pocket in her tunic, and turned to the others.

"And if I say it's the most preposterous thing I've ever heard? Ambros, at his age, to go haring off after a priest of Achrya! You, to let him—!" The Marshal, brows bristling in fury, strode back and forth in the grange, hands thrust into his belt. Paks, Mai, and the other yeomen stood against the wall; Ambros' body lay on the platform, still wrapped in his cloak.

"Marshal, if I may—" Sir Felis looked almost as angry as the Marshal. The Marshal stopped in midstride, balanced himself, and nodded shortly. Sir Felis looked at all their faces before he spoke. "Marshal, when he told me what he planned, I thought as you. A fool's plan, I told him. I think—I think I was wrong."

"Wrong! With him dead, and—"

"Wait, Marshal. I told him he had no experience. I told him that orders were orders. I insulted her"—he nodded at Paks—"and told him he was a fool to go anywhere with a thief and a mercenary. And then he told me, Marshal, that his orders came not only from you but from Gird."

The Marshal's face contracted, showing wrinkles it would not bear for many years. "It wasn't—"

"I didn't think it was Gird. I told him that, too—that too many youngsters thought the gods blessed their folly. But, Marshal—I think I said too much. Gird graces the hard head, as well as the strong arm. He was angry, at me, and that made him—"

"Maybe not." The Marshal sighed. "If it was Gird, if it wasn't just a childish stunt—" He looked at the others. "What do you know about this? Were you all in it with him—did he think it up—or what?" For a moment no one answered. Then Mai, his voice still distorted by the bruises on his face, spoke up.

"Sir Marshal, Ambros was determined to find the priest as soon as he came back from talking to the robbers. He told me then that Paks thought he should wait for you—but he was sure that he couldn't."

"Is that true, Paksenarrion? Did you try to dissuade him?"

Paks nodded. "Yes, sir. When he first told me, on the way back from the keep, I thought he was crazy." She felt the blood rush to her face, and glanced down. "I—he had told me, sir, of a dream, a few days before. He dreamed he was killed, in some battle. It was the day after you left."

"Did he think it was a true dream?"

"He wasn't sure. He asked me—I didn't know. He thought it might be an evil sending to frighten him from doing what he should. That's what finally made him do this, sir, I'm sure. I tried—I tried to tell him it could be a warning from Gird—or something like that—but he thought he had to find out."

"But why couldn't he wait? At least a few days—" The Marshal looked toward Ambros' body.

"He—he thought it must be soon, sir." Paks felt the tears burning in her eyes. She hoped Ambros would not mind her telling the dream now. "He could see—in the dream—the marks I gave him that last night at drill. The cut hadn't healed." The Marshal nodded, silent. Then he looked at the others.

"Did he tell any of you this dream?"

"No, sir." They answered in a ragged chorus. Mai went on. "I knew something was wrong, sir—he didn't say about the dream, but when I said something about not being in best shape to fight, he took me up on it and said I should stay behind."

The discussion had dragged on for hours. Finally the Marshal dismissed them, having, as it seemed, worn out his anger. Paks was so tired she could hardly walk, but her mind kept buzzing at her. She made it to the inn, and up the stairs, without a word to anyone. Stretched on her bed, still wearing her armor, she wondered what she'd done with her horse, and was too tired to get up and find out. She thought she would never go to sleep. Cold air rolled over her from the window. At last she managed to pull a blanket over her and slept.

Dawn was gray and foggy. She had left the shutters open; the floor near the window was wet and cold. Paks looked at the beads of moisture with narrowed eyes; she didn't want to move. She heard noises from the rest of the inn, footsteps and voices. Her legs hurt. Her shoulder ached. Something was poking a hole in her side. It was that which finally moved her—that hard lumpy something that seemed to be underneath a rib no matter how she squirmed. In one rush she threw back the blanket and staggered to her feet. Her boots skidded on the wet floor as she reached for the shutters.

The remains of her clothes hung on the fine chainmail like old leaves on a shapely branch. Only the leather tunic was whole, though scarred by the net as if it had been touched by flame. She ripped the rags free, glad she had worn her old clothes for that trip, rather than the new ones. She slid out of the mail, noticing as she did a lumpy pocket in her tunic. Arvid's present. She reached into it and pulled out a handful of fire.

After a moment, she could see what it really was. A string—several strings, interconnected—of fiery jewels, some white and some blue. It poured through her hand like sunlit waterdrops. The clasp was gold. She stared, openmouthed, then tucked it quickly away. When she opened the door, she nearly fell over Suli, who was curled up asleep outside.

"It won't work," said Paks firmly. She avoided Suli's eyes, tracing a design on the table with one finger. "It won't work because I'm not what you hoped for—and it's not as easy as you think."

"I know it's not," said Suli. "I know—I saw Ambros die—it was terrible!" Paks shot a glance at her; the girl's face was solemn. "I still want it—even though I know—and I don't see why you won't—"

"You *don't* know!" Paks lowered her voice after that. "Suli, if you think that was bad—one man dead, and quickly dead—you don't know anything." She thought of Effa's broken back, of Captain Ferrault at Dwarfwatch. "You think because you've survived a couple of fights—difficult fights, yes, I'll grant you—that you're ready—"

"Just to be your squire," pleaded Suli. "I know I couldn't earn my way yet, as a soldier. But you could teach me—"

"I don't know enough myself. No, don't argue. I know what a private in the Duke's Company knows, and a little more. You think it's a lot—that's because you don't know—" Paks broke off, shaking her head. Would this have convinced her, the year she left home? Would anything convince Suli, now glaring at the table? She could feel that stubborn resolution as if it were a flame. She tried again. "Suli, I do think you can be a good soldier. You are strong, fast, and fairly skilled. More skilled than I was when I left home. I'm not trying to keep you from becoming a fighter. If you don't want to join a mercenary company, try one of the guards' units. Or ask Marshal Cedfer about training in the Fellowship. But all I can teach is fighting skills, and I'm finding out how much more I need. Why, when I first came, I'd never stayed in an inn before—"

"That's why I don't want to join a company," said Suli. "Staying all together, never on my own. I already know how to live on my own—and I can help you with that."

"You fight too much," Paks said. She had heard that from Mai and the others. Suli blushed. Paks went on. "My old sergeant said soldiers were fools to get in brawls. Most folk don't like soldiers anyway, and you get a reputation for causing trouble, they're glad enough to see you in the lockup or sold to slavers."

"We don't have any slavers here," muttered Suli.

"No, but you've got a lockup." Paks drained her mug. "Look, Suli, that's beside the point. It's not you. It's me. I'm not ready to take on someone to train. I was looking for more training for myself. If I were just adventuring, it'd be different, but I'm not. I want—"

"But I'll never have another chance," Suli burst out. "Nobody pays any attention—I'm just a crazy girl, that's what they think. I thought you would help—you're a woman, after all—and I'll never get out of this place if you don't—"

Paks slapped the table. "That's just what I've been telling you, Suli. How to get out and get the training you need. But you don't want to do it the right way. You want it to come all at once. I can see it in your eyes—you look at my sword, and my mail, and that big horse, and see yourself. What you don't see is the years in between, the years it took me to get all that. And there's no other way. Yes, I was lucky—I got some of it by a lucky chance. But the experience, the fighting skill, no. That came from years of just what you say you don't want—daily drill, daily work, battles that you call dull. That's what gave me the skill to take a chance when it came. You can't just leap from being a village girl with a knack for swordplay to—" she paused, uncertain how she would describe herself honestly.

"It could happen," said Suli. "It could. If you had found someone before you joined the company, she could have taught you everything you needed. You might have been rich and famous before now."

"I might have been dead before now, too. And Suli, knowing what I know now, I wouldn't have hired myself back then. It took the Duke's recruit company months to train any of us."

"But I've been training, with the Marshal. You've seen me—I'm not a beginner."

Paks sighed. She wondered if she had seemed so—so young, when she'd joined the Company. All that eagerness. At least she had taken Jornoth's advice, had not just run away to search for adventure on her own. She was trying to frame an answer, aware of Suli's intense gaze, when a shadow fell on her. She looked around. One of the senior yeoman nodded to her.

"Lady Paksenarrion? Marshal Cedfer would like to speak with you in the grange." He smiled at Suli, who reddened. "They say, Suli, that you fought well with this lady."

"She did," said Paks.

"We'll have to see about transferring you to the senior rolls," said the man to Suli. "Might make a yeoman-marshal, might she?" he asked of Paks.

"I—don't know how you choose yeoman-marshals, but Suli is a good swordsman." Paks stood up. "If you'll excuse me, I'll get my cloak—" The yeoman sat down and began talking to Suli; Paks was relieved.

The Marshal's office was slightly cold; Paks wondered why he had lit no fire in the small fireplace. Then she saw that the Kuakgan stood leaning in the corner, quiet as a shadow.

"Come in, Paksenarrion," said the Marshal. "We've been talking about you." She glanced quickly at the Kuakgan, who said nothing. What had they said? The last talks with the Marshal had been painful enough; she knew he no longer blamed her for Ambros' death, but she still blamed herself a little. She sat down when he gestured at a chair; the Kuakgan moved forward to take another.

"You will be wondering why," the Marshal went on. "I, as you know, would like to see you join the Fellowship of Gird. As a Marshal of Gird, I am interested in all soldiers, as well as the cause of right. In your case, something more moves me. It is for this that I contacted the Kuakgan, and talked with him about you."

"Yes, sir," said Paks, when he paused as if for some comment. She didn't know what else to say.

"Before we go on, would you mind telling me whether you have accepted Suli's service? I know she wants to be your squire, or some such—she's been wanting a way out of Brewersbridge for the last three years."

"Marshal Cedfer, I was talking to her when your yeoman asked me to come here. I don't—I know I'm not a knight, and have no way to use a squire. I'm not a wandering free sword—which she seems to think—and I don't need a companion. I told her that."

"Have you any complaint of her?"

"No. None at all. She fought bravely against the hool, as I told you, and did well against the priest's guards. But sir—she's not ready to be a soldier, I don't think. And I'm not the one to train her. I need more training myself, to be what—what I'd like."

"Do you know what that is, Paksenarrion?" asked the Kuakgan.

"No—not exactly." Every time she tried to imagine herself in some noble's troops—even the Tsaian Royal Guard—the picture blurred and blew away. "Not a mercenary—what people think of as a mercenary. Not a caravan guard the rest of my life."

"A knight?" asked Marshal Cedfer. "A captain, perhaps?"

"Maybe." Paks looked at her hands. "I am a soldier, I enjoy swordplay, I want to be in that kind of life. But not just for—for fighting anything, or for show. I want to fight—"

"What needs fighting?" suggested the Kuakgan.

Paks looked at him and nodded. "I think that's what I mean. Bad things. Like the robbers in Aarenis that killed my friends, or Siniava—he was evil. Or that—whatever that held the elf-lord. Only I don't think I have the powers for that. But I want to fight where I'm sure it's right—not just to show that I'm big and strong. It's the same as tavern brawling, it seems to me—even if it's armies and lords—"

The Kuakgan nodded. "You've learned a lot, Paksenarrion, besides what most soldiers know. I thought so before, but now I'm sure. Do you know anything of the rangers in Lyonya?"

"No." Paks frowned. "Why?"

"You have fought with the elfane taig. It may be that you can sense the taigin, and if so you would be able to work with them."

"Master Oakhallow—" the Marshal began. The Kuakgan waved him to silence.

"Marshal, I don't question the sincerity of Girdsmen. You know that. We honor the same gods. But some fighters have abilities Gird does not use. She may be one of them." He turned back to Paks. "Paksenarrion, we agree that you have shown ability to fight evil. You have shown a desire to know more of good, and to fight for it. We both think you have been touched by the evil you've fought—not to contaminate you, but in such wise that you should not go back to ordinary soldiering. Do you agree?"

Paks was too bewildered to answer. Marshal Cedfer spoke up.

"Paksenarrion, when you came you said your Duke had recommended additional training—even toward a captaincy. We are prepared to guide you toward such training, but you must choose. I can give you a letter to the Marshal-General at Fin Panir; she will probably take my recommendation and let you study with the training order there. From that you can become a knight in either of the two Girdish orders—or even a paladin, if Gird's grace touches you."

"And I can give you introduction to the rangers of Lyonya," said the Kuakgan. "If you satisfied them, they might recommend you to the Knight-Commander of the Knights of Falk. That would be a few years away, however. But in either case, you would use your skills only in causes of good. If that way of fighting did not appeal, you could always leave."

"You could not take Suli with you, either way," said the Marshal. "That's why I asked. If you had contracted with her, the gnome merchants have told me that they can get you a contract from the gnome prince of Gnarrinfulk. Something in the way of soldiering, I don't know what. But if you aren't taking Suli, then—" He stopped and cocked his head, waiting for her answer.

"But I'm not Girdish," she managed to say. Nothing else came out.

"No. But I daresay that in Fin Panir, at the High Lord's Hall, after training with others of the faith, that Gird would make plain his interest in you." The Marshal leaned back a little in his chair. "I think he has already, Paksenarrion. When I think of the things you have come through—" Paks thought to herself that he didn't know the half of it. She had not told him all about Aarenis. She remembered what the priest of Achrya had said: "Near enough a paladin... Achrya will be pleased if I interfere in the growth of a paladin of Gird..." And the training at Fin Panir was famous throughout the north. She might become a knight—or even a paladin—she pushed the thought away. It was for the gods to think of such things, not a soldier. But the other way. Rangers—she knew nothing of them. The thought of more powers like the elfane taig daunted her, though she hated to admit it. And years of service, before she might think of the Knights of Falk.

She looked at the Kuakgan again, meeting his dark eyes squarely. "Sir—Master Oakhallow—I honor you—"

"I know that, child," he said, smiling.

"If you have a—" she stopped, knowing what she meant, but not how to say it. If he demanded it, in return for releasing her from guilt for the snowcat's murder, she would go. She saw understanding in his eyes.

"I have no commands for you, Paksenarrion," he said softly. "You have served Brewersbridge well; you have fulfilled my trust in you, and my hope for you. Go with my blessings, whichever way you go."

"Then—" she looked back at the Marshal. Was it for Ambros, who had trusted her with his fears and died beyond her help? Was it for Canna, who had left her the medallion? Or for something else, something she felt dimly and could not define? "I would be glad, sir, of your recommendation," she said formally. The Marshal shot a triumphant glance at the Kuakgan; Paks nearly took her words back. But the Kuakgan's smile was open and friendly. He spoke to her alone.

"Paksenarrion, the Kuakkganni treasure all life created in the first song. We study, we learn, but we do not order a creature from its own way. And the creature itself knows its own way best, unless it is sorely hurt. If the other way had been best for you, you would have known." He turned back to the Marshal. "Marshal Cedfer, we are no more rivals than two men who plant a seed neither of them knows, and argue until it sprouts whether it will be fireoak or yellowwood. The seed knows itself; it will grow as its nature demands, and when the first leaves open, all arguments are over."

To Paks' surprise, the Marshal looked shamefaced. "You're right, Master Oakhallow. I have no right—but I was hoping so, for some good to come of Ambros' death." The Kuakgan nodded gravely. "And yet you know that good has come of it. The webspinner's priest is gone, and you will clean that filthy place from end to end. Ambros has shown that your training prepares untried lads for the worst of wars, and the best of ends. You live in constant combat, Marshal, and it makes you alert to each advantage—but the gods move in longer cycles, as well. Be at peace, honest warrior." He rose and left the room. For a long silent time, Paks and Marshal Cedfer sat in quiet, contented. Then the Marshal shook himself like a wet puppy and snorted.

"Girds grace, that fellow could cast a spell on stone. He may have time enough, but I live a normal span, like any man. Paksenarrion, I will write my letter this afternoon. When will you be fit for travel?"

"In a day or so. I'd like to get everything cleaned up."

"Good. I think you should not linger; winter will close some roads soon, and it makes bitter traveling to the northwest. About Suli—do you want me to talk to her?"

"I told her she should talk to you, but she—"

"She doesn't want it; she knows what I'll say. I've said it before. All right. I'll say it again. I can send her to another grange—a larger one—with more women training. Let her know what she can work towards—yeoman-marshal, or something like that. Tell her to come, if you see her."

Paks wondered if it would help, but said she would.

CHAPTER EIGHTEEN

As autumn darkened into winter, Paks rode north and west, into Vérella of the Bells, and west along the Honnorgat, through one town after another, as the river narrowed. She passed from grange to grange, enjoying the hospitality of each, as the Marshal's letter opened the doors. As she neared Fintha, she tried to think of a more elegant name for the black horse, something suitable for a warhorse, but she had thought of him as Socks from the first, and it stuck in her mind. She thought of turning aside at Whitemeadow, and following a branch of the river north to Rocky Ford, and then on to Three Firs. But had her dowry arrived yet? Would she be welcome? She decided to wait until she had her knighthood, and ride home with Gird's crescent on her arm.

Frost whitened the ground the morning she first caught sight of Fin Panir. She had been on the road before dawn, the saddle cold as iron beneath her, and her breath pluming out before. When the sun rose into a clear cola sky, the ground sparkled in rose and gold; the tree branches interlacing overhead were glittering with frost. It was like riding inside a pearl. A little wind blew the sparkling frost in swirls before her. Paks found herself grinning, and nudged the black horse into a trot. He squealed and kicked out behind before settling down. She laughed aloud.

Then the forest broke apart, and she saw across a bend of the river the spires of the High Lord's Hall, gleaming in silver and gold against the blue sky. Beneath was a tangle of roofs and walls, multi-colored stone, tiles, sliced into fantastic shapes by the sharp shadows of a winter sun. Fin Panir was a walled city, but walled like none Paks had seen, with multiple angles in and out. She rode toward it, yearning.

Within an hour she was near enough to pick out the gates. Between her and the walls, a small company of horsemen rode, armor glittering and banners dancing above. When she was near enough, they hailed her.

"Ho! Traveler! Where are you bound?" The leader was deep-voiced, a man of middle height in chainmail with a blue mantle bearing Gird's crescent.

"To the Hall in Fin Panir," said Paks. "I have a letter from Marshal Cedfer of Brewersbridge."

"For the Marshal-General?" he seemed surprised.

"Yes, sir. Can you direct me?"

"Yes, of course. But you might ask at the gates; she may be abroad this morning. You will have left Tor's Crossing early—or did you camp out last night?"

"I left early, sir."

"Well, the Marshal-General's quarters are in the Hall Courts. Take the first left, after the gate, and then a right—go straight past two turns, and then left again under the arch. Someone will take your horse there, and guide you. But, as I said, ask at the city gates if your message is urgent; they will know if she's ridden out somewhere."

"Thank you, sir." Paks lifted her reins and started forward. One of the other riders spoke to the leader, and he lifted a hand.

"Wait a moment—" He looked closely at her. "Are you a Girdsman?"

"No, sir."

He looked puzzled. "You are carrying something of great worth—is it a gift from the Marshal?"

"Gift? No, sir." Paks thought of the jewels she still had, and wondered if that was what he meant. Somehow she didn't think so.

At the city gates, a neatly uniformed guard waved her through after she explained her errand. When she asked, he said that the Marshal-General had gone to the practice fields west of the city, but that she might wait at the Hall if she chose. Paks followed the directions through stone-paved streets of middle width, and arrived at an arched entrance through a wall. Far above she could see the towers of the

Lord's Hall. A grizzled older man stepped out of an alcove in the arch and asked her business.

"Marshal-General, eh? She'll be out until noon; can you wait?" At her nod, he stepped forward. "Good, then. I'll get someone to take your horse—"

"I can take him," Paks interrupted. "If you'll tell me where."

His bushy eyebrows rose. "A guest take her own horse to stable? What do you think we are, ruffians?" He turned and bellowed through the archway. "Seli! Seliam!" Paks heard the clatter of running feet, and a boy raced up, panting. "Take this horse to the guest stables, Seli. Have the stableboys see to him." The boy laid his hand on the rein, and Paks dismounted. She rummaged in her saddlebags for Cedfer's letter to the Marshal-General. "Seli will take your saddlebags to the guest house in a few minutes," the man said. "Would you prefer to wait there, or in the Marshal-General's study?"

"Could I—" Paks suddenly felt shy. "I—I haven't been in Fin Panir before," she began again. "Could I see the High Lord's Hall? Is it permitted?"

His face split in a grin. "Permitted! Of course it's permitted. Let me find someone for the entrance, and I'll take you in myself. Haven't been here before, eh? I daresay you've heard tales, though, haven't you?" He turned away without waiting for an answer, and yelled again through the arch. This time another older man answered the summons.

"What is it, Argalt? An invasion of orcs?"

"No. A newcomer, who wants to see the Hall while waiting for the Marshal-General."

"And you want to show him—her, excuse me." The man smiled at Paks. "Gird's grace, lady, you've made Argalt's day. He loves to show off the Hall. And you've bright sun for it, too." He waved them away, and Paks followed the man through the arch and across a cobbled courtyard to the entrance of the High Lord's Hall of Fin Panir.

Broad steps led up to a pair of tall bronze doors, cast in intricate designs. Paks stopped to look at them, and her guide began to explain.

"These doors are not the original—those burned, hundreds of years back, the year the Black Lady fought to the steps here. But these were designed and cast by the half-elven craftsman Madegar. The middle of each door bears the High Lord's Seal—it's inlaid in gold, as you see. All around are the seals of the saints, and a little picture of each one doing something famous. There's Gird, with the cudgel, and Falk with a sword and the tyrant of Celias, and Camwyn riding a dragon, and Dort shearing the golden sheep, do you see all that?"

"Yes." Paks traced the designs with her finger, as far as she could reach. She found Torre and her magical steed, Sertig with his anvil. She stared, fascinated, until the man tapped her on the shoulder.

"Come along in, now, and see the rest."

From the great doors, the Hall stretched away, longer than any grange Paks had seen. The grange at Brewersbridge, she thought, would have fit in sideways, and three more with it. The soaring arches that held the roof were lifted from stone columns like treetrunks springing from the floor. It reminded her, in that way, of the elves' Winterhall underground. At the far end, a double platform with a low railing took the place of the usual training platform in granges. On either side a railed gallery with stepped seating offered a clear view of the floor.

But all this she saw later. First she was aware of the great wash of brilliant light, broken into dazzling chips of color, that poured through the great round window in the far end. All along both sides, high windows of colored glass spread fanciful patterns of light on the floor. She turned to the guide, who was chuckling at her reaction.

"How?" was all she could say.

"You had seen glass in windows before?" he asked.

"Yes, but—" she waved a hand at the magnificence.

"It's colored glass, laid in a pattern, and bound in strips of lead. And I'll have you know, it wasn't an elf designed that." Now that the first dazzle had passed, Paks could see that the colored glass made designs—even pictures, in some of the windows. The round window held a many-pointed star in shades of blue with accents of gold. Along the sunny south side of the Hall, she saw Gird with his cudgel striking a richly dressed knight, Camwyn riding a dragon whose breath seemed literal flame, a harper (she could not remember the name of the harpers' patron saint) playing to a tree that seemed to be turning into a girl, and Torre partway through her Ride, with half the stones of the necklace turned to stars. The longer she looked at each window, the more she saw. Each had smaller scenes inset in medallions around the main picture. Paks walked over to Torre's window. There was her home, with its six towers, and that must be her sorrowing father with the wicked king threatening him. Here was the stable, with the strange horse standing loose between the stalls, the ring of coals around its neck. A white flower stood for the first trial of her Ride, and three snowflakes for the next. A fat dwarf held the blue ring, and an elf in green held out the branch of yellowwood in flower, complete with two bees. The wicked king's red banner blew from a tower on a cliff. A sleeping baby in a basket floated on a river. At the very top of the window, the stars of Torre's Necklace blazed out of blue glass just as they did in the sky.

Paks tore her eyes away and looked around again. The shadowed, northern side windows were pictures as well. Sertig pounding on his anvil, and Adyan writing the true names of everything in his book. Alyanya, the Lady of Peace, wreathed in flowers, with fruitful vines trailing around her. Some pictures she did not recognize at all. One seemed to be all animals, fitted into every available niche, all mixed together, large and small. One was simply a tree, whose gnarled roots and branches filled up the space above and below, curling and recurling until Paks could not tell how many little rootlets filled even one small section.

When she finally left the windows to look at the rest of the building, it was equally engrossing. The floor was paved with flat slabs of stone in a subtle pattern. Many of the slabs were engraved with names and dates that meant nothing to Paks—but much to her guide, when she asked.

"That there's Lolyin's marker—he was Marshal-General over a hundred years ago, and converted the King of Tsaia to the fellowship of Gird. That was the great-grandfather of the present crown prince. Under his name is the paladin Brealt. You might have heard of him, since I can see you've been in Aarenis. He freed the captives of Pliuni, and fought two priests of Liart by himself to do it." Paks had not heard of him, but she nodded. The old man went on. "Marshal-Generals and paladins of Gird—and a few others—they have their names and dates put here. Some say their deeds should be added, but the rule is that those who want to know should look them up in the archives. There's not one of them but is worth remembering. Take this—" he led her up near the platform. "This is Gird's own marker, put here by Luap—the oldest we have." The stone was worn in a hollow, and the letters were faint. "In the old way, all that joined the knights of the fellowship, or became paladins of Gird, would spend part of a vigil washing that stone, to keep Gird's name pure. But then they realized they were wearing it down, and only the Marshal-General does it now."

Paks could think of nothing to say. She had never imagined that anything built by men would be as beautiful as the Hall. That soaring space seemed to liberate something inside her, as if it called for wings within. When they came out at last, she blinked in the sunlight, her head still full of what she'd seen.

She had no idea what to expect of a Marshal-General. The Marshals she had met had been matter-of-fact, much like the Duke's captains. But what she'd seen of feudal commanders, and the splendor of the Hall, led her to think that the Marshal-General might be more—she tried to think of a word—impressive? magnificent? As the servant led her through the passages and up a broad stair to the Marshal-General's office, she felt her stomach flutter.

The door was open. Paks looked across a fairly large room to a table set under one of the south windows. Behind it stood two people, a woman and a man, both in blue tunics over gray trousers. Both had Gird's crescents on chains around their neck. They were looking at something on the table as the servant knocked; the woman looked up.

"Yes?"

"A messenger, Marshal-General, from Marshal Cedfer of Brewersbridge." He gestured at Paks.

"Ah yes. Argalt mentioned you—your name?"

"Paksenarrion Dorthansdotter," said Paks, uncertain of the correct address.

"You're not a Girdsman?"

"No—my lady." Paks thought that was safest.

"Then you may not know I'm Marshal-General Arianya. But you're a warrior—that's clear enough." Paks nodded. "Well, then, let me see your message."

Paks walked into the room and handed over the Marshal's letter. The Marshal-General was a tall woman of middle age, her graying curly hair cropped short. She wore no sword, but her tunic was marked by sword belt and scabbard. Her right hand bore a wide scar; Paks wondered how it had missed severing some tendons. The Marshal-General looked up from what she was reading.

"Do you know what Cedfer's written?"

Paks felt the blood rush to her face. "Some of it, my lady. He said he—that you—that I might take some training here."

"He's recommended that you be admitted to a probationers' class in the Company of Gird. And he's said why—" She paused and looked at Paks closely. "It's most unusual, you know, for anyone not of the fellowship to be admitted here."

Paks felt her heart sink. She had only begun to realize, during the trip to Fin Panir, the power wielded by the granges of Gird. When the Marshal had suggested a half-year in the training program, it had seemed like fun. And she had always been able to learn warrior's skills. She said nothing, and met the Marshal-General's eyes steadily.

"What has he said, Marshal-General?" asked the man. Paks glanced at him. He was a little taller than the Marshal-General, and had a short gray beard.

"He recommends her highly—" the Marshal-General paused again, and looked once more at Paks. "You were trained and fought with Duke Phelan of Tsaia, is that right?" Paks nodded. "Cedfer was surprised to find you so good with a longsword; he implies that the Duke himself suggested you seek advanced training. That's so?"

"Yes, my lady." Paks felt very uncomfortable. She knew what was coming next; she still did not want to talk about those last weeks in the Duke's Company. But the Marshal-General's next question surprised her.

"Do you think he would be pleased to have you here?"

Paks knew her face showed her astonishment. "Why—why of course, my lady. Why wouldn't he? It would be an honor—"

The Marshal-General looked away. "Duke Phelan, Paksenarrion Dorthansdotter, is not without his quarrels with Gird and Gird's granges."

Paks thought of the subtle tension between the Duke and the Marshal in Aarenis. His words to the paladin at Cortes Immer came back to her. She shook her head, driving them away. "No—I'm sure he would be glad. He is not a Girdsman himself, but he is a good man—a good fighter—and he would be glad for any honor that came to me. And training here would be an honor."

"Why would you think it so, when you are not of our fellowship?" asked the man quietly. Paks turned to him.

"Sir, it is widely known. The Knights of Gird, the paladins of Gird—all of them train here, and many others beside, who serve honorably in the royal guards of several kingdoms."

"I see." He glanced at the Marshal-General, but she was looking at Marshal Cedfer's letter. After a moment she looked up at him.

"Kory, if you'll excuse us, I'd like to talk to Paksenarrion. Cedfer almost persuades me, but I must see for myself what she is."

"Of course, Marshal-General."

"Paksenarrion, have you had anything to eat?"

"No, my lady. Not since breakfast."

"Then we'll eat together here. Kory, ask them to send something up, will you?"

"Certainly." He bowed, and left the room. Paks met the Marshal-General's gaze.

"Well, Paksenarrion, have a seat—there—and let's find out more about you. Cedfer sent word at once about the elfane taig, but few details. Where are you from, and how did you come to join the Duke's Company?"

"I'm from Three Firs, my lady. My father is a sheep farmer."

"Three Firs! I know that country—far from the Honnorgat, or any city, isn't it?"

"Yes—"

"So you left to join the Duke's Company? Or for another reason?"

"I wanted to be a warrior." Paks thought back to the mood of what now seemed her childhood, when Jornoth had come visiting with a bright sword and his purse full of silver. "My father didn't—so I ran away." The Marshal-General nodded. "I joined the Duke's Company at Rocky Ford, and then—" she shrugged. "I was a recruit, and then a private in the Company."

"You fought in the north, or in Aarenis?"

"In Aarenis. For three seasons." Paks stopped, uncertain how much to say about those years.

"Cedfer says the Duke evidently favored you—had give you some important missions. Can you tell me about them, or would that violate a secret of the Duke's?"

Paks shook her head. "No. Nothing secret—I don't know how much to say. The last year, I was acting corporal for awhile, when Seli was hurt. And I helped capture Siniava."

"Siniava. Then—wait—" The Marshal-General's face furrowed for a moment. "Did you meet a paladin in Aarenis? Fenith?"

"Yes, my lady." Paks didn't want to talk about that, either: the one time the Duke had not lived up to her image of him.

"You're that Paksenarrion!" The Marshal-General stared at her. "Fenith wrote about you—you took on a priest of Liart, and lived! Gird's grace, child, I hadn't heard of such a thing. Neither had he. He sent the High Marshal to your Duke to find out about you, and the Duke nearly took his head off for suggesting you might not be what you seemed."

"He did?" Paks didn't remember any such thing.

"I suppose your Duke didn't tell you. Fenith also said you were the one to spot Siniava in shapechange. He thought it had something to do with a Gird's medallion you carried—a gift of a friend, he said—"

"Yes." Paks did not want to discuss Canna's gift, which she had not worn since the night Siniava died.

"You told him, I understand, that you would stay with the Duke's Company—yet here you are on our doorstep. What happened?" The Marshal-General's eyes were as shrewd as the Kuakgan's; Paks realized that there was no way out of this but the long one—the whole truth. Haltingly, at first, she began to tell of the last year in Aarenis. The Marshal-General did not interrupt, and the pressure of her attention kept the tale flowing. When a servant carried in a tray of food, bowls of stew and a couple of loaves of dark bread, Paks stopped. The Marshal-General spread the food on the table, and waved the servant out.

"Gird's grace be with you, Paksenarrion, and with me, and may we gain strength to serve the High Lord's will. Go on, now, and eat." She took up her spoon and began. Paks did the same. After the stew was mostly gone, the Marshal-General looked up. "I can understand why you left, and why you were reluctant to leave. But I am still not sure why you quit wearing Canna's medallion. Do you know?"

Paks laid down the hunk of bread she'd picked up. "I thought—it seemed that it—it led me into things. Trouble. I never knew if it—if I—how they happened."

"It led you into trouble? And you a mercenary?" The Marshal-General's voice had an edge of scorn. "You had not chosen the most peaceful life."

"No, my lady. But I don't know what it did, or didn't do. I don't know if it healed Canna, or didn't or if it really saved me from the man in Rotengre—"

"Wait. You haven't told me about that yet. Canna is your friend who died and left it to you, isn't that so? What's this about healing?"

Paks felt the sweat cold on her neck as she began to tell the Marshal-General about their flight from Dwarfwatch. Knowing that she would insist on hearing those parts of the journey that made Paks the most nervous didn't help. She had not mentioned the prayers over Canna's wound to anyone but Stammel, and it was no easier now. The Marshal-General seemed to grow more remote and august as she listened.

"You, no follower of Gird, suggested praying to Gird for healing? Don't you think that was presumptuous? Had you planned to join the fellowship afterwards?" Paks had not thought of it like that at all.

"My lady, we had need—I didn't know much of Gird, then, and—"

"Your friend had not told you? And she a yeoman?"

Paks shook her head. "We didn't talk about it much; she was our friend. We knew she was a Girdsman, and she knew we had our own gods."

"You know more of Gird now, I'll warrant—what do you think now, of such a thing?" Paks thought a moment.

"I don't think Gird would mind—I can't see why he would. If he had been a nobleman, perhaps, but—why would it be wrong to try? Healing is good, and Canna was one of his yeomen."

The Marshal-General shook her head slowly, but more in doubt than disagreement. "I'm not sure, child. What happened?"

"That's what I don't know." Paks remembered clearly Canna's yelp of pain, and then the seeming improvement in her condition. "It didn't go away at once," she went on, carefully telling the Marshal-General everything. "But she had been getting weaker, and feverish, and she was stronger afterwards. It looked cleaner and drier the next time we changed the bandage. But you see, we'd found some ointment in that farmstead, and used that too. I don't know which worked, or why."

"You didn't tell this to Marshal Berran or Fenith," said the Marshal-General.

"No—I wasn't sure—"

"Go on, then. What happened with the man in Rotengre?" That, too, Paks told, even Captain Dorrin's remarks afterwards. The Marshal-General nodded.

"Your captain had the sense to see what lay before her. Is she Girdish?"

"No, my lady. Falkian—or that's what one of the sergeants said."

"I see. What did you think then, when two times the medallion had acted for you?"

"I didn't—I was frightened of it, lady. I didn't know what to do."

"Did you not think of speaking to a Marshal?"

Paks shook her head vigorously. "Oh no. I—"

"You were with Duke Phelan. I suppose you had no chance."

"I didn't want to, not then. I—I suppose I wished that it would just—just be over. I kept thinking about them—"

"Canna?"

"And—and Saben. He was my—our friend, that was with us."

"Your lover?"

"No." The old grief and longing choked her again. When she looked up again, the Marshal-General was stacking the bowls on the tray.

"Taking those events with the later ones, Paksenarrion—with surviving the blow of Liart's priest in Sibili, the warning of ambush, and withstanding the enchantments when Siniava tried to escape—don't you think that there's clear evidence of Gird's action in your behalf?"

"I don't—I can't be sure—"

"Gird's teeth, girl, what do you want, a pillar of fire?" The Marshal-General glared at her. "D'you expect the gods to carry you up to the clouds and explain everything in words a sheepfarmer's daughter can understand?"

"No, my lady." Paks stared at her hands, near tears again. She heard a gusty sigh.

"How old are you, Paksenarrion?"

Paks counted it out aloud. "I was eighteen winters when I left home—and then nineteen was in the stronghold, and twenty—twenty-one after Dwarfwatch—near twenty-two, my lady."

"I see. Are you set against the fellowship of Gird?"

"Oh no, my lady! The more I know, the more—but you see, my family was not Girdish. And I still think it's better to abide the gods you know—"

The Marshal-General sighed again. Paks looked up to find her gazing out one of the narrow windows, her face stern. After a long moment she turned back to Paks. "We are not," she said firmly, "a training camp for those who want fancy skills to show off." Paks felt her face reddening again. "If what you want is an accomplishment to display—like someone stringing another pearl on a necklace—you don't belong here, and I won't lend Gird's name to it. Those we train must go out as Gird's warriors, to serve the lands and defend them against the powers of evil. They must care, Paksenarrion, for this cause more than their own fame. Those sworn to the fellowship of Gird I have ways of testing. If you persist in remaining aloof, I must assume that your dedication is unproven. I will not—absolutely not—let you take advantage of this Company, and go off boasting that you trained with the Company of Gird at Fin Panir, unless you can show me what you will pay. Not in money, young warrior, but in your life."

Paks managed to meet her eyes steadily, though she felt as frightened and helpless as she had when a new recruit. She said nothing for some time, wondering what if anything she could say. At last she looked away and shook her head ruefully.

"I don't know, my lady, what I could say to convince you. For me, I have been trained as a warrior, not to argue. I think perhaps you feel what I felt in Brewersbridge—there was a young girl there, who wanted to join me, and be a squire to me. I knew I didn't know enough to be her—her commander, or whatever, but also—I used to think she only wanted the glory she could see. To wear a sword like mine, to have a scar to show, perhaps—but she didn't know what it cost, what lay behind it. I tried to tell her, tried to get her to join a regular company, as I had—"

"And did she?" The Marshal-General's voice was still remote.

Paks shook her head. "Not as far as I know. I tried—but she wanted adventure, she said. It would be too dull, she didn't like people yelling at her; she said she could get enough of that in Brewersbridge." Paks stopped before saying, "She had a very bad father, my lady."

"You ran away from yours."

"Oh, well... he wasn't like that. But I see what you mean—you think I want to—to make a name for myself, from the fame of your Company. That would be wrong. You're right. But—I can't swear to follow Gird until I know—until I'm sure of myself—that I can do it."

"That's coming out differently than what you said before. Then you didn't seem to trust Gird."

Paks floundered, unable to define what she meant. "I don't—I mean, I don't know Gird, but you all say Gird is a saint, and I won't argue. But I don't know Gird—I have known good Girdsmen, but also good warriors following other gods and saints. How do I know Gird is the one I should follow?"

The Marshal-General's eyebrows went up. "You would not believe the evidence of the medallion?"

Paks set her jaw stubbornly. "I'm not sure. And I won't swear to something I'm not sure of."

To her surprise, the Marshal-General laughed. "Gird be praised, you are at least willing to be honest against the Marshal-General. Child, such stubbornness as yours is nearly proof that Gird claims your destiny—but it may take Gird's cudgel to break a hole in your head to let his light in. The gods grant you are this stubborn about other things that matter." She sat forward, leaning her forearms on the table between them. "Now, what sort of training did you look for?"

Paks could hardly believe her ears. "You mean—you'll let me stay?"

"Let you! By Gird, I'm not likely to let someone like you wander the world unconvinced without giving my best chance to convert you. Of course you'll stay."

"But if I don't—"

"Paksenarrion, you will stay until either you wish to leave, or you give me cause to send you away. When—notice that I do not say if, being granted almost as much stubbornness as you, by Gird's grace—when you find that you can swear your honor to Gird's fellowship, it will be my pleasure to give and receive your strokes. Is that satisfactory, or have you more conditions for a Marshal-General of Gird, and Captain-Temporal of the High Lord?"

Paks blushed. "No, my lady. I'm sorry, I—"

"Enough. Tell me what you thought to learn."

"Well—everything about war—"

The Marshal-General whooped. "Everything? About war? Gird's grace, Paksenarrion, no one knows that but the High Lord, who sees all beginnings and endings at once."

"I meant," muttered Paks, ears flaming, "weapons-skills, and things about forts—things the Duke's captains knew about, like tunnels—"

"All right," said the Marshal-General, wiping her eyes on her sleeve. "I see what you mean. Things about forts. Honestly! No, sorry, I see you're serious. Well, then. I'll assign you to the training company. Many of them are younger than you—nobles' youngsters, from Fintha and Tsaia, mostly. They've been someone's squires, and now they're preparing for knighthood. Some have come up through the granges, and have been yeoman-marshal somewhere for three years. You may not know, but all our marshals are trained here, along with the knights. You'll be assigned space in the courts—we don't have open barracks, for you'll need to study alone. You do read, don't you?" At Paks' nod, she went on, now writing swiftly on a loose sheet of paper. "Weapons practice daily—the senior instructor will assign the drills once he's examined you. Riding—do you ride? Yes, because Argalt mentioned putting up your horse. You're a few weeks behind one group they arrived just after harvest. That's when we start the new cycles. But we'll see if you can catch up to them." She looked up from her writing. Although she was smiling, it seemed to Paks that she was even more formidable. "What weapons do you have?" she asked.

"This sword," said Paks, laying her hand on the hilt. "Another one, not so good—"

"That one's magical," said the Marshal-General. "Did you know?"

"Yes, my lady. And a dagger, and a short battle-axe."

"Do you use all of them?"

"No, my lady. Just sword and dagger, and I can use a long-bow, though not well."

"And I see you have mail as well. For the first weeks, though, you will not use your own weapons. The Weapons Master will assign you weapons for training; yours may be stored in your quarters or in the armory, as you prefer."

"Yes, my lady."

"Your clothes—" she glanced at Paks' traveling clothes. "We have training uniforms, but we are not strict, except during drill and classes. We discourage display of jewels and such, but you don't look the type to show up in laces and ribbons."

"No, my lady."

"Very well." She signed the end of her note, and handed it to Paks. "Take this down, and ask Argalt to direct you to the Master of Training. He'll assign your quarters, and see that you're set up with the instructors. You will take your meals in the Lower Hall—by the way, you have no difficulties with the elder races, have you?"

"Elder races—you mean elves and dwarves?"

"Among others. We have quite a few here—you'll be meeting them. Don't get in fights with them."

"Oh no."

"Good. You may go, Paksenarrion. May Gird's grace be on you, and the High Lord's light guide your way." She rose, and Paks stood quickly, knocking her hand on the table edge.

"Thank you, my lady—"

"Thank the gods, Paksenarrion, for their bounty. I have done nothing yet to deserve your thanks."

CHAPTER NINETEEN

Argalt, when she finally located him again, after losing herself in a maze of passages on the ground floor, looked her up and down. "Training Master, eh? So you're going to become a Knight of Holy Gird, are you? Or a Marshal? Or is it paladin you're thinking of?"

Paks felt her ears burning again. "I—don't know, sir."

Argalt snorted. "I'm no sir, not even to the newest member of the training company. Argalt: that's my name and that's what you'll call me, young woman."

"Yes, si—Argalt."

"That's better. You're no hothouse flower of a noble house—where are you from?" Paks told him. He looked at her with surprising respect. "Sheepfarmer's daughter? That's like Gird's daughter herself—barring he raised cattle and grain, so the story goes. But still it means you know what work is, I'll say, and a few blisters on the hands. Where'd you learn to wear a sword like you could use it?" When she mentioned the Duke's name, he stared. "You were in the Fox's Company? And came here? I'll believe anything after that!" He shook his head as he led her across the courtyard, past the Lord's Hall. "I was in the Guards at Vérella when I was young; what I don't know about that Duke—" But Paks asked nothing, and did not expect that he would have answered if she had. He gave her a long look outside the Training Master's office. "If you need someone to talk to, sometime, sheepfarmer's daughter—I'll share a tankard of ale with you."

"Thank you," said Paks, still not sure of his reasons. He nodded and turned away.

The Training Master was a hand taller than Paks herself, a hard muscular man in dark blue tunic and trousers, with Gird's crescent embroidered on the breast. He read the Marshal-General's note, and Cedfer's letter, in tight-lipped silence. When he looked up, his ice-blue eyes were hard.

"If you're to catch up with the others, you'll have to work—and work hard. You'd best not loll about."

Paks repressed a surge of anger. She'd never been lazy. "No, sir," she said stiffly.

"It means extra work for the instructors as well. I shall take you myself for tactics in the evenings after supper. I hope Cedfer's right about your weapons-skills. That would let us chop a glass or so off there, and give you more time in supply—though why the Marshal-General bothers with that, for you, is beyond me." Paks felt her shoulders tighten, and forced herself to be still. He sighed, heavily. "Very well, then. How much gear do you have?"

"Only what was in my saddlebags, sir," said Paks. "I suppose it's—"

"They'll have it brought to your quarters." He glanced for a moment at a chart on his wall. "Let me think. There's a room on the third floor, next to the end of the corridor. You can have that, for now. It's small, but it won't mean moving anyone else tonight. If it's too small, we can change things in a week or so." If you stay that long, his tone clearly said. "You'll need clothes; I'll have the steward send something up. Come along." He pushed past her to the corridor, and led the way upstairs.

The room he opened seemed amply large to Paks—larger than her room at the Jolly Potboy, with two windows looking out over a lower roof to a walled field. Besides a bed and chest, and a curtained alcove with hooks, it had a table, stool, and low chair. A narrow shelf ran along the wall over the table. Several blankets were folded neatly on the foot of the bed. Paks had hardly taken all this in when he began speaking again.

"Students do not wear weapons except at practice," he said, with a pointed glance at her sword. "We prefer that personal weapons be stored in the armory, but the Marshal General has given permission for you to keep yours with you." Paks did not want to let the magic sword out of her control; she said nothing. Just then a servant came in with her saddlebags; behind him was the steward, with an armful of clothing, all dark gray but for the blue cloak. The steward eyed her.

"You said tall, Master Chanis; this should fit near enough for now. What name do you use—Paksenarrion, or Dorthansdotter?"

"Paks is all."

"Paksenarrion," said the steward cheerfully. "I need something long enough it can't be mistaken in anyone's handwriting. Come by for measurements, or if you have something that fits well—"

Paks unstrapped her saddlebags, and pulled out her green shirt. "Will this do?"

"Good—good material, too. From Lyonya, is it?"

"No, but near there. Brewersbridge."

The steward shook her head. "I don't know it. Trousers, too, if you've an extra pair." Paks pulled out the patched ones, which the steward took without comment, and handed over a pair of socks as well. The steward checked the number of blankets, and left the room.

"If you're ready," said the Training Master, "there is time to see the weapons instructors before supper. No need to change now; in the morning is soon enough." Paks set her swords neatly on the shelf, and the saddlebags behind the curtain, before following him out of the room. "You have fought mostly in a mercenary company, I understand."

"Yes, sir."

"Short sword or polearm?"

"Short sword."

"But you carry a longsword."

"Yes, sir."

"Have you used a bow?"

"In training, yes—it's not my best weapon."

"Polearms?"

"Only in training."

"Mace? Axe? Crossbow? Siege weaponry?" At each shake of her head, his lips seemed to tighten. Paks wondered if he really thought all of those important. She had trouble keeping up with his long sweeping strides, and noticed little of the building around them—only rows of doors, open and shut, and the stone flags of the hallway. They came out into a small court surrounded on three sides by stables; a pile of dung centered the court, and two youths were shoveling it into a cart. Past a row of box stalls, each holding a massive warhorse, the Training Master ducked through a narrow archway into another passage. This time they emerged on the edge of the walled field Paks had seen from her windows. On their right, the stone building sprouted a long finger; the Training Master turned toward this.

It was a single room, and resembled a small grange except that it had no platform and no doors at the far end, only the one on either side. It was empty at the moment, but Paks could hear grunts and the clash of weapons from the far side. The Training Master led her through it, and out the other door.

Here were perhaps a score of fighters, all in training gray, practicing with swords and—Paks was surprised to see—hauks. To one side a burly man in blue watched them closely. He glanced over at the Training Master, and waved. Paks followed as they walked around the training area to meet him.

"This is Paksenarrion Dorthansdotter," said the Training Master abruptly. "The Marshal-General has assigned her to this class."

Sharp black eyes met hers. "Ha. She's no novice."

"So I understand. If you can spare her for more time in other studies, Cieri, do so."

"Am I to hood hawks so they may learn music?" Paks thought by the tone that this was an old argument begun again. The Training Master's face relaxed.

"There are other skills of war, Cieri—"

"Oh, and so there are, but none of them any good if you can't keep a blade from your guts." He shook his head. "Never mind, Chanis, I know what you mean, and the Marshal-General, too. If she can spare the time, I'll see to it. But only if, understand that." He cocked his head at Paks, and looked her over.

"See that she knows where to go, when you're through," said the Training Master. He turned to Paks. "Gird be with you, Paksenarrion. If you have any need, come to my office at any time."

"Thank you, sir," said Paks, still ruffled.

"Well, now." Cieri, the Weapons Master, was walking around her. She turned to watch him. "Where have you fought? What weapons? I see marks of a longsword on your clothes." For the third time that day, Paks outlined her training. Cieri, at least, showed no doubt. "That's good. Three fighting seasons with Phelan—that means you know your way with short sword and formation fighting. And you've used a longsword since—very good. Many who come to us with your background cannot fight without the others in formation. Not until I've trained them, that is." He grinned broadly. For all that he was younger and heavier, he reminded Paks of Siger. "What about unarmed combat?"

"I've done it," said Paks cautiously. She knew that Siger himself had mastered only a few of the many styles.

"Can you fight mounted? I know Phelan has infantry."

"I have, some. Marshal Cedfer in Brewersbridge was teaching me, and I fought a little with a sword."

"Without cutting up the horse? Good. I see you're wearing mail—Chanis didn't give you time to change, eh? But we don't wear mail in practice sessions—you must not come to count on it. Today I'll test you, but tomorrow you show up in training uniform, right?"

"Yes, sir." Paks noticed that the others were watching covertly, slowing their own practice to see what she was doing. Cieri noticed that, too, and bellowed at them.

"Gird's gut, may the ale hold out, you dolts keep gaping like that and I'll run you all around the field ten times before supper. D'you think an enemy'd let you gaze all around like a bunch of calves in pasture? Get to your work, or—" But the tempo had speeded back up at once. Cieri picked up two swords from a stack near the edge of the practice area. "Here—we'll start with what you're comfortable with."

Paks took a sword and moved it, testing its balance. It was heavier than her own, and broader across the blade. Cieri stood casually, touched her blade with the tip of his, and leaped in so fast that she almost missed her own stroke.

"Aha!" he said. "If you were that slow with enemies, you would have more scars than you do. Don't hold back, girl—I'm better than Cedfer, if you want the truth of it." Indeed he was, and Paks found herself working hard to keep his blade from clashing on her mail. She had gotten used to the delicate balance of the magic sword—that responsive light spring—and she felt, at first, that she was fencing with a length of iron firewood. Several minutes later, sweating freely, she found her balance, and tried offensive strokes as well as defensive. Cieri countered them easily, but grinned even more widely. "You're learning," he said. "You've got a reach on you, too. And reasonable speed." He tried one of the tricks she knew about, and she thrust it aside, lunging quickly to mark his tunic. "And you know something.

Very good. You haven't wasted your time." But in a flash he shifted his blade to the other hand. Paks, confused, missed her parry, and felt the sharp blow along her side. Another, in the same place, and then she countered with a blow that drove him back a step.

She had forgotten that he wore no mail, until after a fast exchange of heavy blows she caught his arm and blood darkened the tunic. "Hold," he said, but she had already lowered her blade. He glanced at his arm, and then at her with new respect. "You do know something. By Gird, we may have a swordsman in this class after all."

"I'm sorry—" she started to say.

"No matter. In a Hall full of Marshals, little wounds like these are no problem. Look here—" He pulled aside the ripped sleeve to show a narrow jagged wound already closing. "You must all learn to fight, and strongly, and therefore I take a lot of healing."

Paks was startled. "But I thought—"

He looked closely at her. "Oh. You're not Girdish, are you? Most are. With an arm like that, you should be. It's nothing, here—Marshals can heal themselves as well as others, and Gird does not begrudge healing to weapons masters."

"Then you're—"

"A Marshal, yes. You didn't know? Most of your instructors here are Marshals."

"Oh."

"Now put away that sword you obviously know how to use—that you can't learn more—and let's see what you do with staves." Paks had never fought with staves before, and collected a quantity of bruises proving her incompetence. Cieri then tried her in archery; her form, he said, was passable, but her ability to judge windage was abysmal. She could not throw a javelin at all, and when he saw her grip on a battleaxe, he told her to put it down at once. "And I won't have you try unarmed combat in mail just yet—tomorrow will do for that." By this time, Paks was sweaty, tired, and sore enough to be glad of a rest. "You're beyond most of the class in sword handling," he said, after thinking a few moments. "Some of them have had lessons for years, but no actual fighting. That's what makes the difference. You'll need regular practice with the sword, but instead of new tricks with it, I want to improve your other weapons skills. When you finish, you should be able to instruct with at least five weapons. More if you're interested. Tomorrow morning, come with the others for mounted drill—do you have your own horse?"

"Yes, sir."

"Well, you can ride your own horse tomorrow. If it's trained enough, you'll bring it to every session, but we switch around. Marshal Doggal takes most of the mounted classes. Mounted work first thing in the morning, then your other studies, before lunch, then drill here. Is that clear?"

"Yes, sir. But—what about my horse? Where is he, and what about grooming—"

"You've been caring for your own horse? Good, good. You won't do that for a while—this autumn session, we keep the class busy enough without, but in the spring each student is assigned a mount to care for. Just show up at the right time in the mornings, and saddle up."

"Oh." Paks thought of explaining Socks' character, but decided not to.

"Now—" he looked at her closely. "I don't mean to insult you, but the order provides adequate clothing. Leave your soiled things near the door each morning, and they'll be cleaned." Paks nodded. "You look to be in fair condition, but you'll be sore and stiff with the schedule you've got. Hot baths are available each night. Many students prefer to bathe and change before supper—if they have time." He looked around at the rest of the students, and shook his head. "Nearly time to quit, and they know it. As you've come in from traveling, and are wearing mail, I won't send you—but we end with a run most days." He turned to the others, raised his voice. "Rufen!" A young man with dark brown hair stepped back from his partner, and came forward. "This is Paksenarrion; she's a new member. Take her back to the House, and show her where things are. She's got a horse for tomorrow, but doesn't know where it's stabled."

Rufen bowed, giving Paks a quick glance. She thought he was several years younger than she, half a hand shorter, and more slender. As he led her away, back through the empty armory, he looked at her again. "You're not a Girdsman?" he asked. Paks could not place his accent, which seemed slightly melodic.

"No," she said. She was not going to explain everything all over again. Not then.

"You fence well," he said, with another sidelong glance. "I've never seen Cieri move so fast, except against the knights. What kind of horse have you?"

Paks answered stiffly, suspecting a joke. "Just a—a black horse. Warhorse."

They were in the stable courtyard by then, and he asked one of the workers. "That black with the stockings? And a wide blaze? He's in the new court stables."

"That's where guest horses are housed," explained Rufen. "I expect they'll move him in here, if they've got a free stall." He led the way through a tack room full of racked saddles into another, larger, stable complex. Before he could find someone to ask, Paks heard Socks, and saw his wide head peering out over a half-door. Rufen looked startled when she pointed him out. "That's yours? If he's not Pargunese-bred, I'll take up the harp. Look at the bone of him." By this time they were at the stall, and Socks had shoved his nose hard into Paks' tunic.

"I don't have any," she said sharply. He seemed in good shape, and had obviously been groomed carefully; no saddle marks showed on him. Rufen hung over the door, still talking.

"Great gods, what a shoulder. How's he trained? Did you train him? Do you have a pedigree? No speed, I'd say, but a lot of bottom." Paks had no chance to answer; the questions came too fast, and Rufen wasn't paying attention to her anyway. A groom came up.

"This horse yours?"

"Yes."

"He don't like his hind legs messed with, do he?"

"No—did he kick?"

"Kick! Look there at that board—" the man pointed. It was split along its length.

"He was hurt before I got him," said Paks. The groom eyed her sourly.

"That's what they all say," he said. "Hurt before I got him, pah! Could have trained him out of it, couldn't you?"

"I did," said Paks, suddenly angry again. "Look." She jumped up on the stall door. Socks threw his head up and snorted. "Be still," she said firmly, and slipped onto his broad back, then down to stand beside him. She ran her hand over his massive rump, down the hind leg, and chirped. He lifted his hoof obediently into her hand, and she tapped the sole, then put it down. "There, you see?"

The groom nodded. "All right. Now tell that beast to let someone else do it.

"Come on in." The groom opened the stall door. Socks stiffened his ears, and clamped his tail. Paks soothed him with a hand, and the man followed her gesture and picked up the other hind hoof. "I suppose, come to think of it, that no one's handled his legs but me since I got him," she said.

"I hope he'll remember this," said the groom.

"Try apples," said Paks.

"Bribe a horse?"

"That's what I did."

"It works," put in Rufen. "They're such greedy-guts, horses are. We use apples in our training."

"Yes, my lord," said the groom, with a slight bow. Rufen colored, glancing at Paks. When the man had left, and they were walking back across the stable court, he sighed.

"I suppose you know we use only one name here?"

"No—" Paks hadn't thought about it.

"Well, the—the servants and all, they know our full names. But don't worry about it. Just call me Rufen."

"And I'm Paks," she said. He nodded, and led her back into the maze of buildings.

"It's simple, really," he said a few minutes later, after taking her to the Low Hall where they would eat, and then to the bath house and past some of the classrooms. "The High Lord's Hall opens into the Forecourt, and directly across from it is the Marshal-General's Hall. Her quarters are upstairs, but they hold large meetings downstairs. And several other Marshals live there as well. Where you came in—that archway—that's all quarters for the gate guards and some of the servants. The other side of the Forecourt is the Training College—where we live and meet for classes. It used to be quarters for the Knights of Gird, but when the order grew too big for it, they converted it for us. The ground floor is much larger—rooms on the back side look over the roofs. That's because it doesn't have cellars; all the storerooms are above ground."

"Why?"

Rufen shrugged. "I don't know. I never wondered; they just told us when we came. Anyway, the Low Hall is more-or-less behind the

Marshal-General's quarters; you saw where the kitchens were, between the steward's office and the Hall. The stables are really confusing, and I hear they're thinking of redoing them. Most of our horses—those assigned to training—are stabled in that little court just back of us. But the only way from there to the guest stables is through the tackroom—so you'll have to ride out the back of the guest stables, and around the smithy. Then the Knights' horses are stabled on the other side, south of the training armory."

Paks was still confused, but hated to admit it. "There are other armories, then?"

"Gird's teeth, yes. Each order of knights has its own, of course, and the paladins have theirs—and by the way, don't even think of trying to see what magical things they've got. Elis of Harway tried that, a year ago, and was knocked senseless for two days by the guard power they've set."

"Oh."

"And the Marshal-General chewed her out when she came to, and had her assigned to be Suliya's servant for a week." When Paks looked blank at that, he explained. "Suliya's a paladin—she—well, she stays here now." Paks said nothing, since he seemed uneasy. Finally he went on. "Sometimes, they say, even a paladin is defeated. You think of them dying, but sometimes—" He shook his head. "Of course, I've never seen her. Elis said it was—well, she said she'd fight any of us if we tried violating paladin-secrecy. You don't know Elis, of course."

Paks began to think she'd like to know Elis. She was about to ask which of the students was Elis, when Rufen went on. "You won't, anyway, unless she comes back before you leave."

"Was she dismissed?"

"Elis? No, but her father died, and she was the oldest. She had to take his place. As soon as one of the others is old enough, she wants to come back. And she will. In the long run, if Elis wants it, she gets it."

They were now in the passage outside Paks' room. A neatly lettered card fitted into a slot she had not noticed before, so that anyone would know it was her room.

"I'm down four doors, across the passage," said Rufen. Paks finally found words for something that had puzzled her.

"How did you know about Elis? I thought the Marshal-General said the new class had been here only a few weeks."

"Oh, them." Rufen laughed. "There are—oh—a dozen of them. They're all younger than you. I've been here a year and some."

"Were all those in practice with you?" Paks did not want to reveal how unskilled they had seemed to her.

"No—we train in groups according to skill. That's the most basic group, in swordwork. My father, you see, planned for me to be a scholar. I had a badly broken arm, as a boy, and he thought it would never hold up to fighting. I thought differently."

"Oh." Paks found his composure as interesting as his story. He did not sound angry, or defensive—he might have been talking about the training of a horse.

"You won't do your swordwork with us, I'm sure. But then Aris and Seli won't do staves with you. By Gird, I've never seen anything so clumsy as your grip on a staff." Paks flushed, but he obviously meant no insult. "It gives me hope for my swordwork, for I was just as clumsy to start—perhaps you were so with a sword, and yet you've learned great skill."

"Well—I'll work hard," said Paks, trying to copy his calm.

"Oh, you'll learn. Cieri could teach a cow grace, if he wanted to. And he likes you somewhat—not that that will take the sting out of his blows. But if we want baths before supper, we'd best get going. The rest of them'll be crowding in soon enough." He went in his own room, and Paks turned to hers. Already two complete sets of gray tunics and trousers were folded neatly on her bed. She took off her mail, and her sweaty clothes, and put on the loose bath-gown of heavy gray wool. A knock on her door. Rufen called from outside. "I forgot to tell you—lots of us don't wear the uniform to supper. It's up to you, but don't wear mail, or weapons but the dagger."

"Thanks," she called back. She rummaged among her things, and decided finally to wear her second-best shirt from Brewersbridge. Perhaps they would think it strange if she showed up in students' gray at once. Then she thought of the Training Master, and wondered. It seemed that she could be wrong either way. Why hadn't they told her exactly what to do? She was willing to do what she was told. She looked from one stack of clothes to the other, biting her lip nervously, trying to remember exactly what the Training Master had said. At last she took up her own shirt and trousers, and headed for the bath house.

* * *

Bathed and dressed once more, Paks returned to her own room, wondering now how she would know when it was time to eat. No one had mentioned a gong or other signal. Rufen's door was shut; she was too shy to knock. She heard voices in the passage, but could not distinguish the words. Suddenly, a commotion began—shouts, thuds—Paks leaped for her sword, then stopped short. No weapons. She snatched at her door, and looked out.

A black-haired boy in red velvet lay flat on the floor, blinking up at two who had their backs to Paks. She saw Rufen's door open, and his narrow good-humored face peering out,

"And if you come up here again, Aris—" said one of those standing.

"What are you doing now, Con?" asked Rufen.

"Don't bother yourself, Rufen. Just reminding the juniors that they've no right to come up here—"

"I do!" began the boy in red, but the second of the standing pair laughed shortly.

"You do, eh? Then we've a right to dump you on your tail." He took a step forward, but Rufen came out of his room.

"No one has a right to brawl, Jori, and you and Con know it. I don't know where you got the idea that this is your passage—"

"You'd dispute that?" asked Con scornfully. "You? By Gird's toe, Rufen, I can throw you with one arm alone."

"I doubt that," said Rufen. The boy had started to roll to his feet, but Con aimed a kick in his direction.

"Stay there, little boy."

Paks had been growing angrier. Jori sneered at Rufen, and said, "We have to do something—the Master's put one of 'em on our floor!"

Rufen cocked his head. "So?"

"So, we'll have to teach them all a lesson—I don't suppose a peasant girl can be much trouble."

Paks felt her anger like a leaping flame. "You don't?" she asked, trying for a pleasant tone. The two whirled; she saw the shock in their faces as they saw her size and condition. Behind them, Rufen helped the boy in red to his feet. "What kind of lesson," she asked, rocking slightly from heel to toe, "did you think to teach me?" She hoped they would jump her; she wished she had gone for them at once.

"Who in Gird's name are you?" asked Con, glancing sideways at Jori for support.

"Paksenarrion Dorthansdotter," said Paks quietly, still ready to jump. "A—peasant girl, I believe you said, wasn't it?"

"You're the new—?" Con seemed unable to believe it.

"Yes." Paks waited, suddenly finding it funny.

"Paksenarrion," said Rufen pleasantly from behind them, "is a veteran of the wars in Aarenis. I believe she is known to Sir Fenith, as well as Marshal Cedfer of Brewersbridge and others." Paks glanced at him quickly, still balanced to fight. The boy Aris was grinning openly.

Con shook his head. "I'm sorry for what I said, then. You're no novice, barely trained as a squire. I had heard you were a sheepfarmer's daughter, but obviously—"

"I am a sheepfarmer's daughter," said Paks, dangerously quiet. "Does that change your opinion?"

He looked confused. "But you're not Girdish. Where did a—a girl like you learn warfare, outside the granges?"

"In Duke Phelan's Company," said Paks, glad to see the surprise return. "I began there, as a recruit."

"Phelan!" that was Jori. "But he's—" he looked quickly at Con.

"Yes?" Paks let her hand slip to her dagger hilt.

"I didn't say a thing—" began Jori. He held out his hands, palm up. "Look, Pak-Paksenarrion—I don't know Duke Phelan, I only know what I've heard. Don't—"

"And what is this?" The Training Master had turned into the passage from the stairs. Paks, facing them all, saw their faces stiffen at his voice. She stood silent, waiting to see what would happen. No one spoke for a long moment. Then—"Well? Have you set a gauntlet for our new student to run? Aris, I thought you were to escort her to supper, and now I find you all standing about up here as if you had all night to chat."

Even Rufen seemed to have no quick answer to this. Paks moved forward, passing Con and Jori without looking at them. "Pardon, sir," she said. "I did not know the usual signal for supper, and delayed them talking about your customs. You did say, did you not, that I need not change to the student uniform for tonight?"

"Yes—I did." The Training Master looked taken aback. "But—"

"Is it permitted to wear one's own dagger to the table?"

"Yes, of course, but—"

"Then," she said, with a glance back to the others, who were watching in some kind of shock, "I apologize again for making everyone late. Aris, will you show me the way?"

The boy in red seemed the least dazed of them all, and came quickly to her side, nodding respectfully to the Training Master, who looked down at him thoughtfully. "Someone downstairs reported a disturbance up here," he said at last.

"Oh, sir?" Aris managed to look doubtful.

"Yells," said the Training Master.

Paks intervened. "They were expecting a peasant girl," she said, carefully not looking at Con and Jori. "I think I surprised them."

"I see." The Training Master looked them all over carefully. "I will see you after supper, Paksenarrion; we must be sure you understand the rules of the house."

"Certainly, sir. Where shall I come?"

"Aris can show you." Aris colored at this, and Paks surmised that he had been called often to the Training Master's study. With a last nod, the Training Master turned away; they all descended the stairs behind him, silently. When he turned away, and they were alone in the passage between the kitchens and the Lower Hall, Rufen spoke.

"Paks, thank you for not going into all that with him—"

"I thought we were in for it," added Con. Paks looked at him with distaste.

"Soldiers don't complain to commanders about every trifle." Con reddened. "That's not what I meant—"

"It's what I meant." She turned pointedly to Aris, who had not spoken to her yet. "Where are you from, Aris?"

"From Marrakai's House, in Tsaia—do you know it?"

Paks laughed. "No—but I've heard of Duke Marrakai."

"My father," said the boy proudly. "I'm the fourth son."

"And knows it, too," muttered Jori, from behind them. Aris whipped around.

"At least *my* father is a Duke!" he said. "And I have three estates already to my name—"

"Oh Gird's grace," muttered Con to Jori, "did you have to start him off again?" Even Paks was tempted to smile at the boy's intensity. But they were at the doors of the Lower Hall, and looking for a place to sit at the crowded tables. Obviously more than students ate here: it seemed to Paks that a whole village was in the room, and the noise confirmed it. She followed the others between the tables, to a serving hatch. There her platter was stacked with sliced meat, a dipper of redroots in gravy, a small loaf of bread, and a slice of something that looked like nut bread dipped in honey. On a table beside the hatch were mugs; she had seen that each table had two pitchers.

The Hall was so crowded that they could not sit together; Aris found a space for the two of them, and the other three wandered away. Paks was hungry and began eating at once. When she slowed down enough to look around, the crowd was thinning out a little. Aris was chatting with another fairly young boy across the table—he was straw-blond, with gray eyes, and slightly crooked teeth. The person next to Paks had left without her noticing. She mopped up the rest of her gravy with the bread, and looked around the table. Next to Aris was a heavy-set redheaded man in a blue tunic, munching away steadily. Next to him, on the end, was a tall, slender—Paks stopped, and stared.

The elf looked up, and smiled at her. "I did not hear your name, lady—will you share it?" The voice held that strange music that all elves voices shared, a hint of harpstrings or bells.

Paks choked down the last bit of bread. "Paksenarrion Dorthansdotter, sir."

The cool gray eyes sharpened. "Would you be that Paksenarrion who traveled with one Macenion?"

"Yes, sir."

"Indeed. It is my pleasure, then, to welcome you—you are welcome to us, as to the Girdsmen. I am one of the embassy from the Westforest elves to Fin Panir; my elven name would be difficult for you to say, but you can call me Ardhiel."

Paks realized that Aris was staring at her, open-mouthed. He hissed at her. "Paksenarrion! The elf spoke to you? He's never said anything to me!"

Silvery laughter fell around them; the elf's eyes sparkled. "I do not know your name, young sir—and what would I speak with you about?"

Now the man beside Aris was also alert, listening.

Aris changed color. "I—sir, I—I only meant that—that I thought elves didn't talk to—"

"To students, rarely. We fear it might distract you from your own affairs—and your affairs, young sir, are not mine."

"But I—but she—but my father is Duke Marrakai!"

"Oh—you are the Kirgan?"

"No, sir. I'm the fourth son; the Kirgan is my brother Juris." The elf waved his hand, dismissing.

"Whatever, young Marrakai—your father's affairs might march with mine, but yours—no. I mean you no discourtesy, but—"

"I'm not a child!" insisted the boy. Paks had to admit he seemed childish even to her: the elf's face expressed nothing, but she could feel his withdrawal.

"No? For me, young Marrakai, all in this room are but a summer's memory. If you would be comfortable with elves, you must admit this. I have known your family for more generations than you have lived in your House." Aris flushed, and set his jaw stubbornly. When his friend across the table whispered, he rose to go, looking pointedly at Paks.

"The Training Master said I was to show you where to go."

"Yes—thank you, Aris, I'll be right there." She looked back at the elf, whose eyes seemed for a moment sad. "Sir, I thank you."

"Lady Paksenarrion, it is nothing. I hope to see more of you hereafter."

CHAPTER TWENTY

In the next few days, Paks felt that her mind and body both were battered and confused. Her instructors were forthright with both praise and criticism; other students accepted her presence without comment, but tested her skills relentlessly. Yet they tested each other just as freely, and seemingly held no rancor. She found it somewhat like being a recruit at the Duke's Stronghold, with the many hours of required drill. Yet out of class and drill there was no regimentation, no barracks chores. Clean clothes appeared in her room each day, and the room itself was cleaned while she was out. Someone else maintained the jacks and the bath house; someone else groomed the horses and polished tack. She began to wonder if this was the way the nobles lived, playing at war with weapons drill, but with someone else doing the dirty work. She had to admit she liked it.

Once she knew where everything was, and which place to go when, she began to enjoy it as she had never enjoyed anything else. Most of the students cared as much about weaponry and tactics as she did. They sat up late, arguing problems assigned by the instructors: where should a cohort of archers be set, or which order of march was best in heavy forest. At first Paks was shy of speaking up to Marshals and High Marshals, but silence was no protection: they would ask her. For Marshals in Aarenis had brought reports of the last season's fighting to Fin Panir, and the problems set were those she had fought through.

It started with an analysis, in a discussion of supply, of the march from Foss Council territory to Andressat. "Assuming a march of five days," Marshall Tigran said, "what would you need to supply a cohort of a hundred soldiers?" Paks tried to remember if it had indeed been five days. When the others had answered, and she was called on, she simply remembered how many mules they'd used, and blessed Stammel for insisting that she learn how to divide everything by three.

"Mules?" asked Tigran, and someone laughed. He frowned at them. Paks shook her head.

"To carry the supplies, Marshal."

"Aha! That was going to be my next question—how to transport it." Somehow Paks was getting credit for a right answer she had never actually given. But the next one she earned on her own. "Then," he went on, "how you do figure the extra transport for the supply taken up by transport?" Paks knew that, from Stammel's many tirades on the subject. One Tir-damned mule in four, he'd muttered, just to make sure the beasts have enough for themselves. Tigran looked at her with respect, as did the rest of the class. When he found she knew how long fresh mutton or beef could travel in different seasons, and how long it took to grind the grain for a cohort's bread ration, he grinned, and turned to the other students. "This is the value of practical knowledge," he said. "Some of you know in theory, and the rest of you are learning, but here's a soldier who has been in the field, and knows what the ration tastes like."

"Can you tell us if it's true what Marshal Tigran says, about not being able to fight without supply even for one day? I still think brave troops could do without—not for long, maybe, but for a day or so." That was Con, more interested than aggressive. Tigran nodded to Paks, and she thought back to the various campaigns, and the day of the ambush in the forest near the Immer.

Paks described the enemy's apparent retreat, her Company's forced march trying to catch them, and the ambush in the forest. No one interrupted with questions; even Con was quiet. She told them of the damp cold that night, when the wounded had no shelter, and no one had food, when the smell of the enemy's food drifted across the locked squares, making their hunger worse. And the next morning's attack, their allies' arrival. And finally of the sudden weakness that toppled more than one of them, that long march and heavy fighting without food or rest.

"It's not a matter of bravery," she said. "You can live long without food, and stand and fight for a time, but not march and fight."

Tigran nodded at her. "Most of you have never been hungry for long—and since you aren't seasoned warriors, never when fighting."

"I wonder why you came to study, Paks," said Con after that class. "You already know as much as the Marshals—"

"No. No, I don't." She wondered how to explain what she didn't know. "I know what a private knows—the soldier in the cohort—"

"It seems plenty—"

"No, listen. I always wanted to learn, and so I paid attention to the sergeants, and the captains when they talked in my hearing. But I only know it from the bottom. I don't know how to plan—how to think of more than one cohort at a time. You know how to reckon amounts for any number—right?" He nodded. "Well, I don't. My sergeant taught me to divide by three, to find our cohort's share of the Company's supplies. And I can add that three times, to go from a cohort's share to the whole Company. But that's all. He told me one time that Marrakai, when he goes to war, has five cohorts. I can't reckon in fives at all."

"You can't? But it's not hard—"

"No, maybe not. But you know how, and I don't. And in tactics, I know some things not to do, but I don't always know why. I can write well enough, and read—but I can't write a description of a battle, as Marshal Drafin showed us, or read one and make sense out of it. The sand table is one thing, but those books—"

"Huh. I thought after the first night that you knew everything—or thought you did."

Paks shook her head again. "I won't ever know anything—there's not time enough to learn all I want to know—"

"Now that's an interesting sentiment." The Training Master had appeared, as usual, without warning. Paks had begun to wonder if he had magical powers. "Are you serious in what you say?"

Paks was, as always, wary around him. "Yes . . . sir."

"You feel you have much more to learn—even with your practical experience?"

Paks felt an edge of sarcasm in his voice. She stiffened. "Yes. I said that."

"Don't bristle at me." To her surprise, he was smiling. "One thing that worried the Marshal-General was the possibility that you might find these things too boring—"

"Boring!"

"Don't interrupt, either. We have had a few other veterans who found them so—who were so intent on what they had done already that they could not learn new things." He looked intently at Con, who colored. Paks wondered what that was about, but was glad enough he wasn't after her. "How are you coming with your reading?" He was after her. She wondered if he'd heard what she had said to Con. She hated having to admit her weaknesses.

"Not—very fast, sir."

"I thought so." It did not sound too sarcastic. "Paksenarrion, the only way to learn to read faster and better is to read—just like swordplay. You can't learn swordplay from a book, or reading from your sword."

"But if I can listen to someone who knows—"

He shook his head. "Paksenarrion, no one knows everything—you're not alone in that. Writing stores knowledge, for others to use who may never know the writer. You know how tales told change in the telling—" She nodded, and he went on. "That's why writing is so important. Suppose you are in a battle; if you can write well enough to describe it accurately, then others can learn from your experience many years from now."

"It's too late." Paks looked down. She had hated turning in her scrawls when the others wrote neat, legible hands. "I—the ones who can write started earlier."

"And when did you start with staves? And you're already out of the novice class, into intermediate. Work at it. As for you, Con," the Training Master turned to him. "You quit worrying about your standing with the juniors, and start spending your evenings on tactics. And supply. Perhaps if you'll explain reckoning in all numbers to Paks, she'll explain why you can't march a cohort for two days on sixteen measures of barley and a barrel of apples."

"Apples? I meant to write salt beef."

"Your writing is not much better than Paks'—neither Tigran nor I could decide what you really meant, so we called it apples. So might your supply sergeant, someday."

She could not remember when she had felt so at home. Not even in the Company, that last year. Instead of Saben and Canna, she had Rufen, Con, and Peli. They spent hours with pebbles and beans, teaching her reckoning. She taught them all one of her favorite sword tricks, so that Cieri, bested three times in one day, glared at them all, and accused Paks of trying to get his job as Weapons Master. She began to read faster, and understand more complicated books and scrolls. They began to realize, as Rufen explained one night, that the soldiers they might command one day were real people.

"I knew they were," he said thoughtfully, "and yet I didn't. Here we talk about supplying a cohort, or positioning a squad of archers over here, and a couple of cohorts of pikes there. They're just—just bodies. Soldiers. Gird forgive me, being a Girdsman, but I looked like that at my father's guardsmen . . . they all wore a uniform, they all wore the same weapons. But after knowing you—and you were, as you say, 'just a private'—I know they're real people."

Paks looked down, suddenly moved almost to tears. She felt, for the first time, that these were real friends. She could talk to them about the Company—about the people in it—with no betrayal of trust. Little by little she opened up, talking a few words at a time about Stammel and Devlin, Vik and Arne—even Saben and Canna.

She had special status with the juniors—for Aris Marrakai had told his friends about her protecting him from Con's bullying. They did not venture to intrude on the upper floors very often, but she was conscious of shy smiles and friendly greetings from the whole group that Con despised.

Then there were the other races, seen close-to for the first time. The elf who had spoken to her the first night often ate at her table. When he saw her interest, he taught her a few words of elventongue—polite greetings and other courtesies. Some evenings he played the hand harp and sang; Paks and the others listened, entranced. Paks might have thought him a mere harper and wordsmith, but he came to weaponsdrill from time to time, and only the most advanced students fenced with him. Paks lost her sword twice in one session.

The dwarves kept more to themselves, and Paks might not have met them but for an accident with an axe. She had asked to learn axe-fighting, remembering Mai's effectiveness, and Cieri shook his head.

"I can teach axework, but to be honest, Paks, I don't know as I've ever seen a good swordfighter take to the axe. You're likelier to make a good spearman. But whatever you want—as long as you keep improving with staves."

"I still don't understand why that's so important."

Cieri grinned. "You don't, eh? Well, keep in mind that the rest of us are Girdsmen. Gird was a farmer, not a lord's son to have a sword at his side. He won the freedom of the yeomen with weapons they could find or make: clubs, staves, cudgels—and an occasional axe. Every Girdsman learns to use those first; every knight of Gird can not only use, but teach the use of, the weapons you can find anywhere. Then no yeoman of Gird is helpless, so long as a stick is within his reach."

Paks thought about it a moment. "You mean—ordinary farmers—fighting regular soldiers?"

"Yes, exactly. Surely you've heard that?"

"Well, yes—but—"

"But you still don't believe it?" He shook his head. "You were a farmer's daughter—and you wanted to fight—so in your mind you built up what a soldier's weapon can do. When you become a Girdsman, Paksenarrion, I'll show you, wood against steel, how Gird won."

"Why not now?"

Cieri gave her a long look. "Because you are not under Gird's law yet, and I just might lose my temper."

"Oh." Paks was not sure what he meant, and didn't think she should ask more.

"But as for axes, that's a Girdish weapon. Have you ever used one much for chopping?"

"No—we didn't have forest where I grew up."

"And in Phelan's Company?"

"The sergeants said they didn't have time to teach us axework."

"Wise. Well, go get one from the armory, and we'll start."

For a few days things went well; the basic drills were not hard, and Paks soon adjusted to the heavy axe-head hanging on the end of her arm. Or so she thought. Then Cieri set up a roughly carved log for her to "fight." It had a couple of branches for "arms." Paks looked at it disdainfully. She had seen the amusement on the others' faces.

"Isn't this just like chopping a tree?"

"Yes, but you haven't chopped any trees, and we don't happen to need any trees chopped. This will be fuel for the main kitchens later, if you'll get busy and do what I tell you." He took the axe from her, motioned her back, and with two smooth swings took a four-finger-deep chunk out of the log. "Like that," he said. "And remember what I told you about backswing and bounce. Wood is harder than flesh, but softer than armor—at least this wood is."

Paks took the axe, which now felt comfortable in her grip. The basic stroke, he had explained, was much like the sideswing in longs word—but for using two hands. Paks had not used a two-handed sword; she did not think that mattered. She swung the axe back over her shoulder, and brought it around smoothly. Harder than flesh—softer than armor: she put what she thought was the right force into it. Whack! She felt the blow in both shoulders, and the axehead recoiled, dragging her off balance, and missing her knee by a finger's breadth.

"You have to hit harder than that, Paks," said Cieri. "A two-handed blow is a twisting blow; get your back into it."

The next stroke caught the axe-blade in the wood. She struggled to wrench it free, while Cieri described what happened to fighters whose weapons caught in an enemy. She felt the back of her neck getting hot; yet she knew he was right. That didn't help. When she began again, she managed a series of effective strokes, knocking off chips much smaller than Cieri's, but not making any serious mistakes. He called a halt, and nodded.

"You're doing well for a beginner. Now see if you can hit a certain target." He brought out his pot of paint, and daubed red on both of the "arms," as well as two spots on the "body." "Let's see you get the left arm first, then the upper body, then the lower body, then the right arm. Make your strokes work; use as few as you can. Remember, he's got a spear he's poking at you in the meantime."

Paks looked at the targets. "Axe fighters don't carry shields, do they?"

"Not using this kind of axe. There's a light battleaxe for riders that you can use one-handed—you could carry a shield with that. But here it's your quickness."

"I could break the spear with the axe, couldn't I?"

"You'd better. But that's a smaller target than you're ready for. And it moves. You've something to learn before you face a live spearman with an axe."

Paks nodded, and turned to the enemy tree. She had just gotten in position for a stroke at the left-hand branch when Cieri stopped her.

"Now look, Paks—you've got more sense than this. Look where you are."

She was sideways to the "enemy," in easy reach of the right "arm."

"You can't face him directly with that axe—think! Where can you strike, and be out of range."

Paks was annoyed at herself. She moved around the side of the tree, and swung at the left branch from there. She heard the wood creak as the axe sank deep, and was halfway into the next stroke when Cieri yelled again.

"Gird's blood! Do you think he'll stand still while you chop him up? Move, girl!"

Paks felt title blood rush to her face. She jumped, whirling the axe high, and swung again at the branch. It split before taking the full force of her blow, and the axe swung on to lay a deep gash in her leg as she landed from the jump. Furious, she ignored the pain and aimed a vicious slash at the main trunk, straight at Cieri's mark. The axe stopped in midstroke, wrenching her shoulders, and hung in the air.

"Let go," said Cieri mildly. Paks looked at the axe, down at her leg, and then unwrapped her hands from the axe handle. The axe fell with a clang. "If the blade's damaged," Cieri went on, "you can grind it down yourself. I'd thought you too seasoned a fighter to lose your temper for a little thing like that."

Paks said nothing, still angry. Pain from her leg began to demand attention. He came forward, and picked up the axe, running his fingers over the head and blade edge. Then he looked at her.

"You're damned lucky, Paks. Now will you believe me about axes?"

"I can learn." She was surprised at her own voice, furry with anger.

His eyebrows rose. "Oh? How? By cutting off your limbs one at a time? The way you're going, you'll be an axe-fighter about the time you're holding the axe in your teeth.'

"I could—if you weren't badgering me." Paks glared at him, saw the flash of his dark eyes.

"Me! You—not even a yeoman—you're telling me, the Weapons Master, that I shouldn't heckle you? I thought you had more sense—and here you stand flatfooted like a novice, then lose your temper just because I tell you so, and then this! I suppose I should be glad you aren't a Girdsman."

"I—" Paks was suddenly conscious of all the other listening ears. "I'm sorry," she muttered.

"So you should be," he said crisply. "You'll miss days of work with that leg, and I don't think you'll find yourself in the same class when you come back. If you do."

Paks looked up, startled, to meet a grim cold Cieri she had never seen. "Sir?"

"It might pass in a novice, Paksenarrion, but not in someone who claims to be a veteran. Was all that just an act?"

"What?" Now she was completely bewildered. It must have shown, for Cieri's face softened a trifle.

"That even disposition you showed until today. That smile, that willingness. Which is the real you, Paksenarrion? Do you know yourself? Or are you acting a part all the time, inside and out?"

"I—I thought you—liked me," she said. She knew at once it was the wrong thing to have said.

"Liked you? Gird's arm, what do you mean by that? Listen, Paksenarrion, you come here on trial, not even a Girdsman—you come in full of life as a yearling colt, showing off, taking every trick I know, everything the other Marshals can teach you—and teaching your own tricks to the others—and you expect us to like it? Well, any teacher likes a willing student—but that's not enough for us. We're training knights of Gird, Paksenarrion, and paladins, who will go and and die for the justice Gird brought. You—you're playing with us, enjoying a safe, exciting time doing what you like to do. Then you'll go where you please, using what you've learned for your own ends. The rest of us aren't playing a game." He shook his head. "I've let you play; after all, you're a good practice partner for the others. I thought, from the way you seemed to be, that you might join the Fellowship and justify the time I've spent. But I won't waste my time on games anymore. We'll see what the Marshal-General says, before you return." Paks could hardly believe her ears. He was turning away when he glanced at her leg. "Better wrap that; you've bled a lot."

Paks watched him walk without a backward glance toward the other students, who were staring in the same shock she felt. He had them back to their drill in seconds, and did not look her way again. Paks forced herself to think, to move. She took off the scarf she had wrapped around her head against the cold, and bound it tightly around her leg. The bleeding had slowed, but she had left a sizeable stain on the ground. She could do nothing about that, but she did take a few seconds to stack the hacked limb neatly near the rest of the tree before limping back to the armory. Cieri still had the axe.

She looked back from inside the armory. Cieri was fencing with Con; no one looked her way. She felt cold, inside as well as out. She had been stupid—even rude—but was it really that bad? And had they all been resenting her since she came? She tried to think what to do. She took a roll of bandage material from its box beside the armory door, and retreated toward the stableyard, which had a well. It was midmorning; a stable worker trundled a barrow full of dung out the far archway as she came into the yard. No one else was in sight. Paks pulled the scarf away from her leg, wincing, and washed the wound out until the bleeding stopped before wrapping it with clean bandages.

The Training Master, she was thinking dully. I must see the Training Master—and then the Marshal-General. Her leg was hurting in earnest now, throbbing in time with her pulse. She rinsed the scarf in a bucket of water, and wrung it out. Her fingers were stiff with the cold water. When she looked up, two dwarves were watching her.

"Your pardon is it?" said the darker one. "Is it that you can say what way to the training field for the knights?"

Paks worked the meaning out of this. "Did you want Marshal Cieri?" she asked

They nodded gravely. They hardly topped her head, the way she was leaning over the bucket, and she didn't think it would be polite to stand. The darker one carried a double-bladed axe thrust into his belt; the yellow-bearded one carried his in his hand. "It is that we were asked to show something of this skill with the axe," he said. "It is Marshal Cieri who teaches this, is it not so?"

"It is." Paks felt her ears redden. She felt even worse than before. If he had asked dwarves to come and teach her—"It is through that arch," she said, nodding toward it, "and then right, and through the building there." She could not explain; besides, it might be something else.

"What is it that you do here?" asked the darker dwarf, peering into the bucket. "It looks blood."

Paks blushed deeper. "It is—I cut myself, and this wrapped it at first."

The dwarf nodded. "Cut—are you then not a student of the Weapons Master?"

"I—am," Paks hesitated, wondering if she should claim that now.

"But he is Marshal, yes? It is that he heals those injured in training?"

"Not this time," said Paks, hoping they would go.

Four shrewd eyes bored into her. She could not read their expressions. Then the darker dwarf emitted a rough gabble of words that Paks had never heard before: dwarvish, she thought. The yellow-bearded one spoke to her. "I am Balkis, son of Baltis, son of Trok, son of Kertik, the sister-son of Ketinvik Axemaster, the first nephew of Axemaster. It is that you are not Gird's?"

Paks had never met a dwarf, and did not know that this introduction was normal. She was trying to remember it all when the question came, and for a moment did not answer. The dwarves waited patiently. "I am not of the Fellowship of Gird," she said finally.

"But you are here," said the darker dwarf. "How is it that you are here?"

"I was offered a time of training here," said Paks carefully, "because of something I had done."

"Ah." Another pause. Finally the yellow-bearded dwarf, Balkis, asked, "Is it that we might know your clan?"

Paks realized, belatedly, that she had not responded to his introduction with her name. "I'm Paksenarrion Dorthansdotter, of Three Firs."

An exchange of dwarvish followed this. Balkis spoke in Common again. "Please—is it that Three Firs is a clan? We do not know this name."

"No, Three Firs is the village nearest my father's home. It is far from here, to the north."

"Ah. And your father is Dorthan, but of what clan?"

Paks wondered how to explain. "Sir, my father's father was Kanas Jorisson, but I do not think we have the same kind of clans you do—"

Both dwarves laughed loudly. "Indeed, you would not! No—no, you would not. But some men think they have clans as we do, and give themselves names for them, and if you were such then we wished no insult by failing to acknowledge that name." Then Balkis leaned back on his heels watching her. "What is it that you did, to make a hurt the Weapons Master would not heal?"

Paks looked down. "I—cut myself."

"Yes, but—" He stopped, and leaned close to place his face before her. "I would not have you to think that it is our nature to be inquisitive."

Abruptly, Paks found herself grinning. "Oh, no," she said. "I wouldn't think that."

"Good. But we have to study men, who come into our rocks and want things of us. So it is that you will tell us what is that cut?"

"I was trying to use an axe," said Paks slowly. "And I became angry, and struck too hard, and cut my leg."

"Ah. Angry with an axe is dangerous."

"So I found," said Paks ruefully.

"And this the Weapons Master found badly done, is it so?"

"Yes. And I was rude." She wondered why she was telling them, but their interest seemed to pull it out of her.

"Rude—to a Marshal." Suddenly the darker one loosed a volley of dwarvish, and both of them began to quiver. Paks looked up to see their eyes sparkling with mischief. "You fear not Marshals?"

"I—" Paks shook her head. "I should fear them more. I was here as a guest, and my rudeness will cost my place."

"Ha!" Balkis nodded. 'They are as a clan of adoption, and you are not adopted. So it is they can be unjust.'

"It wasn't unjust," said Paks. "It—they think I have been unjust, to take their hospitality without giving in return."

Now they frowned. "You haven't?"

"No." Paks poured the stained water out on the cobbles and watched it drain away between them. "I thought—but I haven't."

"Hmph." The snort was eloquent. "But it is you that are the fighter interested in axes?"

"Less than I used to be," said Paks.

"Would you try again?" asked Balkis. His voice held a challenge.

"I might—if I have the chance."

"If it happens that your Weapons Master refuses you, I will show something," he offered. "It is not every human that will be rude to Marshals of Gird, and be willing to work with axes past the first blood drawn."

"But I was wrong," said Paks, thinking ahead to what the Training Master would say. The dwarves both shrugged, an impressive act with shoulders like theirs.

"It is the boldness of the fighter," said Balkis. "We dwarves, we will not take lessons from Marshals, despite their skill, for they are always insulting us. Did you know any dwarves, where you came from?"

"No," said Paks. "You are the first I have ever met, though I saw dwarves in Tsaia and Valdaire."

"Ah. Then you know not our ways. It involves no clan-rights, but perhaps you would sit at our table some night?"

"If I'm here," said Paks.

They shrugged again, and passed out of the stableyard toward the training fields. Paks gathered up the damp scarf, pushed herself upright, and limped back toward her room. On the way, she saw the Training Master turn into the corridor ahead of her and called to him. He stopped, looking back, and came forward, looking concerned.

"Paksenarrion—what's happened? You're hurt?"

"Yes, sir. I—" Suddenly she felt close to tears. She pulled herself upright. "It's not that, sir, but I must speak with you."

"Something's happened?"

"Yes, sir."

"Well, come along, then." He led the way to his study, and waved her to a seat. "What is it?"

CHAPTER TWENTY-ONE

Paks took a long breath, clutching the sodden scarf in her hands. "Sir, I—I lost my temper, and was rude to Marshal Cieri, and he doesn't want me in his class."

"I see." His face looked almost as cold as the first day. "And you come to me about it—why?"

"I thought I should." She swallowed painfully the lump that had been growing in her throat for the past half-hour. "Sir."

"You want me to plead for you? Without hearing his story?"

"No, sir." Why was everyone misunderstanding what she meant? Paks plunged on. "It isn't that—I thought I was supposed to tell you—"

"He told you to?" That was with raised brows.

"No, sir," said Paks miserably. "I mean—you're the Training Master—if it was back in the Company, I'd have to tell the sergeant—"

His voice gained a hint of warmth. "You're saying that you are doing what you would have done in Duke Phelan's Company? Reporting something you did wrong?"

"Yes, sir."

"I see." His fingers drummed on the desk. "You agree that whatever happened was your fault?"

Paks nodded. Thinking back, she knew that Siger or Stammel would have reacted just as Cieri had—if not worse.

"Well, suppose you tell me about it. And by the way, how did you get hurt?"

"You knew I'd asked to learn axe fighting?" Paks waited for his nod, then went on. "I'd been doing drills with the axe—not hitting anything, and today Marshal Cieri set up a target. A log, with limbs." Paks stopped. It seemed even worse as she tried to think how to say what had happened.

"Yes?"

"Well—sir—I had trouble with it—he'd said I would—"

"And you lost your temper over that?"

"No, sir. Not then. After a while I made some chips of it, and then he wanted me to hit specific targets. Only when I started, he—he got after me for not thinking of it as live, for giving it a chance to hit back." She looked up to see the Training Master's lips folded tightly. As bad as that, then. She went on. "Then I hit a limb—he said to think of it as an arm—and when I went to hit again, he was angry that I hadn't allowed for it to move. So I jumped at it, and hit it really hard, and the limb broke and the axe hit my leg."

"How badly?"

"Just a cut. But then I was angry, and I was about to—to swing as hard as I could, and he stopped the axe." Paks looked up again. "I didn't know he could do that."

"It's not something we demonstrate very often," said the Training Master, in a neutral voice. "Go on."

Paks ducked her head. "Then he said he thought I knew better than to lose my temper, and that I wouldn't be any good at axework, like he'd said. And that's when—"

"What did you say, Paksenarrion?"

"I said—" she paused to remember the words. "I said I could learn if he wouldn't harass me. It—I was wrong, sir, and I know it. I knew it as soon as I said it—"

"Did you apologize?"

"Yes, sir; I told him I was sorry—"

"Did you mean it?"

Paks looked up, startled.

"Were you sorry for being rude, or sorry he was angry with you, or sorry you'd lost your temper in the first place?"

"I—I don't know, sir. I suppose—I was just sorry about everything."

"Hmph. So then what happened?"

Paks told the rest as well as she could, and on being prompted added the conversation with the dwarves. When she had finished, the Training Master sighed.

"So you came to me, because you thought you should, and you expect me to do—what? What do you think will happen now?"

Paks met his gaze squarely. "I think you'll send me away," she said. "If that's what all of you think—that it's unfair to spend the time when I'm not a Girdsman. And even if I were—he said it would be bad—you might still."

"Do you think we should send you away?"

Paks didn't know what to say to this. For a moment she looked away, but when her eyes returned to his face it held the same quiet expectancy. She thought the question over. "Sir, I—I don't know what your rules are—what your limits are. If I do what you don't want, then of course you have the right to send me away. But I can't think what is best for you—for the Fellowship. If it is best to, then you will. Otherwise—I don't know."

"Well, if you are convinced we will send you away, why come to me? Why not simply go pack your things and leave? Or tell us you're leaving, and not wait to be dismissed?"

"But—I couldn't do that. I would be—" She couldn't think of the right words; she knew it would be wrong, and somehow worse than wrong. "Discourteous," she finally said. "Ungrateful. It's my fault, and you have the right; I don't."

He shook his head slowly. "I'm not sure I follow your reasoning, Paksenairion. You agree that we have the right to dismiss you, if you displease us—but you think you have no right to withdraw?"

"If I didn't want to stay—or if something happened, perhaps to my family or something—then I could, but it wouldn't be fair to—to walk out when it was my fault."

He pounced on that. "Fair. You're trying to be what you think is fair?"

"Yes, sir."

"And you said, 'If I didn't want to stay'—does that mean you do want to stay?"

"Of course I do," said Paks, louder than she'd meant to.

"There's no 'of course' to it," he replied crisply. "Many who come here to train don't like it, and don't want to stay. Are you saying that even after Cieri's thrown you out of his class—in front of everyone—you'd still prefer to stay here?"

"Yes, sir."

"Why?"

Her hands twitched. "It's—it's what I always wanted to learn. These weeks have been the best of my life."

"Until today."

"Yes, sir." Then she looked at him again. "If I could stay—today is not much, really—"

"Oh?" His brows went up again; Paks' heart sank. "You call an axe wound, and having the senior Weapons Master refuse to have you in his class 'not much'? We have different views, Paksenarrion."

"I'm—"

"You're sorry. I'm sure." He sighed again. "Paksenarrion, we accept occasional outsiders—non-Girdsmen—because we know that good hearts and good fighters may choose another patron. You have an unusual background; it may be that you have seen that which makes today seem minor to you. But to us it is important. We have all watched you, for these weeks, and been puzzled. You are capable, intelligent, hardworking, physically superior to most of the others. You have gotten along with the others, juniors and seniors both. You don't brawl, get into arguments, get drunk, or try to seduce the Marshals. If you were a Girdsman, we would be more than pleased with your progress. Yet you have reserves, you harbor mysteries, which we cannot fathom. All our skills say these are not evil—yet great evil has been known to masquerade as good, just as a beautiful cloak can cover an evil man. This—today—is the first chink in your behavior. Is it characteristic? Is this the true Paksenarrion coming out? And why have you refused to make any commitment? Marshal Cieri does, in this way, speak for all of us. We would welcome you gladly as a knight-candidate—perhaps more—if you were of the Fellowship of Gird. But until you show us something, some willingness to give in return for what you are given—more than that surface pleasantness you have shown, I must concur with him."

Paks sat still, unable to move or speak. She had never really believed that anyone could think she was evil. She longed to be back with the Duke's Company, where Stammel, she was sure, would defend her against any such accusation. Why had she ever left that safe haven? Into that shock, her leg intruded, throbbing more insistently. She blinked a few times, and lifted her head.

"Yes, sir," she said, through stiff lips. "I—I will go pack."

"Gird's right arm!" The Training Master's voice must have echoed through the entire first floor. "That's not what I said, girl!" Paks stared at him. "You have the choice—make it!"

"Choice?" Paks could not think.

"You can become a Girdsman," said the Training Master crisply. "Has that not occurred to you?"

"No," said Paks with more honesty than tact.

"Then it should have. By the gods, girl, you think better than that in tactics class. You recognize what the problem is: you want to stay for more training, and we are unwilling to give more training without some return. How much do you want to stay? What are you willing to give? And what did you want the training for, if not to follow Gird?"

Paks felt her heart pounding so that she could scarcely draw breath. "You mean I could join—but if you think I'm bad, why would you—"

The Training Master gave a disgusted snort. "I didn't say I thought you were evil. I said it was a possibility. Do you want to join the Fellowship of Gird? Will you pay that price?"

"I—" Paks choked a moment and went on. "Sir, I want to stay. If that is what—but will Gird accept it?"

"We can talk of Gird himself later, Paksenarrion. What we, the Marshals, are looking for is something less than what Gird may ask. Is it something your Duke told you, that makes you dislike Gird so? Or have you another patron you haven't told us about?"

Paks shook her head. "No, sir. It's nothing like that; all I have been told of Gird I admire, and here you teach that Gird is a servant of the High Lord, not a god to worship instead of him. But—" She could not explain the obscure reserve and resentment she felt, and worked her way toward it haltingly. "When I was in the Duke's Company, I knew Girdsmen. Effa was killed in her first battle—but that doesn't matter. I think it was when Canna was captured and killed. She was a Girdsman, but it didn't help. She died, and not in clean battle, even though we were trying to reach the Duke, and tell him about Siniava's capture of the fort. If Gird saved anyone, why not Canna, his own yeoman? Why me?"

"You don't like the notion that great deeds reward the hero with a quick death?"

Paks shook her head more vigorously. "No, sir. And hers wasn't quick, by what I was told. Capture, and a bad wound—that's no reward for faithful service. And she was the one hit at the fort itself, by a stray arrow. Why didn't Gird protect her then? She kept us together, led the way—it should have been her chance, that last day, not mine." She felt the old anger smouldering still, and fought it down. "And more than that—the captain said it was probably Carina's medallion that saved me from death in Rotengre—but I'm a soldier. Why didn't Gird save the slave, or the baby? Why did they have to die?" Now more scenes from Aarenis recurred: the child in Cha, the frightened rabble in Sibili, Cal Halveric's drawn face, old Harek dying after torture. And the worse things, from the coastal campaign. She set her jaw, feeling once more that old sickness and revulsion, that helpless rage at injustice, that had driven her from the Duke's Company to travel alone.

The Training Master nodded slowly; she could see nothing mocking in his face. "Indeed, Paksenarrion, you ask hard questions. Let me answer the easiest one first. You ask why Gird did not save his own yeoman, and the answer to that is that Girdsmen are called to save others, not be saved." He held up his hand to stop the questions that leaped into her mouth. "No—listen a moment. Of this I am sure, sure from the archives and from my own knowledge. Gird led unarmed formers into battle with trained soldiers—do you think they won their freedom without loss? Of course not. Even the yeomen of Gird—even the novice members of the Fellowship—have to accept a soldier's risks. Above that level, as Yeoman-marshal, Marshal, High Marshal, and so on—and as paladin—Girdsmen know that their lives are forfeit in need. Gird protects others through the Fellowship—he does not protect the Fellowship as a shepherd protects sheep. We are all his shepherds, you might say."

Paks thought about that. "But Canna—"

"Was your friend, and you mourn her. That is good. But as a yeoman of Gird, she risked and gave her life to save others—or that's what it sounds like you're saying."

"It's true."

"Now—about those innocents who are not Girdsmen, and are killed. This is why the Fellowship of Gird trains every yeoman—to prevent just that. But in many lands we are few—our influence is small—"

"But why can't Gird do it himself, if he's—"

"Paksenarrion, you might as well ask why it snows in winter. I did not make the world, or men, or elves, or the sounds the harp makes when you pluck the strings. All I know is that the High Lord expects all his creatures to choose good over evil; he has given us heroes to show the way, and Gird is one of these. Gird has shown men how to fight and work for justice in the face of oppression: that was his genius. It is not the only genius, nor dare I say it is the best; only the High Lord can judge rightly. But as followers of Gird, we try to act as he did. Sometimes we receive additional aid. Why it comes one time and not another, or why it comes to one Marshal and not another, I cannot say. Nor can you. Nor will you ever know, Paksenarrion, until you pass beyond death to the High Lord's table, if that happens." He gave her a long look. "And I think that you blame Gird because you are still blaming yourself for these deaths. Is that not so?"

Paks looked down. She could still hear Canna's voice, that last yell: Run, Paks! And she had run. She could still hear the others. "It might be," she said finally.

"Paksenarrion, Gird does not kill the helpless—someone alive, with a sword or club or stone, does that. If you still think, after the time you have been here, that the followers of Gird act that way—"

"No, sir!"

"—then you should leave at once. But if you see us trying to teach men and women how to live justly together, and defend their friends and families against the misuse of force, then consider if that is not your aim as well. Gird may ask your life, someday, but Gird will never ask you to betray a friend, or injure a helpless child. Consider the acts of your Girdish friend, and not her death, and ask yourself if these were good or bad."

"Good," said Paks at once. "Canna was always generous."

"And so you are rejecting Gird because he has not acted as you would—is that it?"

Paks had not thought that clearly about it. Put that way it seemed arrogant, to say the least. "Well—I suppose I was."

"You are not rejecting his principles, it seems, but the fact that they aren't carried out?"

Paks nodded slowly, still thinking.

"Then it seems, Paksenarrion, that you ought to be willing to try to carry them out." His mouth quirked in a smile. "If the rest of us are doing so badly."

"I didn't say that!"

"I thought you just did. However—" He leaned forward, elbows on the desk. "If you don't think we are too corrupt, perhaps you will give us the benefit of your judgement—"

"Sir!" Paks felt her eyes sting; her head was whirling already.

"I'm sorry." He actually sounded sorry. "I went too far, perhaps—I forgot your leg. We'll talk again later—we must get you upstairs and let the surgeon see that."

"See what?" A voice in the doorway interrupted. Paks tried to turn her head, but felt too dizzy. Her ears roared.

"She's got a small wound, Arianya," said the Training Master.

"Not that small," said the voice. "It's bled all over your floor, Chanis. Better take a look."

Paks tried to focus on the Training Master as he came back around the desk to kneel beside her chair. Her eyes blurred. She heard the two Marshals talking, and then another excited voice, and then felt a wave of nausea that nearly emptied her stomach. She clamped her jaw against that, and roused enough to know that they were carrying her along the passage. Finally, the motion stopped, and her stomach quieted. When she got her eyes working again, she was lying flat on a bed, staring at the ceiling. Her mouth was dry, and tasted bad. She rolled her head to one side. That was a mistake. Her stomach heaved, and she hardly noticed the pail someone pushed under her mouth until she was through.

From a distance, someone said, "If she had the sense to match her guts, she'd be fine—"

"I don't call fainting from a simple cut like that guts, Chanis."

"She didn't, and you know it. We all pushed as hard as—"

"Well, however you say it, I still think—"

Closer, someone called her name. "Paksenarrion? Come on now, quit scaring us." She felt a cup at her lips, and drank a swallow of cold water. Her stomach churned, but accepted it. She opened her eyes again to see the Marshal-General's flint-gray eyes watching her. Before anyone else could speak, Paks managed to force out her own message.

"I want to join—the Fellowship—even if you send me away."

Silence followed this. The Marshal-General stared at her. Finally she spoke. "Why now?"

"Because I was wrong about him—Gird. And so—and so I want to join, and do better."

"Even if I send you away? Even if you never go beyond yeoman?"

"Yes." Paks felt as stubborn now on this ground as she had before on others.

"I hope you feel the same when you've remade a couple of skins of blood." The Marshal-General sat back, and grinned. "Gird's ten fingers! Did you have to lose half the blood in your body to learn sense?"

"I didn't," said Paks. She had the curious feeling that her body was floating just above the bed. She knew she understood more than the others, only it was hard to speak. "It isn't lost—it's not in the same place, is all."

"And you're wound-witless. All right. If you still want to make your vows when you're strong enough, I daresay Gird will accept them. But that will be some time, Paksenarrion. For now you must rest, and obey the surgeons."

Not until some days later did Paks hear the full story of that day. She had had no visitors at first but the surgeons, the Training Master, and the Marshal-General. Finally, the surgeons agreed that she could move back to her own room. She was surprised at how shaky she felt after climbing the stairs—from one simple cut, she thought. She sat down hard on her bed, head whirling, and leaned back against the pillows. Rufen and Con woke her some time later when they discovered her door open and looked in to see why.

"Paks?"

She woke with a start; the last sunlight came through her window. "Oh—I forgot to shut the door."

"Are you all right? You look pale as cheese," said Con. Paks gave him a long stare.

"I'm fine. I just—dozed off."

"The Training Master said you were back. He said not to bother you, but your door was open—"

"That's all right." Paks pushed herself up. She wondered what they were thinking about, and felt her ears going hot.

"I've never been so mad in my life," said Con, moving into the room to sit at her desk. "I'd have taken Cieri apart if I could have—"

"Instead of which, he dumped you—how many times?" Rufen leaned against the doorframe, smiling.

"That doesn't matter. Listen, Paks, if they'd thrown you out, I'd have—have—"

Paks shook her head. "Con—it's all right."

"No, it's not. It wasn't fair—we could all see that. I couldn't believe it, the way he hounded you—and you the best of us. Gird's flat feet, but I'd have blown up at him days before."

Paks stared at him in surprise. "But I thought you'd be on their side—I thought you'd agree that it wasn't fair for me to be here as an outsider."

Con shrugged. "That! What difference does that make? I've been a Girdsman all my life, and I never will be as good a fighter as you are. It's not as if you were bad: you don't quarrel even as much as I do. No one's ever found you doing something underhand or cowardly. They ought to be glad you're willing to come here at all. And that's what I told him."

"And then what?" Paks could not imagine that scene at all.

"And then he told me I didn't know what I was talking about, and until I did I should kindly keep to my own business, and I told him my friends were my business. And he said I should choose my friends with care, and I said I'd learned more from you since you'd come than from him since I'd been here—" Con stopped, blushing scarlet.

"And then," Rufen put in with a wide grin, "then Cieri said maybe he should have long yellow hair to catch Con's attention, and Con swung on him, and ended up flat on his back. Cieri asked the others what they thought, and apparently everyone was on your side. I wish I'd been there—I knew I'd regret being in that lower class after you got here. I don't know if I could have done any more, but—"

"But you shouldn't have," said Paks, looking at Con. "He's—he's the Weapons Master, you shouldn't argue with him."

"But he was wrong," said Con stubbornly, his eyes glinting. "Paks, if you've got a fault it's that you're too willing to be ruled. I know what you'll say—you'll say that's how a good soldier is. Maybe so, for a mercenary company. But we're Girdsmen; Gird himself said that every yeoman must think for himself. I don't care if Cieri is the Weapons Master, or the Training Master, or the Marshal-General, if he's wrong, he's wrong, and if I think he's wrong I should say so."

"Just because you think he is wrong doesn't make him wrong," argued Paks. "How do you know you're right?"

"I can tell unfairness when I see it," growled Con.

"How do you know?" Paks persisted. "Sometimes things seem

unfair when they happen, but later you can tell they weren't—so how do you know when something is truly unfair?"

"Well, when it's—I mean—by Gird, Paks, it's easier to know than to say. I know Cieri was unfair to you; he kept picking at you, trying to make you mad, and then when you got mad he blamed you for it. And you were hurt, dripping blood all over, and he didn't even offer to heal it for you."

Paks shrugged. "If he thought I was wrong, he wouldn't."

"But it was his fault. And so it wasn't fair. Don't you know anything? Didn't you ever have brothers or someone in your Company that kept trying to put things on you—surely you know what I mean."

Paks shrugged again. "Con, I know enough to know that looking for the final fault, who's really to blame, just keeps trouble alive longer. I shouldn't have lost my temper, no matter what. If he was wrong to push me that far, it was still my fault. And the Marshal-General told me when I came that they were reluctant to train someone who had given no vows of service."

"But now you're joining the Fellowship, is that right?" asked Rufen.

"Yes. The surgeon says I should be up to a bout at Midwinter Feast."

"How bad is your leg?"

"Not bad. They stitched it up; it's healing clean. It's mostly blood loss; I should have tied it up tighter to begin with." Then she thought of something else. "Con—did some dwarves show up at the field after I left?"

Con looked startled. "How did you know about them?" Then he grinned broadly. "That was something, let me tell you. Two of 'em came marching up, right into the class, in the middle of the row we were—anyway, came into the class, and interrupted us. I can't talk like they do—all that 'it is that' and 'is it that it is'—but the long and short of it was that Cieri had asked them to come and demonstrate axe fighting, and they were ready. Cieri told them he'd dismissed his student, and they grumped about being called out for nothing. So he said they could show the rest of us, and they glared around and said they wouldn't show anyone who didn't have the guts to learn. One of them challenged Cieri himself. Well, we saw some axe fighting let me tell you, and that axe you were using won't ever be the same."

Paks felt a guilty twinge of satisfaction. She tried to conceal it; Con needed no encouragement. "Is Master Cieri all right?"

"Oh, yes. He got a scratch or two, but you know he can heal that—it's nothing to him. Anyway, now that you're joining the Fellowship, you'll be coming back to class, won't you?"

"I suppose. I haven't seen Master Cieri." Paks wondered if he would hold a grudge against her.

"You are staying, aren't you?"

"Yes."

"Then you'll be back with us. That'll be good. And listen, Paks, you keep in mind what I said. As a yeoman, you have a right to think for yourself. You're supposed to—"

"I do," said Paks. "You—"

"You do, and then you don't. I know what you're thinking, about me and the juniors, and you were right, there. You stand against us—the others in the class—when you think differently. But you don't stand against anyone over you—I'll bet you never argued with your sergeant, or captain, or the Duke—"

Paks found herself smiling. She could not imagine Con arguing with Stammel more than once, let alone with Arcolin. But she defended herself. "I did argue with the Duke once—well, not exactly argue—"

"Once!" Con snorted. "And he was wrong only once in three years? That's a record."

She shook her head at him; it was useless to try to explain. She tried anyway. "Con—privates don't argue with commanders. Not unless it's very important, and usually not then. And we don't see everything, we can't know when the commander is wrong."

"So what did you argue—not exactly—about?"

Paks froze. She had never meant to get close to that night in Aarenis again. "I—you don't need to know," she said lamely.

"Come on, Paks. I can't imagine you arguing with anyone like that—it must have been something special. What was it? Was he going to start worshipping Liart, or something?"

Paks closed her eyes a moment, seeing Siniava stretched on the ground, the Halverics at his side, the angry paladin confronting her Duke. She heard again the taut silence that followed the Duke's outburst, and felt the weight of his eyes on her. "I can't tell you," she said hoarsely. "Don't ask me, Con; I can't tell you."

"Paks," said Rufen quietly. "You don't look ready for supper in the hall; we'll bring something up for you." His gentle understanding touched her; she opened her eyes to see them both looking worried.

"I'm all right," she said firmly.

"You're all right, but you're not well. If you're to make your vows at the Midwinter Feast, you don't need to be scurrying up and down stairs again today. It's no trouble—" he went on, waving her to silence. "If we go now, we can all eat up here in peace. Come on, Con." And the two of them went out, closing her door softly and leaving her to her thoughts.

CHAPTER TWENTY-TWO

Marshal-General Arianya headed the table; three High Marshals, two paladins, and five Marshals (three attached to granges, and two from the college itself) completed the conference.

"Will that new yeoman be ready to test for the Midwinter Feast, Arianya?" asked the oldest of the group, Marshal Juris of Mooredge grange.

"I think so. She says she's well enough now, but the surgeons don't want her fighting for another few days."

"That would look good," muttered High Marshal Connaught, Knight-Marshal of the Order of Gird. "Nothing like a candidate feinting in the ceremony."

"She won't feint," said the Marshal-General firmly. Someone chuckled softly, thinking of it, and she frowned around the table.

"It's not that often we bring new yeomen in here," she reminded them. "It's serious to her—"

"I know that," said Marshal Kory, the Archivist. "It just slipped out, Marshal-General."

"Very well. And while we're on the subject, I would like to suggest something else."

"What you and Amberion were chatting about yesterday?" asked Marshal Juris. "If it's what I think, I'm against it."

The Marshal-General glared at him. "You might at least give me a chance to present the idea, Juris." He waved his hand. She glanced around the table. "You know we're desperately short of paladins—" They nodded. "I have word from Marshal Calith down in Horngard that Fenith was killed a few months ago."

A stir ran around the table. Several of the marshals glanced at the two paladins, who stared ahead and met no eyes. Fenith had been Amberion's close friend, and Saer was his great-niece.

"We need to select a large class of candidates, if we can; the paladins in residence here agree that they can each take on two candidates—"

"Is that necessary?" Juris broke in, looking from face to face.

"I think so." The Marshal-General spread a short parchment in front of her, and ran her hand down the page. "Juris, for the past two hundred years or so, the Fellowship of Gird has had from twenty to thirty paladins recorded at a time. Those on quest vary from fifteen to twenty-five at any one time. We now have on quest only five—" She waited for the murmurs to cease, nodded, and went on. "You see? And here in Fin Panir we have only seven who can take on candidates for training. As you know, any of these may be called away at any time. If we can find fourteen candidates—two for each training paladin—it will still be well over a year before any of those are ready to go. And in the meantime, we have no one to train a backup class—"

"I think we should feather that," said Marshal Kory. "If we chose seven now, then they might progress faster, having more of the paladins' time. In a half-year or so, choose more. Then we'd get a few out faster, and have more coming along."

The Marshal-General nodded. "That's a good idea. Amberion, what do you think?"

"I like that better than taking on two novices at once," said Amberion. "But I don't know if that will shorten the time any. Remember that each candidate has had, by tradition, all the time a single paladin-sponsor can give. We dare not test these candidates any less because times are desperate. It is in desperate times that we need most to be sure of them."

"What list do we have?" asked High Marshal Connaught.

"A short one." The Marshal-General rubbed her nose. "I sent word to all the granges last spring, when Fenith wrote that Aarenis would be at war by summer. We talked of this last year, remember? But we've lost eight paladins in the past year—"

"Eight!"

She nodded gravely. "Yes. We all know that great evil has been moving in Aarenis and the Westmounts. Nearer home, we have seen outbreaks again in eastern Tsaia. Some reports indicate serious trouble in Lyonya. Marshal Cedfer, of Brewersbridge, reported that a priest of Achrya had been laired between his grange and the gnome kingdom nearby. Apparently, he had preyed on nearby farms and caravans using spell-bound robbers."

"They'd say they were spell-bound," muttered Juris.

"That may be, of course. I have only his report to go by. But Brewersbridge has been a healthy community for years—since Long Stones, at least. If Achrya can have a priest there, where else may we not expect trouble?"

"What happened to the paladins, Amberion?" asked Marshal Kory.

"We are still finishing the reports for the archives, Marshal," said Amberion slowly. "Chenin Hoka—he was from Horngard originally; he hadn't been north of the mountains for years—was killed by Liart's command, in Sibili, during the assault on that city—"

"I thought that's where Fenith was."

"He was there, yes. Chenin was taken some time earlier, while helping a grange near Pliuni defend itself; a witness thought he was dead. But Siniava's troops got him to Sibili, to the temple—and he was killed, finally, after long torments." Amberion said nothing more, and silence filled the room. Then he sighed, and began again. "I knew him, when I was a candidate; that was the last time he was north. He knocked me flat, I remember, and I lay there wondering why I'd ever wanted to be a paladin. Anyway, Doggal of Vérella was lost at sea; he was sailing east along the Immerhoft coast. He'd told a Girdsman at Sul that he had a call to come north. The ship was seen going onto reefs near Whiteskull, and his body was recovered some days later. We have no reason to doubt the identification. Garin Garrisson was killed in battle at Sibili; Fenith saw that. The two of them were holding light against a darkness cast by Liart's ranking priest. A crossbow bolt got him in the eye. Arianya Perrisdotter held a daskdraudigs away from a caravan in one of the mountain passes in the Dwarfwatch, but it fell on her in the end. Tekki Hakinier was apparently killed by a band of forest sprites—whatever they call them in Dzordanya. The only word we have is from a witness that says he was 'stuffed with pine needles like a pin-pig,' which I suppose is what they call a hedgehog."

"No." Marshal Kory shook his head. "No, a pin-pig is bigger and lives in trees. They call it that because its flesh is sweet like pork. It sounds like those mikki-kekki—they come in waves, hundreds at a time. But what was he doing up there?"

Amberion shrugged. "I didn't know he was there until we got the word he'd been killed. The witness said something about a varkingla of the long house of Stokki, whatever that means."

Kory nodded. "It means Stokki's clan thought they had to move somewhere, the whole bunch. That's not common. Tekki was Dzordanyan, wasn't he?"

"Yes."

"I would guess that they asked his protection, to move the clan through the forest, and the mikki-kekki didn't cooperate. They usually don't."

"Have you ever seen one?" asked the Marshal-General.

"Oh yes. When I was a rash boy, my three cousins and I sailed across the Honnorgat to visit Dzordanya. That was the plan, at least. My uncle had told us we couldn't sail across the river like that; of course, we thought he was just trying to spoil our fun."

"Why can't you?" asked Saer, speaking for the first time.

"You're from the mountains, aren't you, Saer? Yes. Well, any time you sail across the river, you've got its current to consider, just like rowing. But at the mouth of the Honnorgat, it's that and the tide and the sea current, all together. The short of it is that we ended up a long way up the coast. We couldn't even see Prealith any more. The way the current set, we couldn't sail back without going far out to sea. We may have been rash, but we had more sense than that, to sail a skin boat out of all sight of land. We thought we'd walk back along the shore, carrying the boat, until we got to the Honnorgat."

"Carrying a boat?" Saer was clearly skeptical.

"Skin boat. Not as heavy as you'd think. Hard work, though, with the sail and lines and all. Anyway, the forest in Dzordanya comes right down to the sea—and I mean all the way. You can walk with one foot in the waves, and slam into limbs. With a boat, we had to weave in and out as we could. Not easy. Halory, my oldest cousin, thought we should climb onto level ground, back in the forest, and go that way. Seemed a good idea to me. I'd nearly had my eye poked out by too many twigs already, trying to watch my footing.

"For a time everything went well. Not too much undergrowth, just tall dark firs and spruce, spaced so we could make it between them with the boat. Then we heard the first voices."

"The sprites?"

"Mikki-kekki. Nasty whispers, that you couldn't quite identify. Squeaks, little cries like someone sitting on a hot tack. I started to feel my neck sweat, and so did the others. Halory tried to hurry us, and we fell right into one of their traps. A sort of cone-shaped pit, lined with pine needles, and slippery as grease. We'd hardly caught our breath when they were all around it, chittering at us. They're much less than dwarf-tall, with greenish fur all over, and very long arms with long-fingered hands. It was the boat that saved us. When they started with their darts, we got under it and shook."

"What do they use, bows?"

"No. A sort of tube. They blow into it, and the dart flies out. They throw them by hand, too. The darts are poisoned, usually. Inory, my middle cousin, was hit by one and though he lived he was sick for weeks. That night we thought he'd die. If it hadn't been for some clan's long-house nearby—their sentries heard the mikki-kekki laughing and taunting us—I wouldn't be here. They drove them off, and pulled us out. It was two days before we got home, and my uncle—well, you can imagine." Kory shook his head.

"Well," said Amberion, "now we know about mikki-kekki." He went on with his list. "Sarin Inerith went into Kostandan, as you know, because we had word that Girdsmen were held in slavery there. Her head returned to Piery grange; we have no idea what happened, where, or how. Jori of Westbells finally died of the lungfever that's plagued him these four years. And Fenith, as you heard, died in Horngard."

"What of the current candidates? Don't we have any who will finish this year?" That was High Marshal Suriest, Knight-Marshal of the Order of the Cudgel.

"At best we may have five this year, Amberion tells me. Kosta has withdrawn his candidacy, and transferred to the Marshal Hall. Dort withdrew. Pelis may withdraw. And of course we don't know what will happen in the Trials. Because we had so few paladins here to train, we don't have any scheduled for the following year; we would have had Elis, but she had to leave, as you remember. She may be back, but not soon enough."

"Which leaves us with the new list—what have we got?"

The Marshal-General shifted the papers in front of her, and glanced at another one. "We've talked over most of these before. Are you still opposed to the Verrakai squire, Amberion?"

He nodded. "Marshal-General, we cannot define the problem, but we would not be happy with him."

"Nor I," said High Marshal Connaught. "Look at the time we put in on Pelo Verrakai, and what came of that!"

"Well, then, as I see it we've got five good candidates. Four in the knight's classes, and Seddith, the Marshal we spoke of last time."

"And we need seven."

"And we need as many as we can find," said the Marshal-General. "Now—"

"I know what you're leading up to," interrupted Juris. "You want to include that new yeoman."

"What!" High Marshal Suriest turned his head; Connaught snorted. The Marshal-General held up her hand, and they all quieted.

"Juris, you could have let me say it—but yes, I do. Before you say anything, consider. Sne's a veteran of the Aarenis wars—"

"That's a recommendation?" But Kory subsided when the Marshal-General looked at him.

"We had a report from Fenith about her; he thought she should be considered a possibility if she ever joined the Fellowship. Marshal or paladin, he said. Cedfer reports that she freed the elfane taig, in the mountains southeast of Brewersbridge. He checked that report with full elves—and so have I, here. Also she cleared out that nest of robbers, and was able to fight the Achryan priest alongside Cedfer's yeoman-marshal. As far as weapons-skills, she heads the list. Since she's been here, Chanis reports that she has worked hard on everything we've thrown at her. She's even shown skill in teaching; Cedfer reported that from Brewersbridge, and I've seen how the other students follow her here."

"It's too soon, Marshal-General," said Juris, and several other heads nodded. "I grant she may be what you say, but what do we know of her as a Girdsman? Nothing. She's not even a member of the Fellowship yet. How can you think of giving this honor to an outsider?"

"But she won't be an outsider after she takes her vows," said the Marshal-General.

"No, but—" Juris squirmed in his seat. "I know we need candidates. But we need the best candidates. We need to be sure they're strong Girdsmen first, and then—"

"Watch them get spitted by better fighters?" The Marshal-General's voice sharpened. "Right now this outsider, as you call her, can outfight most of the Marshals here, unless they use their powers. I've seen her—Amberion has seen her—ask Cieri."

The Marshal-General folded her hands on the table. "Juris, I know it's not usual. But we haven't found anything wrong with her. Gird knows we've tested, prodded, tried—Cieri had to set her up for days to make her lose her temper even once. And then she agreed she was wrong. Of course, she's not perfect—no one is. Of course we wish she'd been Girdish all along, come up through the grange training. But allowing for that, she's the best candidate on the list. And if anything is amiss, it will come out in the stress of training, or in the Trials. It's not that we're choosing her over someone else—we haven't got anyone else."

Juris shook his head. "Arianya, you're wrong—and I don't think I can convince you. Suppose she is a potential paladin, that Gird will approve and call. But right now what she is, is a good soldier and a novice Girdsman. I don't care if she knows all the answers, can recite the Ten Fingers backwards and forwards; she hasn't experienced a grange. If she's so good, send her to me—or to another grange—for a half-year. Let's see how she does as a yeoman among yeomen. We've had unpleasant surprises before."

"Gird's gut, may the ale hold out! If I had a half-year, Juris, I'd send her. But we don't have it."

The argument went on some time, but the shortage of paladins won over caution. "We must have the candidates," said the Marshal-General finally. "We must. She will be with the others here, under our protection. Unless you can suggest a better, Juris, I must insist—"

"All right." He frowned, sucking his cheeks, but finally nodded. "All right, then. But be sure you do ward her, Marshal-General. Don't rush that one through the training. She's not a knight yet, remember, and she's never had that sort of training."

Paks, called to the Marshal-General's office, knew nothing of the argument. She expected to be told more details of the ceremony that would make her a Girdsman. She found the Marshal-General, the Knights-Marshal of both orders, and a stranger waiting for her.

"Paksenarrion, there are High Marshal Connaught, High Marshal Suriest, and Sir Amberion, a paladin of Gird presently attached to the Training Order. Please sit here."

Paks sat where she was told, her heart pounding. What now? Was she suspected of something so bad that it would take two High Marshals and a paladin to deal with it?

"You have not changed your mind about joining the Fellowship?" asked the Marshal-General.

"No, Marshal-General."

"You are ready to accept Gird as your patron, as you now accept the High Lord's dominion?"

"Yes, Marshal-General."

"Do you feel any particular—um—call, such as we have talked about in the past days?"

Paks frowned. "Marshal-General, I have felt something, something I could not define, for some time. It began in Aarenis, when I was still in Duke Phelan's Company. I felt the need for a different kind of fighting—but I'm not good with words, Marshal-General. I don't know how to say what I feel, but that here it seems right. I feel that it's right for me to join the Fellowship of Gird; I feel that here I will find the right way to be the fighter I always wanted to be."

"You told Marshal Cedfer in Brewersbridge that you didn't want to fight for gold alone—you wanted to fight against 'bad things.' Is that still true?"

Paks nodded. "Yes, Marshal-General."

"Paksenarrion, I have talked to Marshal Chanis and Marshal Cieri about your progress, and with these High Marshals and Sir Amberion about that and your past. They needed to hear what you have said from your own mouth." She looked at the others. "Well?"

One by one they nodded. Paks watched their faces, confused. What could she have said that was wrong? The Marshal-General tapped her fingers on her desk. Paks looked back to her.

"Paksenarrion, you must know—there's no way you couldn't know—that you are one of the best young fighters in the training company. Cedfer was right to send you. You can qualify easily for either of the knightly orders, if that's what you want." She paused, and Paks held her breath. The Marshal-General resumed. "Or—there is another possibility. Ordinarily, I would not make this offer to someone who is not yet a Girdsman—in fact, ordinarily, it comes only to those of proven service to Gird. But from the reports I've received, Gird has accepted as service several of your deeds in the past. The Training Council has agreed to it. So—would you accept an appointment as a paladin-candidate?"

Paks felt her mouth open. She could not speak or move for an instant of incredulous joy. She saw amusement on their faces, felt her ears flaming again. "Me?" she finally squeaked, in a voice very unlike her own. She swallowed and tried again. "You mean—me? A—a paladin-candidate?"

"You," said the Marshal-General, now smiling. "Now—this is not an order; if you don't feel you can say yes, then refuse. We will not hold it against you—indeed, there are those who think you need more experience."

"But—but I'm so young!" Paks could feel the tears stinging her eyes. Her heart was moving again, bounding, and she felt she could float out of her chair. "I—"

"You are young, yes; and you will be a novice yeoman, which is worse. But if we didn't think you could be a paladin, Paksenarrion, we would not suggest this." The Marshal-General turned to Amberion. "Sir Amberion, you might just tell her what the training is like, while she considers this."

Paks turned to the paladin, a tall, dark-haired man somewhat younger than the Marshal-General by his looks.

His open smile was infectious. "Paksenarrion, paladin-candidates receive training simultaneously as knights and as Girds warriors. Each candidate is attached to one of the knightly orders, but spends much of his or her time with a paladin-sponsor. The training is lengthy and intensive; the candidate must be tested in many ways, for any weakness could open a passage for evil. And even then, the candidate may fail, for the final Trials require proof that the gods have bestowed on the new paladin those powers which paladins must have. Of the few who begin this training, more than half never become paladins."

"It means, as well," said the Marshal-General, "giving up all thought of an independent life. Paladins are sworn to Gird's service; they own nothing but their own gear, and must go wherever Gird commands, on whatever quest Gird requires. For many, these restrictions are too onerous; even we Marshals have more freedom. So we do not expect that all to whom we offer candidacy will take it—or complete the training—and we respect those who withdraw no less than those who go on."

Paks tried to control her excitement, but she could not think of anything but her oldest dreams. Paladin. It meant shining armor, and magic swords, and marvelous horses that appeared from nowhere on the day of the Trials. It meant old songs of great battles, bright pictures in her mind like that of the paladin under the walls of Sibili, all brightness and grace and courage. Another picture moved in her mind, herself on a shining horse, riding up the lane from Three Firs to her father's farm, with children laughing and cheering alongside. Her mother smiled and wept; her brothers gaped; her father, astonished, finally admitted he had been wrong, and asked her pardon. She blinked at that unlikely vision, and returned to hear the Marshal-General saying something about opportunities to change her mind later. But her mind would never change, she vowed. When the Marshal-General paused, she spoke.

"I am honored, Marshal-General; please let me try."

The others looked at each other, then back to her.

"You are sure, Paksenarrion?"

"Yes, Marshal-General—if you are. I can't believe it—" She fought back a delighted laugh, and saw by their faces that they knew it. "Me—a sheepfarmer's daughter—a paladin-candidate!"

Now they laughed, gently. "Paksenarrion," said the Marshal-General, "we are pleased that you accept the challenge. Now let me explain why we are taking a chance on hurrying you." Quickly, she outlined the situation: the shortage of paladins, the growing assaults of evil power in several areas. "You see, we must replenish the ranks—as fast as we can—or risk having no paladins to train new ones."

"How long does the training take?" asked Paks.

"It depends in part on the candidate's previous status. For you, it means becoming a knight first, and then a paladin—more than a year, likely two years. It means some isolation—paladin-candidates withdraw from the main training order, sometimes for months at a time, for meditation and individual instruction. Not all the candidates progress at the same rate. Do not be surprised if someone finishes before or after you who begins the same night.

"We will be taking the vows of the new candidates the same night you become a Girdsman," said the Marshal-General. "This is unusual—as I said—but I feel that it is even more important for your vows to be public. Then—if anything happens..." But Paks was determined that nothing would happen—everything would go well. At that moment, she would have done anything they asked, for the sheer joy of having a chance to prove herself a worthy paladin-candidate.

She hardly felt the stairs under her feet as she went down. As she came through the arch to head for her quarters, she nearly ran into Argalt. She had spent a couple of evenings with him and his friends at a nearby tavern. He grinned at her. "Well—so you haven't been sent away, eh?"

"No." Paks felt like bouncing up and down. She wasn't sure if she should tell him; they had said nothing about keeping her selection secret.

"It must be good news. How about sharing a pitcher later?"

"I can't." Paks couldn't contain it any longer. "I have so much to do—you won't believe it, Argalt!"

"What—did they select you for paladin-candidate, now you're joining the Fellowship?"

Paks felt her jaw drop. "Did you know?"

He laughed. "No—but it's what I would do. Well, now, sheepfarmer's daughter, I'm glad for you. And you so stiff when you came—remember what I said?"

"Yes—yes, I do." Paks threw back her head in glee. "I have to go—I have things—"

"To do, yes. I heard. I'll be watching you, now. You'd better show us something."

Paks had never imagined Midwinter Feast in Fin Panir. Back home, it had meant a huge roast of mutton, sweet cakes, and the elders telling tales around the fire. In the Duke's Company, plenty of food and drink, speeches from the captains and the Duke, and a day of games and music. Here, the outer court erupted at first light with all the juniors starting a snow battle. Paks took one look at the fortifications, and decided that they must have stayed out half the night building them. When the Training Master came out to quell the riot, he was captured, rolled in the snow, and rescued only when Paks led the seniors in an assault on the largest snowfort. But by then he had agreed (as, she found later, was the custom) that the juniors had the right to demand toll of everyone—of any rank—crossing the court. Those who refused to pay were pelted with snowballs; some were even caught and held for ransom. The day was clear, after several days of snow, and no one could possibly sneak across the yard undetected.

The feasting started with breakfast. In place of porridge and cold meat, the cooks offered sweet cakes dipped in honey, gingerbread squares, hot sausages wrapped in dough and fried, and "fried snow," a lacy looking confection Paks had never seen. All day long, the tables were heaped with food, replenished as it was eaten. And all day long the feasters came and went, from one wild winter game to another.

Paks had been told that she was free until midafternoon. With that, she joined a group that rode bareback out onto the snowy practice fields, where they jousted with blunt poles until only one remained mounted. Paks lost her pole early, but managed to stay on the black horse for most of the game, winning her bouts by clever dodges, and a quick straight-arm. She did not recognize the woman who finally shoved her off into a snowdrift; she floundered there, laughing so hard she could not work her way out for several minutes. After this, they tried to ride in a long line, all holding hands and guiding the horses with their legs. Soon they were all in the snow again, and after another few tricks they came back for more food.

Now the tables held roasts and breads as well as sweets. Paks piled her plate with roast pork and mutton, a half-loaf of bread yellow with eggs. Four juniors staggered in, their faces bright red with cold. Behind them came the dwarves she had met, eyes gleaming. They saw her, waved, and came to sit across from her.

"Is it that you have recovered, Paksenarrion Dorthansdotter of Three Firs?" asked Balkis.

"Yes, indeed," said Paks. "But the surgeons didn't want me fighting until after today."

"Ah, we have heard that you make adoption into the Fellowship," said Balkis, stuffing a leg of chicken into his mouth. "This will make it that you are blood-bound to the others, is it not?"

Before Paks could answer, the woman who had dumped her in the snow slipped into a chair beside her, and answered the dwarves.

"No—it is not that, rockbrothers. Ask not the child of the father's business." To Paks' surprise, both dwarves blushed. She looked at the woman in surprise.

"You're the one who—"

"Yes." The woman grinned as she took a sweet cake from a tray. "I'm the one who dumped you. I'm Cami, by the way—that's what everyone calls me, but my real name is Rahel, if you need it." She said something in dwarvish to the dwarves; Balkis looked startled, but the darker dwarf burst into laughter. Paks eyed her. Cami (or Rahel) was small and dark, a quick-moving woman who reminded Paks a little of Canna.

"Why are you called Cami if your name is Rahel?" asked Paks.

"Oh that. Well, it started when I came here. They used to tease me that I should have been Camwyn's paladin instead of Gird's—"

"You're a paladin?" Paks had not thought of any paladin being so light-hearted; Cami seemed almost frivolous.

"Yes." Cami stuffed the rest of the cake into her mouth, and then spoke through it. "It was what I did when I was young and wild. I won't tell you; you don't need ideas like that. But they started calling me Camwynya, only that was too long, and then Cami. You're a candidate, right?"

"After tonight," said Paks.

"I thought so. It's good that you know these rockbrothers already—"

"I don't, really—" began Paks, but Cami shushed her.

"Better than many do, I can tell. Balkis Baltisson, I will speak no more dwarvish, for this lady knows it not, but it is not the blood-bond of brethren that she joins this night."

"Not? How so? It is the Fellowship of Gird."

"Yes. The Fellowship is the blood-bond of Gird with each yeoman, sir dwarf; not each with the other."

"But it is that brother of brother is brother," insisted the dwarf. "It is that makes the clan-bond, the blood-bond."

"It is that for dwarves," said Cami. "For man it is other. The bond is like that of the Axemaster for each member of the clan, not between members."

"It is not possible to have one without the other," said Balkis, his eyes flashing. "If the Axemaster accepts adoption from any outlander, the outlander is blood-bound to the clan. All of it."

Cami shot Paks a quick look. "Paks, no one has ever convinced dwarves of this—and I won't—but I'll keep trying." But now the second dwarf spoke for the first time.

"Lady Cami, you know me, Balkon son of Tekis son of Kadas, mother-son of Fedrin Harasdotter, sister-son he of the Goldenaxe, but to this lady I have not spoken in my own name." His voice was higher than Paks expected when speaking Common, midrange for a man, but much higher than Balkis'.

Cami nodded politely, and Paks copied her, wondering if she should state her own name again.

"You say this lady is to be paladin as you are?"

"Yes," said Cami, with another quick look to Paks.

"Last time we saw Paksenarrion Dorthansdotter, she had hurt of an axe, and no healing of Marshal. That I thought was disgrace, or punishment. To be candidate must be honor, is it not? Why this then?"

Now it was Paks' turn to blush. She did not know how much Cami knew of the whole situation. But someone had to explain.

"Sir—sir dwarf," she began, copying Cami's style of address, "I said then it was not unfairness of the Marshal—"

"But we thought it so. It might be you did not know, being *nedross*." At that word, Cami choked on her food, and shook a finger at the dwarves. Paks, confused, waited for a moment, then went on.

"It was not unfairness. I told you they thought I had taken value from them in training, and had not returned value." Now they nodded, and she hurried on. "So they said if I wished to stay I must make a commitment; I was willing to make it, even if they did not let me stay, for the truth I felt of it."

"Truth." Balkon looked at her sharply. "It is that you have that power to see truth itself?"

"She might," interrupted Cami. "And not even know it. Nedross, indeed!"

"What is that?" asked Paks.

"I hope," said Cami severely, "that they're using it in the gnome sense, unwilling or unable to see insult, and not in the dwarf sense of cowardly."

Both dwarves burst into speech, protesting.

"It is not that we—"

"That is not what we—"

Balkon shushed his friend, and continued. "Lady Cami, Lady Paksenarrion, we did not think that this lady, this lady who would use an axe, would be cowardly. No—only that it is not always the same for man and dwarf when words be said, that some should be taken and others not. If it is that we make mistakes, and think someone unfair to this fine lady, who would use an axe, Sertig's first tool, then we ask pardon of the lady, but we are glad to see that she had honor now in this house, and is blood-bound to a clan we honor."

Paks was thoroughly confused. Cami turned to her with an exaggerated sigh. "I'd advise you to accept their good wishes, and apologies, and be glad you have found dwarven friends. They truly did not mean to say you were cowardly."

Paks smiled at them. "Sirs, I know not your words, but I thank you for your good wishes."

They both grinned back. "That is very good," said Balkon. "And if you wish to learn, we still will teach you what we know of axes."

Paks nodded. "If I am permitted, in my training, I will ask it of you."

"Paks!" Aris Marrakai had come up behind her, with several of his friends. He shuffled from one foot to another when she turned. "I—I brought you something."

"Aris—you shouldn't have—" Paks took from his hand a carefully worked leather pouch, fringed and decorated with tiny shells. "It must have cost—"

He shrugged. "Not that much. And anyway, Rufen told me that paladins never have any money and can't buy things, and so I thought maybe you'd keep it and—and remember us."

"I'd remember you anyway, Aris," said Paks. "But thank you—I will treasure this." She knew already what would go in it: Saben's little red stone horse, and Canna's medallion. Aris darted away; Paks met Cami's eyes.

"It isn't quite that bad," said Cami. "We don't get rich, but we can buy a fruit pie occasionally."

"That's good," said Paks. "I like mushrooms, myself."

"Then pray you aren't assigned to the granges west of here for your duty," said Cami, laughing. "Dry and high—not a mushroom for days and days."

"When do we have grange duty?" asked Paks.

"Just before the Trials," said Cami. "You may find it strange; you've never been in a normal grange, have you? No—then it's even more important for you. We all must know what limits Marshals face, and granges, and not think because we are gifted with powers that it's so easy for others."

"Cami!" The hall was filling now, as more and more cold revellers came in for warmth and food. Paks was startled to see the Training Master grab Cami by both shoulders and hug her. "Gird's right arm, I thought you were still in achael!"

"Through Midwinter Feast? Master Chanis, even the High Lord wouldn't keep me in achael through the best day in the year!"

"I suppose not. Are you out, or just on leave?"

"Out. Gird's grace for it, too; if I had missed Midwinter's Feast, and the installation, I'd have burst something."

"And are you fit to sing, Cami?" asked Sir Amberion, who had followed the Training Master into the hall. Cami looked at Paks.

"Ask Paksenarrion—I only dumped her a couple of times this morning."

Paks could not help grinning. "Only once—"

"Ah, but who stuck her foot in your black's ribs, in the line, to make him crowhop? And you flew off then, too."

"Was that you?" Paks joined the roar of laughter.

"It was," said Cami, "and I could do it again. Fit to sing? By the dragonstongue, I could sing and blow the lo-pipe at the same time." Again laughter, and Paks saw someone scurry away, yelling that a lo-pipe was coming up. But as she watched Cami move a tray out of her way and settle onto the table, the Training Master touched her shoulder, and beckoned. Paks followed him away from the hall.

To her surprise, it was already midafternoon. The rest of the day was taken up with preparation for the night's ceremonies. She had to change into the plain gray of the Training Company, but the steward handed her, as well, the white surcoat of a paladin-candidate. She would have to change hurriedly between ceremonies. Paks had lines to learn and, like the Finthan youngsters who were making their final vows that night, she spent some time in the High Lord's Hall in meditation. When spectators began arriving, the group was led away to a small bare room off one end. Paks felt her stomach tightening. Her mouth was dry. The others in this room were not the paladin-candidates, but junior yeomen making their vows as senior yeomen—the honor of taking these vows at Midwinter Feast in the High Hall came to those whose grange Marshals had recommended them. Most were about the age Paks had been when she left home—eighteen or nineteen winters. They eyed her as nervously as she watched them.

The summons came with an ear-shattering blast of trumpets, as High Marshals Connaught and Suriest opened the door and called them out. The High Lord's Hall was brilliantly lit by hundreds of candles. The spectators sat and stood on either side of the wide central aisle. With the others, Paks stood just below the platform. The trumpet music ended, to be followed by an interlude of harps. Then another trumpet fanfare introduced the Marshal-General, resplendent in a white surcoat over her armor, with Gird's crescent embroidered in silver on the breast. Following her were the other High Marshals presently at Fin Panir, all in Gird's blue and white. Behind them came those visitors who would be honored during the ceremonies: two Marshals of Falk, in long robes of ruby-red, with gold-decorated helms set in the crooks of their arms. A Swordmaster of Tir, in black and silver; Paks remembered the device on his arms from Aarenis. Last of all came the seven paladins resident and whole of limb in Fin Panir, each in full armor, carrying Gird's pennant.

Paks watched them come up the aisle, her heart pounding with excitement and joy. This was exactly what she had thought about in Three Firs—the music, the brilliant colors—she tried to take a long breath and calm down. She recognized Sir Amberion and Lady Cami, but none of the other paladins. They mounted the platform behind her, and she heard the footsteps move away to its far side. The the trumpets were still, and the Marshal-General's clear voice called out the ancient greeting:

> "In darkness, in cold, in the midst of winter
> where nothing walks the world but death and fear
> let the brave rejoice: I call the light."

"I call the light!" came the response from every voice. It seemed to shake the air.

"Out of darkness, light. Out of silence, song. Out of the sun's death, the birth of each year." Paks half-listened, knowing the words better than any other she'd heard from the Marshal-General. Just so had her grandfather said them, when she was small, and just so her father had said them, the last Midwinter Feast she was at home.

"Out of cold, fire. Out of death, life. Out of fear, courage to see the day." With the others, she gave the response. And together they all completed the ritual, raising first one hand then the other, and finally both, to defy sundeath and greet the sun. "In darker night, brighter stars. In greater fear, greater courage. In the midst of winter, the world's birth. Praise to the High Lord." This would be repeated between every segment of the ceremonies, until sunrise the next dawn. Paks remembered falling asleep, year after year—and the first year that she had managed to stay awake, the last year of her grandfather's life, to light the first morning fire with new wood. For with sundown, all fires were destroyed—to show respect, her grandfather had said, and to prove their courage to endure. Here, too, the fires went out when the sun fell, to be kindled at daybreak. Only those desperately ill were allowed a fire on Midwinter Night.

"Yeomen of Gird," said the High Marshal then, and Paks pulled her mind back to the ceremony. "We have with us those who seek to join the Fellowship of Gird; by our ancient customs we will test them in their steadfastness, and you will witness their vows."

"By Gird's grace," came the response. Paks felt her neck prickle. She was suddenly cold, and wanted to rub her arms.

"Stand forth, you who would swear fealty to the Fellowship of Gird," said the Marshal-General. With those on her side of the aisle, Paks faced toward the center of the hall. One at a time they would mount those steps and face a Marshal for the ritual exchange of blows. Paks suspected that in her case it might be something more than a ritual. Her leg itched; she resisted the urge to rub it on her other leg.

Before she had time to worry, she heard her name. All at once, she felt eager, and went up the steps quickly. To the questions she made response firmly: she acknowledged Gird as the High Lord's servant, the patron of fighters, the protector of the helpless. She swore to keep the Code of Gird, and obey "all Marshals and lawful authority over you." And then the questioner stepped back, and she faced the Marshal-General, who held out two identical staves.

Paks took one, with an internal prayer that she wouldn't look too foolish. The Marshal-General smiled, feinted, and aimed a smashing blow at her. Paks rolled aside, countering as best she could. The power of the Marshal-General's blows carried all the way up her arms. Ritual exchange of blows indeed, thought Paks. The staves rattled. She took a blow on the thigh, and managed to touch the Marshal-General's arm with a leftover move that carried little sting. Then her staff seemed to twitch in her hands and go flying through the air; the Marshal-General's staff tapped her head firmly before she could dodge. And the Marshal-General stepped back, bowed, and greeted her.

"Welcome, yeoman of Gird, to Gird's grange." As she spoke, she placed a Gird's medallion over Paks' head.

Paks bowed as she had been instructed. "I am honored, Marshal-General, to be accepted in Gird's Fellowship." Then, dismissed, she left the platform and returned moved to a space behind it, where the Training Master waited to help her on with the candidate's surcoat and her new Gird's medallion.

The paladin-candidates were presented just before dawn, after ceremonies honoring Marshals and paladins killed in the past year. It seemed to Paks a very plain affair: the candidates were simply named and shown to the spectators, and assigned to one of the knightly orders and a sponsoring paladin. After the events of the day before, Paks had hoped to get Cami as her sponsor, but instead Amberion led her before the crowd. Cami was sponsoring a yeoman-marshal from somewhere in the Westmounts, she heard later. Paks knew none of the candidates well, and only four of them at all; the others had been sent from distant granges after earlier selection.

She had one more day of freedom—for the second day of Midwinter Feast was as lively as the first—and fell into bed that night completely exhausted and as happy as she could ever remember being.

CHAPTER TWENTY-THREE

Paks' first experience as a paladin-candidate was a familiar one—moving into new quarters. These were south of the main complex, in an annex to the Paladin's Hall. She was surprised to find that she would still have a room to herself, but Amberion explained.

"You will spend time in solitary exercises; you will need the privacy. Later, you will learn the skills of meditation even when surrounded by noise and upheaval, but for novices it's easier to learn in solitude."

Paks nodded silently. She was still shy of her paladin-sponsor; it was hard to believe that he and Cami were in the same order. He seemed more somber, far less approachable. She unpacked her things quickly, wondering a little at the requirement that her sponsor must see everything she owned. But for that, too, he had a reason. Paladins must be willing to go anywhere, anytime—able to endure hardship, not just discipline. Those who clung to treasured possessions, favorite foods, even friends, might make fine Marshals or knights, but not paladins. So in the early days of training, they must do without accustomed possessions. Those who withdrew would have theirs restored, but those continuing had to face the possible loss of items deemed too luxurious. Paks understood the reasoning, but could not imagine anyone preferring fancy clothes or jewelry to being a paladin. She said so, and Amberion grinned at her.

"I've seen it myself. And there is always something hard to give up. If not material things, habits and ways of thought. This may be a trivial test for you, but there are others. No one passes through this training without struggle." He looked over her gear as he spoke, and told her to keep Saben's red horse and Canna's medallion. Aris' gift, her weapons, the shining mail the elfane taig had given her—all these went into storage. Then he said, "What about money? Do you have any gold or silver?"

Paks handed over the heavy leather sack she'd brought from Brewersbridge. "This, and some on account with the Guild in Tsaia."

His eyebrows went up. "Did Marshal Cedfer know how much gold you had?"

"I don't know." Paks thought back to Brewersbridge, already distant to her mind. "I told him the elfane taig had gifted me; he saw the jewel I gave the grange, and knew I had money for food, lodging, and clothes."

Amberion frowned, and Paks wondered what she'd done wrong. "Did you know that most orders of knights charge a fee for their training, which is waived for poor applicants?" he asked. Paks shook her head. She had assumed that the Training Company was maintained by the Fellowship of Gird, through contributions from the granges. "Perhaps Cedfer expected you'd become a Girdsman, as you have, and didn't bother to mention it," Amberion went on. "As a paladin, you may not hold wealth. We are bound to keep this for you, and restore it if you fail, but if you are called as a paladin . . . well . . ."

"You mean I owe the Training College?" asked Paks.

"Not precisely owe. Cedfer sponsored you here, at first, and you accepted this chance freely, as a gift. It would be ill grace on our part to ask alms of you now. On the other hand, while we would ask nothing of a farmer's daughter who had nothing, we would ordinarily ask a fee of someone who could pay. And that gold, that fee, would not be returned, whatever happened." He shifted the bag from hand to hand. "What had you planned with this?"

"Well—" Paks had trouble remembering the clutter of plans and dreams with which she'd ridden from Brewersbridge. "I had sent money to my family, to repay my dowry, but I'd planned to send more if I became a knight, for then I could always earn my own way. And I'd thought of a new saddle for Socks—my black horse."

He nodded slowly. "You thought of warriors' needs ahead, and your family. Are they poor, Paksenarrion?"

"Not really poor, like some I've seen. We had food enough, if not too much; we always had clothes and fire in winter. But there's no money, most times. It took me years to save up the copper bits I left home with. And all the other children to be raised and wed—" Paks shook her head suddenly. "But now I'm here—and if I'm a paladin, I won't need a saddle, will I? Someone else will take Socks. And I won't be looking for work. Tell me what the fee is, sir, and I can send the rest to them and be done with it."

Amberion smiled at her with real warmth. "You choose well. Would you agree to give this bagful to the Fellowship, and send whatever is on account to your family?"

"There's more on account," said Paks.

"No matter. We are not here to fatten ourselves at the expense of farmers. Now—what's this—?" He pushed at the little bundle of scuffed and tattered old scrolls left in her saddlebags. "I thought you weren't a scholar."

"I don't know," said Paks. "I found them in my things after the elfane taig. I was going to ask Ambros about them, but that's when the caravan was attacked, and after that I forgot. I couldn't read them then—maybe now—" She started to unroll one of them; the parchment crackled.

"Here—wait—" Amberion took it from her. "These are old, Paksenarrion—we must be careful with them, or they'll go to pieces." He peered at the faded script. "Gird's arm, I can't—what do you think that is?" He pushed it back to Paks, who leaned close.

"I'm not sure. 'For on this day—something—Gird came to this village where was the—the—' is that word knight?"

"I think so," said Amberion. "I think it's 'knight of the prince's cohort, and there they—' something where that's rubbed out, and then 'and as he said to me, that he did, and called the High Lord's blessing on it'—" Amberion looked up at her for a moment. "Where did you say you found these?"

"I didn't find them, exactly," said Paks. "After the fight underground, the elfane taig got me back to the surface—somehow—and then had me pack up a whole load of things. I was too sick to notice much, but the elfane taig insisted. A day or so later, when I looked through the packs, the scrolls were there. I tried to read them, but—" Paks flushed. "I didn't read that well—and the script is odd."

"Yes—it is." Amberion seemed abstracted. "Paks—this has nothing to do with your training, but I believe these scrolls may be valuable.

They're old—very old—and I've read something like this in the archives. Would you let the Archivist see them?"

"Of course," said Paks. "I'd be glad to know what they are and why the elfane taig gave them. I almost threw them away, but—"

"I'm glad you didn't," said Amberion. "If they're really an old copy of Luap's writings—"

"Luap? Is that Gird's friend?"

"Yes. Most of what we know about Gird comes from the Chronicles of Luap. This—" he nodded toward the scroll he held, "seems to be part of that—it's talking, I think, about the battle at Seameadow." He put the scroll down and looked around the room. "That's all, then? Good. Now about your horse—what do you call him?"

Paks felt herself blushing again. "Socks," she mumbled. She had had enough comments to know that it should have been something grander. But Amberion did not laugh.

"Better, to my mind, than some long name you can't shout at need. You know that if you pass the Trials you'll have a mount?" She nodded. She had heard more than once of the paladins' mounts that appeared after their Trials, waiting fully equipped in the courtyard outside the High Lord's Hall. No one knew whence they came; no one saw them come. "But in the meantime, you can use Socks for training. Doggal says he's good enough. In fact, the Training Order would take him when you pass the Trials, unless you want to sell him elsewhere."

"Yes, sir."

"Take the things you won't need back to the steward, and then come back here; you'll meet the other paladins and candidates."

For some days after that, Paks heard nothing more about the scrolls. Her schedule kept her too busy to ask. It was unlike any training she'd had before. Instead of weapons drill or military theory, she found herself immersed in history and geography: which men had come to which area, and when, and why. She learned of their laws and their beliefs; she had to memorize article after article of the Code of Gird. Gradually she built in her mind a picture of the whole land about, and the beliefs of the people. She could see, as in a drawing, her father's family perched on the side of a moor north of most trade routes. They had believed in the High Lord, and the Lady of Peace, but also in the horse nomad deity Guthlac, and the Windsteed. Their boundary stones, and the rituals for keeping them, came from Aarenis;

the well-sprite for whom she had plucked flowers every spring was called the same—Piri—from Brewersbridge to Three Firs, and south to Valdaire. But in Aarenis proper, the well-spirits were multiple, and called *caoulin*: they had no personal names.

She learned that elves claimed no lands: the elvenhome kingdoms cannot be reached by unguided humans anyway. In Lyonya, where elves and humans ruled together a mortal kingdom, human land-rights were held provisionally, and any change of use had to be approved by the crown. Dwarves claimed daskgeft, a stonemass, but cared little who traveled the surface. Gnomes held all property by intricate law, and to step one footlength on gnomish land without legal right could bring the whole kingdom down on the criminal. Even in human lands, the laws of property differed. In Tsaia, where land was granted by the crown in return for military service, those who actually formed rarely owned the land they worked—but in Fintha nearly all farms were owned by the farmer.

High Marshal Garris taught them the lore of the gods—all that was known of the great powers of good and evil. Paks learned that Achrya, the Webmistress, had not been known in Aare—proof, according to Marshal Garris, that Achrya was a minor god, for the great gods had power everywhere in the known world. Liart, on the other hand, had been known in old Aare, but not to the northern nomads or the Seafolk until they met the men from Aarenis. She learned that her fear of the Kuakkganni came from mistaking them for kuaknom, a race related to elves but devoted to evil; the Kuakkganni, Garris insisted, were never wholly evil, and often good. Of the greatest evils, Marshal Garris taught only their names and general attacks: Nayda, the Unnamer, who threatened forgetfulness, and Gitres, the Unmaker.

"They are one in destruction," he said firmly. "They try to enforce despair, and convince you that nothing matters, for they will wipe out all. Never believe it. The elves call them A-Iynisi, The Unsinger who unravels the Song of the Singer, but they know as well as we that the Singer lives, and living must create."

"But are they really one, or two?" asked Harbin, the yeoman-marshal sponsored by Cami.

High Marshal Garris shrugged. "No man knows, Harbin; no man needs to know. I think—but it is only my thought—that it is only one, but one who appears in the guise you most fear. One fears the loss of fame, of being unknown and forgotten, and another fears having all his works unmade. All mortals have some form of this fear, and in search of immortality among men may do great evil without intention. It is hard to trust that the High Lord's court will remember and reward a good life, hard to risk fame or lifework when those are at stake."

Along with this, all the candidates were encouraged to learn languages. Paks had already found, in her travels, that she was quick to pick up new phrases. Since she had made friends among the elves and dwarves in Fin Panir, Amberion urged her to spend her evenings with them, speaking elven and dwarvish in turn. At first this went quickly: she could ask for food and drink, and greet her friends politely, after only a few lessons. But the more she wanted to say, the harder it got. A simple question, like "Where are you from?" would bring on a flurry of discussion. Paks found the dwarves more willing to explain than the elves, but she could not follow their explanations.

"It is simple," said Balkon one night, the third time of trying to explain dwarf clan rankings. "Let us begin with the Goldenaxe." They had begun with the Goldenaxe before, but Paks nodded. "The Goldenaxe has two sons and a daughter."

"Yes, but—" Paks knew that something difficult was coming.

"Wait. The Goldenaxe that was, before this, had a sister who had a son, and so this Goldenaxe is the sister-son of the Goldenaxe that was."

"His nephew?" ventured Paks.

Balkon scowled. "No—not. In Common that is son of either brother or sister, yes? And this is only for sister-son. Brother-son is mother's clan."

Paks started to ask why, and thought better of it.

"Now—this Goldenaxe has no sister, only brother, and brother has no sons. But a daughter. It is clear?"

Paks nodded. She still had a thread to follow. The current Goldenaxe had a brother, with a daughter, and two sons and a daughter of his own.

"So will inherit to the title either the son of his brother's daughter, or his oldest son, or the son of his daughter."

"But why not just his son?" asked Paks.

"Because that is not his blood," said Balkon. "His son's son is not his clan, you see that—only his daughter's son—"

"Then why not his daughter?" asked Paks again.

"What? She be the Goldenaxe? No—that would rive the rock indeed. No dwarfmaid wields coldmetal—"

"They don't fight?"

"I did not say that. They wield not the coldmetal, the weaponsteel, once it is forged. You, lady, would not stand long against a dwarven warrior-maid in her own hall."

Paks went back to asking the names of common objects after that. With elves the trouble was different but equally impenetrable. Some questions were simply ignored, others answered in a spate of elven that drowned her mind in lovely sound. Ardhiel gladly taught her songs, and encouraged her to learn the elaborate elven courtesies, but as for learning more about elves themselves, it was, "Lady, the trees learn water by drinking rain, and stars learn night by shining." Paks found individual words easy to speak and remember, but her best efforts at stringing them together sounded nothing like Ardhiel's speech, though he praised her.

She had also much to learn of paladins, as did the other candidates. Most of them had thought, like Paks, that being Gird's holy warrior meant gaining vast arcane powers—they would be nearly invincible against any foe. Their paladin-sponsors quickly set them straight. Although paladins must be skilled at fighting, that, their sponsors insisted, was the least of their abilities. A quest might involve no fighting at all, or a battle against beings no steel could pierce.

"Paladins show that courage is possible," Cami said to them one day. "It is easy enough to find reasons to give in to evil. War is ugly, as Paks knows well," she nodded toward Paks, who suddenly remembered the worst of Aarenis, the dead baby in Rotengre, the murdered farmfolk, Ferrault dying, Alured's tortures. "We do not argue that war is better than peace; we are not so stupid as that. But it is not peace when cruelty reigns, when stronger men steal from farmers and craftworkers, when the child can be enslaved or the old thrown out to starve, and no one lifts a hand. That is not peace: that is conquest, and evil. We start no quarrels in peaceful lands; we never display our weaponskills to earn applause. But we are Gird's cudgel, defending the helpless, and teaching by our example that one person can dare greater force to break evil's grasp on the innocent. Sometimes we can do that without fighting, without killing, and that's best."

"But we're warriors first," said Paks before she thought. She wished she'd kept still. She had already noticed that the others, with their years in the Fellowship and service in the granges, had different views. Now they all looked at her, and she fixed her gaze on Cami.

"Yes," said Cami slowly. "Some evils need that direct attack, and we must be able to do it, and to lead others in battle. Did you ever wonder why paladins are so likeable?" It seemed an odd remark, and threw Paks off balance. Apparently, by the stirrings in the room, others were confused as well. "It's important," said Cami, now with that grin that pulled them all together. "We come to a town, perhaps, where nothing has gone right for a dozen years. Perhaps there's a grange of Gird, perhaps not. But the people are frightened, and they've lost trust in each other, in themselves. We may lead them into danger; some will be killed or wounded. Why should they trust us?" No one answered, and she went on. "Because we are likeable, and other people will follow us willingly. And that's why we are more likely to choose a popular yeoman-marshal as a candidate than the best fighter in the grange."

Paks dared a sideways glance. From the thoughtful and even puzzled faces around her, the others had never considered this. She herself, remembering the paladin in Aarenis, realized that she had trusted him at once, without reservation, although the Marshal with him had annoyed her.

"But you see how dangerous that could be, if someone wanted to do evil," said Cami, breaking into her thoughts. "We choose from those with a gift for leadership, those people will follow happily. Therefore we must be sure that you will never use that gift wrongly. Another thing: because we come and go, we make demands on those we help for only a short time. It's easier for them to follow us quickly, and then go home. Never scorn Marshals: when we have left, they must maintain their yeomen's faith. Perhaps we showed them what was possible—but we left them with years of work."

As for the powers legend had grafted onto paladins, in reality there were four.

"We all have powers, but not all of us have them equally," said Amberion one day. "Any paladin can call light—" A glow lit the end of this finger. "It is not fire, which gives light by burning, but true light, the essence of seeing. There are greater lights—" At his nod, Cami suddenly seemed to catch fire, wreathed in a white radiance too bright to watch. Then it was gone; all the candidates blinked. "More than that," Amberion went on, "some paladins—but not all—can call light that will spread across a whole battlefield." Paks remembered the light in Sibili. "It is the duty and power of a paladin," said Amberion, "to show the truth of good and evil—to make clear—and that is what our light is for. It is a tool. Sometimes we use it to prove our call, but it must never be used for the paladin's own convenience or pride."'

"But how do you make the light?" asked Clevis, one of the other candidates.

"We do not make it. We call it—ask it, in Gird's name. Later in your training, we will graft this power onto you, for a while, so that you can learn to use it—but it will not be your power until you are invested as a paladin, in the Trials, and the gods give or withhold your gifts."

"You mean we won't know until then?" asked Harbin.

"You knew that, surely?"

"Well, yes, but—" He shook his head. "It seems a long time wasted, if we don't become paladins. Can't you tell earlier?"

"We can tell if you are doing badly," said Amberion. "But we have no power over the gods' decisions, Harbin. We prepare the best candidates we can find as well as we can, and then present them. Then they choose—why, we do not know. That's one reason the failing candidates are honored: it does not mean they are not worthy; they are the best we could find. Even those who withdraw from training are honored for having been chosen to attempt it. Any one of you—" he looked around the small group. "Any one of you would make a fine knight in any order.

Most of you would make a fine Marshal—one or two, perhaps, are too independent of mind—but you would all do. But to be a paladin requires more than weapon skills, a gift for leadership, the willingness to risk all for good, the deep love of good and hatred of evil. Many good men and women share these with you. Beyond that, you must have the High Lord's blessing on that way for you, as shown by the gifts you receive in the Trials." They thought that over for some minutes in silence.

Saer, a black-haired woman with merry blue eyes, explained the gift of healing, second of the paladin's special abilities. This too was a gift, to be prayed for; the gift might be withheld at times. As well, it required knowledge of wounds and illness, the structure of the body and its functions. Paks would like to have asked her about Canna's wound—had she healed it, and was that any proof of Gird's favor?—but she was shy in front of the others. After a short discussion, in which she took no part, they passed on to other matters.

Sarek, who reminded Paks of Cracolnya in the Duke's Company, with his stocky body and slightly bowed legs, explained about the detection of good and evil. "A paladin can sense good and evil directly," he began. "Now you might think that makes everything simple: on one side are the bad people, and you kill them, and over here are the good people, and they cheer for you." Everyone laughed, including the other paladins. "It would be nice," he went on, "but that's not how it works. Normally you will experience people much as you do now—liking some, and not liking others. Most people—and that includes us, candidates—are mixtures, neither wholly evil not wholly good. But if you are close to someone intent on evil—an assassin, Achrya's agent, whatever—you will know that evil is near and be able to locate it.

"That's not the same as doing anything about it," he said, again waiting for the laughter that followed. "You must learn to think. Suppose you are trying to decide whom to trust in a troubled town. An evil person may lie, but he might tell the truth, if truth serves his plan. A good person may lead you wrong, being good and stupid. You, young candidates, are supposed to be good—and smart." Again they laughed. "But more of this later. Only realize that like any gift, it is a tool—and you must learn to use it carefully, or it can slip in your hand." He gave them a final grin, and waved Cami up.

"Most important of the gifts," said Cami, now more serious than Paks had ever seen her, "is the High Lord's protection from evil attack. Of course you can be killed—we are human, after all. But as long as you are Gird's paladin, your soul cannot be forced into evil by any power whatever. All magical spells that assault the heart and mind directly will fail. No fear or disgust, no despair, can prevent you from following the High Lord's call if you want to follow it. Moreover, you can protect those with you from such attacks. This is one reason our training is so long and so intense—for this, of course, we cannot test in training. We must be sure you do want this with a whole heart, that you are indeed under that protection, before you go out to battle the dark powers of the earth."

For that reason, they were told, their every act and word would be scrutinized; even small faults could reveal flaws too dangerous to be granted such power.

"But would the High Lord grant the powers to someone unfit to bear them?" asked one of the candidates.

"No. But evil powers might grant a semblance of such. It is hard to explain—though you will understand if you succeed—but during your training you are more open to evil influence than before. We must so harrow your minds: and as in a harrowed field both sun and frost strike deeper, so in your minds both good and evil can strike a firmer root. That is why you are kept apart from the others, once you begin the final training, and why you are always in the company of your sponsor, who can sense any threat and protect you from it."

"But we're supposed to be more resistant anyway," grumbled Harbin. Paks agreed, but said nothing. It almost sounded as if they were weaklings.

"You are—you were—and you will be," said Cami. "But right now, and for the time of your training, we are looking for weakness—searching for any crevice through which evil can assail your hearts. And we will find things, for none of us is perfect, or utterly invincible, except in the High Lord's protection." Paks wondered uneasily what weakness they would find in her, and what they would do about it.

"And," added Sarek, closing that session with a laugh, "remember that while a demon can't eat your soul, once you're a paladin, any village idiot can crack your skull with a rock. By accident."

Other such discussions followed. They learned that paladins never married unless—and this was rare—they retired from that service to another. Yet although celibate on quest—Paks saw someone frown, across the room, and wondered if he would drop out—they might have lovers in Fin Panir or elsewhere, as time allowed. "But those you love most are in the most danger," pointed out Amberion. "Choose your loves from those who can defend themselves, should Achrya's agents be seeking a weapon against you. We are here to defend the children of others—not to protect our own. And if we had children, and were good parents, we would have no time for Gird's work."

Soon Paks knew the paladins as people. She knew the room would bubble with excitement when Cami arrived, that Saer brought with her an intensity and mysticism almost eerie to experience, that Sarek's jokes always had a lasting sting of sense, that Amberion was the group's steady anchor. She, like the others, opened up under Kevis' warm and loving regard; and like the others she found her determination hardened by Teriam's stern logic. Garin, last of the seven, left on quest shortly after his sponsored candidate withdrew—the first of their group to fail. Paks had not known Amis well, and did not know why he had left. She knew less of the candidates than she'd expected, for when not in classes together, they were each with a sponsor or learning to meditate alone.

But even so she was conscious of a difference between these young Girdsmen, long committed to their patron, and herself. Matters that she thought trivial were cause for hours of discussion, and the simple solution she always thought she saw never satisfied them. They picked away at the motives they claimed lay behind all acts, creating, Paks thought, an incredible tangle of unlikely possibilities. She had imagined herself committed to the defense of good . . . but was good this complicated? If so, why was Gird the patron of soldiers? No one had time to think of definitions and logic in the midst of a battle. The way Sarek had said it first made the most sense to her: here are the bad people, and you kill them; there are the good ones, and they cheer for you. Surely it was only a matter of learning to recognize all the evil. She prayed, as Amberion was teaching her to do, and said nothing. She was there to learn, and in time she might understand that other way of thinking. She had time.

Busy as she was, Paks had almost forgotten the mysterious scrolls when she received a summons to the Master Archivist, Marshal Kory. She found him at a broad table set before a window, with the scrolls all open before him.

"Paksenarrion—come and see the treasure." He waved his hand at the array. "Amberion tells me you had no idea what you brought?"

"No, sir."

"Well, if it were all you ever brought here, Paksenarrion, the Fellowship of Gird could count itself well repaid. We have all examined these—all those of us in Fin Panir with an interest in such things. I believe—and so do many others—that these scrolls were penned by Luap himself, Gird's own friend. How they got where you found them I doubt we will ever know for certain."

"But how can you know what they are?"

Marshal Kory grinned. "That's scholar's work, young warrior. But you would know a sword made in Andressat, I daresay, from one made in Vérella—"

"Yes, sir."

"So we have ways to know that the scrolls are old. We have copies of Luap's chronicles and letters; we compared them, and found some differences—but just what might have come from careless copying. And these scrolls contain far more than we have: letters to Luap's friends, little sermons—a wealth of material. We think the writing is Luap's own hand, because we have preserved a couple of lists said to be his—and one of the letters here mentions making that list of those who fell in the first days of the rebellion."

Paks began to feel the awesome age of the scrolls. "Then—Luap really touched those—I mean, he was alive, and could—'

"He was a real person, yes—not a legend—and because he writes so, we know that Gird was real, too. Not that I charge you with having doubted it, but it's easy to forget that our heroes were actual men and women, who got blisters when they marched, and liked a pot of ale at day's end. Luap now—" His eyes stared into the distance. "That isn't even his name. In those days, luap was a kinship term, for someone not in the line of inheritance. The military used it too. A luap-captain had that rank, for respect and pay, but had no troops under his own command: could not give independent orders. According to the old stories, this man gave up his own name when he joined the rebellion. There are several versions with different reasons for that. Anyway, he became Gird's assistant, high-ranked because he could write—which few besides lords could do in those days—and he was called Gird's luap. Soon everyone called him 'the luap,' and finally 'Luap.' Because of him, no one used luap for a kinship term after that; in Fintha the same relationship now is called 'nik,' and in Tsaia it's 'niga' or 'nigan.' " The Archivist seemed ready to explain the origin of that and every other term, and Paks broke in quickly, sticking to what she understood.

"And he speaks of Gird?"

"As a friend. Listen to this." Marshal Kory picked up one of the scrolls, and began to read. " '—and in fact, Ansuli, I had to tell the great oaf to quit swinging his staff around overhead like a young demon. I feared he would hit me, but soon that great laugh burst out and he thanked me for stopping him. If he has a fault, it is that liking for ale, which makes him fight sometimes whether we have need or no.' And that's Luap talking of Gird at a tavern in eastern Fintha. I'm not sure where; he doesn't name the town."

Paks was startled. "Gird—drunk?"

"It was after their first big victory. I've always suspected that the reason several of the articles in the Code of Gird dealt with drunkenness is that Gird had personal knowledge of it." He laid that scroll down and touched another with his fingertip. "We have had the copyists working on these every day. It is the greatest treasure of the age—you cannot know, Paksenarrion, how it lifts our hearts to find something so close to Gird himself. Even when it's things like that letter—that just makes him more human, more real to us. And to have in Luap's own words the last battle—incredible! Besides that, we now have a way to prove whether or not these scrolls are genuine. Have you ever heard of Luap's Stronghold?"

Paks shook her head. "I had not heard of Luap until I came here, sir."

"There's been a legend for a long time that Luap left the Honnorgat Valley and traveled west, to take Gird's Code to distant lands. For a time, it was believed, he had established a stronghold, a fortress, in the far mountains, and some reports had Girdsmen travelling back and forth. But no one has come from the west with any reports of him for hundreds of years, so most scholars now think it was just a legend. But in one of these scrolls, sent back, he says, at the request of the Marshal-General of that day, he gives the location of that stronghold. If someone were to go there, and see it, that would prove that these are, indeed, the scrolls of Luap."

Paks thought of it, suddenly excited. "What are the western lands like?"

"All we have are caravan reports. Dry grassland for some days' travel, then rock and sand, then deep gouges in the rocks, with swift-running rivers in the depths. Then mountains—but they don't go that way, skirting them on the south, to come to a crossways. North along that route is a kingdom called Kaelifet; I know nothing about it. Southward is more desert, and finally a sea."

Paks tried to imagine those strange lands, and failed. "Will you go, then, Marshal Kory?"

"Me!" He laughed. "No, I'm the Archivist—I can't go. Perhaps no one will. Some think it is an idle fancy, and the trip too long and dangerous to risk with evil nearer to hand. But I hope the Marshal-General sends someone. I'd like to know what happened to Luap—and his followers—and why they left Fintha. Perhaps there are more scrolls there—who knows?" He looked at her. "Would you go, if you could, or does this seem a scholar's question to you?"

"I would go," said Paks. "A long journey—unknown lands—mountain fortress—what could be more exciting?"

CHAPTER TWENTY-FOUR

The early spring flowers were just fading when Paks rode west up the first long slopes above Fin Panir. She still thought nothing could be more exciting. With the caravan, the year's first, rode Amberion, High Marshals Connaught and Fallis, and four knights: Joris, Adan, and Pir, from the Order of the Cudgel, and Marek from the Order of Gird. A troop of men-at-arms marched with them, and a number of yeomen had signed on as drovers and camp workers. Most of the caravan was commercial, headed for Kaelifet, but Ardhiel and Balkon rode with the Girdish contingent as ambassadors and witnesses for their people.

Paks continued her training under the direction of the paladin and High Marshals. If she had thought the trip would provide a respite from study, she was quickly convinced otherwise. By the time they reached the Rim, a rough outcrop of stone that loomed across their path, visible a day's journey away, Paks had passed their examinations on the Code of Gird and grange organization. She began learning the grange history of the oldest granges, the reasons for locating granges and bartons in certain places, the way that the Code of Gird was administered in grange courts and market courts in Fintha. Now she knew how the judicar was appointed in Rocky Ford, and why the required number of witnesses to a contract varied with the kind of contract.

Their encounter with the horse nomads was a welcome break. She had been marching along muttering to herself the names of the Marshal-Generals who had made changes in the Code when one of the wagonmaster's sons came pelting along the line, crying a warning. As he neared the Girdsmen, he yelled, "Sir paladin! Sir paladin! Raiders!"

"Where, lad?" Amberion was already swinging onto his golden chestnut warhorse.

"North, sir! The scouts say it's a big party."

Paks felt her stomach clench as she hurried to untie Socks from the wagon. Socks was tossing his head, and she scrambled up, uncomfortably aware of her awkwardness. At least she had her own armor and sword for the journey. She swung Socks away from the wagons, and unhooked her helmet from its straps. Amberion was already helmeted, shield on arm.

"Paksenarrion!" he called. "Bring spears." Paks unfastened her shield from the saddle and slid it on her arm. At the supply wagon, she called for two spears, and a young yeoman slid them out the rear. Paks locked them under her elbow, whirled Socks, and rode off to find Amberion. To the north she could see a smudge of dust. The caravan itself was suddenly alive with armed troops. Their score of men-at-arms marched as a rear guard; the regular caravan guards rode atop each wagon, crossbows loaded and cocked. High Marshal Connaught carried a bow; he, Sir Marek, and Ardhiel rode toward the head of the caravan. The other three knights waited on High Marshal Fallis, whose bald-faced horse was throwing its usual tantrum. Paks grinned to herself. She'd had to ride that horse a few times herself; she could imagine the struggle to get helm and shield in place while staying aboard.

Then a bellow from the wagonmaster bought Amberion back. He shrugged at Paks, and she followed him to the cluster of mounted fighters. High Marshal Connaught was glaring, but the wagonmaster never looked up.

"You can't do it, I say, and you agreed when I took you on that you'd be bound by my orders."

"Thieves and outlaws—" began Connaught. The wagonmaster interrupted.

"Horse nomads. Horse nomads I've met before, and will every year, whether you ride with me or not. Maybe you could hold them off—if it's one of the half-decent clans like Stormwind or Wintersun. But what about next year? We skirmish a little for honor's sake, pay our toll, same as a caravan would on the long route through Tsaia, and that's it. None of your Girdish sermonizing here, Marshal: it'll get me killed."

"And if they attack?" said Amberion. Paks noticed that the wagonmaster's fixed glare softened a little.

"We fight, of course: that's why I have guards. But they won't, with you in sight. I'm glad enough to have the extra blades and bows, and that's truth, but for the rest of it, I'll pay toll." Connaught started to speak, but Amberion caught his eye, and he closed his moutn. Amberion smiled at the wagonmaster. "Sir, we agreed to follow your command while we traveled with you; forgive us for our eagerness to defend you."

It was not long before they could see the advancing warriors clearly: a mass of riders armed with lances, on shaggy small horses. Paks watched the war party ride closer—and closer. Now she could see the shaggy manes, the glitter of bridle ornaments, the colors of the riders' cloaks. On tall poles long streamers of cloth fluttered in the wind: blue, gray, and white. She could hear the drumming of those many hooves.

The wagonmaster had insisted that all but the parley group he led stay near the wagons, but he had invited Amberion to ride out with him. Paks followed, at his nod. As they moved toward the nomads, the wagonmaster gave them his instructions. Finally they faced their enemy only a bowshot away. Amberion waved his spear slowly, left to right. The nomads halted. Several of their horses whickered.

A single figure in the front of the group waved one of the streamered poles and yelled something in a language Paks didn't know.

"Parley in Common!" yelled Amberion.

The figure rode forward ten yards or so. "Why we halt?" he called. "Yer on our pasture, city folk. On the sea of grass, only the strong survive. Can ye stop us taking all you have, and feeding ye to the grass?" His speech was thickly accented, a mixture of several dialects.

"Aye, easily enough." The wagonmaster sounded confident.

"Ha! Five against fifty? Are ye demons, then, like that black one that walks north?"

"We are servants of Gird and the High Lord," said Amberion. The wagonmaster shot him a glance, but said nothing.

"Well met here, servant of whoever. Go tell yer master that those who travel our lands must pay our tolls—unless ye'd rather fight."

Amberion turned to the wagonmaster, brows raised. The wagonmaster nodded. "Oh, these aren't bad. These are Stormwinds—that's old Carga out there; he don't torture prisoners at all. Keeps slaves, of course, they all do, but if there's a good horse nomad, it's Carga. He'll take our tribute and leave us alone. You notice he changed his demand, that second time?"

The wagonmaster had assembled a bale of striped cloth, a small keg of Marrakai red wine, several skeins of red and blue yarn, a sack of river-clam shells, and a bundle of mixed wooden staves of a length for arrowshafts. Now he waved, and some of the drovers carried the goods toward them.

The nomad leader rode forward slowly, alone, close enough that Paks could see the curl of hoof on its thong around his neck, the spirals tattooed on his cheeks, the clear gray eyes under dark brows. He rode without stirrups, in knee-high boots whose embroidered soles had surely never been used for walking, clear as the colors were.

"Ye ride with strange powers, cityborn trader," he said. "Yer men I know, but him—" he pointed at Amberion. "Wizard, is it?"

"A paladin of Gird," said Amberion. The nomad shrugged and spat.

"Never heerd of him, nor paladins neither. But ye stink of power." He watched closely as the goods were displayed before him, and finally nodded. "Go yer way, scarfeet riders—" It took Paks a while to understand this reference to their stirrups, and the marks those left on boots.

She hardly had time to enjoy the memory of the nomads before High Marshal Connaught had her hard at work again. Spring passed quickly into summer, the hot windy summer of the grasslands. At times it seemed they rode in the center of a bowl of grass, and Paks wondered if the world might be turning under them, so that they would never be free. Then the green turned grayer; the grass hardly reached their horses' knees. The dry air rasped in her nose, chapped her lips. Paks could see the ground's color showing through, as if the grass were a threadbare rug over the land, and then the grass failed. The trail went on, a deep-bitten groove of dust and stone.

They moved from water to water. Paks learned to ride with a cloth over her face, and keep her mouth closed against the dryness. The horses lost flesh, despite their care. The caravaners showed the Girdsmen how to turn over every rock before sitting down: Paks loathed the many-legged creatures that lurked in that cool shade and carried poison in their tails.

It took days to cross the first deep canyon: first to ease the wagons down that steep trail without losing control of any of them, then to warp them across the roaring river, red with ground rock, then to drag them back up, foot by foot. And when they came out on top again, Paks could see little of where they had been. After another such canyon, the caravaners pointed out a line of purple against the northern sky. Mountains, they said. Elves, they said also, with sidelong looks at Ardhiel.

Paks asked him, and Ardhiel answered that those mountains were home to elves, but not of his family. He seemed troubled by something, but Paks knew better than to ask. Baikon, looking north, muttered eagerly about stone. He had confided to Paks that his family, the Goldenaxe clan, was looking for more daskgeft, more stonemass for the increase of the family. He hoped to find some; the descriptions Luap had written of the land made him think the stone there might be "dross," or suitable. Paks wondered again how dross could have so many meanings in dwarvish: courage, wit, strength—almost anything good, it seemed to her, was dross.

Day by day, the mountains seemed to march nearer their flank. Ahead was only the rolling level of the desert, broken by watercourses. Paks began to feel a pressure from those mountains; she understood why the caravaners would go around rather than through them, for that alone. Then one morning an edge of red rock showed ahead. As they marched toward it, it rose higher and higher. By the next afternoon, they could see the lighter rock below, great sweeping curves of white and yellow—the same color, Paks thought, as the walls of Cortes Andres. And two days later, marching under those great stone ramparts, the Girdsmen turned aside.

Here a river emptied itself from those stone walls into the sand and rubble outside. The caravaners muttered and made gestures, but finally moved on, while High Marshal Connaught examined the map again. When the caravan was gone, he mounted his bay horse and led them up the watercourse, the horses lunging through the dry sand. Ahead, Paks could see towering white walls closing in. She wondered how they could ride in such a narrow space if the water came up.

"Bad place for an ambush," said Amberion beside her.

"Yes, sir."

"By the map, we'll be leaving this soon, and climbing into another stream's valley. I hope the route can be climbed by horses."

Paks had not thought of that, but looking at the sheer walls of stone, she realized what they might face. "If they can't—"

"Then we'll leave them. Build a stout camp, leave the novice yeomen and most of the men-at-arms.'

Before the canyon walls closed completely, High Marshal Connaught turned left away from the river, leading them onto a rough slope of broken rock. He seemed to find a trail; Paks, far back in the group, could not see anything ahead to guide them. Socks heaved upward, stride by stride. They stopped often to rest the animals; the warhorses were curded with sweat. Amberion's horse, alone of all the animals, never showed the marks of hard riding, always slick-coated and fresh. Paks had noticed that about all the paladin's mounts in Fin Panir. Far back she could see the mules, head down, picking their way delicately and almost without effort over the rocks. Below, the canyon they had come from disappeared into a jumble of shadow and light. Now she could see far to the right, more swooping curves of stone, patterned by dark cracks. Far up on the heights, she thought she saw trees.

By late afternoon, she could see a strange shape against the sky: a dark cone with a scoop out of the point. Amberion pointed to it.

"That's marked on the map. Blackash cone, it said: we must bear left of it." As they came nearer, always climbing, the rock changed abruptly from white to red. The trail led through a break in that vertical red wall. Suddenly the black cone was close; it looked like a loose pile of dark rock sitting on the red stone around it. Paks stared. Had someone—some giant, surely—built a cairn? Long shadows streaked the land, making weird shapes of the windblown rocks around them. Now they could see that the canyon they had climbed from was only a small section of something much larger that extended far to the east, ending at last in a higher rampart of white topped with forest. South, the land dropped abruptly into that hole. It was hard to believe they had climbed anything so sudden. Westward the land dipped to a rumpled plain of sand, and that again dropped sharply: Paks could just see against the setting sun the distant mountains beyond that drop. Northward, their view was blocked by the black cone and the higher land behind it. Red cliffs, these, with fortress-size blocks lying at their feet. Paks wondered if the others felt as small as she did.

That night they camped on the sandy plain just southwest of the black cone. A cold wind brushed the camp; stars blazed brighter than Paks had ever seen them. She woke several times to hear Ardhiel singing. Dawn came early on that high place. Paks saw the white stone below begin to glow even before she was aware of light in the sky. Then the high wall to the east stood clear against a green dawn. First light turned the red peaks north of them to fiery orange; then the light crept down to meet them, throwing blue shadows below.

They had some trouble to find the trail from there. Just to the left of the black cone, layers of stone like those that peel from a boiled egg curved downward, but the horses skidded and slipped. High Marshal Connaught sent Thelon ahead; he reported that the stony way ended in a drop four or five men high. Then they searched for a way around. Paks decided that walking in deep dry sand was harder than any marching she had ever done. The wind increased, blowing sand into their eyes. The horses flattened ears against it. The first three trails they tried led to sheer cliffs, and it was early afternoon before the scout found a safe route.

It began in a narrow grove of pines, where broad low boles rose from drifted sand, old trees bent by strong winds into a tangled thatch of branches. Below the trees, the trail followed a twisting ravine, its bed choked with boulders of garish red and black on a bed of sand; they radiated the heat like coals. Across the ravine, as they went down, they could see outcrops of red rock. Suddenly the cleft they traveled angled back to the left, then crooked right again. They were on a narrow platform above a small valley that led straight away toward a tangle of cliffs and canyons. On either side sheer cliffs rose hundreds of feet, rose-red and orange, striped with black. To the right, an arm of the valley angled back away from them. Down the valley a stream reflected the sky; it looked wider than Paks had expected.

As they rode down into the valley, Paks heard conflicting opinions.

"What a farm that'd make," said one of the yeomen with the mules. "Wind-shelter from those cliffs—water—must be good soil with all that grass."

"A long way to market," said another. "Unless you founded a grange out here, Tamar."

"Marry me, and we might," said the woman, laughing.

"Marry—I'd have married you in Fin Panir, but you wouldn't have it."

"And miss this? Come on, Dort, you weren't any more ready to settle down than I was. But couldn't we make a farm here?"

"I'll tell you that when I find the nearest market." Paks heard them laughing for some moments after.

"It is not good," muttered Balkon, who had turned his pony aside from the others to look closely at the rock wall nearest them. "See—" He poked at it with his axe-haft. "It is soft here. Good rock there—" he pointed at the east wall of the valley, and at great cliffs beyond it. "But something is wrong here. With those cliffs, it must be deeper."

"Strange," murmured Ardhiel as Paks rode by. "It has an odd feel—very strange."

But most of the company liked its looks—green grass and water, walls far enough apart to allow maneuvering, yet close enough for protection. Then they rode out of the last rock-strewn mouth of the ravine, and found themselves once more in deep sand—this time wet sand.

"Ah," said the dwarf, eyes gleaming. "It is that this valley is choked with sand—something blocks it there—" he pointed at the far end. "The side rock goes down, very far below this; I feel it meet under our feet."

"Find us firm ground," said High Marshal Connaught to the scout. "These horses can't handle boggy—" He threw himself off as his horse sank hock-deep by one leg. They all dismounted. Close up the valley was smaller than they had thought; the hills were low dunes rising above the level. The stream was only a trickle across the sand surface. "But plenty if we dig," the High Marshal assured the others. "It's like those waterholes in the low desert."

While the scout and several men-at-arms searched for a firm path to the north end of the valley, the Marshals and knights looked at the angled canyon that wound away to the right. That way the ground seemed firmer, and the little stream, though narrower, gurgled ankle deep over fine gravel.

"It's too bad we aren't going this way," said High Marshal Fallis. "I suppose it's blocked at the far end by another cliff."

"Let's look at it," said Marek, one of the knights, and the only member of the Order of Gird. "We ought to learn the shape of the land, in case of trouble."

"In case of trouble," said Joris drily, "nothing in this land offers comfort. We should have been born with wings."

"I agree with Marek, though," said Connaught. "We should know, and mark the map."

They set off on foot, the High Marshals, Amberion and Paks, the knights, and Ardhiel and Balkon. In a few minutes an angle of rock cut them off from sight of the others. On either hand the cliffs rose straight out of the sand, as if carved by a knife. Paks noticed a great arch set into the northeast wall. Under it a dark shadowed space looked large enough for a building. She looked from cliff to cliff, uneasy. In several places the stone seemed to have broken away leaving an overhanging arch, some much smaller than others. She nudged Balkon.

"Why does the rock do that? Is it natural? Did something shape it?"

"What—oh, it is the arch you mean? That is stone itself. I have not seen before, but I have heard. It is good stone that can take an arch; the arch is the drossen shape—" He saw her puzzled look, sighed, and tried in Common. "The shape that stone holds when it is sound—strong—healthy. Not nedross, like that stone that we came by, where the wall broke to let us in. Look in the High Lord's Hall—you see that even human masons know the right shape, the good shape, for stone holding stone. The longer the arch, the better the stone."

"Oh." Paks shivered. She did not like this valley; it was hard to judge how high the cliffs were, how far they had come from their friends. She looked back, to see someone leading a horse across the stream, heading down the valley. She could not see the other men-at-arms or horses at all; only a narrow view remained of the main valley. She craned her neck to look at the large arch again. Surely the whole party could shelter there—if you could get horses up the cliff. She started to laugh at that idea, and suddenly stopped. Something was moving in the shadow. For an instant she could not speak, but then she called to Amberion.

"What is it?" he asked, turning. Before Paks could answer, Ardhiel cried out in elven, swinging his bow from his shoulder and snatching arrows. Paks pointed upward, then staggered as an arrow slammed into her helmet.

"Keep your faces down!" bellowed High Marshal Fallis. "Eyes—" But Paks knew that, and had already dashed for a leaning rock. Pir and Adan were huddled there, too. More arrows clattered on the rocks around them. She heard a high-pitched cry from above, and then the terrible smack of a body on rocks. Another scream from across the canyon. Then silence.

"That won't be all," said High Marshal Fallis. Paks looked around. Ardhiel was close to the cliff on the far side; she saw Fallis near him. Connaught, Amberion, and Joris had taken shelter behind another rock near her, and Marek and Balkon behind yet another. She risked a quick glance upward, but could see nothing for the overhang.

"Beware!" Ardhiel's voice rose again, and he yelled something in elven. Paks saw a swarm of black-clad figures leap from cracks in the rock, turned just in time to meet more of them attacking on her side. She and the two knights leaped to their feet.

At first it seemed they might be cut down in their separate groups. The attackers were skilled with their narrow blades, and had numbers and height on their side. Adan staggered; a blade had gone deep in his leg. Paks covered his side; together she and Pir managed to fight their way back to High Marshal Connaught, half-carrying Adan between them. Fallis and Ardhiel dashed across to join them, and the group locked into a unit, back to back with Adan in the center. From her position, Paks could not see if any of the others, far back down the valley, had noticed any disturbance. She was fighting too hard to have breath to yell. She did not even recognize what she was fighting until the top of Pir's sword flicked back one of the hoods.

"Elves!" she cried; the fine-boned face, the long graceful body now seeming the same as Ardhiel's. But the elf called to them.

"No—not elves. Iynisin—unsingers—once of our blood—"

"And we are still the true heirs," called one of the enemy, in elven. Paks could just follow the words. The voice held the same music as Ardhiel's, but was colder. "We have not changed; you have fallen, cousin, making alliance with mortals and rockfolk, to the insult of your blood."

"Daskdusky scum," muttered Balkon, swinging his axe wide from his corner position.

Though outnumbered, the little group was able to shift slowly back toward the main valley. High Marshal Fallis, facing that way, told them he saw the men-at-arms coming. Paks, Pir, and Amberion, holding the rear, stepped back cautiously, keeping the enemy blades at bay. Then Marek called a warning. Paks glanced up at the nearest cliff. There, moving swiftly on the sheer wall as if it were level, a great many-legged thing dropped down on them. At the overhanging ledge it stepped into the air and fell, swinging on a shining line behind it, leaping from its first touch on the ground to arc high above their heads. Pir swung and missed; Paks twisted, trying to strike behind her; her sword clashed on Fallis', and the thing leaped out to whirl and attack again.

While they were still shaken by this creature, from overhead a loud voice cried a single word. Paks stopped short, hardly able to breathe. She felt as if she'd been dipped in ice. Her eyes roved, following the great monster. Now she could see it had almost the form of a spider, many legs around a bulbous body. She felt her hand loosening on her sword.

But with a ringing tone like that of a great bell, white light glowed around them. Paks could move again; she felt her heart beating wildly, but her hand clenched on the sword. As the monster leaped, she hacked at its head. Her sword skidded off the hard surface, but Pir's severed a leg. Paks thrust again, for the eyes. It reared back, aiming small tubes along its belly at her. Amberion shoved her aside. A gout of grayish fluid missed her; she heard Adan cry out behind. But by then Amberion's sword had severed the head, and the thing lay twitching on the ground.

"Stay close," said Amberion. "It is a spell of fear laid on us." Paks felt no fear, now, and fought on.

In the space of the monster's attack, more enemy fighters had come from the cliffs to cut them off from the rest of the party. These were bowmen, close enough that their arrows could wound even through armor. Between them and the bowmen were two ranks of swords. Paks took a deep breath. She had not expected to have such a short career as paladin—not even paladin yet, she reminded herself—but she thought she would as soon die in this company as any other. She saw Balkon bend to kiss his axe. High Marshal Fallis had done something for Adan; he was standing more steadily. Connaught frowned at the enemy, lips folded. Amberion touched Paks on the arm.

"It's only five to one," he said, smiling. "Your Duke has faced worse than that."

Paks grinned. "Oh well—we'll win through easily, then."

"You stay close, though. You have no protection of your own against that fear." Paks thought she had, but wasn't going to argue the point. She saw Connaught draw breath to send them forward; she wondered why the archers hadn't shot yet. Then Ardhiel moved, taking from his side the old battered hunting horn he had carried from Fin Panir. He set it to his lips.

Whatever Paks expected, it had not been the sound of that horn. It began sweet and tender, swelling louder and louder to a triumphant blast that nearly shattered her bones. Wind swirled into the canyon, a great column of whirling air funneling into and from the horn's throat. A roiling mass of pink and gold-lit cloud blotted out the hard clear blue of a desert sky. Paks could not see the cliffs—the enemy—or Ardhiel himself. The cloud shimmered, steadied, became a piled and rumpled staircase of gold. Down it came a brilliant shining creature, winged with rainbow colors, so bright she could hardly stand to see it, and so beautiful she could not look away. On its back was Someone in mail brighter than polished silver, wearing a blinding white cloak. He spoke: the language was elven, the voice rang with authority and troubled the heart like elven harps. And Paks saw Ardhiel bow, and move to his side, and saw him mount that fabulous beast, and saw them rise once more into the clouds.

When the clouds blew away, in the last throbbing notes of that horn-call, the enemy was gone, though the rattle of their flight through the rocks echoed from wall to wall. Ardhiel lay unconscious on the ground, smiling, and the horn in his hand showed its true nature: the finest horn Paks had ever seen, jeweled with rubies and emeralds, shining gold.

With no delay, Connaught had them carry Ardhiel back to the others.

"It's an elfhorn, it must be," he said over his shoulder. "I'd heard of them, but Gird knows I never expected to see one. Let alone hear one. By the gods, this is a bad place. You were right, Balkon. Bad for an ambush, and I walked right into it. I hope it doesn't kill Lord Ardhiel. That'll take some explaining. 'Old hunting horn,' indeed. No wonder he wouldn't play on it for our dancing that night. It makes my skin itch to think of it."

"It's Gird's grace he brought it," said Amberion. "I wonder why they didn't shoot at once? They could have gotten us—"

"Or thought they could." Fallis grunted as his foot turned on a rock. "Damned treacherous ground. Probably a damned kuaknom behind every stone."

"Kuaknom?" asked Paks.

"That's what we call them—kuaknom, tree-haters—as elves are tree-lovers. The elves call them iynisin, the unsingers. Remember, it's the kuaknom that used to be confused with Kuakkganni."

Paks wondered how anyone could confuse those horrible parodies of elves with a Kuakgan. Confuse with elves themselves, yes—for her mind held the memory of the same beauty, the same grace. "Were they the same as other elves once?"

"Aye," answered Balkon, before anyone else could. "And some say they are still, the blackheart rockfilth. The elves like to pretend all the kuaknom failed away many years ago. But here we see the truth of that! By Sertig's Hammer, all the fair-spoken ones would rather have a tongue of silver, though it lied, then tell iron truth at need."

Amberion shook his head. "Your pardon, sir dwarf, but in this I judge you wrong. The kuaknom parted long ago from the true elves, in a quarrel that began before men—"

"Not long before," muttered Balkon. "The Kuakkganni—"

"If they are truly men, then it was not before—but it was before other men. And the cause of that quarrel—"

"Was the Tree. Aye, I've heard that. But it seems a foolish quarrel to me. Would a dwarf enact rage because iron bends to any smith, or stone to any chisel?" He shook his head, and challenged them all with his look. "No, I deem not, and you know the truth of it. But I call no harsh name on Ardhiel's head, for his call saved us, and he has paid for that. The best of elves are fair indeed—aye, though we grumble, being made rough and ugly as rock and iron, we honor them for their grace. Well they name their lord the Singer of Songs; the best of them are true songs, well sung; but we are other, hammered on Sertig's anvil to bear the blows of the world. Our songs are the ring of steel on stone." Paks was astonished; she had never heard any dwarf speak so. He bowed stiffly, and was silent thereafter until they reached the men-at-arms, now coming forward in battle order.

The High Marshals led them swiftly out to the trail the others had found, and the whole company moved down the main valley while it was still light. Here the walls were nearly a bowshot apart. Thelon, sent ahead once more, had found a trail leading out: not where the valley seemed to end, for that was a jumble of house-size stones ending in a twenty-foot cliff, but climbing again over a shoulder of the western wall.

"But it is no trail you could take in the dark, Marshal Fallis," he reported. "Even the near part will tax the horses; after that it is easier, but the first of the trail going into the canyon beyond is worse. I could not go far enough to be sure they can get down. We may have trailwork to do; I judge you will not want to leave them here."

"By no means," said Marshal Fallis. "We had thought of that, when we saw this fertile valley, but we can leave no one behind to suffer attack of the kuaknom. And it is by no means so fertile as it seemed." For they had found all the valley floor to be sand, dry or wet or boggy; the green growth was sedge, not grass, and only a few trees dared that sandy expanse.

They made their camp near the foot of the trail, watering the beasts in a hole dug downstream. Paks helped with that, for it took two to dig away the sand that slithered into the hole while the horses and mules drank. The High Marshals ordered a line of fires between the camp and the eastern wall, the one they expected the kuaknom to use. Paks wondered briefly if the kuaknom might infest the western cliff as well, but she could see no holes or caves for access. By this time the valley was in shadow, lit by the sky. Gradually it faded. Paks had the late watch, and she rolled herself in a blanket against the surprising chill. The sand made a comfortable bed. She slept soundly almost at once.

Thelon, the scout, woke her for her turn at watch. Paks stretched, stiff from sleeping in armor, and took off her helmet to scratch her head. When she replaced the helmet, she let it sit loosely on her braid as she came to the main fire for a mug of sib.

"Nothing so far," reported Thelon. "I wandered across the stream—if you can call it a stream—far enough from the fires to see better, but I saw nothing. But it feels strange, and I don't like it."

Paks yawned. She took a long swallow of sib, aware of sand sifting through her clothes, itching. "I don't mind it feeling strange, as long as those kuaknom, or iynisin, or whatever they are, let us alone."

"Iynisin is the better word," said Thelon seriously. "Elves are the sinyi, the singers of the First Singer's songs, and these scum are those who not only refuse to sing, but who unsing the songs, going against the Singer's will in everything. So, being created as the sinyi are to love trees and flowing water, these hate them, and burrow in stone, fouling bright water with their filth, or choking it—like this one—with stone dust. For the daskin race, the dwarves, it is right to live in stone; they are the dasksinyi, the stone-singers, whose song is stone and its metals. They honor the stone. But these iynisin defile it. So Balkon will tell you."

"Yes, but he calls them something else—"

"In dwarvish, yes—but dwarftongue is not truesong; for the right names, the truenames of things, ask an elf. The singer is known by some as Adyan, the Namer of Names—"

"I thought that was different," said Paks.

Thelon laughed lightly, in the elven way. "Some also say that the god of men should be called the Sorter of Beads, for men worry more of such division, and not right and wrong." Paks scowled at him, but he held up his hand. "Indeed, you call your god the High Lord, and speak of his Hall as a seat of justice. What is justice, then, but judging and choosing—sorting fact from fact, and laying on one side the true, and on the other side the false? Now I, being but half-elven, have less pride of race than elves: my own thought is that the great king is one only: He Named the first Names, and Sang the first Song, and He rightly judges all things as true or false, good or evil. I would even say that Sertig the Maker is but another name for him—for surely one only came first, and did these things. Now we spend one time singing, and another time fighting, and another time learning or praying—but we are mortal—and even the immortal elves live mostly in one line—we divide, therefore, like a man who says that this mountain is gnomeland on one side, and his land on the other. But it is all one mountain."

Much of this Paks did not understand, but she liked the idea that the High Lord might be the same as Adyan and Sertig. She finished her sib, and went to her post, on the south end of the camp.

The nearest watchfires burned low, scarcely more than a heap of coals, for they had found little wood to burn. High Marshal Connaught had told them to keep wood back, in case of trouble. A chill wind drifted down from the higher land; Paks heard a distant moan where it poured over the lip of the valley into the lower canyons beyond. One of the other watchers coughed; a horse stamped. She thought of Socks, tethered with the others at the north end of the camp, just under the bluff they would climb in the morning. Against the bright starry sky, the eastern cliff loomed, a black presence. It was strange to camp so near a stream and hear no water sounds, but the sand-choked flow moved silently. Something hissed along the sand near her; Paks jumped and looked around. Nothing. Her scalp itched; she pushed her helmet back again to scratch.

All at once the night was full of dark fighters, striking at every post. Paks yelled, with the other sentries, and the camp crashed into wakefulness. Someone threw wood on the nearest fire; by that light she saw the iynisin eyes gleaming under their hoods. She could not tell how many attackers they fought. Blades swept toward her out of the dark; she felt the force of their blows stinging along her arm as she countered them. Something struck her head. Her helmet, still loosely set on her head, bounced off, and her long braid thumped on her back. She had no hand free to find the helmet; several swords faced her. The iynisin cried aloud in their beautiful voices, words she should know—but she was fighting too hard to translate. She was forced back—and back again. Then her foot came down on something that rolled beneath it, and she fell, trying desperately to tuck and come up, but the heavy sand caught her. A great weight fell on her, forcing her face into the sand. Before she choked, she felt a blow to her head, and nothing.

The attackers fled as swiftly as they had come. When High Marshal Connaught called the roll, four failed to answer. Sir Joris was dead, with an arrow through his eye. Two of the men-at-arms had suffered mortal wounds. And Paksenarrion had disappeared. They found her helmet, and her sword, but no trace of her.

CHAPTER TWENTY-FIVE

At first, Paks was hardly aware that she was aware. It was dark and cold and the stone beneath her was hard and slightly gritty. She wondered vaguely if she was dreaming about the cells under the Duke's Stronghold. She tried to move, and a savage pain shot through her head. Not a dream. It was hard to think. Dark. Cold. Stone. She felt about with one hand. It met a wall rising from the surface she lay on. Fighting nausea from the pain in her head, she struggled to sit up and feel about her. Wall—another wall—yet another. All were stone; she could not feel any joints. Solid stone? She could not remember what might have happened—where she might be.

As she moved, she realized that her skin itched and stung as if she had rolled in nettles. She reached up to see what she had on—a tunic of some kind. It felt scratchy. She grew aware of something uncomfortable around her throat—something heavy, and slightly tight. And cold uncomfortable bands around her wrists and ankles. She reached to feel the thing at her throat. Pain stabbed her fingers, and she jerked them back with a gasp. Her throat tingled; it was hard to swallow.

For a few moments, she held very still, fighting a rising panic. She tried to remember anything at all that would give her a clue to where she was. She thought again of the Duke's Stronghold. That wasn't right. A caravan. A caravan where she was riding, not walking. A tall black horse with white stockings and a blaze. My horse, she thought. All right... what next? She thought of gold, and at once remembered Amberion on his chestnut, remembered his name and the nature of the quest. She pushed at the cloud across her memory. They had been—coming into a canyon. No, they were in it. A day later—smoke from the cliffs, arrows—but nothing more. She remembered Ardhiel saying something about the black cousins, the iynisin the elves did not like to remember.

Suddenly, she thought where she must be. Underground, taken by the iynisin. She felt around frantically for her weapons. They were gone. Of course, she thought. No sword, no battleaxe, no armor—and no medallion of Gird. All gone.

She found herself breathing rapidly, almost gasping, and tried to regain control of herself. Think about it, she told herself. No, think about the others. Do they know? Will they come? Can they come? They will come, she thought hopefully. They won't leave me here; they will come. She tried to picture them, fighting their way down tunnels to find her. What if they fail? her mind asked suddenly. What if we all die under these rocks, and no one ever knows what happened? She tried to call on Gird, but something about the place—the quality of the silence, perhaps—stopped the words at her lips, and she could not say Gird's name aloud.

Yet thinking about Gird and Amberion helped. Whatever happens, she thought—and forced back the imagination of what might happen—I am a warrior of Gird. Whether I can fight my way free or not, I can fight to the end. She remembered Ambros falling as he gave the death-stroke to Achrya's priest. That would not be so bad. Any soldier expected to die someday. She had heard tales enough, in Fin Panir, of paladins and knights fighting against impossible odds, for the glory of Gird. For a moment, she saw herself, fighting alone against—what?—she imagined many black-cloaked swordsmen—in a blaze of light.

Paks leaned on the wall and pushed herself up, dizzy as she was. Much better standing. The darkness was more than absence of light; it had a malign and bitter flavor. She edged around the walls, feeling her way along the stone. Wall. Wall—and something other than stone, colder than stone, and smooth. She felt along its edge. A door? Yes. Iron, she thought. She could find nothing but a smooth surface: no bars, no grille, nothing but the smooth metal itself until it met stone. Panic rose again. Suppose they just left her there forever?

You're not a silly recruit any more, she told herself firmly. Don't think of that. And if it happens, it happens. She moved past the door, feeling for hinges, but found none. Without that clue, she could not tell which way the door would open—could not even try to surprise someone coming in. She went on around to the next corner, and the next—which would be opposite the door, she thought—and leaned into it. It was hard to keep her eyes open in the dark. She felt herself slipping down the wall, and straightened with a jerk. Whenever they come, she vowed, they will find me on my feet.

Despite that vow, she woke on the floor of the cell when she heard scraping outside the door. She made it up before the door swung open, but her heart was racing, shaking her body, and her mouth was dry. She squinted against the light that poured in—a lurid yellow-green blaze. Something stank. Facing her was a tall slender figure, caped and cowled in black, face hidden by the shadow of its cowl. Evil radiated from it as it entered the cell. On its chest was a silver carved spider, a handspan across, hanging from a silver chain. Paks moved her hand in the warding sign she had learned as a child. The figure laughed, a liquid sound that would have been beautiful but for the evil aura.

"That won't help you," said the silvery voice, lovely as all elves' voices are, but utterly cold. "Surely they are not sending children, now, with children's little superstitions?"

Paks said nothing. She glanced past the first figure to see two torchbearers; the green-flared torches smelled like rotting flesh—the stench rolled from them in heavy waves. A third attendant, also black-hooded, carried a wood and leather case. "We were informed," the first one went on, "that you were a warrior of some importance—even a candidate for the order of paladins, or some such nonsense. I find that hard to believe, as easy as you were to capture, but we shall see." It came closer yet. Paks braced herself, whether to take a blow or give one she could not have said. "No, mighty warrior," it said. "You cannot touch me if you try." Suddenly it threw back its cowl to reveal a face entirely elven but the reverse of Ardhiel's: the same fine bone structure, but expressing only evil, its nature cruelty and lust. She was instantly convinced that it was male.

Despite herself, Paks shivered as he reached out a slender long-fingered hand and touched the band around her throat. She could not move back; the band tightened just slightly.

"You see," the iynisi continued, "you wear already the symbol of our lady, and while you wear it you cannot harm any of her servants. Nor can your puny saint—whatever his name is—aid you. You have only yourself, your own abilities—if you have any—to help you here. If you amuse us, and learn to serve us, you may yet live to see the sky again. But, of course, if you prefer to starve alone in this cell—" he looked at her, waiting for an answer.

Paks tore her gaze from his eyes, and looked around the cell, in the green light. It was stone, cut out of living rock: just long enough to lie down in. Nothing else. Her glance flicked down her own body. The tunic she wore was black, and looked slightly fuzzy. The bands on her wrists were black, with hasps for chains. There were no chains in the cell. Yet. She tried to think of Gird, of Amberion, but her mind froze, clouded.

"Perhaps you need to partake of our sport before you can choose," said the iynisi. "You are already familiar with this cell. Since we want no foolish uproar—" he beckoned to the attendant with the case, who opened it. The first iynisi took out what appeared to be a hank of gray yarn. He unwound the stuff, which seemed slightly sticky, and reached for Paks' wrists. "One of our lady's arts," he said. "Not so cumbersome as chains, and of course, no use to you as a weapon. But you'll find it strong enough; it will bind dwarves, let alone humans. I advise you not to fight it. For now, I am using the wristlets, but if you are troublesome, I'll wrap your bare flesh with it, and this"—he laid a strand against Paks' arm; it burned like a coal, like the strands of the net in the Achryan priest's stronghold—"is what that feels like."

Paks shivered again, but made no sound. The iynisi nodded. "So there is something warrior-like in you after all. That is well. We should lose our amusement were you entirely craven. Come along, now." The iynisi turned to leave; Paks felt a tug at her wrists, now bound closely together. For an instant, she thought of resistance to the pull, but the other attendants showed the long knives in their hands, and she knew it would be futile.

"Excellent," said the iynisi, as she took the first step to follow. "We had heard you were capable of thought and planning. It is so important for a warrior to know when fighting is hopeless."

No, thought Paks; it is never hopeless. You can always die. But she was already walking down a stone passage as she thought this, between the first iynisi and a torchbearer in front, and the other torchbearer and attendant behind. She thought of lunging at the one in front, tried to gather herself for it, but her body ignored the thought and kept walking. They passed a branching passage, then another. She tried to look around her, tried to pick out directions and openings, and orient herself, but the speed at which she was led, and the peculiar green light, made this impossible.

They turned into a wider corridor, dimly lit by a greenish blur along the angle of wall and ceiling. Paks could not see what it was, but it gave off a sour smell different from the rank stench of the green torches. Here were other iynisin, that hissed as they saw her. All wore black, but not the cape and hood of her escort, or the great spider emblem. They melted from her path—or from the iynisi with her. As they went on, she thought she heard more and more following behind.

Her escort turned into a narrow passage that sloped downward to the right, falling away from the roof. Ahead of the iynisi, Paks could see a wider opening, and brighter light. She was led through it into a wide flat area, slightly oval. Surrounding it were tiers of stone seats, already half-full, and filling with more iynisin. On one side, a dark gaping maw replaced the first two tiers. As the torchbearers of her escort moved around the oval lighting torches set on brackets, she realized that the dark space was not empty. Eight eyes as big as fists reflected chips of green light. A vast bloated body hung in the web that stretched across the opening. Each of the eight legs, Paks saw, was as long as she was tall.

Paks was hardly aware of the chill that spread over her as she stared at the great spider in horror. Was this Achrya herself? Beside her the iynisi chuckled. "I see you have noticed our ally. No, that is not our lady—merely one of her representatives, you might say. But do not let fear of her make you less nimble. While you wear her symbol, she will not pursue you." By this time, the torchbearers had finished lighting the whole circuit; now more green light flared from above. Paks looked up to see a great hanging framework, also made in the likeness of a spider with legs outspread on a web, holding more torches. By this light she could see that the seats were almost filled, and not alone with iynisin. Hunch-backed orcs clustered in one section; grotesque dog-faced beings in another. All stared down at her, eyes glittering in the flickering light.

"Your reputation has preceded you, Paksenarrion," said the iynisi, with a mocking smile. "You were involved in the loss of our friend and ally Jamarrin in Brewersbridge." His voice rang out, now, and the rest of the chamber was silent but for the sputtering torches. "We would see for ourselves what skill in arms, what brilliance of strategy, defeated so fair a servant of our lady." Paks did not answer. She tried to think what this was leading up to, besides a miserable and public execution.

"We could, of course, simply kill you here," he said, echoing her thought. "Our lady would be pleased to see the—inventiveness—of our methods, and the torment of one who destroyed her servant Jamarrin. But such sport lasts briefly, with you human folk. Perhaps, also, you have been used by those you think your friends. Certainly the elves have not treated you fairly, stealing from you and clouding your memory." He reached out quickly and laid a cold, dry hand along her brow. As suddenly as light springs into a dark closet, she remembered the Halveric's scroll that she had sworn to take to his wife in Lyonya—and remembered the elves who had sent her instead to Brewersbridge, to take their messages, while they took the scroll. The iynisi smiled and nodded. "They 'healed' you, as you thought—indeed, yes, and cast their glamour on you, to turn an honest soldier into their errand-girl, made oathbreaker and faithless by their enchantment. Was that well done? I see you have doubts of it now, and so you should. How much of what you said and did was their bidding? Perhaps you have never acted of your own will yet. We shall give you a chance, therefore, to earn your next day of life." Despite herself, Paks felt a leap of hope. If they would let her fight, even outnumbered—even unarmed—that would be a better death. Surely if she fought, Gird would come and help her, would protect her from the worst. She pushed the thought of the elves away; later she could worry about that, if later came. No doubt they had merely meant to save her trouble. But a faint doubt lingered, souring her memory of them.

"There are many here who would be glad to prove your reputation unfounded," the iynisi continued. "I myself think you do have some skill. We shall see. For your first trial you will face but a single opponent. Hardly a test of your ability, but he will be armed, and you not. If you dispute the fairness of it, you may always forbear to fight, and be cut down without resistance." The other attendants had gone away while he was speaking; Paks looked around as the iynisi stepped back. With a swift stroke of his knife, he cut the strands that tethered her wrists, and stepped farther back, bowing. Then he turned to the surrounding seats, one arm upraised. "Let the sport begin!" he cried. The spectators rose in their ranks and cheered. The caped iynisi ran lightly to the web across the arena, bowed to the huge spider, and swarmed up the web to the seats above.

Paks, alone now on the floor of the arena, looked about for her opponent. She tried again to call on Gird or the High Lord, but could feel nothing when the words passed through her mind. It was like calling in an empty room. For the first time, she wondered whether Gird would even listen. Surely, if he could hear, he would help—in something like this—but the words she'd been taught echoed in her head, unanswered. She heard the scrape of the boots from the passage by which she had come, and turned to see an orc stride into the lighted space. He wore leather body-armor and helmet, as well as the boots, and carried a short-thonged whip in one hand, and a curved knife in the other. Paks took a deep steadying breath and rocked from heel to toe, loosening her muscles. With her own weapons, such an opponent would have been no problem at all; without even a dagger, she was at a severe disadvantage. Still, she could fight—she reached for the spark of battle anger, and welcomed it.

The orc came to her slowly, with a low, smooth gait unexpected in such a bent shape. Paks crouched slightly, up on her toes, ready to shift any direction as chance offered. The orc grinned at her, and screeched something which the watching iynisin understood, for they laughed. She supposed it was a challenge of some sort. She felt a rising excitement, hot and joyous. Perhaps this was Gird's gift, instead of his presence.

"Come on, then," she said to the orc in Common. "Many of your kind have I killed; come join them."

Closing abruptly, the orc swung the whip at her head; Paks ducked to save her eyes, watching its knife hand. Sure enough, as the knotted thongs bit into her neck and shoulders, the knife thrust toward her belly. She pivoted away from the thrust and caught the orc's wrist with one hand, jerking him forward. He went to his knees, and she tried to make it to his back. But he rolled as he fell, and she met another slash of the whip. This time the thongs wrapped her legs, and she fell heavily, narrowly missing another thrust of the knife as she twisted away from his hand. He was on his feet an instant before her, aiming another blow of the whip. She scrambled away from it; the iynisin above her tittered.

"Sso . . . we . . . teach . . . to . . . humanss . . . what . . . iss . . . mannerss," said the orc in barely understandable Common. He grinned again. "For thiss one . . . no sswordss . . . just whipss enough." He swung the whip around his head; the thongs hummed. Paks kept her eye on the knife blade. He edged toward her again. Paks took a deep breath from the belly, summoned up all the anger she could rouse, and charged an instant before he did. The whip was still in backstroke; she threw all her weight on him, both hands on the wrist of his knife hand. To her delight, he sprawled backwards. She tucked as they hit the stone floor and rolled on, still digging her thumbs into his wrist. The knife clattered to the stone. He had already recognized the danger, and dropped the whip to grab for it with his free hand. Paks kicked it away; it skittered across the arena. The orc squealed and grabbed her leg, then sank its teeth in her ankle. Paks let go of the wrist, and reached for the whip. Again, the orc anticipated her, and snatched it up an instant before she reached it. She rolled away, taking another hard lash of the whip before she was scrambling for the fallen knife.

This time she reached the prize first; she turned to face the orc with a weapon in her hand. She scarcely felt the whip welts or the bite. She grinned back at the orc as he came. Even now it would not be easy—the blade was short, and the orc's armor tough—but she, at least, was sure of the outcome. The orc paused, and screeched again in its unknown tongue. The iynisin were silent, except for one voice that by its tone denied a request.

"Did you wish to quit, orc?" asked Paks. "Have I endangered your soft hide too much?" It was the worst insult she knew, for Ardhiel had told her that the orcs' name for themselves meant iron-skins.

The orc glared at her, baring its fangs and running a tongue around its mouth which was stained with her own blood. Paks spared a quick glance to see where she was. Nearly in front of the spider's web—not where she wanted to be at all. She slid sideways in a crouching glide. The orc turned to follow her, more slowly this time. She led it around the arena until its back was to the spider. By then the orc was beginning to grin again. She watched how it moved, decided where to strike.

Suddenly she stood at full height and stretched her arms upward, like someone just arising from a comfortable sleep. As she expected, the orc darted in and aimed a vicious slash at her exposed torso. She sidestepped left, taking the force of the blow without pausing, and rammed her suddenly lowered right arm into the orc's neck. She had shifted the knife blade in that instant to a side-hold, and it slashed his throat from side to side, catching edge-on in the neckbone. The orc fell, blood pouring over her arm as she tried to free the blade. Above her, the silvery voices clamored for an instant and were still. Paks rolled the dead orc on his back, and levered the knife free. It had a notch, where the bone had chipped it. She crouched, looking up at the circle of faces, as she tried to catch her breath.

"Well enough," called the caped iynisi from above the spider's lair. "It might have been done with more artistry, but the final stroke was admirable. Continue to amuse us so, and you may yet survive. For your next trial, you may keep the knife you have earned. For now, stand against the wall—" he gestured to the wall behind her.

Paks rose, not to comply, but found that the entrance to the arena was filled with heavily armed iynisin. They fanned out around her and forced her back with their pikes. She could not have touched them with the knife, and did not resist. She watched as two of them dragged the orc's body across the the spider's web, and bowed as they placed it just beneath the lowest strands. With horrible quickness the vast bloated body came down and grasped the corpse, the huge abdomen bending around it so that Paks could see cords of silk from the spinnerets twisting around and around. Soon the orc was a neatly cased packet hanging in the web. Paks swallowed against a surge of nausea. So that's what would happen if she failed—she thrust that thought aside hurriedly. Holy Saint Gird, she thought, just help me fight.

As the battle anger left her, she began to tremble. She was terribly thirsty; the orc-bite on her leg throbbed; the whip welts spread a cloak of pain about her. She wondered again how long she had been imprisoned underground. Surely they knew she was gone—surely Amberion would come looking for her. Her vision blurred, and she leaned on the wall behind her. She had not noticed that the pike-bearing iynisin were gone until the caped one spoke again.

"I hope that is not weakness we see," came the silvery voice. "Surely such a champion does not think the trial is over after a trifling altercation like that? No, no . . . we must see more of your vaunted skills. Even now your opponents approach; do not disappoint us."

Paks ran her tongue around her dry mouth. How could she fight again without water or rest? She forced herself to straighten, to look toward the entrance tunnel. Get out in the open, she told herself. You've got to have room. She had stiffened, even with that brief respite, and now she limped on the bitten leg. I have to keep fighting, she thought. I have to.

Out of the dark entrance came two orcs, this time armed with short swords and shields. Holy Gird, she repeated to herself. I can't fight two of them, two swords, with only a notched knife! But Siger's words, spoken long ago in Aarenis, trickled into her memory: the enemy's weapon is your weapon if you can take it. Two swords—if I can get one, then it's one to one. Even a shield will help—

As the orcs came forward, she edged back to the wall. Until she got one of them down or disarmed, she wanted something at her back. She noticed that these two did not seem as eager as the first. One of them held its sword awkwardly. A trick? She waited, and let them come to her, heedless of the iynisin catcalls.

The taller, more skillful orc came in on her right hand, her knife hand. The other edged to her left. Again she noticed that this one held the sword like a stick. The tall one thrust at her. She parried the thrust with the knife, thankful for her long arms. From the corner of her eye, she saw the small orc rush, sword extended stiffly. Paks leaped back to the wall, slamming against it, and grabbed the awkward one's wrist. The orc fell forward as Paks jerked, and she caught a glimpse of a terrified face under the helmet. This one's no fighter, she thought. She dug her thumb into the pressure point, and the orc's sword hand opened. Paks reached for the sword as the taller orc aimed a slash at her over the struggling body of its partner. She ducked. The orc she was fighting tried to slam the edge of its shield into her arm, but she had the sword hilt, as well as her knife, in her right fist. She kicked the orc, hard, and danced back to the wall, switching the knife to her left hand. A surge of triumph gave her momentary strength—that would show them!

The tall orc howled at her and charged, trying to force her sideways into the other one. The shorter orc tried to move in, staying low. Paks slid sideways along the wall, countering the furious thrusts and slashes as well as she could. She felt herself slowing; exhaustion clouded her vision. Only the reflexes developed under hours of Siger's instruction kept her blade between the orc's sword and her body. She had the reach of him, but she could not get past his shield. She tried to force him back, with quick thrusts of her own, but failed. The other orc closed in again, this time grabbing at her knife hand. Paks aimed a kick at the orc's knee, but it snatched at her foot and threw her off balance.

Paks fell heavily on her side, trapped close under the wall. Just over her, the taller orc's blade clanged into the wall. She stabbed at his feet with her knife, rolling towards him to get inside his stroke. Again he missed her. This time his blade landed on the shoulder of the smaller orc, who was trying to grapple with Paks' legs. The little orc screeched and sat back. Paks jerked her legs into a curl and launched herself straight up at the tall orc. She had both blades inside his shield; the sword rammed through his body armor into his belly, and the knife slid into his neck.

Before Paks could free the blades, she felt a weight hit her back, and a strong arm wrapped around her neck. Then the smaller orc's teeth met in her shoulder. Paks threw herself backwards. The orc grunted as it hit the ground, but did not release any pressure of hand or teeth. Paks saw its other hand groping toward the sword the tall orc had dropped. She swiveled, pushing hard with her legs, to get the orc out of reach of that blade. Her own knife was free, but the sword stuck fast in the dead orc's belly. She felt herself weakening, her left arm useless with that grip on her shoulder. The orc began to heave up from underneath; if it once got on top, she would have no chance.

Paks shifted her grip on the knife and struck back over her shoulder, feeling for the orc's eyes. She felt its jaw loosen even before the screams, and stabbed again. Then she raked the knife along the arm around her throat, feeling for the tendons. The grip softened. Paks worked the knife deep into the orc's elbow and twisted. The grip was gone. She rolled quickly and thrust into the orc's throat, trying not to look at its face.

She tried to push herself up from the dead orc. I must get that sword, she thought. I must be ready. But her breath came in great gasps, and she could not see. She felt herself slipping into nothingness, and fell back across the orc's body. With her last scrap of consciousness, she tried to call on Gird, but the name rang in her head, empty of meaning.

★ ★ ★

She woke in a cell, whether the first or another like it she could not have said. A torch burned in a corner bracket; by its light she saw a pitcher, mug, and platter near her. Her wounds smarted as if they'd been salted, but the bleeding had stopped, and she felt much stronger. She reached for the pitcher, then paused. Someone had said something about the danger of taking any food or drink from the iynisin—or was that something from a child's tale she'd heard long ago? She tried to lick her dry lips, but her tongue was swollen and sore. If she had to fight again, she would have to drink something. And if they poisoned her, she would not have to worry. She shook her head, and winced at the pain. Was she thinking straight? But she had to be able to fight. Gird honored fighters. She was going to die here, almost certainly, but she had to fight.

She took the pitcher and looked into it... in the green torchlight, she could not tell what the liquid was. She poured it out, her hands shaking. Whatever it was, she thought, it was still liquid. She raised the mug to her lips, sniffing, but the torch stank so much she could smell nothing else. She took a swallow. It burned her throat all the way down, but she wanted more of it. She drained the mug. On the platter was a slab of some dried meat and a hunk of bread. Her stomach knotted, reminding her of the hours since she'd eaten. The bread was hard, and tasted salty and sour. The meat was salty too; not until she'd eaten most of it did she think what the salt would do. Thirst swamped all other sensation; she drained the pitcher at one draught, only to find that it gave strength without easing her thirst. She felt the burning liquid work its way along her body, stinging it awake. She was afire all over, with thirst and the wounds and that terrible itching she had felt since the first.

She found herself growling softly. Fight, she thought. Oh, I will fight by holy Gird, I will fight exceedingly. She thought of the combat past, the unfairness of it, the knotted whip, the orc's teeth in her leg, her strokes, the orcs' strokes. For a moment she grimaced at the thought of the last encounter, when she had stabbed the orc's eyes, but she forced the revulsion down. I had to, she thought. It wasn't fair; I was outnumbered, I had to do—whatever. She drew grimness around her like a cloak. Saint Gird of the Cudgel, she thought. If that's what you want, putting me in a place like this, that's what I'll do—I'll fight. Protector of the helpless, strong arm of the High Lord: I will be true. I will fight.

But a moment of doubt had her frowning. Gird was not for fighting only—she thought she remembered that. Fairness—truth—she shook her head, trying to think. She seemed to see Stammel's face, telling the recruits not to brawl, then the look he had given her in the cell when Sejek had banned her. Something was wrong; she should know something better. But of course something's wrong, she thought irritably. I've been taken by iynisin; I had to fight three orcs unarmed; the stuff they gave me was poisoned—

When she heard scraping outside the door, she sprang to her feet, a little surprised at her body's quick response. She felt ready—even eager—for what was to come. They wanted to see fights, did they? She would show them fighting such as they had never seen.

"I see you have recovered from your shameful collapse." The caped iynisi entered the cell. It flicked a glance down at the pitcher and platter. "Ah—refreshed yourself, have you? I fear you may find our ale a bit thirst-provoking, don't you? But it is strengthening. And if you are successful this next trial, we might give you water as a reward. What do you think, eh?"

Paks felt her lips draw back in an involuntary snarl. The iynisi laughed. "I suppose we must not expect to find fighters courteous," he said. "But how you humans do reveal your needs. It is a weakness of yours, which the elder races have learned to control." The iynisi snapped his fingers and an attendant brought forward the box from which he took another hank of the gray stuff. " 'Tis a pity this is necessary," he said. "If we had your word that you would cause no trouble—no? Discourteous. Perhaps we shall have to teach you manners as well. Hold out your hands, and pray that I remember to cut the bond before your combat begins." Paks found that she had extended her hands without thinking about it, nor could she jerk them back when she tried. She wondered if the iynisi used a spell—a ring?—surely something to control her.

As before, she was led into the small arena; this time the seats were full when she came in. A sword, dagger, shield, and helmet were stacked in the center. "You earned these last time," said the iynisi. "Possibly the body armor as well, but we differed on that. Convince us, if you can."

The combat that followed was a whirling confusion that was never after clear in Paks' memory. How many she fought, in that bout or another, or what arms they had, she could not say—only that she fought at the limit of her strength and skill again and again. She had no memory of individual strokes, how she won, or what wounds she took. When she won, she was rewarded with a dipper of water, a short rest, a weapon to replace one that had shattered. When she collapsed, of wounds and exhaustion—and she did not know how many times, or how often, that happened—she would awake in a cell, her wounds no longer bleeding, but afire with whatever had been used to treat them. She was given food and drink that did nothing to ease her hunger and thirst, but gave her strength to fight once again.

Soon she could think of nothing but the opponent at hand, the weapon that menaced her, the hands that wielded it. For a long time, she tried to call on Gird before each onset, but she could never bring the name out aloud. At last it drifted from her mind while she lay unconscious between encounters. She fought grimly, then, to the shrill squeals of the watching iynisin and their allies, and never knew what she fought, or how. There was only pain, and danger, and the bitter anger that kept fear at bay.

That anger grew after every bout; it spread to include all she thought of. The High Lord should never have made the world to include iynisin, she thought bitterly, and if elves could turn so to evil, he should not have made elves. Now the distrust of true elves the iynisin had sown flowered in bitterness. She remembered the elf-lord laired deep under stone, bound to some power of evil, and drawing her to his side with irresistible enchantments. Macenion's lies, his greed and cowardice with the snowcat, his arrogance. Even at their best, elves toyed with humans, clouded human memory for their convenience, sent them into dangers they could not assess, with that glamour upon them. Were a few tinkling songs and flowery compliments in a sweet voice a fair exchange for all this disdain of human lives and needs? Hardly. In a world where such evil existed, it ill-behooved elves to sit aside and cast human lives like dice for their pleasure.

It was monstrous that such evil existed—that innocents were tormented in dark places—that she was alone and helpless and frightened. But she wasn't frightened, she reminded herself. Death was the end of all things, and darkness surrounded all light, but she was no child to be frightened of what must come. If Gird wouldn't help—or didn't exist—she would get along without him. She would fight until the end, and then grapple death itself. That would show them.

When she thought at all of her friends, in bits and scraps of memory, she saw them standing idly in the sunlight while she was fighting against impossible odds underground. She had an image of Arne and Vik, charting peacefully in Duke Phelan's barracks—of the other paladin-candidates, safe in Fin Panir, looking forward to their own tests—of the rest of the expedition, feasting around a fire, leaving her behind with a shrug. For awhile she knew this was untrue; she reminded herself that her friends were better than that. But in the end that truth slipped away as well. They would find out, she thought grimly, and enjoyed imagining their grief and their pride in her deeds. And if they never knew—that might even be better. She was no longer angry with them; they could not understand, it was not their fault. It was their weakness, all those silly thoughts of right and wrong, the rules made for gentler combats: if they had been where she was, they would know that only the fight itself mattered, the enemy's death, the anger sated by blood.

She awoke, once more in a narrow cell, to find the caped iynisi standing over her. She blinked, still under the influence of the healing methods they used. He beckoned one of his henchmen, who quickly raised her head and held a mug to her lips. She swallowed: the same burning liquid. As always, she wanted more. With every swallow, strength flowed back into her. She gulped down two mugs full before he moved away, then she rolled easily to her feet.

"You have given us good sport, Paksenarrion," said the iynisi. "Such sport that we are minded to reward you greatly—even to risk the displeasure of our lady. You remember your friends, don't you? Your friends outside?"

Paks felt her forehead wrinkle, as she tried to remember. Friends. Yes, she had friends somewhere—she could not remember their names, but she had friends. She nodded.

"Your good friends," he coaxed. "Such good friends." Paks felt a surge of anger. Why was he being so tedious? "Your friends are worried about you; they have come to find you. To free you."

Paks growled, then stumbled over the words. "Can free myself. Can fight."

The iynisi smiled. "Yes, that's right. You can fight. You can free yourself. We will let you fight, Paksenarrion. Just one more fight, and you will be free. You will be with your friends."

Suddenly Paks' mind cleared for an instant; she seemed to see Amberion, Ardhiel, and the Marshals before her. Those were her friends. Were they here? Mingled worry and hope rose in her. She glared at the iynisi: what did he mean, fight herself free?

"Ah—some memory coming back. This is well. Now listen to me. You must fight once more, fight your way through some of our lesser servants, to reach your friends. If you can do this, you may go free. Otherwise, you will die, and so will they. We will arm you in what you have won."

Before she could reply, he waved into the cell several iynisin carrying a suit of black plate armor, a black helmet crested in black horsehair, and a handsome longsword with a curious design at the crosshilts. Paks had no time to examine it. The iynisin began to fit the armor on her, she found, as always, that she could not move when the caped one commanded her to stand still. The armor had a strange feel; it made her uneasy. The helmet was even worse. As it neared her head, she felt a sudden loathing for it, and tried to duck aside. The effort was hopeless. Down over her head came the helmet, close-fitting around her ears and cheeks. She felt breathless. Someone pulled the visor down. She squinted through the eyeslit, but found that everything wavered as if seen through a blowing mist.

"I can't see!" she said.

"That's all right," the iynisi answered. His voice echoed unpleasantly in the helmet. "All down here are your enemies, yes? All are enemies. Here—take the sword." She felt the sword hilt pressed into her right hand. She hefted the blade. It felt good. "All enemies—" said the iynisi's voice, now behind her. "Go—fight—fight for your rights, Paksenarrion. Fight your enemies. Fight—"

She hardly needed that encouragement. She was walking down the corridor, away from the cell, walking alone and unguarded for the first time. At first she could barely see well enough to stay away from the walls, but then her vision cleared a little. She saw iynisin ahead of her, all running somewhere. Those who looked at her screamed, and ran faster. Behind the visor, she smiled. Soon. Soon she would show them. She was no longer helpless; now she had the power she had longed for in all those dark hours. She wondered which way to go, heard a confused clangor from a wide cross passage, and turned to see what it was. A fight. A big fight. She saw the passage choked with armed figures: iynisin, orcs, others. She drew breath and stalked forward, sword ready.

She struck the back of a confused mass, hating the black-clad iynisin who had laughed at her. Wide sweeps of her sword parted heads from shoulders, and cleared a space around her. Those in front turned to face her; she leveled the great blade and swiped from side to side, laughing. The black cloaks melted in front of her. Beyond them were greater ones, huge to her eyes. Hatred and anger flared together in her mind. You too, she thought. I will fight. I will fight through all of you, whatever you are. Fight through to my friends. By Gird—the name leapt into her mind, and she opened her mouth to yell it out loud. This time, at last, the sound passed her lips: not as a yell, little louder than a whisper: in the name of Gird.

A vast space opened in her mind, and out of it a voice like stone said, "Stop!" She froze. One arm held the sword up for another swing, one foot had nearly left the ground. At once she was bereft of vision and hearing, and plunged into darkness.

CHAPTER TWENTY-SIX

Paks woke to darkness. She lay a moment, feeling cool air—living air—wash over her face. She lay wrapped in something soft, on something more yielding than stone. She blinked. She could see something glittering overhead. Stars. The current of air quickened; it smelled of pine and horses and woodsmoke. She could not think where she was. Her mouth was dry. She tried to clear her throat, but made a strange croaking noise. At once a voice—a human voice—spoke out of the darkness.

"Paks? Do you want something?"

Tears filled her eyes, and ran down her face. She could not speak. She heard a rustle of clothing, then a hand came out of darkness and touched her face.

"Paks? Are you crying? Here—" The hand withdrew, and after a sharp scratching noise, a light flared near her and steadied. She thought: lamp. Her tears blurred everything to wavering points of light and blackness. The hand returned, a gentle touch, stroking her head. "There, Paks, it's all right. You're safe now; you're free."

She could not stop the tears that kept flowing. She began to tremble with the effort, and the person beside her called softly to someone else. Another person loomed beside her. "The spell's going, I think," said the first voice.

"About time, too. Can she speak yet?"

"No. But she's aware. I hope we can get her to drink; she's as dry as old bone."

"I'll lift her." The second person slipped an arm under her

shoulders; Paks felt herself shift as she was lifted to lean against a leather tunic. "There now. Paks? You need to drink something. Here—" She felt a cool rim at her lips, and sipped. It was water, cold and clean. She swallowed again and again. "Good," said the voice. "That's what you need."

"I'll get more," said the first voice, and she heard the rasp of footsteps. She drank another flask full. Tears still ran from her eyes. She did not know who these people were, or where she was, or what had happened. Only that it was better now. At last she slipped back into sleep, still crying.

She woke in daylight: light blue sky overhead, red rocks against the sky. She turned her head. She lay on a sandbank above a stream. She could see horses across the stream, and men in chainmail grooming them. Nearer was the pale flickering light of a campfire. Around it were three men, a woman, and a dwarf. One of the men and the woman left the campfire and came toward her. They were smiling. She wondered why.

"Paks, are you feeling better this morning?" That was the woman. Paks felt her way along the words, trying to understand. This morning. Did that mean that it was last night, the voices and the crying? Better? She tried to roll up on one elbow, but found she could hardly move. She felt utterly weak, as if she were hollow from the bones out.

"Can you speak at all, Paks?" asked the man. She looked at him. Dark hair with a few silver threads, short dark beard. Chainmail under a yellow tunic. They wanted her to say something. She had nothing to say. They were smiling at her, both of them. She looked from face to face. The man's smile faded as she watched. "Paks, do you know who I am?" She shook her head. "Mmm. Do you know where you are?" Again the headshake. "Do you know who you are?"

"Paks?" she answered softly, tentatively.

"Do you know your full name?"

Paks thought a long moment. Something seeped into her mind. "Paks. Paks—Paksenarrion, I think."

The man and woman looked at each other and sighed. "Well," said the woman, "that's something. How about breakfast, Paks?"

"Breakfast—" she repeated slowly.

"Are you hungry?"

Again Paks thought her way to the meaning of the words. Hungry? Her stomach rumbled, answering for her. "Food," she murmured.

"Fine," said the woman. "I'll bring it." She strode off.

Paks looked at the man. "Who is that?" she asked.

"The woman? Pir. She's a knight." His voice held slight coolness.

"Should—should I know her?"

"Yes. But don't worry about that. Do you remember anything of what happened?"

Paks shook her head before answering. "No. I don't remember anything much. Did I—did I do something bad?"

"Not that I know of. What makes you ask that?"

"I don't know." Paks turned her head to look the other way. She was looking up a narrow valley or canyon walled with red rock on both sides. Nothing looked familiar.

The woman returned, carrying a deep bowl that steamed, a mug, and a waterskin slung from one wrist. "Here—stew, bread, and plenty of water. Can you sit up?" Paks tried, but again was too weak. The man propped her against a pack he dragged from a few feet away. The woman set the bowl on the sand, poured water into the mug, and offered it. Paks tried to wiggle a hand free from the blanket around her, but the woman had to help her even with that. When she took the mug, her hand shook so that much of the water slopped onto her face and neck; it was icy cold. But what she managed to drink refreshed her.

"I'll help you with the stew," said the woman. "You're too shaky to manage it." She offered it spoonful by spoonful. Paks ate, at first without much interest, but with increasing relish. She began to feel more alert. A thread of memory returned, though she could not tell if it was recent or remote.

She looked at the man. "Is this Duke Phelan's camp?"

His face seemed to harden. "No. Do you remember Duke Phelan?"

"I think so. He was—not so tall as you. Red hair. Yes—I thought I was still in his Company. But I'm not. I don't think so—am I?"

"Not any more, no. But if you remember that, then your memory is coming back. That's good."

"But where—? I should—I should know you, shouldn't I? You asked me that. And I can't—I don't know you—any of you—or this—" Her voice began to shake.

"Take it easy, Paks. It will come back to you. You're safe here." The man turned away for a moment, and waved to someone Paks could not see.

"But if I—when I was with the Duke, I was a soldier. I must have been. And you're wearing mail. What happened?" Paks tried again to push herself up; this time she got both arms out of the blanket around her. She had on a loose linen shirt; below its sleeves her arms were seamed with the swollen purple lines of healing wounds. Her wrists were bandaged with strips of linen. She stared at them, and then at the man. What is this place? Did you—"

He reached out and took her hand; his grip was firm but gentle. "No, Paks, I did not deal those injuries. We brought you out of the place where that happened." He turned to another man who had just walked up to them. "She's awake, and making sense, but her memory hasn't returned. Paks, do you know this man?"

Paks stared at the lean face framed in iron-gray hair and beard. He looked stern and even grim, but honest. She wanted to trust him. She could not remember him at all. "No, sir," she said slowly. "I don't. I'm sorry."

"Don't apologize," said the second man. "I wonder," he said to the first, "whether we should try to tell her what we know."

"Names, at least." said the dark man. "Or she'll be completely confused. Paks, my name is Amberion; I'm a paladin of Gird. And this is Marshal Fallis, of the Order of the Cudgel."

The names meant nothing to Paks, and the men looked no more familiar with strange names attached. She looked from one to the other. "Amberion. Marshall Fallis." They looked at her, glanced at each other, then back at her.

"Do you remember who Gird is, Paks?" asked Marshal Fallis.

Paks wrinkled her brow, trying to think. The name woke a distant uneasiness. "Gird—I—I know I should. Something—it's—what to do—to call—when—" She stopped, breathing hard, and tried again. "When you start to fight—only—I couldn't say it aloud! I tried—and it wouldn't—something on my neck, choking—No!" Paks shouted this last loud enough to startle the entire camp. She had shut her eyes tightly, shaking her head, her body rigid. "No," she said more softly. "No. By—by Gird, I will fight. I will—not—stop. I will *fight!*"

She felt both men's hands on her shoulders, steadying her. Amberion spoke. "Paks. Listen to me. You're out of that. You're safe."

Then, more quietly, to Fallis. "And what do you suppose that was about. Surely she wasn't free to fight them?"

"I don't know," was Fallis' grim reply. "But I suspect we'd better find out. Considering how we found her—"

"I won't believe it," said Amberion, but his voice had thinned.

Paks opened her eyes. For a moment she stared blankly at the sky, then shifted her eyes to look at Amberion. She could feel patches of memory coming back, unconnected still, but broadening. "Amberion? What—"

"You were injured, Paks. You don't remember much."

"I feel—strange. Will you tell me what happened?"

"We don't know all that happened. And it might be better to let you remember it for yourself."

Paks looked around. "I don't recognize this place. But the color of the rocks—something—is familiar."

"We moved the camp after you—after the fight."

"Are we in Kolobia yet?" Paks saw Amberion's face relax a little.

"Good. You are remembering. Yes, we're in Kolobia. How much do you remember of the trip here?"

"Some of it—we were in a caravan, for a long way. We saw the horse nomads, didn't we?" Amberion nodded. "And I remember a bald-faced red horse, bucking—"

"That's my warhorse," said Fallis. "Do you remember why we were coming to Kolobia?"

Paks shook her head. "No. I wish I didn't feel so peculiar. Did something hit my head? Was it a battle?"

Fallis smiled at her. "You've been in several battles. Both on the caravan, and here as well. I think you'll remember them on your own when you've rested more. Your wounds are healing well. Do you need anything more?"

"Water, if there's enough."

"Certainly." The Marshal walked away and returned with a full waterskin. He set it beside Paks, then he and Amberion walked upstream, looking at the cliffs on the far side. Paks managed to get the waterskin to her mouth. She took a long drink, then looked around again. The dwarf was looking her way, talking to the woman. When he caught her eye, he rose and came toward her. She tried to think of his name.

"Good morning, Lady Paksenarrion," said the dwarf. His voice was higher and sweeter than she'd expected. She wondered how she knew what to expect. "How fare you this day?"

"I'm all right. A little—confused."

"That is no wonder. Perhaps even names have escaped you. I am Balkon of the House of Goldenaxe."

The name fit; Paks could almost think she remembered it. As she looked at the dwarf, the distant silent scraps of memory came nearer and seemed to fuse in his face. "Yes," she said slowly. "Master Balkon. You came with us from Fin Panir. You know about rock, where it will be solid or weak. You are a cousin of the Goldenaxe himself, aren't you?"

"Eighth cousin twice removed," said the dwarf with a smile. "I think you must be recovering very swiftly. We are glad it should be so, who saw you in such dismay."

"Dismay?" Paks felt a twinge of fear.

The dwarf's face constricted into a mass of furrows and then relaxed. "Is that not the correct term? You must excuse me, Lady Paks. I have not the skill in wordcraft as were I an elf. Dismay? Distress? Dis—oh, I cannot find the word, plague take it! But you were much hurt by those blackhearts, and that your friends sorrowed to see. And you are now much better, and we are glad."

"Thank you, Master Balkon," said Paks. She did not understand what he was talking about, exactly, but his kindness was welcome.

"I wanted to ask you—if it will not be too great a sorrow to speak of it—what those rockfilth used on your injuries."

Paks stared at him. "Rockfilth?"

"They corrupt the very stone, good stone, by living in its heart. Those blackheart elf cousins, I mean, who took you."

"Took me?" Paks shook her head, as a sudden chill ran over her. "I have no memory of such a thing, Master Balkon."

"Ah. Magicks, then." The dwarf muttered rapidly in dwarvish; Paks caught only one or two words. He stopped abruptly and looked sharply at her. "You remember none of it at all?"

"None of *what*?" Paks began to feel a prickling irritation. Everyone else knew something about her, but wouldn't tell what it was. It was unfair. She glared at the dwarf.

"Tcch! Be still. That Lord Amberion, your paladin, and the Marshal

Fallis, they will not have you told too much, for seeing what you shall remember in time. Do you make noise, they will come to see what we speak."

"Will you tell me?" asked Paks with rising excitement.

The dwarf smiled, a sly sideways smile. "And should I say what such men of power want not to be said? I am no prince or lord to rank myself above them. But they did not say to me what not to say—it is a point on which it is possible to differ. So—" he looked at her again. "I will say what I think should be said, as it would be done in the House of Goldenaxe."

Paks forced herself to lie still, remembering this much about dwarves, that they cannot be hurried in the telling of anything. The dwarf pulled out his curved pipe, packed it, lit it, and drew a long breath. He blew three smoke rings.

"Very well, then," he said, as if he had not paused. "You were taken by those blackheart worshippers of Achrya," he spat after saying that name, "such as elves like Ardhiel do not like to admit exist and are of elvish origin—despite having their own word for them. That was when they attacked our camp, the second night in this canyon, and they carried you away down their lairs, under that cliff yonder—" he jerked his head to indicate the cliff across the stream. "And there they held you, some days. We know not what befell you in that dark place, save the marks you carry. Dire wounds enough, they must have been, to deal such marks. We had some trouble to follow your path and find you—do you truly remember nothing of this?"

Paks had been listening in rising horror. She stared at the cliff, the rust-red and orange rocks streaked with black, and shook her head. "I don't—don't remember. Yet—as you talk—something comes back. Like—like seeing a valley from a hill, faraway and hazy."

"That will be the magicks, I don't doubt, or the knocks on your head that left such lumps. Well, then, when we found you, that was a strange thing, too. We had fought several times in the dark ways, and came to another band of the enemy. None of us knew what was that black warrior so tall behind the others, all in black armor. You—but we didn't know then it was you—were killing them, the ones we faced, and when they parted seemed like to kill us too. Then—" he paused to puff on his pipe and blow more rings. Paks waited impatiently, a feeling of pressure swelling her head. "Then, Lady Paksenarrion, you were still, all at once, sword arm so above your head. Very strange. Very strange indeed. Lord Amberion and Marshal Fallis went to look—being careful, too, for any treachery. Then they lifted the visor of the helmet—and a nasty, evil thing that was, that I could sense from where I stood—and there was your face behind it, pale as cheese, and your eyes seeing nothing. All that bad armor was magicks—enchanted—your paladin and Marshal had their way with Gird. It split, finally, lying around you like a beetle's wingcases, then it shrivelled and was gone. But that wasn't all. Around your neck—"

"Master Balkon!" Neither Paks nor Balkon had noticed Amberion's approach. He looked more than a little displeased. "Is this well done, to tax her beyond her knowledge?"

"Tax her? I but tell her what things are lost to her."

"But you knew we thought it wise to tell her nothing."

"That you thought it wise, yes—but you never forbade such telling to me. And of the ill-doing of elves and their kindred we dwarves have more knowledge than those the elves would make their allies. To my wisdom it seems right that she should not be left to anxious wondering."

Paks felt a wave of irritation that they would talk over and about her as if she were not there. "I asked him, Sir Amberion, as I asked you. And he chose to think me whole-witted enough to answer me as one fighter to another, not as if I were a witless child." She surprised even herself with the bitterness in her voice.

Amberion looked at her, brows raised. "Surely, Paks, you realize that we do not think you a child—you, of all people. We were concerned that if we told you what we knew, you might never again regain your own memories, which must include much that we cannot know. Have you so forgotten the Fellowship of Gird, that you mistrust a paladin this way? It must be your wounds that make you so irritable."

Paks felt herself flush at the mild reproof. "I'm sorry," she muttered, still angry. "I—I was worried." Her voice trailed away, and she looked beyond Amberion to the cliffs beyond.

"Are you in much pain?" Amberion went on.

Paks realized that she did, in fact, ache all over as if with a fever; her head throbbed. "Sir, I do ache some."

He felt her forehead, and frowned. "It may be fever—and no wonder with your wounds—yet you feel cold. Let me see what I can do." He placed a hand on either side of her head, and began to speak. Paks felt she should know the words, anticipate the phrases, yet she could hardly concentrate enough to hear them. Her vision hazed. For a few moments the throbbing in her head merged with her aching body in one vast rhythmic pain, then it eased. As it disappeared, she knew how much pain she had felt, and wondered for an instant why she had not known it—had it been even worse, that she could accept it as normal? Her vision cleared. She felt Amberion's warm palms leave her head.

"Does that ease the pain?" he asked.

Paks nodded. "Yes, sir. Thank you. I had not realized how much it was." Now her outburst of a few moments before seemed unreasonable to her; she could not understand why she had said such a thing to Amberion.

"Good." Amberion sighed, and sat beside her, across from the dwarf. He looked tired. "Master Balkon, I heard but the last of what you told her. Was it just the tale of her capture and our pursuit?"

"Aye, it was, and scantly told, at that. I did not speak of the capture itself, since none of us saw it, only that she was taken. Nor did I speak of the debate when she was found missing, or—"

"Well enough," Amberion interrupted. The dwarf scowled at him. "Paks, has any of that come back to you as he was telling it?"

"It seemed, sir, almost as if something were trying to break into my head. Something I should know. But as I told Master Balkon, what I do recall seems faraway, dreamlike."

"That's not unusual. By Saint Gird, I wish that elf would wake!"

"By his face," said the dwarf sourly, "that one is enjoying some rare dream such as elves delight in, too rare a dream to wake for our need."

"Elf?" asked Paks.

"Ardhiel," said Amberion. "From the embassy to Fintha—"

"Oh!" A live memory flashed into Paks' mind. "I remember him. In Fin Panir, when we—" she looked at Amberion, then went on more slowly, with dawning comprehension. "When we planned this expedition—I remember that now. I was there. I was taking training, and then—" In her excitement, Paks tried to sit up, but could not.

"I'll get another pack for you," said Amberion. He brought a fat blanket roll, and propped her higher on it. For an instant she was dizzy, but recovered.

"I do remember," she said eagerly. "On the caravan, and when we turned off—those canyons with the white stone high above. A black hill with a dip in the top. Is this farther down the canyon we went into, the one Master Balkon said was not as deep as it was meant to be?"

"Yes, lady," said the dwarf. "This is the canyon choked with sand. I have not yet had the time to look, but I expect something—some rock fall, perchance—has blocked the downward end."

"And at the high end—that's where the cliffs were that the smoke came from?"

"Yes, in a branch canyon to this one. Do you remember the fight?"

"Something of it. One of those black fighters called out, and it was hard to move after that."

Amberion nodded. "It affected most of our party, save Master Balkon and me."

"Then you did something, and it eased; they were shooting arrows down. Ardhiel and Thelon were shooting back—"

"Yes," said Balkon. "And then that black scum who called down the fear on us came down the cliff in the shape of his lady—" the dwarf spat again. "That one."

"Like a spider," said Paks. "I remember. It was horrible—he just came down the rocks, straight down, and then more and more of them swarmed out of holes in the walls, and Ardhiel blew that old hunting horn he carries, only it didn't sound like a hunting horn."

"No," said Amberion. "And after he blew it, its own shape returned. It was under some enchantment. It's an elven horn, the only one I've ever seen, and a rare treasure. Whatever or whoever it was who appeared when the horn sang, I know not, but great goodness and power were allied in him."

Paks shook her head. "I don't remember anything but the sound of it."

"Pretty enough," grumbled Balkon, "but I'd like to know what it means."

Amberion stretched and sighed. "It meant trouble for our enemies that day, and a long sleep for Ardhiel. Paks, I think your memory will come back; as it does, I'd like to know about it." She nodded. "Master Balkon, we still think it would be best to let her recall these things on her own."

"I worry about those wounds," said the dwarf frankly. "The elves have some means of speeding and slowing growth. Something like that must have been used by those rockfilth—she'd still be bleeding, else. It's dangerous. I would know what was used on her, and would wish you to think what may be done." He grinned at Paks for an instant and went on. "Besides that, it is this talk which has brought her memory so far. Surely more would be better."

"It is that," said another voice, "which distinguishes dwarves from more temperate folk—they always think more is better." Paks looked over to see a dark man in stained leather clothes; she remembered that this was Thelon, a half-elven ranger from Lyonya. Master Balkon bristled at his words, but Thelon laughed gently, and lifted his hand. "My pardon, Master Balkon, but I could not resist. It has been long in this camp since anything seemed funny."

"I don't see—" began Balkon; Thelon shook his head then, and bowed.

"Sir dwarf, I am sorry. I had no intention of insult; I'll say so before all, and confess a loose tongue."

Balkon shook his head, and finally smiled at Thelon. "You are but half-elven, and a ranger—which is another word for hardy, as we dwarves know. And I confess I am as fond of plenty as you are of enough. Let it pass, Thelon; I will not bear anger to you."

Thelon bowed again. "I thank you for your courtesy. I came to ask Amberion to attend the Marshals. Ardhiel may be rousing from his sleep, and they asked for you."

Amberion looked sternly at the dwarf as he rose. "Master Balkon, we are as concerned as you, but if Paks doesn't remember, she can't tell you what they used. It would be better to let it be."

Balkon nodded. "If the elf is wakening, he might know far more than I—only he should be told at once, if he can listen."

"Then—?"

"Then I will but bear her company, and no tales tell, until you bring word of Ardhiel," said the dwarf. And with that Amberion had to be content, and he turned away. Paks watched the dwarf, hoping he would resume his talk, but he did not meet her eyes. He poked and puffed at his pipe, until the smoke rose steadily. Then he looked at her. 'I am not one to break my word," he said fiercely, "even so little of it as that. Bide still; the time will come, and you will hear it all."

* * *

Paks slept again while waiting for Amberion to return, and woke hungry. She was able to feed herself this time. With the wizard's help, she managed to stand and stagger a short way to the shallow sand pit that served the camp for jacks. But that exhausted her, and she fell into sleep again as soon as she came back to her place. It was evening when she woke, with sun striking the very highest line of the opposite canyon wall.

No one was beside her at the moment. She saw the dwarf, hunching over the campfire. Pir stood at a little distance, staring up at the sunlit rock far overhead. Off on her right, Amberion and the Marshals stood talking to another taller figure. Paks recognized this as Ardhiel, the elf. She stretched, slowly. She felt a vague ache again, not so strong as before, and wondered at it. The only other time she had experienced a paladin's healing, the wound and pain had disappeared at once and forever. Perhaps she'd been lying awry.

She pushed up her sleeves to look at the marks on her arms. Ordinarily she'd have said the wounds were several weeks old; the scar tissue was raised and dark. But the others had said she'd been missing only a few days. She tried to remember what had happened. What Balkon had told her seemed to fit, yet her memories gave no life to his words. Captive—underground—that almost made sense. But what about the wounds? Had she actually fought? And who had she fought, and how? The marks gave her no clues—they looked like any healing cuts, could have been given by knife or sword or pike. The only unusual thing about them was the number—more scars than she had collected in three seasons of fighting with Duke Phelan. She could not understand how she had fought at all—how she had survived—with so many wounds, all given at once. Yet something about them seemed to convey that they'd been given in combat, rather than inflicted on a bound and helpless prisoner.

Amberion's voice interrupted her thoughts. "Paks, I'm glad you're awake again. Ardhiel is with us now, and he examined you this afternoon." Paks was suddenly angry. What right had they to stare at her while she lay helpless? She fought the anger down, surprised at its strength, and tried to conceal it. She knew they would not understand. Amberion went on. "He would like to talk with you, if you feel well enough."

"Yes, of course. I'm just—" she decided not to mention the aching to Amberion; he would think it weakness. "I'm still confused," she said finally. Ardhiel sat beside her; he seemed thinner than she remembered, but his face was alight with some joy.

"Lady Paksenarrion, I sorrow that I was not here to defend you. I did not know that when I blew the elven horn I would be carried away—"

"Carried away?"

"In spirit. I had always been taught that elves have no souls, that we are wholly one with our bodies; I had no idea that I could be plucked out, like a hazelnut from its shell, and be gone so long. It did not seem long to me—only a day at the High King's Court—but when I returned, I find that you have spent many dark hours with the iynisin."

"So they say." Paks looked away, frowning. "I can't remember."

"Not at all?"

"Only vaguely. Balkon told me some, and it seemed to make sense—I had the feeling that he was right, as far as he knew. But I don't remember it, clearly, on my own."

"Ah." Ardhiel leaned back on the sand, staring skyward at the glowing blue that deepened as the sun lowered behind distant mountains. "I wish I knew more. We elves prefer to ignore the iynisin—even to pretend they do not exist, or are not distant kin. But at such times as these, that way is proved dangerous, for us and for our allies. I do know that they have the same magical abilities that we have, and share in the powers of those they worship: Achrya and Nayda, Gitres and Liart."

Paks shuddered as the four evil names seemed to foul the air. A face swam before her: elven, but evil. Frightening. "I—don't remember," she said.

"If it is truly wiped from your mind, by a blow on your head, for example, that is one thing. But if the memory has been blurred by the iynisin or their deity, then we must do what we can to bring it back. I could not tell, this afternoon—I was still half-enchanted by my own experience." Ardhiel sat up, stretching. "Amberion. Did you want to do this before or after eating?"

"Do what?" asked Paks, alarmed. Amberion turned from watching the distant line of mountains, and smiled at her. She thought his face looked flat and featureless in the dimming light. He sat on her other side, and reached for her hand.

"We need to find out what magic the iynisin used on you, Paks. Surely you realize that. Ardhiel and I will each try what we know—"

"But—" Paks tried to think of some argument. "Isn't it—didn't you tell me that—that paladin-candidates must not submit to spells?"

Amberion frowned. "Usually, that's so. But this is a special case—you have already been spelled, we think, by the iynisin. And you were assigned to my care. Gird knows, Paksenarrion, what I feel that I did not save you from that capture. But now—we must do what we can for you."

Paks nodded, meeting Amberion's eyes with difficulty. She could tell that he was concerned—even worried. For herself, she felt more annoyance than anything else. In time she would heal, as she always had, and be strong again; the memories would come, or not come. She wanted to hear what they knew—wanted them to trust her enough to tell her, as Keri and Volya had told her about the sack of Sibili.

"Amberion tells me that these wounds were already so healed when they found you, Paksenarrion." Ardhiel laid his long-fingered elven hand on her wrist. Paks tried not to flinch. "You were missing so short a time—either the wounds were never what they look like—that is, they were not real wounds, but created in this half-healed state—or they were magically healed."

Paks looked at her arms again. "Could they be—made that way? I never heard of such—"

"No. It's not widely known that it can be done, and it would only be done by evil intent. But the other is bad, too. To force flesh to such healing, out of time—that has its own hazards. I have known an elf, one of us, who could speed growth and healing. He used the gift on plants, but told me once it could be done on animals. What I would like to do, Paksenarrion, is try to lift the cloud from your memory. If it is what I think it may be, Amberion and I can do so—and you can then remember what you need."

As much as Paks had wanted to know what happened, she still shrank from this. The elf's glowing eyes seemed dangerous as coals. She looked at Amberion. He nodded. "Ardhiel has convinced me that this is best, Paksenarrion. The iynisin powers should be countered as soon as possible."

"Then Balkon was right—" she murmured.

"Right in his way," said Ardhiel. "You do need to remember, but you need to remember for yourself. It is this I will try."

"Well, then—go ahead." Paks looked from one to the other of them. "What should I do?"

"Think on Gird and the High Lord," said Amberion. "They will guide your thoughts—and your memories, we hope—while we free them."

Paks closed her eyes and lay still. She could not keep from pushing at the dark curtains in her mind, and felt more and more breathless and trapped as she lay there. She was hardly aware of Ardhiel's hand when it moved to her brow, or Amberion's firm grip. Ardhiel began chanting something in elven—she did not even try to follow the meaning.

Shadows moved in her mind. Some were darker—some moved away from her, and others menaced her. She saw again an elven face, pale against a dark hood. She felt a burning pain at her throat, and tried to raise her hand, struggling. The shadows seemed to harden, thickening into reality. Sounds came, faintly at first, then louder. Shrill cries, mocking laughter, the clatter of weapons. Bitter fluid stung her throat, the stench of it wrinkled her nose. The faces came clearer out of the darkness: orcs, their fangs bared, their taloned hands holding swords, knives, whips. Other fighters, whose kind she did not know, in armor of leather plate. The light was green, a sickly shade that made spilled blood black.

Gradually she was able to remember the bargain the iynisin had made: she had to fight, fight for their amusement against opponents of their choosing, fight with whatever weapons they gave her, for the chance to live a little longer. As it had happened, so in the memory Ardhiel's treatment roused: she could not remember how long these fights had gone on, or the intervals between them. But she could remember, as if reliving them, the pain of her wounds, the hunger and thirst and exhaustion, the fear that she would never see daylight again. When Ardhiel took his hands away from her brow, she was aware. And the memories she had lost lay in a cold heap in her mind. She hated the thought of them, of stirring through them, but she had no choice. That, too, she resented: she had had no choice with the iynisin, and no choice here. It seemed unfair.

CHAPTER TWENTY-SEVEN

For of course Amberion insisted on knowing what, if anything, she remembered. She replied as quickly as possible, surprised at her own distaste, with an outline of the iynisin bargain and her fighting. She remembered even the black armor, and her reluctance to wear it.

"And you called on Gird before each encounter?" asked High Marshall Fallis, who had come up to listen.

"I tried. I couldn't—couldn't say it out loud." Paks hoped he would say nothing more about it.

"But you tried—you intended to?" Amberion's eyes held hers.

"Yes—sir." Paks looked away with an effort. "I tried. At least, all the times I remember—"

"That should be enough—" But his tone lacked conviction, and he looked across her to Ardhiel.

"I don't understand. What's the matter?" Even Paks could not be sure whether irritation or fear edged her voice.

Fallis sighed. "Paksenarrion, you had no way to tell—but if you handled cursed weapons, and in a cursed cause—"

"And that black armor was definitely cursed—"

"But I killed orcs—some iynisin—and they're all evil—"

"Yes. I know. That's why we think it may work out." Amberion shook his head, nonetheless. "I wish you hadn't touched those things…"

"But—" Paks felt ready to burst with the unfairness of it. She had been trapped, alone, captive, far underground—she had fought against many enemies and her own fear, to survive—and now they said she should never have touched a weapon. I'm a fighter, after all, she told herself. What should I have done—let them kill me without lifting a hand? Bitterness sharpened her voice. "I thought Gird would approve—fighting against odds like that."

"Gird does not care for odds, but for right and wrong." Fallis sounded almost angry. "That's what we're trying to—"

"Then should I have stood there like a trussed sheep and let them cut my throat?" Paks interrupted, angry enough now to say what she felt. "Would you have been happier to find my corpse? By—by the gods, I thought Gird was a warrior's patron, in any fight against evil, and I did my best to fight. It's easy for you to say what I should and shouldn't have done, but you were safe in the sunlight, while I—"

"Paks!" Amberion's voice, and his hand on her arm, stopped her. "Paks, please listen. We know you had little choice; we are not condemning you. You are not a paladin. We do not expect such wisdom from you. And now you are still weak and recovering from your injuries. We shouldn't have told you our worries, I suppose, but we did. I think myself that you will be all right when your wounds heal, and you have rested. Eat well tonight, and sleep; tomorrow we need to move camp again, and be on our way."

Paks stared at him, still a little angry, but appalled at her own words when she remembered them. Had she really spoken that way to a paladin and a High Marshal? "I'm sorry," she said quietly. "I—I don't know what—"

"Anyone," said Amberion firmly, "anyone coming from such an ordeal, would be irritable. Can you walk as far as the fire to eat, or shall we bring food here?"

"I'll try." Paks was able to stand with Amberion's help, and made it to the fire, walking stiffly but alone. She said little to the others, concentrating on her own bowl of food. Master Balkon eyed her from across the fire, but said nothing. She wondered how much the others knew. She felt empty and sore inside, as if she had been crying for a long time.

After the meal, High Marshal Fallis asked Ardhiel to tell the company about his experience. The elf smiled, sketched a gesture on the air, and began. Paks, listening, recovered a little of her first enchantment with elves. The intonations of his voice, even in the common tongue, gave it a lyrical quality. His graceful hands, gesturing fluidly, reminded her of tall grass blowing in the wind. He caught her eye, and smiled; she felt her own face relax in response. The story he told, of being taken away on the flying steed they'd seen, and feasting in the High King's Hall, was strange enough. Paks was not sure whether Ardhiel thought the High King was the same as their High Lord—or whether that was someone else entirely—but she did not ask.

When he had finished, full darkness had fallen, and the stars glittered brightly out of a cloudless sky. Paks began to wonder if she could make it back to her place; she did not feel like moving again. Someone else began to talk with Ardhiel; she was too sleepy to notice who it was. Then she was asleep, hardly rousing when someone draped a blanket over her.

She roused again before dawn. One cheek was stiff with a cold wind that flowed down the canyon; the sky was pale green, like a bruise. She could see both rock walls clear against the sky, but down in the canyon shadows hid all detail. She rolled her face inside the blanket, and warmed the cold side of it with her breath. She felt stiff and sore, but much stronger than the day before. A horse whinnied; the sound echoed from the walls. Another one answered, louder. Now several of them called. Paks thought she could pick out Socks' whinny from the rest. She pushed herself up. Cold air swirled under the blanket and she knew she'd have to get up to get warm. A dark shape crouched over the fire, muttering. This morning she recognized one of the men-at-arms.

When she came to the fire, he handed her a mug of sib, grinning. "'Tis cold, these early mornings," he said. "It must be the mountains; I've always heard it's cold all year round in mountains."

"That's true of the Dwarfmounts," agreed Paks. She shivered, and spread her hands to the flames. She had on a linen shirt over her trousers; the wind seemed to go through it as if it weren't there. Where were her clothes? Which pack?

As if he had heard her thought, Amberion dumped a pack beside the fire. "Your pack," he said, and reached for a mug of sib. "Glad you're up. We'll be riding today."

Paks found a wool shirt to cover the linen one, then paused. "Should I wear mail?"

"Yes—better not take a chance. Oh. That's right—yours is gone. We'll have to find you some." He finished his sib and stood up. Paks donned the wool shirt, and unrolled her cloak. She was still cold. She moved around near the fire, trying to warm up. Gradually the stiffness eased, though she still felt a deep aching pain along her bones. It was much lighter. Someone had started a pot of porridge for breakfast; when she looked for the horses, she saw several men at work, tacking them up. Socks was still bare, tied to a scrubby tree. Paks walked toward him.

"Will you be riding him today?" asked one of the men.

"I suppose so." She had no idea what sort of trail they would take, but if they had to fight, she wanted Socks. He stretched his neck when she neared him, and bumped her with his massive nose. She rubbed his head and neck absently, scratching automatically those itchy spots he favored. The man reappeared with her saddle and gear. Paks thanked him, and took her brush from the saddlebags. When she tried to lift the saddle to the horse's back, she was surprised to find she could barely get it in place. Every muscle in her back protested. She took a deep breath, and fastened the rigging. Foregirth, breastband, crupper, rear girth. Saddlebags. She was panting when she finished. Socks nosed at her. She fitted the bridle on his head, and untied him.

By the time they had ridden out of the canyon, onto a shoulder of the heights to one side, Paks felt she had been riding all day. Socks and the other horses toiled upward. Paks tried to take an interest in the country once more rising into view—the great cliffs of raw red stone, the fringe of forest on the plateaus above. Far to the north an angular gray mountain, dark against all the red, caught Balkon's attention.

"There! See that dark one? Not the same rock at all—that one comes from hot rocks, rocks flowing like a river, all fire-bright. It will be sharp to the feet if we come there."

"We shouldn't," said Amberion. "The map gives us a cross-canyon next, deeper than the last, and Luap's stronghold is somewhere nearby."

"Nearby, eh," grumbled the dwarf. "Nearby in this country can be out of reach." They were riding now through a little meadow of sand, carpeted with tall lupines in shades of cream and gold. Ahead the trail led up toward a curious spire of rock that looked, to Paks, as if it were made of candle drippings that had been tilted one way and another while still soft.

"Is that some of your rock that flowed like a river?"

"No." Balkon grinned at her. "Rock that flows doesn't look like it afterwards—this is all sand-rock. Like that below, in the canyon."

All this time, the distant cliffs that Amberion and Fallis were sure lay beyond the cross-canyon drew closer. Paks could not believe that much of a canyon lay between them and the cliffs—until they reached the spire, and the rock fell away beneath their feet. A thin thread of trail angled back and forth down the rocks.

"Gird's breath, Fallis—we can't get the horses down there." Amberion took a few steps down the trail, stumbling on loose ledges of rock. "It's as steep as a stair. Mules, mayhap, but the warhorses—"

"We can't leave them here." Fallis looked around, frowning. "Those kuaknom, or iynisin, or whatever could come back—and you know the scroll mentioned dragons, as well."

"Yes, but—" Amberion slipped again, and the dislodged rock rattled down the trail several lengths before stopping.

"I'll scout ahead," said Thelon, pushing his way forward. "This may not be the best way down—"

"By the map it's the only way down."

"Still—"

"You're right. Take someone with you." He glanced at Paks, and she thought herself she should go—but her legs felt soft as custard. Amberion's gaze slid past her to one of the men-at-arms. "Seliam—you're hill-bred, aren't you?"

"Yes, sir." The man slipped by Paks and together he and Thelon disappeared down the trail, quickly out of sight. Meanwhile everyone dismounted, and moved the sure-footed mules to the front of the line.

"Though I'm not sure that's best," said Connaught. "This way the horses can fall on the mules. Of course, they're as like to fall completely off the trail as down it."

In the end it took the rest of that day to get everyone down to the bottom. They had only the one trail; Ardhiel and Thelon might have been able to take another way, but no one else. They took everything that could be carried down by hand, climbing back up for load after load, and then led the mules down one at a time. The horses were last and worse; Paks was ready to curse their huge feet and thick heads by the time she had Socks down beside the stream that flowed swiftly and noisily in the canyon.

Here at least they had good water and plenty of wood. That night's camp, on an almost level bank some feet above the water, brought no surprises—Amberion and Ardhiel both thought the iynisin had been left behind. Paks said little. She could not understand why she was so tired, when Amberion and the High Marshals had done their best to heal her. She had found the strength to work with the others, but it had taken all her will to do it—nothing was easy, not even pulling the saddle off Socks.

The next day dawned clear again, and the two High Marshals began looking for the clues in Luap's notes. Paks forced herself to rise when they did, managed to smile in greeting, and almost convinced herself that nothing was wrong. Others were groaning good-humoredly about their stiff joints; she had nothing worse than that. She brought deadwood for the fires, and thought of washing her hair and bathing. Thelon reported a bath-size pool, only a few minutes' walk downstream, already sunlit.

But when she stripped and stepped into the pool, the cold water on her scars seemed to strike to the bone. She shuddered, seeing the scars darken almost to blue against her pale skin; she felt suddenly weak. The current shoved her against the downstream rocks; they rasped her nerves as if she had no skin at all. She crawled out, gasping and furious. What would the others think, if she couldn't take a cleansing dip like anyone else. Her vision blurred, and she fought her way into her clothes. Let them think what they liked—she shook her head. No one had said anything. Maybe they wouldn't. She felt an obscure threat in her anger, in everything. By the time she climbed back to the camp, she could hardly breathe; her chest hurt.

But Amberion had gone with the High Marshals, and no one spoke to her. Paks crouched by the fire, worried but determined not to call attention to herself. They had enough other problems. When the scouting party came back, jubilant, having found the mysterious "needle's eye of rock" through which the detailed map of the stronghold could be seen, she was much better. She ate with the rest of them, and that afternoon they all prepared for the next day's journey. That night Paks slept better, and woke convinced that nothing but fatigue was wrong. She was even able to saddle Socks without great effort. They started on their way soon after daybreak.

Very shortly they came to a side canyon, emptying into the main one at almost right angles. They turned up this, clambering over and around great boulders until the horses could go no further. Here there was a glade, and a deep pool of water. Connaught left Sir Malek in command of half the men-at-arms, the other two knights, and the other yeomen, and told them to keep the animals out of the main canyon.

"The scrolls mention a dragon—and I've never seen country that looks more like it should have a dragon in it. But in this narrow cleft, you should be safe. Gird's grace on you. If we are successful, we can open a closer entrance from inside. Wait for us at least ten days before giving up."

The rest of them made their way around the pool, and began climbing the rock on the far side. It seemed to Paks like a great stair, each step perhaps ankle high and an arm deep, but with the treads tilted downward. She looked up and gasped, forgetting her pain and exhaustion.

There, far overhead, a great red stone arch hung in the air, spanning the distance from one massive stone buttress to another. Behind her, she heard Balkon mutter in dwarvish. Everyone stopped for a moment in amazement. Connaught called back to the yeomen below, and Paks saw them come around the pool and look up.

"I see it," shouted one. "By the High Lord, that's a wonder indeed."

They kept climbing. The stone slope, roughly shaped into tilted stairs, curved below and under the arch. Connaught led them toward the nearer, southern end of it. As they neared the vertical buttress walls, it was clear that someone had shaped the natural stone, flattening the increasing tilt of the treads. They reached the vertical cliff, and moved along it. Now the stairs were hewn clean, like any stone stair—except for the crescent of Gird chipped into the rise of every other one, alternating with an ornate L. The stairs steepened. Paks fought for breath; her chest burned and her eyes seemed darkened. She nearly bumped into Amberion, in front of her, when he stopped.

"Now we'll see if we have understood the message," said Connaught. "This should be a door—if I can open it—"

Paks could not see, from her position many steps down, what he did. But suddenly those in front of her moved, and she climbed wearily to a last small platform before an opening in the rock.

Inside she saw with a pang of dismay that the steps continued—even steeper, they spiralled up into darkness. Light flared above her; it must be Amberion lighting the way. Paks bit her lip and started up. When she reached a level again, her legs were quivering. The stairs had come out in daylight, on top of the cliffs. Amberion touched her shoulder.

"Are you all right, Paks?"

"I'm tired," she admitted, hating that weakness. "I shouldn't be, but—"

"It's all right," he said. "Let me try to help." Paks did not miss the looks the men-at-arms shot her, as Amberion's hand touched her head, but the warmth of that touch and the strength she felt dimmed her embarrassment for the time.

They had come out on the clifftops; from below, Paks would have thought that the top of the mountain, but now she could see another lower row of cliffs and a rounded summit, heavily forested. A trail led south, along the edge of the cliffs; Thelon reported that it ended at a small outpost, a simple rock shelter carved into the stone. Another led west, toward the forested heights, but the main trail led north—out onto the rock bridge that they had seen from below. Paks felt her stomach heave at the thought. Others, she saw, had faces as pale as hers felt.

"Are we goin' out on that?" asked one of the men-at-arms.

"We must," said Connaught. "It is the only way to Luap's stronghold."

"And where is the stronghold?" asked the man, looking around that wilderness of great rocks in confusion.

"There." Connaught pointed to the opposite buttress. "Inside that mountain."

"I give them praise," said Balkon suddenly. Paks looked back to see his eyes gleaming. "That is a worthy stone; such a place would suit our tribe."

Despite her fears, when they walked out on the stone arch it was not bad. Wind was the worst problem, whipping past their ears from the southern desert and moaning in the great pines below. But once on the bridge they could not see below; it was too wide for that. It seemed, in fact, wide enough to drive a team on. They were almost at the far side when they were faced with a huge man in shining mail, who held a mace across his body. They stopped short.

"Declare yourselves," said a strong voice. "In whose name do you invade this place."

"In the name of Gird and the High Lord," answered Connaught. The figure bowed, and stepped aside. As Connaught's foot touched the stone beyond the arch, it vanished as suddenly as it had come. Paks felt a cold shiver all the way down her back.

On the far side, the trail was clear, a nearly level groove in the stone leading east along the buttress to its eastern end. From here they could see far to the north, to distant red rock walls, and that irregular gray mountain that Balkon insisted was fire-born. Eastward a still higher plateau broke suddenly into the maze of canyons they had wandered. On the very point of the buttress, another guardpost carved into the rock gave a clear view.

The way into Luap's stronghold was a circle carved in the rock, with Girds crescent and Luap's L intertwined in its center. When High Marshal Connaught stood there, and called on Gird, the stone seemed to melt into mist, revealing a stone stair. They clambered down, with sunlight pouring in the well. Paks could not tell how far the steps went down. They seemed to spiral slowly, after the first straight flight, around an open core where the light fell. Finally they ended in a square hall with four arched entrances leading from it. Over each was a symbol, lit by its own fire: Gird's crescent, the High Lord's circle, a hammer, and a harp. Through each a passage could be seen, but nothing else. In the center of the hall a circular well opened to the depths.

They stood a moment, bemused by the designs, then without a word moved slowly toward one or another of the arches. Paks saw Balkon strut through the one under the hammer, and Ardhiel stepped under the harp. She and most of the others stepped under Gird's crescent.

They entered a Hall, as large as the High Lord's Hall at Fin Panir, its great stone columns carved on the living rock. Gentle light lay over it without a source that Paks could see. The floor was bare polished stone, the same red as the rest, except for a wide aisle where some polished white and black slabs had been set in, forming a pattern that Paks found compelling but confusing. Far up at the other end, rows of kneeling figures, robed in blue, faced a shallow platform. Paks looked around at the others, and met Balkon's surprised gaze. Beyond him was Ardhiel.

"I did not come with you," murmured Balkon. "I went under the

Hammer, and saw—and saw great wonders of stone, and yet am here. This has the Maker of worlds shaped well."

Paks nodded, speechless. She had not thought she would like being so far underground, with the whole mountain's weight above her, but she could feel no fear. The Hall seemed to cherish them, protect them—Paks could not even feel the ache along her bones that was becoming familiar.

The two High Marshals walked slowly up the aisle; the rest of the party followed. As they neared the rows of kneeling figures, Paks was suddenly seized by fear: would they turn and attack? But they did not move. She could not see even the gentle movement of breath, and then feared they were dead. Ahead, High Marshal Connaught turned to look into the faces of the rearmost row. He said nothing, and passed on. The silence pressed on them; it reminded Paks of the silence of the elfane taig, but it had a different flavor, at once more familiar and more majestic.

When she reached the platform with the others, and turned to look, she saw rows of faces—perhaps a hundred in all—that seemed to be in peaceful sleep. Each held a weapon—most of them swords—point down, with hands resting on the hilts. Paks shivered. She saw the men-at-arms eyeing the figures, and then one another.

"Gird's grace, and the High Lord's power, rest on this place of peace," said Connaught softly. The words sank into the silence. And then as if a drop of dye had fallen into clear water, the silence took on another flavor, and shifted, pulling away from them to drape itself around the sleepers, protecting their rest, while leaving the company free to talk. It was as if a king's attention had passed to someone else, setting the pages free to whisper along the walls of the chamber.

"Well," said High Marshal Fallis, with a little shake of his shoulders. "I never expected to find this sort of thing."

"Mmm. No." Connaught had stepped onto the platform. "Look at this, Fallis." The platform was itself stone, apparently all one great slab of white stone, and into the upper surface a brilliant mosaic was set, unlike anything Paks had seen. "I wonder where he found someone to do this—" He turned to Paks. "You were at Sibili, weren't you? Didn't they have work like this?"

Paks shook her head. "Sir Marshal, I don't remember—I had a knock on the head and don't remember anything. But—let me think—someone in our Company mentioned pictures made of chips of stone."

"Yes. I thought so. Along the coast of Aarenis they do this work; I've heard that it was used a lot in old Aare."

"It could have come from Kaelifet," said Amberion. "I've seen bronze and copper ware from there ornamented with bits of colored stone; perhaps they do stone mosaics as well."

"It might be." Connaught walked slowly from one end of the platform to the other, looking at the design. It spread from a many-pointed star in shades of blue and green to an intricate interlacement of curves and angles in reds and golds. "I would like to know what it is."

"It is a place of power," said Ardhiel suddenly. They all looked at him.

"I feel power in all this," said Amberion. "But what do you mean?"

Ardiel nodded toward the pattern. "That is a pattern of power. This place is made of many such. That—" he pointed to the black and white of the aisle, "is another of them."

"What do they do?" asked Fallis.

Ardhiel smiled, a quick flash of delight. "All—you men! You hear that I am saying more than elves are wont to say, and you hope to learn great secrets. So—listen closely, and I will say what I can in Common. And in elven, for those who can hear." He threw Paks a smile at that. "This place is sustained by patterns of power, else those sleepers would have died long since, and the dust of time half-filled this chamber. How was it we each saw and followed the symbol of our lord—Master Balkon, I daresay, saw and followed the dwarf's secret symbols, and was met and welcomed as a dwarf, just as I saw and followed the Singer's sign, and was met and welcomed as an elf. Is it not so?"

"It happened," said Balkon.

"Yes. Then together we found ourselves in this Hall. A pattern of great power. I think more than men had the shaping of it."

"But—" began Fallis, and the elf waved his hand for silence.

"I will be as brief as the matter allows, Sir Marshal. In haste is great danger; the right use of power requires full knowledge. This pattern, on the platform, is much like one placed in every elfane taig, in the center of every elvenhome kingdom. I do not know if I can explain how—and I know to you that means much. We elves—we think that as the Singer sang, and we are both songs and singers ourselves, we both are and make the Singer's patterns. So our powers grow from the patterns of our song. We do not enjoy putting these aside—outside us." Paks could tell he was having a hard time saying what he meant in Common; for once an elf's speech seemed halting and out of rhythm.

"You mean, as men do in machines?" asked Amberion.

Ardhiel nodded. "Exactly. We have—we are—the power—as you paladins are: and I know what you will say, that it is the High Lord's, and he but lends it. That is also so of us, though we are given more—more—" he faltered, waving his hand. "We can choose more for ourselves, how to use it," he said finally. "But on occasion we have used built things—patterns of stone or wood, or growing things, to make patterns of power that any elf can use, even if he lacks a certain gift."

"At the elfane taig—" Paks spoke without intention, and Ardhiel looked at her sharply. "The stone's carving—if I looked at it—it held me—"

"Yes. Instead of having some always on guard, elves have used such to bemuse and slow an enemy. This pattern, though, is used for other things." He seemed reluctant to go on, but finally sighed and continued. "I might as well tell you, since it is clear that men used it before. With such a pattern, it is possible for a small group to travel a great distance all at once."

"What!"

Ardhiel nodded again. "Look here—and here—you will see that each of the high gods and patrons is included by symbol. This pattern draws on all their power, and can be used by a worshipper of any of these: elf, dwarf, gnome, those who follow the High Lord, Alyanya, or Gird, Falk, Camwyn, and so on."

"But how do you know where you'll go?" asked Fallis.

"I am not sure. If it were exactly the same as the elven pattern, you would go where you willed to go. You would picture that in your mind, and that you would see, and that is where you would go. It would be possible, however, to set such apattern for a single destination."

"And to set it off?"

"An invocation of some land—I do not know. Perhaps you will find guidance somewhere else in this place." Ardhiel was reverting to the more usual enigmatic elven reticence.

"In that case, I think we can wait. Perhaps we will find some guidance elsewhere." Fallis gestured to a narrow archway leading out of the Hall behind the platform. "Perhaps we should take a look?"

The group followed the High Marshals across the platform—Paks noticed that they skirted the pattern gingerly—and through the arch into another stone passage, well-lit by the same sourceless light. At intervals they passed arched doorways into rooms hollowed from the stone; most were empty. But one chamber, when they came to it, was very different. A desk and two tables were littered with scraps of parchment and scrolls. Shelves along the walls held neatly racked scroll-cases as well as sewn books; a brilliantly colored carpet on the floor showed the wear of feet, but no touch of moth. A hooded blue robe hung from a hook. And a pair of worn slippers, the fleece lining worn into little lumps, lay under a carved wooden chair, just where the wearer must have slipped them off to put on boots. Connaught touched them with a respectful finger.

"These—must be his. Luap's or his successor's—Gird's grace, I can hardly believe it—"

"He might have stepped out only moments ago," said Fallis softly. "There's no dust—no disarray—" He glanced at the loose sheets on the worktable. "Look, Connaught. Supply lists—names—and here's a watch-schedule of some kind: south outpost, east outpost, north—"

"I wonder what happened," murmured Amberion. "I feel no evil here at all, only great peace and good, but—some sleep, and others are gone—

Connaught sighed. "Amberion, we wouldn't know if Falk himself slept out there with the others. Who knows what he looked like? The legends say he was thinner than Gird—and none of us ever saw Gird. I don't suppose," he said, turning to Ardhiel, "that you happen to be of an age to know what Falk looked like—"

Ardhiel shook his head. "Sir Marshal, I am sorry that this is not a mystery I can solve for you. Only I agree with Sir Amberion, that this is not a place of evil. Whatever happened here, happened for good."

"So—now what?' asked Fallis. "I feel strange, rooting around in these things that seem untouched. If it were a ruin, and everything half destroyed—but here, I feel like a—a—robber, almost."

"We asked Gird's grace, and the High Lord's power, Fallis. They know our need, and the needs of this place. We will be warned, I daresay, if we trespass where they do not wish us to go."

Fallis nodded. Connaught turned to the others. "Amberion, if you don't mind, you might lead a group looking for a lower entrance. They must have had a way to get animals in and out, and heavy loads."

"With all the magic this place holds," said Amberion drily, "perhaps they simply wished them inside." Connaught chuckled, then sobered abruptly. "By Gird, Amberion, I hope you're wrong."

Before Amberion got out of hearing, however, Fallis had found a map of the complex, in the wide desk drawer. They called Amberion back.

"Look—this is the main Hall—"

"And this is Luap's office, as we thought. So that corridor, if we'd gone on, would lead to the kitchens—"

"I wonder what they do for firedraught, so far down," said Fallis. "Master Balkon, do dwarves have any trouble with that?"

"Firebreath? No, it is important to make a hole for it, that is all."

"Look at these red lines, Amberion—could that be shafts?"

"It could be anything until we go and look. Let me—ah. Look here. Is there another sheet?"

"Yes. Two more; I put them on the table there."

"Good. Let me see—yes, look at this. I thought so. This keys to the other sheet, and this must be the ground level—if this mapmaker followed Finthan tradition, then this sign means a spring."

"But we saw springs coming out of the rock very high," said Connaught.

"Yes, but look—isn't that a trail sign? And it's twisting here, as in natural land, not straight or gently curved like these corridors."

Paks, looking over their shoulders, could make little of the brown, red, and black lines on the maps. She had found the Hall easily enough, and Luap's study, but the maze of corridors, and the strange marks that Amberion insisted meant ramps or stairs, confused her.

"I only hope," Fallis was saying, "that your trail isn't like that rockclimb we had."

Amberion laughed. "No—I'm sure it's not. Well go down that way and see. How many would you like left with you?"

"Who has a good writing hand?" asked Connaught. "We should make copies of what we find." Paks and one of the men-at-arms, who was known to write clearly, stayed with the High Marshals.

Paks heard later that day how Amberion had led the little group through echoing passages of stone, ever deeper, down gentle ramps. They had found a stone stable, clean but for a few ancient bits of straw, and the deep-grooved ruts of the carts that had carried in fodder and carried out dung. They had found great kitchens, three of them, and Balkon had told them why—that whatever way the wind blew, one of the hearths would draw perfectly. They had found storerooms still full of casks and bales—but across the doors lay a line of silvery light that Amberion would not try to pass. And finally, when the last wide corridor ended in a blank face of stone, Amberion had touched it with one glowing finger, and the stone vanished in a colored mist. The cold, pine-scented air of the canyon blew in, swirling a little dust around their feet. Some of the men were reluctant to go out, fearing the passage would close again, but it stayed open like a great grange door behind them.

Paks spent that time copying what seemed to her a very dull list of names. She supposed that the High Marshals had some reason to need a complete list of Luap's followers, with the years of their coming, but she could not understand it. Behind her she could hear them at the shelves, gently taking down one scroll or book after another, and murmuring to each other. She used up the small amount of ink that Fallis had had, and asked him for his inkstick. He reached over to Luap's desk, where a bowl of ink sat waiting, as it seemed, and handed it to her.

"Use *this*?" Paks asked.

"Why not?" He hardly looked at her, face deep in a large volume bound in cedarwood.

"But it's—it might be—"

"It's just ink, Paksenarrion. What else could it be?" Paks felt her shoulders tighten at the sneer she thought she heard in his voice, and ducked her head. How did he know it was just ink. Ink doesn't stay wet for years—all the years this place had been—whatever it had been. She stabbed at the ink with the pen, and felt vindicated when it clicked on the surface.

"It won't write," she said. "It's dried up."

"Oh?" Fallis put the book down, picked up the bowl, and tilted it. "That's odd. It looked wet, and I'd have sworn it shifted. Hmm. Well, here's the inkstick and—yes—here's a bowl for it."

Silently, Paks mixed a measure of ink with water from her flask. She pushed it over so that Elam could use it too.

★★★

Amberion reappeared to say that he had found the lower entrance, and had started moving the animals and others toward it.

"It's nearly dark, though, so I thought it better to camp for the night—that trail is barely passable in daylight. Will you come out, or shall I have food sent in?"

"We'll come out," said Connaught. "Everyone needs to hear all about this, and we should be together."

"I thought you might want to set sentries on the old guardposts."

Connaught shook his head. "Until we know more about how this place works, that would simply call attention to us. Paks—Elam—that will do for today. Let's go have some supper."

And Paks, rising from her seat, realized how stiff and hungry she was. She followed the others out without a word.

In the next two days, some of the party explored as much of the old fortress as the light would allow. One rash yeoman tried to pass a doorway barred with silver light, and fell without a cry. Amberion touched his head, and did nothing more.

"He'll wake with a headache, and more respect for these things. Someone stay with him, until he wakes."

Paks spent her time copying records. She wished she could roam around, seeing the things others spoke of in the evenings; it didn't seem fair that she had to act as scribe all the time. But no one had asked her what she wanted to do, and she refused to bring it up. Surely they could tell, if they thought about it, she thought bitterly. Finally, when one of the yeomen was describing a long climb up a narrow corridor to an outlook on the very top of the mountain, among the trees, Paks exploded.

"—and you could see so far," the man said, gesturing. "North of here, and west—what a view. Of course it was cold up there, and after climbing all that way my legs quivered like jelly." He grinned at Paks. "You're lucky, lady, that you get to sit all day in the warm, just wiggling your fingers with a pen."

"Lucky!" Heads turned at the bite in her voice. "Lucky to sit all day? I'd give anything to be where I could see something besides another stinking scroll! How would you like to travel all the way out here and then be stuck in a windowless room? I've already been underground as much as I care to—" She stopped short, seeing the worry in Amberion's face, the High Marshal's stem expressions.

"You could have asked, Paks," said Fallis mildly. "We thought it would be easier for you, with your wounds still healing, than climbing all over."

"I'm sorry," she muttered. Now that she'd said it, she felt ashamed, and still somehow resentful. She shouldn't have protested—she shouldn't have felt that way. Yet she did, and it was unfair.

"Take some time tomorrow," Amberion said. "I'll show you some things if you wish." But Paks felt that he was humoring her, as if she were still sick.

When she tried to follow Amberion around the stronghold the next day, she found that in one thing the High Marshals were right. She was too weak to climb for. She pushed herself, determined not to show what she felt, but when Amberion turned back toward the lower levels, near midday, she was glad. That afternoon she copied lists without complaint, and that evening the High Marshals announced their decision to try to use the pattern on the Hall's platform.

"We won't take everyone; enough must stay here to go back, as planned. The maps show another way out of this canyon, down through the western cliffs, and a clear trail to the trade route from Kaelifet. We suggest that, instead of the trail that would take you past the kuaknom again. But if the transfer works, we will return and the rest of you can travel easily that way. Wait ten days for us to return before you leave; Ardhiel assures me that if we can use the pattern at all, we can return in that time."

Paks was elated to find that they wanted her to try the pattern with them. High Marshal Connaught, commander of the expedition, was staying behind; those returning were Amberion, High Marshal Fallis, Ardhiel, Balkon, and herself. With Connaught watching, they mounted the platform, standing as near the center as they could. Paks watched Balkon; he had confided to her that if he was to travel like this, he might as well go home if he could. Then the High Marshals together lifted their voices, calling on Gird and the High Lord. Ardhiel's silvery elven song joined them, then Balkon's chant in dwarvish. Paks thought she heard a faint and distant call of trumpets.

CHAPTER TWENTY-EIGHT

As the Hall of Luap's Stronghold faded around them, the sound of trumpets seemed to come nearer. Abruptly they were standing on the lower dais of the High Lord's Hall at Fin Panir, facing the Marshal-General as she came forward between the ranks of knights: the fanfare had just ended. The Marshal-General stopped in midstride, her face a stiff mask. Behind her, the knights drew sword; others burst into shouts, questions, even one scream, chopped off short. The Marshal-General's arm came up, paused... the hubbub stilled, no one moved. Then Amberion spoke, a formal greeting that Paks hardly noticed because she'd realized that Balkon was not with them, and grinned to herself. She had no doubt that he had chosen to return to the Goldenaxe, and hoped his magic worked.

In moments, the Marshal-General had reached the dais, touching each of them, eyes bright. And again the Hall was full of sound: greetings, whispers, comments, the scrape of feet, the rasp of weapons returned to scabbard and rack. To Paks, it seemed noisy as a windstorm after the calm of Luap's Stronghold. She felt at once submerged in it and remote, a solitary stone washed by contending waves. Eventually, the noise receded, the crowds dispersed, and she went to her quarters, hardly noticing the shy greetings and questions of those few students who spoke to her.

A few hours later, the Marshal-General summoned her. When she arrived in the study, she found the Marshal-General and Amberion waiting.

"I have been telling the Marshal-General," began Amberion, "about your capture and ordeal with the iynisin—the kuaknom—" he said quickly, after a glance at the Marshal-General.

Paks nodded, at once alarmed and defensive.

"I wondered what your plans were, Paksenarrion," said the Marshal-General. "From what Amberion says, and the way you look, it seems that you may need a rest. Such wounds would slow anyone. Have you thought of it?"

"No, Marshal-General. I did not know if—I mean, I am tired, yes, but I don't know about rest. Do you mean you want me to leave?"

"No, not that. Amberion thinks you are not fit for a full schedule of training; he thought several weeks of rest would help. There are many things you could do here, without much strain, or—"

"I know what I would like," said Paks suddenly, interrupting. "I could go home—visit my family in Three Firs. It's been four years and more." As she spoke, the longing to go home intensified, as if she had wanted this for long.

Amberion frowned. "I don't think that's a good idea," he said slowly.

"Why not?" Paks turned to him, annoyed. "It's not that far, by the maps. I'm surely strong enough to ride that far—and there's no war—and—"

"Paksenarrion, no. It's too dangerous, as things are with you."

Paks felt a wave of rage swamp her mind. She was not weak, just tired from the fighting and the trip. They kept trying to make her believe something was wrong—"There's nothing wrong with me!" she snapped. "By Gird, just because I'm tired—and you said anyone might be—you think I can't ride a few days to see my family. I traveled safely alone on foot, with no training at all, four years ago—why do you think I can't do it now? You keep trying to convince me something's wrong—and whatever it is, it's not wrong with me!" She glared at them, breathing hard.

"It's not?" The Marshal-General's voice was quiet, but hard as stone. "Nothing wrong, when a paladin-candidate feels and shows such anger to the Marshal-General of Gird? Nothing wrong, when you have not thought what what such a visit could do to your family?"

"My family—what about them?" Paks was still angry. She could not seem to fight it back.

"Paksenarrion, you have attracted the notice of great evil—of Achrya herself. Do you think you can travel in the world—anywhere in the world—without evil knowing? Do you think your family will be safe, if you show Achrya where they live, and that you still care for them? Gird's grace, Paksenarrion, be on your mind, that you think clearly."

Paks sat back, stunned. She had not thought. She shook her head. "I—all I thought was—"

"All you thought was what you wanted to do."

"Yes—"

"And you resented any balk—any balk at all—"

"Yes." Paks stared at the tabletop; it blurred as her eyes filled. "I—I thought it was over!"

"What?"

"The—the anger—Amberion can tell you. I thought it was past—that I had—had beaten it—" Paks heard the rustle of clothing as the Marshal-General moved in her seat. She heard Amberion clear his throat before beginning.

"Immediately after we got her out, she had a—I don't quite know how to describe it. Fallis and I thought we should let her memories return naturally—at least until Ardhiel awoke. But Balkon—the dwarf, you recall—he disagreed, and began telling her some of it. Anyway, I stepped in and interrupted, and Paksenarrion became angry. Very angry. I thought at the time it was the pain of her wounds, and attempted a healing—"

"It did help," said Paks softly, trying not to cry. "It eased them—and then I could see I was wrong—"

"But whatever it was recurred. A couple of times, in the next days—nothing bad, if it had been someone else, someone more irritable to start with. But it just was not like Paksenarrion not the Paksenarrion we knew. We spoke to her of it, and made allowances for the wounds which Ardhiel said had been healed so far by some kuaknom magic—and she seemed to have recovered, but for the weakness and exhaustion I spoke of to you."

"I see." The Marshal-General was silent a long moment, and Paks waited, as for a blow. "Paksenarrion, what do you, yourself, think of this anger? Is it just the wounds? It's not uncommon for people to be irritable when recovering from illness or wounds."

"I—don't know. I don't feel different—except for being tired. But if Amberion says I am, then—" She shook her head. "I don't know. In the Duke's Company, I didn't get in trouble for fighting, or anything like that, but I did get angry. I can't tell that it's any more now than it was then."

"Our fear," said Amberion, "was that the type of fighting she did, with the iynisin—the kuaknom—would open a channel for Achrya's evil—"

"I would hate to think so," said the Marshal-General. "I would hate that indeed. Paksenarrion?"

"I don't feel that, my lady. Truly, I don't—and I care for Gird, and for his cause, as much as ever I did. The anger is wrong—to be angry at you, I mean, but I can control it another time."

"Hmm. Amberion, had you any other concern?"

"No." He smiled at Paks. "She has not begun beating horses, or cursing people, or telling lies—it's just an uneasiness. Ardhiel feels the same."

"Paksenarrion, I hope you agree now that you should not travel to Three Firs—" Despite herself, Paks felt a twinge of irritation at this; she masked it with a nod and smile. "Good. Take a few days to rest; let our surgeons look you over. It may be that rest and good food will bring you back quickly. Don't start drill again until I've talked with you. We may want you to help instruct a beginner's class."

Paks left the Marshal-General's office with mixed feelings. The thought of instructing was exciting—she could easily imagine herself with younger students, as she had worked with recruits in the Duke's Company—but the prescribed days of rest were less attractive. Though tired and jaded, she was restless, and could not relax.

"I'm about to do a dangerous thing," said the Marshal-General, pulling out a blank message scroll.

"What?" Amberion watched her closely.

"I'm going to write Duke Phelan of Tsaia." Arianya trimmed her pen, dipped it, and began.

"Phelan? Why?"

"I think you're right. I think this child is in serious trouble. And I think we don't know her well enough. Phelan commanded her for three years; he will know which way she's turned."

"Then you sensed evil too?"

"Yes. Not much as you said. But deep, and so rooted that it will grow, day by day, and consume her. By the cudgel of Gird, Amberion, this is a sad thing to see. She had so much promise!"

"Has still."

"Maybe. Right now—we must keep her from leaving, and from hurting anyone else. If she leaves us—" She shook her head. "The only thing standing between Achrya and her soul is the Fellowship of Gird. Ward her, Amberion."

"I do, and I shall."

It was some days later that Pak came into the forecourt to find familiar colors there: three horses with saddlecloths of the familiar maroon and white, with a tiny foxhead on the corners, and a pennant held by someone she had never seen before. She lingered, wondering if the Duke himself had come to Fin Panir, and what for, but she had urgent business with the Training Master, and had to go. Upstairs, in the Marshal-General's office, she herself was the topic of conversation—if such it could be called.

Duke Phelan faced the Marshal-General across her polished desk, his eyes as cold as winter seawater. "And you want me to help you? You, who could not protect, for even a year, a warrior of such promise?"

Arianya sighed. "We erred, my lord Duke."

"Tir's guts, you did, lady! Not for the first time, either! I thought I'd never be so wroth with you again, as when my lady died from your foolishness, but this—!" He turned away, and paced back and forth by the window, his cloak rustling, then came to lean on the desk again. "Lady, that child had such promise as I've rarely seen in thirty years of fighting. Your own paladin saw that in Aarenis. You could not ask better will, better courage, than hers. Oh, she made mistakes, aye beginner's mistakes, and rarely twice. But generous in all ways, willing—we hated to lose her, but I thought she'd be better off in some noble service. She had a gentle heart, for a fighter. I was glad to hear that she'd come here for training. She'll make a knight, and well-deserved, I thought. And then—!" He glared at her.

"My lord, we thought—" began Amberion.

"You thought!" The Duke leaped into speech. "You never thought at all. Make her a paladin, you thought, and then you dragged her into such peril as even you, sir paladin, would fear, and without your powers to help her. You think me gray, Girdsmen, compared to your white company, but I know better than to put untrained raw recruits into hot battle. 'Tis a wonder you have any paladins at all, if you throw them away so."

"We don't, Duke Phelan," said Marshal Fallis. "They do not go out untrained. But in her case—"

"She did. Do you even know how young she is? What years you have wasted?"

"Duke—" began Fallis angrily.

"Be still!" roared the Duke. "I'll have my say; you asked me here for help and you'll hear me out. I have no love for you these fourteen years, Girdsmen, though I honor Gird himself. Protector of the innocent and helpless, you say—but where were you and where was he when my lady met her death alone and far from aid?" He turned away for a moment, then back. "But no matter. If I can help this girl, I will. She has deserved better of us all." He looked around for a chair, and sat. "Now. You say she was captured, and is now alive but in some trouble. What is it?"

"My lord Duke, a paladin-candidate can be assaulted in spirit by evil powers; that's why we normally keep them sequestered. We think that in defending herself during captivity she became vulnerable to Achrya's direct influence. This is the thought of Amberion and Fallis, who observed her at the time they brought her out, and also of Ardhiel the elf, who knows how kuaknom enchantments might work."

"I see. Then you think she is now an agent of Achrya?"

"No. Not yet." Arianya met his eyes squarely. "My lord, all we have noticed so far is irritability—unusual for her, for we have known her to be always goodnatured, willing, and patient. It would hardly be noticed in another warrior—indeed, many expect all fighters to be touchy of temper."

The Duke grinned suddenly. "I am myself."

"I noticed. But she has not been so since we've known her. You have known her longer; we thought you could tell us if she has changed."

"You want me to tell you if she has become evil?"

"No. She has not become evil, not largely. That I could certainly sense for myself. I want you, if you will, to speak to her—observe her—and tell us if she is changing in the wrong way. Becoming more violent, less controlled—that is a sign of contamination."

"And if she is? What then will you do?"

The Marshal-General paused long. "I am not sure. She is a member of our Fellowship, and a paladin-candidate—as such, she is under my command. As she is, she cannot be a paladin—"

"You're sure."

"Yes. I'm sorry, but so it is. What is of no account in another may be a serious flaw in a paladin. If she had gone over to Achrya, it would be my duty to kill her—"

"No!" The Duke jumped to his feet.

"Please. Sit down. She has not—I am not saying she has—I am saying if that were true, which is not true. Yet. But if she is changing in the way—if the evil is growing—then, my lord Duke, we cannot tolerate an agent of evil among us. We cannot. Somehow, before that happens, we must prevent it."

"What can you do? Can you heal her, as you heal wounds?"

"Unfortunately not. Her wounds, indeed, have not yielded to our healing. The elf, as I said, says that this is because of some kuaknom magic used on them. As for her mind . . . I think that we might be able to destroy the focus of evil—if, indeed, I am not misnaming it—but like any surgery it would leave scars of its own.

"You speak of magic?"

"If you consider the gods' powers and magic in the same light, my lord, which I do not. The High Lord has given us—Marshals and paladins both—certain powers. With them I might try to enter her mind and cleanse it."

The Duke shifted in his seat. "I don't like it. I don't like it at all, Marshal-General, and that's without any rancor for the past. It's bad enough that she had to bear such captivity, and such wounds as you describe. That she had to have that filth trying to corrupt her mind. But then to let someone else in, to stir the mess further—"

"Believe me, I don't like the idea either. But what else is there? If we are right, and the evil is rooted there, and we do nothing, she will come to be such as even you, my lord, would admit must be destroyed. Could anything—even death now—be worse than that dishonor?"

"No, but—I dislike being the means of it. She is—she was, I should say—my soldier, under my command and protection. She has a right to expect more from me—"

"Now?" asked Fallis.

"Yes, now. By the gods, Marshal, I don't forget my soldiers when they leave. She served me well; I will not serve her ill."

"My lord, one reason I wrote you was that she had so often spoken of her respect for you. We are not looking for an accuser, my lord, but a friend who knew her in the past—"

"And do you think I will condemn her to you, having known her?"

"I trust you for that. You have always been, by all repute, an honest man—and so she thinks of you."

"I will not persuade her to your opinions—"

"We don't ask that. Go, talk to her, see for yourself. If you come and tell me I'm a fool, I will be best pleased by that. I don't think you will—but do your best for her."

The Duke ran his hand through his hair. "I'll tell you what, Marshal-General, you have set me a problem indeed. But you have one yourself. All right. I'll see her. But I think perhaps I'll have a new captain for my Company out of it, and you'll be a paladin the less."

"That may be so."

Paks came from the Training Master's office in the black mood that had begun to seem familiar. She was not to ride out with the others to hunt the following day, and she was not to plan on taking part in the fall competitions. She lengthened her stride, hardly noticing when several students flattened themselves out of her way. At least, she was thinking, I can take Socks out to the practice field. She turned hard right into the stable courtyard, and nearly bumped into a tall man in a maroon cloak. Before he turned, she knew who it was.

"My lord Duke!" She fell back a step, suddenly happier.

"Well, Paks, you've come far in the world." He looked much the same, but he spoke now as if she were more his equal.

"Well, my lord, I—"

"They tell me that's your horse, the black."

"Yes, my lord—"

"Will you ride with me? I'd like to see how the training grounds are laid out."

"Certainly, my lord." Paks turned toward the tack room, but a groom was already leading Socks out, ready to ride. The horse had recovered his flesh, and showed no ill effects of the expedition. The Duke's own mount waited, and after they mounted, he rode beside her.

"We were glad to hear," he began, "that you'd been accepted here. I had two years with the Knights of Falk, and I understand that the training here is as good if not better."

"It's thorough, my lord," said Paks. He laughed.

"Fortification? Supply? Field surgery?"

"Yes, my lord, and more."

"Good. And you enjoyed it?"

"Oh yes. Last winter was the happiest time of my life—" she stopped suddenly and looked at him. "I mean, my lord, after leaving the Company."

"Don't be silly, Paks—you weren't happy with us, that last year. Few were. Of course you'd like this better. Now—what's that?" For some minutes they rode in the training grounds, the Duke commenting and questioning on the equipment and methods of training that they observed. Then he turned to her again. "Did they teach you such riding here?"

"No, my lord. That was Marshal Cedfer in Brewersbridge, where I got my horse."

"Brewersbridge—that's in southeast Tsaia, isn't it?"

"Yes, my lord." Paks wondered if he would ask her about the details of her journey across the Dwarfmounts, but he said nothing for a bit. Then—"What's this journey you've been on, that they talk of so? And they said you were captured by some kind of elf—is that so?"

Paks shivered, unwilling as always to remember that too clearly. "Yes, my lord. We had gone to the far west—a land called Kolobia—to find the stronghold of Luap, who was a friend of Gird himself. It goes back, sir, to when I left your Company: in the journey over the mountains, a traveling companion and I were enchanted by the elfane taig, and had to fight a demon-possessed elf underground."

"By Tir! And you lived?"

"Yes, my lord. And the elfane taig rewarded me with great riches, and gave me also a scroll. It seems that the scroll was written by Luap—it's very old—and contains much about Gird and his times that was not known, for the scroll had been lost. It was in this scroll that the stronghold of Luap was mentioned, and a map besides. So the Council of Marshals, and the Marshal-General, declared a quest that search should be made for this stronghold, and the rumors of lost powers."

"But why did you go? You were but a student here, isn't that so?"

"Yes—but they asked if I wanted to. Because I'd brought the scrolls, you see: it was a reward, an honor."

"I see."

"They didn't know, my lord, that I would have such trouble."

"No, but they might have thought." He shook his head. "Well, enough of that. How did you come to be captured?"

Paks told the tale as best she might, and the Duke looked grave, but listened without comment. When she finished with Ardhiel's treatment, he sighed. "Are you well, then?"

"I think so. They—" Paks looked aside, but no one was near. "My lord, they seem to think not, but I don't know why. I have lost my temper once or twice—even spoke sharply to the Marshal-General—"

"That's nothing," said the Duke quickly. "I've done as much."

Paks grinned, thinking of it. Then she sobered. "My lord, I don't want to be bad; you know I never did." He nodded. "I don't think I am, yet they don't trust me anymore. Just today, the Training Master told me not to ride out hunting tomorrow—and not to join in the autumn competitions, either. Is that fair? I haven't done anything—I've been careful—I do all they ask me—I don't know what more I can do!" Her voice had risen; she took a deep breath and tried to continue more calmly. "They—they say that evil begins as a little thing—too little for me to sense. That it will grow, and consume me, until I become one of Achrya's minions. But sir, you know me—you've known me all along. Am I so bad?"

Phelan looked at her, a piercing gaze that she found hard to meet. Then he shook his head slowly. "Paks, I see you much as you were: a good soldier, loyal and courageous. You bear scars that I would not care to have, and you have suffered under both enchantments and blows. I do not see evil." Paks relaxed, but he went on. "But Paks, I am no Marshal or paladin to discern evil directly. The gods know I have no great love for the granges of Gird, but they are not evil. I think perhaps you should submit yourself to their judgement."

"My lord!"

"And if it is not fair, or if you do not agree, leave them. I will not forsake you; as you were my soldier, so you can be again. As I recall, you held the right to return when you left."

Paks said nothing, and after a while they rode back silently. She suspected that the Duke had come to Fin Panir because of her—and this was confirmed when she answered a summons late that afternoon to the Marshal-General's quarters. She was shown to a study she had not been in before, a level higher, with windows on three sides. Amberion, Fallis, Ardhiel, and Duke Phelan, as well as the Marshal-General, were all in the room. The Marshal-General began by explaining what they thought was wrong, and what she thought could be done about it, a sort of surgery of the mind.

Paks nodded gravely, trying to pay attention through a numb haze that fogged her mind. Arianya paused, for that nod, then went on.

"So much we think we can do. But that is not the whole story; I want to be fair with you. We are sure that if you live the evil will be destroyed, but some good may be destroyed as well."

"What—what sort of good?" asked Paks, her mouth drying with fear.

Amberion looked away, at a tapestry on the outer wall. Arianya glanced down, then met Paks' eyes squarely. "Paksenarrion, the flaw, being made of an excess of your best qualities, is bound tightly in them. You may not be a fighter afterwards—"

"Not a fighter!" Paks felt the blood leave her face.

"No. I will not lie to you. You may be weak, clumsy, uncertain. You may lose your will to fight... your courage."

"No!" Paks clenched her fists, anguish twisting her face. "I cannot! You cannot want me to be so!"

"Lady Paksenarrion," said Ardhiel, "what we want is that you be healed and whole, and free of any taint of evil. But our powers are limited, and it is better to be free of the dark one's web than be a prince under her control."

"But—" Paks shook her head. "But you ask that I give up the only gifts I have—chance them—and if I survive a weakling or a coward, what good is that? To you or anyone? My lady," she said to Arianya, "the granges would not let me in, if I were a coward. I would be better dead, indeed. You say I am not so bad, yet. If I cannot be a paladin, I can still fight your enemies. Then if—if I go wrong, then do your treatment, or kill me."

Arianya started to speak, but Duke Phelan interrupted. "Paks, when you were in my Company, you learned that wounds must be treated at once, lest corruption begin. And if the surgeon cuts away good muscle, it's better than leaving the least infection to spread and engulf the whole body."

"Yes, my lord, but—"

"Paksenarrion, the Duke speaks truly. If we thought the evil would not spread, or would spread but slowly, we would not try such a drastic cure. But it is the nature of such to spread with awesome speed. You yourself, being damaged already by this poison, cannot perceive how far it has gone already."

"But my lady—to lose all—and think how long I might live—what could I do? So long in disgrace—"

"It will not be disgrace, Paksenarrion, however it turns out. You have already won honors beyond your years. Nor will any grange of Gird be closed to you; that I promise. And if you have these troubles—and you might not—we will help you find another way to live."

Paks thrust back her chair and rose abruptly, striding to the window to stand braced against the embrasure, looking out at evening sunlight yellow on the cobbled court and the roof of the High Lord's Hall across the way.

"I always dreamed of being a warrior," she said softly. "Silly, childish dreams at first, of being the hero in old songs, with a silver sword. Then Jornoth came, and I was going to be a mercenary, a good one, and earn my living with my sword, and see strange lands, and win honor serving my lord. So I joined Duke Phelan's Company, and prospered as well, I think, as any recruit. You've heard they thought well of me." She glanced at the Duke, who nodded gravely, then turned back to the outside view.

"I stayed three seasons, but—no fault of my lord Duke, who's as fine a leader as I ever hope to fight under—I saw things I didn't want to be part of. So I left, thinking I'd go north and home, and join some castle guard. You know what happened with the elfane taig, and near Brewersbridge. Marshal Cedfer . . . Master Oakhallow . . . they showed me fighting, but for cause, not for a person. My dreams grew—more than being a guard captain instead of a sergeant, I dreamed of fighting as Gird fought—for right, for the protection of the helpless. And you encouraged me: you, Marshal-General, and you, Marshal Fallis, and you, Sir Amberion. You said learn: learn languages, art of weaponry, supply and surgery, fortification—you said all these things were right." Paks' voice broke, and her shoulders shook. The listeners were silent, each with his own memories, his own visions. Paks took a deep breath, then another, and turned to face them, tears filling her eyes.

"And then you honored me, sheepfarmer's daughter, poor commoner and mercenary, beyond all dreams I'd dared. You, my lady, offered me the chance to become a paladin. A paladin! Do you—can you—have any idea what a paladin means to a child on a sheep farm at the for edge of the kingdom? It is a tale of wonder, all stars and dreams. A—a fantasy too good to be true. I had met paladins! And you said 'Come, be one of them. That is your destiny.' " She stopped for breath again, then went on, looking from one to another as she spoke.

"I could not argue, my lady. I felt you must know; you wouldn't say it if it weren't true. I wondered, and rejoiced, and then—to go on quest, with Amberion and the others! I was glad to chance all dangers in such company. And all of you were most courteous to so young a warrior. You remember, Amberion, the nomads' attack? You said I did well, then."

"Paks—" he said, but she went on heedlessly.

"And then we met the iynisin, and—then I was taken. No, my lords!" She said as both Amberion and Ardhiel started to speak. "I blame you not; I said so before. The evil ones wanted me; it was my weakness or flaw that drew them to me. How could I blame you, who followed into the rocky heart of their lair to free me, outnumbered as you were? No. And while I was thus, in their hands, I tried to pray to Gird and the High Lord for aid, but I had to fight against their servants lest they kill me. I was alone—in the dark—I thought that to fight so—Gird would approve. I thought that was right."

She looked down, suddenly, and shuddered. "It wasn't—wasn't easy." Then she faced them again. "Now you say that because I fought them, because I didn't just die, I have opened a passage for great evil. I can't feel this myself; I don't know... But to chance all I can do, to chance losing all I've learned, all I am—that you helped make me—and to think how long I must live if it goes badly... Could such a one as I be a—a potter, or a weaver? Oh, better to kill me, my lady, and quickly."

Silence followed her words; Paks turned again and stared blindly out the window. Then Arianya took breath to speak, but Ardhiel forestalled her. "Lady Paksenarrion, elf-friend, may I tell you a true tale?"

Paks gazed at him, white-faced and desperate. "Yes, Ardhiel; I will listen."

"We elves, milady, know not death from age, and thus our memories are long, and we see slow processes in the world as easily as you might see the start and finish of a meal. Once, long ago, before ever this Hall was built or even started, I walked the green forests with an elf known for the beauty of his voice and the delight of his songs. From him I learned that very air I taught you, milady, when we first met. It was his craft to shape his instruments of living wood—a delicate business, to urge the growth of linden or walnut or mahogany so that it grew fitly shaped for harp or lute or lo-pipe. And to shape it so that in time the complete instrument could be separated from the tree without harm to it or to the creature it grew from. Long years of growth and shaping were required for a single instrument, but long years we elves have, and delight in.

"In that time, he was growing a harp: not a lap-harp, as might be grown from any angle of applewood or pear, but a great harp, on which he hoped to play before the throne of our king. If you think of the shape of a great harp, you will realize how difficult this would be, for if the harp frame were strong enough to withstand the tension of the strings, removing it would cause severe damage to its tree. I cannot tell you how it was done—it is not my craft—but he caused a part of the tree, the part between the instrument and the main plant, to withdraw, as it were. This process must be complete when the instrument was grown, else it became gross and unmusical, and required shaping with tools, which he abhorred. But if it was begun too soon, the withdrawal weakened either instrument or tree, and could allow woodrot and other decay to attack both.

"It happened that he had just begun shaping his harp-tree when our king determined to wed. Not immediately, for that is not our way; but the courtship and preparation began, and in twenty years or so, the wedding day was announced to all elf-kind. It would be another forty years, for the beauty of elf-maidens does not fade or wither, and the king's subjects would have time to prepare all good gifts for the festival.

"When he heard the news, my friend determined that his wedding gift would be the great harp he was then shaping, a kingly gift indeed. He brought me to see it growing, though little I could see, and he had to point out which twig would grow to make the fret, and which root-sprout would form the shorter leg. The frame, you see, was to be grown all in one piece: trunk, branch, root, and sprout top-grafted to the branch. In twenty years, I happened by again, and the shape was far clearer. But my friend was concerned. By his craft, he knew that as it grew, it would grow too slowly—it would not be ready for the king's wedding. I laughed, I recall, and reminded him that elves have no need of hurry. For such a royal gift, the king would be well content to wait. He laughed with me, and seemed reassured.

"But though elves are not by nature hasty folk, we are proud of our crafts, and love ceremony. And ceremony means things done fitly, and in time, and by that love and desire that his gift might be the means of great pleasure at the wedding feast, my friend was betrayed into haste.

"I know not when he did it, or exactly what he did; he had ways of speeding and slowing the growth of all plants he worked with. Indeed, I've seen him grow a lo-pipe in but one season. If it cracked in ten years, what matter, if it served the need to gift a dying man? But somehow he tried to speed the growing of his harp, and the withdrawal of the parent tree, and out of this haste a flaw came into the wood. A part of the withdrawal moved into the harpwood, and weakened it, and the great post that would have to bear the greater strain of the stringing grew awry.

"I well remember the day he showed me, sorrowing, what had gone wrong. Fifty years and more of work, and a little space where the rot crept in had ruined it. To heal that, and reshape the post, would not only take time—years of time—out would also require that the weak part be burned out, regrafted with live wood, and supported while new growth took over. And, he said, 'twas more than likely that it would never grow true in shape, but be clumsy and crooked even if strong enough. Yet to ignore the woodrot would doom the harp and the tree that bore it. I asked him what he would do. He looked at the tree a while, and said, It is not the fault of the wood, which grew true to its nature. I will amend what I can, and tune it as it will bear.'

"Lady Paksenarrion, it is not through your failure that this trouble has come, but we who should have been wiser tried to rush your growth into that beauty we saw possible. Yet now we cannot leave you to perish by our mistake; we must try to mend, though mending is not sure."

Paks had watched his face as he told the tale, but found it as mysterious as all elven faces; it held surmise but no answers. "Sir—you have always been kind to me," she faltered. "But—but need it be now? Could I not go to the green fields, just once, to be a—a memory?"

"Lady, I have known you—I, an elf, who will not die except in battle. You are in my memory and the memory of my people, and there you will not fade in all the years to come when men may forget. We will make songs of you, lady, whatever happens.'

"That's not what I meant," said Paks miserably.

"Paksenarrion, we cannot force you to this," said Arianya. "It would be better to do it quickly, but we cannot—and would not—force you. But you cannot wander alone, with this peril on you. Nor, I think, should you be much abroad with others. Whatever you decide, and whatever happens, it need not become common gossip."

Paks looked from one to another of those in the room, meeting troubled eyes everywhere, doubt and wariness where once she had seen delight and encouragement. Cold despair assailed her heart, more bitter than she'd felt in captivity. Then she had only enemies against her; these were friends. At last she looked at Duke Phelan, leaning against the wall in one corner, arms folded. He gazed back at her, holding her with the intensity of his gray eyes. After a moment, he came to her, still holding her glance at rest.

"Paksenarrion Dorthansdotter," he said. "I will trust you. I will trust you with my Company, the one thing I have built in my whole life, if you desire it. You may come with me, in spite of them, and take command as a captain, and I will trust you, who never failed my trust before, to decide if you can do so in good honor. By my faith, Paksenarrion, you are a good soldier and a good person, and worthy of the trust you have had, and the trust I offer you. You will not fail in this. You have never railed me, and here's my hand on it." And Paks felt her hand swallowed in the Duke's as her face flushed scarlet in relief and joy.

"Tir's gut, you fools!" the Duke went on to the stunned group. "You'd think you were dealing with a weak, witless chit of a girl who couldn't do the right thing without being led in strings. Whatever she decides, whatever she is when you wise folk get through with her, she's got courage enough now, and wit enough now, for the lot of you. If you didn't think she could be trusted, you shouldn't have been trusting her." He turned to Paks. "Don't cry, captain. My captains don't cry before outsiders."

Paks, her hand still clasped in the Duke's, struggled against a wild mixture of emotions. Joy in the Duke's trust—that someone still trusted—came to her as a flash of light that let her see what lay within. Her arguments of minutes before showed false as tinsel, though she had believed herself true as she spoke. In a few moments she had mastered that turmoil, and the sudden change of her expression brought silence and attention to the chamber.

"My lord Duke," she said. "You have given me more than you offered, for by the light of your trust I can see what honor requires. I may never come to serve you again, my lord, as I should to thank you for this gift, but you will lie in my memory, however short it may be."

"Paks—"

"No, my lord. You know what it must be; I would not forfeit your trust. Sir—I would ask your blessing—" Even as she spoke, a prickle of anger stung her; she fought it away.

The Duke wrapped his arms around her and held her close for a moment. "My child—may all good be with you, wherever, however, whenever—may all evil begone from you forever. And if ever you come to me, Paksenarrion, in whatever state you are, I will help you as I can."

"Thank you, my lord."

"And," he added with a growl, "I will stay until I see how you fare with these—"

"Thank you, my lord. Marshal-General—?"

"You are ready, then?" Arianya's eyes were wet, but she rose steadily, and waited the answer.

Paks stepped away from the Duke. She was trembling, but kept her voice firm.

"Yes, my lady. It must be done, and, as you say, will be no better done for waiting."

CHAPTER TWENTY-NINE

A circle of light centered the world. Paks watched it change color: first golden yellow, then glowing orange like coals, then red, deepening to violet, then bursting into blue and white, then back to yellow. After some time, she wondered where and why and similar things. She was sure, looking at a circle of red, that it would darken to violet and blue, then burst into brilliant white. Distant sound disturbed her: ringing, as if bit chains, chainmail, herd bells. The crash of stone on stone, or steel on steel. Voices, speaking words she didn't know.

She opened her eyes at last to find a finger of sunlight across them, and blinked. She felt as light and empty as an eggshell. She had no wish to move, fearing pain or loss. A shadow crossed her vision: a shape she should know. A person. She felt the shifting of what she lay on, a draft of cooler air and easing of pressure. Something damp and cold touched her skin, then warm hands, then warmth returned. She blinked again, seeing, now, a Marshal she had met casually the previous winter, but did not know well. The face was remote, quiet, contained. Paks stared at it without intent. It was a puzzle she had to solve.

The face turned to hers; she saw the surprise on it, and wondered vaguely. "Paksenarrion! You're awake?"

Paks tried to nod. It was too hard; she blinked instead.

"How do you feel?" The Marshal leaned closer. Paks could not answer, closing her eyes against the strain. But a hand touched her forehead, shook her head with what she felt as immense force. "Paks! Answer—"

"Wait." Another voice. "We don't know yet—" Paks opened her eyes again. The Marshal-General, robed in white, stood by the bed. She smiled. "Paksenarrion, Gird's grace be on you. The power of Achrya is broken; she cannot control you. You are free of that evil."

Paks felt nothing at these words, neither joy nor fear. She tried to speak, but made only a weak sound. The other Marshal glanced at the Marshal-General, and at her nod fetched a mug from a table.

"Here," she said. "Try to drink this." She lifted Paks against her shoulder, and pressed the mug to her lips. Paks drank. Water, cold and sharp-tasting, cleaned her mouth.

"Can you speak now, Paksenarrion?" The Marshal-General pulled a stool near the bed and sat.

"I—think—yes, my lady."

"Very good. You have been unconscious some days, now. We were just in time, Paksenarrion, for the kuaknomi evil had invaded deeply, spreading throughout your mind." The Marshal-General touched her head; Paks shivered at the touch, then quieted. She watched those eyes, wondering what the Marshal-General was seeing. Finally, the Marshal-General pulled back her hand and sat up with a sigh. "Well," she said to the other Marshal, "we've done that much at least. It's gone." She looked back at Paks. "How do you feel?"

Paks was beginning to remember what she'd been told before; she tried to feel around inside herself, and found nothing. Nothing strange, nothing bad, nothing at all. "I don't feel bad," she said cautiously.

"You aren't." The Marshal-General sighed again. "You weren't bad anyway, Paksenarrion, any more than someone with an infected wound is bad. Evil had invaded you, as decay invades a rotting limb. We have destroyed it, all of it, but I cannot yet tell what else we may have destroyed. Remember that we are your friends, and your companions in the Fellowship of Gird. Whatever happens, we will take care of you." She rose, and arched her back. "Gird's grace, I'm tired! Haran, get Paksenarrion whatever she wants to eat, and keep watch until Belfan comes. If she feels strong enough, Duke Phelan would like to see her."

"Yes, Marshal-General." Marshal Haran glanced back at Paks, and followed the Marshal-General to the door. Paks could not hear the low-voiced question, but heard the answer. "No. By no means. An honored guest, Haran."

When she had gone, Haran came back to the bed. Paks tried to focus on her face, tried to understand what was going on. They had done something to her: the Marshal-General, Amberion, the elf

Ardhiel, others. She felt no pain, only great weakness, and wondered what, after all, it had been.

"Are you hungry?" asked Haran abruptly.

Paks flinched at the tone. Why was Haran angry with her? She nodded, without speaking.

"Well, what do you want? There's roast mutton—"

"Good." Paks looked around the room. "It's not—my room—"

"You didn't think you were with the other candidates, did you? After that—" Haran looked at her, another look Paks could not interpret. "You're in the Marshal-General's quarters, in a guest room. When she's sure—" Her voice trailed away.

"Sure of what?" Worry returned, a faint icy chill on her back.

"Sure that you're well. I'll be back shortly with food." Haran left the room, and Paks looked around it. The bed she lay on was plain but larger than the one in her quarters. A window to her right let in daylight sky, a smooth gray. Several chairs clumped around a small fireplace opposite the bed.

Haran returned with a covered tray. "Have you tried to get up? If you can sit at the table—" But Paks could not manage this. Haran packed pillows behind her shoulders with a briskness that conveyed disapproval, put the tray on her lap, and went out again. Paks struggled with the food and utensils. She could not grasp the fork properly; it turned in her hand. By the time Haran returned, with a tray for herself, Paks was both annoyed and worried.

"Marshal, I'm sorry, but I can't—" as she spoke, the fork slipped from her grasp entirely and clattered on the floor. Haran stared at her.

"What is it? Can't you even feed yourself?"

"I—can't—make it work." Panting, Paks fought with the knife and a slice of mutton. She felt as clumsy as an infant just learning to reach and grab.

"You're holding that like a baby," said Haran, with exasperation. "All right. Here—" She put down her own tray and came to the bed. "I don't see why you can't—" And with a few quick motions, she cut Paks' meat into small bites and retrieved the fork from the floor. "Now can you do it?"

Paks stared at her. She could not understand Haran's hostility. "I—I hope so."

"I, too." Haran strode back across the room, shoulders stiff, and began eating her own meal without another word. Paks tried again with the fork. Her hands felt as big as pillows, and it was hard to get the food to her mouth. After a few more bites, she stopped, and lay watching Haran eat. When the Marshal finished her own meal, she came to take Paks' tray.

"Is that all you'll eat? I thought you were hungry."

"I was. I just—"

"Well, don't decide you want more in an hour or so. Finish your water; you need it." She stood over Paks until the mug was empty, then snatched it away. In a moment she had left the room, carrying both trays. Paks sank back on the pillows, still confused. What could she have done while unconscious to anger someone she'd only met once before? A knock on the door interrupted her musings. She spoke, and recognized the Duke's voice.

"Come in, my lord."

He opened the door and entered quietly. "Where's your watchdog?" Paks could not think what to say, and he went on. "That Marshal who keeps your door. Haran, I think she's called."

"She's taking trays back." Paks felt, as she had when a recruit, the menace of the Duke, the sheer power of the man. He prowled around the room like a snowcat, tail twitching.

"I've been wanting to see you, and they keep saying wait." He turned to her. "Are you well? How are they treating you?"

"I don't know. I just woke a little while ago. I can't feel much of anything..."

"That's for the best, I'd think, after what they—I tell you, Paks, I came near to killing the lot of them."

"What?"

"To see you like that, with all of them working over you. I feared for you."

"My lord, they had to—" Now she remembered more, and fear grew in her.

"Hmmph. Have you been up yet?"

"No, my lord. I couldn't get up to eat."

He shrugged. "It's been some days; the weakness is normal after so long asleep."

"I wish I knew—" In his presence, still more of the warnings came clear, and the emptiness inside was no comfort at all.

He looked sideways at her. "What?"

"If I will be all right again. I don't know how I'll know. And now that I remember what they did, I can't think of anything else."

He sat near the bed, and laid a hand on her arm. "Don't fret about it. You remember that worries before a battle don't help. When it's time, when you're stronger, then you'll find out."

"But what do you think, my lord. Do you think it's gone?"

He sighed, and did not ask what she meant. "Paks, from what I saw, they stirred the very roots of your mind with powerful magicks. From such stirring nothing would be safe. You don't look different, bar being pale from days in bed, but I can't tell by looking. The test of a sword is not its polish, but its temper."

"I want to be . . . myself." Paks whispered the last, thinking.

"You are yourself, Paks, and always will be. Yet people change with time, with age—"

"Not like that. I can't stand it, my lord, if I can't—if I become—"

"Paks." His grip on her arm tightened. "Look at me." His face, when she looked, was as grim as ever she'd seen it, his eyes hard. She feared him suddenly. "Paks, you are yourself, and you can stand whatever comes. I swear to you. I was not always a duke, I had—"

"But you were always brave, always a warrior!"

"No." His gaze slipped past her into an immeasurable distance. "I will not tell you that tale now, but no, I was not always brave. And you do not yet know you have lost anything. Take heart, Paks, until the time comes."

"But why does Haran dislike me so?"

"Haran?" His face relaxed, puzzled. "I don't know. The Marshal-General assigned her here; perhaps she'd rather be elsewhere. Has she been unkind?"

"No. But she seemed not to like me, or something I'd done."

"My lord Duke!" Haran's voice, from the doorway, was indignant. The Duke turned slowly. Paks saw the muscles bunch in his jaw.

"Marshal Haran." His tone would have warned anyone in his Company.

"What are you doing with her?"

"I? I came to see how she was, and found her awake and willing for company. Have you any objection?"

"No. I would have sent, later, to tell you she was awake—"

"Thank you. As you see, I found out for myself."

"I had to take the trays back—" Paks realized Haran was defensive.

"No matter." The Duke waved, as if a squire were apologizing for an overdone loaf of bread. "Tell me, if you can—is the Marshal-General satisfied with her recovery?"

Haran bristled visibly. "I can't speak for the Marshal-General. She knows best. But she did say—" a sharp glance at Paks, "that the evil was safely destroyed."

"And at what cost?"

"That she did not say." Marshal Haran sat down near the fireplace. "Whatever the cost, it would be worth it."

"Whatever?" The Duke turned to her, his hand still on Paks' arm.

"Duke Phelan, I am a Girdsman. A Marshal. The most important thing is that evil be defeated—destroyed. Nothing else matters. Whatever stands in the way—"

"A life?" asked Phelan softly.

"Yes." Haran looked stubborn, her brow furrowed. "I have risked mine. Any Girdsman knows the risk: we are to serve good, and only good."

"Ah, yes. Good. Are you sure you know good?"

"Of course." Her chin was up; she met his look boldly.

"Yes. Of course. You are sure, Marshal, that you know what is good, but I am not so sure." He paused, as if waiting for her comment, but she said nothing. "I have not been sure, for some years, that you Gird's Marshals really do know good from evil, and as yet nothing I've seen here has convinced me." His hand left Paks' arm; she could feel the taut control of that movement. "You do not, perhaps, think I have any such standards myself. But I assure you, Marshal, that a professional soldier, as I am, has had more combat experience than you. I have seen men and women under great stress, repeated stress. And I know those soldiers more thoroughly than you ever will." He paused again. Haran looked furious, but still said nothing. "Paks is one of them."

Paks stirred, and said, "My lord—"

"Paks, this is not your argument; you but furnished the opportunity. What I am saying, Marshal, is that you have known her but a short time; I have known her for years. You have seen her in one trouble; I have seen her in many. I know her as someone trustworthy in battle, in long campaigns, day after day. You see some flaw—some little speck on a shining ring—and condemn the whole. But I see the whole—the years of service, the duties faithfully performed . . . and that is good, Marshal. Is there one of us with no flaws? Are you perfect, that you indict her?"

"I don't—I never said—"

"Not you personally, but the Girdsmen here. You're one of them; you said so."

"Well—I—" Haran looked at Paks, then back at the Duke, clearly gathering herself for an attack. "She's supposed to be so special—"

"What!" Paks flinched at the Duke's tone even though he spoke to Haran.

"She came only last fall; she was paladin-candidate after Midwinter Feast. That's different, if you like! Promising, they all said. Remarkable. Chosen to go on quest, when she's not even past her Trials. And then she gets herself captured, like any half-wit yeoman without battle experience, and rather than die honorably, as most yeomen would have done, she cooperates with the kuaknom and is contaminated by Achrya." Haran slapped the table and drew another breath. "And now they made this fuss over her—I can understand it from you, who aren't even Girdish, but the others! It makes me sick!"

"Haran!" None of them had noticed the Marshal-General's arrival. She looked almost as angry as the Duke. Haran paused, then shook her head.

"Marshal-General, I'm sorry, but I don't care. It's true. Paksenarrion should never have been accepted as a candidate; she wasn't fit, she hadn't served long enough. Of course the evil had to be rooted out; if something was lost, she'll just have to live with that. It's nonsense anyway; if she had had sufficient courage, there would be no danger of losing it. I don't see all this pussyfooting. It's not that she's special, it's that she's had special treatment. And far too much of it!" Haran turned on her heel and stalked out. The Duke moved to follow, but the Marshal-General held up her hand.

"Please, my lord Duke! Hear my apology first, and allow me to discipline my own."

"I'm listening," he said grimly.

"I am sorry—I did not know Haran felt that way, or I would never have had her here. I wanted Paks to have marshals, whose oath of secrecy I could trust, caring for her. I knew Haran was a bit prickly—

she always has been; it's why she has no grange—but she has always been fair before."

"Well, then. And what of Paks?"

The Marshal-General came past him to Paks. "To you, as well, I apologize for Marshal Haran's words. May I ask if she has done you any harm?"

"No, my lady." Paks still felt numb from the force of Haran's attack.

"No harm but to bully and insult her," put in the Duke.

"My lord, I understand that."

"Good. Marshal-General, I came hoping you would be here as well as Paks. Can you tell yet what has happened to her?"

Paks watched the Marshal-General's face, hoping for reprieve from imagined dooms, but it was still and unreadable. "No, my lord," she said to Phelan. "I cannot tell. It is early yet, and she is still recovering." She turned to Paks again, her expression softening. "Paksenarrion, you must have realized, from what Haran said, that some fear you have been badly damaged. I would not lie to you: as I warned you before, great loss is possible. But I think we will not know until you have regained your strength. We worried because you lay senseless so long, but that may mean nothing. Please tell me if you feel anything different in yourself at any time."

"I—I couldn't eat—" Paks said softly.

"Couldn't eat? What was wrong?"

"I couldn't—couldn't hold the—" Suddenly she began to cry, and tried to smother it. "—the fork—I couldn't cut—I dropped—"

"Oh, Paks!" The Marshal-General took her hands. "Don't—It will get better. It will. You are weak, it's too soon—"

"But she said—like a baby—" Paks turned into the pillows, ashamed.

"No. Don't say that. She was wrong. It will come back, faster than you think." The Marshal-General looked aside; Paks watched the line of her jaw and cheek. "If you keep trying, Paks, it will come back."

"All of it?" asked the Duke softly, echoing Paks' thought.

The Marshal-General's lips thinned. "My lord Duke, please! We cannot know yet. It will do her—or you—no good to worry about that now."

"But she cannot help it, Marshal-General. Nor could you, if you were in that bed, and she beside it. I, too, tried to tell her not to worry about the future, but that's empty wisdom no one can follow. What can she think about, save this? Nothing but knowledge will ease her."

"I have no knowledge," said the Marshal-General. She shook her head, and met Paks' eyes again. "But believe this: I do not think as Haran does, nor do your other friends. And Haran will not think that way long. Only someone of great courage and strength could have held off that evil so long, once it entered."

A knock on the door interrupted them again. Marshal Belfan, whom Paks had known before the journey to Kolobia, put in his head. "Now or later?" he asked.

"Come on in, Belfan." The Marshal-General got up. "Paksenarrion is awake, but weak."

"So Haran said. Gird's grace to you, Paksenarrion, my lord Duke. Old Artagh says first snow by morning, Marshal-General."

"Winter starts earlier every year," grumbled the Marshal-General; Belfan laughed. He had an easy way with him, and hardly seemed a marshal most of the time.

"You said that last year," he said. "It comes," he said to Paks and the Duke, "of having a Marshal-General who grew up in the south."

"In Aarenis?" asked the Duke, clearly surprised.

"No. Southern Tsaia." The Marshal-General was smiling now. "Around here they call any place where it doesn't frost the Summereve flowers the south. Gird knows I like hunting weather as well as anyone, but—"

"You're getting older, Marshal-General, that's what it is." Belfan stuck his hands in his belt, chuckling. She gave him a hard look.

"Is it indeed, my young Marshal! Perhaps you'd like to trade a few buffets in Hall and find out just how old I am?"

"Perhaps I'll throw myself down the steps on my own, and not wait for you."

They all laughed, even Paks. Belfan came over to her. "You look enough better that I expect you'll be throwing the Marshal-General down the steps in a few days yourself. What a time we've had! The long faces around here looked more like a horse farm than Fin Panir's grange and Hall."

"What about something to eat?" asked the Marshal-General. "I can have something sent up for all of us."

"Good idea." The Duke smiled down at Paks. "If we stuff her with food, she'll soon feel more herself."

And when faced with a bowl of thick soup, Paks was able to spoon it up with few spills. No one commented on the mess; the Marshal-General wiped it up matter-of-factly, while talking of other things. When they had all finished, she helped Paks sit up on the bed: she could not lift herself, but could balance alone.

The next time she woke, the Marshal-General and Belfan helped her stand, wavering, between them. She walked lopsided and staggering, but with their aid could make it across the room. Several days later she could walk alone, slowly but more steadily. Her improvement continued. When she could manage stairs, she went outside to the Marshal-General's walled garden. After that came her first walk across the forecourt, to the High Lord's Hall. The glances of the others pricked her like nettles; she looked down, watching the stones under her feet. Haran had claimed that others felt as she did: some of them saw cowardice on her face, with her scars. But she hoped, while fearing her hope was false, that with the return of physical strength she had nothing else to fear.

She had grown strong enough to fret at the confinement of the Marshal-General's quarters, and had begun taking walks on the training fields, usually with the Duke, or one of the Marshals. She did not question their company, noticing that they rarely left her alone, but not wanting to know why. One crisp cold day, she was with Belfan when a thunder of hooves came from behind. They turned to see several students galloping up, carrying lances. Paks felt a wave of weakness and fear that took the strength from her knees. Sunlight glittered from the lance-tips, ominous as dragons' teeth; the horses seemed twice as large as normal, their great hooves digging at the ground. She clutched Belfan's arm, breathless.

"Paks! We thought you were going to be shut up forever!" It was the young Marrakai boy, waving his lance in his excitement. "I wanted to tell you: I've been put in the higher class! I can drill with you now—" As his horse pranced, Paks tried not to flinch from the sudden movements. Another of the students peered at her.

"You've got new scars. They said—"

"Enough. Begone now." Marshal Belfan spoke firmly.

"But, Marshal—"

"Paks, what's wrong? You're shaking—" The Marrakai boy's sharp eyes glittered; she could see the curiosity and worry on all their faces.

"Go on, now." The Marshal took a step forward. "This is nothing for you."

"But she's—"

"Now!" Paks had never heard Belfan bellow like that, and she jumped as the students did. They rode away, looking back over their shoulders. He looked down at her. Only then did she realize that her legs had failed her, and she had collapsed in a heap. "Here—let me help you up." His hand, hard and calloused, suddenly seemed threatening in its strength; Paks had to force herself to take it. She felt the blood rushing to her face. What would the students think? She knew. She knew what she thought. She had never felt such fear, never been mastered by fear like that. Her eyes burned with unshed tears. She heard Belfan sigh heavily. When he spoke again, his voice was still cheerful, though Paks thought she heard the effort behind it.

"Paks, don't think one time means anything. Some days back you couldn't take a single step alone. Now you can walk around the wall. This is the same; this weakness can pass, just as the weakness of your legs passed. What frightened you most?"

But this she could not say. Noise, movement, speed, the sharpness of the lances, the memory of old wounds and what that speed and sharpness could mean, in her own flesh—all these jumbled in her mind, and left her speechless. She shook her head.

"Well, it came suddenly, all at once. Like a cavalry charge, and here you were unarmed: no wonder." But to Paks, his voice carried no conviction. "I daresay it will be better, when you begin training with one weapon at a time. Your skills will be slow to return, perhaps, as you were slow to walk, but they'll come back, and so will your confidence."

"And if it doesn't?" She spoke very low, but Belfan heard her.

"If not, then—something will come for you. Most of the world is not fighters, after all. If you'd lost an arm or leg, you'd have to learn something else. This is not different. Besides, it hasn't come to that yet."

Paks returned to hauk drill, in a beginning class: clumsy, as she now expected, in the first days. When someone lost the grip, and a hauk flew through the air, she flinched, and tried to hide it. Afraid of a hauk!

She forced herself on, exercising early and late, and the strength and coordination came back. But that only hastened sword drill.

When she first gripped a sword again, it felt odd in her hand. Marshal Cieri looked curiously at her, and adjusted her grip. "Like this," he said. It felt no better. She looked down the length of dangerous metal—for he had seen no reason to try her with a wooden practice blade—and tried not to show her fear. The edges, the point, stood out in her eyes; she was afraid to move it lest she cut her own leg. He faced her, and lifted his own sword. Paks stared at it, eyes widening. It seemed to catch the sunlight and throw it at her in angled flashes that hurt her eyes. She blinked. "Ready?" he asked.

Her mouth was dry; her reply came as a hoarse croak. He nodded and moved forward, lifting the tip for the first drill movement. Paks froze, her eyes following the sword.

She tried to force her own arm to move, to interpose her own blade, but she could not. She saw the surprise on his face, the change to annoyance, and then some other emotion she could not read, that terrified her with its withdrawal.

"Paks. Position one."

She struggled, managed to move her arm awkwardly. His blade touched hers, a light tap. She gasped, whirled away, tried to face him again, and dropped her sword. As it clanged on the ground, she was already shaking, eyes shut.

The next time, and the next, were no better. If anything, they were worse. Soon she feared anyone bearing arms, even the Duke when he came to her room with his sword on his belt. As she felt herself weaker and more fearful, she saw the Marshals and paladins and other students as stronger, braver, more vigorous. Despite the Marshal-General's protection, she had heard enough to know that many agreed with Haran. Their scorn sharpened her own.

At last even the Marshal-General admitted that she was not improving. "But as long as you want to try, Paksenarrion—" she said, eyes clouded with worry.

"I can't." Paks could not meet her gaze.

"Enough, then. We hoped the contact would help, but it hasn't. Well see what else can be done for you—"

"Nothing." Paks turned her head away, and stared at the pattern of the rug. Blue stars on red, white stars on blue. "I don't want anything—"

"Paksenarrion, we are not abandoning you. It's not your fault, and we'll—"

"I can't stay here." The words and tears burst from her both at once. "I can't stay! If I can't be one of you, let me go!"

The Marshal-General shook her head. "I don't want you to leave until you have some way of living, some trade or craft. You're not well yet—"

"I'll never be well." Paks hated the tremor in her voice. "I can't stay here, my lady, not with real fighters." She would not, she told herself, tell the Marshal-General about the taunts she'd heard, the mocking whispers just loud enough to carry to her ears.

"Through the winter, then. Leave in spring, when the weather's better. You can study in the archives—"

Paks shook her head stubbornly. "No. Please. Let me go now. To sit and read all day, read of others fighting—I can't do that."

"But—Paks—what can you do? How will you live?"

Nor would she admit she didn't much care whether she lived. And she had thought of a reasonable plan. "I came from a sheepfarm; I can herd."

"Are you sure? Herding's hard work, and—"

Paks drove the thought of wolves away—she would not be alone, on a winter range—and steadied her voice. "I'm sure."

The Marshal-General sighed. "Well. I'll see. If we can find a place—"

Before she left, she had a last talk with the Duke. He showed none of the anger she had feared, and no scorn; his voice was gentle.

"Take this ring," he said, tugging a black signet ring from his finger. "If ever you need help—any kind of help—show this ring to anyone in the Company, or anyone who knows me, or send it. I will come, Paksenarrion, wherever you are, whatever you need."

"My lord, I'm not worthy—"

"Child, you did not throw your gifts away. They were taken from you. For your service to me—for that alone—you are worthy of my respect. Now put that ring on—yes. You must not fail to call, Paks, if you need me. I will be thinking of you." He hugged her again, and turned to go. Then he swung back. "To my thinking, Paks, you have shown great courage in consenting to risk its loss, and in trying so hard to regain your skills. Whatever others call you, remember that Phelan of Tsaia never called you coward." Then he was gone, and Paks turned the ring nervously on her finger. It was loose, and she took it off and stuffed it in her belt pouch.

Two days later, the Marshal-General walked with her to the archway. "Remember, Paksenarrion: you will be welcome in any grange, at any time. I have already sent word. Gird's grace is on you, and our good will follows you. If my parting gift is not enough, you can ask more, freely." But Paks was determined not to spend that roll of coins, wound in a sock in the midst of her pack. "Right now you are unhappy, and reasonably so, with the Fellowship of Gird—"

Paks shook her head. "Not so, my lady. Not with you. I think Marshal Haran had the right of it, in part. My error let Achrya's evil in, and my weakness could not withstand what you had to do—"

The Marshal-General stopped and looked at her. "That's not true, and I've told you before. By Gird's cudgel, I hate to let you go, thinking that. All paladin-candidates are vulnerable, and anyone with less strength than you would have been taken over completely far sooner. You must believe in yourself." She paused, rocking from heel to toe, arms crossed. "Paks, please. Promise me that if things get worse, you will come for help."

Paks looked away. She did not want to say what she thought, that more of such help as she'd had would leave her bedbound as well as craven.

"My lady, I'd best go, to be in the market on time." Paks kept her eyes stubbornly on the ground. The Marshal-General's sigh was gusty.

"Very well, Paks. You are sworn to Gird's Fellowship, and Gird the protector will guard your way. All our prayers are with you." She turned back through the gate, and Paks walked on, determined not to glance back.

CHAPTER THIRTY

With that walk down to the market in Fin Panir, where she was to meet the shepherd who would hire her, a pattern was set that continued all that hard winter.

"Eh, you took your time," grumbled Selim Habensson, when she found him talking with several other sheepmen. "Hated to leave the Lord's Hall, I suppose. Let's see—" He looked her over as if she were a ewe up for sale. "The Marshal-General says you're fit, and you've handled sheep—is that so?"

"Yes, sir. My father raised sheep."

"Good enough. Get in there and find me th' three-tit ewe w'the scarred hock and a double down-nick offside ear." As Paks paused to look over the pen of sheep, trying to see a likely earmark, he barked, "Get on, there—get in—I want to see you in with 'em."

Paks swung over the low railing, among the crowded sheep. She had not feared sheep since she had been able to see over their backs, but the shoving of woolly backs and sides made her feel strange. She saw one offside earmark, but it was a single notch. Most of this pen was nearside marked. There—on the far side—was a double down-nick, offside. She pushed her way slowly through the sheep, careful not to startle or disturb them. A quick look told her this was a normal ewe, not hock-scarred; she looked again for the right earmark, and found it in a corner. A ewe, a three-tit, and scarred on the near hock. She looked up to see the shepherd just outside the rail.

"Very well—you do know somewhat about sheep. But you haven't worked 'em lately, I'll warrant."

"No, sir."

"I thought not. Those clothes belong in a shop, not on drive." He spat on the cobbles outside the pen. "I hope to Gird you don't mind getting dirty."

"No, sir."

"All right. When market's over—another glass, say—we'll be moving this pen and those two"—he pointed—"out to a meadow for tonight. Tomorrow we start for the south. Follow us out—make sure none of 'em stray in the city—and you'll be watching tonight."

Although bothered by the noise and bustle of the market, Paks had no trouble with the sheep on the way out—to her own and the shepherd's surprise. The sheep settled well in their temporary grazing ground, and Paks took up her assigned post on the far side while the other shepherds made camp and cooked supper. She had not thought to bring anything for lunch, planning to buy it in the market, so by evening she was hungry. When the first group had eaten, Selim called in the others to eat. Paks was given a bowl of porridge and a hunk of bread. She ate quickly, hardly noticing the others until she finished. Then she looked up to find them watching her.

"You eat like you thought there was more coming," commented Selim. She had, indeed, assumed there was more. He turned to the others. "Been living in a city for a while, she has. Fine clothes. Eating well. Listen, now. We're sheepfarmers, not rich merchants or fancy warriors. We work hard for what we get; you'll get your fair share, but not a drop more. Understand?"

"Yes, sir." Paks nodded, and cleaned her bowl. She was remembering that when she first joined the Duke's Company, the food had seemed rich and plenty—she had forgotten, in the years since, how her family had lived, and how she had longed for bakers' treats on market days.

"Good. You'll take first watch. Jenits, you relieve her at change. We'll start out at dawn."

In the next few days, Paks became acquainted with hunger again. She felt cold and hunger as a force that dragged on her legs, making her labor to keep up with the flock. When a sheep broke free, and ran, she struggled to chase it, fighting a stitch in her side and leaden legs that would not hurry. Selim scolded her about it.

"By Gird's cudgel, this is the last time I'll hire on the Marshal-General's word! I've a half-grown lass that could do better!" Paks forebore to say that she herself, as a half-grown girl, had done better. She saw clearly that excuses would only make things worse. She ducked her head and promised to work harder. And she tried. But Selim and the others never came to trust her, always saw her as an outsider who had been forced on them by the Marshal-General. In addition, the wounds she'd received from the iynisin began to swell and redden again. They had never faded much, but now they looked and felt much as they had when she first came out in Kolobia. The shepherds looked at the marks they could see and muttered.

So it was that when the flocks were safe in the winter pastures of southern Fintha, Selim turned her away, and refused to hire her through the winter.

"I'm not saying as I think it, mind. The Marshal-General, I expect she'd know the truth of it, and she said as how you was not to blame for any. But they all think you're cursed, somehow. Never saw the like of those marks on your face turning dark like that; it's not natural. We've plenty of young ones in the village that need work can look after the sheep well enough. Here's your pay—" It was not much; Paks did not count it. "And I'll wish you well."

It was a bitter morning, gray with a sharp wind. Paks shivered; she was, as always, hungry. "Is there an inn, here, where—"

"No, not here." His voice was sharp. "We're not some rich town. On that way—" he pointed to a side lane. "You could make Shaleford by tonight if you get a foot on it, or back the way we came." Paks looked from one to the other, irresolute. "You won't make it shorter by thinking on it," he said, and turned back into his own house, shutting the door.

Paks put the coins he'd given her into her belt pouch, biting her lip. The way they had come was north, into the wind, and the nearest town more than a day's travel. She took the lane to Shaleford.

The lane dwindled to a track, and the track to a hardly visible trail that led up over a rise open to the wind. All that day Paks fought the wind, leaning on its shaking shoulder. She had nothing to eat, and nothing in the bare countryside offered shelter or sustenance. When she topped the rise, she looked into a country already softened by coming night; behind her the sun fell behind heavier cloud to a dull ending. She saw nothing that looked like a town, and wondered if the shepherd had lied. But the miserable trail wound on, and she saw sheep droppings nearby. Sheep meant people, she hoped, and kept on. At least it was downhill.

She was stumbling in the gathering darkness when she saw the first light ahead. Thinking of warmth, food, being out of the everlasting wind, she missed her footing again, and fell flat, jarring every bone. She lay sprawled, listening to the wind's howl, and wondering how far the light was.

Shaleford had an inn, if a three-room hut with a lean-to kitchen could be called an inn. Paks handed over most of her earnings for a pile of straw at one end of the common loft and a bowl of soup. The other customers drank ale, heavily, and eyed her sideways. She paid another of her coppers for a second helping of soup and some bread. She was tempted to spend one of the Marshal-General's coins for a decent meal, but was afraid to show the others that she had anything worth stealing.

The next day she found that no one in Shaleford had need for an extra hand over the winter. By the time she'd asked for work every place she could think of, it was too late to make the next town by nightfall. She could not stay another night at the inn without using some of her reserve. But Shaleford had a grange—she'd seen it, first thing in the morning. She decided to see if they would let her stay there.

The Marshal, said the stocky yeoman-marshal, was out. He'd been to Highfallow barton for their drill, and wouldn't be back until the next day. Yes, there'd been a recent message from Fin Panir, but that was the Marshal's business, and he couldn't say what it was. If she had something from the Marshal-General herself—Paks pulled out the safe-conduct, and the yeoman-marshal pored over the seal. She realized suddenly that he could not read.

"A message for our Marshal? Is it urgent?"

"It's to any marshal—about me." Paks felt herself redden under his gaze. His glance flicked to her visible scars.

"You're a yeoman?"

"Yes—well—not precisely—"

"Well, then, what?"

"I was at Fin Panir—"

"The training company?"

"Yes."

"And they sent you on a mission?"

Paks was torn between honesty and the likelihood that he would not understand what she really was. “I don’t think I can explain it to you,” she said finally. “I need to speak to the Marshal, but since he’s not here—”

“Even if I went, he couldn’t get back before tomorrow.”

“No, I understand that. Can I wait for him here?”

“In the grange?” The yeoman-marshal’s frown deepened. “Well—I suppose. Come along.” He led her through the main room to a tiny sleeping chamber off a narrow back passage. “You can leave your pack there, and come back in for the exchange.”

Paks had forgotten that custom. In Fin Panir itself, the exchange of buffets whenever a visitor came to the grange had been abandoned because of the number of visitors. But in outlying granges, it was still usual, and the test of someone who claimed membership in the Fellowship of Gird. She froze.

“I can’t.” Her voice was thin.

“What!”

“I can’t. I—it’s in this—” she waved the Marshal-General’s letter.

“Hmph.” His snort was clearly one of disbelief and scorn. “I see you’ve been wounded recently—is that it?”

Paks nodded, taking the easy way out, as she thought.

“I’d think if you could travel at all you could exchange a few blows—but—” He shook his head. “You hear all sorts of things from Fin Panir. All right, then. I’ll just go put more meal in the pot.”

Paks sank down on the narrow bed, frightened and discouraged. Was this the sort of welcome the Marshal-General intended? But of course the Marshal was away. She could not take it to heart. She got up with an effort and looked around for the jacks and the washroom. At least she could be clean.

Her spare shirt smelled of sheep and smoke, but was, she thought, somewhat cleaner. The yeoman-marshal gave her a pail of water and soap for the dirty clothes, and she came to supper feeling more respectable then before. She had oiled her boots and belt, and the sheathe of her dagger. The yeoman-marshal was obviously making an effort to be friendly.

“So tell me—what’s new in Fin Panir? Is the quest back from the far west yet? Did they really try to find Luap’s lost Stronghold, as we heard?”

"Yes. And found it, too." Paks told a little of the quest, hoping to stave off questions. Luckily, the yeoman-marshal was tired, and when she had told what she thought would interest him, he was yawning.

The next day, when the Marshal returned, he nodded when he heard her name. "Yes—Paksenarrion. I've heard of you; the Marshal-General mentioned that you might come this way in her last letter. Where are you bound next?"

"I—I'm not sure, sir."

"You could take a letter to Highgate, if you would. And I know there's traffic there—you might find work on the roads."

"I'd be glad to." Paks found herself almost eager to go. This Marshal, at least, had no scorn for her.

"If you stay a day, you'll be here for drill—oh, I know you can't bear arms, not at this time, but surely you can tell the yeomen about Kolobia, can't you? They like to hear a good tale, and finding Luap's Stronghold would interest any of them."

Paks didn't want to face a crowd of strange yeomen, but she felt she couldn't refuse. She nodded slowly. The rest of that day passed easily: she was warm and well-fed for the first time in days, and she dozed most of the afternoon. The Marshal offered a mug of herb tea which he said might ease the ache of her wounds, and it helped. But the next night, facing the assembled yeomen, was difficult. She had told them about the trip west, the fight with the nomads, the brigand attacks in the canyons they crossed, but the closer she came to describing the iynisin attack, the worse it got. The Marshal had said she ought not to mention her own capture—not that she wanted to—but she could hardly talk of any of it. Finally, she raced through it, skimping most of the action, and went on to Luap's Stronghold. When she finished, they stamped their feet appreciatively. Then one of them, a big man she'd seen in the inn, spoke up.

"If you're one of that kind, what are you doing here?"

"Any Girdsman is welcome in our grange," said the Marshal sharply.

"Aye, I know that. But I saw her come in two days ago, cold as dead fish and smelling of sheep. Hadn't eaten in days, the way she started on her food over there—" he jerked his head toward the inn. "You know's well as I do, Marshal, that knights and paladins and such don't travel like that. The way she talks, she wasn't walking the wagons out to Kolobia—she talks like she fought alongside that Amberion and that elf. So I just wonder why she's—" His voice trailed away, but his look was eloquent. Paks saw others glance at him and nod.

"Yeomen of Gird," said the Marshal with emphasis. "It is not my tale to tell. I can tell you that the Marshal-General has commended her to every grange—every grange, do you hear?—and to all the Fellowship of Gird. I daresay she travels where she does, and as she does, by the will of the High Lord and Gird his servant. I will not ask more—and you would be wise to heed me."

"Well," said the big man, undeflated, "if you ask me, she looks more like a runaway apprentice than a warrior of Gird. No offense meant—" he said with a glance at Paks. "If so be I'm wrong, then—well—you know how to take satisfaction." With that he flexed his massive arms, and grinned.

"You're wrong indeed, Arbad," said the Marshal. "And I'll take the satisfaction for your discourtesy to a guest of the grange on next drill night, or hear your apology now."

Evidently, the Marshal's right arm was well-respected, for Arbad rose and muttered an apology to Paks. The meeting broke up shortly after that. A few had come to speak to Paks, but most huddled together in the corners, looking at her and speaking quietly to each other. The Marshal stayed near her, stern and quiet.

At Highgate Paks delivered the Marshal's letter to the Highgate Marshal, and shared a hot meal at the grange. He introduced her to a trader, in town on his way south and east, and Paks hired on as common labor. The rest of that day she unloaded and loaded wagons, and harnessed the stolid draft-oxen. With the other laborers, she slept under one of the wagons, and the next day they started on the road.

Keris Sabensson, the trader, rode a round-bellied horse at the head of the wagons; he had a drover for each wagon, five guards, and two common laborers. Paks was expected to do most of the campwork, load and unload the wagons at each stop, and help care for the animals. She found the work within her strength, but was terrified of the guards, who tried to joke with her.

"Come on, Paks," said one of them one night when she jumped back from a playful thrust of his sword. "With those scars you've got, you've been closer than this to a sword. You know I'm not serious. Here—let's see what you can do." He tossed the sword to her. Paks threw out her hand, and knocked it away; it fell to the ground. "Hey! Stupid, don't do that! You'll nick it!" He glared at her.

"You can't tell me you haven't fought—what happened, lose your nerve?" Another one had her by the arm.

"Let her alone, Cam—suppose you ended up—"

"Like her? Never. I'll be a captain someday, with my own troop. Who'd you fight with, Paks—tell us."

"Phelan," she muttered. She could not break free, and was afraid to try.

"What? I don't believe it." Cam dropped her arm. "You were in the Red Duke's Company? When?"

"A—a couple of years ago." They were all watching now, eyes bright in the firelight. She swallowed, looking for a way out of their circle.

"What happened? Get thrown out?" Cam's grin faded as he watched her.

"No, I—" She looked into the fire.

"Tir's gut, Paks, you make a short tale long by breathing on it. What happened?"

"I left." She said that much, and her throat closed.

"You left." The senior, a lean dark man who claimed to have fought with the Tsaian royal guard, confronted her. He looked her up and down. "Hmm. You don't get scars like that from not fighting, and you're too old to have been thrown out as a recruit, and not old enough to be a veteran. But you're scared, aren't you?"

Paks nodded, unable to speak.

"Is that why you left Phelan?" She shook her head. "When did you—no, those scars are too new. Something happened—by the look of it, within the past few weeks. She closed her eyes to avoid his gaze, but felt it through her skin. No one spoke; she could hear the flames sputtering against a sleety wind, and the hiss of sleet on the wagons.

"All right," he said finally. She opened her eyes; he had turned, and faced the others. "I think she's told the truth; no one lies about serving with Phelan and lives long to tell it. She's got the marks of a warrior; something's broken her. I wouldn't want to carry that collection myself. Let her alone."

"But, Jori—"

"Let her alone, Cam. She has enough to live with. Don't add to it." With that he led them away to one side of the fire. Paks went on with her work but spent most of that night awake. She began to realize that she could not pass as a laborer; her scars would always betray her past. People she met would expect things—things she no longer had—and each meeting would be like this.

Two days later, a band of brigands struck the wagons. They were deep in a belt of forest, where the guards could not see far, and they had dragged Keris Sabensson from his horse and cut the traces of the first team before the guards got into action. The drovers reacted quickly, defending their teams and wagons with the long staves they carried; the other laborer ran forward and caught Sabensson's horse. Paks froze where she was, terrified. She could not move, could not help or run. And when the fight was over, and the trader, head bandaged, was settled in the first wagon, he fired her.

"I'm not having any damned fools here," he said angrily. "Stupid, cowardly—by all the gods I'd rather have a drunken swineherd to depend on. Get out! Take your pay—not that you've earned it!" He threw a few coins out of the wagon; one hit Paks in the face. "Go on—move!" He poked the drover, who prodded the oxen into motion. Paks stepped back, ignoring the coins at her feet. On the second wagon, Cam smirked at her, but she hardly noticed. She stared blankly ahead as one wagon after another passed her, and the oxen blew clouds of steam.

At the last, Jori, now riding the trader's horse, stopped. "Paks, here." He handed her a small leather bag. "It isn't much—what we—I mean—" He touched her head. "I know what kind of soldiers Phelan has. You be careful, hear?"

She stood a long time in the track, holding the bag, until she finally thought to tuck it into her belt and start walking.

At the next town, they had heard of her from the trader, still angry. She trudged past the grange without looking at it, and went on, going the way that the trader had not gone. She had not dared enter an inn, but had bought bread from a baker. At the town beyond that, after a night spent in a ruined barn, she found work in a large inn.

"Not inside," said the innkeeper after a look at her face. "No. You won't do inside. But if you're not afraid of work, I can use someone in the yard. Haul dung, feed, clean stalls—you can do that?" Paks nodded. "Sleep in the shed—in the barn if it's not full. You get board and a copper crown a week." Paks thought dully that she must be back in Tsaia—Finthan coins were crescents and bits, not crowns. "Can you work with big horses?" She shook her head, remembering the disaster in Fin Panir when she had been unable to groom Socks, let alone ride him. Somehow her fear transmitted itself to horses, and made them skittish. "Too bad; it's a chance for tips. Well, then, stay out of the way. The grooms'll be glad to have the dirty work taken off them."

So they were. Paks hauled dung from the barns twice a day, pitched straw, bedded stalls, carried feed. Work began before daylight, and continued as late as the last person came to the inn. The shed she slept in was by the kitchen door, and half-full of firewood; it backed on the great fireplace, and she thought she could feel a little warmth in the stones, but that was all. She had no place to wash, and no reason to—the innkeeper was clearly surprised when she asked. She did not mention it again. As for board, the innkeeper was more generous than many: bread, soup, and porridge, and a chance at the scraps. Not that much was left after the kitchen help, indoor help, and the rest of the stable help took their share. She hid her own pack behind the firewood, and half-forgot it was there or what was in it.

She noticed that her scars from Kolobia had begun to fade again, as mysteriously as they darkened. This time, however, the pain did not fade with the color. It continued as a bitter bone-deep ache that sapped her strength. She did not think about it; she didn't think of anything much, but whether she could lift another shovel-full. Winter's grip strengthened; even within the courtyard there were days when the wind blew snow into a white mass that made it hard to breathe. She wore all her clothes, and still woke stiff in the mornings. Trade slowed, in the bitter cold, and the innkeeper told her she could sleep in the barn, now half-empty. It was warmer there, burrowing in straw, with animals heating the air.

She hoped to stay there all winter, but one night two drunken thieves drove her away. It began when they arrived and handed their mule's lead-rope to one of the grooms. The tall one caught sight of Paks and nudged the other. She saw this, and ducked behind a partition, but heard their comments. Late that night, they came out to the barn, "to look at our mule," as they said. The grooms were gone; one to the kitchen, where he had a lover, and one to a tavern down the street. Paks had gone to sleep in a far stall, carefully away from the mule. They found her.

"Well, well—here's a pretty lass. Hello, yellow-hair—like a little present?" She woke to find them standing over her. The tall one whirled something shiny on a ribbon; the other one carried a branched candlestick with two candles. She looked around wildly. She was trapped in a corner stall; they stood in the door, chuckling. She scrambled up, backing away from them.

"By Simyits, I think she's scared. Surely you aren't a virgin, sweetling—why so frightened?" The shorter man came nearer. "Kevis, are you sure of her? It's easy to tell she works in the stables."

"Oh, I think so. It's the ugly ones and poor ones that appreciate presents. See this, sweetheart? It's a nice shiny ring. All for you, if you just—"

Paks jumped for the gap that had opened between them, trying to scream. As in a dream, little sound came out; the tall man grunted as she bumped into him, and grabbed her. His hand clamped over her mouth. "Now that's not nice, pretty lass—behave yourself." She struggled wildly, but the other man had set the candlestick on the stall partition grabbed her as well. "Quiet down, girl; you're not going anywh—Damn you, you stinking—" Paks had managed to get a finger between her teeth, but his other hand gripped her throat. She choked; the shorter man twisted her arms behind her.

"What, Cal?"

"She bit me, the stupid slut." Paks heard this through the roaring of her ears as he kept the pressure on her throat. "If we didn't need her, I'd—"

"Let up, Cal. I've got her." The tall man gave a final squeeze, and loosed her throat. Paks gasped for air; it seemed to scrape her throat as it went in. She could not stand upright with the pressure on her arms. The shorter man increased it, and forced her to her knees. The tall man bent near her; she could smell the ale on his breath.

"Listen to me, sweetheart—you're going to help us, and you're going to give us a good time. If you do it right, you'll get a little reward out of it—maybe this ring. If you act stupid, like you just did, you'll die hurting. Now—do you understand?"

Paks could not speak for terror and pain. She was shaking all over, and tears sprang from her eyes.

"I asked you a question." A knife had appeared in the tall man's hand; it pricked her throat. Paks heard herself moan, a terrible sound that she did not know she could make.

"Simyits save us all," muttered the shorter man, behind her. "It's no wonder they have this one in the stable. No wits at all."

"No wits, the better lay."

"Kevis—"

"Well, Cal, you know the saying. It tames wild mares and witches. Why not a stable hand?"

"What about time?"

"So how long does it take?"

"You may be right." Paks heard the grin in the voice behind her, and saw the man in front fumble with his trousers.

"I'll go first."

"Greedy—you always go first." The man behind her let go her arms, and Paks fell facedown in the straw. She rolled away, trying to escape, but they caught her. The tall man backhanded her across the face, knocking her into the back of the stall.

"That's for the bite, slut. Now don't cause trouble." He grabbed her shirt, and ripped it open. "What a beauty!" His voice was cold. "Where'd you get those scars—somebody whip you once?"

"More than once," said the other one. "By the dark goddess, I never saw anything like that outside of Liart's temples in Aarenis. Kevis—"

"Don't bother me, Cal." The tall man tugged at her belt. "I'm busy."

"Kevis, wait. If this is Liart's bait—"

"Cal, I don't care if it's the crown princess of Tsaia—"

"But Kevis—" The shorter man pulled at his companion's arm. "Listen to me. I know what I mean—Liart won't like it if that's one of his."

"Liart can go—" He had broken the belt, and forced his hands between her thighs. Paks tried to struggle, but he had her wedged against the wall where she could not move.

"Don't say that!" The shorter man used enough force to pull the other's arm away. "Kevis, it's serious. Liart is a jealous god; he'll kill—and I know how he kills—"

"Don't bother me!" The taller man turned away from Paks and pulled his knife. "Hells blast you, Cal, you're as craven as she is. Get back—"

"No! I'm not having any part of this if she's Liart's—"

"Then go away. Don't—I don't care—but don't—" He swayed a little on his feet, and the shorter man took his chance to pull him away from

Paks. She watched through a fog of fear as they began to fight. They stumbled into her and away; she took stray blows and kicks, feeling each of them as a shattering force that left her still less will to move, to escape. Finally they staggered into the partition, and knocked over the candlestick. Light flared up from the neighboring stall; the man stopped short, staring.

"Hells below! See what you ve done?" The shorter man, breathing heavily, glowered at the other.

"Me! It was you, pighead! Come on—run for it!"

"What about her?"

"Leave the stupid slut." Paks heard their feet on the passage floor, heard the crackling flames in the next stall. She could not move, she felt her body was a mass of pain. She heard more yelling, and more, in the distance, but was hardly aware when someone grabbed her legs and dragged her out of the burning barn. By the time she had realized what had happened, she was already being blamed for it.

"I let you sleep there, out of the kindness of my heart, and what do you do? You not only whore around in the stalls, but you take candles—candles, open flames, Gird blast you!—into the stable and start a fire! If it hadn't been for Arvid coming back in, we'd have lost five horses. We did lose all that hay. He should have left you there."

"It wasn't—I didn't—" Paks could hardly speak, with her bruised throat, but she tried to defend herself. "They—they tried to rape me."

The innkeeper snorted. "I don't believe that! No one would pick you—gods above, I have comely girls in the house they'd likelier try. You've been using my barn—my barn!—for your tricks. Now get out! Where do you think you're going?"

"My pack—" said Paks faintly.

"I ought to take it for the damage you've done. All right, take the damn thing—it's probably full of lice anyway, dirty as you are." He hit her hard as she tried to leave, and drove her out of the gates with another blow and a kick. She fell heavily into the street, but managed to clamber up as he came toward her, and limped away.

It was dark and bitter cold. She followed the street by touching the walls along it, stumbling into them, choking down sobs. She felt as if a great vise were squeezing her body, twisting it to shapes of pain she had never imagined. When she thought of the past—of last winter—it seemed to recede, racing away into a distance she could never span.

A last little bright image of herself at Fin Panir, happy and secure, gleamed for moment in her mind and disappeared. She stopped, confused. She had no wall to touch, and all around was a howling dark, cold and windy. It was one with the void inside.

CHAPTER THIRTY-ONE

Marshal-General Arianya
High Lord's Hall
Fin Panir
To all Marshals of Gird, Greetings:

In the matter of Paksenarrion Dorthansdotter, recently a member of Gird's Company here, I request the courtesy and charity of your grange. Paksenarrion was a member of Gird's quest to the Stronghold of Luap; without her defense the quest would have failed more than once. Through the malice of Achrya, she has been left unfit for battle, and has chosen to work her way in the world rather than accept grange gift, which she was offered freely. Marshals, this is not weakness; she was assailed with such power as even you or I might fall before. Give her any aid she needs; report any contact to me in Fin Panir for reimbursement; defend her as you can against malice and evil, for she can no longer defend herself. On my honor as commander of the Fellowship of Gird, she has no taint of evil herself, and Gird's grace is on her.

She is tall, yellow-haired, and gray-eyed, and has many fighter's scars, including some that look recent, still inflamed. She carries a safe-conduct from me, but I fear she may be too shy to present it. Look for her. She is under our protection.

* * *

Marshal Keris
Shaleford Grange
To Marshal-General Arianya, Greetings:

As you requested, I am writing to report that Paksenarrion Dorthansdotter has been here. I was away when she came, but Yeoman-marshal Edsen took her in overnight. She seemed in good health; she seems to me a pleasant young woman, very willing to please, though not steady of nerve. She spoke to our yeomen about the quest to Kolobia, which they had not heard. I sent her with a message to old Leward at Highgate Grange; I know there is much traffic along the way there, even in winter, and thought she might find work. No one is hiring here.

I must say that with the little you wrote, it's hard to explain her to the yeomen here. Even Edsen wondered about her. Perhaps in more traveled areas, they'll be more understanding. If I understood you correctly, she has had her mind damaged by a demon—right?

It looks like another hard winter; I'm having trouble getting all the grange-gift without cutting the farmers too short. I'm sending the rolls; note that Sim Simisson died, and his widow has remarried into Hangman's barton. Their farm was split between the three boys, but Jori and Ansuli have moved away, and young Sim is farming it all. Gird's grace to you.

★ ★ ★

Leward of Highgate Grange
To Marshal-General Arianya
Greetings, Arñe!

Did you hear that old Adgan finally died? Kori Jenitson told me a few weeks ago, when he rode by this way. I told him to write you, or send word from Vérella.

Keris sent that Paksenarrion Dorthansdotter to me. What is the Fellowship coming to, after all? I know, I know. You had your reasons. But such things should happen to those of us with years enough to know better. She's nought but a young sprout, I don't care how many years she fought with Phelan. By the way, someone told me he'd been to Fin Panir. Is that true? Is he coming back to the Fellowship?

Anyway, I found the girl a place with a trader I know.

She looks strong enough, though much disfigured with those scars. Loading wagons should put a little muscle on her—then maybe she won't find swords so frightening. Keris, the trader, promised to keep her on all the way to the south if she earns her keep. Can't see any reason why she won't. She's certainly polite and better-educated than most. If she weren't scarred as she is, I'd be tempted to find a husband for her.

Remember me at Midwinter Feast. I will roast a pig in the honor of Luap's Stronghold.

★ ★ ★

Sulinarrion
Marshal of Seameadow Grange
To Marshal-General Arianya, Greetings:

Arñe, I have sad news about your stray. Keris, a small trader, came storming in to complain of her. Leward of Highgate had placed her with him as a laborer, and according to Keris, she ran away, or fainted or something when bandits attacked his wagons. I know Keris of old; we see him in grange-court every few years when he either complains of short weight or gives it. He's a hasty, hot-tempered man who will cling to a mistaken idea until the nomads build walls. Anyway, he says he fired her on the spot—somewhere in the woods of Lowfallow, if I can tell by his tirade—and left her there. According to him, she was unwounded, and the bandits were all dead, so perhaps she has made it somewhere else. I asked to talk to his guards, and the senior, a Falkian named Jori, from Marrakai's domain, told me that she had simply frozen, neither attacking the bandits nor defending herself. He said some of the guards made up a small sum for her, and he gave it to her. He felt bad about it, he said, but he couldn't leave the wagons. I think it's the best we could hope for.

I've told my yeoman-marshals and my yeomen to keep looking for her, but no one has turned up yet (though they did find a tall blonde thief we've seen before; she's enjoying our hospitality in a different way, awaiting the Duke's Court). I told Keris what I thought of him, but it didn't do much good. He's so used to covering fear with bluster that he doesn't want to admit anyone can't.

I'm sorry I have no better news. On the bright side, we have had an unusually good year in all the eastern bartons, and the grange-lands themselves, and can help those west of us who are short. I've heard that some granges can't make their Hall share; you can see from our rolls that we can help out. I hope to come in sometime next spring—do you still have that dappled gray? I'll make an offer you can't refuse.

★ ★ ★

Sulinarrion
Marshal of Seameadow Grange
To Leward of Highgate Grange
Greetings.

Leward, why on earth did you place Paksenarrion with Keris? You must know what sort of rough clod he is! He came ramping in here complaining of her cowardice, and the dishonesty of Girdsmen, until I nearly hit him on the head to shut him up. Didn't you warn him that she couldn't fight? He fired her after a bandit group attacked the wagons and she didn't defend them. Of course she didn't defend them. I know plenty of men—some of them, unfortunately, yeomen—who would run like rabbits in an unexpected attack. When I finally got the whole story out of one of his guards, it turns out Keris himself simply fell off his horse and bellowed the whole time. Now she's disappeared, and Gird alone knows what's happened to her. Next time you need something handled with delicacy, don't go to Keris.

★ ★ ★

Sim Arisson,
Marshal of Lowfallow Grange
To the Marshal-General of Gird
Greetings:

In accordance with your request for information about the whereabouts and welfare of Paksenarrion Dorthansdotter, I am writing you a full report of recent events in this area.

Several weeks ago, I was touring the bartons and was not in Lowfallow for some days. When I returned, the innkeeper of the largest inn called me to attend one of his grooms, who had been badly burned in a barn fire. The short of it is that the innkeeper blamed one of the stablehands for the fire, and claimed she had been in league with two thieves, who had robbed the inn on the night of the fire. I think this person was Paksenarrion, from the description and name given by the innkeeper. Apparently she sought work there a few weeks before the fire, giving her name but no reference to the grange. She worked well, according to Jessim (the innkeeper), and slept in a shed near the kitchen. A few days before the fire he had said she and another stablehand might sleep in the barn, trade being slow. When the fire broke out, the groom discovered her in the barn, with her clothes as much off as on. He could see a candlestick in the midst of the fire. Jessim assumed she'd been whoring, and either set the fire as a distraction for the thieves or made it carelessly. Jessim drove her out that night, being angry, as he said. No one saw her leave town; it was bitter cold and windy, and most were fighting the fire. The next day he reported her description (but not her name, which he had forgotten until I questioned him) to the Duke's militia, as an accomplice of the thieves.

After I spoke to him, he withdrew the charge, and I have cleared her name with the militia, though I have asked them to look for her, and let me know if they find her. I asked the grange here, and none of the yeomen knew her, or remembered having seen her. I swear to you, Marshal-General, that she did not come to my grange for aid; I would have given it gladly. We found no sign of her in Lowfallow or in the farmland around. You will understand that it took some time to look, for I was afraid she might have been hurt in the fire and unable to travel. I had my yeomen look in every ditch and bramble. We were heartened to find no body, but we did not find her.

I delayed writing you because I hoped to have more certain news. Jessim promised to ask any travelers that came in, and I have spread the word to the distant bartons of my grange. Two days ago, one of my yeomen from Fox Barton reported a stranger living with an old widow in an outlying cottage. By the time we rode there, she was gone, but I am sure it was Paksenarrion.

The old women is not a Girdsman, but has a name for honesty and hard work. She is a widow (her husband died of fever; he was a woodsman) and supports herself and a crippled daughter with weaving and spinning. At first she did not want to talk about it, but after we convinced her we meant Paksenarrion no harm, she told her tale. It seems that Paksenarrion appeared one morning (she could not be sure of the date, but that it was a clear day after a cloudy one) in her shed. She described her as nearly frozen, half-naked, and hurt. Apparently, one leg was injured, for the woman told us she limped for most of the time she stayed there. Anyway, the old woman took her in, mended her clothes, and fed her, though that was hard—which I could well believe, looking around. They found Paksenarrion to be, in their words, "gentle—she never said a rough word—" and she seems to have helped them by fetching water, finding wood and breaking it up, and so on. They said she offered to pay for her keep, but the old woman could not use her Finthan coins without walking into Lowfallow to change them—which was too far, she said, in winter. I suppose that means she still has the money you gave her in Fin Panir.

They had hoped she would stay, as she seemed strong to them, but she was unable to spin or weave, though apparently she tried to learn. Without extra help, they could not earn enough to keep three. Paksenarrion decided to leave, although they protested, and she insisted they keep a few Finthan coins. The old woman asked me if I could change one for her in Lowfallow. I told her to keep it; that the grange would aid to those who helped Girdsmen. I find that Fox Barton was already providing meat from time to time, but have put these women on the grange rolls. They need someone young and strong to board with them, and learn care of the daughter, who will never walk; we are working on that. In the meantime, I have sent supplies, and an order from the grange for two rugs a year. With your permission, I will name them on the Year Roll. They are not Girdish, but we owe them that.

Anyway, that's all I could find of Paksenarrion. Before I could extend the search, we had a thaw which left every road a quagmire. I have written neighboring granges, but it seems clear that she is avoiding granges. From the descriptions given by the women and by the innkeeper, I doubt that she will be recognized as anything but a vagrant. However, we will keep watch, and report anything we find.

I know you will be disappointed in this report. I think it hopeful that she is clearly still able to serve others weaker than herself. Perhaps some day Gird and the High Lord can restore her trust in the Fellowship and in herself.

* * *

Seklis, High Marshal
Marshal-General Arianya
Greetings:

While traveling from Valdaire to Vérella, I met a party on the road who spoke of an ex-Girdish warrior named Paksenarrion. When I reached Vérella, your waiting letter mentioned such a one. My news is meager indeed. At the time I was with the traders, I did not know of your interest, and did not question them as I might have. They said something about meeting an unusual sight—a Girdsman afraid of her own shadow, of barking dogs and horses. One of them said she'd been cursed that way, and gave it as proof that she was lapsed from the Fellowship. I do not recall where they said they had seen her, or where she was going—if they even said—but I report this because of your interest.

More important, I believe, is the continued conflict in Aarenis between the Guild League cities and the old nobility; trade is completely disrupted, and famine this year has been widespread . . .

Thus ends Book II of *The Deed of Paksenarrion*.
Paksenarrion's adventures continue in Book III, *Oath of Gold*.